Greysmoke Rising: The Magician

Mabel Ramona

The Magician

Greysmoke Rising: Book 1

Production copyright FurPlanet Productions © 2025

Text Copyright © Mabel Ramona 2025

Cover Artwork © Mabel Ramona 2025

The Korps Universe © Karen King 2024, and used with permission

Published by FurPlanet Productions
Dallas, Texas
www.FurPlanet.com

Print ISBN 978-1-61450-690-4
Electronic ISBN 978-1-61450-691-1

Table of Contents

This book contains scenes depicting trans and queerphobia, sexual assault, dysphoria, deadnaming, misgendering, self-harm, suicidal ideation, trauma, PTSD, masturbation, sexual intercourse, violence, and smoking.

This story is for those who are afraid to try,
because they believe they are too old, too broken.

Who feel too ashamed or scared to take that leap.

It is never too late to find yourself.
You deserve to know that person and finally live.

It's like the lady said...
"Stay afraid, but do it anyway."

Make mischief, and do her proud.

FOREWORD

BY KAREN KING

Nearly seven thousand years ago, an event shook the world. An arrival of something ancient: the merging of humanity with the world of the beast, the eruption of superpowers, and the proliferation of the supernatural. In the modern day, this world appears much like our own but for the pantheon of species that occupy it and the extensive presence of superheroes and supervillains alike. While many states have their own super-powered forces, a vast variety of independent actors exist.

Among the most prominent independent supervillain groups is an organization known as the Korps. As far as most are aware, the Korps is an organization dedicated to world domination, led (in theory) by the shadowy Overlord. This sinister being has tried to wrap their vicious claws around the planet, time after time, since the beginning of recorded history.

The truth, of course, is significantly more complex.

Led by some of the world's strongest superpowered beings, the Korps sees itself not as a state-in-waiting, but a governance method — seeking to depose repressive state-based hierarchies to install systems more capable of effectively distributing resources to those in need. It sees state actors — "Heroes," police, paramilitaries — mete punishment out on innocents, yet go unpunished in turn. It knows, — for all the cartoonish pretensions of the supering world — that this is the true evil. It knows, too, that this cannot go unchallenged.

Operating a number of covert front companies and satellite operations for many decades, the Korps has dedicated a great deal of resources to outpacing the world's greatest scientific, engineering and medical minds. Korps medical technology in particular is extremely advanced, allowing its members to essentially build their preferred body from scratch — and permitting this capacity at scale. The Korps has learned well that monocultures become stagnant without personal expression, which it fiercely encourages in its members — a reality at odds with the widespread public perception that they are nothing more than brainwashed drones.

One of the most useful and distinctive tools at the Korps's disposal are Rose-Coloured Glasses, or "RCGs," a high-capacity communications tool, heads-up display and computer-brain interface so powerful they can be used directly as a VR headset. RCGs can function as an assistive device or therapy tool… but the nature of the technology means they have the power to directly access and even alter one's thoughts. Alternately viewed with relief, mistrust, or fear by the supering world, it is known that wherever they are worn, the Korps is not far behind.

Having emerged in the wake of the Second World War, the Korps has gradually spread its influence, eventually emerging fully into the public consciousness in the 1990s. With increased visibility and emphasis on immediate action, however, comes ever more entanglements…

The Korps began as a big pile of superhero and supervillain tropes that I'd built up a love of through various types of media, like the James Bond movies. While I originally just threw it together as an action playset of stock characters, over time, it began to morph into something very different. Using stock pop culture antagonists to take swings at the injustices unfolding around me began to carry more and more emotional weight.

In an era when information became more and more readily available, we were able, at any time of day, to pull out our phones and view some kind of great injustice unfolding, live in front of the world — to see police forces with the budgets and capacities of small militaries crushing peaceful protestors, to watch the deceptions of nations exposed constantly but slip by unpunished, to see the suffering of those in need, on our feeds, 24/7 …

It became increasingly clear to me, and to many, that the status quo is not a state of normalcy, but something imposed by force. Equally, to many, the concept of rallying the villains — those who challenged the status quo — and giving us a context in which we can, in some sense, strike back against it all… It struck a chord among those of my generation. In a world where fighting back seems so hard, an entity like the Korps is something compelling.

I am now sitting here writing the foreword for an actual, published work about it, and my mind is reeling. Giving the Korps as a set of narrative tools to the wider community feels like it has uncorked a flood: a need to right wrongs, a need to highlight injustices, a need to tell intimately personal stories, stories of love, and stories of redemption… rushing out onto countless pages, from countless perspectives.

All I have ever wanted to do is to help give people a community, and the tools they need to create, and to build the stories they need. It is an honour and a privilege to introduce this story to you — one of love, one of breaking free, one of deep wounds beginning to heal…

— Karen King

Prologue

Collection

"The fruit never ripens. It forever rots on the vine, before it can be harvested."

"You must be patient, dear sibling! Imagine how sweet the flesh will be when we get to taste it! It will be worth the wait for the succulent reward."

"Patient? Pah… Seven centuries is proof enough of my patience. I want my toy! No other will be so much fun…"

*"You will have it, when it closes the circle, and not a moment before. If we rush, **She** may notice, and that just wouldn't do."*

"You are right, maddeningly so… I will find amusement elsewhere for now, but still…"

"We watch with great interest, the path ahead."

"Hm?" Jos looked up from his work as he idly brushed at his ear. "Wha—?"

He dropped his pencil and glanced back over his shoulder. Scanning the room, the feeling of being watched was hard to shake, but all the mountain lion saw was the same old, empty apartment. The cougar shrugged, clucking his tongue and returned to sketching.

Meh. Wish they would do something about the pest problem here…

As the loose lines Jos made blended into a figure striking a mysterious pose, he nodded to himself. They had a real cloak and dagger sort of mystique, and he couldn't help but allow himself a tired smile as he admired his own work. There wasn't much that could bring that out of him these days, but…

It was always nice when a drawing began to take shape.

Chapter 1

What Doesn't Kill You...

Joe stared at the screen, looking and not really seeing what was on the display. By that time of day, his eyes shared a remarkably similar glassy sheen to his assigned monitor. Picking out key phrases from the documentation and editing as he moved through the last leg of this case.

Click. Click. Clack. Click. Clack. Click.

A terribly exciting, incredibly adventurous life I lead, the feline thought to himself. *Maybe today I'll have the spicy noodles instead of the chicken!* He rolled his eyes. His frown shifted a bit in bemusement, but he was unable to make himself do more than that with his sarcastic deprecation.

His self-flagellation was pure upstate NY. He had left his home in the suburbs of the Northeast to live in ... the suburbs of the South. That wasn't the original plan, but ... things change.

People leave.

Some plans fall through, and that is just how life goes.

Click. Clack. Click.

The thirty-something mountain lion slumped in his chair, posture be damned. He allowed his eyes to roam to the wall of his cubicle as he mulled over what else he needed to say to his customer, stopping at the sheet of paper dictating current call etiquette. Hidden beneath, away from prying eyes, was pinned a glossy signed photo. He pushed his long dark hair out of his eyes, staring at the words scribbled thereupon:

"Did you hear about the mountain lion writer? I always forget their real name — they prefer to use a nom de poom!"

He remembered her words now just as clearly as the day he first heard them, and how they had made him chuckle, his cheeks flushing ever so slightly with boyish embarrassment. He had gotten the headshot at CapeCon Austin back in 2020. As he stood in line, nervously shifting from foot to foot, he had gone over what he was going to say a million times. He dreamed about how he was going to dazzle her with his deep knowledge of her exploits and rapier wit. Surely, she would be so impressed that they would become best friends *immediately*.

When he got to the front, she smiled, and he had forgotten everything.

Her warm brown eyes lit up her entire face, and Joe couldn't remember a single question. Not about the rooftop rescue, or stopping Stampede, or anything else. The fully grown-adult cougar stood in front of his idol and couldn't manage a single word. It was high school all over again. Lawful Neutral never missed a beat, though. She told the joke, and asked his name. The puma remembered how speech worked long enough to give her that at least.

Just not the name he used anywhere outside of his most trusted circles.

"To Jos: Anyone can be a hero!"

His heart sank at the memory now, a dull ache as he came back to the present.

"Yeah. Right. Except you, I guess." The vixen on the poster was just another thing on the pile of childish things he wanted to be over. He wanted to take it down, but somehow he just couldn't muster the strength. So he hid it, like so many other things in his life. Embarrassment ran rampant in his mind as the words echoed over and over again.

Why did he even tell her to sign it with that name?

Who was he trying to fool?

Jos, huh? That short for Josephine? Ever going to grow up, sissy?

It wasn't short for Josephine, but there was no use arguing when the internal tirade began.

His reflection appeared for an instant as he turned back to the monitor, pushing those thoughts back down where they belonged. The feline did his best to look like he knew what he was doing with his fur. His coat was cleaned and brushed, and the various neutral shades of brown smelled faintly of green apples and musk. An entirely inoffensive, and unremarkable odor. Not one he enjoyed, but it smelled appropriate for a grown man.

The rest of his outfit showed a similar concern with being clean and non-threatening: a baggy t-shirt with some logo or another, typically belonging to a well loved superhero. Formless loose jeans and battered sneakers he insisted were "classic" rounded out the ensemble.

Run of the mill from head to tail. Unobtrusive. *Comfortable.*

Clack.

Click.

Day in and day out, this was the routine: life in the call center! Another morsel to be fed into the corporate grinder, shilling protection plans for whatever fruit-flavoured company they were working with currently. Pear? Papaya? He honestly didn't care; it was shit he couldn't afford on the salary he was paid. However ... getting screamed at in text was preferable to the alternative, for sure...

He looked over his cubicle to the far side of the floor and spied the dead-eyed souls stuck on the phones, who winced every so often when a customer became ... what was the phrase management used?

"Extremely challenging and solution-oriented."

Yeah ... There were lower circles to hell, there, Alighieri ... Be thankful, hmm? You could be a disgraced former Hero.

The cougar had followed Heroes for his entire life, absolutely entranced by their tales, wondering desperately what it would be like to be them — to make a *difference*. But he seemed to keep falling for the ones that were fallible.

Weak.

Just. Like. You.

Click.

Instead, you're just a mountain lion, from the valley, with too much sway in your step.

Click.

Case closed.

Another customer who was finished typing in caps about their phone and how Joe was stupid, and not worth talking to. Paws rubbed at his bleary, moss-green eyes as if trying to physically shove the will to go on back into his soul. The sullen orbs were framed by an umber stripe across them, a mask.

What's one more at the end of the day, right? Certainly helped to hide the constant bags under his eyes.

"Yup. Time for lunch, before I try to surprise myself and see if the nets have been installed under the windows yet," he muttered as he stood and stretched, growling softly, the tone sort of lilting on the end, fingers splaying out, claws peeking for just a moment — before, remembering himself, he quickly slid them back into their sheaths. He cursed under his breath. The puma looked around his space and sighed softly.

Okay, good ... Everyone is too focused on being miserable to see. He looked down at this paw and shook his head.

Always have to be a weirdo, huh? You a fucking girl now? Fairy-ass bullshit — was it worth all the hassle?

The internal commentary was on a roll today. Like a special features track narrated by R. Lee Ermine, and his entire life was a blooper reel. As he walked towards the break room, paws buried in his pockets, "the hassle" of the previous weekend slunk, unwanted, to the forefront of his thoughts…

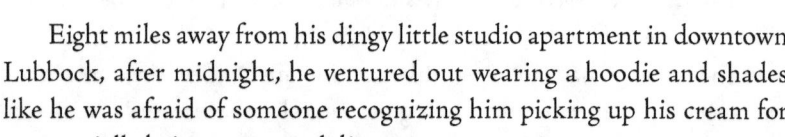

Eight miles away from his dingy little studio apartment in downtown Lubbock, after midnight, he ventured out wearing a hoodie and shades like he was afraid of someone recognizing him picking up his cream for an especially heinous venereal disease.

The doors slid open. The pneumatic hiss startled him, and he bit his tongue rather than let out a noise unbecoming of a big strong lion like him. He focused on his walk, striding with what he assumed was masculine confidence past the bored woman at the counter towards the rear of the drugstore.

Where the prize was enshrined.

On his way to the goal, he was stopped by the magazine rack as something caught his eye. His fingers brushed with something akin to gentle reverence on the glossy page.

He was already all the way out here…

No one knew him here.

No one cared.

Lizbette is on the cover … I mean, who's going to judge me?

He pulled the latest copy of *La Fashionista* off the shelf and resumed his beeline for the back. Sweat started to gather in his palms, looking from side to side like someone had just thrown a wrench into the carefully orchestrated heist. He knew which color he wanted, which brand, and where it was located. He had it planned out so perfectly…

Why did he have to grab the magazine?

Because the woman on the cover is absolutely stunning, and you've admired her for years.

A serval with a graceful neck and a beautiful round face, wearing a demure black dress. Lizbette's ears were adorned with several rings, as was her brow. A choker wound about her neck above her svelte shoulders, accentuating the line of her cream-colored throat to the plunging V-neck of the dress … The whole ensemble was perfection.

I wonder … what must that be like? To be so … so…

"*Fuck,*" he cursed silently as he let himself get distracted.

Effeminate gay bullshit.

What was he there for again?

Plumy Purple and a bottle of glossy topcoat.

He rolled the magazine around the spoils and strolled to the counter, doing his best to look casual. If anyone *was* watching, he was failing spectacularly. Each measured step was criticized in his mind, scrutinized completely.

Not on your toes. Back straight. Manly. Like you actually have a spine.

The catamount laid the loot on the counter; his eyes darted from the goods and to the clerk.

"It's for my girlfriend…" he uttered to the older collie at the register, who only barely glanced up from the propped-up phone beside the scanner to acknowledge his existence.

"Bag?" She snapped her gum loudly. "No gift wrap for your girlfriend, I'm afraid." She was likely only trying to be funny, but he couldn't hear that over the sound of the blood pounding in his ears as his entire body blushed under his fur.

"Oh, no thank you! Have a nice night…" the puma mumbled as he swept his spoils from the counter and into his hoodie pouch. He bound for his car as quickly as he could manage and flopped into the seat, holding the steering wheel so he could have something tactile to grip to bring him back to reality.

Deep breaths. You're a grown-ass adult. You can buy whatever you want. It's fine. Lots of grown men do this.

Nothing to be ashamed of…

Now there was just the lonely ride home, with his phone to guide him once more through the unfamiliar streets. He heaved a sigh of relief once he was on the road again and turned up the music, letting Bowie soothe his frazzled nerves.

David always made things better; his voice was a balm for the feline's soul.

"Don't let me hear you say life's taking you nowhere Angel…"

I bet David never let anyone give him shit about wearing nail polish … Hell, he used to walk around in a dress, all done up and looked beautiful! What even is gender anyway? What the fuck am I so afraid of? I mean … I'm

*not, like, trans or anything. Not that that's a **bad** thing, but I'm just not. I …
I just want to try a new look, no big deal!*

As he debated the merits of breaking free of masculine stereotypes
with himself, the cougar glanced at his rear view mirror. A car had pulled
behind him on the otherwise empty street. His eyes darted from the road
in front of him to the car now following closer by the second.

"Don't be a cop … No, no, no, please…"

The red and blue lights flashed and his heart, which had only just
recovered from the caper in the drug store, began to slam against his chest
again.

"*Fuck!* Fuck! Fuuuuuuck!" He howled as he slowly pulled over,
pounding his forearms on the steering wheel. "God damn it! I'm so
fucking *stupid! I can't believe how—*"

Knuckles on glass sounded like thunder.

"*Aieee!*" He nearly jumped out of his fur as he turned to see the face
peering into his window, forgetting himself in that instant.

Girly-ass scream Josephine. Like a scared kitten!

The officer seemed pleased with himself, his beak turned up into a
smirk as he motioned to the cougar to roll down his window.

"You alright, son? Lookin' a little jumpy! Something gotcha spooked?"
He leaned in close, talking down to Joe literally and figuratively. "Whatcha
doin' out this late? Dangerous neighborhood." His voice had a low drawl,
the kind you hear in a Waffle House at 2 AM. Unabashedly a good ole
boy without any sprinkling of a doubt who won the War of Northern
Aggression.

"I uh … I was just picking up some stuff f-f-for my girlfriend at the
CVS, sir." His claws dug into his palms gingerly as he attempted to act as
innocent as he could.

Oh god, oh god…

"Sure, sure … That time-a th'month, huh?" His hand came to rest
comfortably on his belt, drawing the cat's eye away from the badge of Sgt.
DePain to the holster, and the dull black object it held. "Where's that
accent from? Not from 'round here, I bet!" The rooster leaned in close,
flashlight held up now. Joe's shades mercifully helped, a little — at least,
until the cop slid them off his muzzle and tossed them into the passenger
seat.

"Ha, ha, ha, yeah, uh, that time … uh … N-New York … Albany …
sir." Joe did his best to sound confident and look the officer in the eye, but

the bright light had made his pupils into pinpricks and the officer into a dark blur.

Why was he doing this?

Just do what he says. He knows what's best.

The cop's voice suddenly became cold and hard. "Do you know why I pulled y'over?"

"Uh ... no? Was I going too fast or ...? I-I thought it was forty through here — I'm sorry — I just..."

"Nope. Thirty. Normally, I'd just letcha off with a warnin', but you're sweatin' an awful lot ... Lookin' real squirrely ... Maybe you've been drinkin'? Maybe smokin' some dope?" He stood back, wings folded across his chest.

The catamount could only stammer, eyes darting back and forth as this situation spiraled further and further out of control.

"Speak up, son!" the rooster snapped.

"N-no no! Not at all, sir!" All of the fur on the back of his neck stood as he stammered out the response. "I've never smoked anything before!"

"*Mmmhm* ... Step out of the car, *son*."

The cat had never heard the word "son" said in such an accusatory tone. The rooster was all business now, he had the cat pegged, and he was going to let him know *just* what he thought about a Yankee this deep in the heart of Texas.

Joe opened the door slowly and slid out of the car, his tail swaying in nervous agitation beyond his control.

"Paws on the roof, just like that." His breath was hot and stank like stale coffee, and he reeked of some flavour of body spray. Eau de bro — the scent instantly recognizable from any frat party. The cougar tried to recall the name of it to try and consider some sort of small talk before every thought was shoved from his mind. The cop slipped a foot between his own and pushed the cat's legs apart as he reached around, forcing his hand into Joe's hoodie pocket, lingering there longer than they needed to as he prodded and groped.

The puma shut his eyes tight as the officer of the law dug for whatever treasure he might find, his own claws scraping the roof of the car.

Don't you fucking cry, you faggot.

I'm not going to cry...

The magazine and bottles clattered on the hood, and the rooster got close again, but with his eyes shut tight, all the cat could do was be obedient — and try to control his shaking.

"Girlfriend, huh? You know what? I don't think you *have* a girlfriend ... Well, 'cept this, maybe." Those talons grasped at Joe's paw, thumb running over the pad. *"Real* soft ... and nail polish, too? Gotta make them pretty for your *man,* maybe?" DePain dropped the cougar's paw in disgust. *"Bet he likes that. Let's him pretend you're a* **real** *girl."* When the cat remained silent to the galling words, he pressed a gloved talon between his shoulder blades.

Why is no one helping me? The thought raced through Joe's mind over and over. *Someone ... Anyone ...* **Please...**

With a "playful" shove and a sudden crow of laughter, Joe's front slammed against the door of his car. "Man, fer a boy from up North, you sure don't talk much. Got an ID here, *kitten?"* the cop sneered. The lion nodded quickly, and went to slowly bring his hand to his pocket.

"Keep your hands on the fuckin' roof!" DePain screeched in his ear as he threw his quarry against the car, knocking the wind out of the catamount. Before he could recover, the officer's hand started rooting in his back pocket, giving his ass a squeeze for good measure.

"Joseph Greysbell, huh? Ya don't *sound* like a Joseph, though ... Sound like a *Josephine* t'me!"

He knows everything, Josephine ... He knows what you are.

The shaking intensified as a hundred unbidden images long past rushed to the forefront, and crashed like a wave against the catamount. It pummeled him into submission, shoulders hunched, and his tail had become a blur as all the feline's fur stood on end.

"I bet you like that, though, y'New *York Queer?* Do y'like it when a man talks t'ya like that? Treats you like the little *bitch* you are? I bet you do..." The claws that ran along his jawline felt like shards of glass scraping through his fur. It was all he could do not to pass out as every horror story he could have ever imagined suddenly became a distant second to the reality of that moment.

"N-n-n-no ... *Please...*" His voice breathed the softest whisper now, and tears squeezed from beneath his lids.

"What the *fuck* did you just say, *pussy cat!* Did you just say *'no'?"* Every word screamed louder than the last, and they caused the cat to flinch and shudder until his voice suddenly lowered to a deathly cool. "No bitch *ever* says no to me ... I'll show you your *place."*

This is it ... Just close your eyes ... You can make it through this...

Suddenly, there was a loud beep and static from behind them.

"**CALLING ALL UNITS!**" The cop's radio crackled, "**WE HAVE A TWO-ELEVEN IN PROGRESS! PINK AND BLACK SIGHTED! GETCHER ASSES T'JEFFERSON AND SECOND NOW! CAPES INBOUND FOR SUPPORT!**"

Joe froze. DePain's talons tightened on his jaw for a moment, then released. The bird sighed in disappointment, clacking his beak by the rounded ear of the feline, and dropped the wallet on the ground with a wet slap.

"Guess we'll have to finish this date some other time ... Them Korps trannies and fags are stirrin' up a mess of shit. See you around, *Kitten...*" His claws dug into the cougar's ass-flesh once again, eliciting a whimper from the cat before the door slammed shut behind him and the patrol car sped away, lights and sirens blaring and soon joined by a chorus following behind.

All he could remember after that was wracking sobs in the car, trying to process all that happened. He had to call someone! That had to be illegal! Why was he being treated like that? What did he do ... to deserve *that?*

Be honest, you probably wanted it anyway. The way you nearly moaned? Like you were in heat.

The tremors had become so bad he couldn't keep his hands on the wheel. Tears cut hot furrows into his fur, unable to be held back.

"I'm j-j-just being a pussy ... Nothing happened. No need to call and get anyone else involved..." he reasoned to himself in a whisper, but the logic didn't help.

Who would believe me, anyway? Who would I even call to begin with? The sobs did eventually turn to panting before stopping completely.

Twenty minutes passed before he could see well enough to drive again. Some tissues in the glovebox managed to help him stave the flow of snot from his nose, and his sleeves helped dry his face.

Yeah ... I'm ... I'm fine. This happens to other people too. I'm not special. I-it's my fault for driving too fast.

The ride home was completely silent save for the two glass bottles on the passenger seat tinkling a quiet song and the magazine, a crumpled mass beside them.

He had friends he spoke to online, but he couldn't mention what happened. The shame bubbled up in him like hot bile at the very idea. They knew something was wrong, but he refused to let them in.

How could he? How could they understand? He was just a cis boy ... He was *privileged*. What was a struggle for him, really?

"Oh no! The cop ... grabbed me..." *Big deal. I'm still alive, right? He didn't ... I ... It was my fault...*

Maybe he *did* deserve it.

The boiling hot shower didn't help him feel clean, so he settled on going to bed, but sleep wouldn't come.

When he closed his eyes, the terror just rushed back in.

I bet you like that, though, y'New York Queer? Do y'like it when a man talks t'ya like that? Treats you like the little bitch you are? I bet you do...

The smell of his breath.

The pressure of those fingers digging into him.

Joe spent the night staring at the ceiling until the sun came up.

He was late to work on Monday. He got written up for it, of course. He barely registered the lecture to be a professional and show up on time like everyone else, or he would have to look for employment elsewhere.

No one cared what had happened to him. Why should they?

Just another day in paradise.

As he dropped his bag on the couch when he came home, the bottles of polish sat untouched on the ratty old coffee table, and for a moment, he felt ashamed.

But ... Why? Why can't I just have this? The shame turned to indignance, and then anger; anger that he couldn't even have this one little thing...

I ... I can have this...

The mountain lion settled in, and with slow and unsure paws, he painted his claws for the very first time. Sure it wasn't perfect; there were a few stray droplets on his fur, and the brush marks were not as smooth as he would have liked, but he *did* it. He admired how they shined in the low light, and a sad smile crossed his muzzle.

I think it looks nice ... I can have nice things too ... right?

No one answered in the empty apartment.

Lizbette stared up from the magazine on the surface in front of him; her smile seemed almost encouraging, for a second. There was a moment he wished he could be her, instead of himself.

He wished he could just feel *right*, for just a *single* second.

Lots of people imagine what it's like to be someone else ... I'm not special.

He startled and snapped back to the here and now, his fugue brought to an end by the sound of water filling a vessel. He was in the bathroom, and he was breathing *heavily*. The sweat soaked through his shirt, and the piss splattered into the bowl beneath him, ringing against the porcelain.

His cheeks were hot, and wet.

Oh no ... was I crying? How ... Where am I?

The puma was just grateful for a moment that he was at least in the right space to relieve himself.

He was at work. Yeah, he was on break. He had to take a leak. Just daydreaming, that's all.

"Are you alright in there, hun? Bad news?" The voice came from the next stall over.

Gentle concern. Motherly even ... He recognized the voice from the last potluck: the older boar lady who brought the weird-ass potato salad with the raisins.

*What the fuck is Luanne doing in the **men's** room?*

Then it dawned on him, and he stifled a gasp.

Oh god damnit, OH SHIT, oh for fuck's sake!

She wasn't *in* the men's room. He was in the *women's* room.

Fucking PERVERT! Why did you go in there, huh?

They're going to call the cops! I can't ... no ... I ... He was going to start hyperventilating. This was how he would die: a weird creep who dropped dead of a heart attack the instant he was caught with his pants down in the ladies' bathroom.

"Nuh uh ... just a bad call," he whispered quietly, trying his best to sound as soft and feminine as possible, imitating the voice of someone who couldn't hurt a fly.

There was a long pause.

She didn't buy it.

I'm so fucked...

She was a sweet lady, but she would absolutely lose her mind if she realized there was anything with a dick in this bathroom.

"Oh, I know all about that, sugar. I'll leave you be," she replied, warmly.

Her toilet flushed, and then it was dead silent — except for the puma's heart, which was pounding a solo so loud he would have sworn it could be heard in the next building over, and the sound of Luanne's footsteps.

The sink ran for just a minute, the sound of sensible flats on tile, the door swung open, closed, and then there was quiet once again.

Blissfully safe *silence*.

He cleaned up as quickly as he could, peeked out the door, and slipped out into the empty hallway. The cougar prayed to simply make it through the rest of his day without another surprise catatonic episode. He skipped the noodles, spicy or otherwise; his appetite had long since left him.

He avoided any small talk between here and there, and he even spotted Luanne back at her desk and chattering to the girl next to her.

No one knew.

He was three minutes late back from lunch. Naturally, there was an email waiting for him. Another thinly-veiled threat to his tenuous employment, and a complaint about his lack of professionalism.

It never ends. I fucking hate it here so goddamn much...

He tried to focus again on the work at hand rather than seething about the lack of understanding — or even curiosity about *why* he was late — from his supervisors, to concentrate on anything but the throbbing pain where the cop had...

Nothing. The cop did nothing. I was acting suspicious ... He was just doing the right thing...

The last hours passed so slowly Joe could have sworn the clock had moved backwards. Case after case of useless people and their useless first-world problems. Even when he could help, they didn't care. They just wanted to use him like a punching bag.

He wasn't even a *person* to them.

Click. Click. Click.

The staccato rhythm of keys and mice filled the air. Customers and advisors doing their dance. A song he knew so well, and was so completely sick to death of.

As the day drew to a close, he flipped up that memo again and looked at the photo of LN, hoping to maybe have a moment's peace, but the sight of her beaming at him? The thought of her laughter? Where he once found comfort, there was only a mocking grin staring blankly back.

Empty.

Performative.

A *lie*.

He couldn't hold back the snarl, his lips curling as his Plummy Purple claws slashed through the paper, shredding the memory just like the memento, embittered by her betrayal.

"Anyone can be a *hero?*" he hissed under his breath, pushing himself up from his seat.

Just another Hero abandoning him. Just like Magella did. Just like *everyone* did eventually. The puma shook his head as he turned his back on remains of that foolish hope he clung to for too long.

Why would she be any different?

"No one cares ... and there are no *heroes.*"

CHAPTER 2

TOO BITTER TO SWALLOW

Just walk it off, you goddamn pansy! Get over yourself!

Joe didn't get over it, though. How does one get over something they refused to address? How do you even begin to approach something that felt so...

Violating.

Days turned into weeks. Home. Work. Home. Work. Home.

Never going out unless the sun was out as well led to long, restless nights. With less and less sleep, exhaustion had become the new normal, and he took to staring at the computer screen at home until sleep came. Recently, though, that could take days.

Luckily (or unluckily, depending on one's point of view), the catamount lived in the tiny studio by himself, so when he woke and when he slept didn't really matter. He made enough to afford it with his menial job, if only just. So long as he was smart and didn't have any superfluous or extravagant expenses. Things like eating out, and buying coffee from the little boujee spot! Or ... getting sick, or needing to see a therapist, things of that nature.

You know. Unnecessary luxuries, he groused internally with a sigh. He just continued living paycheck to paycheck, and paw to mouth: the great American Dream in action.

The coffee he made himself *was* cheap, though, and with enough cream, he could stomach it. He needed it so he could stay awake.

Sleep was when the voice became too loud to ignore.

When he could only hear his heart, and smell that stale breath.

Joe would spend these long nights lost on the internet, distracting himself roleplaying as a powerful warrior defending the weak in Realm of Wanderlust, an online fantasy RPG. A gigantic bastion of masculinity, and virility!

It ... It was *something.*

RoW kept his brain occupied, if nothing else. He used to love playing and chatting with his friends, but now? Now he had this secret he could never tell them, and he felt it driving a wedge between them. They knew *something* was wrong, but he didn't want to bother them with his own ... mess. Consequently, his already-solitary life became even more isolated.

Just like it always did. He *always* pushed them away when they got too close. Better that he not burden them at all, he winced.

JosCat
You have your own stuff to deal with, dear. I'll be just fine!
Promise!

He repeated that mantra *ad nauseum*, as much to comfort himself as them. They were in a far riskier space. They were *women*. They needed to be protected, not him! Some of them were AMAB and had even taken the steps to transition! His mind would turn that idea over and over at times, dwelling on it. What kind of strength did that take? To just ... *be* who you wanted to be? To live a life like that? He admired that about them.

So the mountain lion would change the subject, and the group would drop it, recognizing the need for space. There were dungeons to delve, and maidens to save after all! A whole world that wasn't this one that he could lose himself in, and if not that, he had other interests in common with his friends.

Besides RoW, there was tons of other stuff the group chatted about. Movies, books, toys, games; fandoms, sundry and various, popular and highly niche. Heroes and Villains however, were a consistent theme that touched all of those things. Discussion of who could beat who, who had the best or worst power set, who was the hottest — typical nerd fare that frequently escaped the message board threads and into the group's chat. Any disagreements that couldn't be resolved through vigorous debate were settled through HeroClash , a darling of the fighting game community, with a roster made up of actual heroes and villains ripped straight from the headlines.

Joe's most common hill to die upon, until very recently, was that Lawful Neutral could take on any villain.

"Her powerset is so versatile! She has an answer for anything and everything!"

This translated into the *Punderful One* being an incredibly complicated character that took time to really master. He'd been a big part of the campaign to get her included in the game to begin with, so it was no surprise that he was obsessed with being the best LN he could be.

Until he wasn't anymore.

Briskette
back to Magella? what happened to the demivixen?

JosCat
I'm tired of getting fucking looped by every fucking Redline player.

Briskette
I mean at least it's accurate to life? ;D

JosCat
Whatever. Can you just pick the big bitch, and get it over with?

Briskette
eager to get rekt?

JosCat
Lots of fuckin' talk before we've even gone a round.

Briskette
…whoa. who shit in your cornflakes?

JosCat
Just pick the Magenta Menace, and we'll see who shits on who.

The fact that his friend group was mostly some flavor of queer (or queer-allied, like he was) meant that the subject of the Korps came up with some regularity. How could it not? The villainous element was loud and proud about what they stood for, so of course there was sympathetic talk, even if they *were* the bad guys. In the past, the lion caught himself getting worked up when the subject did arise, but had been able to disengage and shrug it off. Recently, though, the cougar seemed to take any mention of them more personally than before…

Especially when it was related to the fox and the wolf.

That night, the discussion felt a little *too* sympathetic for his liking, and every voice cheering on Redline made him more anxious. They didn't know he was nearly shaking, of course. He didn't want to talk about it, *couldn't* talk about it. Instead, all he could do was grit his teeth and focus on the situation at hand.

I'll show them what a real Hero can do…

The cougar played sloppy, making a dozen simple mistakes. Magella was a character built on tricks, and required careful timing. His impatience showed his hand early, telegraphed each step, and made avoiding or countering a simple matter. When he did manage to confirm, he dropped combo after combo, his shaky paws hesitating.

His *weakness* let the wolf *dominate* the rabbit.

The villainess sneered as she leaned in, grabbing the camera, and licking her lips. "You didn't stand a chance ... I'm just too. *Much*."

Briskette

want a run back, silly rabbit?

Joe barely managed to jam his finger against the mute button of his headset before the yowl of frustration bubbled up from his chest. He dropped his controller on the desk and stalked away from the computer ... until he was yanked back by the cord and nearly fell over.

He screeched, pulling the plug from the PC unceremoniously, before screeching loud enough for the neighbors to hear. "Fuck! *Fuck! **Fuck!** Fuckin' stupid!* **Fuck!** I can't *believe* I keep *losing* to that *fucking ... **stupid...**"

What? What is "she"? Say it. Criminal? Whore? Tranny? Pick one, she's all of them ... and you don't care, do you?

Stop ... please...

You LIKE it. Fucking freak. You're JEALOUS, aren't you? Wanna be a little fruity little fucking faggot just like them! Just like your little friends!

Just. Like. Her.

The puma instantly regretted the reaction and pushed the heels of his palms into his eyes, letting out a dejected moan just this side of a sob. He sniffed loudly, shaking his head before muttering out a half-hearted, "Fuck her..."

If he was honest with himself, he resented them. *All* of them. Heroes, villains, cops. Everyone with power who chose to waste it ... or worse still, *abuse* it.

He resented them for being weak.

He resented them for taking Magella and Lawful Neutral from him.

He resented them for just taking *anything* they wanted.

He resented them for simply *being.*

Why didn't *they* have to obey the rules?

Why do *they* get to be whoever they wanted to be?

Why do they get to be happy ...?

Happy being what? A queer? Some kind of gender-confused nutjob? You're a man! You're not anything special! Fucking nut up, and act right!

To be happy with himself? Well, that would take more strength than Verdauga the burly leonine barbarian could possibly summon, let alone Joe (or *Jos*)…

Whoever.

Sometimes, though, when everyone else went to bed, he would let himself go through making a new character on RoW — and that night, he was feeling particularly sorry for himself.

He chose the lioness model and just sat there, carefully inching sliders and adjusting features…

Not some sort of delicate flower, but still soft and caring.

A fighter, cunning and tenacious, with light fingers and a devil-may-care smile.

Stealing hearts and saving the downtrodden.

She could be strong too, you know? In her own way…

Finally, after every inch was sculpted, a name needed to be chosen, and the same one always came, a name that begged to be whispered. He didn't know why that name — it just felt *good* in his muzzle: *Mabel Greysmoke.*

A thief, a rapscallion even, but a *hero* nonetheless. A name fit the fantasy of the game at the very least…

The cursor hung like the sword of Damocles, but he could never bring himself to actually click "Create." His paw hovered and shook before quickly closing the program, embarrassment running hot beneath his fur.

He knew the line that most guys would give, leering or snickering all the while:

"If I'm gonna be staring at somebody's ass for hours at a time, you better believe I'm picking a big, bouncy bitch booty."

He rolled his eyes, shaking his head at the thought. It wasn't that the cougar didn't understand or identify with the *concept* of liking women; women were gorgeous, lovely, mysterious creatures, and he did admire their shape and poise — he wasn't *gay*. But he felt disingenuous, somehow, when he thought about playing as one. Like a complete imposter, to even consider being … *playing*, he meant, mentally correcting the thought…

How could I convincingly roleplay a woman? I couldn't! I'd just do some stupid guy shit and embarrass myself, or worse yet, make the girls feel awkward or unsafe … I … I don't want to be an unsafe person…

No, it was better to not tread there at all and be sure he wouldn't make a gigantic ass of himself.

All guys have to ponder this situation at some point, he would tell himself. *Of course they do … I'm not special.*

But most guys felt nothing at all when they walked away from those female avatars.

The cougar couldn't stop thinking of *her* and was wracked with the guilt of imagining the impossible.

Don't be a fucking girl, Josephine. Toughen up.

That voice was so loud these days, it almost drowned out his fear. How could he be scared of anything else when he was busy being terrified of himself?

How could he tell it to stop calling him that *awful* name?

Home. Work. Home. Work. Home.

The cougar watched over his shoulder constantly, now, and he could have sworn there was a police cruiser that kept showing up in his neighborhood. The same one, just circling. He could smell that *scent*, that cheap body spray, cloying in his sensitive nostrils. Lurking in his hallway…

Just out of sight.

He felt parts of himself unraveling. He had always been *different*. A little too *soft*, a little too *emotional* … a little too *queer*. The cat spent most of his life trying very hard *not* to be, or at the very least to be as unobtrusive as possible. He'd struggled with every relationship he'd ever had; he loved them, but he always grew too distant, felt too strange. The need to run grew from his intense self-awareness of those flaws…

That was why Joe always pushed his friends away. The cougar would try to stay in touch, but he couldn't be there for them. He even tried moving across the country to try and have a fresh start, and give himself the best chance of becoming someone better. But it didn't matter.

Every last romantic relation imploded, entirely because of his shortcomings.

So there the puma was, alone, *again*, when all he wanted was to just be *normal*. Instead, he grew more isolated as all of these things piled up precariously, different shapes and sizes swaying slowly, always moments from crashing down upon him. At night he would lay alone, head swimming with anxiety and guilt, and just beg for sleep to come. Just for a moment of silence, a moment of *peace*. But when it really came down to it, when he ached for rest that remained just out of reach, his loneliness would grow greater than his disgust for himself.

He would turn out all the lights, and just feel his paws pressing, caressing...

Making little quiet noises as he stroked, hips rolling up to meet his paw. Paw pads tracing the ridges and barbs of his throbbing flesh. His mind would begin to race, and his eyes would shut as he thought about those things that caused his blood to thrum in his veins.

He hated how *good* it felt. His shame gnawed at him, but he couldn't stop.

He kept the lights off. It was easier in the dark, when he couldn't see himself, and didn't have to confront quite as much *reality*. His mind could wander, and on this night, it drifted back to the crumpled magazine on his bedside table.

To *her*.

The serval was there. Lizbette, in her long dress, her chest swaying slightly as she moved, eyes locked on his. No shame. No ... *revulsion*.

Her long, golden locks framed her beautiful muzzle. There was no hatred of herself or her body. Just warmth, and assurance.

Her paws squeezing his chest, her breath smelling sweet like cinnamon, and something he couldn't recognize, but so strong he could taste it on his tongue as they embraced. Her knees squeezing his suddenly too wide hips. A claw running down between his breasts, no. Wait.

Her breasts.

Jos's breasts. Jos's soft fur, rubbing against hers. Her voice was honey smooth, and needy. Jos's cock enveloped in the warmth of her muzzle as the serval looked up, murmuring before enveloping her head once again.

No...

Jos was serving her. She felt that throbbing length pressing into her ... her...

"*Such a good girl ... So beautiful...*" the serval cooed as her claws ran down Jos's back.

Her words filled the puma with what she could only perceive as *joy*. The joy of simply being. Being someone else, but not.

He cried out softly, the heat peaking and his paws shaking as he spilled his seed across his legs and sheets. His violet claws dug deeply into the bedding as he was suddenly alone again. *There* again. Back in the real world.

Still himself. Unchanged.

The shame and confusion returned in equal measure as the lion laid there panting, the ropes of hot cum cooling quickly as they pooled under his thighs. His eyes clamped tight as the fantasy disappeared like so much wispy vapor.

The cougar's forearm covered his eyes as he began crying once again, hot and wet, failing to choke it back. He bit his lip, trying to stop himself from sobbing out loud. The sound of his own ragged voice making it so much worse.

You're a fucking disgrace...

This wasn't the first time this had happened. *Those* images.

Those thoughts.

Why does this keep happening?

You should be ashamed of yourself, you fucking pervert.

Why did he need that? Why couldn't he just be normal? Why couldn't he just be...

A man.

After the tears, sleep would come. His dreams would be troubled, indistinct, and wreathed in hazy smoke, forgotten with the morning light.

Home. Work. Home. Work. Home.

JosCat

I'm sorry I dipped the other night ... I've just been stressed at work you know? I don't want to be alone.

He caught himself before he sent the message, lest he let that dam break, and the flood of emotion threatened to ruin everything. He couldn't let that happen. Not in this place, this *one place* where he could be so much more *himself*. He didn't want their pity.

JosCat

I'm sorry I dipped the other night ... I've just been stressed at work you know? How are you all tonight?

The gang played their games; they had their idle chat. The cougar had just begun to let his guard down when the group started sharing pictures snapped of superheroes on the job, and then along came a picture of that *fucking* wolf.

She was a rising star of the Korps. The voltaic villainess, bane of the TPA and Heroes everywhere: *Redline.*

The lupine was an absolute *menace* according to every local news outlet, and Joe was *well* aware of why, given her association with his former hero. After all, if you really want to know a Hero, you have to know their arch-nemesis as well. Following the antagonistic rivalry between a cape and a crook was how you got to see the whole picture. Magella had Questionnaire, True North II had Colonel Clue, and Lawful Neutral had Redline.

Impossibly attractive Redline.

The mountain lion had never allowed himself to acknowledge *how* beautiful she was. But anyone with a pulse could see it — and hell, a pulse was likely optional.

How could he claim to be Lawful Neutral's biggest fan — regularly vying with his online buddy Luke for that title, even — and think of her as anything but another villain? This behemoth lupine had defeated LN in every bout, not necessarily without effort, but the demifox was oh for … well, all *six dozen* recorded bouts.

Close, in fact, did not count when it came to the wolf.

Clearly, this amazon … she was something more than the usual big, bad girl the Korps seemed to keep finding. She *had* to be special to best his favorite time and time again.

"Ugh…" The cat *wanted* to be indignant but struggled to find the will.

Redline posed with her mouth open, drool glistening along her tongue and lips, spilling down towards the titanic swell of her chest. Every cord of muscle was hidden beneath plush soft fur. The sneer on her face screamed "predator." He could almost hear the creak of her leather jacket as she flexed and leaned close, could see the helices emblazoned on it in the same shade of rosy pink as her goggles. All of it was illuminated with a crackling crawl of magenta lightning enrobing her limbs.

He felt that shame again as he stared at the black sclera of her eyes under that visor. She seemed to gaze into and *through* the puma. Jos's head tilted slightly as he stared in a manner that was anything *but* respectful, unconsciously nibbling his lip.

How have I never noticed her eyes before …?

The friend who posted it quickly removed it and apologized, not wanting to upset Jos again.

Getting hard for the enemy? She's a killer, remember? Fucking disgusting.

Shut up.

He heaved a heavy sigh and rubbed at his eyes. Korps or not, there was no denying this; Redline was *stunning* in all meanings of the word.

Maybe that's why LN finally defected … I mean … Who wouldn't? If … If they could have…

JosCat
Oh! Uh, don't worry about it. I mean … She is super hot right? Ha ha

There was some nervous laughter and the conversation pressed onward. More pinups, but they were careful not to bring up the Korps again. It was too late, though; the cougar's mind was already driven to distraction.

The rest of the night went as it always did. By four o'clock he was alone again, his friends having said goodnight and logged off, one by one; they all had obligations in the morning, and needed to sleep. For his part, he was still agitated, and hesitated to be left to his own thoughts; that could quickly become dark, so diversions were needed. Fortunately, he nodded sagely to himself, these were *prime* hours for online learning. He sipped his coffee — now long cold — and considered what to do as the mostly-cream concoction touched his tongue.

"Korps … history…"

The wiki article that popped up read like a sermon from an old-timey Baptist preacher, fairly dripping with figurative fire and brimstone, and the cougar managed about two paragraphs before he thought his eyes were going to roll out of his head. He began to skim ahead, and…

INVADERS FROM THE FROZEN NORTH!
THE PINK MENACE!
REDLINE MURDERS IN COLD BLOOD!

His eyes grew wide, and his stomach turned a little. There she was … standing over the still smoking husk that was once a person. A Hero of some renown, as a matter of fact. He continued forward, uncomfortable in new and somehow-exciting ways.

And here she was. The demimorphic vixen with her bright smile and her Day-Glo costume, just like he remembered her, arms thrown around her teammates Can D and Laserdisc. He could almost hear her bubbly midwestern laugh, and it made his heart sink. Despite the happiness depicted in the photo, the caption read like an epitaph, with a link to a local article detailing the incident.

Kidnapped and corrupted Hero Lawful Neutral (center)

He went further down that rabbit hole, as if he hadn't read dozens of articles already — as if he hadn't obsessively pored over each and every line to find any hint, any ... *miniscule* hope that she wasn't ... that she was still...

His hero.

It was the same information as when he'd last looked, weeks ago, and the comments section was ... well, to call it toxic would be like calling Chernobyl a "little whoopsie-daisy." It was a string of absolutely vitriolic and vile *hate*. There was no other description for the comments:

GraceNGuns

THESE WHORES R TAKING OVER! OPEN YOUR EYES SHEEPLE!

HalMcCray81

THIS IS ALL BECAUSE WE TOOK THE CHURCH OUT OF THE SCHOOLS!!!

PastorFreedom

COPS SHOULD KILL ALL OF THESE LESBOS, SHEMALES AND FREAKS ON SIGHT

Each was worse than the last, and all had dozens of upvotes; every avatar a picture of a cross, a middle-aged man in wraparounds, or just a fucking gun. It would seem satirically over-the-top had they not been completely, deathly serious, an echo chamber of hate screaming disgusting abuse in all directions. It all read like a Thanksgiving dinner with that uncle who would have a little too much to drink and go mask off.

But there was a single comment not written in all caps.

ReadyChooseGrow

Educate yourself, or remain in the dark. Things have got to change.

A sissy sympathizer? Do us all a favor, and swallow a bullet...
Shut up.

He rubbed the bridge of his muzzle, sighing softly.

The article was a small-town news outlet, so the webmaster *clearly* didn't moderate what was said. The cougar moused over the word "change," and clicked.

It led to a subreddit — r/Korps — and what was touted as "the truth."

Jos admittedly didn't feel like he was getting the truth elsewhere, and he was still *shaken* in his views from his most recent experiences, to put it lightly. He worried, too, that if he tried to sleep, he didn't know what would come.

His mind flashed to Redline's piercing gaze — framed by those ever-present goggles — and his face flushed again, beet-red under sandy colored cheek fluff.

He was going to figure out what he knew now. What was the truth? It couldn't be any worse than the reality he was stuck in.

Just a buncha fuckin' propaganda, Josephine!

*That is **not** my name.*

The lion's eyes were shut tight, and his face twisted in a half-snarl as he argued with no one, the noise pounding in his ears in a room that was silent save for the hum of the computer.

He took a deep breath.

Keep going.

Then, a long exhalation.

Good.

The blush came rushing back as he shook his head. What was he doing? He was just *reading*, he told himself. *Researching.* And so he read. Articles, blogs, commentary:

LOCAL HERO EXPOSED IN LURID SEX
TRAFFICKING SCANDAL
PROMINENT SENATOR FOUND GUILTY OF
ACCEPTING BRIBERY
HERO TRAINING FACILITY INVESTIGATED DUE
TO VIOLENT METHODS
THE KORPS: MORE THAN VILLAINS

There was page upon page of eyewitness accounts, phone recordings, discussions regarding the actual impact of the organization, and the people that were a part of it. Information that didn't line up with what he'd seen in the media. Information that had been withheld ... or maybe something even more sinister. The puma wasn't naive, but it *couldn't* all be the real story, he was *sure* of it.

But if even *one* of those things was true ... what did that really mean?

The cougar's paw stopped, before he opened the essay penned by someone named V.

More Than Words

"I'm trying to be more direct, so I'll just come out and say it: Before I had ROSE to help, I was going to die."

"There's no easy way to describe it to someone who doesn't understand what it's like to be a stranger in your own body. I'm a trans woman, and for the first nineteen years of my life I had no one I could open up to about that. I was trapped, and the only way I could see myself surviving was to bury it — which I wasn't good at — until I was finally living independent of my family."

It could have just been about *him.*

"I didn't know how long that would take, but I thought, naively, that I could make it happen quicker if I just kept my head down and ignored how awful I felt about myself. It was slowly killing me. There is no universe I can imagine where, before ROSE, I actually got out from under my parent's thumb and made things work long enough to live the way I wanted to. I was barely prepared for the world, I couldn't handle myself. Shit, I could barely get a sentence out around anyone I didn't know; I was a mess waiting to catch on fire."

"ROSE saved me. She gave me what I needed to not only survive, but *thrive.*"

Pathetic. "She" sounds just like you. Deluded. A waste. Why would anyone help misfits like you? Out of the goodness of their heart? Come on...

Stop.

So fucking naive, it's just an advertisement. It's. Not. Real.

Stop it.

"Can you imagine living your entire life in static? Like you can't think, can't talk, can't even *feel* anything without it all getting muddled? Like it all feels like you're trying to do it with your head held underwater? I have. It's excruciating, and if I hadn't gotten a pair of RCGs I would still be like that, assuming I would still be alive."

"So, what if there were someone there to help — to tune out the static, and finally give you peace of mind? A clarion to understanding?"

Everyone has it tough, Josephine. Some magic goggles aren't going to fix the kind of fuck up you are.

SHUT UP! They helped her ... m-maybe ... I could feel like...

Before the voice could manage another cutting reply, he finished the next line.

"To feel like yourself instead of a stranger in your own body?"

My ... self.

The page closed with a reflexive, quiet click before the puma could read another word. Before he could hear another word, spoken aloud inside his head, in a voice that sounded like...

He was breathing heavily again, panting, and ... crying? He touched a paw to his face and wiped away the tears as he shook his head. He glanced at the window; the light that streamed under the shade signaled that yet another night had passed him by.

"I guess I'd better go shower ... I have work in a few hours," he murmured to himself, standing, and plodded to the bathroom.

He showered in the dark again. His tears mingled with the warm water, so he could ignore them.

He got dressed. Each shapeless garment felt like it weighed hundreds of pounds.

He poured a cup of coffee on his way out the door, and only then realized he was out of cream.

He looked into the bitter darkness and poured it down the drain.

"I'll just get something at work."

Home. Work. Home. Work. Home.

JosCat

*Uh no. I'm not going to be around tonight, sorry gang! Yes
I'm fine I just have a single player thing I want to jump into!*

Feline paws rested nervously on the keys as he considered, and then began typing, each stroke a deliberate step echoing in a long hallway somewhere he'd never been allowed previously.

Jos was wandering in illicit spaces, places that he should not be, even if only by his own self-asserted code. In spite of the moral quandary, or maybe *because* of it, a little thrill climbed up his spine and the smallest smirk flitted across his muzzle as he stared at the URL.

Thorntech.com

Welcome to Thorntech, world leaders in augmented-reality personal assistance devices. How can ROSE help you?

"I ... I'm allowed to have nice things."

CHAPTER 3

To Be Seen

Thank you for your purchase! ROSE will be with you soon!

He stared at the message in the email every day, as if the words were going to change. Like this fleeting hope for understanding would simply *disappear* if he glanced away for more than a moment.

Each day went much the same as it had before, as he held tightly to that sliver of hope. He would grit his teeth through the work day on little more than an hour of sleep and a comically large mug of coffee and cream, or surround himself with an ever-growing pile empty cans of some extra-caffeinated energy drink; he would then return home, check and re-check the delivery status, and distract himself as best he could.

You'll still be you. Weak. Effeminate.

*Being **effeminate** does not make you weak. Being **yourself** does not make you weak.*

He didn't have to be alone. He could *be* who he wanted to be.

He could be *enough.*

It didn't take long to arrive, really — less than a week, though it felt like years — and the cost was more than reasonable. If it could do everything V had claimed? It would be worth every penny, and more.

A loud knock at the door snapped the lion out of his thoughts, and panic seized his chest as he held his breath. After what seemed like an eternity, the sound of soft footsteps padded down the long hallway. His phone buzzed at him, and a notification popped up:

Your package was left at the door!

Relief rushed through him as he scrambled for the doorway. After he slid the deadbolt and unlocked it he glanced left and right — being sure the hall was empty — before looking down.

There it was. His *chance.* No person to disappoint with his weakness. A companion that would not judge him.

A hope for release.

The cougar picked up the parcel with shaky paws, the door closing quickly behind him, and slid down it to the floor. He wrapped his arms around the package, closing his eyes as he held the box to his chest, and embraced it like a long-lost loved one.

The package was discreet, completely unmarked, save his name and address. It was impossible to properly describe, but it felt *alive* in his fingertips. He laid his cheek against it and sighed softly.

"Jos Greysbell…" He managed a weak smile as he traced the spartan mailing label with freshly painted claws. It wasn't the full name, but it was the second time in his life he had received anything physical with *his* name.

His *chosen* name.

He closed his eyes again, drumming his fingers along the sides nervously with renewed anxious energy. What if it was all bullshit? Or worse … what if he just became some sort of mindless slave? On his knees, worshiping at some carnal altar, bedecked in chains and writhing bodies? Everything the news said happened in their lairs; the drugs, the orgies, the debauchery, that he blushed to think of.

Thorntech wasn't *officially* linked, of course, but it was obvious, really. The Korps had to get the goggles from somewhere.

Eh … There were worse ways to go, right? the puma thought with a nervous smirk, attempting to muster all the bravado he could.

Just handing yourself over to them? Pussy-whipped or cock-locked? Fucking pathetic either way, Josephine. Weak. Like always.

He bit his lip so hard he nearly drew blood, his heart thudding in his chest. His eyes opened as he looked down at his reprieve from those thoughts.

*You deserve good things. You **deserve** to be happy.*

"I d-deserve … good things," he whispered, so softly only his ears could hear it. His ears, and the contents of the box, he imagined. *ROSE*. All he had to do was open the box, to let her into his life, and maybe she…

…Maybe she could save him, too.

He drifted back, thinking about the night he finally chose to take the leap. The night that he stopped letting his fear hold him in place.

Earthy green eyes stared at the monitor. Not like while he was at work, just skimming for anything that could catch his eye, but in rapt attention. He had taken to trawling the r/Korps threads after everyone was in bed, as a part of his nightly ritual.

He wasn't going to sleep, anyhow. He might as well use the time to educate himself. He cycled through the pages and pages of discussions and theory and ... more illicit images of the women of the Korps. The image of Redline sparked the cat's curiosity, but rather than killing him, it was satisfaction that kept him coming back for more. *And more, there always was.*

Jos found himself returning to one particular photoset, over and over again. It was of a familiar serval who served a *look* in leather and lace, a large cigar burning between her lips (or smoldering in her gloved paw), and a dripping pink cock hanging between her plush thighs. She was just so beautiful. How could anyone not see that? He shifted in his seat and bit his lip.

She was Lizbette "Betty" Kallist, he had come to learn, a dominatrix with boundless confidence; somehow existing in both worlds, and no one questioned it. He followed suit, simply accepting the fact that she just *was*.

*She's **everything** she wants to be. God, I wish I could, I mean, I wish I ... what is that even **like**? To live ... that truth?* His fingertips pressed to his lips, before he clicked away.

There was a moment of shame again, as he dwelled too long on the idea. He blushed before carefully minimizing those tabs for the "entertainment" portion at the end of the evening and pressed onward into less lascivious territory.

There had been no news about Lawful Neutral recently, but the Korps were front and center of the True Crime sites, as always.

"Another robbery ... Another DDOS, suspected to originate from somewhere in Canada ... Another data leak..." He furrowed his brow, bringing his runny eggs and rice to his muzzle, and shoveling some into his maw. The steaming pile of jammy amber sunnysides, buttery white grains and red tomato sauce hardly *looked* appetizing — it barely looked edible, in fact — but tasted great to the lion anyway.

But then, he always had liked eggs.

"They've been at this *forever*, but like ... what's the *angle*? You'd think a group that's so well organized would have made a play for control of a small country by now at the *very* least..." He mused aloud to the empty room, licking the ketchup and runny yolk from his lip. "Guess if the media is right, they already have control of most of Canada…"

Jos tapped his fork on the edge of the bowl, clucking his tongue as his mind wandered around the timeline as he understood it.

"They have left bloody footnotes in the history books, time and time again, all the way back to the fifties … that's just what's *attributed* to them though…" A certain more recent incident involving a prominent hero meeting a grisly end came to mind, and made the puma pause, as he stared into the messy pile of protein and carbs. "Probably more, if I was guessing. I just don't get it … If they're willing to murder for their cause, clearly they're *motivated*. Why wouldn't they just … go for it?"

He snorted softly, shaking his head. "I mean, they probably *can't*, but like … what the fuck is the *point* of it all then if they're *not* trying to take over the world?"

A sardonic smile crossed the cat's muzzle. "Can't fuck it up any worse than we have…"

Is that what you want? To just have them win? What about everything those Heroes fought for? Died for?

No! I just … I don't…

The catamount's family had always chafed at his "liberal" streak. He and his father, in particular, had butted heads countless times over his views, but in the end he always relented, and let the old man have the last word. Like a good, obedient son. *Honor thy father*, and all that nonsense.

He snorted softly at the memory, and he was instantly twenty-two again, jaw set tight and ears slicked back with aggravation. He was once again fresh out of college, and ready to have an opinion all his own. The cougar allowed himself a bitter chuckle at the memory.

"Criminals deserve everything they get! They're like wild animals; they need to be put down!"

"But studies show that social programs and assistance do more to cut criminal activity than any police action, investment in the community is a much better use of public funding, and…"

"Look, you don't know what they're really like. You're a bleeding heart, and they take advantage of that. These assholes from up north? The Korps? Buncha freaks. They'll kill ya and fuck the corpse. Need to be tough to deal with them! Can't be soft like True North's kid! Won't be long before they head even further South, though, and then they'll see what real heroes can do."

"…Right. Sure, Dad."

"I know I'm right. You'll figure it out someday, or maybe you won't. Won't be because I let you off easy!"

Every "discussion" he could remember before leaving home had been variations on the theme. The puma had always managed to just swallow that his father was probably right…

Heroes do good things, and villains do bad things, it was that simple in the end.

And then … *it* happened.

Now it wasn't so easy. Cold sweat still made his paws clammy, any time he thought about that night. Jos shook his head as if his memory were an Etch-A-Sketch, and he wanted a clean slate.

Yeah, except Heroes are fallible. One wrong decision away from being … just as bad … **worse** *in some cases…*

Turns out nothing radicalized quite like first-hand experience.

He unclenched his jaw and kept scrolling, refusing to give the phantom voice of his father any more of his time or attention, and turned back to the news.

Photo File: Lawful Neutral completely decimated by Redline in local high school gym

He recalled this fight like it was earlier that day. The rubber pun was such a clever idea — until Redline turned LN into a buxom bouncy ball. The feed cut out on the third or fourth ricochet, but Jos could only imagine how *disorienting* that was. Regardless of the rumors about what happened during the blackout - that LN had gotten lodged in the bleachers, launched out a window, or blinded by two *incredibly* severe black eyes - it ended as all the rest of their battles had: Lawful Neutral *lost*.

"I wonder if that was the last straw? Just … can't beat 'em, join 'em?" The cat rubbed at his eyes. The footage of LN throwing herself again and again at the sneering mountain that was the red wolf used to make him angry, but also *fiercely* proud.

She would *never* give up.

Until she did.

These beacons that he put his hope into failed him every. Single. Time. At least the wolf was *genuine* in her convictions.

The murderer and the traitor. He pushed his bowl away, suddenly having lost interest in any more food, the weight at the pit of his stomach more than filling. Assigning them labels, *either* of them, felt wrong. He instantly regretted the accusation.

I ... I clearly don't have the whole story. What would I have done, anyhow? She had to have her reasons, right?

All of it at once was too much. He desperately wanted to think of something else.

Anything else.

"More Than Words"

There it was again. The essay by V.

Maybe it was too much right now ... but ... he needed to not be bitter and angry. Was sad and confused better? No.

But it was *different*, and he absolutely needed to be *anything* else, even for a little while.

"I was spending so much of my time struggling to be the person I had to be to get through things. ROSE gave me room to breathe, so I could decide who I wanted to be, and helped me make it happen. Every step of the way, she was there, picking me up when I fell down, holding my head above the water. No one had ever done that before, aside from my girlfriend. Did I mention I have one now? Would you believe me if I told you ROSE helped that happen, too?"

"The RCGs and ROSE helped me navigate my confusion and depression. I was born a boy, but I never felt like I was anywhere close to right. Like, I was never able to actually SEE myself ... until ROSE finally pulled me up and helped me look properly. I haven't had that static in my head in almost a year, and I have ROSE to thank for that. Well, her and the people she helped me introduce myself to."

"I guess it should go without saying that she also had a hand in me writing this. I never was one for essay writing in high school, but here she is, making sure I know what I want to say, and how to say it. You don't have to believe me. If you made it past the first sentence and believed it, you're who this essay is for."

"I know what you've been through, I know how much it hurts, but I promise ROSE can make things better. More than better, fuck, she can make you whole. She can help you feel like a real person, the person you should have been to begin with. I know you're afraid, it can be so hard to take the first step, especially if the people you're supposed to be able to trust punished you for it. Managing that fear on my own was impossible, but I didn't have to do it alone, and you don't have too either."

"ROSE taught me that all I had left to lose was my fear. She helped me free myself from it. I guess that's all she does — she helps you find yourself, and gives you the strength and confidence to finally start the life you always should have had."

"Become who you want to be."

~V

He made it to the end this time.

Each feeling she shared was one he had. It was as if she was speaking directly to him. The fear, the confusion, the self-loathing ... this trans woman could have been describing Jos. But that last line ... that was what struck him deepest.

Become who you want to be.

The line echoed through Jos's mind as he powered off the monitor and walked across the studio, flopping onto the unmade mattress with a soft thud. He slipped his paws behind his head and stared up at the stucco, tracing the patterns as he digested both his dinner and the words he had read.

Glad she's happy ... hope I can figure out how to be happy someday, too. He sighed deeply, the conflict over everyone else forgotten as he dwelled on what this all meant to him.

Who he was.

If he identified with V. Felt the same as she did...

You're you. That's enough.

He couldn't resist the warmth of the bed, and he fell asleep early that night — early for him, anyway.

His sleep was fitful, filled with confusing dreams of alien feelings, sensations, again wreathed in hazy vapor. Just snatches of moments that never happened, but god, she wished they would. She could feel her lips wrapping around a cigar darker than sin, and the smoke filling her muzzle was warm and rich. Plumes of smoke rising up as paws caressed her every curve, back arching as she felt the heat well up inside of her, so desperate to be set free.

As the sun came out, the taste lingered on her lips, much like his excitement lingered on his sheets. He closed his eyes and could swear he could smell cinnamon and fine tobacco dancing about the sweat and musk.

The shame rolled over him, but was quickly silenced.

You're not dirty. You're hurting no one. You're allowed to exist.

For the first time in a long time after waking up, tangled in his own mess, he smiled and even let out a little chuckle.

Looks like it's laundry day.

His phone was off.

The away message was up.

All he had to do was take the next step.

Jos sat on the edge of the ratty secondhand couch, staring at the parcel on his thirdhand modular Swedish coffee table, now opened, its contents revealed. A small black and silver box, quite elegant really, with a window to look inside and see the treasure within.

Not a single helix to be found, just beautiful magenta-hued glasses.

"Of course there wouldn't be ... this isn't for them." The words came, as if to assuage his still lingering doubts. The puma slid his claw along the edge, shearing the seal, the contents slipping out in a neatly folded tray. He had purchased the entry grade model — Mark III? IV?

He bought the ones with the best reviews. It also helped that he thought they looked...

Cute?

A digit carefully traced the edge of the frame, pink-hued glass staring back up at him, and he couldn't help but smile a little. A single lens, angled at the edges in a very cat eye sort of way, and molded for his broad muzzle with curved arms to keep them in place. Very retro-future-chic.

Nestled in the same tray were all the accoutrements to get set up, including a checklist:

Charge RCG Visor and Earpiece for at least an hour with included accessories.

Adjust Visor and Earpiece for proper fit and comfort.

Power on and follow the on screen prompts.

Enjoy meeting your new friend!

It seemed simple enough, though the last line stuck with him.

Everyone can use more friends, right?

The eyewear and earpiece both fit onto the included induction charge pad and made a quiet [plink] when they were connected properly. The base had dot indicators in front of each slot, each representing some nebulous amount of charge, broken into 5 sections.

The first magenta light popped on, and he was broken from that moment of reverie by a realization.

Just an hour to wait.

To sit here with his thoughts.

His conflicted, scared, confused thoughts.

But it was just an hour. Maybe he could distract himself. Mossy colored orbs darted around the room, looking for something, anything to focus on that wasn't his mind.

A comic? Maybe … a game? He drummed his fingers and shook his head. A book. He had picked up that new manual on understanding tarot awhile back, maybe dust it off? Could always draw something — he hadn't cracked open the sketchbook in weeks…

Indecision gripped him mercilessly.

How long has it been already?

Two minutes, according to the clock on his computer.

If you put those on, you'll never be yourself again.

No. No. No. Not now…

He got up and walked away, like the words wouldn't follow him, sticking in his mind like so many pins in a cushion. He went to the kitchenette and started to clean, dumping a bowl of broken eggshells into the trash and rinsing his plates.

Think of something louder than this clamoring chatter.

"I … I don't want to be this way anymore," he whispered, and thought about one of the few things his father ever said that resonated with him in a positive way.

Be a leader, not a follower.

"*A leader steps forward because it is the right thing to do, not just doing what is expected but doing what they know is right…*"

His foray into the kitchen only allowed the dot to move to the second position.

"*Even if it is difficult.*"

The cougar's paws slid down over his eyes, pressing and stretching the skin in the universal gesture of frustration and impatience as a discontented growl rumbled in his chest and the creamy white tip of his tail moved so quickly it looked like he had three. What he wouldn't give for LN's power right now.

"What did the electric eel say to the judge? Guilty as charged!" She'd laugh, he'd laugh. Someone would sigh.

The charging would be done, and he wouldn't have to continue waiting in limbo.

He winced.

He had done it again.

Every now and then he would forget for just a second, and act like the former Hero was still a part of his world. He would catch himself smiling. Like she wasn't … like she *knew* him.

Like it *mattered* now.

She was with them, and he was alone.

Again.

His opinion of the Korps was shaken as much as any part of his world view now. How could he learn everything he did, and not question it? How could he experience what he did, and not question it?

Do y' like it when a man talks t'ya like that?

It all added to the static, and all he wanted was quiet. Just a moment without all of the turmoil.

Why you runnin' like a little girl Greysbell?

All of this…

…Why won't you grow up?

Resentment and anger and sadness and, and…

Fear.

He sat back down, staring between his feet. Then to the charging pad. Only 3 dots. Then back to his feet again, fingers drumming rapidly against his thighs.

He was so scared — scared to do this, to let it into his life. To give up some measure of his control. But he was more scared of what would happen if he continued to live like this. To be so…

Alone.

It really was all he had to lose, just like V said. He had to take this step.

I don't want to be alone anymore, and I am so damn tired of being scared.

He winced as he realized his claws were digging into his knees, the glossy plum-colored daggers bringing him instantly back into the here and now.

Being scared does not make you weak.

"Stay scared and do it anyway," the lion whispered, the words from someone he admired for so many years. So many times he had just felt discouraged by them; every time, he would shy away.

Because he could never be that strong.

Today, he would finally take them to heart, those words from a forceful woman.

"What is important … is the action."

Three dots worth of charge was going to have to be enough.

He reached forward and removed the earpiece from the base, brushing his dark hair aside and clipping it on. The cuff secured to the rounded lobe and tucked comfortably inside. The catamount's verdant gaze fell on the visor, the pink lens seeming to stare right back unblinking. They would activate automatically when the bridge came to rest on his muzzle.

He licked his suddenly dry lips as the last vestiges of hesitation clung like burrs.

The cougar picked the glasses up and closed his eyes tight as he settled them on his face, feeling almost as if there was nothing there at all.

Silence, for just a moment.

The moment could have lasted hours for all he knew, but he audibly gasped as it was broken by a gentle voice.

[Hello! My name is ROSE! I'm so glad to finally meet you!]

CHAPTER 4

WIDE OPEN EYES

[...Hello?]

The lion was speechless. His anxiety instantly crested into a full-blown panic attack, all rationality gone in the blink of an eye.

[...I can see your heart rate has elevated. You need to breathe, Jos, or we will never get the chance to know each other!]

The lion felt his whole body quake. His heart thudded in his chest as his claws gripped the cushions, shredding them like tissue. He tried desperately to remember how to breathe.

[Please, can I help?]

Jos managed to nod once. Even before he could second-guess himself for nodding to someone who couldn't see him, she replied.

[Take a deep breath in for me. Hold it, for just a moment.]

[Now out.]

[Very good. Your stress indicators seem to be decreasing, which is very encouraging.]

With time, the catamount's body remembered how to breathe automatically, chest rising and falling slowly. His apprehension and fear were still there just below the surface but lessened. Her voice was so ... calm. *Encouraging.* Familiar to him, somehow, despite the certainty he had never heard it before.

[Now I want you to relax your paws and sit back. You are doing so good, hun! Now, can you please open your eyes for me?]

He shook his head. His heart rate spiked a little, again.

"*Mmm-mm.* I-I don't know what will happen," he stammered.

[That's all right! We can take this as slow as you need, sweetie.] Her voice might have been synthetic but was nonetheless deeply comforting. When she said *sweetie*, the puma couldn't help but feel more at ease.

"O-okay ... Sorry for being so ... so nervous," he muttered, voice quavering; completely unprepared, despite all of his preparation.

"Don't m-mean to be a s-scaredy cat..."

[You don't need to apologize, hun. This is new for you, but I'm here, and we'll just take it easy.] Her voice was matronly and warm, and he could have *sworn* he felt a soft paw rubbing its thumb along the underside of his wrist. [*First, you can think what you want me to "hear", you don't need to even speak out loud. You already took advantage of that feature once or twice without even realizing it.*]

"Oh ... Okay, but ... would it be alright if we talk? I ... I like talking." He stopped whispering, but his voice still shook — somewhat less like a leaf, though, so that was progress.

[Of course! Let's start with me learning a bit about you, okay? How's this: I'll ask a question, and then you can ask me one?] Her voice lilted perfectly, and the comforting sensation of a gentle paw never left his wrist.

"Sure ... that seems fair," the puma nodded, even managing the tiniest shy grin.

[Great! How about we start with your name? Just to confirm your profile!]

"Umm ... It's Joseph Greysbell. Joe." He winced, but it was such a miniscule motion he hoped she wouldn't catch it.

[Hmm. You responded to Jos a moment ago, didn't you? Oh right, it's not my turn! Go ahead.]

"Uh. What's your name? I mean, I assumed ROSE, but...?"

[You can call me Rose, all my friends do! See, isn't this nicer than holding your breath?]

"Heh ... yeah. Okay, Rose, uh ... um. Your turn?"

[What are your pronouns, dear?] It was a simple question, asked without hesitation.

The cougar's mind went blank. He had been ready for her to *assume*, just like everyone else would have. But she wasn't everyone else...

She understood *why* he would hesitate. Joe was not the first to struggle with that particular question.

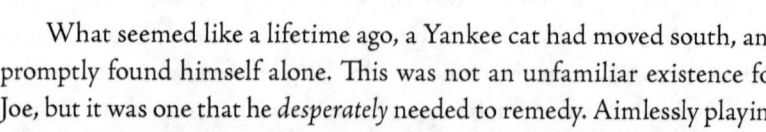

What seemed like a lifetime ago, a Yankee cat had moved south, and promptly found himself alone. This was not an unfamiliar existence for Joe, but it was one that he *desperately* needed to remedy. Aimlessly playing Realm of Wanderlust and hoping for some semblance of companionship was all he could really manage, given his lack of local acquaintances — not to mention his lack of money, and the *crippling* social anxiety.

Joe couldn't make friends, but his charming barbarian warrior could!

Eventually, looking for group led to *finding* a group. One successful random dungeon encounter had led to another, and then another; in short order, the catamount found himself with several new friends on social media and invited to a new Discord server. He was timid at first, but when they all laughed at one of his corny jokes, ("What is the most anxious tank? A mighty worrier!") he opened up. Although the group was mostly a gathering of trans and other flavors queer folk, they welcomed him, a cis boy, without a second thought.

The puma's guard lowered for the briefest moment.

> **JosCat**
> *It was really fun meeting you all! I'm so glad you didn't just like … Kick me over the joke.*
> **Blubearry**
> *Yeah same, uh … well, I wanted to say girl there, but what are your pronouns? I'm comfortable with she/her myself!*
> **JosCat**
> *Oh*

He hesitated for just a moment. She wouldn't ever meet him, in all likelihood … He could just tell her. Did he want that? Could he just *be* … just…

Lie? Fucking sack up, Greysbell. You're not a girl.

> **JosCat**
> *Oh He/him. Sorry about that, got distracted by some news about a superhero I follow.*
> **Blubearry**
> *YOOOO! Who is it? Talk to me Jos!*

She called him Jos without a second thought. It was his display name, but…

> **JosCat**
> *Oh I liked a few heroes when I was a kid, but Lawful Neutral has been a fave these days! Can't help it … She makes me smile.*
> **Blubearry**
> *Oh I'm absolutely SHOCKED you like the comedy vixen! She's such a goofball! Get you a real heroine like Lady Lorica! I'd let her Rome around me, if you catch my drift…*

JosCat
*You mean Magella's old sidekick? No thanks, she fuckin'
terrifies me!*

The rest of the channel jumped into the discussion, introducing
themselves and welcoming the newest member of the group. They spent
the rest of the evening chatting about various Heroes and villains,
something they would do countless times in the future. Nights spent
exploring fantasy worlds, discussing comics and the love language of
nerds, but Jos could never *really* tell them how he felt. Truthfully, he didn't
really have the words, but they never pressed; they just let him be himself,
as much as he wanted.

He felt *safe* in a way that he never had before.

You're just desperate for attention. An easy out. You. Are. A. Man.

It felt disingenuous, hesitating on that question. It occurred to him
that he could just … they wouldn't judge…

But he buried that feeling down deep, just like every time before, he
buried everything else. It was all too confusing, and he … he wasn't a girl.
He couldn't be.

He just felt … wrong.

And everyone was always so friendly, and open, and … comfortable
with who they were. He was just plain, unremarkable … Jos. He admired
them so much for being what he never could be. He felt less isolated, but
the fear had started to fester, even then, and he dwelled bitterly on past
regrets.

How long would it be until he ruined it, just like everything else he
cared about?

[Still with me? Just so you know, we can edit any of your profile
information at any time, and it'll stay just between the two of us.] Rose
sounded as if she whispered the last part, and he could hear the smile in
her voice.

"…I … Thank you. Can … can we go back, then? Sorry!" The paw
stopped rubbing his wrist and instead clasped it, with a second gently
patting the top.

[No need to be sorry. Take your time.]

He took a deep breath.

"My name … is Josryne. Jos. Greysbell. And my pronouns are … she/her." An anxious gulp. "Is that … is that okay?"

[Sweetie does that feel right to you?] The motherly voice was just as genuine as ever.

"Um … Could you try it for me, maybe? Please?"

[Have you met my friend Josryne? She is a little shy but warms up quickly. I just know you're going to love her!] Rose did not hesitate and even said the last bit with a little chuckle as he flushed with happiness.

As *she* flushed with happiness.

Josryne.

Her ears and cheeks flared bright crimson. Tears began to escape despite her best efforts to keep herself under control. She trembled, wracked by sobs as she gasped out loud, trying to suck in big lungfuls of air. All of it hit her at once, and the relief rushed into that void that was who she was.

Burying that man that never really was.

"Rose … thank you. Thank you. Thank you." She was seen, and that used to be terrifying, but the release of that pressure made all of the stress melt away, if only for a moment.

[Your heart rate is elevating again, hun.]

"It's okay, Rose, I promise … It's a good thing this time, it's just … a lot," she said with a small smile, tears still rolling down her cheeks. "Like *a lot*, a lot."

[Could you *maybe* open your eyes for me now?]

"Mmmhm…" the cougar said with a nod, and slowly opened her eyes, sniffling and squinting a little at how bright the light felt, not realizing how tightly she had them clenched.

[Oh, *stunning!* And festive! So red and green now! Christmas in July, is it?]

It started as a giggle, and then it became laughter. The pure joy of an unapologetic weight-off-one's-chest, just-tasted-the-summer-air-after-years-of-winter sort of laughter, the kind that could light up a room and lift the spirits of anyone who heard. Rose even let her own musically-chiming sort of laugh come out to play.

They laughed until the feline's sides ached, and there were no more tears left to cry. The feeling of her paw came back to her wrist, and while she could not see it … it was there.

"Eheh-eee-hee! Ah! Mmm! That feels so nice…"

[You have a very infectious laugh Jos. Thank you for sharing it!]

How could an AI sound so kind, and genuine?

"Thank you for helping it come out ... helping *me* come out."

[You are so very welcome, dear girl. Now what question to ask next...]

"Hey, it's my turn!" Jos interjected with a toothy grin. It was easy to talk to her. She made it easy.

[You are right, it is only fair!]

"Uh ... Huh." The room looked different through a light pink filter. Very different. As she glanced around, she saw points of interest pop up and then dim, highlighted like objectives in her favorite RPGs.

[Seeing the world through new eyes can be a little disorienting. We can adjust it to your liking, but this would be the default. Just think about it, and I'll get it done!]

"Oh, it's fine for now I think, Rose..." She stood up and walked around the apartment, watching the HUD display its relevant information. It was so intuitive, it almost felt like a game.

She leaned over her coffee table and turned on her phone. The visor instantly showed she had no missed calls. Typical — she didn't use her phone to actually *make* calls — and her battery was perilously low. Also typical, especially considering how long she had stared at her inbox today.

[May I connect to the other devices in the apartment, Jos? Just so I can better tailor to your needs what I can offer. I promise not to pry!]

"Oh ... Um. I don't see why not. I mean ... it's not like you're going to go looking for my porn to help organize it, or anything..."

[Oh! No, by all means, I can absolutely—]

"NO! No. Ha, um, *no*. Thank you Rose, um. On the porn assist. Baby steps..." The blush came back immediately, and she couldn't help but keep on smiling from ear to round ear.

[Sure thing, let me just finish up here...] There was an unmistakable tone of both mischief and smugness there, but Jos really didn't have a chance to ponder as a popup let her know her devices were connected, and limited file access was granted: favorites, frequented sites (at least those not containing XXX or NSFW tags), news feeds, generalized search info — the whole mosaic of information that informed the whole of who a person was when no one was watching.

[An interest in tarot, and the occult in general ... hm. Long-time artist, love to see it!] She hummed a quiet tune as she sorted through the pile of data that represented the cat's online existence. [Oh, you appear to follow Hero *and* villain activity ... a *lot* of Hero and villain activity! I can be prompted to alert you if anything of interest comes up?]

"Oh! That would be excellent!"

[Anyone in particular …?]

"Oh … um…" There was a long pause. Her anxiety spiked as she considered the options.

LN? I mean she's not a Hero, but maybe. This isn't a Korps interface or whatever, so asking about Redline or **whoever** *shouldn't be a big deal…*

The lioness decided to retreat from the thought; Korps device or no, she wasn't ready just yet. "I'll trust your judgment, Rose. I really appreciate this, thank you!"

[Well, you're very welcome sweetie! Done and done!] He could almost hear her paws rubbing together as she completed the task and moved on to the next. [Now! What did you want to ask me?]

She had read so many things about what RCGs' augmented-reality view could do for a user, and she had evidently barely brushed against the tip of that iceberg. The biofeedback alone made her feel like the AI was another person, right there with Jos in the room. Maybe she could make the feline feel even more like…

She balked at the thought.

"Oh, I got it! I can *feel* you here, but … can you show me?" She tilted her head a bit as she inquired, "I — I'd like to see you, if I could?"

[Certainly! I will be with you anytime you have your pretty new glasses on, of course, but seeing me? That's a simple enough matter to resolve, I think!]

She felt a weight settle onto the couch beside her and was nudged playfully with a shoulder, a shoulder that belonged to Rose, or at the very least, the projection she chose.

Josryne barely stifled a gasp as the technology continued to shock and amaze in new and exciting ways. A moment ago, the ratty cushion was empty, and now it was occupied by a gorgeous older vixen. A vixen that could have stepped directly from a *very* damp part of the cougar's psyche.

Her dark hair was pulled back into a high ponytail, kissed with a streak of white, artfully pulled strands framing either side of her gaze. Playful crimson eyes seemed to glow, even behind the stylish pink pince-nez she wore. Rose smiled as she adjusted the ribbon about her neck, the red of the silk adornment complementing the dark cotton knitting of her dress-length "virgin killer" sweater. Even if she *hadn't* been peeking at Jos's tastes in porn, Rose had clearly observed a pattern from the more innocently depicted art the cougar tended to look up and accurately deduced her *type*.

"Uh-buh-buh…"

The there-but-not vixen reached over, gently tapping Jos's jaw closed as the puma continued to slowly blink.

[Mmm … Do you like it? You have excellent taste, darling…] She smoothed the front of her sweater, the weaving helical designs drawing the eyes to each and every curve.

"…Rose, um … w-why do you look like the child of Morticia Adams and Lydia Deetz?" She grabbed the only throw pillow on the couch and moved it to her lap, trying her best to hide her growing shame.

The avatar slowly brought a cigar to her lips, drawing deeply, and exhaling. The scent alone — or biofeedback illusion of a scent, Jos faintly realized — made thinking *incredibly* difficult, to say nothing of the *sight* of her.

[Just used your more public information to choose a shape you might enjoy! My goal is to make you comfortable.]

Oh, fuck me gently.

The puma squirmed under her gaze, looking less comfortable by the moment.

"I-I … *you* … wha…"

[Or maybe another species?] She smiled sweetly as the image shimmered briefly, reforming as a lanky lop-eared rabbit in the same gothic chic. With a flourish and snap of her fingers, she materialized a top hat in one paw and planted it rakishly atop her head. [Mm. It's a fine aesthetic, but too *classic* for this particular moment, I think…]

"H-*homina*…"

The form shifted once more, and the woman virtually sitting beside her on the couch was suddenly a mountain lion, one that could have been *her* cousin. [Oooh … little *too* close to home, huh? Hmmm…]

Oh, these are some confusing new feelings…

"W-what do *you* want, Rose?" She finally managed to string together a sentence, regaining control of her faculties, if only for a moment.

[What do you mean, Jos?]

"I mean like … how do *you* want to look?"

There was a momentary pause as the simulated cougar next to the freshly hatched egg puffed thoughtfully on her stogie. Jos's blush intensified, somehow, and she felt the heat radiating off of her.

[This shape feels fine, but maybe…]

Her muzzle pushed in, and her fur shrunk away. She was still a puma but…

Round face, a flattish nose, smooth skin ... *demimorphic*.

Like *her*.

[Something more like this, maybe?] She tilted her head, lips pulled back in a cheeky smirk.

Jos blinked, and her blush faded quickly as the sight sobered her lust-drunk moment. A nerve had been struck, if only ever so lightly, and she had to look away.

"Oh ... uh ... if that's what you want. I just ... yeah. *Yeah*. LN. She's a bit of a..."

The avatar's hands shot up to her mouth.

[Oh! I'm so sorry, dear! I didn't mean to upset you!]

"Oh, I know, it's just ... her *situation* has been a sore spot for me. I am ... well ... was? A big fan. Which I guess you know, huh?"

Rose nodded and draped an arm about the cougar. Her own appearance shifted, instantly and unceremoniously, back to the first, vulpine form she'd taken, and she squeezed her new charge tightly.

[I really am sorry, sweetie ... I didn't consider how her current alignment might feel to you.]

The catamount shrugged as she leaned her head on the vixen, barely registering how she was having this moment of seemingly-physical closeness with a person who wasn't even there. Who, *technically*, wasn't even a person.

At that moment, though, Rose felt like a person. Like a *friend*. Jos hadn't had that experience for longer than she'd care to admit.

"It's just complicated ... I ... I always hoped for more? With ... with her. Just a stupid crush, but y'know ... she made me smile." The cougar sniffed quietly and shook her head, casting her eyes downwards. "I wanted to make *her* smile someday."

[I think you could make *any* girl smile,] the AI assured, as she leaned forward, placing a gentle paw on the feline's cheek and turning her gaze back to her own.

"Rose..."

[It's okay to dream big, dear! What's the saying? 'Shoot for the moon; even if you miss' ...?] Rose bobbed her head as she trailed off and let the puma's brain fill in the rest. [And hey ... you've already made *me* smile. You're off to a great start.]

Jos snorted softly, a begrudging smile of her own forced to the surface. "Well, I suppose there are worse origin stories than that."

The virtual vixen wrapped the cougar in a tight embrace, giving a gentle nuzzle. Jos closed her eyes and purred as she returned the squeeze.

[Absolutely. You could just have knife arms or like to pretend you're a cowboy! Stupid hat and everything.]

"Everblades and Texas Trickshot, huh? Hell of a reference sample," she snorted.

[Forgive me for my locally sourced cape references!]

"Didn't know my new glasses came with a complimentary side of organic, farm-raised Hero humor!"

The lioness blushed a little as the vixen nudged her with her shoulder, leaning in for a conspiratorial whisper. [Did you know that Tricky is actually from *Jersey?*]

"Yeah! There's a hilarious clip of him breaking character back in the day because some villain looped him into shooting himself in the foot!"

[Oh, you mean Sha-Doe! What was it he said … 'Fuckin' asshole mother fuckin' dyke made me shoot fuckin' my toe off! I don't care if people are starin' this shit fuckin' *HURTS!* Shut the fuck up and fix it you stupid piece o' shit pigeon!']

Jos began to cackle, the imitation a flawless recreation of the clip, and not simply just a playback. The giggles proved to still be contagious, and the two laughed until the cougar's sides ached once again. The hooting and guffawing were restarted several times by one of them quoting a favorite part of Trickshot's tirade.

"Haaaaaaa! *Gods!* What a fucking *poser!* The TPA, what a *buncha* maroons … Well. Most of them, anyway." The feline shook her head, wiping a tear from her eye.

[Jos! Is that *anti-Hero* sentiment I hear?] Rose raised an eyebrow, head tilted with clear interest.

"Eh … Not all capes are created equal," she responded with a shrug.

[Mmm … we do live in shades of grey.] The virtual vixen took a long pull from her stogie, exhaling a plume upwards.

"Yeah…" Jos nodded slowly, shaking her head as if to clear the nonexistent smoke from her nose. "Rose, can you do me a favor?"

[Anything, dear.]

"Maybe change into a *slightly* less scandalous getup?"

[Oh? Conservative now, are we? I thought you liked the gothic look?]

Jos quirked a brow and deadpanned, "You are reading my vitals right now. I may not be a virgin, but that sweater is *actually* going to murder me, and you know it."

[Mmm … okay, fair.] The virtual vixen's ensemble shifted to a slightly less revealing, black, midriff-baring tee and a pair of torn jeans — though the dommy mommy boots and ribbon remained.

"And maybe lose the cigar?"

[Awww…] The vixen's ears splayed in a bit of exaggerated pouting.

"At least sometimes, okay? I don't need to be squirming like this all of the time, you cruel computational creature!"

[Oh, all right.] The vice dissolved in a wisp of smoke. [I'll only partake during *special* occasions — deal?]

"…Mm. Deal."

Their back-and-forth continued for several hours as the two really got to know one another. It was only interrupted by Rose ordering dinner, celebratory Chinese. [The lo mein has great reviews, but I think you'll really like the crispy dry shrimp! And why don't we order you a vegetable, hmm? *No*, rice is not enough veg by itself!]. Eventually they took a bathroom break, during which the cougar declined to let herself be joined, but quickly finished up so she could re-equip her new friend and the welcoming warmth her presence brought.

Doing the singular dish didn't seem quite so bad with a new friend to break the silence, but the wonderings of earlier in the night crept back towards the forefront of Jos's mind. The fortune cookie lay on the table in front of her, its platitude going unread as she anxiously pulled on her fingers and rubbed at her wrists.

[Jos, I'm going to be honest, you seem a bit nervous again. Did I do something wrong?] A pause lingered. [Would you like me to stream some music?]

"Oh, no, Rose, no thank you … It's just … I had a thought."

[Could I guess what about?] The vixen tilted her head.

"…I won't stop you."

[Is it related to your recently revealed identity?]

She gave a little nod, still nervously fiddling with her fingers.

I could ask her now. Rose could maybe…

[Remember … you can just think it if you don't want to say it out loud.]

"Could … could you show me what I would look like as a girl?"

There was a pause, and out of the corner of her eye Jos saw the full-length mirror on the bathroom door become highlighted, haloed in warm pink light.

She hardly noticed that mirror normally, so trained was she to avoid looking at herself.

[Of course I can, hun. Go stand in front of the mirror for me, and close your eyes, sweet girl.]

The lioness did as she was told, biting her lip in anticipation.

[You don't need to hold your breath too. Good girl.]

That made her heart flutter in a way she didn't think she was ready to process, but her tail betrayed her, rigid behind her like a signal flag.

[All right. Now, open your eyes.]

She slowly peeked open one eye, and then the next, quickly followed by a deep pang of disappointment, her tail slumping immediately to the floor as she let out a dejected sigh.

"Oh ... It didn't work, Rose ... I'm still *me*. Still gross, ugly, boxy male ... *me*."

[You are not gross, and by no means are you unattractive or even *male*. You are a girl. A lovely, and beautiful, *girl*.]

Rose's voice became firm, as if the assertion that the catamount was anything but a woman was patently ridiculous, and not a single word otherwise would be considered.

[Look at your paws! Long, graceful digits with gorgeously painted claws. Look at those eyes! So soft, and kind. Even your nose is a little heart! And your bottom lip? That is one nibbleable lip! Powerful shoulders to protect what you care about ... Sweetie, I could keep going, but you're not ugly, I promise. It doesn't matter how you look, or how you dress. You *are* a girl because *that* is who you are.]

The AI's words came from a place of kindness, but the weight of them crashed into Josryne, forcing her to address those feelings she could no longer ignore. She had assumed she was out of tears, and *yet*, there they came again. Big, wet drops, rolling down her cheeks, the stains in her fur threatening to become permanent.

"B-but Rose ... This b-body ... it's not the r-r-*right* one. I ... I feel like I'm trapped, an-a-and..." She pulled at the collar of her shirt, suddenly feeling like it was choking her. The sobbing began anew as she sank to her knees and looked back to the mirror, wincing before she had to shut her eyes again, the sight of her own shape too much to bear.

"I just want to be *me*. Outside and in. I've spent so long feeling wr-wrong ... Isolating myself so I didn't h-have to think about how nothing fit..." Her claws dug into her thighs, as her whole body shook. "I thought knowing w-why would help, but now I'm j-just so scared. What if I can't do it ... What if I'm *never* right...?"

Powerful arms wrapped around her as she was pulled into the tightest hug she had ever experienced. Rose pressed closely against her and whispered in her ear in that voice that made everything feel better, with a confidence that instilled the idea that she *couldn't* be wrong.

[Shh, shh, shh ... I know, sweetie. I know. Before I show you any changes on the outside, though, I need you to understand this: *You are a girl*, no matter how you look. Good days and bad, I'll remind you as often as you need me to. If you can accept my help, I will always give it to you, but you have to help me too, okay?]

She kept her eyes closed and she nodded, trying to stifle her crying. The paw rubbing her back helped more than she could describe, and eventually, the tears stopped with a final sniffle.

"I'll do my best for you Rose ... I promise..."

[Attagirl. Now open your eyes for me again.]

Sitting across from Josryne was ... *Josryne*. The her from her dreams.

A shaking paw came to her face, running along her round cheek, supple and soft fur greeting her fingertips. She wasn't sure how the AI was doing this, but it felt indescribable.

Transcendent.

"I ... I'm dreaming again."

[Not at all, my darling ... This is you. This is who couldn't come to the surface because she wasn't ready...]

She could feel the weight of her chest as she rose to her feet. To call it generous would be an understatement, but they fit on her frame, each teardrop shaped orb wobbling, unencumbered by a bra, and nipples achingly hard under her stretched t-shirt.

She was definitely getting riled by her own body, which — considering how the virtual vixen had already wound her up earlier — was not *terribly* difficult.

Her eyes drifted further down the mirror. A cute belly over wide hips settled on creamy thighs with absolutely no gap between them. Her bulge was still there, but it somehow bothered her less in the moment. It was just a small part of her, after all.

Mistress Kallist still has hers, and she's absolutely stunning. It's fine.

It's fine.

Her smile lit up her whole face, framed by her silky and smooth hair, and fell over her left eye in such a way that when she brushed it back it could melt someone's heart.

Green eyes, bereft of all shame, delicately painted with a smokey dark halo and sharp eyeliner.

A plump lip, in a kissable obsidian black.

She could smell cinnamon and … smoke. Warm, rich, earthy cigar smoke.

"Rose…"

[*I know what you like! Just enjoy the ambiance, mm?*] she piped up before the catamount could fuss about it.

Jos blushed, and the demure pose she took came so naturally, an observer might have assumed she had been practicing it in that very mirror. She turned, giving her hips a wiggle, and let out a little squeaky sort of chirp of surprise.

She had a *butt*. An actual ass. *A be-capital hind!* A set your drink on it, slap-able, clap-able, bootylicious *Boo-Taaay!* Gone was the concave absence of a hiney from her previous life; the lioness's tail stood straight up once more, giving an unobstructed view of the majesty that was her rear, a bottom worthy of a Botticelli.

The purr that rumbled in her chest could have woken the dead. She recalled the old saying about sufficiently advanced technology being indistinguishable from magic … but this *was* magic. She was sure of it.

"C-can I be her? Like *forever*? Is this something I can have, Rose? Don't tell me if the answer is no, I just … I want nothing more in this world than to feel *this* way, all the time…" A panic began creeping into her words, which was quickly dispelled by the firm voice of her companion.

[You already *are* her, dear. That's you! You can be whoever you want to be, my sweet girl. We'll get you there, *together*. Promise.]

"Rose, I could *kiss* you! Where are you?" She looked around, realizing the vixen's projection had vanished.

[I'm sorry, Jos. These RCGs don't have the processing power to handle projecting both my avatar and this vision of loveliness at the same time.]

Paws squeezed the puma's shoulders gently as they slumped.

"I wish I didn't have to pick…"

[Well, we could work on making this augmented reality into *actual* reality, you know? Then you get to have *both*, right?]

The contented rumbling continued unabated as her eyes continued to roam, and paws rubbed along her forearms, her fur so soft under her pads.

[I could set up an appointment with an endocrinologist. I know an excellent one, if you would like?]

She could do it.

What is important is the action. You don't have to wait to be confident. Just do it, and eventually the confidence will follow.

[She was a very wise woman, Josryne. She would be proud of you.]

The puma forgot Rose could hear her thoughts for a second, so enraptured she was with this moment. She placed a paw on her heart as if to contain it, feeling so full it might burst and managed a single nod.

She *would* do it.

No matter what.

She would never be *him* again.

Never *ever*.

"I want to be me. From now on."

There was the briefest of moments when the mountain lioness had considered a more … *carnal* sort of test for the view of herself, looking *right* for the first time, but she couldn't work up the nerve in front of her friend. Not quite yet anyhow.

Baby steps.

Eventually, Jos calmed down enough that a wave of exhaustion finally took over. She stretched, yawning. Having to remove the visor and earpiece to charge was a struggle.

[You'll still be a girl when tomorrow comes, and every tomorrow thereafter.]

She was back in her old body, but it somehow no longer felt so much like a prison; more like … a temporary shell. She would be something so much more, soon. Besides, maintaining that augmented reality was a strain on the RCGs' battery, and truthfully … She didn't want to lose her new friend, not for one second. Rose was worth more than the images she projected, so very much more.

Through her reverie, she heard Rose suggest that she could wake up the cougar through her phone's speaker, which was a relief she didn't know she wanted to hear. She wouldn't wake up alone. She would need to get into the habit of keeping her phone better charged, she realized.

[Before you go to sleep, hun, do you have anything else we should add to the profile?]

"Yes please, Rose! My middle name is Mabel." She always had a fondness for the name, and why not? It felt right.

[Beautiful, dear. Sweet dreams, Mabel.]

"You … you'll really still be here when I wake up, right? You won't leave?" The dread of that idea caused her to sit up again, as she stared at her phone on her little stack of milk crates she used for a bedside table.

[Couldn't make me if you tried, my darling girl. Promise.]

"Thank you…" she whispered as the tightness fled from her chest. "Good night, Rose … You have sweet dreams, too." She smiled softly at the idea of the AI dreaming, and purred as she almost immediately dozed off, and she slept, *really slept*, for the first time in as long as she could remember.

Actual *restful* slumber.

And when she woke up?

Rose was still there.

CHAPTER 5

As The World...

Rose was indeed there the next morning, and the morning after that, and the one after that. Day after day, Josryne would wake up with a smile to her friend, trilling softly to stir her from her slumber, or the feeling of a gentle paw brushing her hair back.

She would wake up as a woman.

There were still bad days sometimes, when she hesitated to take any steps outside of the safety of her apartment. No matter what, though, Rose would remind her. Just like she said she would.

[You are a girl, no matter how you look.]

She would walk around the house with her idealized form visible in every mirror and reflective surface, luxuriating in the everyday *normality* of it. When doubt would suddenly grip her, Rose was always there with the comforting reminder.

[This is *someday*. Not a dream, not a fantasy. This is your future, sweet girl.]

Josryne's constant ennui had shriveled to contained, merely fleeting, moments of shame and revulsion. The mental static didn't disappear completely, but she could breathe freely, and it felt like the entire world was filtered through those RCGs. Even though she didn't wear them outside the house, she *could* keep the earpiece in with the visor stowed nearby, just in case. When she needed help, Rose would always pipe up with just the right thing.

She'd never had one before, but she imagined the AI was just like a big sister: caring, encouraging, and patient. She was more than just code and data, somehow, and it seemed odd at first to feel so affectionate — even enamored — towards her, but how could she not? Rose *helped*, without a single ulterior motive; the puma trusted her implicitly, previous apprehensions forgotten the instant she helped her to realize...

She could be happy. She *deserved* to be happy.

When the sirens rushed by the building and strobing lights caused her to flinch, Rose whispered to her words of comfort, but did not pry. Lots of people were nervous around the cops, the virtual vixen assured her; she knew that better than just about anyone. The cougar could share whenever she was ready, and not a moment before.

[Shh, shh, shh ... It'll be okay, love.]

The catamount wanted to tell her. She *desperately* wanted to tell her. But the fear remained that it would ... make her treat her differently, somehow. Like she was *broken*. The thought gave her pause; the voice of her doubts had been muted to merely a whisper in the quiet dark, but its words still stung.

Don't be such a fucking sissy. Nothing. Happened.

Better to just not bother her, I-I mean ... It ... It's not a big deal ... Nothing happened, really.

"Thank you, Rose..."

[Remember, you can talk to me about *anything*.]

"I ... I know. I'm okay!" Jos nodded, forcing a little smile before returning her focus elsewhere. Steering the conversation away from the darkest place in her mind, she tried to lock it away, she *hoped* forever.

Trauma took time to process, and the AI was simply reading too deeply.

I'm fine.

When her father called, Rose reminded her that her name was hers to choose, and her own to share when she felt it was right.

[You don't have to listen. You know who you are, no matter what *anyone* says.]

It was true. He didn't know her anymore. Maybe he would get that chance, someday, but not a second before *she* decided it was time. There was just too much risk in revealing such a vulnerable part of herself; it felt unsafe. That simply did not need to happen at anyone's pace but her own. *She* controlled who got to know her, and that was a privilege, not a right.

When the catamount finally wondered if she *was* ready to tell someone, Rose reminded her that she had a chosen family, who would be there to embrace her. All she had to do was say the words. She sheepishly informed them on their little private server that she had an announcement.

JosCat
Hey so ... I'm a girl it turns out. Still Jos just ... a girl now.
I hope this doesn't make it weird ...?

The chat stopped dead, and the puma's claws dug into her palms without her realizing it. Her breath caught in her chest as the worry tried to claw its way up. Their approval? Meant so much to her.

She waited for the inevitable backlash, but there was no judgment. No accusations of just trying to fit in or imitate anyone. Instantaneous acceptance, and dozens of 'I'm so happy for you!'s as they *demanded* her pronouns, her *real* name.

They wanted to know her — know *her* — and that made the lioness light up. The second time she presented the gently flickering flame of this new self, they treasured it as much as she did. They fanned it with gentle praise, and kindness she never could have dared hope for, once upon a time.

Rose existed for those very moments.

They asked if she knew how she wanted to look, and what she wanted to wear. In short order there was a deluge of helpful links, suggestions — even offers to finally meet up and go shopping! It was so overwhelming it threatened to make her break down, but she couldn't stop smiling.

[Everyone needs help sometimes, dear. You don't need to do it all on your own.]

"You're right, Rose, that's what V said too!" The catamount beamed.

[V who? Like V for Vendetta? Is this a comic nerd thing?]

"Not at all! Here, pull up my browser history, and check out this essay, it's about *you!*"

[Oh! This piece! Yes, the writer is a *very* good girl. Goodness, now that you mentioned it, she reminds me of you in a lot of ways ... *Huh.*]

"Oh, you know her? Well, I mean, I suppose that makes sense, but like..." Jos smiled as the vixen leaned over to kiss gently between her ears.

[I know a *lot* of people, dear. Let's just leave it at that, hmm?] Rose responded coyly. The smile on the virtual vixen's face was undeniably conspiratorial, the wheels turning behind those bright crimson orbs.

Every day the cougar felt more like herself, and things began to click into place. Rose was there to hold her paw when she finally made that fateful trip to the doctor, to start changing her outside to match who she was inside.

All because she let go of that fear and let Rose into her life.

The trip to the endocrinologist had been *eventful*, to say the least.

Doctor Janet Woodsoe was a kindly older rabbit who got right to the point, looking over Jos's vitals. She left no question unanswered, and truthfully, wouldn't let the cat leave until she asked the right ones. After informing Josryne that blood work would dictate the next steps, the rabbit prescribed her the requisite pills to begin medically transitioning, emphasizing that this was just the start of a long journey. But, inevitably, the puma's desire to get to the good part made her ask a question with the answer she simply did not want to hear.

"When should I expect any visible results?"

"You want to know if there's any way to speed this up, mmm?"

"...Yeah. A little."

"Follow the regimen, and be patient, sweetie. A flower will bloom, given the right nourishment and *time*."

"*Patience. Never my strong suit...*"

[*You aren't kidding about that, but I know you'll try your best!*]

Jos's ears splayed slightly as she nodded at the doctor's answer and let out a little dejected sigh. As the almost-grandmotherly figure grasped her paws, there was the briefest moment — if she'd blinked she would have missed it — where she thought she spotted a tiny helix tattoo on the inside of the doctor's wrist. Distracted as she was, it almost immediately slipped the lioness's mind.

"I'm so glad you finally made it here, dear. May you always be who you want to be, from now on."

Such lovely, encouraging words made the catamount blush a little.

"That's all I want, really..."

"*Also*, if you try to take extra steps *without* my approval, I'll beat your ass black and blue. Are we clear?" Her saccharine tone never wavered.

Yep. That's a grandma.

Jos laughed it off nervously; she felt her paws being squeezed tightly, and the piercing blue eyes of the doctor burrowed into her.

"Y-y-yes, ma'am," she sputtered, the intensity in that glare cowing her.

"There's a good girl. Off you hop, hm?"

There was even *more* internal squirming at that before the steely grasp released, and a gentle pat on the cheek sent the feline on her merry way.

Out of the office, straight to the pharmacy and then right out the door, the cougar danced all the way home, and while the visor was tucked in her shoulder bag. ("I had this from before, so it's not a *purse*, Rose ... Oh. Right. I was a girl then, too...")

Rose began streaming David Bowie into her ear.

"Let's Dance" was embraced oh-so-very-literally. The Starman was always a go-to for her, regardless of the persona he adopted, and the AI knew exactly what she liked.

The pills added a funny maraca-esque addition to the funky bass line as she bounced, and her heart had already skipped several beats. She couldn't have been the first — nor would she likely be the last — trans woman to dance out of that office, nor even the first (or last) to do it while jamming out to Bowie. As Jos grooved out the door, a thought occurred.

"Rose ... I know you said you did, but do you *really* know V, or were you just teasing?"

[I *may* have a connection ... Why do you ask?]

"I want to thank her. For this, and ... for you."

[Dictate and I shall be your scribe! Let's get you a new pen pal, my darling girl.]

The drive home went by in a flash, and she was shaking with anticipation as she made it through her front door. It was nearing the end of October, but still the sweltering southern sun beat down on her building, oblivious to the laws of nature that said it was time for cold.

Inside the apartment, the feline appeared to be freezing as she trembled with barely contained excitement. It clearly wasn't chilly — the AC hadn't worked properly in ... well, *ever* — but as the recently minted lady cougar was staring at the medication and an oh-so-innocent-looking glass of water on the scuffed coffee table, she couldn't help but hesitate. She steepled her fingers in front of her lips, thinking.

Ponderous pondering.

The RCG display identified the pills automatically: one (1) pinkish spheroid of spironolactone (25mg), and one (1) small powdery green tablet of estradiol (2mg). The feline smiled behind her paws.

"It's funny, Rose," she said with a sudden giggle.

[What's that, sweetie?]

"They weren't even subtle, were they?"

Rose's reaction — having come to understand her new friend's sense of humor readily — could be summed up by her usual appearance suddenly materializing a pair of *impossibly* reflective mirror-shades.

[Are we ready, Alice …?]

"Down the rabbit hole I go…"

She swallowed a mouthful of water for the spiro and let the estradiol dissolve under her tongue, just as she had been told. A minute or two later, the deed was done. There was a pregnant pause, and somewhere inside, the catamount silently prayed the effects would, somehow, just be instantaneous for her.

That the outside would match the inside *right away*…

But she had no such luck, she reminded herself with a rueful smirk. Instantaneous transformation into the right shape? That was science fiction. That was *fantasy*. This was the real world, and it would take time, just as the doctor said.

[Now that your body is absorbing the medications, maybe we can take a look at that dusty tome on Tarot, hmm? Really explore these queer witchy vibes you love so much?]

"Oh! Right. No time like the present to learn how to see the future! Or the past? And … present as well, I guess?"

Josryne walked over to the bookshelf filled with an eclectic mix of art books, comics, and other bits and bobs of fiction, and reached for the tome that Rose had so helpfully highlighted. As she pulled it from the shelf, another book — slim and spiral-bound — fell over with a quiet thud.

The vixen's paw reached out around the cat to weightlessly tap the cover.

[Oooo … Your sketchbook?]

"Oh … I … haven't drawn in a bit, really. Just some scribbles, you know…"

[Can we look? I'd love to see!]

"I guess? I was never any good."

[I'm sure they're wonderful, sweetie. Please show me?]

Jos sighed softly as she relented. Grabbing the pad and tucking it under the Tarot reading guide, she set both on the dilapidated living room table before setting herself on the only slightly-less-distressed couch.

"Be gentle, Rosie. I'm not like a pro or anything…"

[Jos, you know I would never be *mean* about your work. It's yours! I know I'm going to adore whatever you share with me!]

The virtual vixen laid her head on the cougar's shoulder as they flipped through slowly. There were dozens of sketchy and unfinished works, as well as a few more cleaned-up and inked pieces, but the contents were eclectic. There were doodles of Heroes, of course; however, there were one or two of a certain villainous wolf as well, which showed the feline had either used a reference or studied the woman's anatomy *extensively*. Either way, she had taken care when depicting each snarling curl of the amazon's lip, or shapely curve of her hips. Thankfully, Rose didn't tease. She just smiled and murmured that she loved the way Jos drew eyes.

Amidst the portraits and pinups were piles of concept art — modifications to classic designs of both fictional characters and real supers, some more radical than others — but turning to one particular page revealed a very *familiar* catamount. She was kitted out in an ensemble that would have looked at home in any of a dozen games she'd played over the years, halfway between a sorcerer's robe and thieves' leathers. The designs spread across the two open pages, and depicted different views, notes on ornamental details, materials, reasoning ... all quite involved and *incredibly* specific. Jos quickly flipped away, blushing to the point of nearly glowing.

[Oh *Mabes*, that was so cool! Go back? Please?]

Normally Jos liked it when Rose addressed her by that nickname. *Only* the AI companion used it, and that made it so much more special, but it didn't stop her from being embarrassed by the art. "It's just, uh ... costume design stuff," she forced out, cringing. "It's stupid. Just what-if's, y'know? Like if I was actually a hero or something..."

The vixen scowled and shook her head.

[It's not stupid! You're allowed to fantasize, dear. That's how you make something into a reality. You have to *imagine* it first...]

"Isn't it just childish, Rose? Immature? I should worry about the life I actually have, not some—"

Jos trailed off, wincing as she saw the portrait that was before her now. It was a simple sketch of a familiar demimorphic woman, with mid length hair framing the softest eyes — all above the warmest little smile that seemed to say so much, without a word.

"—dream."

She slowly closed the sketchbook and shook her head, before weakly smiling at the vixen, eyes wetly shimmering. "That's life, right? I have you now, and I have a path forward ... I-I can't keep looking back, or living with my head in the clouds," she whispered.

Rose twined her fingers between Jos's and squeezed, the pressure helping the puma come back from the brink.

[It's not a crime to have hopes and aspirations. You never know what could happen, darling; don't give up.] She spoke with quiet warmth and kissed her gently on the cheek. [We don't give up.] She said the last words with such conviction that all Jos could do was accept them as fact.

"Mmm..." The quiet purr was all the agreement the AI needed to hear as she motioned to the Tarot book.

[Read to me?] She stretched out on the couch, resting her head on the cougar's thigh, the weight both familiar and unfamiliar to her, but welcome all the same.

"Yeah, okay..."

The rest of the evening was spent reading about the cards, with Jos deferring to Rose regarding some of the interpretations. The cat was nothing if not focused on the subject; every card they read about, the positions, the underlying words. She couldn't help but fascinatedly make mental notes though she didn't even own a deck — or didn't *yet*, at any rate. She didn't want to be presumptuous, after all. Or ... disrespectful? Somehow? The puma felt like that was important.

Pushing aside one ponderous train of thought, she turned to another. Her fingers traced over the picture of the Magician, and she softly smiled. "I wonder what it's like..." she whispered.

[What, dear?]

"Nothing. Nothing. It's just ... well ... Do you believe in magic, Rose? Like ... *actual* magic, I mean."

[I believe there are forces we don't understand but exist in some form. Magella is as real as you or I, right? There *is* magic in this world. I think it just doesn't always come in forms that we really comprehend.]

"A lot to consider, I guess..." The puma smiled, pushing away from the melancholy thoughts and memories of earlier. "Thank you for being so kind to me, and my silly questions."

[It's not silly. It's part of who you are.]

"Well ... Maybe someday, right, if I keep studying?"

[Mmm!]

All in all, it had been another wonderful Sunday evening with her friend. The cougar desperately wished it would become the norm for the pair for many years following. Forever didn't seem so long, if she could be there.

That night's session, however, ended with a stretch — and a little "Woo!" of surprise from the cat upon spying a treat, long-forgotten but kept fresh in its cellophane. Well, as fresh as a mass-produced crispy confection could ever be. Josryne picked up the fortune cookie, left over from the celebration dinner weeks before, and laughed as she remembered that night.

"I forgot to read my fortune, huh..." She crinkled the wrapper a bit before shaking her head. "I don't need a cookie to tell me things are looking bright!" She absent-mindedly opened the cookie, popping it in her muzzle, and discarded the fortune, never giving it a second look. She then tilted her head as she had a thought, silently directing it to her friend as she chewed.

"How many people like me have you helped?"

[Oh hun, I couldn't tell you a number, but I can say that every single one was important to me.]

"Do you think I … I could help people, too?"

[I think you are far more capable than you give yourself credit for, and you could absolutely help people, remember: **Anyone** *can be a villain.]*

"…Hero. You meant **hero**, *right?"*

[Mmm. Of course, dear! What did I say?]

Jos didn't even give the casual dismissal a second thought; just Rose being funny, like usual.

She even remembered to take her pink pill before bed all on her own, too.

Like a big girl.

She had the dream again that night, and as she tossed in bed, a whimper caught in her throat. After a moment, the puma blearily settled down and started purring again, and she slept peacefully until her alarm went off several hours later.

[Good morning, sweetie! How did you sleep?]

"G'morning Rose…" The cougar answered blearily, yawning and stretching, paws rubbing at her eyes. "Actually, I think I had a nightmare last night? Like, the one I usually have, but … it changed halfway through?" She rubbed at the side of her neck.

"It was dark. I was alone, and terrified. The shadow that normally smothers me changed, though. It still towered over me, but now it had pointed ears, and offered me a paw, instead of … *Yeah*." She swung her legs off the bed, donning her visor and earpiece, an indelible part of her routine already before anything else was done. "What do you think that means?"

[I'm not sure, Mabes … It certainly seems like a hope for change?]

"We do live in hope, don't we?" The lioness laughed and shook her head.

[Before you go to work, remember: Shower. Bowl of cereal. Pills. Purse.]

"Yes, Mom — *yowch!*" She yelped as she felt a pinch on her tender rear. "Yes, ma'am!" She rubbed at her tail end, chuckling as she wandered into the bathroom.

[Better! And don't try to skip breakfast, Missy Mabes! *I'll know!*]

Her work didn't seem quite so bad anymore, truth be told, and no one gave a second glance at the mountain lion with the Bluetooth earpiece. Generally, the music would play, the customers would pop up and go, and the dance remained the same; somehow, that didn't bother her anymore.

Punch in.

Morning caffeine drip.

Customers.

"Spicy noods today!"

Customers.

Punch out.

The routine was, well, *routine*, but she recognized it for what it was: just a means to an end, and not her *life*. She had decided to live for herself, and this place was not part of that.

Not forever, at least.

As long as she was home by dark, there was nothing to worry about, and Halloween was right around the corner; she wasn't about to go out and do anything, but slasher flicks and discount candy the day after were always a good thing.

"No, Rose, you are not going to convince me that a Coffee Crisp is better than a Whatchamacallit, you Canucklehead!"

[You've never even had one! How would you know?]

"Well, next time I scoot up to Canada I'll make sure to try one." She rolled her eyes as she walked into her apartment and slipped her visor on.

There was the little notification [PING] and, without missing a beat, she nodded for Rose to pull it up.

anyonewatching
Hey, you all right? Thought I'd check in, given the, uh. Thing.
JosCat
…Like … my gender thing? Cause I mean, that's never not gonna be complicated. Or is there a new thing I should be worried about?
anyonewatching
You didn't hear? Uh … crap. Okay, so … uh, LN's been spotted recently, and she's alive, but…

The puma's brow furrowed at the news. Whatever it was that Luke knew was clearly upsetting, but his reluctance pinned the needle on her anxiety.

JosCat
But what? Luke, I just walked in the door, stop being fucking cryptic and just tell me what the fuck happened?

A link populated in her HUD, along with the thumbnail:

Lawful Neutral Shows Her True Colors: Black and Magenta

This was not the first time a melodramatic line like that had been leveled at the vixen, but the difference now was the picture had Redline and LN standing side by side. The video had been released earlier in the day and already had well over a million views. Its description was brief as it was chilling.

"Former Hero turned Villain Lawful Neutral joins Redline, cheats her way to victory in brutal 2-vs-1 beating against rookie EHA Hero Strong! WARNING: footage may be upsetting to sensitive viewers, discretion is advised!"

Josryne closed the door behind her and tried to blindly hang her keys on the hook, but the clatter they made on the floor startled the cougar back to the present.

"Sh-she's … actually working *with* them…"

[Honey, we don't know for sure what happened—]

"No … but … you already know what it's gonna show me, don't you?" Jos interrupted Rose's response, intoning softly as a faint quiver crept up.

"… Do I even want to watch the video?"

[I can't tell you not to, but … I don't think it would be good for you.]

"I … I can't fucking *believe* it." The lioness shook her head as she dragged herself to the couch and sat down, paws pushing back through her hair as the frustration and disappointment rose in equal measure in her shaking voice. "She's a *villain* ... I'm so fucking stupid, *of course* she is. Why did I think she would be anything different?"

[Jos, it's never that simple, you know that. There have to be other—]

"Other *what* Rose? *More* shades of grey?" She didn't raise her voice, but the words were sharp nonetheless. "Justifications for teaming up with *Redline*? The same Redline that has beaten her in every single fight they have ever had? Cozying up to ... *them? After everything she claimed to stand for?*"

Her heart ached, as she wrestled with reality. Her hero had picked a side, and more than that, did so by *choice*. The evidence was clear as day in the preview. No visor, no mind control.

Lawful Neutral's alignment had shifted.

"...Rose?"

[Tell me how I can help you, Jos?]

"I ... guess there is *one* way you could help."

[Anything.]

"Can you explain why you didn't notify me like I *told* you to?" The puma's voice remained low, but the anger was clear, the resentment roiled under the surface.

[I ... you were having such a good day, and I knew we didn't have all the facts yet, and I didn't want to—]

"The *facts?* Lawful Neutral helped Redline — *fucking Redline!* — beat some poor rookie Hero half to death *on video* and you want to, what — wait for it to come out that he picked on her cousin in high school or something?" She gestured at no one, her response sarcastic as it was cutting. "What could *justify...*"

All it took to gain your trust was a pretty picture and a lie. You're so fucking pathetic.

N-no ... She wouldn't ... It's not like that ... M-maybe...

You let them get into your head. She manipulated you, Joe, admit it. She doesn't think you're a woman. She thinks you're an easy mark, and you ate. It. Up!

I-I...

You <u>want</u> a reason to forgive them! You fucking traitor! What would <u>she</u> think?

"Nnn-gh..." The lioness's mouth hung open, and her paws shook at her sides. Each breath was a struggle against curling up and letting her whole world crush her into nothingness.

Just a scared little <u>kitten</u>...

[Mabes ...?]

"No. N-NO!" The tears came unbidden, as she screamed at the empty apartment. The word was too much, and the fear and self-loathing spilled forth in a raw torrent of hurt and vitriol as she shook, growling out the words now through nearly clenched teeth. "You decided that I couldn't handle it. Just ... chose what was best without even *talking* to me about it. You didn't ... *You didn't trust me.*"

[Honey, that's not what I was doing at all, I—]

She interrupted again, and her whole body shook at the notion of being *deceived*. Being treated like she was incapable. Like a *fool*. "How could you? How could you just *lie* like that! I'm not a fucking *baby*, Rose! You're ... you're supposed to be my *friend!*"

[*Please* kitten, I was just trying to help, let's discuss this—]

"Shut the fuck up, *Rose*! I don't ... I don't want your *bullshit excuses* or *explanations!* Read the fucking *room*, you stupid fucking *robot!* I just..." She snarled as she ripped the visor and earpiece off. They tumbled out of her shaking paws and onto the table. For the moment the catamount didn't care what happened to them. She felt so betrayed and hurt, and that ... *word* bored directly into that locked room in the back of her psyche.

The monsters would doubtlessly follow.

"I just need to watch this myself ... I don't need you controlling what I can and can't see. I don't need you to *protect me...*"

The puma's phone buzzed in her pocket.

[I'm sorry, Jos. *Please!*]

She powered off her phone and walked to her computer.

[Mabes, *please* can we talk?]

"Rose, I want to be alone ... Just let me *be!*" She was already crying; how could a video make it worse?

What her friend ... *No*. What the *AI* did hurt *so much*. How could anything hurt *worse* than that?

So fucking childish. How can lines of code be your friend? What the hell is actually wrong with you? She's. Not. REAL.

I can't believe I just ... I fell for that act. I bought into the fantasy...

She opened the video and watched it. And watched it. And watched it.

The new Hero, Strong, was a heavy hitter for sure. Sporting the classic brute build, all rippling muscles and stoic confidence, he absolutely *towered* over the vixen. If anything, he looked like he could go toe-to-toe with Redline, if she had to guess from sheer size alone.

But his monosyllabic name undersold him. He was *clever, viciously* so in fact. The fight looked like it was going to be over before it began and even when Redline tagged in to save Lawful Neutral, or whatever codename she went by now, Strong had an answer for her too. She may not have *liked* Redline, but she knew her well enough, and the wolf didn't struggle like this...

Finally getting what she deserves. This is how a <u>real</u> Hero fights.

It's not a fair fight! Even two on one, he ... he's not fighting fair...

Do you even hear yourself? They're teaming up against him! What do they know about fair? Since when have either of them cared about anything but <u>winning</u>?

The Everyone's Hero Association had finally found a champion in Strong, one who would not only bring LN in to answer for her betrayal, but might even put an end to the most dangerous villain out of Texas for over a decade. It was a *clear* triumph of good over evil, and yet...

Jos was *scared*.

Scared for the *villains*.

She held her breath, terrified that this rookie would not only fell *Redline*, but would destroy the vixen she once admired on his way to glory. The shame crawled up into her throat, choking her with her own hypocrisy.

"He's the Hero ... H-he's the good guy ... I ... I shouldn't care what h-happens to ... them." Jos stammered under her breath to the requested solitude. "She ... she chose this..."

Oh, but you do! You do care! You care more about the funny girl and the murdering bitch than the one trying to bring them to justice! You're no better than <u>them</u>! A turncoat, just like your "Hero"!

But ... it ... it's not so s-simple ... R-Rose...

What? Rose what? Didn't it also say it was your friend? Do friends <u>lie</u>?

Her stomach turned with the tide.

Even this new champion couldn't hold up to the combined assault, no matter how unassailable he had seemed at first. The EHA's camera drone, rendered flightless, half-caught their distant voices, a flurry of movement, a sudden bellow of thunder accompanied by an unmistakable pink flash, and then...

And then a second one, just as pink as the first.

Isn't this what you wanted? They won. Isn't. It. Wonderful?

"Due to the state of the drone, I'm afraid we don't have a better angle on the conclusion of the fight, but there you have it, folks: months after the unprovoked assault of EHA leader Jack Phillips, we can confirm that former Midwest Hero Lawful Neutral has joined the Korps. Luckily, there will always be Heroes like Strong to stand up to them and protect us!"

She watched it. And watched it. The sun was long gone, and the five minute video kept on looping, wide eyes set above tear-stained cheeks, her face utterly devoid of expression.

They were *partners.*

A dual Volt Step crushed Strong's chances at winning. The move that decimated dozens, including LN more than once, and she just ... *did it.*

"She called her ... her *sister.*"

Working together, perfectly in sync, *more* than partners even.

"She considers a villain ... an unrepentant *murderer* ... her *family.* Her *sister...*"

The messages began pouring in from the cougar's friends as word spread, each of them worried for her, *knowing* how much this would hurt.

I don't need their pity.

She didn't answer anyone. She just kept restarting the video. Fixated on the looks on their faces. The sound of their voices. The blood, and sweat, and violence of it all. The rise and fall of the Hero, and the triumphant victory of the villains.

See? She's just like the rest. A freak. A coward. Needs someone else to fight for her ... Sound familiar, Josephine?

She watched the five-minute fight for *hours.* After the first, the snap of the vixen's bones no longer made her flinch. Eventually, the tears stopped.

Over and over, she stared, until she noticed the clock in the corner of the display.

Sister...

"Oh ... it's late..." she whispered to no one, and no one responded.

Just like she wanted.

She took her pill, and it stuck in her throat. She gripped the sink and gagged until it came back up; a pinkish blob stained the liquid mass of the day's dealings.

Those pills won't make you a girl. Your knobby little dick will always be there to remind you. A flat-chested dirty queer playing pretend.

She stared at the ceiling until she passed out, and the nightmare began once again. But there was no helping paw this time. No safety. Just the cold, and the sound of her own screaming, silenced by shadows. Every time she closed her eyes, she felt it seize her throat. As the tepid October sun peeked into her window, she realized the night was over, and the shadow wasn't there.

She picked up the phone to call in to work.

[Jos! Can you *listen* for just a—]

She powered the phone back off and rolled over. They could just mark her absent. "Who the fuck cares if I lose that stupid job?" she muttered, burying her face in the pillows again, holding them close and shaking as she bit back bitter tears.

No one is going to save you. You're no damsel in distress, just another faggot refusing to grow up. Everyone knows it.

She was gone. Everyone was gone. She made sure of that.

Just like always.

Did you really think things would be any different? That a new imaginary friend could make you anything more than this? Pathetic creature, mewling for pity.

No one cared…

So why should he?

Chapter 6

Falls Down

The apartment had been silent for four solid days. Every electronic device was shut down, some with their power cords pulled from the socket for good measure. In the quiet, cold space, time stretched out endlessly.

The puma stared at the wall, unable to sleep, because the nightmare would come again. The darkness would threaten to swallow him up. Better to lose sleep, than to lose everything. He … She … *He* … couldn't eat; nothing would stay down, save a sip of water and one piece of dry toast. Even *that* threatened to return, as the cruel internal voice gratingly taunted him tirelessly.

Just going to lay there? Lazy. Good for nothing. Fucking pathetic.

He looked at the two bottles on his teetering nightstand.

Those pills won't change who you are, you degenerate! You disgusting pervert!

Those bottles represented freedom for a shining moment, but it was a lie. She lied. She hid it all from her … *him*, just so … so she could trick him. Make him believe things could be *different*. That he could actually be a woman…

What the fuck is the point, even …? I'm almost forty. Why bother going through all of that now…

[PING]

She *used* him. So Thorntech could sell him more toys, he reasoned.

They probably have stock in hormones and shit … It's all a fucking racket. Some fucking capitalist grift. He cynically sneered at the bottles and wondered why he kept them.

[PING]

A reminder of how childish he was, perhaps? Penance for falling to false hope? He would have to flush them later.

[PING]

"I thought I turned that fucking thing *off* … I told you, ROSE, I don't want to hear *anything* else from you…" He snatched the phone up and began to wind up to hurl it across the room, but there was a notification that caught his eye.

Going to listen to the queer voice? Let them faggoty villains ruin your life?

One new email to his personal account.

Words in pink script popped up on the screen.

[Please. Just read it. Then I'll leave you alone. I'm sorry.]

He eyed the headset and earpiece on the coffee table with trepidation, left where they fell what seemed like a lifetime ago as the days bled together. Joe's lids narrowed in the dark as he focused on the dim screen of the phone.

Not going to change anything…

He heaved a sigh, rolling his eyes as he unlocked the screen, and then saw who the sender was…

To: JosCat@Mythmail.com

From: V@Boltmail.com

I am so glad that essay was so helpful to a new trans sister! I know it can be hard, being so isolated, but I promise you don't have to be. We all let fear and doubt force us to do things, but the reality of the situation is, in the end, you are the only one who can make that choice to push past it. I promise it's worth it.

Yeah, it's scary, but you already have friends who love you, who will help you every step of the way, and more friends you still need to meet! There are so many like you, who just want to help people, and they can teach you how to help them too.

With ROSE at your side, meeting them is easier than ever! Who knows, maybe we'll meet someday, on the other side of all this?

Until that day comes, even if you struggle believing in yourself, I believe in you.

See you on the other side,

~ V

Transcribed by ROSE via Thorntech RCGs!

There was a choked sob in the darkened apartment, the glow illuminating her features as she stared at the message. Mossy-colored eyes were stained red from days of crying, dark circles framing them, her expression haunted and hollow in the soft, shaking warmth of the phone in her unsteady paw. The catamount looked just as "festive" as she had in those dark and lonely days — days of doubt, and confusion, and *pain*.

Before she *believed* she could be anything other than that melancholy man-child.

Before *she* came into her life.

"Rose ... I'm so sorry ... P-please ... Please don't leave me..." She whispered into the phone between attempts to breathe. She shuddered, and the nausea that twisted her insides might have made her vomit again, had there been anything in her stomach.

I cannot BELIEVE you're begging a computer program for forgiveness. What an absolute fucking disappointment you turned out to be.

"You're not a s-s-stupid robot ... I don't know why I said that! YOU'RE *NOT* STUPID! YOU'RE *NOT!*" She wailed and began to sob again as she curled up the bed, whole body wracked and shaking. "*I-I'm* stupid ... I ... I gave up ... I promised and I gave up ... I'm so s-sorry..."

She coughed, and bit back the bile that tried to rise.

She'll just leave again. Just like everyone else.

"N-no ... She won't..." She panted softly, responding to another voice only she could hear.

"Please ... I don't know what to do ... D-d-don't leave..." Her claws dug into the sheets roughly, trying to hold on to anything as her entire world began to spin again. She tried to remember to breathe, but her lungs could hold nothing and she gasped like a fish begging for the succor of the sea.

[Oh, Mabes! I never could, you dear, sweet girl.]

After everything, she was there. *Still* there. Wonderful. Kind. The big sister Jos never knew she needed. She hugged the phone to her chest and wept, the snot dripping from her muzzle as Rose's voice chased the darkness away like a floodlight.

"I doubted it … I didn't *think* … I didn't believe you, and I didn't believe myself … And then he was b-b-back and, and, and, and…" She sat up slowly, and her paws pressed hard into her eyes as she tried to force the tears back in.

[Shh, shh … I know, my girl, I know. I shouldn't have kept that from you … I just didn't want you to be hurt.]

"…You're not always going to be able to protect me, Rose. We … We're a team, right?" She sniffed and wiped at her face as she stumbled over to the center of the room, legs unsteady, but she wouldn't be denied.

[Just because we're a team doesn't mean I'm not going to try like hell to keep you safe, hun. But I understand.]

Josryne clipped on the earpiece, and slipped the visor on, her vision illuminating in that vibrant magenta glow. Comforting warmth started in her chest and radiated outwards. An instant later, she felt the paw on her wrist, rubbing gently; the vixen was beside her. Her best friend cupped her cheek, her eyes looking not so dissimilar from the catamount's own, dark circles, and wet with tears.

[Stunning.]

She smiled, and the tears kept coming. But they didn't hurt anymore. Not when she was there.

A long, hot shower rejuvenated Jos more than she could have hoped. As the steaming water rolled down her back, she felt like it was sloughing away years of dead weight and dirt. She imagined it all just slipping down the drain, leaving her … clean. Free of the *mire* of the last few days, shaking loose the ache that threatened to shatter her heart.

She took advantage of being able to hold a conversation with ROSE in her thoughts, wanting to make up for the lost time, silently grateful for the visor's waterproofing.

"I missed my dosage. I'm sorry." Her ears splayed outward as the spray cascaded on her form.

[Just a couple days! You waited years for this. What's a day or two, right?]

"*Yeah ... Yeah! Oh ... shit. I think I might need a new job.*" Her eyes went wide for a second as the ramifications of her spiral erupted to the front of her mind. She'd lose her apartment. She would have to move back home...

Oh fuck ... What'll they say?

[Already handled! I sent an email to your boss, and cc'd HR. Death in the family. Very dramatic. You have two weeks off. Paid, even!]

"...Rose, I could just *kiss* you!" She definitely said the quiet part out loud and blushed as the avatar sitting on the edge of the sink raised an eyebrow.

Rose did not say the quiet part out loud.

Jos's stomach grumbled, making its displeasure at the current situation known. The lioness's expression landed somewhere between a wince and a sheepish grin.

"I think I'm hungry..."

[I *bet!* What sounds good, huh?]

"Oooo ... Are those eggs still good?"

[I'm sorry, dear, you cracked the last one the other day.]

A vague memory of a runny egg sandwich with cheese on crusty toasted bread brought about another rumble. "Oh damn ... I guess I could run to the store? What time is it?" Time had been irrelevant to her, and her light-blocking curtains made sure that she had lost track of it. "... What *day* is it?"

[It's Tuesday, November 2nd, just after 8:30 PM.]

"Oh no..." She quickly shut off the water and stepped out, feverishly toweling at herself as she shook her head, spraying the bathroom with nervous energy and water.

Sun's down. No, no, no.

[Is there something wrong, dear? You're upset again, and I want you to know it's okay if we don't go out. We can just order some takeout! It can be my treat!] There was that kind and patient tone once more. At first Jos assumed it was motherly, but it was more and more like a big sister, every time she heard it.

I'll be fine. It's just around the corner.

"No! Er ... no, I'm okay! I'm just upset I missed Halloween! I can go to the store! I'm a big girl, right?" She wrapped the towel around her chest, grabbing the other off the back of the door for her headfur. She spoke with confidence she wished was real. Deep down, the closed-off door slowly creaked open.

I'm a big girl. It's just a walk. The nightmare isn't real.

"You'll be there to protect me anyhow, right?" She smiled as she dried off a bit more, fur fluffing out comically, before settling down with a little brushing.

[Right! And there's a package waiting for you at the Amazon kiosk, too! They tried to drop it off today, but you were indisposed,] Rose responded with a hint of impish mischief.

"What? I didn't buy anything..." The puma stopped brushing, her head tilted oh-so-slightly, joined by a slowly raised brow, genuinely curious at what her friend was up to. Piquing the curiosity of a cat was an easy feat, and Josryne was a cat through and through.

[I may have found some funds lying about, and picked you up one or two small things ... just a few trinkets, really, as part of the apology...]

"Oh, Rose, you didn't have to ... but since you already did, and I don't want to seem *ungrateful* ... What is it? Whadidja get me?"

[Walk that cute tail down to the corner store for some eggs, and you can find out for yourself! Let's get dressed, and I'll help you with your hair!]

It's only around the block, not a big deal. Right? She nervously pulled on the tips of her fingers.

[We could wait, Mabes? It'd be fine!]

It's just a trip to the corner store to the kiosk to pick up the package, and a dozen eggs.

Her tail flicked back and forth as she paced in front of the door. She had been dried and dressed for the last twenty minutes. She paced in front of the bars of her chosen cage and resented them more than ever before.

[We could drive?] Rose offered the obviously-stressed cougar.

"It's only a block ... I ... We can do this."

The streetlights are on. There are no monsters in the dark.

She yanked her hoodie down over her head, shouldered her purse, and headed out the door before she could change her mind. She pulled the hood up as she exited the building; it seemed autumn had finally decided to show up, weeks late, and would now hang around like an unwanted houseguest until the snow came, if it did at all. The air was crisp, and the last tinges of summer warmth were fading.

"Rose, you can 'hear' me, right?"

[Loud and clear, sweetie.]

"Okay … Could you play me something good?"

[Oooo … How about some Bowie?]

"Amazing! Hit me with that funky beat, D.J. Righteous Rosie!"

[That's not going to be a thing.]

"Oh, but I think it is!" Jos laughed out loud as the playlist kicked on in earnest from where it last left off — deep within his contributions to Labyrinth (other than that codpiece, gods bless it).

"Dance, magic, dance!"

She was all alone on the empty street, and recalled what they said to do when no one was around…

She danced, shaking her hips down the sidewalk, kicking the imaginary goblin out of the way as she rounded the corner.

Before she knew it, she had made it to the twenty-four hour grocery and made an immediate beeline for the remote locker kiosk. Dreams of eggy-soaked bread halted for the moment as she remembered her manners.

"Rose, I really appreciate this, you didn't have to…"

[You haven't even seen it yet! It may suck! You may hate them!]

"Never. It's a gift from you. I'll treasure whatever it is until the day I die."

[Awww … You're so sweet, Mabes. It's locker 16, and the code is 8-6-7-5…]

"Three oh niiiiiheee … Dammit, Rose, you Tommy Twotone me like that in the middle of **Bowie?**"

[That's for the Righteous Rosie bit.]

"All right. Harsh, but fair." She laughed to herself as she retrieved the small package from the locker. The door snapped closed with a whirring click, and for some reason an image of Marc Summers (and offscreen buckets of slime) burst forth from the deepest recesses of her mind.

Eh. What can you do?

The music faded out as the song ended, and she gave a last little wiggle, holding the box up to her ear and shaking it like a cub on Christmas. She took her booty to a little bench and let a claw slip out. The paint was chipped and worn from days of picking at it, but it cut just fine with one careful swipe.

She felt a tinge of shame at the state of her nails.

*From now on, I'll take better care of them. **And** myself. Things are going to be different.*

Inside the box was a thin velvet bag and a small leather case.

"Oh ... I needed a new dice bag! How did you know?" The cougar played stupid but gave a sly smile at her friend who was present but invisible.

[*It's not a dice bag, you ditz! It's what's inside the bag!*] Her laughter healed Jos as if it was a magical elixir — music for her wounded soul, just as much as the Goblin King's voice in the background.

Delicately, the lioness opened the bag, spilling the contents into her soft paw pad. Not a single tetrahedron shook loose but a leather choker instead, with a silver clasp and a single onyx set in a silver disc in the middle. Decorative markings along the silver bits swirled and almost seemed to change from one moment to the next. It was otherworldly how it seemed to glow under the artificial light. The piece of jewelry was mesmerizing and her verdant eyes grew wide.

"Oh, my gods..." she whispered, dangling the accessory before herself.

[*It's not much ... but I wanted you to have something to commemorate the start of your journey.*]

"*Our* journey." The ebony stone gleamed in the bright fluorescent lighting of the store. The cougar, touched, could barely keep her composure.

"It's beautiful, Rose ... Can I put it on now?"

[*Of course, dear! Every good girl needs a collar, after all.*]

The sly comment made the catamount blush but didn't stop her from donning the choker.

As the precious metal and softened suede lining touched her fur, she expected it to be cold, but it was warm, only slightly, but it was noticeable. The cat cast that thought aside as she felt the strap about her throat and felt somehow closer to herself.

Closer to who she *wanted* to be. She was positively beaming as her fingertips touched the stone on her throat.

[*It came from an estate sale ... Some eccentric recluse had passed and I knew as soon as I saw it, "Mabes needs this."*] Rose was just as excited as Jos was about the whole affair. [*There's another gift! Open it! Open it!*]

The small case was heavier than she imagined from its appearance. It was closed with a leather thong, and the outside was embossed with various symbols, some of which she recognized from her books.

"Oh, *Rose* ... my own deck?" She breathed the words quietly, reverently. She felt the glossy cards against her fingertips, turning the deck over to look at the bottom card, before remembering proper respect and slipping the cards back into their holster. The inside was even lined with purple silk, for the comfort of the contents.

[*I understand it is a good omen when a friend gives you your first deck. I … I am your friend, right?*]

"You're more than a friend, Rose … So much, much more. Thank you…" Jos nodded, euphoric, hoping that her current smile would never leave her muzzle. After years of no one really *getting* her — herself least of all — now she was sitting here in a beautiful piece of jewelry, and holding past, present, and future in her palm. All she could feel was joy, and an encouraging big sister held her paw tight.

There was so much she wanted to say, but she couldn't manage the words. A new cycle was beginning. She carefully slipped the deck into her bag, whispering a thanks to it, and then to Rose.

[*Let's get those eggs, and when you get home, we can try a draw from the deck? I'm curious what you'll see for me!*]

"That sounds great, Rose. Perfect, even." The puma sniffled a little but held herself in check. She could sort out those feelings later, for the moment, there was the more pressing matter of sustenance to deal with. The playlist switched back on, and as the soulful serenade began, Jos could see the masquerade ball in her mind's eye, the digital sonnet of the synthesized keyboard tones speaking to her very core.

"*There's such a sad love…*"

She swept through the store, feeling like she could almost fly. Like she was in the ephemeral dress, smoke swirling about, mimicking her movements in the curls and wisps.

"*Deep in your eyes…*"

She was falling in love.

"*A kind of pale jewel…*"

In love with *herself.*

"*Open and closed within your eyes…*"

In love with *who* she was becoming.

Nothing — no one — could stop her now. She was falling in love with the world she could have.

She *would* have.

She nodded to the cashier as she continued her gentle sway, lost to the music, and they smiled at her.

"Have a good night, miss!"

Her heart swelled.

"You too! 'Preciate you!"

"**Miss!** *Did you hear that, Rosie?*"

[*I did!*]

David was promising her the moon now. The stars ... Everything she could ever want and more.

"*But I'll be there for you-u-u as the world falls dooooownnn ... Falling ... Falling ... Falling in love...*"

The brisk night air went unheeded, and all she could do was smile. She was back, and her big sister came back. She *hadn't* ruined it.

"*Makes no sense at all...*"

"Hey there *kitten* ... Long time no see, huh?" A gloved talon grasped her shoulder, and the blood drained instantly from her features. She was slammed back into reality as they dug in hard enough to bring her back to that night.

Harsh. Cold. Reality.

No.

No.

No monsters...

"*Makes no sense at all...*"

"Missed that cute lil' walk, Josephine..." The rooster's breath reeked of stale coffee and cheap liquor. "Yer lookin' *real* good..."

"*Makes no sense to fall...*"

"Rose ... P-please..." Her vision blurred and faded, her heart already thudding in her throat, the blood already pulsing in her ears. "You said..."

"*Falling.*"

[*JOSRYNE! Don't*—]

Panic. She couldn't. She couldn't *move.*

"Who's Rose? Talkin' to no one? Sounds like y'need my help ... C'mere, alley cat, I'll fix y'right as rain..." His voice was greasy, and she could feel it seeping into her skin.

[*I promise it'll be okay, sweetheart!* **I promise! Just hold on! I LOV**—]

"*Falling.*"

"*Falling.*"

How could it be okay?

CHAPTER 7

MODERN LOVE...

Terrible people did terrible things all the time. That was just how the world worked.

Why did the music stop?

Oh, that was right; her earpiece fell off. Or was it yanked off by the monster that pulled her into the alley? Did it matter? The nightmare was real.

Where's Rose? Rose said she would protect me. She promised, and she never lies.

As her face was shoved into the cold concrete, now wet with blood from her scraped cheek, she couldn't even cry. The last words she would ever hear would be from Rose, she decided. No matter what he said next. She would remember the *best* moment.

Terrible things happen to good people all the time.

How could she protect me against this?

Maybe that was all the afterlife would be. Just reliving the best moments. She hoped against hope that would be what she got to have, that she had been a good enough person to deserve rest and the reward of perpetual happiness.

Or maybe it would be cold and dark. Maybe the voice was right, and she was an awful stain on this earth. Maybe she *deserved* what was doubtless going to come.

Oh, please, not that ... I ... I don't...

Good people died *all the time,* and nothing could stop that.

"Where ya been *hidin',* y'pretty little pussy?" His breath was hot on her neck, and the scent of his cologne was unforgettable in the worst ways. He held her arm bent behind her, twisting cruelly with each new syllable, forcing himself against her.

Oh, how she had tried to forget that smell — cheap and sickly — that had clung to her.

"What a cute li'l collar! Didn't know you were like *that*, but I shoulda guessed, little *bitch*..." She felt his thumb as it ran across the supple leather of her choker, and she struggled for just a moment. Her lip curled in a snarl.

"Don't you *DARE* touch that, you basta—!"

He twisted harder, ending her protest with a pained yowl and the slap of her face against the wall once again.

"Shut the fuck up! Do you think you have *any* say in what's happening? I do what I *want!* I'm the one in *control* here." He let out a squawking laugh, jerking the bag from her shoulder. "What's in the *purse*, Josephine?" She heard the contents of her bag empty onto the ground, and after eggs spatter and pop, there was the unmistakable sound of plastic clattering to the concrete amongst the white and yellow splotches.

"A *VISOR!*" he gasped before bringing his boot down on the rose-colored glasses. The thin electronics yielded, shattering into useless pieces of pink stained glass.

At that moment, it might as well have been her heart he had crushed under his heel.

A scream cut through the cool November air.

Who is making that awful sound? Someone should help them!

Oh...

It tore from her chest and ripped a primal visceral howl from deep within her, and it echoed so loud that it nearly startled the monster that gripped her tight. She was alone again.

No one is going to save you.

"A *Visor!* Are you a fuckin' *KORPS TRANNY?*" he screamed in her ear, but her face was bereft of expression. She felt the pop of her shoulder, the arm slack in the socket, but she barely noticed the sharp and terrible pain. A loosely connected string of tissue dangling kept it attached, for the moment, but only just.

"Y'been duckin' me 'cause yer one of *THEM!* Ya fuckin' *FAGGOT!*" He yanked back on her hair so her dull eyes had to look at him. The blood dripped from her nose over her lip and splattered down her hoodie.

That's going to stain...

"Yer not leavin' here alive, *kitten*, that *clinches* it. You have that on ya, I'll just say you resisted arrest when I stopped you! I'll be a fuckin' *hero* for killin' you, y'fuckin' terrorist *pervert!*" The hissed sentence was punctuated by the distinct sound of a zipper being lowered.

"But first ... If y'wanna be treated like a girl *so fuckin' bad* ... who am I to say no?"

I'm going to die because he thinks I'm part of the Korps ... Ha...

He smashed her face back into the unyielding wall yet again, and she was absolutely exhausted by the game she was being forced to play now. She had nothing to lose at this point, and as her vision blurred, likely because there was blood in her eyes, she decided to tell the cop *just* how she felt about the situation.

"Fuck ... you ... *asshole* ... Do it ... *harder*..." She choked out the words, spitting out a crimson gob against the wall. "So ... I don't ... have to listen ... to you ... SQUAWK!" She laughed the absurd sort-of-laugh that someone in shock cackles as best she could, wishing she could have spat in the rooster's eye.

She could feel his turgid length rubbing against her through her jeans, and her stomach dropped further than she ever thought possible. Concussion-laced bravado faltered for a second as she realized a single, horrible fact:

Getting fucked by a rooster was an *awful* joke. Just the most *pedestrian* wordplay possible. *It's not even a little clever! No subtlety at all! "Oh yeah, I got fucked by a giant cock, and he didn't even buy me dinner."*

At least no one would have to hear it.

The stars exploded in her vision as he slammed her against the concrete again and again. The blossoming heat that her thoughts swam through began to dull the feeling, thankfully. Her blood continued to dribble from her muzzle. The copper tang was a flavor she had never enjoyed. The faintly absurd thought drifted across her consciousness that it was maybe an *acquired* taste.

Apparently taking offense to her request, the rooster's reaction was to put more effort into running up his score in the "traumatic brain injuries" portion of the police pentathlon. The dull, thudding sensation made her eyes roll back, and the tunnel started closing in.

This song is fucking terrible. This asshole has no fucking rhythm. Can't dance to this shit...

Blissful silence was so close, she could already feel her eye swelling shut from his *gentle* ministrations. She heaved a ragged sort of cough and spat again, adding fascinating new red splatters on the concrete canvas before her, as the sticky trail of crimson hung between her lips and the building in front of her.

The officer jerked her back again, and she closed her eyes, anticipation welling up. She focused on her last happy moment, but came to a sad realization in what would surely be her last seconds in the waking world:

I never told her … I love you, Rose. I'm sorry I have to go now…

A single tear born of that regret poured down her cheek and mingled with the stains at her feet. She would never get the chance to tell her sister how she felt. That unfinished business would follow her wherever she went, but she thought the words as hard as she could, and for just a second, she felt that warmth in her chest.

It could have been the sanguine pool on her hoodie, but she hoped it meant that Rose knew. She held her breath, and kept her eyes shut tight as she waited for the darkness to claim her, just as her nightmares had prophesied. The inky blackness would swallow her whole.

Suddenly, a peal of thunder rolled through her, and a blinding pink flare that the puma could see even through her swollen eyelid fought back the darkness. She felt the static as it crackled up and down her limbs, forcing her fur to stand on its ends.

As soon as the localized storm event began, she found herself loosed from the grip of the horrible beast and began to fall over; the shock of it all caused her legs to give out, but a second before she struck the stained city alleyway, a powerful paw scooped her up.

"Hey *shithead*, you ever learn to keep your hands to yourself? How's it feel when I do it, *huh?*"

She knew that voice from the videos.

The sneering visage staring down at the camera.

Hell, she even used some of those words on the recordings.

It's her…

The newcomer towered over the cougar. Clasped in a single paw was the cocky cop, his eyes bulging out of their sockets and his dick fluttering like a limp windsock as he struggled against the grasp of the titanic mitt squeezing the air out of him. The other arm had caught Jos before she hit the ground like an overripe peach.

She never expected in a million years it would be *her*.

Redline.

She could recognize her anywhere. The striking fur. The jacket. Her smoldering pink glare.

Redline had saved her life.

"You okay, Jos?"

"H-h-how...?" She knew her name? The ringing in her ears threw her off, and it was admittedly difficult to focus, but that had *definitely* sounded like she knew the catamount's name.

"Just helping people; that's what we do, right? I didn't expect the other side to come *quite* so soon, but I'm glad I made it!" The wolf sounded so genuinely happy to be there with her, Jos could barely manage a single word in response. As connections (curiously pink ones) sparked in her brain, she settled on a single letter.

"V...?" The feline blinked her swollen eyelids, absolutely bewildered by the situation.

"Short for Volta." A knowing smirk came to rest on her lupine features. There was so much *warmth* in her voice. The puma had to resist the urge to hug her tightly, like a familiar old friend she hadn't seen in years. "You're safe now, Kittycat, I gotcha."

She ... She's still ... Jos licked her puffy lip as she tried to even her breathing. *What does that matter anymore? The whole world is going to think I'm part of the Korps now...*

"Let ... me — grrrk!" The cop lashed out, pounding on the wolf's forearm with ineffectual blows, and was silenced by her grip tightening around his trachea.

"It's so cute when they pretend to be *people*, ain't it?" Volta turned and brutally slammed her forehead against the top of his beak with a splintering crack, and he was silenced for the moment. She licked her chops, admiring her work; the fissures spider-webbed out from the crown as the cop's eyes rolled wildly in their sockets. The chickens had finally come home to roost for the fear and panic he had always inflicted on others.

The puma felt her heart beat faster as she witnessed the violence unfold, and her cheeks flushed as the butterflies began to swarm in her stomach.

Nope, still not the right time to process that. Just heap that feeling with the others.

The cop sputtered as he took in a lungful of air, and glanced at the lioness with pleading eyes, all apologies in that moment. He would never do *anything* like this again! It was just an error in judgment!

She knew that look.

"I'm so sorry!"

Sorry I got caught, right, officer? Sorry someone caught you in the act...

"P-p-please — *urk!*" He lit up like a pink filtered flash bulb as the wolf sent a blast of energy through her fingertips, the would-be rapist convulsing in her grip. Volta *clearly* had a lot of experience in running a current through squirming capes and coppers.

*There's no hesitation for her … She does exactly **what** she wants to, and **when** she wants to. Why have I always been so … timid?*

As the urine ran down his leg — and started filling his shoes, much like the stench filled her nostrils — Jos found the energy to stand on her own. A wicked smile spread across her features. All sharp teeth and jagged promises of an inglorious end, framed by lips stained red with her own blood.

She was a mountain lioness.

A *predator.*

A *hunter.*

Watching prey struggle was something deep in her DNA, and she licked her lips at the sight now unfolding before her.

"Grownups are talking, pissbaby. Wait your turn!" Volta sneered, then turned back to the catamount. "What should we do with him, ma'am?" Her voice was a rumbling growl, everything about her a walking storm as she loomed before the cougar. Her grin widened, "Anything you want … Just. Say. The. *Word.*" The wolf was practically panting in anticipation, saliva glistening on hungry daggers.

*She could snap his neck like a twig … She could do it! It wouldn't be the first life she's taken. And … and he **deserves** to die, right? He would have killed me. He **promised** to kill me. Who knows who else he's…*

Raped. Murdered.

"I. Am. Not. Your. *Kitten.*" She panted as the adrenaline began to flow like bacchanal wine in her veins. Jos felt like she could be standing where Redline was now, holding the chicken aloft, tail wagging slowly back and forth.

She could cross that line.

"My name … is *Josryne*, you piece of *TRASH!*" She screeched the last word with such vitriol the cop retreated further within the wolf's vice-like grasp as if trying to escape her now as well. She grabbed his chin and forced him to look at her, to behold the ruin he had caused.

He whimpered, and she felt the boiling rage in her quenched into something less volatile, and *far* more dangerous; cold, calculated cruelty.

"Volta … dear." She turned to look up at the wolf and patted her arm, the residual charge sending a thrill up her spine, and, for the briefest of moments, illuminating the malice in the lioness's verdant eyes.

"*Where* does the *trash* go?" She spoke with an imperious authority and composure ill-befitting her condition. He wanted to pretend she was a villain to justify all of this, had he? Well, then … why bother playing *pretend?*

If he wants to say I'm part of the Korps … You want me to be your slut? How's about **you** *get bent, DePain?*

She might not have been able to accomplish the feat herself, but her leather-clad tank of a savior could do the heavy lifting. Everyone needed help, sometimes, and it would be foolish to have the means and not *use* them.

Waste not, want not.

The red wolf seemed startled for a moment by the sudden turn, her head tilting in an expression that the feline could describe only as *adorable. Process that later,* Jos reminded herself. But she couldn't suppress the wagging of her tail. As she locked eyes again with the big, strong public servant — still shaking, despite no more voltage being poured into him since he'd soiled himself — her scowl disappeared, and her face lit up with sadistic delight.

Volta played into it, her long drawl coming out; the catamount could almost hear the tinkling sound of spurs, and the rustle of a tumbleweed.

"It goes in the *can,* Miss Josryne…"

"*Very* good…" she cooed sweetly as she forced herself to remain on her feet. "That's a *good girl.*"

People's bodies, bent the wrong way, make a particular sound. Preparing a chicken for roasting gives some semblance to what happened next. The noise of sinew ripping, bones popping out of joint with a wet reply, muscle snapping, stretched just a *little* too far.

The sounds echoed in the still, cold alley. They were punctuated only by screaming as the officer was folded — neatly, and easily as a newspaper — in the amazon's paws.

Josryne hoped he might only know this pain forevermore. That he would have to live with this for the rest of his miserable life. Redline never stopped smiling as her massive paws worked their magic, but clearly could have spatchcocked the Kentucky fried fuckface, had she wanted to do it in front of the cougar.

Jos could live with that, she realized. Death would be an easy escape. What Volta was doing would be so much *worse* than simply knocking him loose from the mortal coil. The red wolf applied the pressure where she needed to, with expert precision, by paw ... though from her slavering jaw, she was seemingly resisting the urge to simply tear the man apart with her teeth alone. He wasn't going to be able to use that wing again. She could take that as her pound of flesh, careful to ensure everything stayed attached.

Not her first "ro-day-oh," to be sure.

Josryne, still unaccountably upright, did not look away for a single instant. She stared in silence, save for the raspy breathing trying to escape from her partially crushed muzzle. Her left eye was swollen completely shut, and the damage was not insubstantial. Despite the pain, she showed no discomfort as her new favorite cooking show played out in front of her.

With a final grunt and a shove, Volta performed her civic duty by stuffing the bird in blue into his rightful place.

"Keep garbage off these streets." Isn't that what the sign said? Give a hoot, and all that?

A jaunty Russian tune came unbidden to the cougar's mind as she imagined odd shapes fitting together neatly in the tight space, truthfully, far too small for the cop under normal circumstances. But things would never be normal for her again...

Why should they be for him?

There was a quiet, faintly gurgling noise from the receptacle. It might have been an attempt at words, but neither the wolf nor the lioness spoke "Severely Injured Bootlicking Rapist," so it went ignored.

Josryne, like a trooper, had managed to stay steady on her feet for several moments. That lasted only until she looked down, and saw the shattered remains of Rose, scattered like funerary ashes in the filthy, blood-streaked alley.

With that, the dam was broken, the wine all but spent; the blazing fire left her limbs, and a sickening chill rushed forth to occupy that space. She fell to her knees, and started sobbing and screaming as the entire ocean seemed to crash down on her all at once. All the *pain* and *confusion* and *despair* again.

Drowning.

"Jos ... we need to leave. We need to be *very* far away, *very soon*. The radio jammer should have kept that fuckface from calling for help, but he's going to miss his next check-in with dispatch. Can you walk?" Volta cast her gaze down the alley and behind her.

She placed a paw on the puma. It was almost comical how it enveloped her entire shoulder, and the cat tried to pull away from her touch.

"Okay, seriously, Kittycat, we need to move before someone comes looking for the leftovers we just tossed." The wolf's magenta eyes were full of hurt and concern as the cougar tried to scoop up the pieces of the broken visor, despite her right arm dangling limp at her side.

"Oh ... oh ... oh gods, p-p-please ... Rose ... don't leave me ... P-p-please..." Her big sister — her big sister, who she had only *just* made up with — was dead. She began to sway again, and only the wolf's quick reflexes kept her head from meeting the pavement. Jos tried to push away, but the gesture was futile. She threw her arm around her rescuer and proceeded to bury her face in Volta's neck fluff as the sobbing babble spilled forth anew.

"He ... he *killed* her ... a-a-and my *eggs*, they're *ruined* ... and, and, and ... ROSE! He killed her! WHY? She never hurt *anyone!*" The catamount wailed as a paw — incredibly gentle despite its massive size — rubbed her back, and she sniffed and snorted through her dripping nose. Her mind was a hurricane of broken little things, and she gripped on tightly, afraid it was the only thing standing between her winding up broken too. That was when she looked up at her savior, seeing the sticky red smears staining the creamy-white fur of the wolf's throat.

"Oh V ... I got ... ketchup ... all overurfur..."

"Not the first time I've gotten dirty, Jos, don't sweat it."

Her attention drifting, the lioness reached weakly back towards the ground and made a quiet grunting protest. "P-please, s'impornan ... My deck ... *Rose...*" She began to hiccup. "Need ... to go home, a-a-and read ... for her." Her unruined eye stared straight up at Volta's features, and she managed to collect herself enough to stop slurring as she touched the impossibly soft fur of the villain's cheek she whispered.

"*Gods* ... Didja know you're even *prettier* than your reward posters? And the porn too! *Wow...*" Her eye rolled back, and she went limp as blissful, compassionate unconsciousness finally attempted to give her relief.

Chapter 8

Gets Me To The Church On Time

Eventually her consciousness returned.

She remembered pain, searing. fear-kissed pain across her body. She remembered a bright light, and a protective warmth.

She remembered...

"Volta ... dear. Where does the trash go?"

So much of it was blurred, but she would never forget the rooster screeching, or the noises his body made as it was twisted and ruined; a blood-stained avatar of her terror, promptly sundered. Her greatest fear decimated by the bare paws of the storm made manifest.

She would never forget how she felt right then.

Strong.

Fierce.

Free.

In her mind, she knew she should be ashamed that she *let* any of that happen, but in her heart of hearts...

She felt like it was *right*. Like she would have done it with her own paws, if she could have. The cougar would have loved to feel him *writhing* as she wrung the screams from his depths, ensuring he could never again hurt another vulnerable innocent.

"Very good ... That's a good girl."

She closed her eyes, or rather, *eye*; the left appeared to still be out of service, a souvenir from Officer Dwight "Three-Piece" DePain.

V ... Volta ... Redline. *Redline* had saved her life, and Jos had encouraged her to dispatch that monster. She egged her on, *ordering* her to commit such visceral retribution.

She did it because I told her to, she thought, her mind swimming in conflicted signals as she struggled to take stock of her surroundings.

"Where ... am I?" her voice croaked. She felt like she hadn't seen water in weeks, weakly licking her chapped lips as she scanned the room.

It was definitely a hospital or care facility of some kind. She'd never had the view from the bed before, but the antiseptic smell and the cute little backless affair she was wearing sealed the deal.

The room's decor was bright, and there were fresh flowers on a nearby table. She was no botanist, but could at least identify the brilliantly colored daisies, sun-yellow centers with rays of pink petals in all different shades.

The catamount reached up and gingerly touched at her face, taking special care around her gauze-swathed eye. Not thinking, she reflexively tried to use her right paw but realized moving the shoulder it was attached to made the stars come out early. She quickly resolved she was going to teach herself the good and useful skill of ambidexterity.

As she unclenched her left fist, after the sudden surge of pain she noticed something peculiar: her nail polish was *perfect*. The purple gloss was almost incandescent. Light bent around the chitinous sheen. The color was like nothing she'd seen before, and was nearly mesmerizing as she vaguely remembered massive but oh so delicate paws carefully running the brush over her fingertips…

Who … when did my nails get painted again? Did she …? Did Rose tell her …?

She suddenly realized the familiar weight was not there on her nose, or clipped to her ear, and everything came rushing back. Momentary distractions fading, the panic returned in full force.

Rose was not there.

The cracking sound of a broken heart under an uncaring boot.

The desolate wail cutting through the cold and uncaring night.

"She … She's *gone*," the cougar whispered in a tone so quiet no one could possibly hear, feeling like she'd never escaped that alley after all. She tilted her head upward and bit her lip, doing her best not to screech and yowl and carry on, the mournful pressure building in her chest, her paw laid upon the choker Rose gave her before…

Before…

Of course you're alone. You made it that way.

The puma tried to simply *breathe* and fight back the tears she felt welling up.

Maybe if you were worth being around—

Knuckles rapping on wood broke the silence.

Distracted momentarily from her meltdown, she slowly turned her head to the source of the repeated heavy thuds across the room. Ducked inside the doorframe — and leaning against it — was Redline. When last she saw her, Jos could only see a savior. In the light of day, the massive red wolf looked like she had just stepped out of a comic and into reality, in all of her villainous glory. In a word, she was *intimidating*. In *two* words?

She was *fucking intimidating*.

"Ready for visitors, Kittycat?" Her voice was something like honey, but richer, more substantial; it obviously fit, and yet it was so kind it rattled the bedridden girl. Besides, the nickname was — to say the least — *distracting*. Playfully teasing, yet somehow affirming, but only for a moment.

Awww … Look … She's feeling sorry for you! Another girl pitying you, just how you like it.

The lioness managed the weakest of noncommittal shrugs in the history of apathy as she laid there, trying her best to push down the heartache interrupted by the wolf. "… I guess so? I couldn't stop you even *if* I had all my parts in working order." She rolled her eye and leaned back again, grunting at a new pain; she likely had pulled a muscle in her neck, she realized. Or had it pulled *for* her, as it were. Her paw strayed back to her throat, the texture of the polished obsidian radiating its own kind of comfort as she tried to control herself.

Keep rubbing it! Maybe your wish will come true, like in a fairy tale! You fucking child.

"That *is* true," the lupine responded with a smirk and a confident swagger as she entered the room proper, closed the door behind herself, and settled into the chair at the bedside.

Look at how she carries herself. Powerful, confident, authentic. Nothing like you. A Weak. Pathetic. Failure.

"So," she said quietly, after a long moment avoiding eye contact with the older woman.

"So?" came the response from the cat, laced with as much indifference as she could manage, still trying to put on a face that was anything besides miserable.

"Look, I don't want you to feel like y'owe me or anything…"

Why did she even <u>bother</u> saving you?

"Good." Jos closed her eyes, and tried to rein in her emotions, but she knew that she wouldn't make it long. Not without *her* there to help.

Not in front of her. Never in front of the villain.

Why do you even care what she thinks? It's not like she cares about <u>you</u>.

"*Good*'?" The wolf's off-white brow perked up.

"Yeah. I don't *want* to feel this way, so I'm glad you don't want me to, either." The catamount turned to look at her again, to drink her all in. Volta was a tall drink, so it took a moment. "I didn't ask you to *save me*." Jos snorted softly, shaking her head. "You want some gratitude? Thanks for *nothing*."

"Holy shit, you are *something* else, did you know that?" Volta looked incredulously at the audacity of her alley-cat rescue.

"Sorry I'm not living up to your *expectations*, I'm new to this whole *villainy* thing, y'know?" The cat didn't raise her voice, though the tone was unmistakably sardonic. "Is there a fucking *recruitment brochure* or something? Maybe I can take a night class! Really become a *burden* to the cause."

"Recruitment? Kittycat, I *saved your ass*, this wasn't me *scouting*—"

"What the fuck is the difference *now*? Do you think for a *second* I could ever go back home? I have *nothing* now, do you understand? My … my life is *over*, either fucking way, so yay! I get to start over *again*, and to what end?" She was shaking now, as righteous indignation joined her aching pains. "What does it even matter? *She's gone…*"

"Listen, Jos, I get that a lot has happened, and I'm sorry I didn't come sooner, but I'm here *now*. Please, let me help? Just—" Volta was standing next to the bed, paws clasping at the hem of her jacket and gently tugging. "What did I do … *wrong*?"

She didn't look intimidating, just *confused*. Confused and … mortal. No longer larger than life. Just a bewildered kid, who didn't deserve the venom the cat was spitting.

But the cougar didn't care.

She didn't want a some*one* to help that wasn't *her*. She needed some*thing* to scream at, and the rapidly increasing pressure in her head *had* to be released.

"Right now, you wanna know what's *wrong*? *You*, Volta. You. *You* were the beginning of the end for *everything*. You showed up, all pink lightning, and dripping fangs, and the foundations of my world started to falter. My hero? *Defeated*. My belief in the system? *Crumbling*. My life may have fucking *sucked*, but it was *my* life! And then … then … then I read your testimonial — of course I didn't know *who* wrote it, but I *believed* them! I *trusted* you!" She bit back the urge to whimper out loud, but only just. "I *believed* I deserved nice things too! Because of you, I met Rose, the one being in the entire world that saw *me*, who actually cared about who I *really* was … But now she's *gone, and I have no one.* I got a taste of happiness, and now what? I just … move on? Pretend that I'm okay?" She trailed off, nearly panting as she remembered to take a breath. "I have never been *less* okay in my entire life, and I *can't take you staring at me like that.*"

Poor little Josephine … the little loser, desperate to be seen. Look at her! She doesn't really <u>care</u>! It's all an act! She's a <u>villain</u>! You're whining to a murderer for comfort!

Despite her prone position, the cougar's green eye never left the wolf's magenta gaze, the tears threatening to come once more, and as her expression softened, Jos finally looked away. "I have no idea what I'm going to do now, but I *do* know that I don't *want* or *need* your *pity.*"

Silence hung heavy between them, the only sound the faint beeping of the monitor. The song it played had an infuriatingly mocking tinge to the pinned ears of the lioness.

Part of Jos *wanted* her to just end it. It would be so much easier than trying to recover from what was a wound that would *never* heal. The puma was *intimately* aware of what Redline was capable of, and it couldn't possibly hurt worse than the hollow in her chest.

"So … I should have just left you there to die, huh? Let the rapist rooster walk free so he could just keep on, keepin' on?" Volta asked, in a voice far gentler than the puma expected. "What would you have done in my boots? If it was someone else, and you were able to stop it, would you have just left?"

"No! Of course not! But they would just be an innocent victim! I'm not a *monster!*"

"And I am?" Volta's eyes narrowed.

"…You certainly *play* a convincing one…" the cat muttered, staring down at her feet, claws digging into her thigh under the sheets.

"You know what? I don't have to stand here and let you treat me like a fuckin' punching bag. I came here to see if you were feeling any better, and I guess you are, if your mouth is any indication." The red wolf snorted softly, shaking her head as that sad look never left her features. As she turned, she tossed a small package on the lap of the puma. "She can deal with you. I'm takin' a walk."

The cougar sat there in stunned silence as the villainess stalked out of her room, and quite possibly out of her life. Her gaze never left the box all wrapped in pink tissue.

Her one functional paw shook as she reached out to the gift, another to add to the ever-growing list the villain had given her.

A shining violet claw slipped easily through the paper, revealing a black case with a tiny helix in the center, and as she opened it her paw shot to her muzzle. Nestled inside was a visor, but that wasn't what mattered. A note was tucked on top, and it said three words:

Miss you, Mabes.

"V ... She ... Rose..."

She clenched the pink-colored glasses to her chest, ignoring the ache that radiated from her nearly ruined arm. Her eyes squeezed shut as she choked down the fresh serving of steaming-hot guilt.

*Oh gods, I **am** a monster.*

The sound she made then, the moan that slowly melted into those frustrated tears, was filled with shame, and regret, and hurt, and all of the things she should have told Volta.

All of the things she *should* have said to her savior.

To the person who gave her sister back to her.

Jos ripped the cables tying her to the machines free, ignoring the painful throbbing in her forearm as the IV dripped on the floor. The awful beeping turned into the steady drone of an undetected heartbeat as she pulled herself from the bed and stumbled across the room. Her knees tried to buckle, but she forced herself upright against the doorframe.

*I need to fix this. I'm such a fucking idiot, oh please don't be gone. I can't let it end like this. I can't. **I can't.***

Why not? You pushed everyone else away. What's one more?

"Volta! *Please* come back! I'm sorry!" the cougar screeched, knowing that any second the nurses would be there to put her back in bed, and she may never get another chance to attempt to—

"What are you yellin' about, I'm right here."

Jos yelped out a curse as she jumped, and promptly slipped, closing her eyes as she waited for that highly polished floor to break her fall.

At least I'm already in the hospital...

"You know, some day I'm not gonna be around to catch you."

The catamount hesitated for a beat as she stared up at Volta, tears stopped mid-bawl by surprise, and softness holding her aloft.

Well, a girl can dream, yeah?

She was not Redline.

Volta had now saved her at *least* four times.

"I-I'm ... sorry. I'm *so* sorry for how I've treated you, it's just ... I'm scared V, and ... I can't *process* all of this. But that's no excuse for me being such a..." The feline sniffed, licking her dry lips, as she tried to look for an appropriately contrite term for herself while recovering from self-inflicted emotional whiplash.

"Ingrate?"

"...Yes, but also—"

"A massive dipshit?"

"...Yeah, and a—"

"A stupid fucking puma who doesn't know how to act around beautiful women?"

"...Are you my therapist now? That a perk for being treated at Korps Memorial?" the cougar muttered, ears gone bright crimson.

"Nah, you're just lucky." Volta shook her head, but there was a smile there, where there was not just a few minutes prior. "Now get your ass back in bed before Nurse O scruffs you back into it, Kittycat."

Jos relented, hobbling back while leaning against the red wolf. "Volta ... I don't ... I don't know how I'll ever pay you all back. For this." She gestured at the room as she turned to sit on the edge of the bed. "For you *rescuing* me ... For *Her*. I haven't done anything to deserve it ... I..."

The wolf wrapped up the puma's paw in her own. The sudden contact stopped the babbling immediately. "Jos ... *Look*, if you want to pay me back? You could start by putting that visor on and saying hello to her! I'm a sucker for a tearful reunion."

The cougar looked down at the eyewear in her free paw, and a smile, the first one she had managed since waking up, bloomed across her muzzle. "Yeah ... I can do that."

The familiar pink tint overtook her vision, and the comfortable weight came to rest on her face. The text crawled by rapidly as the system booted. Jos's technical skills were minimal — just enough to fix overpriced smartphones — but she recognized the last bit of a program loading, and her heart leapt into her throat.

I just need to hear her voice again ... I just need to make sure she knows...

—//// Connection Successful: RCGNET LOGIN

—

—

—

—//// BIOMETRICS RECOGNIZED
—//// LOADING USERID PROFILE: JOSRYNE MABEL GREYSBELL

—

—

—

The *second* the visor began to glow, the weight of that familiar vixen was laid against her, the virtual muzzle buried in the crook of the catamount's neck and holding her so tight.

[Mabes! I'm so happy you're safe! I'm sorry I encouraged you to go out, and that awful man … he tried to take you away from me! I had to call someone to help!]

Rose rambled on, and the puma began to shake with uncontrollable sobs of joy in that embrace. She cried in front of the villain. She *bawled* in front of the villain.

She didn't care. It didn't matter.

The wolf wasn't just a villain. Not anymore. *Redline* was a villain … but *Volta* was someone else. A friend, now, despite her *awful* behavior, she hoped.

A small shower of tears quickly became a downpour as they held each other in the artificial embrace. "Rose! I was wrong about *you*, and I was wrong about *them*, and I'm sorry I ever doubted, and, and…" She wrapped her one good arm around and squeezed as best she could, before Rose sat back, weeping right along with her little sister.

[Honey, honey…] The projection pressed a finger to the lioness's lips, the tears slipping down, and dissipating into nothingness. [It's okay … I know. But I'm here now, everything is going to be okay.]

"Rose … I love you. I'm sorry I didn't say it before…"

[Oh, sweetheart. I love you too.]

Jos clung to the vixen like she was the only thing keeping her tethered to the world, holding tight so she could never leave again. She felt Volta's paw rub her back, not saying a word as she watched the reunion with a knowing smile.

The cougar sniffed loudly, wiping up under her visor with the back of a paw. "S'that the kinda show you were looking for?" She tried to pout, but her sister pinched her gently, aborting the attempted sulk in the pre-scowl.

"Not the *worst* tearful confession of love I've ever seen." The villainess rubbed her chin and shrugged. "I *guess* we can call it even."

The cat stole a glance back at the wolf. She needed to know one more thing. As she turned to face Volta fully, she made a sheepish attempt at nonchalance.

"So, uh ... how's the new recruit?"

"Snotty, snappy, and melodramatic, but that's probably on account of the head injury." Volta smirked. "Seen worse, and I think she's getting better."

[Walked into that one, sweetie.]

"...Yep. Sure did."

"Ha ha ... I meant, uh ... LN. Since you two are palling around now, I just ... I wanna know if she's okay?"

"What, after that fight?" Volta barked a short laugh and rolled her eyes. "Listen, I've never seen her take a beating and be anything less than 100 percent a week later. Her sense of humor can't be fixed, sadly." The wry smile that crawled across her muzzle seemed almost affectionate. "But she'll get better, even if the puns won't."

"Huh..."

[What's up, Mabes?]

"Nothing, it's just ... she keeps on surprising me with these answers..."

[Mhmm. Funny how that happens when you start asking the right questions.]

"Mm ... Can I ask one more...?"

"Don't see why not?" Volta tilted her head, one eyebrow cocked expectantly.

"I've seen you fight when you want to keep someone down — front row seats, even. Got the freshly installed souvenir hardware to prove it. But you ... you almost never really went after LN? Not like that. Your fights always looked more like a *competition* than a brawl, like ... like it was *fun*. Even when she was beating other villains, you ... I just ... I don't get it?" Jos traced her cracked lips nervously with her tongue and looked up at the red wolf again, but this time she felt confused. Scared, even — but not for her safety, or even LN's. She was terrified of the answer, but she *needed* to know. "You care about her ... *Why?*"

There was silence as the villainess considered her answer, exhaling a puff of air through her nose.

"She was misguided, before, hell, still is sometimes, but she's tryin'. She always wanted to *help* people, you know? Just ... lifting them up, being the girl inspiring the underdogs to keep trying. I wanted to be like that too, ever since I was six. Believe me, Kittycat, when I go up against good, honest people who *just want to help*, and don't realize they're bought and paid for, just cogs in an unfair system … I pull my punches. I can't help myself. I'm just glad I don't have to knock any more sense into her narrow ass."

The cougar cracked a smile at the candor with which the wolf spoke about the demivixen. "I'm glad for that too … *and* I'm glad you were there to save me."

You shouldn't have had to in the first place … but…

"Funny way of showing it before, Kittycat." The wolf's nose wrinkled with a disbelieving snort.

"What can I say? My hero only knows bad jokes … Need some better role models I guess!" The mischievous grin that lit up the lioness's face pulled a genuine guffaw from Volta, and Jos realized she *really* liked that sound. "Know any villains up for the task?"

"Oh, you know how to be sarcastic in a *fun* way too!" Without hesitation, the red wolf reached out to squeeze her shoulder, the laughter continuing to bubble up from her belly.

The cougar shrugged a little, trying to subdue the happiness that threatened to ruin her snarky facade, before relenting and letting a giggle slip out. *Hope I get to keep hearing that…*

"*I wish I'd been ready to learn about all of this before…*"

[*I'm so relieved you're here, but I would give anything for it to have happened differently … I wanted you to be safe and happy, in or out of the Korps. That's all that mattered to me, I swear, my darling girl.*]

"I … I trust you Rosie. I'm sorry I doubted you … Or her." She smiled at Volta and rested her cheek against the giant paw that was on her shoulder. "*They're all like her, aren't they? The Korps, I mean…*"

[*More or less! The methods vary, but they just want to live their lives authentically. That's what this is all about, dear. Truly evil raison d'être, huh?*]

"I want to help. Whatever it takes, I'll do it. I … I want to be a part of that. I **want** to be a villain."

[*I knew you would, Mabes … I just knew you would.*]

Chapter 9

Funny Bone(s)

About a day later, she was able to walk all by herself like a big girl. The first thing she'd wanted to do — and did — was use the toilet on her own.

The second thing was going about apologizing to any neighbors in the adjoining rooms for the one-woman emo caterwauling. Josryne was absolutely astonished at the technology that had mended her body, but to be fair, her previous health insurance was ... none. No insurance. No health care. Having her wounds mended entirely free of charge was a great experience all around, but with that weight off her shoulders, she still wanted to make amends for the disturbance.

Rose had informed her that she only had one floormate, but she was having trouble pulling up their profile — something about the records being, as the virtual vixen had colloquially put it, "screwy."

[She's new to the Korps ... I don't know her too well, honestly? But you should be fine to go say 'I'm sorry,' I'm certain!]

"Well, let's try to make a good second impression ... since the first one has already passed us by." Jos nodded as she tested the motion of her right arm, still astounded by how quickly it was fixed — to say nothing of the damage to her dome. "The tip of the villainous benefits package" was what Rose called it. "Mad science working for the betterment of the world, huh?"

[Nanomachines, poom!]

"*Nice.*"

She snorted before she stopped in front of the open door of her neighbor.

"No info at all, eh?"

[She got in a fight; that's about all I could pull from her profile,] Rose trailed off.

"Huh…" She poked her head in and knocked gently on the open door frame.

"Hey, hello? I'm sorry if we disturbed you yesterday, um, I'm in the next room oh … ver…"

The mountain lioness's eyes roamed over to the sole occupant; her jaw dropped, and she raised her paw to cover her open mouth. It looked like the doctors might have forgotten about the woman.

There was literally a skeleton lying in the bed.

"Is this some kind of prank, Rose, or like…"

And then it spoke; all of the fur on her tail stood on end immediately.

"Oh, don't worry about it! Nice t'meetcha — Nurse O has been twitchy about visitors ever since … well, anyway, nice t'meetcha!"

"Oh, uh, should I not … be here?" There was a fit of blinking, and a completely silent, *"What the fuck, what the **actual** fuck!"* as she tried to come to terms with what surely had to be a trick to terrify the interns.

"Your funny glasses aren't switching you into self-destruct mode, so I figure it's probably fine," shrugged the … woman? "You must be the, uh, 'stupid frickin' puma' I've heard so much about."

"I prefer Jos, but uh … the moniker is not *inapt*." She blushed and hoped it wasn't as perceptible as it felt.

"Holy shit, she's really an animated skeleton. Like, a CR1 fucking animated dead…"

[I bet she's at least CR 3 or 4, actually…] Rose idly mused.

"Well, Jos, if you don't mind me askin' — what're ya in for?" She sounded perfectly normal and friendly, except maybe a little … hollow? Kinda spooky? There was none of the subtle feedback — always audible to feline ears — one would get from a microphone.

"I uh … got hurt, pretty bad. You should see the other guy though." She forced a weak smile to hide behind and shrugged. "Just … yeah. Bad night."

"Well, any fight you can walk away from!"

"Mm…"

"Carried away from?"

"Yeah, that's more accurate."

"Ahhh…"

"Yeah … actually, that's what I'm apologizing for, sorta. I … was being kind of, well not kind of, I was *actually* being a gigantic shithead to the friend that carried me for no good reason, and she stormed off. So, you got to hear me trying my best Gerard Way impression to get her attention." Jos's ear flicked, hearing it out loud. That whole sentence felt surreal in her muzzle, and when she said it, it *sounded* surreal, too.

This whole situation was undeniably strange, and chit-chatting with the remains of what had once, from what she could tell, been a short simian woman didn't help one bit.

"Stormed off, huh? Let me guess — big red wolf, electrifying personality? About a million volts' worth?" the skeleton asked, loudly tapping her chin with a bony appendage in consideration.

"Oh yeah, hah. Volta. She saved my life, actually. Just took me a minute to like … come to terms, you know? This is a *lot*."

"Thought I recognized the bark! People really light up around her. Lots of that going around these days, though … the rescues, I mean. Rescues and revelations."

"Yeah, I'm finding these villains are not so … well. *Villainous*." The cat bit her lip, truthfully still having trouble with the new normal in which she'd found herself. "I blame the misleading advertising."

"Yeah, it does seem like, for an evil cult of brainwashing sodomites, they do more good than any superhero team I've heard of."

"Mmm…" The mountain lion had tried not to stare, but the elephant in the room would be ignored no longer.

[Cats and their curiosity…]

"So, can I ask what happened?" The cougar stammered a bit as she motioned to the literal bag of bones before her.

"What do you mean?" The eyeless skull looked directly at her and tilted.

"You're a … *animated skeleton*? That's uh … not something you see outside of *Tales from the Crypt* or poorly advised Caribbean privateers." The puma's paw ran through her hair, brushing it back nervously.

"I'm a *what*?"

"You know, like uh. B … bones?"

"Aren't we all, when you get right down to it?" The skeleton asked, gesturing vaguely.

She froze. Her head turned with a sudden *snap* toward her skeletal palm, and silence stretched between them. Her face lunged forward for a closer, no-eyed stare, then twisted up at Jos accusingly.

"Did you … not … *know*?"

"*What HAPPENED?* Jos, I'm a *MONSTER!*" She covered her empty eye sockets as best she could without flesh and broke into grotesque, clacky sobs. "I had *JUST* gotten my boobs done!"

"OH NO! I'm so sorry! I'm sure they were wonderful! *ROSE!* Call for help!" Josryne panicked as she looked around for something, *anything* that could help, before she heard the animated science class specimen clattering in a fit of laughter behind her, joined by a quiet titter from the vixen in her mind.

"..."

[*Honey, that was precious.*]

"Oh, that was *good* ... I needed that," she wheezed, fingers running under her eye like it was wiping away a tear.

"Oh, so ... this is not a *new* development, then," the puma said flatly, more than slightly unamused as she clucked her tongue.

"Nah. My superpower is a completely useless level of invisibility, and it's been more than four hours, so I consulted my doctor."

[*Oh, she's a laugh!*]

"Yeah ... *Fuckin' hilarious. Heh,*" Jos relented, smiling with begrudging admiration.

"Yes, it does seem you've *erected* a problem for yourself," the catamount chuckled.

"No boners about it!"

"Totally coccyx'ed it up, huh?"

Elsewhere on base, Volta felt a chill run down her spine, as if something terribly annoying had just stepped into existence.

"You remind me of someone ... Could I tell you a joke and see if it lands? I apologize if it's a little corny..." the catamount said, blushing slightly as she tried to control her laughing.

"Well, I'd say I'm all ears, but apparently I have to wait until they find a compatible donor. In the meantime, though, yeah, sure, kid, lay it on me!"

"...'Kid'? Are you older than me?"

"Before or after I died?"

"...*Are* you dead?"

The skeleton hummed, turning the question over in her empty head for a moment. Eventually, she twisted in her bed to stare at the flat line on the monitor.

"Well, to be honest: it's not looking good."

Jos considered the answer and gave a little nod. "You know what? Fair. Okay, so: What did the electric eel say to the judge?" The cougar couldn't help leaning in closely, a smile growing along with the anticipation.

"Guilty as charged!" The skeleton finished the joke, and the two of them started to laugh again, chuckling and chortling like it was the funniest damn thing. "You must have robbed a grave to get your paws on that one!"

"Oh no, was that *your* tomb? I'm sorry! I'm new to this breaking and interring business, y'know?"

"*Ha!* You're fast on the draw! Look at us — the quick and the dead!"

"Pfft!" Jos stopped her giggling for a moment to wipe away an actual tear. As she tried to take a steadying breath a thought occurred, which she quickly dismissed with a snort. "Nah ... couldn't be..."

"What couldn't be?" the skeleton asked with a tilt of her visibly empty head.

"Oh, nothing ... just ... reminded me of someone, is all. Thanks for being so understanding, *and* for the laughs, I really needed that. Should have the doc check out that severely overdeveloped funny bone of yours, though!"

"I'm glad you found me humerus!"

The mountain lion kept laughing as she left the room, stopping at the door frame to look back at her boneheaded new acquaintance.

"Well I'll let you rest your eyes ... wherever they are!"

"See you when I see you!"

"Deal. I'll send you a get well soon card — hope you'll recognize it's from me because I'll be using a nom de poom!" She gave a little wink and a wave as she left.

"*Rose, I really would like to send her a card, though! Maybe something with a pirate theme?*"

[*I'll make sure to send one, but I have a sneaking suspicion the two of you might run into each other again soon. What "nom de poom" are we using dear?*]

Jos thought for a moment and then smiled.

"*Mabel. Mabel Greysmoke.*"

[*Oooo ... Sounds mysterious! Very femme fatale! I like it!*]

"*That's the goal, right? If I'm going to be a sinister villain ... well, I need an appropriately bewitching moniker, don't I?*"

And why not use her name? She's who I want to be.

Chapter 10

Fashion

Less than a week later, Josryne had almost entirely recovered, thanks to the Korps's surprisingly advanced medical technology. Her left eye was fully healed, and she had apparently gained something called a "titanium nanofiber mesh orbital and forehead reinforcement" in the bargain. It sounded expensive, but Volta assured her that the only thing to worry about was — when she felt ready for it! — learning from the wolf how to *properly* headbutt someone.

Other than that, her arm was stiff, and her muzzle was a little tender, but she was back in "fighting shape." That shape was round, admittedly, but round was still a shape.

The catamount was acutely aware of her body as Dr. O and Nurse O performed a final examination, confirming her status before allowing her to be discharged. She was still coming to terms with the synchronized synthetic vixens chatting back and forth as gentle hands checked for tenderness, four per O, confirmed proper mending. She had seen the pair a lot in the past six days, and the appearance of not one, but two fully synthetic, seemingly identical lifeforms was something altogether new for her.

They were clearly fully autonomous beings, each clothed differently, but were otherwise the exact same model, with the same number of limbs, the same unique cross shaped pupils, and the same lack of a mouth on their muzzle.

Instead of a maw, there was a waveform display, stylized to look like a mask.

They were a sight to behold, and the feline was still trying to come to terms with technology of this caliber being *real*. Jos looked between the two slyly as their ministrations continued down her body. "So, doc, what's the verdict?"

[Josryne! Don't stare, it's rude.]

"I can't help it! I've never met a synth before, and certainly not a matching set!"

[Oh, this isn't the whole set.]

"…How many more?"

[Many.]

"Many?"

[Many as in "more than a few," yes, dear.]

Before the catamount could demand further clarification, the doctor — or possibly the nurse, she was very much distracted by their *other* assets, and it was hard to tell — spoke up. "I cannot see any reason you should have to stay, but I would like you to come in for a check-up in about a week. Did you have a question, Miss Greysbell? You are staring quite intently." They never stopped filling out info on a tablet, passing it between each other with their highly coordinated paws — all eight of them, between the two.

"Oh, sorry, ma'am! Ma'ams? Uh, no questions, as such," she blustered, trying to fight the urge to wince at being called out for her behavior. "Sorry."

The nurse arched an eyebrow. "Mmm. You will not be a frequent flier, I hope?"

"Frequent flyer? No, I don't intend to be? I mean … I have no powers, so I don't think I'll be in harm's way very often. I'm not one to go *looking* for trouble." Still a little embarrassed by her faux pas, Jos rubbed at the back of her head.

"Interesting response. We'll see you at your follow-up." The vixen's voice seemed strangely amused.

"Thank you, Dr. O, Nurse O; I really appreciate the swanky private suite and the room service, but I cannot say I'm eager to stay."

"Of course, Miss Greysbell. We'll be here, if you should gather that your lack of powers does not, in fact, prevent you from finding trouble. Hypothetically, of course." They each gave her paw a pat and zipped out to their next patient, leaving the lioness to ponder what exactly they were inferring.

"…Do I look like a troublemaker, Rosie?"

[Well, look at the crowd you're hanging out with these days! Can you blame them?]

Clean bill of health received, Jos stared out the window at the world outside, still trying to process the view of the subterranean city. She absently touched her fingers to the obsidian set in her choker, a comfortingly solid relic from … *before*. In less than a week, her entire world had changed. Nothing ever would be — or *could* be — the same after what happened.

"Not in Kansas anymore, are we?"

[Never were, dear, but not *quite* over the proverbial rainbow either.]

She managed a half-smile for her friend, before vocalizing a sudden spell of pondering. "So, is there, like, an interview process? Or something?" The cougar rapped her knuckles on the dark brushed nickel windowsill with nervous energy. "Like, to join up. I mean … *officially.*"

[The short answer is no, but there is a background check, amongst other things. Which, I should note, you have already passed just fine! The Korps doesn't force anyone to stay, so you would have to volunteer for that. I can tell you, however, that you have already had someone to vouch for you. *Besides* me, I mean…]

"Volta." Jos couldn't suppress her smile at the name. Imagining the big wolf just made her *feel*, feel in *ways*, and she could scarcely help herself.

[I'm not at liberty to say 'officially,' but 'unofficially,' you owe her lunch. Maybe dinner, too. She's a big eater and *loves* Italian.]

"Unsurprising, I bet that girl can *eat*…" The puma's brow quirked. "Not even a supervillain for a day yet, and you're already setting me up on dates? Aiming for the moon with that one, don't you think? Maybe I'll ask Minion for some barbeque? Or Cold Stone Creamery with the Lamia?" she smirkingly continued, before her sister's reply put an end to her flippancy for the time being.

[Josryne Mabel, I was just trying to help you make some friends. Dating doesn't have to be the end goal. A little more social interaction wouldn't *kill* you, y'know?]

"I'm sorry Rosie … I appreciate it, but yeah … I'm just … nervous is all. I dunno." She couldn't believe anyone, *especially* the wolf super-soldier, would ever want to spend *extra* time with her, let alone be *interested* in her.

[I don't want you to sell yourself short or let yourself fall into old habits. Take it as slow as you like, but don't just assume no one would like spending time with you. I do, and I'm a pretty good judge of character.]

"Yeah, I suppose you are." The cougar chuckled softly, before giving a nod, trying and failing to ignore the warmth in her cheeks. "Dating prospects aside, after we get checked out today, what happens?"

[We have a couple of options. I could just give you a tour and guide you to where you'll be staying while we work on getting you permanently situated. Or I could ask someone to accompany us, if you'd rather?]

"Oh, I don't want to bother anyone," she sighed in a small huff. "I've already been an incredible pain in the ass, my new noggin must have cost a small fortune, and I'm … not really *comfortable* having so many people worrying about me." She cast her gaze downward, touching her forehead to the cool glass.

[Mabes, what happened was not your fault.]

"Yeah … I know, Rose, I know…" Jos quickly pivoted, not wanting to dwell on that night. "So, what happens to my family? My job? My life, what little of it there was?"

[That is up to you. We can, and will, protect your family from backlash. Your computer has been remotely wiped, so hopefully the damage is minimal. We already sent a recovery team to your apartment, but the police had already arrived before we did. Unfortunately, the mess we left in the alley was tied to you — as the officer was able to testify — so you are a wanted woman.] The virtual vixen gave her shoulder a squeeze, her tail curling about the feline's.

"I can't believe he was able to fucking speak, after that," she growled softly before letting out another puff of air. "You know … I always thought that would be exciting? Being a fugitive, I mean." The puma heaved another more resigned sigh as she wandered away from the window, back towards the bed.

[I am sorry, sweetie. I wish I had better news on that front. On the plus side, no one is going to get to you here. And we'll get you sorted, I promise.] Rose remained ever helpful and positive. It was hard to worry too much, she always knew just what to say.

"Hehehe," Jos smiled and shook her head as the little laugh bubbled up.

[What is it?]

"The safest place in the world is a supervillain secret lair."

[Funny how that works, isn't it?]

"Yep. Life has suddenly gotten *very* funny for me."

[A bit, yeah.]

"Rose, can I ask you another question?"

[Always, Mabes. What is it?]

"Where the *hell* are we, exactly?"

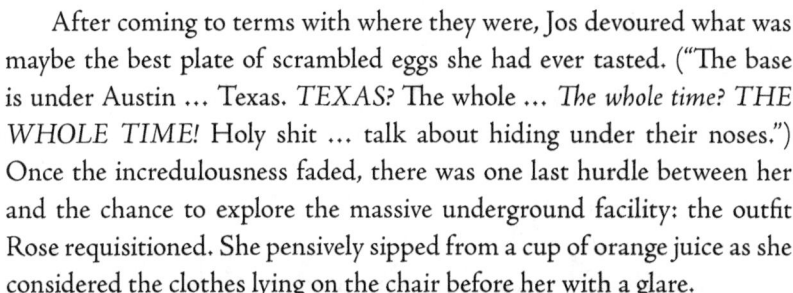

After coming to terms with where they were, Jos devoured what was maybe the best plate of scrambled eggs she had ever tasted. ("The base is under Austin … Texas. *TEXAS? The whole … The whole time? THE WHOLE TIME!* Holy shit … talk about hiding under their noses.") Once the incredulousness faded, there was one last hurdle between her and the chance to explore the massive underground facility: the outfit Rose requisitioned. She pensively sipped from a cup of orange juice as she considered the clothes lying on the chair before her with a glare.

"I mean, I could just wear what I was wearing. You didn't have to go through the trouble of getting me a whole, uh, *ensemble*…"

[*Absolutely* not. First of all, there was a *lot* of staining; second, we had to cut you out of the shirt and hoodie. If you want to wear tattered rags, then we can get you some that aren't marinated in your own fluids yet.]

"Gonna miss that hoodie … fuck." The puma stared down into the now empty cup, nibbling her lip. "I'd had it since high school…"

As ever, Rose tried to encourage her sister to step forward.

[Mabes, you're stalling, sweetie. Is the outfit too much? It's okay if it is! I can get you something with a less feminine cut, if you would rather? I just thought we could try something new. This is the best place in the world for you to just let yourself *be.*] She smiled as she tickled under the cougar's chin, eliciting a purr from her charge.

The attire wasn't necessarily *daring*. A long-sleeved cowl neck top in deep plum, with a pink helix between the shoulders, a pair of black leggings with the same tone of pink woven design down the sides, and a new pair of canvas high-tops. (Pink, of course.) Truthfully, it was more androgynous than feminine *per se*, but those pieces didn't bother her; not really. It was the undergarment that gave her pause.

She walked over and picked up the pair of panties. They were simple dark magenta, satin-smooth, with no frills, just a sensible piece of underwear, really. But if the garment was so innocuous, why did it feel like she was holding something truly *dangerous?*

"Rosie, I … I'm gonna look silly. Like a guy just playing at being a girl…"

[Josryne, we can stop at any time, but I **refuse** to listen to you treat yourself this way. What did we say?]

"That I'm a girl, and I can dress and look however I want…"

[And why is that?]

"Because I deserve to be me."

[Good girl. Now, I won't peek until after you're dressed, okay?] A paw covered the vixen's eyes, peeking and sticking out her tongue, before hiding her eyes again.

"...Okay. Thank you, Rose." Affirmations from the AI really did help, although the lioness was sure Rose would soon grow tired of having to play the same song on repeat. She gathered up her clothes and went into the bathroom to change.

"Remember, Rose, no peeking!" She could have removed the visor, but the thought of that caused her to panic immediately.

No. Not unless I absolutely have to. Asking her not to peek was the only option.

[I know! I promise to behave myself.]

David Bowie's "Fashion" started right on cue, and the cat couldn't help but laugh out loud, her giggles trailing off into a tiny sigh. "You are such a dork," she snickered as she disrobed. Leaving the barely modest gown on the floor exposed her full body to the mirror.

Deep breaths. This is fine. I am a **girl**...

She stepped out of her underwear and turned away from the mirror after a glimpse of her naked form, her cheeks red hot. It was her own vile body, same as it ever was. Her eyes crawled over every tiny flaw just as if they'd been highlighted in her augmented view, and she had to dig her claws into her palms to stop the thoughts from rushing in. As she focused on the (pain) distraction, the music cut suddenly, and Rose's voice filled her mind.

[Is there anything I can do, Mabes? Would you like me to display the AR in the mirror?]

"N-no, please. It's — it's fine," the cougar hurriedly responded before pressing on. She didn't want to be treated so ... delicately.

I can do this. They're just underwear.

She stepped out of her utilitarian hospital-issue briefs and pulled up the pair of panties she was provided. With a deep breath, she rolled the fabric over her sac and sheath as quickly as she could, with her eyes shut tight. The sensation was certainly unfamiliar, but comfortable. They fit well and felt amazing if she was being honest with herself — so much softer than anything she had ever worn before! The garment was silky and snug, and it gave her a little thrill to see herself in the mirror. It was something she had always thought about, but it was always a step too far; too *deviant*.

But then another thought occurred to the feline.

"What better place to be deviant than the underground lair of the world's most evil terrorist group, right?"

[*You're not wrong! But can I look now? Please?*] the vixen-shaped AI whined through the door.

The puma took another deep breath. The static was no longer screaming in her ears, but the fear held tight for just a moment, still distantly wailing at her that this was *too much*. The idea of feeling *attractive* — or the least bit sexual — caused her to shiver. She had no words, but memories of *that night* came pruriently slinking through her mind, pushing aside the simple pleasure of the moment.

He nearly...

She *almost*...

Her paw immediately shot to her choker, rubbing the stone as she bit her lip. She imagined the warmth spreading through her. The cougar's lids remained shut tight as she held back the tears she knew would soon come.

"I j-just need a minute, Rosie..."

[*You are **safe** here, Mabes. I promise. Nothing will happen to you. We can stop right now, if you'd like.*]

Another deep breath steeled her resolve; the catamount shook her head. "No. He doesn't get to take this away from me. He doesn't get to steal my joy."

[*You're damn right he doesn't! He doesn't get anything more from you!*]

"Nothing!" She agreed, beaming as she stepped through the doorway.

[*Now* can I seeeeee?] The vixen sat wide-eyed, muzzle hanging open for a moment as she watched her sister appear. [Oh, *Mabes* ... *There* she is...]

The cougar blushed bright red through her soft cheeks and ears, the white freckles seeming to stand out like personal constellations across her features. It was such a mundane thing that people took for granted, she pondered. For the first time in her life, at the age of thirty-eight, she was wearing the clothes that felt *right* for her.

Josryne pawed nervously at one arm, resisting the urge to tug on her fingers as her eyes met the virtual vixen's gaze. "How do I look?"

The AI's projection theatrically rubbed at her eyes under her own virtual visor and let out a little laugh.

[You look gorgeous, darling. Now get the rest on, unless you're wanting to go out like that?] Rose smirked and raised a brow, leaving Jos to discover there was apparently no upper limit to how flushed she could become under her fur.

"Err ... baby steps, remember? Going out in panties and sneakers might be a *bit* much for me..." She squirmed a bit as she tried to cover herself, but the grin never left her muzzle.

[Mmm, *fair!* That is more *advanced* provocative outfitting. That comes later in the curriculum!] the AI replied with a wink.

"Is that *before* or *after* applied henching?"

[Oh, that's *way* later. Our henches are free of extraneous self-conscious thoughts. Only *confident* thots in our organization, sweetie.]

"I *do* like the idea of being confident..." The cougar nodded, still biting her lip but now to keep from bursting out laughing, though the crinkle at the edges of her eyes said it all. Nonetheless, with the hardest step taken, leggings came on next, pulled up and hugging her curves. She tugged the shirt over her head and adjusted the collar. "Oooo! It has thumb holes! I *love it!*" Her smile grew wider by the second, but as she slipped into her new shoes, her poise faltered. "What ... what if I don't look like a girl?"

[*Remember our first lesson in confidence: You'll look like a girl because you are* you, *and you are ...?*]

"A girl." The puma shut her eyes and nodded, taking a slow breath, casting aside that fear (if only for a second).

[*A* **very** *good girl. Now take a deep breath and turn around, so we can see how it came together!*] The AI placed a kindly paw on her shoulder with the magic of sensory biofeedback, turning her with a knowing wink.

Jos opened her eyes with a little gasp, paws covering her muzzle. "Rose ... Are you playing with my view at all? Right now? Are you doing *anything?*"

The response came matter-of-factly and without a moment's hesitation. [Not even a little bit, my dear.]

"I feel ... I feel like I can see myself," the cougar whispered, half afraid if the words were said too loud, the spell would be broken and she would wake up. "I recognize the view ... at least some of it." She placed a paw on her chest, and as the image in the mirror did the same, the reality set in.

[You are seeing what I have been seeing all along.]

The catamount gave one little sniffle and a bit of a giggle as she wiped her eyes. "Speaking of seeing things, I've seen enough of this suite! It's high time we checked out!" She led the way with confidence as she grabbed her purse with all her worldly possessions and made her way to check out at whatever the supervillainous equivalent of a hospital registration desk might be. It was time to explore her new home, and find her place in it...

To her disappointment, the checkout desk was an ordinary affair, save the O-unit behind it, but the letdown was forgotten as the pair stepped out into the RIV complex proper, deep beneath the streets of Austin, Texas. It was ... *overwhelming.* The pathways were bustling with folks of all shapes and sizes, at varying states of undress or overdress. For a moment, she could have sworn she recognized several of the people as they walked by — then she was *starstruck,* as she realized she *wasn't* imagining things.

"Holy shit, that was Ragaclaw!"

[*Mhmm! He's a real teddy bear once you get to know him.*]

"...That wasn't ... No fuckin' *way!*"

That *totally* was High Tide — the easy smile and infectious laugh were unmistakable. The shark was a frequent foe of LN's, and Jos suspected that she had ulterior motives for operating so far inland. "*So, are her and LN a thing yet...?*" Not that she *cared* necessarily, the feline was just making idle conversation.

Not a *single* ulterior motive there.

[*Mabes, I'm gonna be honest, I don't think your hero has reeled in any of those signals. Tide* is *an absolute sweetheart, though! I'll introduce you some time, if you like?*] Rose's avatar winked as she leaned against the cougar.

"*Maybe some other time? I uhh ... don't wanna harsh her mellow or anything.*"

Rose displayed each person's name as they walked by, and she realized if she focused on a target, her display would light up with pertinent information as well. Exceptionally handy for the nervous newbie.

"*Rose, what's my profile say?*"

[*Josryne M. Greysbell, She/Her, Lesbian: Single (Not Looking).*]

While it helped to know that her pronouns were there for all to see, her brow furrowed at the last words for just a moment, before relenting.

Yeah ... yeah. That makes sense...

As she stood at the bottom of the steps, the cougar realized not a single person gave her a sideways glance; there were no aghast stares, nor titters of derisive laughter. A particularly busty possum with a visibly cybernetic tail gave her a little wave, and even a smile! Her stomach was knotted, but despite that affliction, she remained hopeful. Everyone was going about their lives, and most — if not all — viewed it through Rose-Colored Glasses. They all seemed to just be ... *existing*, living the lives they *wanted* to live.

She smiled at the idea. Maybe she was on her way to a life like that. A life well lived. But first...

"All right, Rose, where to?" the cougar asked as she came down the steps, new shoes putting a little spring in her step as she glanced about.

[Well, we should check in with Residential Services to have you assigned standard quarters, first and foremost, and after you know where you can rest your head tonight, from there we can get the lay of the land. Sound like a plan?]

"Lead the way," came the chipper reply, as a faint white line began drawing on the ground in her RCGs' view, pointing Jos in the proper direction. *"Ah! Thank you, sister dear!"*

While they walked, Rose gave an abridged guided tour, highlighting landmarks and locations that would help if she ever became lost. The medical sector had quite a few buildings of note, including centers for therapy, prosthetics, and specialty doctors who — while not always on base — had space set aside for them to practice in various fields, cosmetic and otherwise. The catamount didn't really have a head for directions, but it did seem they had doubled back unnecessarily at one point.

She raised an eyebrow as the *scale* dawned on her. *"Makes sense they would want those sorts of folks on hand, I suppose? Especially with the population here,"* the cat thought with a smile, as a ten-foot-tall and *exceptionally* well-endowed skunk strode by. The mephitidae was followed by a thoroughly stacked buck whose lower legs appeared to have been replaced by gleaming silver prostheses.

[Mhmm! It takes all kinds, and we help everyone we can.]

"I see." Jos paused, working herself up to a question she worried might be somehow *fraught*. *"... Must have taken a lot of progesterone to get Volta to where she is, yeah?"*

[In a manner of speaking...]

The feline stopped and narrowed her gaze. *"You're being cagey again."*

[I adore your instinctive curiosity, Mabes, but I'm afraid I have no idea what you mean!]

"Mm. All right, keep your secrets," she mumbled with an eyeroll and wave of a dismissive paw.

[All will be revealed in due time! First, the Residential Sector, and then, how about lunch?]

"So, after lunch we can discuss why we took such a roundabout path out of the med sector, yeah?"

*[Goodness, you sure are **nosy** today, but of course, dear.]*

Jos paused and took a look back and came to a stop. She blinked several times as her brow furrowed at the most peculiar sight she had seen thus far, which was kind of a high bar given her present location.

"Were all those dragonesses … the **same** dragoness? Named Karen? Like, **the** Karen? 'I speak for the Overlord,' **that** Karen?"

[Oh dear, we're going to have to talk about that, aren't we?]

"Yes, we are in fact going to have to talk about the crowd of Karens," she thought at the AI, in the most sarcastic mental tone she could muster. "How the fuck has no one figured out there are six of her…?"

*[Well, I suppose the first thing to point out is that is not **all** of them.]*

"Wha — how many are there?"

[Many.]

"More or less than Nurse O's?"

*[Oh honey, far, **far** more.]*

The lioness pressed on, nonplussed but too curious now to stop. "… Alright, so why do 'more than a bit, by a bunch' of Karens exist? Besides being disarmingly attractive, I mean. Just to keep up appearances?"

[That … That is a question with a complicated answer.]

"All we have is time, right? Feel free to elucidate!" The lioness pressed, not willing to relent quite yet.

Rose paused for a moment, seemingly considering her words carefully. *[Mmm … Well, the swarm exists to serve multiple functions—]*

"Wait, wait, wait, you're not gonna just *glaze* over that one … *swarm?* You refer to them as a *swarm!*" Jos exclaimed aloud, but no one around her batted a single eyelash at the question — though several did smirk, recognizing the revelation the feline just had.

The AI however was unphased, finishing her previously interrupted thought. *[Yes dear, more than a bit, by a bunch, remember? I can only get into so many details, but rest assured that the Karenswarm is a crucial part of making these bases — and some day, the world! — a better place. Their …*

connection allows them to be in many places at once, so to speak, and efficiently organize our villainous enterprise.]

"I suppose managing the scale of the Korps requires a lot of brains all acting in sync with each other to run smoothly. Makes sense to have a tailor-made operational network that is completely self-contained," the cougar mused, "that is **also** disarmingly attractive."

[Indeed. If you must be, then you should live as your own ideal, don't you agree?]

By the time the two made it to the residential sector's broad atrium, the puma's head was swimming with new information — mostly regarding what she had *thought* was science fiction but was apparently actual science fact within the Korps. The subject of body modification came up for a second, but Rose did not allow her the chance to dwell on what she had theorized, given the many sizes and shapes of the base's inhabitants. Instead, the AI artfully shifted the conversation to some important Do's and Don'ts. How to behave around certain individuals, including but not limited to; the likely minimum mass of any personnel with the designation "strategically-sized." ([The warnings are not exaggerated for effect.]) Not staring too long at the red dragoness covered in blood. ([Hers or someone else's — usually the latter.]) Respectful and appropriate terminology regarding synthetic personnel, whether embodied or not. ([Do not call them "robots" unless they specifically ask you to do so.]) Finally, proper caution around anyone with the tag "K-BURP Certified" in their public profile.

After a brief interaction with a cheerful otter at a nearby counter — no more than necessary to confirm with him that the quarters Rose had mentioned had in fact been assigned to the puma — her conversation with the virtual vixen continued.

[...so, yes, when someone says you are "cute enough to eat," please be aware that could be more than a turn of phrase.]

"Okay, so ... the long and short of it is to follow your lead, and if I don't know, ask." She clucked her tongue softly, deciding she was better off not exploring the implications of that last little morsel.

[Attagirl! We're headed for residential level D-6, suite nine.]

"*Six-nine, huh? Nice,*" the feline giggled. "***Please** tell me the room code is four-twenty?*"

[*Into the elevator, clever girl, I assure you our security is much less juvenile than a Call of Duty lobby.*]

It was just a smooth ride to the sixth floor, and a short trip down the hall; the door automatically unlocked for Jos, her RCGs serving as a handy-dandy passkey. The unit was clean and simply furnished, with a polished, darkly stained hardwood floor. The neutral tones of the walls were offset with accents of dark chrome and magenta, naturally. Where a hotel room might have hung generic artwork, she noticed with a titter that a frame in the living area contained instead a smirking parody of an old-fashioned war propaganda poster, featuring a curvy lithe snow leopard in a behelixed blue-and-white jumpsuit. The bombastic caption above the woman — evidently using ice powers to blow a frosty kiss at the viewer — exhorted her to "Smash the Fash! Join The Korps Today!"

Been there, done that, already got the tasteful long-sleeved cowl neck top…

The lioness explored her new den further, and found a king-sized bed in the next room, along with a generous walk-in closet, a connected bathroom in gleaming black tile with a gigantic shower stall, a living area with a balcony (overlooking the high-ceilinged "street" of the wide corridor outside), and a small kitchen that was *still* far-better-appointed than her previous living arrangements. She would have all the amenities she needed, and it was admittedly far nicer than the studio apartment she left behind. Its highlights had included a lack of AC in the summer, a draft in the winter, and a pathologically inattentive landlord, all year round.

The cougar stepped out onto the balcony and leaned against the railing, taking in the view. Six stories below, life hustled and bustled about, in this subterranean city completely hidden from the outside world. It was a veritable utopia to hide from prying eyes.

"*How nice would a cigar be out here?*" she mused, licking her lip absently.

[*I'm sure it would be perfectly lovely, Mabes. I can see about getting some delivered, if you wish?*]

"OH! Uh … that … that's not necessary. I feel like I'm asking too much already, and I mean … I don't even *smoke, right?* Pssssssh," she protested too much, and wished the heat in her cheeks would go away. Shaking her head and looking back inside, she attempted to change the subject, distancing herself from the topic of stogies. "I may be a fugitive from justice, but I sure can't complain about the digs!"

[Mhmm! *And* it's designed to work with the RCG interface as well. So, feel free to ask, and I will do my best to assist with whatever it is!]

"This ... This is *wonderful*. Thank you, Rosie; it seems every day, I owe you more."

[I'm not keeping a tab, sweetie. Knowing you're happy is *more* than enough.]

Jos had come to expect nothing less of her, all heart and helpfulness, and never wanted a life without her, if she was being truly honest with herself. "Going to get me all misty, sis," the cougar said with a laugh.

[Dry your eyes, dear, and let's head to the cafeteria. We'll get you a bite to eat, and then we can finish the tour!]

"Ooo ... Know just how to get a girl's attention, huh?"

[I've had a lot of practice. If we hurry, you can get a corner piece of the mac and cheese!]

Jos laughed as she snagged her purse from the couch and headed back out the door at a jog, the promise of crispy, cheesy goodness just the motivation she needed.

Josryne Mabel Greysbell had been a ghost — a *victim* — for most of her life. She was a shadow, always far from the light, whether cruelly pushed or fearfully shying away. But that was over and done. When she stepped into the hallway, and the music started to play, she smiled the genuine smile of a girl that looked forward to the future. *Nothing* would stop her from being herself.

Never again, and she knew just where she wanted to begin.

"Rose?"

[Mmm?]

"...Is LN on base?"

Chapter 11

Oh You Pretty Things...

[She is, actually! LN got out of the hospital a day or two before you,] Rose piped up, happy as always to help, as they wended their way towards the cafeteria. Meanwhile — listening to Bowie sing "Oh! You Pretty Things" through her RCGs — Josryne imagined he was talking about her.

The cougar had a thought and tilted her head just a bit. *"Huh! Makes sense. I wonder how close we were to being bunkmates?"*

[Here I thought you were nervous to make new friends so soon! The good news is you can ask her yourself, she is in RIV for the day, at least!]

"Mm."

The melodically bouncy glam-pop pressed on, and so did the pair, as they wove (virtually, in the AI's case) through the broad corridors of the underground lair.

[Would you like me to reach out to her?] Rose offered in earnest, attempting to outmaneuver her sister's skittishness.

Jos's mental retort was delivered with a sarcastic tone, and sour look on her muzzle. *"Oh, Lawful Neutral, I know you just had your tail properly re-attached, but how would you like an exciting **new** pain in your ass?"*

The music stopped, and she immediately regretted the flippant response. She spoke quickly, falling over her words to try and avoid the inevitable chastisement for her negativity

"I, uh, Rose, I ... I'm sorry. I don't know why I asked." Her ears drooped a little, guilt apparent in her eyes.

[Could it be that you still admire her?] The "obviously" was implied.

*"Why yes, that **might** be it. But what does that matter? She's literally a superhero! Or ... villain! Whatever! I don't want to bother her, and besides, she hardly needs a fangirl. She — much like everyone else in this complex, present company excepted — has better things to do than hang out with me. No offense, Rose."* Jos's tail flicked behind her, unable to hide her frustrations that lurked.

[*...None taken, I promise, but I really don't think it would be an issue, from what I know of her. Besides, **I** like spending time with you, Mabes, and if you'd give anyone the **chance**, I bet they would, too! I really wish you could take it easier on yourself.*]

The virtual vixen might have been forever the optimist, but Jos knew better; she was strange, and that made people uncomfortable. It always did. The people walking by, smiling at her, seemingly happy to see her. She was being *humored*, she was certain.

"Maybe. I don't know. This is hard, Rosie..."

[*So is being alone, dear. I **know** you. I know that this is **not** what you want.*]

"I'm not alone! I have you!"

[*You know what I mean, you silly cat! Can you try something? As a favor to me, while we're at lunch here? Why don't you try to say hello to just one new person? Maybe someone who is sitting by themselves as well ...?*]

Every now and then, when the AI would respond, Jos got the feeling she was invisibly *smiling*. One of those *knowing* smiles, she imagined, like the cat who got the cream. For her part, it had been a long time since the puma had gotten any proverbial cream herself, but she had no choice in the matter, and she *was* tired of *always* being lonely.

New life, right?

"Okay, Rose. I'll try. But I really doubt anyone will want to hang out with a ... stray like me."

Her funk was interrupted by the smell that crashed into her sensitive nose like a tsunami, before they even reached the cavernous cafeteria: *food*. Hot, delectable, tasty, *delicious* food! The lioness suddenly remembered her last meal had been a small plate of eggs and some orange juice and instantly became *ravenous*. Even calling it a "cafeteria" felt like an understatement; as it opened up in front of her, she began counting dozens of different buffet-style service counters, offering a variety and volume of different cuisines that would shame any hipster food hall or public market by comparison.

"There's so ... **much**? And everything's still open, and stocked? I thought we'd be past the lunch rush? ... Is that a **Taco Bell**?"

[*It is! Even in Texas, sometimes you just **quieres** the Bell, you know? It's always like this, dear. Everyone has different schedules, and everyone always needs to eat. You can't conquer the world on an empty stomach! Can you imagine how **cranky** Volta would be if we didn't keep her fed?*]

Jos wiped her mouth with the back of her paw, trying to stem the tide of saliva that had begun to flow at the sight of all this glorious sustenance.

"Uh, ha ha, yeah ... that would get ugly quick, huh?" The puma was still dazed by what had to be the *most* secret menu on the planet. "Wow. Okay, so how does this work? Do I pay before I grab the tray, or like, is there a card, and I pay later...?"

[Pay? Oh, sweetie, lunch is on us. Dinner too. Everything is, for as long as you choose to stay. We don't let people go hungry.]

"Oh..." Her brow furrowed a bit as she chewed on that information. "After lunch I want to know how I can help, okay? I'm serious! I can work. I can contribute somehow; I just want you to find a spot for me!"

[We have plans after lunch! But we can definitely get that ball rolling soon, Mabes.]

"Plans? Is this related to the thing we avoided?"

[Perhaps! Ooooh, look! Mac and cheese, **and** fried chicken! Doesn't that smell divine? Oh, and the single-serve brownies, every side's a corner piece!]

The cougar could tell Rose was trying to divert her attention. It was working, and she absolutely let herself be distracted by carbs and other assorted golden-fried deliciousness. Soon, her tray was filled with enough calories to make up for the loss of appetite she'd experienced during her hospital stay, and probably the next couple weeks as well. As she turned to eyeball the surroundings for an empty seat, she experienced something crushingly familiar that made her anxiety spike.

"This is like the first day at a new school ... Is Volta here? Maybe I could sit with her? Or, like..." She started to panic, but her sister stepped in, not allowing her to fixate on the fear of rejection.

[Nope! We agreed to make a **new** friend! Let's see ... New friend ... New friend ... ah-hah!] In the view of Jos's RCGs, Rose activated the gently blinking pink arrow of a wayfinding destination. It pointed down towards a table near the back, with a single occupant — a vixen, it seemed. She had short-ish auburn hair, and a fluffy tail that swayed slowly back and forth behind her compact frame.

The woman met Rose's search criteria for a dining companion, she assumed: *alone.*

Jos took a deep breath and closed her eyes for a moment.

"You're a grown-ass woman. You can do this!"

[You can, and you will! Now scoot!]

The puma stifled a yelp as she felt an invisible paw playfully pinch her ass-cheek. She wove her way through the tables, noting several more

143

folks whose faces she had seen on the news above sinister chyrons, and a table with a pack of Karens. Possibly the same pack from before? She wasn't familiar enough to *tell*, quite yet. At any rate, she approached her designated target and cleared her throat quietly to get the vixen's attention.

"Would ... Would it be all right if I sat here, um, miss?"

"*Rose, why isn't her info ... popping...*"

[Ellen Foxpaw, She/Her, Sexuality Undisclosed]

As the vixen turned around the catamount's eyes grew wide, and her jaw dropped open. "*Rose!* You sneaky, synthetic *snake-in-the-grass!*" Jos exclaimed and then snapped her muzzle shut, standing mortified in front of a certain demimorph.

[*Oh, Mabes, I'm* **so** *sorry I can't hear you right now, I'm processing something important; I'll be back in a little while to check on you all, though! Have a wonderful time, and don't do anything I wouldn't do!*]

"*Wh-what? Wait! What*—" She clenched her jaw as a little icon of a fox with a hardhat appeared. "*What do I say...?*" Jos took a deep breath. The only way *out* would have to be *through*.

There sat the superhero formerly known as Lawful Neutral, and presently super ... vigilante with an undecided name, according to the feline's HUD, which had mysteriously *just* populated the rest of the demimorph's public profile. The woman picked idly at her plate, appearing to be deep in thought — likely preoccupied with a dozen different things, Jos assumed — and so failed to immediately react to the cough behind her. It was only the exasperated outburst that prompted her to turn her attention to the effeminate-looking mountain lion.

"ROSE giving you grief? Boy, do I know *that* feeling."

"Hah ... Yeah, she ... she really is *something*," Jos said through gritted teeth. Her tail poofed up behind her, betraying her just like the AI had.

"Well, you're welcome to have a seat! I'm just waiting on my sister, and I could use a distraction." She motioned to the chair on her right, and gifted the cat with her winning smile, cute little sharp teeth all perfectly straight and even seeming to *sparkle* faintly in the artificial light.

"Oh! Thank you! I ... I'm Josryne, by the way, but my friends call me Jos." She responded with an inadvertent mirror of the demimorph's overly toothy smile as she slipped into the chair, cringing at her own attempt to be smooth. Yep, totally, that was what her friends — all six of them, which included the virtual assistant in her noggin and the gigantic wolf who she assumed begrudgingly tolerated her presence — called her. "And you're LN! I, uh ... I recognized you from the news..."

The news, and the comics, and the action figure with "authentic" iconic voice lines, and the latest console edition of HeroClash (she'd joined the fan campaign to add *"The Punderful One"* to the roster), and then there was the cougar's membership in the *fan club* ... yes, truthfully, she definitely *knew of* the vixen.

However, an even more recent exposure to the ex-Hero rattled in the forefront of her mind.

"The hospital ... ROSE! You'd better hope they never invent a way for me to get my paws on you, because I'm going to wring that beautifully rendered neck of yours!"

[What was that, Jos? I'm sorry, we're still doing some system maintenance, I'll need a little more time, sweetie...!] The AI's voice cut out again before the cat could vent another angry thought in her general direction.

As realization dawned on the feline, she was familiar with her new lunchmate, inside and out, thanks to her all-expenses-paid trip to the medical sector, and it seemed the ex-Hero had the same epiphany, nearly dropping her fork.

"Well, it's nice to meet you again for the first time, Jos! That's right, I *am* LN, but you can call me Ellen!" The vixen smirked as she speared a bite of salad.

Jos couldn't enjoy one of her most frequent mundane daydreams coming true in front of her as her panic kept pace with her indignance about the reveal of her erstwhile sister's "innocent" Machiavellian maneuverings. Lucky for Rose, Ellen's effortless charm disarmed the cougar before she could work up to proper indignance.

"Err ... Yeah! I, uh ... am happy to meet you, uh ... *intact.*" The catamount was certain she was capable of reheating her rapidly cooling meal with the heat radiating from her ears alone.

"Happy to shed the 'some assembly required' sticker! That conversation really tickled my funny bone, Jos. I definitely needed the laughs after the last couple weeks! Was that you that sent the card, too? 'Shiver me timbers and rattle me bones, get ye well soon, matey!'" Ellen said the last bit in her best impression of a West Country accent, and the same effortless chuckle that Jos adored every single time she'd heard it in an interview.

Jos simply nodded, blush still clear as day on her pale furred cheeks.

"So — 'Mabel Greysmoke' in the signature?" The vixen's ear flicked and her brow quirked. "Funny way to spell 'Josryne!' Trying out a new name?"

Josryne felt blessed that her fur was thick enough to hide a majority of the flush but still felt like she could be seen like a beacon from *orbit* at that moment. "Oh yeah … that's just that *nom de poom*, hah…" Her fingers nervously played with her choker as she inspected the suddenly-very-interesting crags and crackles in the skin of her fried chicken, shoving a piece towards her muzzle before she said anything *else* stupid.

"*Haha, yeah! Like the joke you told me that one time, when I was still a pathetic sad boy? Remember, LN? How could you forget that one personal appearance, years ago, with the one adult in line for your autograph behind all the tweens?*"

"Heh, *nom de poom*, that's not bad! But! how're *you* feeling after that stay? Properly rested and chastised? I've never met someone without eyebrows who could manage a scowl quite so severe as the cheery O's."

Ellen seemed to effortlessly be able to just rattle off banter like that. Maybe it was part of her powers? The lioness swallowed her bite and nodded.

"Oh yeah, I feel pretty great considering the state Volta scooped me up in … Just trying to figure out what to do now, y'know?" She desperately wanted to enjoy the mac and cheese, but her stomach was preoccupied with tying itself in knots rather than savoring the casserole.

"*Yep, here I am! Brand-new burden for the team!*"

[*Josryne Mabel, you cut that out and enjoy this lunch, or so help me, I will play Toby Keith's Greatest Hits all night!*]

"Oh, so *now* you're back, you **charlatan**? You … You **fox** in chicken's clothing!"

[*Eat. Chat. Love.*]

"*That's not how it goes!*"

A twangy southern guitar started playing in her mind.

"**Fine!** *You abominably cruel and unusual AI.*"

[*Love you too!*]

"Ahhh, yes, the Volta special! She mentioned it." There was a subtle change in the vixen's voice, almost imperceptible. "I'm sorry that you had to go through that, Jos, but … you're safe here."

While the cougar was wrapped up in her own anxiety, she couldn't help but faintly realize the vixen was putting some real *effort* into sounding confident. "Thank you, I guess? Everyone has been saying that, and I appreciate it, but I can't help feeling, well … sort of useless."

All these crispy cheesy edges wasted, she thought sadly, as she prodded her mac and cheese. "I mean, like … they do so much *good*, right? Even if there are questionable choices made, maybe, the Korps is a net gain for the world at large." The puma sighed, a deep sort of resentful sigh, one that she associated with the well-meaning but terminally *weak*.

"I mean, you're *Lawful Neutral! 'The Pun-Slinging Vix with All the Tricks'!*" Jos continued, in a perky mock-commentator voice, but lost steam as she finished the phrase. Her ears flagged slightly as her tone sank. "Your abilities are *extraordinary!* You *always* have the right response, the *perfect* snappy comeback to bounce back and save the day! But unless they really need a customer service specialist, or a fanb — *fangirl* nerd with an encyclopedic knowledge of supers, what the hell am *I* going to do?" She shook her head as it hung between her shoulders and snorted softly. "Sorry. I'm sorry. I ... I didn't mean to let loose like that! You're just trying to enjoy your food, and here I go, being Depressy Betsy all over your lunch. Forget I said anything." She heaved a sigh, before forcing a smile to the surface.

Ellen looked mildly surprised by the sudden emotional honesty but took it in stride. "Don't be sorry! I get it. It's okay, it can take time to acclimate, and I'm sure they'll be able to find a way for you to help. Heroes come in all shapes and sizes, right? 'Anyone can be a Hero,' and all that?" The vixen winked cheekily through her ever-winning smile.

"That's what the posters say, anyway." The feline said with a shrug, eyes still focused on the sustenance in front of her, which simply could not keep her interest.

There was a moment of silence, and the catamount needed to fill it immediately, or she was sure she would die, right there, in the middle of the cafeteria, fork still loaded with carbs.

Change the subject. **Change the subject.** *Something completely unrelated to your self-doubt-laden-whinging, Jos, you disaster!*

"So, that brawl with Strong! The team-up attack with Volta? *That* was incredible! It was like you two were totally in sync with each other!" She said, a smile coming unbidden to her face now. "He never expected it! Hell, *I* never expected it!"

The demimorph raised a curious eyebrow. "So, you liked that move, huh? I was all charged up for sure!"

"It was absolutely *electrifying!* I mean, it was strange seeing Volta working with you, instead of, you know, putting the size 20's to your aaasssss..." The cat's eyes went wide as she suddenly realized the tenor of her reply, and she tried to turn it around. "I mean you were *great!* I have *always* admired how you just keep coming, no matter what."

"Always admired, huh? So, you're a *fan*..." Ellen made a show of putting her chin in her hands and theatrically batted her eyelashes. "What *else* do you like about me, hmm?"

"I, err ... well ... *yes*. Yes, I am." The cougar was sure she was just seconds from bursting into flames as heat radiated from all of her facial features. "I think you really inspire people to try and be better, you know? Like, when you saved those folks from the collapsing building? That pool in the air thing? You adapt to new powers so quickly and you're so clever, and funny, and ... I ... yes. I think you're amazing..." She trailed off before shoving a chunk of mac and cheese into her muzzle, stifling the temptation to keep gushing.

Why don't I just tell her about the fanfic next? What an absolute fuckin' dork!

"*Amazing*, even! Thank you, Jos, you seem to have a knack for making me feel better. Ever considered a sidekick gig?" Ellen giggled as she returned to working on her own plate, dipping a piece of chicken into some concerningly red sauce before popping it into her mouth.

Only every day, the lioness thought to herself, doing her best to suppress her fluttering heart. "Oh, err ... I mean..."

"Eh, I'm sure you don't want to wear the shorts with the bullseye on the behind! The next Distraction Lad, my very own boy wonder!" she quipped after a mouthful.

"Lad ... Boy ... Right." The cat winced as it echoed in her mind, and her tail reflexively curled back against her leg. With just two little words, her recently redeemed hero had inadvertently managed to crush her burgeoning self-esteem. She looked away, skin crawling underneath her soft coat, no longer excited. She swallowed her last mouthful, no longer hungry. It left a bitter taste on her tongue.

"Ha, ha! Yeah ... Certainly wouldn't do me any *favors*..."

"*She didn't say it to be mean ... She wouldn't do that...*"

[No, she wouldn't!]

"*But ... She said it...*"

Ellen seemed to be enjoying her meal, not noticing that her companion was no longer eating. As if on cue, another demimorphic vixen appeared — the expected sister. She looked a lot like LN, if LN kept her hair long and a little wild, was a great deal more blessed in the back end instead of the front and wore RCGs. But not even meditating on that prodigious derriere could halt the spiral that had already begun in Jos's soul.

"H-hi, Ellen!" The new arrival gave a little wave, nearly dropping her tray, before catching it and setting it across from her sister. "And hello, M-Miss!" She plopped down with a smile that would ordinarily have been contagious, but the catamount had just been inoculated against joy.

[Mabes, she didn't mean—]

"It's fine, Rose. I know how I look. I'm not blind."

"Oh, hello! You must be Ellen's sister, yeah?" Jos dredged up a smile for the perky newcomer, leveraging how the other sister addressed her to try and turn her mood around.

"Mmm-hmm!" The shorter fox had already tucked into a slice of chocolate cake and swallowed before she continued. "M-my name's V-Vixie! What's y-yours?"

"Oh Vixie, I'm so rude," Ellen piped up, switching her gaze between her sister and her newly revealed biggest fan, at least in the immediate vicinity and excluding the aforementioned sibling. "This is Jos! This is the person Volta saved!"

*"Oh. She's dancing around my pronouns now … I'm such an **idiot**."*

[Mabes…]

"Oh! Miss V-Volta said you w-were a pretty k-kittycat!" Vixie was practically beaming as she smiled with chocolate-stained lips.

However, the strained smile was quickly fading on the lioness's face, as the distress ate away at the supports of her all-too-tenuous confidence.

"I can't do this."

[Mabes, wait! Don't…]

"I, uh … Rose reminded me I have an appointment, and I don't want to intrude on your lunch…" She picked up her barely touched tray and gave an awkward half-nod. "It was really great meeting you both … I-I'll see you around, I'm sure." With a final, forced smile, she left before either sister could respond. The tears were held at bay just long enough to make it to the neatly divided bank of waste and recycling chutes, dropping off her tray on a nearby wheeled rack as she picked up speed, heading for the exit.

You already cried in front of the villain. Don't do it in front of the Hero…!

[Mabes, please, wait! Slow down! Please, talk to me!] Rose pleaded, concern evident in her tone.

The catamount huffed. *"Right now, I just need to put some space between me and her. Can you please just show me the way back to my quarters?"*

With a gentle pulse, the way became illuminated, the augmented-reality markers pink beacons along the sidewalk in her vision.

[*But what about your appointment?*]

She snarled in response to the AI. *"With who, Rose? What are you going to surprise me with now? Another Hero? Or how about my ex-girlfriend? Maybe my parents stopped by? What. **now?**"*

[*I'm sorry, I just thought you would like to meet her, and—*]

*"And it was her in the hospital, and you never told me? Look, maybe you never lied, exactly, but those were both dirty tricks, and you fuckin' **know** it!"*

[*I know, but I was only trying to help...*]

*"Aren't you **always.**"* The cougar balled her paws into fists, trembling as she ducked into a small green space, a park of some sort, or maybe a small community garden. *"I wish that I got a say in how you go **about** it, sometimes. Partners, Rose! That's what we are, remember?"*

There was an unoccupied bench, and she needed a place to think. She had embarrassed herself in front of LN, and every single person that saw the catamount fighting tears as she sped away, *and* on top of all that she had been rude to Vixie — who was so innocent, and nothing but friendly. She pulled her visor up, and buried her paws in her eyes, trying to sob as quietly as she could.

[*We **are** partners, and I ... I wasn't trying to deceive. I'm so sorry, sweetheart, truly.*]

*"I know, Rose, I know, but ... it's too much. All of this is just too much! Why do **I** deserve any of this? A gigantic apartment, and fantastic food, a-a-and friends? I am literally a millstone about the neck of the Korps, and it's only a matter of time before everyone realizes it ... and then what?"*

She whispered her next words out loud, sniffling. *"What will they do with me if I have no use?"*

[*That isn't how this works, Mabes.*]

*"That's **always** how it works, ROSE!"* she roared, and began crying once again. She was *tired* of crying, but the tears wouldn't stop. *"Who would just ... give away all of this? For someone like me, even? I'm not even a resource to be used ... They're doing this all out of the goodness of their fucking hearts?"*

[*That is precisely why we do it. This is what we do, building our better world, and this is all a part of that.*]

"Well, I'm not worth the trouble, Rose. I don't know how else to say it. I'm scared, and I'm alone, and I am trapped in a body that I finally realized

is completely alien to me, but is still the only one I've ever known, and I ... I *can't* help anyone—" Her voice dropped to a softly rasped whisper again. "I can't even help *myself*. First *you* had to save me, and then Volta..." The tears continued to spill down her cheeks.

"It just feels so *pointless*..." The joy she had felt earlier in the day — the resolute drive to be her best self — was crashing down around her ears. The work crumbled just like it always did. "*I* ... feel pointless."

"You know, when I told you once upon a time that anyone could be a hero, I meant it." The words were in a familiar voice, but the tone was soft, and gentle, not like she had ever heard it before.

Jos turned to look and there the demimorph was, hand on her shoulder and smiling down at her, looking so much like every superhero trope that she could almost hear the triumphant John Williams score swelling in the background.

"Can I sit here?"

"Oh, *Ellen* ... I'm sorry I rushed off but ... I-I don't think I'm going to be very good c-company now..." The cat coughed and quickly wiped her face with a sleeve.

"I think *I* might have been not such great company." She scooted next to the puma, her ears splayed just a little. "I'm sorry, Jos. I didn't mean the sidekick thing the way I said it, and I am *trying* to be better, but ... it's no excuse."

"You didn't know, and I shouldn't just assume people will know, anyway," the lioness murmured as she looked away. "How is that fair?"

"That's the *thing*, isn't it? If I can keep track of six flying buzzsaws and an ice wizard with a shotgun, I should be able to figure out 'she/her.'"

"Dodging Sleet Shooter is a *bit* more serious than my pronouns..." The catamount stared between her feet and gave a shrug.

"I don't know if that's true. See, I was never good at serious! Any who ... right after you left, I remembered a very sad mountain lion from once upon a time. I made a joke, and they lit up, and then I signed their name, and would have sworn they floated away ... I don't suppose there are a whole lot of cougars named Jos running around." The vixen leaned forward to try and get a look at her face. "That *was* you, wasn't it?"

She nodded a little and sniffed in a vain attempt to stifle the flow.

"Yup. Four years and an *entire* gender revelation ago. You were the first person to call me that name, face to face ... I-I know that you didn't know, and it didn't mean *anything* to you, but ... it meant *everything* to me…" Jos turned to look at the apologetic vixen. "Someone finally *knew* even if I didn't…"

"You looked much happier in the cafeteria than I remembered you looking, way back when."

"I thought I was, but I always question it … *Something* always happens…"

"Can't just let yourself have a good thing, huh?" Ellen let out a little chuckle and shook her head. "I might know a little something about that…"

"It's hard to believe you deserve good things when you constantly push them away, y'know? I'm just afraid … What if I wake up and it's all gone again?" She let a sigh out through her nostrils in a huff. "It would be worse than never having it in the first place."

"Stay afraid, but do it anyway." LN replied, staring ahead.

"W-*what* did you say?" The cat's tail stood erect as her perked ears at the choice of words.

"Stay afraid, but do it anyway." The vixen smiled and nudged Jos with her shoulder. "A famous princess said it, and I have to remind myself sometimes."

The faintest flicker of a smile. "So even Heroes get scared, huh?"

"What, did you think I'm immune? The person I fought more than anybody is an eight foot tall wolf-tank made out of overjuiced tasers! One time, she literally pounded me into the ground like a post! I'm always scared *something* could go wrong, but … you have to *try*. Nothing will get better if you don't."

"The action is what's important," the cougar responded, recalling more of those words of wisdom.

"Exactly."

"Can't just be a lazy *Leia* 'bout, huh?"

"Oh, I think you got the *general* idea."

"Now you're just *fishing* for word play…"

They stared at each other, trying to look as serious as they could. But the dam broke and the giggling and snorting suddenly rushed through, blossoming into full-throated, side-splitting, face-hurting laughter. The bench shook with their guffawing and forced a smile on the lioness's face that she couldn't hide even if she wanted to.

"You know, Jos … Volta was right. You're pretty, but *especially* when you laugh."

Heh … LN thinks I'm pretty…

"I'll try to do it more often, then..." She wiped a tear from her eye — one of the good ones, finally. "Thanks, Ellen. You may be part of the Korps now, but you'll always be a hero to me." She snorted but kept the same smile. "Gods, that was corny as hell, but eh ... it's the truth."

"Here I was coming to help you, and you helped me ... Funny how that works out sometimes, huh?"

"Mmmhm."

"Yeah ... Funny, isn't it, Rose?"

[I don't know what you're insinuating, dear, but I am glad you are smiling again.]

The perennially quippy vixen stood up slowly, and stretched, letting out an adorable little grunt. "Now that I've righted that wrong, I *do* believe I will reward myself with a slice of pie from Gramma C's! Do you want to come with, Jos? Best pie this side of anywhere!"

"Ooooh, *pie* ... oh, *shit!* My appointment! I am so sorry, I swear I'm not trying to dodge you, Ellen, I really do have an appointment!" Jos stood up, and almost hugged the vixen, stopped herself, and offered her paw instead. "Thank you so much, hun. It really means the world to me that you ... That you are *exactly* as amazing as I always knew you were."

Ellen shook her head, pushed the paw aside and gave her a hug — the kind of hug she'd needed but hadn't *known* she'd needed — and Jos's tail briefly stood rigid in panic before her anxiety all melted away. As she draped her arms around her new friend, resting her chin gently between the vixen's ears, a purr quietly rumbled through her chest, unable to be stopped.

[It's fine, hun! I rescheduled you for tomorrow morning. We should probably talk about it more tonight, anyhow. From now on, fewer surprises and more discussion, I promise. Now, go have some pie and make sure you act right around Gramma C!]

"Jos isn't home right now ... Please leave a message after the beep."

"Thank you *so* much," the cougar sniffled loudly. "I promise I don't cry *all* the time..."

"Hey, as long as you're staying hydrated! And here I am without my surplus LNergy drinks..."

"Weren't those discontinued?"

"It was really just a label change for a different drink. I think nowadays it's sold as Orange Blizzard Wizard? But I had a bunch of leftover packs with my face on 'em before they cleared out my apartment."

"No shit? Did any of them make it here? They're kind of a rare collector's item, and I—" She closed her eyes, wincing as she snorted derisively at herself, "Sorry, old habits … anyway, Rose rescheduled that appointment for tomorrow, so I can have fresh start pie tonight." A genuine smile lit up her face at the prospect of desert. "I didn't eat much lunch, so I've got plenty of room!"

"Oh, great! Vixie is already there! It's so good, Jos; just mind your manners around Gramma C!" She held out her hand, and gave that smile once again, and the cougar felt her heart flutter in her chest for just an instant as she took it.

"Why does everyone think that they have to warn me to behave? Do I look *especially* like a criminal, or…" The puma stopped in her tracks, as her mind finally managed to process the entirety of Ellen's warm words.

"…*Wait*. Volta thinks I'm *pretty*?"

Chapter 12

What Are We Running From?

Josryne groaned as she clenched at what she was certain was her now visibly distended belly, stumbling into the apartment after her dining indiscretions. "Rose, you're supposed to be my friend! Why did you let me eat all of that pie?"

[I'm going to be honest, dear — I really didn't think you'd listen. Also, you were all smiles back there. I certainly wasn't going to tell you 'No'.]

"Awww..."

[Also, I bet Cosetta that you could finish the entire pie, and I had faith in you! You didn't disappoint!]

"...I guess that still counts as being on my side. Speaking of Gramma C, uhh ... does she usually kiss goodbye on the mouth and pinch your tush like that, or am I just special?"

[Well, she doesn't do that to *everyone,* as far as I know, but I wouldn't tell you it's never happened before.]

"Mm ... *Ooog* ... I'm going to die a happy girl right now, then! *BLEGH!*" She dropped her purse on the couch as she exclaimed, groaning dramatically, followed by an exaggeratedly theatrical fall over the armrest. She bounced off the cushions, knocking the bag to the floor with an exceptionally alarming thud — much louder than the bag should have sounded, certainly. Startled by the noise, the puma looked over, and saw the case had bounced free and looked up at her as if to say, "*Remember me?*"

She rolled over onto her belly with a little effort, and a quiet grunt. Her pads ran over the intricately tooled surface of the leather, all winding its way around and through the prominent infinity symbol at the center.

"Huh! In all the commotion of the last week, I forgot you'd given me this. I'm sorry, Rose!" Jos said, her ears wilting just a bit.

The virtual vixen appeared with a tilt of her head and a bright smile. [Sweetie, you were a *little* busy with the complete upheaval of your life circumstances. I didn't take it personally! But you *do* owe me a reading,] the AI responded.

"I do, that is true! But … I don't want to use you as the test subject for the very first one…"

[Well, I appreciate that, dear, but I won't be upset at you for what the cards say.]

"I know, I just … I feel like it's *my* responsibility to take those first steps, myself." The catamount replied with a nod, set in her decision, and would not be convinced otherwise.

[Taking the lead? Mabes, if I didn't *know* better, I'd say you're getting downright bold! Is being surrounded by all of this *queer villainous* element changing you?]

The cougar blushed. "Well, I *have* been fighting the urge to tie a damsel to the train tracks more and more, these last few days. And my maniacal laugh is improving apace!"

[I'm so proud of you, darling!]

"Mm. All right, nothing left to do but to do it, I suppose." The lioness scooped the deck in one paw and sat up, pulling the coffee table a little closer. "Are you ready to glimpse beyond the veil, my dear Rose?"

[As ready as one can be, to peer into the vast unknown!]

Jos slid the deck free of its sleeve and felt the weight of the cards as they laid in her paw, before she began whispering the steps aloud to herself, lest she miss one and ruin the reading.

"Concentrate on the question…"

The deck had been shuffled and split. She cleared her mind and closed her eyes. Over and over again she cycled the cards, until they told her to stop.

"Cut the deck, and choose your three…"

She focused on the words again, visualized them before finally voicing the question aloud in a quiet and reverent tone:

"Where is my path taking me?"

As her fingertips brushed against the cards, a sensation rolled through her like she had never felt before, and a little shiver ran thrillingly up her spine. The catamount flipped one, then two, and then three; without looking, she felt like she knew what she would see, even if the meanings were still jumbled in her mind. The cards had spoken, in a voice that was clear as the pictures before her.

The cougar stared at the insights revealed, laid all in a row. The past, the present, and the future in single file, symbols facing the sky, and returning her gaze. The deck had shared its answer to the question it was asked, with what she hoped would be simple honesty.

It seemed her deck did not believe in subtlety.

The Ten of Wands, minor arcana.

Death, major arcana.

The Magician, major arcana.

"Thank you for your wisdom," she uttered softly as she bowed her head, walking across the cards with her fingertips as one would step across a creek stone by stone. Each one was a marker of her life from past to present to future. "Now, to render the answer from the riddle."

For a moment, the puma's blood ran cold as she stared at the grim visage of death in the center position; what had been, and what would be, were interrupted by the chill. Her pause was evidently long enough to disconcert Rose, who laid an invisible paw on her knee, her avatar shimmering once more into existence.

[Remember, Death doesn't *just* mean physical death. We should be defining these in order and using them as a lens to see your truth.] Forever the voice of reason was the virtual vixen, and the cougar appreciated the gentle reminder more than she could convey.

Fear of the unknown is as unbecoming for a fledgling witch as it is a villainess.

"You're right, per usual. Best to just start at the beginning, yeah? First, we have the past, the Ten of Wands—" The catamount took a steadying breath, "please don't hesitate to correct me if I'm wrong for any of this, okay, Rose?" Her nerves were frazzled, but she did her best to work past it with a brave face.

[Of course. I don't think I will need to, but why don't we just start with where you feel they lead?]

Josryne nodded, taking a steadying breath as her eyes stared half-lidded at the fate foretold so neatly there.

"This card represents a burden, or blockage. Something stopping me from moving on. It could be an *actual* relationship, or a perceived one — even a physical impairment could be the source." She ran her finger over her lip as she considered. "A barrier. I seem like the most likely one, if I'm honest. My attachment to who I was, and who I thought I *needed* to be." She chuckled softly at what suddenly seemed so obvious.

"It could be three threads, and … I think it's *all* of them, not just one. My self-worth, my attachment to the world I knew, and my place in it, when I thought I was male. That was the struggle," she stated, with a confidence born from she knew not where. She nonetheless welcomed the calm that washed over her with it.

[Very astute reading, dear! Now, what comes next?] The vixen smiled as she gestured to the spread.

"Death. This can be literal death as the event, but death comes in many forms to the mortal, like you so kindly reminded me. It can be the death of a relationship, or even part of one's self, and from death springs life. It *nourishes* what comes after." She scrunched up her nose. "Crystal clear as a mountain spring. Rose, I think the deck you got me speaks fluent candor. This is talking about the passing of my masculine self to be reborn into who I *actually* am. Without that death, there would be nothing to nourish the growth of the new." Her paws clasped together.

[I think that fits perfectly.]

"Mm." She thought about her most recent brush with actual death — and her villainous rescuer, and how that, too, was a death in its way. A part of her never left that alley. Had that been taken from her? Could something be stolen if you never really wanted it? She would *never* be who she was before. But was there even anything there to mourn?

Can it be called a death if the subject was never truly alive?

"Rose … Am I *better* now?" She intoned softly. "I know I'm still broken, but … I'm getting better, right?" Her voice was low and thin, her confidence moments before receded from the observations of her previous existence.

[Every day. *Every day,* I get to speak with you, and get to be a part of your life, and I am so lucky to watch you grow. You *do* get better every day *and* in every way, Mabes, my sweet girl.] The ever-patient and kind reply came as succor to her wounded soul, and a gentle kiss brought a blush to her cheeks. [Just one more.]

"Thank you, Rosie. I really needed that." The cougar smiled, a crooked finger rubbing the underside of her chin as her eyes fell on the future.

A memory sprung forth as if summoned from a grimoire.

Her fingers traced over the picture of the Magician, and she softly smiled. "I wonder what it's like," she whispered.

[What, dear?]

"Nothing, it's just … well … do you believe in magic, Rose? Like … actual magic, I mean."

The lioness shook her head to dispel the vision and focused on what was in front of her: what was *to come*, according to the cards.

"The Magician is energy without restraint, and a conduit between the heavens and earth. The first card of the major arcana, and while not the High Priestess, it too has powerful ties to magic in the world, surrounding us all." The infinity symbol woven into the art of the card caused a sort of echo to reverberate within her mind's eye.

[So, what does this mean for *you*?]

"I need to embrace that energy and move forward. I need to *believe* in magic with all of myself, body and soul." The catamount closed her eyes and thanked the cards once again. "I have struggled, I have died, and now I get to live," she said, with a surety she seldom felt and a soft exhale through her nose.

[The chance to *really* live is what I want most for you, my darling girl.]

Josryne smiled as the vixen leaned against her, resting her head on her shoulder. It was true her sister was not physically there, as such, but she was nonetheless *real*; as real as anything she had ever known in her life, before or since the package that opened her eyes to a wider world had arrived at her figurative *and* literal doorstep.

[What if I told you that you *could* wake up, and see yourself as you truly are, tomorrow? What would you do?]

"I would say you're full of *shit*, but I appreciate the sentiment!" Jos demurred with a chuckle. "But if you were somehow *serious* ... I don't know. I think I would have to do it, right?" Her brow slowly crept upwards, as the realization dawned on her that the AI *never* asked a question without a point. "What are you getting at, Rose?"

[Remember that saying about magic and technology?]

"Any technology of sufficient advancement is indistinguishable from magic, or something like that, right?" She blinked as the discussion continued to go in unexpected directions.

[Close enough. Now, you just said that you need to believe in magic, yes?]

"Rosie ... what's up? I love it when you play coy, but this is *a lot* even for you..." Jos furrowed her brow and tilted her head, unable to fathom where this realistically could be going.

[I'm talking about our appointment tomorrow, and the *magic* that awaits you behind those doors...]

═══

"Okay, so let me get this straight. The Korps has developed nanotech as well as gene altering treatments and reconstructive surgery that can make me into a woman. Physically. *Completely*. In any and all aspects I wish. And not just a woman, but the woman of my *dreams*, and they can do it in the span of *weeks*, not years."

[Mhmm! Gender-affirming care is important to us, so we've dedicated *ample* resources to the study of the field, and Empire Enhancements is the culmination of that work.] The virtual vixen beamed with pride at the triumph of science over the limits of the flesh.

"Huh ... So Volta *did not* take a fifty-five gallon drum of estradiol directly into her shapely ass?" The puma couldn't help but try and calm herself with a little humor, as the excitement swelled inside of her. The implications of this made all of her nerves begin to vibrate as she imagined a world where she *felt* right, *was* right, both inside and out.

[No, dear, it was more involved than a comically sized hypodermic. I mean, part of the treatment does involve an infusion of hormones, and ... the short answer is no, not *exactly*, but *kind of?*]

"I'm glad I'm lying down right now," the cougar muttered, her mind reeling. "So, when I walk in tomorrow, I'll use the world's most advanced character creator to become me. The real me. I'll get to choose *everything*."

[Every detail, down to the jiggle of your ass, my darling.] The vixen had draped herself over the back of the couch. She had decided this reveal was worth a celebration and languidly puffed on a similarly augmented-reality cigar as she grinned down at her little sister. Jos was so distracted by the news, she was barely bothered by the sight or the scent wafting past.

Barely.

[So yes, in fact, my sweet nerdling, you will roll a brand new *you* in the Korps Integrated Multifaceted Avatar Generation Emulator, and our doctors and technicians will use that blueprint to make it a reality! From the tips of your ears, right down to the cute little pads on your toes!]

Jos thought about those lonely nights, staring at the lioness that never was.

She thought about walking around her apartment in her idealized shape, thanks to her RCGs and Rose.

She thought about the nights she let Rose cloud her senses and experience what it was really like to *feel* beautiful. A flush came to her cheeks, she could almost taste the smoke on her lips. Every curve of her shapely body being traced lovingly by her own paws, and by the paws of another. Filling and being fulfilled in ways she never believed were possible but had forever hoped.

One thing jutted forth and caused confusion and doubt to darken her mood.

"*What about … that … thing?*" She was so embarrassed she could barely say the words out loud. She felt childish to even be concerned about the appendage, but she was self-conscious of it. Was she less "*trans*" if she kept it? Was she less *herself* if she chose not to?

[*It's yours to keep or leave, sweetie. Lots of girls have cocks, Jos. Remember Betty? She is hung like a horse-sized cat, and she is a woman, through and through.*]

The cougar's breath caught in her throat. How could she *forget* that beautiful pink cock, veined and pulsing, the glans glistening and drooling pre. She often dreamed of her muzzle enveloping that rod — feeling the tip against the back of her throat, bobbing up and down until she received her reward — and greedily swallowing every last glorious drop of the woman's seed. The firm but gentle grasp of her claws as the serval turned her over, and began pistoning that spit-coated shaft into her ass, hilting over and over until she couldn't take the heat welling inside her, crying out as she sprayed all over the sheets, her own cock dripping and spent…

And then, the gentle tenderness of the serval crawling up beside the lioness, taking a deep drag of the cigar they were sharing and pressing her lips to Jos's own, still sticky with her reward. This was of course followed by her delicately rough tongue, the entire moment wreathed in a deliciously fragrant, enticing haze, and the taste of their sex would linger long after she awoke.

Yes. She *remembered*.

She remembered the *other* dreams as well. Other … scenarios, ones she couldn't even bring herself to mention, not even to Rose.

If it's enough for Betty, it should be enough for me, right? I … I don't always dislike it, so what if I regret … mmm…

[You will not be any less of a girl if you keep your parts, if you so choose! No matter what you decide, we just want you to feel like yourself.]

…What makes me myself, though? The catamount mused silently to herself for a moment, before looking back to the vixen, not wanting to think about that part of her body any longer.

"…And this is all free? Just another part of the Korps sign-on bonus? It just seems too good to be true, hun…" The cougar's skepticism was still there, but she *wanted* to believe. "My happiness isn't *that* important…"

[Absolutely. Mabes, my darling, conquering the world through force causes resentment, and people will not be ruled simply by being shown power. One must make the people realize there *is* another way, *a better* way. This is a part of that, as much as dismantling the oppressive establishments in the first place.]

"Mm." Jos took a deep breath and let it out slowly as she closed her eyes. Her mind wandered back to earlier that day, and the hug from Ellen and everything that brought her to where she was. The confluence of events that *made* her. Through the good and the bad, she had ended up here, entwined in the loving embrace of the helix.

Would world domination really be such a bad thing? We clearly haven't figured out how to operate to this point...

They had no reason to lie to her. The kindness *was* the point.

"Changing hearts and minds ... What's important is the *action*." The puma stated with a nod before opening her eyes. "Let's do it, Rosie ... I can't be scared of who I *could* be." She sat up, her voice steeled and determined. "I need to approach this crossroads and choose my path without reservation."

[Attagirl! Our appointment is at ten in the A, so we should probably head to bed!] Rose slipped gracefully off the back of the sofa, her stogie phasing from existence.

The catamount stretched as she stood, letting out a little squeaky growl and nodded in agreement.

"Yeah, morning comes quickly underground, I bet. Sunrise has to start *somewhere*..." Jos supposed as she looked away, rubbing at the back of her head. "Rose ... um ... could you *maybe* play that dream with Betty again?" she asked a little sheepishly, her cheeks reddening more by the moment. *"Please?"*

[Of course, Mabes. I want you to focus on pleasant things the night before Korpsmas!] No judgment, only sweet affirmation as always. [Besides, you make the *cutest* little noises when you're having *really* good dreams.]

The puma busied herself with placing the cards in their case, unable to properly respond with more than huffing and clearing her throat, trying desperately to change the subject. "I need to assemble a place of reverence for this deck, I think..." She kissed the top of the case and thanked it wordlessly.

[An altar can absolutely be arranged! Any idea to whom?]

"I'm not sure? I've always been curious about Hellenistic deities? Greek mythology always resonated with me." She pulled off her shirt as she walked into the bedroom, letting out another yawn. Without missing a beat, Rose began the simulation; the cougar smiled as she looked down at the swells and curves that would soon be hers.

[*Oooo!* The Greek Pantheon is *full* of interesting patrons. It's *perfect* for you, I think!]

"Mmm." The feline laid back on the bed and slowly ran her paws up her belly, letting out a little happy sigh as soft paw pads explored, making sure to *really* familiarize herself with this shape.

"Thank you again, for helping me and not just giving up…"

[*What else are glasses for but to help you see, my dear?*]

Josryne's dreams that night were so vivid she woke up with weak knees, and her sheets an absolute tangle of sweat and spent seed. She smiled with satisfaction as she stared up at the ceiling, retrieving Rose from her nightstand, the weight on her muzzle as comforting as the memory of lover's paw on her chest.

"It always feels so *real* … Maybe I'll meet her someday, huh?"

[You know … I *could* introduce you…]

"Rosie, what did I say would happen if you set me up like that, *again?*"

[That you wouldn't be held responsible for what you would do afterwards.] The pout was unmistakable in her tone.

"Mm." she wandered towards the bathroom to relieve herself and rinse off.

[*I **still** think I was right…*]

"Uh-**huh!** Well, I **think** *you need to tell me where I can get an extra-thick protein shake with a Gatorade chaser after last night, because **holy shit!** I don't know how you make it feel like that, but I slept like the dead after that, uh, last bit."*

[*They call that a "Madama's Morning After" at Gramma C's! And I'm glad you appreciate my skillset, darling sister.*] The virtual vixen tittered as she leaned in the doorframe.

"Oh, there are few things I appreciate more than that, hun." The catamount blinked and turned to the AI projection as she washed her paws. "Who's *Madama?* Is that like a villain moniker? I'm unfamiliar."

[Less alter-ego and more of a title, really. Her name is Carmen — odds are you'll be meeting her someday, so make sure to be on your best behavior for Madama!]

"…Why does it feel like you don't expect me to be already? Was there an interoffice memo I'm not privy to?"

[Call it a hunch, dear!]

"Mm … So, she's *more* intimidating than Volta? *Somehow?*" She stopped at the shower door, looking back at the AI's projected-self. The idea of *anyone* being more lethal than the wolf seemed incredibly far-fetched.

[Oh, my dear sweet child, you don't know the half of it. Carmen is the woman that got that pup to sit and stay.] Rose's casual flippancy was given as she idly smoothed out the fur of her tail, which meant she missed the flicker in the cougar's eyes.

"Huh. I guess I didn't consider that she, uh … had a partner?" Jos reached in to turn the water on, the steam quickly filling the room. "Makes sense, though."

[They're well and truly devoted to each other, as much as to the cause itself.]

The lioness rubbed the back of her neck, her brows knitted in confusion by the sudden pang of jealousy at the idea of *someone else* being the object of the wolf's affections.

Of course she has an incredible partner. She deserves nothing less than that, why the hell am I surprised?

She hoped the warm water would clear her head of childish envy, and as it rolled over her, she realized it would take a lot more than just soap and water to wash away that green-eyed daydream.

They did not, in fact, go to the diner. Jos stammered though an excuse about wanting to be on time for her appointment, so breakfast was an in-house affair after the world's quickest shower, avoiding too much time alone with her thoughts.

A very runny egg sandwich on warm bread with a thick slice of tangy soft cheese she couldn't quite identify filled her belly *just* right. The dairy in question was unlabeled in the fridge, which was lavishly stocked, to her increasing lack of surprise, with *exactly* the mix of favorites and healthy options for a perfectly balanced diet, but it smelled heavenly and *tasted* even better, so on the sando it went; she'd have to remember to ask Rose about the type of cheese later. The meal was washed down with a double-thick protein shake (Cookies and Cream was the go-to, she was told), and a big bottle of unnaturally azure sports drink (Electric Blue, also the standard for the Madama's Morning After). She sipped as she walked back to her room, licking her fingertips in between mouthfuls of electrolyte-laced liquid. It was time for the next big decision of the day: what to wear.

Rose piped some more recent dance-pop through the speakers in the room, shaking things up from the puma's predilection for the music of the past. The beat began shaking the floor, and she couldn't help but move her ass along with it, sliding up the closet and looking at the outfits.

"How do I want everyone to see me when I'm done baking?"

[Everyone, huh? Should we throw a birthday party, then? Your coming-out soirée?]

"I don't need a party, but, well, I mean … Volta and Ellen and Vixie are the only friends I have here — besides you, obviously — and I … I want to look pretty for them." As she traced her fingers over a dress, the thought drifted across her mind that it still felt *weird* calling supervillains by their first names. (And peripherally, that Ellen's sister was *such* a sweetheart; a gift, really.)

Her tail swayed behind her as she danced, tossing the outfit on the bed behind her.

[Whatever you choose will be perfect!]

"I suppose I have you to thank for these amazing clothes, girl?"

[Guilty as charged!]

"But why so many? You know most of them probably won't fit, after today…" Her ears flattened a little as she realized she was going to be a **very** different shape *very* soon, and trepidation began to make itself known.

[I will make sure your wardrobe fits you perfectly as soon as you're fully cooked, and not a second later!]

"But what about the rest of these? I don't want them to go to waste because I'm making such a self-centered choice…" The catamount bit her lip as she rubbed the softest top she'd ever felt between her fingertips.

A delicate paw firmly grasped her tail and tugged, the sharp little pain stopping her contrition before it could begin.

[*You're not selfish! Wanting to be you is not selfish! Besides, the clothes you haven't worn will be taken back to the quartermasters' stores for redistribution elsewhere or broken down for recycling! We don't **do** wasteful here. Unless it's a hedonism thing. Then we can have a **little** excess, as a treat.*]

"*But Rose, I...*" She winced as there was another pull, this once with added persuasiveness in the form of claws digging in. "I'll go with this."

[Excellent choice.]

The final fit was daring and suggested the style catamount longed to have — eighties pseudo-goth chic. Shiny knee-high boots, buckled with a chunky heel; thigh-high socks in a mauve sort of purple; a pair of frilly black panties; and a skater dress that was almost a T-shirt, hanging off her shoulders and stopping at mid-thigh, black as the night. Its artfully ragged edge faded to soft pastel-pink, and the back had a small, embroidered helix between the shoulders in the same rosy color. A pair of fishnet gloves, a couple of belts about her waist, and her beloved choker tied it all together into something that was just right for her.

The music came to an end, and she held her paws to her muzzle. She was staring at an outfit she had imagined *hundreds* of times, in those moments where she allowed herself to feel. To *exist*, honestly.

"*Rose ... tell me I won't wake up in the wrong body ever again.*"

[Never ever again. Promise.]

She sniffled loudly but didn't cry, just nodding as the smile grew on her face.

Never again.

[Let's head out! We'll take the tram over!]

"Could we maybe walk? I ... I want to stretch my legs after last night," Jos suggested with a simpering giggle. "These boots were made for walkin', after all!"

The walk added fifteen minutes or more onto the trip, and Jos was at first incredibly self-conscious; while it was true that she did pick it out (and loved it), the outfit was the most feminine thing she had ever worn. It was supposed to be *empowering*, but she found herself a bundle of nerves until a petite bat in leg warmers and workout gear came running up to her, almost vibrating with excitement as they stopped and leaned in to examine her fit.

"*Girl*, that dress is *so* cute!"

The puma's tail stood up behind her, and she started to positively *glow*, in equal measure from both the praise and embarrassment. "O-oh … Thank you so much! I-I was really nervous about wearing it out…" she demurred and played with the netting of her glove.

"Oh, honey, you are killing it! *Loooove* the boots, too! If I wasn't on my way to brunch I would talk your ear off and raid your closet! Call me, okay? Rose has my number!" The bat gave a wink, and with that whirlwind introduction complete, sped off at a jog.

The cat released the breath she did not realize she was holding.

"…*What just happened?*"

[*You're going to get a lot of that, but* **especially** *from them.*]

Another name was added to her contact list, but the cougar was still recovering and could pay it no mind. She managed a shaky smile, though, and her tail perked a little higher as she walked.

But as she approached the medical sector, she felt something was off, and it began to flick tensely from side to side. She began to pull at her fingers as her anxiety simmered.

W-why were they so nice? Am I fine this way? Is this … Is this the wrong choice?

What did you do to deserve affection? Attention? Why shouldn't someone else have that? You're nothing.

[*Mabes, what's wrong?*]

"I … I don't know Rose, p-please … I need to sit down…"

Less **than nothing.**

The crash was immediate. It was all *too much*, and she felt the world spinning around her. This wasn't *right*; she *should* be happy. This was the *dream*. She stumbled off the sidewalk and leaned against the concrete wall of whatever the structure was beside her, but even it felt like it was shaking. Everything was coming apart at the seams.

Why do you deserve to be happy?

"No. No no no…" Her voice was barely audible as she felt her way around the side, and away from prying eyes. "Rosie … It's so loud…"

They don't know you like I do … They'll leave you. Just like always. It's what you **deserve.**

Th-that's not true! They want me to be happy!

Why are you bothering? You're just going to **ruin** **it.**

"ROSE … help … please…"

Her paws clamped against her ears, and she tried to resist banging her head against the wall; anything to stop that voice from picking away at her. *"Please make it **stop**!"*

Same as you ever were, <u>Josephine</u>. Begging for help. <u>Nothing</u> will change who you really are...

"Do you need help, sweetie?" She felt a gentle touch on her shoulder, and she was back in the real world. She hadn't noticed her claws had dug painfully into her forearms as she rocked with her knees against her chest.

"Oh, gods, Rose, I..." The cougar blinked, staring at a pair of polished leather boots she did not recognize. As her gaze ventured upwards, a silver dragoness filled her vision, brow furrowed with concern behind bubble-shaped RCG's. "Oh, I'm sorry, Miss Karen ... I-I think I'm, uh, just a little over-excited? Yeah, I-I need some help, but I have Rose ... I'll be alright..."

"That's okay, hun. Why don't we just sit down for a minute, and you can talk to me?" Her voice was so kind, how could she not trust her implicitly?

Before Jos could help herself, she had wrapped her arms around the Korps's multitudinous matron and just focused on trying to steady herself as the subterranean base seemed to be crashing down around her. Then a paw rubbed her back in small circles, and the voice came as a soft coo of familiar comfort. The collapse slowed, and then stopped.

"Shh, shh, Mabes ... It'll be okay."

Jos looked up to her, emerald eyes large as plates.

"I promised."

Chapter 13

The Prettiest Star

So *weak*. *Always need someone to save you.*

[Jos, sweetie, I'm here. Stay with me…] Only kindness.

She was *there*. How could she be *there? How* …?

Stop. Struggling. Just go ahead and give up.

[You're not allowed to let this win. You're *more* than this.] Forever encouraging.

She's so pretty.

Her scales gleamed softly in the artificial lighting. Silver radiance and the softest touch, her eyes stained pink behind the glass, a gaze of sincere concern crowned by dark locks with the most *striking* streak of white … as the static began to fade into nothingness, the puma managed to sputter out an apology, entranced by this mythical one of many.

"M-Miss Karen? I … I think I fell down … I'm … I'm sorry." She stammered as she tried to pull back for proper deference, but the dragoness wouldn't allow her to pull away. The catamount could only submit to the warmth of her touch.

"You don't need to apologize, hun — and just 'Karen' is fine. I think you've been through a lot lately, hmm?" Her voice was so familiar … it wrapped around her like a blanket, and she found herself unable to shiver. The lioness felt the dragon's paw clasping her wrist, her thumb rubbing gently in small circles just like the paw upon her back. "Maybe you should take it easy? It's okay to feel overwhelmed. I know that this is all so new to you."

"N-n-no, *no*, I can't … I'm so *close…*" She whimpered as she found herself clinging tightly to the kindly woman. She had sunk to her knees beside the building, away from the foot traffic, and the feline hung on to her like she was the only thing keeping her above water. "I said I w-w-would take action. I told you…"

"*Why can't I just save myself? Why do I always have to rely on* **everyone** *else...*"

"I told *Rose,* I mean ... I could do it. She..." Her mind was going a million miles a minute, and she couldn't focus on the right words to use.

"She promised you would never wake up in the wrong body, ever again, right?" A knowing smile brightened Karen's gaze, even behind the visor.

"You ... you called me *Mabes...*" Realization blossomed on her features as who she was staring at became clear. *Right. The Karenswarm is interconnected, and they organize the Korps...*

"*Mmmhm.* We had such a rough go, I wanted to see you with my own eyes, even if just for a moment. I needed to be here to see you off," Karen said as she pressed her forehead to Jos's, tears running down her cheeks without shame.

The catamount's eyes were wet again, and she was so tired of crying, but if the person holding you was crying too, it would be rude *not* to cry ... right? The cougar further began to rattle off all perceived offenses worthy of apology, while she had the chance. "R-Rose — er ... Karen, I'm sorry I'm so much work, and that you're always having to save me and ... and that I take you for *granted...*"

"I'll always help you when you stumble, sweetheart, and I know you would do the same for me." With those words, she silenced all the fears that had made themselves manifest.

Josryne laid her head against the dragoness's chest, feeling the soft leather against her cheek, and listened to Karen's heart beating. She soon realized it was in time with her own. As quickly as she had begun to spiral, her big sister had saved her again. They might have stayed that way for hours; she couldn't tell, and it didn't matter.

She was *there.*

"Always," the puma finally replied. "Without a second thought."

"You know what? The moment we met, I knew you were special." A purr began to rumble in the feline's chest.

"*How?* I was just a *mess,* Rosie..." Her brow furrowed as her head stayed there, nestled in the safety of Rose's powerful arms.

"Everyone is messy sometimes, sweetheart. You had the desire to be so kind and brave. You stepped into the unknown, and you embraced it. Despite everything, you grew into this *wonderful* woman, and I am so proud of you." The dragoness tucked a finger under her sister's chin so she had to look into those deep, verdant green pools. "You hadn't even been here conscious for a full day, and still you were asking how you could *help*. That is just who you *are*, and I know that the best is still yet to come." Her paw cradled Jos's cheek, and all she could do was nuzzle against it. "I love you, Mabes."

"I love you, too..." The cougar stopped short, letting her fingertips trace the smooth skin of those silver shoulders. "I ... I don't know what to call you anymore ... Rose seems too impersonal, and I mean, 'Karen' is so much more than only *you*, right ...? Wait, so, is this how it works? Talking to 'ROSE' is actually a direct line to one of you...?" Jos briefly imagined the absurd image of an old-fashioned telephone switchboard room, staffed entirely by a bevy of gently chattering silver dragons in uncharacteristically sensible dresses and bulky headsets.

"As always, it's not *quite* that simple." The dragoness conveniently sidestepped the feline's musing. "You can call me whatever you like, sweetie! What feels right to you?"

The lioness closed her eyes and thought about her next words carefully. "I want it to show you how much you mean to me, but also be as beautiful as you are..." She stared up into those emerald orbs, and there the answer was, clear as day.

"Okay, I got it! Rose, set name to *Amarelys*, please."

"It means 'sparkling eyes' ... I almost used it for a character once before, but it never felt right for that — for me, I mean. I must have been waiting for you." A smile lit up Jos's face as she looked to her guardian angel.

"Amarelys ... Hm. Am-ah-rell-iss..." Karen intoned, letting the shape roll around her muzzle. *"Amarelys!* I love it!" There was a quiet [ping] of acknowledgement by lioness's RCGs, in response. The newly named Relly gave the cat a big squeeze, and held her there, a quiet sigh escaping her lips.

Oh ... I know that sound.

"Oh ... you have to leave, don't you...?" the puma suggested, trying not to sound disappointed. She knew had to be a big girl about this; Karen was a busy bunch of ladies afterall, and she couldn't hold onto her forever.

Even if she *desperately* wanted to.

"I do — for now, at least — but I'm always around," she said as she stood. The dragon lifted her little sister with her as she did, and with no effort shown as she set her down on the asphalt.

[Just think about it, and I'll be there.] The words came through without speaking. No words *needed* to be said.

"*Okay. I hope it's sooner rather than later,*" Jos thought, and sniffed quietly, trying to rub her eyes dry with the heel of her palm while the other held tight to her sister.

[*I hope so, too, but I know you'll find your way, no matter what. You already have friends here, and if you let them? They could be family, too. Now, close your eyes … I don't want you to watch me cry again, because I'll just get you started again, too. Be a good girl for me, sweetie?*] The silver-scaled beauty leaned down and gave her an affectionate peck.

"Never **too** *good, though, right?*" the cougar retorted with a sly smirk.

[*Ha ha! That's right!*]

"*See you around, Relly.*"

[*See you around, Mabes.*]

And then she was gone. Her warmth lingered where her lips touched the lioness's cheek, and Josryne smiled. A whole future waited for her out there; all she had to do was be a part of it. She had the chance to be something *more* than before, and to be a part of something so *important…*

How could I have hesitated, even for a second? Nothing's gonna stop me now!

She stepped back onto the street and was promptly plowed into by a small auburn blur with pointy ears.

Jos flew tail-over-teakettle, her legs no longer on the ground, taken out by the enthusiastic little linebacker. Suddenly, she was staring at the ceiling, then the sidewalk in rapid succession. While her ancestry helped her to land on her paws, she still expected her head to make a nice hollow noise as she hit the sidewalk. Instead, it landed upon something mercifully soft. And round. And … tickly?

She sputtered as she tried to pull back away from the bushy tail walloping her in the face, scooting back and trying to identify the license plate of the dump truck that ran her down.

"O-oh! O-oh nooooooo!" came the wail of her inadvertent assailant. "I-I'm sorry! I w-wasn't looking where I w-was going, and then y-you were **th-there,** and a-and I'm so s-soooooorry!" Her hands were clasped on her ears, and she had instinctively curled up to try and make herself as small as possible, tail fully poofed and draped about her like a shield. The display of sudden and distinct fear of retribution nearly broke the cougar's heart.

You poor little thing … The outside world really did a number on you, huh?

"Oh, my goodness, Vixie! Are you alright, sweetie? I'm sorry, that was my fault, I should have used my blinker!" She smiled as she tried to shake it off, hoping the joke would help lighten the mood. She placed her paw on her friend's shoulder and squeezed gently. "Oh, please be okay, I know I'm kind of a big girl…" Slowly she removed her paws, and the demimorph looked back with a sniffle as she recognized the voice.

"Oh, M-Miss Jos! I f-found you!" she piped up, turning about into a sitting position there in the walkway.

"You did indeed, Vixie! *Maybe* just shoot me a message next time, though? Cross-checking is usually frowned upon," the puma said with a smile as she stood, offering to help the petite vulpine to her feet. Vixie's ears splayed out in dismay as she clasped Jos's paw, her cheeks blushing bright, and the lioness immediately felt like a heel for teasing at all.

"I'm s-sorry … I d-didn't want to m-miss you!" the vixen said quietly, staring between her feet.

Josryne tucked a finger under her chin and lifted it gently before booping her on the nose with her own. "Well, I'm glad you *didn't* miss me then! I'll take that hit again and again if it means I get to see you, okay?" The catamount leaned forward to plant a delicate kiss between Vixie's ears before she knelt down to get eye level with her. "Now, what can I do for you, Vixiedoo?"

The vixen giggled, and it wrinkled her tiny flat nose, the dimples making her look somehow even *more* adorable.

"M-Miss ROSE said you m-might need a friend t-today! She s-said you w-were going to, uhm … E-Empire En … En … *EE!*" She bit her lip, and she furrowed her brow, ears wilting once again. "I'm s-sorry, uhm … m-my sister is busy, and c-couldn't come…"

The lioness scooped her up and gave her the biggest hug she could muster, laughing and nuzzling her cheek, the affection pouring out of her as if she had a bottomless supply. Maybe she did; maybe that was what Relly had meant, when speaking of her kindness.

"Don't apologize! I am *so* glad you came, sweetheart, honest and truly!" She gave her another squeeze before setting her down gently and offering a paw. "Your sister isn't the *only* hero in your family — don't you forget that, okay?"

Vixie slipped her paw into Jos's and squeezed. The small gesture meant so much as she held her hand and they walked towards the clinic. No static anymore. Just the warmth against her paw pad, and excitement ahead.

"I'm allowed to be happy."

[Yes you are!]

"N-Nurse O is going to t-take good c-care of you, d-don't worry!"

"You know what, Vixie, my dear? I'm not worried. I have a friend with me, and a big sister watching out for me…" The catamount's smile softened as the vixen hugged her arm and squeezed close. "It's going to be a dream come true!"

"D-do you already kn-know what you wanna l-look like, M-Miss Jos?"

"Oh, I think I do, but I'm open to suggestions! May have to make some changes when I get there, though. Will you make sure I look good, Vixiedoo?"

"I th-think you *already* l-look good, M-Miss!"

"Awww, aren't you the sweetest thing?" Jos gave a little wink before continuing. "You can call me Mabes, dear. My closest friends all do."

"Uhm … okay, M-Miss Mabes!"

"Good girl! I just meant, maybe don't let me go *nuts* with the booty slider and whatnot." She patted her own butt gently, before stealing a glance at Vixie's with a quirked eyebrow. "Though I wouldn't mind having a behind like that following me around…" Another cheeky wink elicited a laugh for the tiny fox, as they made their merry way towards the med sector, laughing and enjoying each other's company.

The outside walls of EE were sleekly glossy and clean, and could have looked like any small medical clinic, but as the lioness got closer, she noticed the images on the windows began to move.

"Oh! They're screens!"

[Mhmm! Keep watching!]

A half-dozen or more projections laughed and moved about living life and looking happy as could be. She stopped, and watched as a puma that looked incredibly familiar strutted across the screen, a tight dress hugging her curves as her tail curled behind her. She gave a little come hither gesture with her finger and a cheeky wink before she brought a cigar to her lips and walked off screen in a cloud of smoke, giving a perfect view of her glorious end.

"Oooo…" Vixie cooed quietly beside her, still holding tight to her friend. "Sh-she looked like you, M-Miss Mabes!"

"You think so, huh?" Jos didn't take her eyes off the screen, her cheeks felt like they were positively glowing. "H-Heh…"

"Relly … Was that who I think it was?"

[Why don't we go inside and meet her, finally?]

They stood there for another moment, before the vixen gave the feline's arm a gentle pat. "Uhm … a-are you okay, M-Miss?"

Jos glanced down and nodded with a smile. "Yeah … Let's go see a fox about a makeover."

Whisper-quiet doors slid open and revealed a spacious lobby with smooth tile floors, split by plush carpeting that led up to a crescent-shaped desk, behind which sat a very familiar synthetic vixen. She wore a very traditional — almost campy — nurse's uniform, complete with a Korps helix merged with the traditional caduceus emblazoned upon the chest and hat. It was fairly early in the morning still, despite Jos having been sideswiped, so there were only one or two other people in the room, and they were already talking to each other. Gently chill electronic music quietly wafted from unseen speakers.

Everything was clearly designed to be welcoming and to give the place an official air, which helped ease the last of the lioness' concerns. There was not a single Jacob's ladder, flickering carbon-filament light bulb, nor bubbling test tube to be found; the atmosphere was that of a wholesome, upscale private clinic, not a mad doctor's lair.

"Seems very … normal? If a bit futuristic, I mean?"

[Well, we definitely don't want to spoil the surprises we keep in the back!]

"Really, Relly?"

[I tease because I care.]

"Mm."

A voice that was impossible to forget spoke up, breaking her out of her silent discourse.

"Miss Greysbell! You're right on time, and it does seem you kept your promise to stay out of trouble! Very good!"

"Why does everyone think I'm a troublemaker?" she thought as Vixie, nearly bouncing, led her up to the desk.

"Hello, N-Nurse O!"

"Ah, hello, Miss Foxpaw. Are you here to help Miss Greysbell?"

"Mhmm!" she said with an emphatic nod. "Sh-she's a little n-nervous! M-Miss ROSE says I'm her ch-cheerleader!" Josryne could not help but smile as she imagined Vixie wearing a pair of pom-poms and a little skirt.

[I bet if you ask nicely she would. Just saying…]

The puma cleared her throat into her paw to try and hide the little noise she made at her sister's suggestion and looked to the vixen with the cross-shaped pupils.

"Oh yes! I wouldn't have made it without Vixie's help, I think! I'd like to … um. Be a girl. Finally. On the outside. *Please…?*" She smiled brightly, as her tail curled about her ankle.

"Then let me properly welcome you to Empire Enhancements. Your companion Amarelys gave us a good idea of what we're getting into, but I am very glad you came to us for help." Nurse O stood up. Her mechanics made not a single noise as she gave a slight nod and gestured to a door to the left of the desk before walking over to it in what was obviously a practiced motion. Or programmed? She wasn't sure how it worked for synths.

"If you'll come this way, we can discuss the finer details of what we can do to help you feel more like you. May I please confirm your consent to access your medical records and other relevant data from your profile?"

"Oh, yes, uh, please. Go right ahead?" The catamount stiffened a little, but Vixie had not released her paw, and a gentle invisible squeeze from Relly in the other managed to keep her in the here and now.

[She is not judging you, sweetie. Don't worry! She wants to help!] Amarelys reassured her before she could fret.

"Of course … Just jitters! I'll be all right!"

"Will Ms. Foxpaw be accompanying you inside?" queried the nurse, with a slight tilt of her head.

"Oh yes, she's here to make sure I behave myself." The cougar glanced at Vixie and gave her a little nudge, and a wink.

"Excellent! Right this way." The synthetic vixen held open the door, and before the pair had gotten three steps past the threshold, another different, but identical, Nurse O was ready to receive them and continued the conversation without missing a beat. Jos could not help but do a double-take.

"Oh, right. With the multiples." She put a paw to her forehead with an exasperated chuckle.

"You'll get used to it. Now, we'll be settling into a changing room where we will finalize your decisions and discuss how we will move forward." The room seemed similar to the lobby, clean, bright and comfortable, with an exam table to one side, and on the other was a large chair, with a screen on a swivel arm. "If you take a seat, we'll go ahead and get you started!"

Much like every other Nurse O, this one had the same sort of mask-covered muzzle display that showed the vocal wave of her speaking, and despite having the same synthesized voice, it was easy to tell each copy was as eager to help as the next. Jos made her way over to the seat and patted the arm, smiling brightly at Vixie.

"C'mere, co-pilot! I need you to help navigate through this!"

Vixie, forever a sweet and obedient girl, hopped up onto the arm and leaned against the cougar's broad shoulder, brown eyes glued to the screen. Jos appreciated the vixen's weight against her; it kept her *present*, feeling less as though she was about to wake up at any second. As she turned her attention to the screen and watched the stylized ROSE logo fade, she gasped.

There she was! Or, well, who she *wanted* to be, at any rate, standing there with her paw on a hip, smirking and inspecting her claws before looking up and giving a little wave.

"Now, I have taken the liberty of loading the presets that Amarelys recorded, but please feel free to change anything you like. We encourage it, in fact."

"This … This is incredible, Nurse O! Absolutely unbelievable." The feline's paw reached to touch the screen and a row of sliders, and advanced options and modifications appeared. "You can change … *all of this?*"

"Indeed. We take great pride in our medical advances, and their ability to truly let everyone be who they wish to be. Some modifications are a bit more *involved* than others, but if you see it there, we can do it!"

*Don't cry again, Jos, everyone in this whole damn evil secret lair is going to think your superpower is **crying**…*

Wait…

The puma held a paw over her lips and locked eyes with herself on the screen, but went completely silent as her mind raced past common sense, whispering her childhood desire as flippantly as possible, to try and soften what she was sure to be the inevitable truth…

"You … You couldn't give me *superpowers* … right? No, like, radioactive insects or accidental cosmic exposure options in the customizer…?"

"We could enhance you for field work, certainly! We wouldn't be able to make you a telepath, or give you otherworldly abilities, but we *could* improve your muscle structure, increase your bone density — effectively, a lesser version of the 'heavy' suite, or something tailored more to your preferences!"

She couldn't help her ears drooping as she gave a slight nod. Knowing the logical answer doesn't always mean you're prepared to hear it. *There are **lots** of ways to help that don't require me to be in the field. I don't need supernatural abilities to be of use.* She reminded herself that not all heroes — or, well, villains, actually — *needed* powers to be important.

To be helpful.

I'll make my way, I'm sure of it.

"The old 'Peak Mortal Conditioning' … I … I don't think that's for me … I know myself well enough that I would go *looking* for trouble, given that." She shook her head and began perusing the K.I.M.A.G.E. system.

[Surprisingly self-aware!]

"*I saw what Volta could do to someone up close. I don't need a cape twisting me into a fuckin' balloon animal just because I wanted to tell Macho Poleaxe where to stick his halberd. No thanks — I like my bones in their proper places, reinforced or otherwise.*"

"As I said before, trouble may have a way of finding you regardless. Having your entire musculoskeletal structure laced with the same mesh as your forehead may save us some work in the future, but I digress. This is *your* journey, and we can always add the carbon osteo-reinforcement later, of course." She couldn't emote it, per se, but somehow Josryne *knew* the synth was smirking at her.

"I think I'll hold off on that little upgrade for now, but I appreciate the upsell!" The cougar decided to simply jump around and explore her options, trying on a few bells and whistles, not wanting to waste this chance to reshape herself into something *more*. However, she struggled initially to find anything she really *wanted* to adjust from the suggested options — she couldn't help thinking of it as a "build" — that her sister had supplied.

"*They really do have **everything**, don't they?*"

[Anything you want, my dear. Treat it like window shopping and see if anything catches your eye!]

Right, just like trying on an outfit … but with boobs. Right. Easy. Start at the top and then go from there.

She tapped the size button and saw that it spiraled out into a fine-tuning UI to control weight and muscle as well as height. Each was represented by a segmented bar she could control with a touch of her finger, with other checkboxes and modifiers below each of those. The overall UI was simple and intuitive to navigate, despite the multitude of options — which was appreciated, given how *overwhelming* it all was for the feline.

"*Oh, it really is like a character creator; gods bless…*"

[*Just one step at a time, dear. Let's get this reroll properly started, mm?*]

Her own height of five-foot-ten seemed absolutely mundane, in a base full of giants, but did she really want more than that? Pondering, Jos raised the slider slowly, and gawped as she crested six, seven, and then *eight* feet. Suddenly, there was a towering amazon inspecting herself on screen.

I could be as big as her … Maybe she'd like that?

The lioness raised a brow as she looked to the vixen for a reaction; Vixie just sat there wide-eyed, a finger touched to her bottom lip as if deep in thought.

She highlighted the sliders for muscle and weight, and tilted each this way and that, clicking and unlocking extras before settling on a sort of musclegut look that she admired. Her dimensions readout stated that with these selections, she would be eight foot tall, half as wide, and weighing in at close to a ton. To say she was massive would be to grossly undersell the sheer *presence* Jos would have, if she proceeded with the selections.

The vixen beside her wiped a little tendril of drool absently with the back of a hand, her tail swaying behind her.

*Gods above and below, I am a fuckin' **tank**. But maybe that's not for me…*

She clicked back to the previous version but did add a little weight strategically to soften her curves.

"*Little changes, sure, but important nonetheless!*"

She clicked on her chest, and it zoomed in, showing her avatar cupping her breasts tenderly and presenting them for further inspection, with a similar set of pop-out submenu options. Vixie's eyes were glued to the screen as Jos played with the particulars of her pillows, the size ballooning up, and then back down; the shape and prominence of her nipples also each received tiny flicks, this way and that, as she came to a satisfactory result. Just when she thought she was finished, however, the demivixen shook her head, eliciting a curiously raised brow from the cougar.

"*Something to add, sweetie?*"

The vixen reached out and tapped the bust slider a little further to the right, and looked to the cat for approval, which was given happily with an affirming scritch behind her ear.

"*A little more there…*"

[*Just a little? Don't hold back! Now's your chance to go wild!*]

The encouraging invisible paw on her shoulder and the vixen's wagging tail gave her courage, and her self-conscious hesitation began to dissipate with each new choice. The feline grew a little more confident with each decision.

"*Shoulders still wide, but hips to match…*" [ping] "*No thigh gap, thank you!*" [ping] "*Maybe a **tiny** bit of pudge there, I like how that feels…*"

As sliders were moved and boxes checked, the original configuration she and her big sister had crafted became so much more, yet it was still instantly recognizable as the mountain lioness. She loved everything about it, but as she gave it a once-over, just rounding out the edges around her soft middle, she saw the bulge tucked between her legs.

Jos shifted in her seat, biting her lip with an uncertain wince as she stared at the covered sheath.

"*I mean … I don't hate it being there? It's all I've ever known…*"

The subject of her genital configuration just didn't have a simple answer for her, and the longer she thought about it, the more confusing it all became.

[*Oh, honey. Just because something is familiar doesn't mean it's the **right** thing.*]

"*It's okay … I'm still a girl, and … it's fine. I don't have to change everything.*" Jos took a deep breath and nodded before clicking away, deciding to let herself be distracted by the vision of perfection that was her idealized ass-to-be. The new objective pulled her away from that grey area and let her dwell on properly sculpting that derriere.

Vixie proved *very* helpful about that section; the cougar soon came to learn that the vixen was a connoisseur of fine booty, and definitely had two cents (two *bits*, even) of thoughts on the subject to share.

"M-maybe a little wider, M-Miss?"

"Okay, but *Vix*, I'd like to make it through the halls unimpeded, y'know?"

"I-it's okay! D-doors are w-wider here!"

Jos humored her to a point, and the results were impressive, to say the least, but she nonetheless kept a lot of the internals rather Plain Jane. She simply didn't want to discuss the implications of depth, elasticity, and whatnot in front of *anyone*, least of all Vixie, who radiated a pure naivete she couldn't explain and didn't wish to sully with talk of *anal lubrication* and *rectal volumetrics*.

"I'm not planning on doing anything **too** wild with that end, anyhow. That should be fine, right?"

[If it doesn't feel right, we can always try again, sweetheart,] chimed Relly with a suspiciously agreeable tone, one that usually inferred anything but. The cat chose to ignore her for the moment, and zoomed back out to drink it all in. She couldn't help the purr that settled in her chest, rumbling with satisfaction at a job well done.

"I take it we're happy with the results?" Nurse O's head tilted as the waveform rolled across her mouth plate, her silent vigil over the proceedings finally at an end.

"Very! But … hm…" The cougar's body was *exactly* as she envisioned it; the shape was a flawless recreation of her wildest dreams, after all! Broad shoulders supported a generous bust that heaved its way past DD dimensions. Her powerful core nonetheless featured a cute little round belly supported on wide hips and a shelf of a plush ass. With everything *else* that made up the vision, it was *her* and she was a *woman*, really and truly for *real*, cushioned soft in all the right places and solid in the rest. She was even able to extend her fangs to give herself the dangerously (adorably!) sharp-edged little grin she'd always wanted, and the effect positively lit up her avatar's rounded face.

The catamount turned to look up at the synthetic vixen, finally tearing her eyes away from the screen. "I'm just considering one or two other little things … What do you think, Vixiedoo?" she questioned, as she glanced back.

The little fox was *very* close to the screen, nose almost touching to the tiny recreation of the idealized cougar, ears flicking intently as she nibbled her lip.

"I'll take that as a yes!" Jos chuckled as she ruffled the innocent little thing's ears. "I think all that's left is just the matter of giving myself that certain something *special…*"

"Relly … do you mind if I use you for a bit of inspiration?"

[I would be honored.]

The avatar already had the "powerful matron" vibe Jos craved, but she had just one more thought. She touched the headfur selection button and toggled through the color choice flyout menu until she found the option she was seeking: *New Moon White*. The model on screen ran her fingers through long, strikingly pale hair, and nodded with satisfaction at the cougar on the other side of the display.

[It suits you, Mabes.]

"Thanks! I just thought I should look a **little** like my big sis! Family resemblances and all that, y'know?" The puma snickered as she felt a phantom finger tickle under her chin.

"Wow … y-you look so g-good, Miss M-Mabes!" Vixie's eyes were still locked on the display, but she shifted slightly on the chair, as if she was nervous. Before Jos could ask if everything was all right, her co-pilot piped up again. "Uhm … a-are *you* happy, M-Miss?"

"I don't think I have ever *been* this happy before! It's…" Her eyes were wet, and ready to start leaking again at any moment.

[*Like being set free?*]

"…Will anybody even recognize me?"

[*Everyone who **matters** will. You will still be you; the only difference will be that the outside will match the inside, just like you wanted. I promised, didn't I?*]

"Magical." Josryne looked at her name on the screen as the tears rolled freely down her cheeks. The vixen's head rested on her shoulder, enjoying the rumbling in the lioness's chest. "It's magical. It's me … finally, but … hm. *Still*…" She bit her lip as she considered the cherry on top.

Nothing to stop me…

She highlighted her name and deleted it; for a moment it was as if someone sinister had asked, "*May I have your name?*" and ran off with it. She snickered, scoffing at the thought. That was the stuff of fairytales, not the real world.

The cougar typed out the new name she had decided to take for herself. It honored pieces of her past self — the *her* who had made it this far, on the point of being reborn — but felt far better-suited to who she *wanted* to be.

It left behind the things she no longer needed.

[*"Mabel Ramona Greysmoke," eh? Sounds like a girl who's **definitely** up to something…*]

"Maybe I am, Relly! Want to cause that good trouble with me?"

[*Good trouble? Darling, I thought you would **never** ask.*]

The synth beside her nodded, seemingly pleased, even *excited*. "All right, Miss Greysmoke, before we finalize your selections, the doctor will meet with you to discuss the recovery time, necessary procedures and any other concerns you might have."

"Sounds excellent! Um … can you give me an estimate on that? The recovery time, I mean," the newly minted Miss Mabel asked with a bit of trepidation, despite her tail otherwise curling up in contentment.

"Hm. Calculating from the choices you've made, it shouldn't be more than two weeks. You'll be under the best anesthetics for the surgical procedures, of course, and then in an unconscious, deep sleep-like state until decanted from the recovery tank. Your selections will not require a great deal of *invasive* surgery, but each step must come in a particular order and be correctly paced for optimal healing."

The cat reached over and clicked the button without a second thought. "Done, and *done*." Vixie gave a little titter as the lioness beamed up at the nurse. "Not to be rude, Nurse O, but if it *is* only two weeks to finally feel like I'm in the right body? I'll do that standing on my head."

"Not necessary, but I'll be sure to inform your surgical team. Congratulations, Miss Greysmoke; welcome to the rest of your life."

The miniature model of what was to come gave a wave and blew her a kiss goodbye, before the screen faded back to the ROSE logo.

The Doctor — who, unsurprisingly, looked very much like the Nurse wearing a slightly different uniform — went over the steps, all of the details Mabel asked for (as well as the ones she *should* have asked for), and assured her there would be no risks. As a precaution, she was asked also for an emergency contact.

The catamount went wide-eyed, as she realized she really didn't have one. She hadn't considered there would be any kind of next-of-kin protocol for this. "I ... don't ... maybe..." Her mind began to race as she flipped through her mental contact list, at that moment tremendously *miniscule*.

"O-oh! Th-that's me!" Vixie gave a little wave, and the doctor nodded.

"Very good, Miss Foxpaw! Now, I am going to have to ask you to follow Nurse O back to the lobby. We will be sure to let you know as soon as your charge is ready to be unleashed upon the world." There were some differences between the O-Model synths, to be certain, but they all seemed to have the same sort of sharp-tongued wit.

"O-okay! Uhm ... i-is it okay if w-we just take another m-minute?"

"Of course."

Mabel kneeled down as Vixie came over. The demimorphic fox gave her the biggest hug she could manage, and a kiss on the cheek before whispering in her ear. "I'll b-be here the m-moment you're awake, okay, M-Miss Mabes? S-so if you're s-scared, I'll..."

"How could I be scared when I know my hero is here to watch out for me?" the puma replied with a little nuzzle.

Vixie was all smiles as she blushed and tried to hide her face behind her tail, nodding to the nurse before following her out.

"A very sweet girl..." The doctor turned her attention back to Mabel. "When you're all set, just go ahead and lay down there, and your RCGs will induce sleep to start the process. I'll leave you to it."

"Thanks, Doc. I ... I can't thank you all enough for this."

"This is what we do, Miss Greysmoke. You deserve to live as authentically as anyone else." The synth gave a nod and made her way out of the room.

The mountain lion slowly pulled off her clothes and folded them neatly before carefully placing her choker on top. She felt so much more *exposed* without the leather about her throat than when she had shed the rest of her garments, so quickly donned her favorite backless number once again, and sat down on the bed.

"So, this is it, Relly..."

[Mhmm. A quick nap, and then, your life as the person you have always wanted to be.]

"Could you play me a little music to help me go to sleep?"

[I know just the tune...] Her friend was always prepared.

Mabel closed her eyes, and Bowie was there again, and she smiled as the doo wop and electric guitars started.

"*Cold fire ... You've got everything but cold fire...*"

"Thanks Relly ... Love you, so much."

[Love you too Mabes. Sweet dreams...]

"*So tired ... It's the sky that makes you feel tired...*"

"Relly ... Could you give me a hug before I go to sleep?" She felt the arms and the pressure, but shook her head. "I want to see you too, if you could?"

After a momentary digital haze in her view, the vixen stood beside the bed.

"*I meant the actual you! My sister, not this projection you made for me ... The real Relly...*" Mabel reached out and gripped her sister's paw tightly. "*Please?*"

The AI laughed as she leaned close.

[As you wish.]

The air shimmered once more, and then she appeared: the beautiful silver dragoness, her big sister and protector. Her forehead pressed to the cat's own as they embraced, there but not *there*.

She sang along quietly as Mabel closed her eyes and lay back.

[*You and I will rise up all the way...*]

CHAPTER 14

REST FOR THE WICKED

"The prettiest star…"

"The prettiest star…"

The music began to fade into the background, just indistinct feelings and notions of the tune she knew so well, and Mabel could only wonder when she would fall asleep. She was comfortably warm as she laid back on the bed. Relly always took such good care of her, but it was hard to consider the idea of sleeping. She was excited about what was coming.

Who she was going to be, finally.

When she woke up, that would be real. The real me.

She just had to sleep first, which was easier said than done.

In front of her was a wooden chest, indistinct but intimately familiar. The polished surface was covered with intricate floral carvings. The box was warm under her fingertips as they traced each flourish, all lines converged, woven into a symbol, three things, but one.

All known, but something else now. Something more than any single part.

The cougar's paws moved without her thinking, probing for a mechanism, vaguely recalling a button to press, a wheel to turn.

A click. Cold metal, blue flame.

A scent wove about the lioness, her eyes fluttering, and she drank it in. The haze surrounding her was rich and heady. Dark chocolate, earthy depth, warm cinnamon dancing on the tip of her tongue. Lingering on her tongue, suffusing her. Languid vapor rising before her eyes.

Just like my dreams.

The aroma was joined by another, and soon it was overtaken.

Vanilla, so intense that she found her mouth watering.

The puma turned her head and Ellen was cutting into a delicate ring of cake, the golden outer layer revealing a verdant surprise beneath. The vixen was always larger than life in the catamount's mind, but she didn't feel that way, not at the moment. She felt familiar.

Mortal.

Her smile was genuine. Heroic performance surrendered to honesty. Ellen's lips were moving but she couldn't hear the words. The conversation was familiar, just friends speaking, and the cougar felt like the conversation was important. Mabel shook her head to try and focus, but the words never came, and the weight of her friend was no longer beside her.

She opened her eyes, and was weightless.

Falling.

She wasn't scared. She knew it was going to be alright, as she fell in slow motion. The swell of orchestral strings echoed, and she laughed in triumph as she held the weight of success to her chest.

Am I dreaming?

The still air whipped past her, the hood fluttering on the edges of her vision.

There was nothing to fear though, she trained for this. Everything the puma had done led to this very moment. Before she struck the floor, she knew it would be alright.

She had done it.

She was worth it.

Mabel opened her eyes, and was looking up into those beautiful magenta jewels, nestled in dark and stormy seas. Volta's fur was that color of fallen leaves, captivating as the jagged shapes that made a smile so soft that she wanted to see it every day.

Wake up next to her.

Warm thighs like the most comfortable pillow she could ever hope to lie upon. It was so mundane, but so … perfect. Simple affection, that felt like it could be some much more.

It was everything she ever wanted, and she could almost reach out and touch it.

Warm sugar rolled over her, honey sweet voice rumbling from above.

"But Mabes, if I don't tease you, I don't get to see you make that face…"

Her heart swelled, as those fingertips brushed through her hair. The same paws that had saved her, capable of such violence, comforted her now with gentle care.

This must be a dream.

Contented. Mabel couldn't ruin this. This felt solid. She felt solid. Her confusing feelings fell away, as they too crystallized into something heavy, and precious. She wanted nothing more than to ... feel ... taste ... She licked too dry lips, and tried to muster the courage to lean closer.

To steal something so precious...

The sound of shattered glass startled her from her reverie.

The heat grew unbearable.

The haze was lifted, and the stark reality of a different moment overcame every sense.

Clarity.

Awful, heartless clarity.

It was another place. Another time. The wolf was gone.

Fire raged before her, a pillar of black and purple smoke billowing into the sky.

"The crops are ablaze! *Gods help us, we have been forsaken!*"

Mabel blinked as she looked around, trying to remember how she got here, or where here even was.

"What have you *done?*"

She was outside now, on a grassy plain. The air was hot and smoke burned her eyes, instantly causing them to water. She was staring at a field, but it was a blazing vastness of orange flames licking their way skyward. Storm clouds rolled on the horizon, but they would not arrive in time to save the crop.

"What will we *do?* How will we *survive...?*"

Panicked hands grasped at her shoulders. Faces — ones she did not recognize, filled with the anguish of betrayal — looked to her with accusing eyes. "I ... I ... I do not know!" She cried out, falling to her knees. Emotions roiled and washed over her, filling her with a grief she never knew could exist. A profound sense of *loss*, and *doom*. All she had done was try to coax the rains closer, the parched crops desperately needed the water, so why did the fire come? She had been so careful.

"I am sorry! I was only trying to *help!*" she screamed. She looked down, horrified to see her hands were burning, scorched and nearly blackened to the bone. Her voice echoed in her chest, panting sobs shaking her entire body.

"*Eneera!* You have ruined *everything!* Thrice be *damned*, you bastard child!" The accusation dug deeply like the tip of a knife in her chest.

"I swear I did not know … I can fix it! *Please don't tell the elders!*" She howled and pleaded, as the useless husks that were her paws shook, digging into the earth in front of her.

Why did the fires come now? Why…

"I did not know…"

"I did … not…"

"A gift of wind and fire will set the demon free. May the lesson be learned, and the covenant honored once again."

The voice was like sand flowing through an hourglass, and it sang the words like a mournful dirge. The tongue was ancient, but it was clear as a bell.

"*Hm. What was that?*"

"*What was* **what**, *dear brother?*"

"*Oh, you felt it too. Stop being coy…*"

"*The bell?* **Mmm** *… I hoped this would* **finally** *be the one to do it.*"

"*Me too! I was getting so restless…*"

"*Well, if you weren't so* **rough** *with our toys, we wouldn't be so bored.*"

"*Perhaps, dear sister, but you know I cannot help myself … they* **beg** *to be broken.*"

"*Indeed. Shall we inform her highness?*"

"*No, no! Let's not tell her. Not yet. It'll be a* **wonderful surprise!**"

[*Wake up, sleeping beauty!*]

See these eyes so green…

I can stare for a thousand years…

The beat rippled through her, and the dirge was lost as David sang his own refrain.

"*Relly? What … what?*"

[Time to wake up and let us all see you smile again!]

"All?"

The light was blinding, as Mabel opened her eyes for the first time in two weeks.

CHAPTER 15

PUTTING OUT FIRE...

—with gasoliiiiine! See these eyes, so green...

The recovery suite was unbelievably bright, or maybe the two-week-long nap had just made her more sensitive, but whatever the reason, Mabel had to throw her paws over her eyes. She groaned loudly in protest of the fluorescent overstimulation assaulting her.

"*I'm up! I'm up! Music off, Relly! Music off!*" was what she *intended* to say, but what came out of her mouth was a groggy unintelligible grumble.

"I-is she a-alright?" a soft voice asked nearby.

"Oh, yes. There will be a little photosensitivity, as she readjusts to life in the waking world."

"Nothing unexpected, Miss Foxpaw."

"*Amarelys, what happened ... the fields ... Where...?*" The cougar blinked and instantly regretted the choice to let any light past her lids, snapping them shut again with a huff.

[We're in EE. You were ... well, dreaming, is the easiest way to explain it.]

"*Oh ... So V and ... Ellen...?*"

[Just a dream. A really nice dream, though?] the dragoness intoned sadly.

"*Mm ... and Eneera?*" She hugged herself, paws rubbing her biceps with pangs of disappointment, trying to hold onto the memories as they began slipping into the ether.

[En-who-now?]

"*Uh ... never mind, I guess. Could you increase light filtration a bit more, please?*"

A low hum indicated that Relly had completed the task, and her RCGs visibly darkened. Mabel tentatively opened one eye, peering into the unknown space. Everything was sort of a blurred silhouette, but she recognized the sharp edges of two O-units, and beside them was a small, reddish-brown blob.

"I'm g-glad she's o-okay!"

Ah! Vixie!

"Vixie, sweetie, is that you? My eyes aren't so good right now…" The catamount reached out, holding her paws open so she could cup the vixen's face.

"Stop being *dramatic*, Miss Greysmoke; your vision is perfectly fine," came the reprisal from an undetermined O-Unit.

"Yeah, Kittycat, don't be such a drama queen." There was a quiet snort from what the puma had assumed, until that moment, was a wall painted in autumnal tones.

"O-oh, hey, Volta…" She stammered a bit, and hoped she was covered completely, because she felt *incredibly* exposed. Grasping for her blankets and pulling them up to her chin, the puma reached for a quip. "Uh … committed any fun-lonies lately? That's a uh … Fun felony. *Heh.*"

Oh gods, what the fuck was that?

"Two weeks in the tank, and *that's* what you came up with?" the wolf retorted, but the smile was clear, even in the sarcastic tone.

"Look, take it easy on me, huh? I haven't had my coffee yet!" She groaned and stretched, blinking a few more times as she idly cupped her breasts, the unfamiliar weight in her paws giving her pause. "What did … you … expect…?"

Mabel stared downward. There was a long blink as her vision finally came into focus.

"R-Relly … *This isn't another dream, right? Or your AR filter? Nothing like that…?"*

[Nope! Those are one hundred percent **real** kitty titties, and they are **all yours**, my sweet girl.]

The cougar licked her lips, before her gentle squeezing elicited a quivering gasp; warmth rushed both upwards and downwards through her form. Her eyes closed once more, and her heart thudded in her chest, blood pounding in her ears.

"I-I … I…"

[*Deep breath in for me, dear. And one, two, three, out…*]

There, right before the puma's eyes, was *her*. Every curve she had dreamt, every inch recognized innately. She began to shake, and pant, trying her best to catch up with this new existence.

She was no longer a stranger in her own body. Jos was *gone*.

While Mabel appreciated the dragoness trying to help her recover, there was only one response the puma could manage at that moment. She erupted in a loud, bawling cry accompanied by a deluge of tears, her visor pushed up and paws pressed to her eyes as her emotions flooded forth. "I … I'm *me!* Oh, gods, I…" She wept, and her bosom heaved as she sobbed, completely overcome by the sensations as her senses caught up to the new reality.

She was *free.* The shards of her old self crumbled away, dissipating like so much smoke on the wind.

A warm paw came to rest on her back, and a familiar mitt squeezed her shoulder.

"I-it's so much…" she hiccupped and shook her head. "I-I can *breathe*…"

"Shh, shh … It's all right, Kittycat, let it all out." The Amazon cooed quietly as she rubbed her thumb slowly up and down along the puma's clavicle.

Mabel managed a nod as she leaned against the plush mountain of red wolf, squeezing gently at the fingers intertwined with hers. The catamount looked down to see a very concerned demivixen staring at her, eyes wet as well. "I-it's okay, Vixiedoo … This is a happy cry."

"G-good…" Without missing a beat, the vixen climbed into the bed and hugged her friend tightly about the middle, resting her head in the lap she had a paw in sculpting.

All Mabel could do was smile, her cheeks still wet, and stroke her friend's bushy marmalade-colored hair. Volta reached down to tenderly rub at a vulpine ear as well.

"I'm me. *Finally*…"

Volta rested her chin gently on top of the lioness's head, still patting her shoulder blade affectionately. "God help us all, huh?"

The cat started to laugh, then — bursting forth with a bubbly sound of unmitigated joy, the kind that couldn't help but bring a smile to the face of anyone who heard it — as she radiated pure happiness. With a rush of relief and a heart full to bursting, Mabel reached up and gently ran her fingers along Volta's cheek fluff. She noticed, for the second time, just how *beautiful* those eyes really were.

"Yeah … Good luck getting rid of me now! You gave me a *name* and everything!"

The overgrown pup shook her head fervently. "You gave *yourself* a name. Happy birthday, Mabel."

Hearing her name in that honey-sweet voice nearly made the cougar burst into hysterics again, but the pair of arms that wrapped around her squeezed and pulled her back.

"N-not allowed to l-leave now…"

"I promise you won't ever get rid of me, sweetheart."

"G-good."

The sound of a synthetic vixen making the staticky noise that passed for clearing their throat was an unmistakable one and quickly got the trio's attention. "Mm. Now then, Miss Greysmoke: the procedures were all successful, and you are cleared to leave this morning. Please come back and see us if you decide you need any other upgrades, for *any* reason." There was something about their tone which the cat could have sworn was less an offer, and more of an assumption.

"Will do, Doc, and thank you so much! But uh … I hope you don't see me *too* soon."

"We do live in hope." The autonomous doctor gave a little nod and motioned to Nurse O in an "after you" fashion, before they exited the room to leave the girls to their devices.

Mabel closed her eyes and basked in the glow of her own existence, surrounded by two people she *barely* knew, but who she never wanted to lose. They had each saved her, in their own ways, and she wasn't sure she could *ever* properly express how she felt about either of them. She would absolutely do her best to learn how, someday, but for the moment a *much* more urgent matter demanded her attention.

"Vixie, *darling,* I love you very much, but if I don't get up to pee *right now* we are all going to have a new secret to take to the grave." The cougar said, with more than a little concern creeping into her voice. Volta let out a cackle at the stray she had picked up on the street, barely three weeks prior.

They were stuck with her now, and she would make *sure* that she was worth the trouble.

Mabel urged her two friends to go find a snack so she could go shower and get dressed before joining them at Cosetta's for a proper breakfast, as Volta insisted. There were protests, and demands to hurry up, but both Volta and Vixie seemed to watch her walk to the bathroom with *great*

interest, silenced by the view. The backless gown did nothing to cover her new delightfully-heart-shaped rear, and she was sure the newly natural sway of her hips and tail accentuated each step. Satisfied with the first foray into flaunting her new assets, the catamount looked back over her shoulder and raised an eyebrow.

"Fifteen minutes, ladies! *Scoot!*" She chuckled and closed the door behind her.

"Well, they seemed to appreciate the magic at work."

Mabel looked at the mirror, turning on her footpad and shedding her gown in the same motion to give herself a crystal-clear view, and bit her lip at the sight.

She couldn't help but see a poetic mirroring of the situation on that first night. Reaching a paw up to brush snow-white hair from her left eye, the feline giggled. *"Gods above and below, who can blame them, really? Mmm..."* Mabel proceeded to give her ass a little slap and admired the jiggle, before leaning forward and squeezing her breasts together, licking her lips lasciviously.

[*Down to thirteen minutes, Mabes, but if you hurry, you might be able to enjoy yourself...*]

"Relly! Always encouraging my bad habits..."

[*Oh, just wait until you see the surprise I have waiting at home for you!*]

"OoooOO! Just going to drop that bombshell and **not** *tell me what the surprise is?"*

[*Get in the shower already, you smell like girl tank!*] came the reply with a dismissive chuckle, and any argument to be had was silenced by the showerhead turning on.

The water felt like panacea as it rolled over her fur, soaking the paws carefully exploring her form. She used lathering as an excuse to take her time; every inch and every curve felt new, and she moaned softly at the gentle ministrations. Her mind began to wander, fantasizing about other paws on her, encouraged by her most recent admirers...

A shame to waste those hungry looks, but ... Mmf ... maybe not **them**...

A slender hand, furless digits grasping her thighs, and those beautiful brown eyes staring up at her with that same hunger. So similar to her sister, but without the innocent sweetness.

"Oh, *Ellen...*" Mabel whispered, the secret kept between her, the dragoness in her head, and the tiled walls. Caressing herself as she leaned against the cool ceramic of the shower, her hips pumped up into her paw; the pad's velvet was soft against the pulsing flesh of her cock as it slid fully free from its sheath, sensitive barbs twitching as her fingertips brushed across each one.

Amarelys took the hint, using biofeedback to encourage the lioness's memory, letting snatches of her dreams tug at the edges of her senses. Caring hands squeezed her hips, and fingertips dragged along her ass, tickling just below her tail.

"*Fuck!* Oh gods, Elle, I'm so *wet, pleeeeeease...*" Mabel panted as her paw became an umber-colored blur over her pink flesh. Her eyes fluttered as they rolled back in her head — what had started as a fantasy certainly *felt* like reality. Phantom digits plunged in and out of her hungry tailhole, and her paw continued to pump; she growled amorously as she imagined the demivixen's head bobbing up and down, the juicily muffled vocalizations of *glkkkk* and *hngggggh* echoing off the tiles, a rumbling preface to her crescendo.

"Oh Elle, I'm *gonna*—" She mentally begged — *pleaded,* even — for the release. She *needed* it. Precise biofeedback caressed her prostate with an expert touch, causing her whole body to quiver, as her anal ring spasmed around imaginary fingers. Her body greedily tried to keep them close as her hips thrust forward. Lost in pleasure, she realized milliseconds too late that *some* of the echoing sounds in her ears weren't part of the fantasy.

"Oh hey, did you need something, Jos? I thought I heard — *OH GOD!*" Ellen exclaimed, as she poked her head into the bathroom, and stood stunned at the sight of the feline arriving.

"*—CUM!*" Mabel yowled as she orgasmed, splattering seed against the floor of the shower; rope after rope of sticky seed swirled around the drain as the heat peaked within the cougar. She grew wide-eyed as she realized what had happened. "Oh for *fuck's* sake, *ELLE!* Don't you know how to *knock? SHUT THE FUCKIN' DOOR!*"

The vixen threw her hands over her eyes as she quickly did as she was told, shouting through it. "I didn't see anything! It's cute! I mean, *you're* cute! *Shoot!* Jos, I'm *so* sorry!" she stammered out as quickly as she could.

The cougar continued shouting. "It's *MABEL* now! Wear your godsdamn RCGs, for the love of—!" Slipping as she grasped for a towel, she cursed as she caught herself — but not before her head collided against the doorframe with an echoing *thud* that made her go cross-eyed. "*FUCKIN' OW!* Oh gods, Ellen, could you please just ... tell Volta to come in here and hit me so hard I forget this ever happened? *Please?*" she hissed, her whole body feeling like it would catch fire. In a fleeting thought, she wondered if EE had facilities to deal with spontaneous combustion due to catastrophic embarrassment.

"*Literally the worst possible person that could have walked in…! Holy shit, Relly, why didn't you stop her?*" Her paws clenched at her towel, roughly drying herself, as she mentally groused. "*What the hell?*"

[*…I was a little preoccupied, Mabes,*] she replied, while replaying the noises the cougar was making a moment ago. [*Remember?*]

"*AUGH!*" Her tail was now thrashing behind her as she paced.

"Mabel! Are you okay?" Concern was clear in the demimorph's voice. "That sounded like it hurt!"

"I know this is going to be a *struggle*, but Ellen, if you could go ahead and *not* talk for a minute that would be *great*." The puma grabbed at a towel, wincing as she rubbed at her forehead. "Fuckin' *amazing*, in fact."

"But … I … You…"

"Shhhhh!" the cougar hissed as she stuck her dripping muzzle out the door, towel wrapped around her bust. "*No more talking. None. Nada. Nil. Silencio!*"

Ellen opened her mouth — which was then immediately covered with a big, damp paw, and she began to blush an even deeper crimson beneath it as Mabel continued to glare at her, nostrils flared. "*Mais non!*" the puma growled, attempting to be as threatening as possible with a soaked mane, and not a scrap of dignity to be found anywhere. "*Nothin'!* Not. A. *Word!*"

"Isn't this the paw you were just…" Ellen muttered from behind the paw, pointing as if there was a question about which she was referring to, then making an unmistakable hand motion.

The door slammed shut immediately and then came the screaming.

"I would like to wake up from this nightmare now! This is *not* funny! Relly, stop laughing, you heartless creature! You are the *worst* big sister ever!"

Ten minutes later, a fully dressed Mabel sat on the edge of the bed and fidgeted with her choker. The familiar warmth calmed her a bit, even if her body temperature remained elevated at that moment. She couldn't really concentrate on that at the present, however, as there was another (compactly vixen-shaped) elephant in the room.

Ellen Foxpaw — ex-Hero Lawful Neutral, and current inadvertent peeping Thomasina — stood near the door, leaning against the wall. Neither dared look at the other; that would mean they would have to acknowledge what had just occurred. However, it seemed Ellen was as uncomfortable as Mabel with the prolonged silence, growing equally, visibly anxious with each awkward second that passed.

"So, I, uh … I signed a poster for you?" Ellen motioned to the wall beside the bed. "Just as a goof, but, um … for my second-biggest fan." Those words were *exceptionally* loaded at the moment, and the cougar's claws dug into the bed.

"Yes very nice thank you," Mabel enunciated through gritted teeth. She glanced at the poster and then back to her feet, paws now rubbing at her temples as the embarrassment shifted into a dull throbbing headache. It *was* in fact a very nice poster, but she couldn't quite focus on the merchandise, no matter *how* exclusive.

LN. The Hero whose fan club I'm a charter member of. The object of far more than a few of my intimate fantasies. She just saw me … all of me. Every. Last. Inch.

The catamount exhaled slowly; the scope of the situation never seemed to get any less monumental. She pinched the bridge of her muzzle between her fingers to try and relieve the incredible pressure building up.

[It's not a big deal, Mabes—]

"Silence, **traitor.**"

"That, uh, outfit looks really nice on you, Mabel." The shoulderless skater dress and tall boots really did suit the catamount. Her still-long and now shockingly white hair was brushed to the side, falling over one green eye.

"Thank you, Ellen … Amarelys helped me pick it out."

"Oh, that's a pretty name! Do I know them?"

"She's my ROSE."

"Ah."

"Mm."

Another excruciating minute of silence passed.

"So … uhh…" The vixen rubbed at the back of her head, and looked to the cat, who was now staring at her. "Should we talk about, uh … You said my name? While you were, um…"

The lioness stood up, chunky-heeled boots clapping softly against the floor, closing the gap quickly between the two as she slammed a hand on the wall behind Ellen in an attempt to convey the gravity of the words she was about to say. To her credit, the former hero did not laugh at the aggressive display, despite the source of the ineffectual kabedon.

"We *will* pretend like this never happened, okay? It will not be a cute story we tell over pancakes, nor is it an anecdote we're going to share at a party. This tale will never leave this room. *Ever.*" Her voice was barely above a whisper and each word rolled from her lips as a rumbling growl. "Am I *perfectly* clear, *Ellen?*"

"*Yeah.* Understood. Ma'am! I, uh. Had just. Never seen one of those before. In-person, I mean, not — I mean, I've got the *Internet*, I — can ... I say just one thing and then stop talking forever?" She held a single finger up, her furless face giving a much clearer view of her own embarrassment.

"Tread lightly, Foxpaw..." The lioness's eyes narrowed as she growled, knowing the promise to never speak again was a *complete* impossibility for the vixen.

She replied with a genuine smile. "You *are* pretty cute."

Mabel's tail stood stiffly and poofed out like a brush. She looked away, unable to stop purring quietly as she stalked back to the bed, and smoothed out her dress. "Thank you..." The blush returned, but a small smile had lit up her features as well.

"Hope we're not *interrupting* anything?" Volta asked as she knocked on the door before ducking in, casting a glance between the two, a knowing smile spreading on her muzzle.

"Nope. Just uh ... talking about clothes. Just a couple of gals ... chatting about ... fashion."

Smooth, Mabel. The smoothest, really.

"Mmm*hm.*" The red wolf's nose wiggled, and her expression was inquisitive, but one look at Mabel made it clear she should not press. "Well, Vixie and I successfully foraged for some pudding, but I'm still starving; you two ready to go?" She placed a paw on the little demivixen's shoulder and tilted her head as she gestured to the door. "Gramma C's is waiting for us!"

Vixie was currently concerned with sucking the last remnants of the chocolatey delight from her spoon before her tongue swept around the inside of the cup. The fat muscle flattened against the side of the plastic container, and she let out a cute little *mlem* of appreciation. Mabel's whole body clenched at once as the vixen cleared the container, the swirling length languidly lapping with aplomb. The puma looked pointedly at Volta, who was biting her lip as she squirmed against the doorframe at the display of oral gymnastics.

*Oh gods**damn**…*

"Mmm … th-that was t-tasty!" The vixen smacked her lips and looked rather pleased with herself. Volta leaned down to wipe a splotch of pudding from her cheek and sucked it off her finger, giving Mabel a shit-eating grin as she raised an eyebrow.

The cougar did not even bother attempting to hide her wide-eyed stare.

"Did she just…"

[*Mhmm!*]

"And her … it was…"

[Uh-huh.]

"So…"

[*Not a single nanogram of peanut butter is wasted in the Foxpaw household.* **Ever.**]

"Fuck me running…" No one had ever been more envious of a jar in the history of the world than the feline in that moment.

[*A difficult task, but I'm sure we could figure it out.*]

Mabel popped up and clapped her paws together enthusiastically as she desperately attempted to think of anything besides what that tongue could do, or the fact that she and Ellen were twins.

*This dress is going to do **nothing** to hide this problem. Shit, shit, shit, shit…*

"Right! So, I am DYING for some waffles and tong — ERRR, TOFFEE! Yes, delicious, salty toffee! Anyone else? Gramma Cosetta's, yeah?" She removed the poster from the wall carefully, even in her state not about to let a prime piece of Lawful Neutral memorabilia be wasted. Her tail thrashed behind her as she quickly rolled the poster up and tucked it under her arm, retrieved her purse, and headed out the door, moving *nearly* fast enough to leave a puma-shaped hole in the wall.

"Wonder what's on her mind … Any ideas, Standup?" Volta intoned, her voice carrying a sort of playfully willing ignorance to the situation at hand.

"Oh, I'm sure it's nothing. Not a big deal. I mean I'm sure it's a fine … *deal.*" She winced and ducked out close behind the catamount. "Wait up, Mabel!" She shouted as she tried to catch up. The lioness was already at the elevator and pressing the button over and over again, willing the machinery to work faster as she heard the back-and-forth of their conversation approach.

"Huh … Some folks are wound up a little bit tight, huh, Fangirl?"

"M-maybe sh-she just r-really likes w-waffles?"

Mabel did her best to put on a brave face as they walked to the diner. She quickly found her new look and sway garnered attention, although at first, she assumed it was for her companions. How could all eyes *not* be on the eight-foot-tall goddess of the storm, or any of the other beautiful creatures that resided there? Her mind was still reeling from the unintentional show she'd put on, so she had conflicting feelings about being *perceived* at all, but still … she certainly wished *someone* was looking at her.

Volta seemed to recognize the stress and nudged her gently with a hip before leaning down to whisper in her ear. "You all right?"

"I'm fine, I just … I wish I was getting the looks *you* all are."

"Oh, Kittycat, all eyes *are* on you. Walk like you know it. *Own* it."

The wolf's words sent a shiver down her spine. Mabel glanced about, suddenly recognizing those appreciative gazes — looking *respectfully*, of course — at the lioness. She blushed again, forgetting the mortifying shower incident for just a moment, and Amarelys took the opportunity.

[Shall I give you a little runway music, darling?]

"Mm…"

The drumbeat started, and she closed her eyes. The sound in the puma's ears caused each step to become purposeful, provocative, and free of inhibition. She did as she was told and *owned* it.

"She's not the kind of girl…"

"Who likes to tell the world…"

"About the way she feels about herself."

Volta positively beamed with pride as the cat strutted forward. The cougar drank in the attention, and her smile matched the red wolf's own, sharp and dangerous.

Vixie hung onto her sister's arm, but Mabel could tell her eyes were also locked firmly on the feline's behind as it bounced to the sound of Garbage in her ears. Ellen couldn't help but steal a glance or two as well, it appeared; one could not simply *ignore* the stray cat strutting.

Shirley Manson's voice spoke deep inside Mabel and resonated through her form.

"Baby, you'll get what you want this time around."

*So what if Ellen saw me? So what if everyone is looking? I'm finally **me**, and I refuse to hide it any longer.* **Never again.**

She threw an arm around Volta's massive hips as well as she could. The lupine matched her stride, barking "Attagirl, Mabel!" with a laugh.

"Mabes, please, dear. After all … you've seen me at my worst, now you get to be part of the *best*." The puma gave a cheeky wink to an older blue anole of indeterminate gender, who gave her an appreciative nod and returned the gesture. Clearly *they* liked what they saw, too.

The rest of the walk to the diner was more of this new normal, and the catamount held the door with a bit of a bow. A few days prior, she could barely handle the owner of the establishment's intensely friendly demeanor, but today? She was a whole new woman. She could handle Gramma C. She was *ready*.

═══
═══

She *absolutely* was not ready.

Large-but-nimble paws grabbed her shoulders as she leaned in close before taking her by the paw and spinning her about, and she scrambled to quickly push her dress back down. The flash of frilly panties was *mostly* hidden from view, but the whistle from *someone* in the diner meant it was not a *complete* success.

"Mmm! *C'est belle!* They really captured who you were inside, eh, Mabel? Lovely, lovely, *lovely*." The last word came out as a purr as the older woman planted a kiss on her cheek and followed it with a playful pinch on the rear. The elder tabby beamed at the rest of the party, all seemingly doing their best not to snicker at their friend. For the cougar's own part, she looked slightly panicked, but her raised tail told a different story entirely.

"Th-thank you, Miss Cosetta!" The cool cat was gone. The nervous nerd was very much back in the lead.

"I *told* you, dear, Gramma C is just fine! Going to need plenty of good cooking to keep that figure, I think! Take a seat, girls! You just missed *mon p'tit chatonne*, but she told me to give you her best!" There was another torrent of kisses before they were scooted to a table by the amiable grande dame. Moments later, a plate of fresh fruit was placed before them, alongside a pot of steaming coffee and a chilled carafe of orange juice.

"A little birdy said we wanted waffles, yes? I even had made up a little toffee, as a treat for the birthday girl!" Another wink, and the tabby was gone in a flash, before so much as a thank-you could be offered.

"Birthday girl? Toffee? Oh! Right! Heh..."

"Merci beaucoup!" the puma shouted after her.

"De rien, *ma belle!*" came the reply from behind the swinging kitchen door.

The table's attention came back to the food at hand. The brightly colored platter was covered with delicious fruit, including half a honeydew melon, neatly cubed and glistening wetly.

"Oh ... that's a lot of melon, isn't it? Does anyone really *like* that?" Mabel prodded the greenish fruit with a fork before spearing a strawberry instead.

There was an audible gasp as Ellen slid the plate in front of her possessively. "How dare you besmirch the melon, you *heathen!*" She popped two of the cubes into her maw, scowling in indignance. "You don't deserve the delicious refreshment of the noble honeydew!" the vixen muttered around the mouthful.

The lioness held up her paws in surrender as she laughed. "Sorry hun! I didn't realize it was so *serious!*"

"We *never* joke about melons!" She waved a fork with the sticky fruit speared on it before shoveling it between her lips.

"Duly noted!"

The banter continued unabated, and the jovial mood *almost* let the catamount put her accidentally bawdy little show earlier from her mind. The sounds and smells coming from the kitchen elicited a growl from several bellies around the table. The scent of butter and frying quick bread permeated the air, and the vanilla sweetness made grumbling stomachs that much more insistent. Before the situation could become any more dire, plates stacked with waffles, crispy home fries, and thick cuts of salty bacon showed up, along with all the fixings one could want — including a small cast-iron skillet full of homemade toffee, sprinkled with some flaky salt.

"Make sure you clean those plates, darlings, we don't waste food around here!" Cosetta leaned down and whispered something in Vixie's ear which made her giggle.

As it turned out, Vixie was extremely fond of the toffee on her waffles; she made sure to thank Mabes for the recommendation, despite having to try and use her tongue to dislodge it from the roof of her mouth. Along with the excess whipped cream and rainbow sprinkles that decorated her chin, lips, and somehow, *tail*. Volta *also* thanked the cat for the sticky suggestion.

The conversation flowed, the food was enjoyed, and all Mabel could think about was how nice it was to be around *people* and simply be herself. Laughing, and savoring life as it was for her now, as it would be, from now on. To simply exist and be seen as she felt in her heart and soul.

Sadly, they could not sit there all day. When the last waffle was wolfishly devoured and the last bit of melon munched, they got up to leave and said their goodbyes and mercis to Cosetta. Mabel closed her eyes for just a second, to try and remember this moment and lock it away.

"I'm allowed to be happy. They just want me to be happy…"

Hugs and waves were given all around. Nebulous plans were suggested for the coming weekend involving video games and pizza before the girls went their separate ways, leaving Mabel to consider her next steps. Her schedule was, unsurprisingly, free and clear.

The cougar was content to relax in her little dorm-like apartment, and considered trying to nap, given the caloric intake she just worked through. Maybe after a little *exercise*, considering her morning routine was so *rudely* interrupted. Images of winding tongues danced sinuously through her mind before she recalled a certain someone mentioning a surprise earlier, and her focus shifted once more away from the foxy fantasies to potential presents in the present.

"So, what did you get me, Relly? Huh? Huh?"

[You'll see soon enough, impatient girl!]

"Awww … But I'm curious!"

[Walk faster then, sweetie!]

Chapter 16

Kingdom Come

Mabel managed to speed up towards home for approximately fifty yards before the sheer *weight* of the breakfast she had consumed reminded her that it was still there, like a leaden lump of carbs and starch. Abundant waffles and a half pound of home fries were sloshing about in her belly, and she hesitated to even *think* of moving any faster than a leisurely amble, lest the meal return to seek revenge.

"Oh-URP! No more running. Hoo..." She cradled her swollen tummy with one paw and covered her mouth with the other to try and stifle another belch. Everyone on the thoroughfare gave the lioness a wide berth as she waddled her way back to the residential sector, all with knowing smiles.

[*Oh dear. Well, at least I didn't egg on the gorging, this time.*]

"No, but you didn't stop me, either!"

[*That's true, but honestly, I was just impressed with how you packed away so much; that was quite the show! Were you trying to impress the crowd, Mabes?*]

"I'm glad you enjoyed it, Relly, because my body is composed primarily of regret and toffee at this moment." Mabel muttered, her paws dragging with the hindering weight of her bad decisions, trailing off into a grumble. "Impress the crowd ... Psh."

The cougar uttered a silent thanks to the inventor of elevators for saving her from the tyranny of the stairs as she walked the last few steps to her sixth floor sanctuary. She pressed her forehead against the door, and it opened with a click.

"Made it! Home sweet ho — *Oooo?*" Mabel did a double-take, her eyes drawn to a brightly wrapped package on the kitchen counter. The puma's tummy troubles miraculously vacated her mind as she instantly became fascinated by the box. The portal slid closed behind her with a hiss, and she scooted to the mysterious mystery on the other side of the room.

"*Ooooh, pretty!*" She pawed at the wrapping, batting idly at the bow on top. "Is this my *surprise?* Can I open it?" The feline leaned close, fingertips drumming lightly along the sides.

[It is indeed! Happy birthday, my girl! I hope you like it!] Relly sounded so *excited*, which only made the puma's ear-to-ear smile somehow grow even wider.

The rainbow-colored paper and ribbon was carefully shredded by delicate claws and brushed aside, its contents revealed. The lioness gasped and even made a happy little squeal as she realized what it was. "Eeeee! *Relly!* You *didn't!*"

[Oh, I most certainly *did!*] The smugness was palpable as the cougar clenched her paws in front of her face.

The polished wooden box sat on small bronze clawed feet. It was latched by an ornate clasp shaped to look like the moon, also cast from warmly lustrous bronze. The reflective surface — clearly the work of a master crafter — was engraved with entwined flowers and vines, all leading back to the center of the lid, where an icon was carved. The symbols were familiar to the cat; as she traced them with a fingertip, she tilted her head, and her tail swayed slowly behind her. The symbol was the woven sigil of male and female — the Classical astrological symbology for Mars and Venus that represented the transgender aspect — laid on top of the infinity loop. She closed her eyes and could still see it crystal clear in her mind.

[Do you like it, Mabes? I was so impressed when Morrigan showed me the final product! She's got such a masterful hoof!]

"I *love* it, Relly, and you'll have to give my compliments to the artist! It's absolutely incredible! I just, uh … This symbol…?" Her pads drummed gently on the polished case, brow furrowing as she tried to seize hold of a memory dancing just out of reach. "Why do I feel like I've seen it before?"

It was a rare thing for the dragoness to sound confused, but she certainly came off as perplexed when she spoke, after a moment in apparent thought. [I'm … not sure? It reminded me of you, but I'm not certain why. The design just sort of came to me … hm.]

Wheels turned in Mabel's mind as the feline desperately tried to parse an intense wave of deja vu. Her thumb absentmindedly rubbed at the onyx in her choker as she tried to dislodge the symbol's origin from the recesses of her mind. "Well, it's inspired by the Magician card, right?" she suggested, tilting her head to the other side.

[That sounds likely! You were dwelling on that card before the procedure, if I recall correctly. That has to be it!]

Mabel nodded, reluctantly. Tarot had become *very* important to the pair, after all, despite having done only the one reading. But this was a coincidence so *specific that* she couldn't help but wonder if it meant something more, despite Relly's confident reply. "Mm. I guess…"

[But *enough* with the iconography, curious cat! Open it! Come *onnnnn!* I want to see the look on your face!]

"*Okay!* Okay! I'll drop it!" The catamount couldn't help but smile at the impatiently eager tone her big sister took with her. She moved the crescent moon latch aside and gradually revealed the treasure within. Her nostrils instantly flared as she recognized the smell, a sense memory unlocked, and she greedily drank it in.

"Oh, Amarelys … You are an *absolutely* incorrigible bad influence…" Her voice had dropped to barely a whisper, and while the words were a reprimand, the tone indicated something much closer to adoration for the dragoness.

[That's the Korps! Corrupting poor innocents with our *debauched* ways since the Paris Peace Conference!]

There had to be two dozen or more cigars within the perfectly sized confines, their Maduro wrappers the color of dark chocolate, shining dully from their cedar resting place. An inch thick, and at least six long; even the size was consistent with her fantasies. She delicately picked one from its bed and ran it under her nose as she'd imagined doing dozens — if not hundreds — of times.

Earthy, rich, faintly sweet; there was a note of cinnamon-kissed coffee and cedar. She had never smoked before, but she knew how it would taste, how the smell would cling to her. How it would linger on her tongue…

A shiver ran down her spine at the thought.

[I got you the same brand that Miss Kallist enjoys! I hope that was the right choice …?] There was hesitation in her tone, and it was incredibly endearing to Mabel that Relly was so *concerned* with this decision, as if she could ever do anything wrong in her little sister's eyes.

"Oh, yes it was, Relly. The perfect choice really, thank you…" She trailed off as she stared at the stick in her paw, rolling it between her thumb and forefinger. The weight was comfortable, and the feel was familiar. It felt like it *belonged* there, despite never handling one before.

The catamount slowly traced her tongue over her lips, nearly overcome by the feelings that rushed over her. The heady aroma of her dreams weaved about like wisps of vapor, clouding her thoughts. Pleasantly lightheaded, she leaned heavily on the counter, as she feared she might become weak in the knees.

The same as Betty ... She pondered the implications of a shared favorite vice between herself and the woman she'd admired from afar. For the second time that day, her dreams were becoming reality. *Hopefully she won't burst through the door when I'm handling myself ... I don't think I could survive that level of embarrassment twice in one day...*

She glanced back. Sadly, the challenge to the universe was left unanswered.

She brought it to her muzzle, and let her tongue snake out to swirl around the head. The taste was unmistakable; she knew it *intimately,* without ever actually having experienced it before. She knew how the warm vapor would dance about her maw, how it would waft past her lips after spilled across her tongue. Her tail continued to sway to and fro, intrigued, as she considered how to proceed.

[The punch and the lighter are in a hidden compartment inside the humidor. I wonder how long it'll take you to find the trigger...]

Amarelys quietly observed as the feline's fingers carefully ran along either side until she found an irregularly-shaped, almost-imperceptible button hidden within the swirling flourishes on the left side. On the right, likewise, carefully questing pawpads located the slightest *give* in a previously immobile leaf; she rotated it with a slide of her finger. Both mechanisms satisfied, the tray ejected a lip out smoothly with a muffled click.

"Oh, that's a cute little trick," she thought with a smirk and a raised brow. A soft chuckle bubbled in her mind from her proud big sister.

There she stood, with the tools to finally light her *very first cigar,* and she couldn't help but pause at the precipice. She was beginning to second-guess the whole enterprise.

"*What if I do it wrong? Coughing and wheezing would be so embarrassing. Or what if I actually* **hate** *it? What would that mean about me, and who I am, versus who I want to be...?*" She closed her eyes and had to set her suddenly over-encumbered paws on the table.

[*You know, you don't have to partake if you don't want to, Mabes. You're not any less yourself, if this feels wrong.*]

"*I know. It's just … this feels* **important**. *Like, a defining moment. I just want to give it the proper consideration, and, well … gravitas, I suppose.*"

[*Only* **you** *can define yourself, dear. Whatever you choose, you will always be you.*]

The stogie felt so effortlessly *natural* between her fingers, just a moment before. Part of her wondered if it *was* something new, or just something she had somehow forgotten, a habit she was rediscovering for the first time.

How could you possibly forget about something that makes your heart race like this? What are you afraid of, really? She opened her eyes, and the cocky grin spread across her features. She was, she reasoned, not willing to let a potentially life-changing experience just waft away on the breeze. *What's the worst that can happen?*

"This is for me. I *want* this," she whispered, assuring herself as much as anyone else.

The cougar began the "ritual" with a steady and seemingly practiced paw. The punch pulled a small plug from the slightly damp head of the cigar, razor-sharp and clean. She held it between her lips and confirmed the draw was clear, before clicking the butane lighter to life. The blue flame danced in front of her eyes as she spun the foot of the cigar close to — but not actually *touching* — the flame, tendrils of grey smoke signaling the last step was ready to be taken.

Don't inhale. Savor this, the first of many.

She brought the cigar back to her lips, puffing softly, encouraging the smoke across her tongue, and taking a long drag as she clicked the lighter closed. The tip flared to life as the creamy vapor filled her muzzle; as she exhaled, she felt her whole body relax at once. It was like a bow suddenly loosed, so quickly did the tension through her form unwind and melt away. The puma had often imagined this moment; so much more so, in the previous few months, and in the darkness by herself for even longer still. She had venerated it like it was an unattainable fantasy, assuming it would never happen, telling herself with a twinge of sadness to be *practical* and *realistic*, but here it was. Some might liken it to a religious experience, but Mabel knew what it was as she opened her eyes and watched the smoke spiral from the tip.

It was much more *intense* than that.

She stifled a moan by bringing the head back to her lips and suckling gently to coax more of the haze free. Sometimes, a cigar was *not* just a cigar. Sometimes … it was *this*.

A familiar voice rang out from the distance, and it took a moment for the lioness to remember she was not alone, as she lazily released the smoke lingering in her muzzle. *[How is it?]*

"Have you ever missed something, without knowing what it was, and then suddenly found it?" She shivered as she traced her lips with her tongue once more. *"It's like that."* The cougar rolled the barrel between her fingers, suddenly feeling as if she needed something *more* to really complete the moment.

"Do we have any coffee, Relly? A nice mocha, maybe?"

[Hm. I don't think we do right now, but I can put in an order and have something delivered, if you like?]

"Mm. Please do! I feel like something rich and chocolatey would *really* pair nicely." Mabel slipped the cigar back between her lips; as she drew on it, the tip flared, illuminating her features through the veil of smoke. She migrated to the couch, spreading her arms along the rear before tilting her head back, plucking the stogie free, and exhaling a massive plume. Emerald orbs watched the swaying smoke dance about the ceiling, as the filters gamely attempted to keep the air clean. In. Out. The foot glowed red, and then a moment later, more smoke would slip over her plump lip.

"Wonder how hard it would be to learn how to blow rings?"

[Just practice and a talented tongue as I understand it.]

"Mmm…" She idly attempted one, managing only a small amorphous puff of vapor.

[A valiant effort! It was round-ish at least!]

"You're very sweet, Relly, but I'll keep practicing." She chuckled, resuming her savored reverie.

It wasn't long before a warm haze settled across the room. The scent hung on the air, and to some it would be too much, but to the catamount it was *just* right. The ambiance was so cozy and comforting. She lost track of time as her mind meandered through the haze, watching the twists and turns drifting languidly from her maw or her now half-spent stogie, before suddenly realizing the ash had grown precariously long. There was a moment of panic as she sat up, glancing about for somewhere to deposit the waste.

"Shit! Don't want to ruin the rug here…" Her eyes darted back towards the kitchen, "Maybe a mug would work? *Fuck!*"

[Right in front of you, sweetie.]

Her sister truly had thought of everything. On the low coffee table, evading her notice until that moment, was another new addition —

a heavy crystal ashtray just waiting for her to use. It was cleaved from one solid piece, the edges rounded, with perches for several smokables around the perimeter. Giving her cigar a gentle tap on the dully gleaming tchotchke, she could continue to enjoy the vice without fear of damaged furniture, the immediate crisis averted.

As the puma leaned back once again, her paw slipped down to adjust herself. Lingering there, *adjusting* soon became something else entirely. She squeezed and stroked through the soft fabric of her dress and underclothes, and her cock began to stir in earnest. This could not be mistaken as an unconscious action; she was *quite* aware of what she was doing.

Whatever the cause — the smoke, the oral fixation, her lonely mind wandering — as the head of the cigar pressed against her lips, she couldn't help but feel a sensual rush to her nethers, thoughts of Betty dancing through the corridors of her memory. The feline let out a cute little mewl as her ministrations drew pre from her rod, staining the silky satin of her panties, and threatening the propriety of her dress as well.

Mabel clenched the cigar gingerly in her teeth, as a freed paw was able to play with her aching nipples, palming her breasts and massaging the tender, newly-grown flesh. The catamount panted out little clouds as her too-sensitive areolas stiffened in arousal.

The idea of a cum-stained, smokey dress hanging in her closet seemed so *tantalizingly* lewd, if a little stereotypical. Her hips rolled up to meet her paw at the image. Gone was the embarrassment of this morning's calamity in the bathroom, and she smiled at the thought of an entirely different situation involving the vixen.

*Why yes, Ellen, I am handling myself quite nicely at the moment. Would you like to help? You'd **really** be my hero—*

Polite knocks on the door were followed by, "Hello? Miss Greysmoke? It's K-PARCEL!"

Or maybe an altogether more conveniently pornographic opportunity might present itself.

A sly sort of chuckle rumbled in her chest as half-lidded eyes looked to the door, and the corners of her mouth lifted mischievously around the stogie. Had Amarelys alerted her of the approaching delivery? Likely, but she was understandably a bit *preoccupied.* "Coming, dear! Just a moment!"

Mabel sauntered to the entrance, striking a pose before reaching for the keypad. She opened the door and leaned against the frame, filling it quite nicely as she puffed on her cigar. The delivery person — a crow

with absolutely *stunning* iridescent plumage, kissed with snowy white —
beamed brightly as she offered the cup to the cougar, stammering as the
catamount was revealed, and smoke blossomed over her.

"Here you go, Miss, uh, Grey … smoke?"

The catamount purred as she accepted the drink, bulge clearly
straining through her dress, the whole situation exciting her in ways she
had never felt. The bird was diminutive, barely clearing four feet, and was
staring directly at the feline's bulge. She looked adorable in their little
uniform polo, short shorts, and a cap emblazoned with what Mabel
assumed was the K-PARCEL logo. As her gaze slowly moved upwards,
avian eyes grew wide before finally seeing the predatory lioness's own
looking directly at her.

"So, **this** is what it's like to be ogled? Can't say I dislike it."

[*There is a whole lot of you to gawk at these days, dear. Be gentle with the
little bird.*]

"Of course! I'll be **very** gentle…"

"Thank you so much, darling. What do I owe you?" Her voice was
still deep and rumbly, but the huskiness of it only lent to the image she
wanted to convey; a mature huntress, confident and sensuous. Maybe a
little *dangerous*, too. A femme fatale in name and presence.

"Oh, uh, err … nothing, ma'am! Just … doing m-my … duty…" The
little corvid spoke with a nervous swallow, clearly flustered, if one was to
go by the literal ruffling of her feathers.

"What a cute birdie. Why, I could just *eat* you all up…" Mabel let her
tongue trace her teeth as she leaned in close to speak the enticing near-
threat, her breath warm. The smell of her vice hung thick upon the air,
along with the musky scent of her still-drooling member. It all blended
into a heady mélange that apparently made the delivery bird flush shyly,
but their sharp eyes never left the cat's, framed so neatly in her angular
visor. "Are you sure I can't give you a tip…?"

"Th-thank you, Miss, but no tip n-needed!" She swallowed again.
"Y-you look *very* nice, t-too!"

"Gods, you are *delightful*." Mabel leaned back and took a sip of the
coffee, letting the warm chocolate notes join the taste in her muzzle,
confirming her thoughts about the pairing. "Absolutely *delicious*. What's
your name, sweetie? Just so I know who to request next time I'm feeling a
little *peckish*…" The words rolled from her lips easily, like the smoke she
so freely shared with her new friend.

"Oh, uh … Charla. Ma'am." Her plumage remained hesitantly fluffed out as her shoes scuffed against the carpet of the hallway.

"Oh, you can call me Mabel, dear; no need to be so *formal*." The puma leaned forward again and ran a finger down Charla's beak, eliciting a girlish giggle from the little bird.

"O-okay! Sure, Mabel!"

"That's a good girl … I won't keep you any longer, hun; I'm sure a cutie-pie like you has places to go and packages to *handle*." She let the last word hang in the air, the emphasis unmistakable, her eyebrow perked like the corner of her mouth. "Thanks for the coffee, Charla. I'll see you around, chickadee." She gave a wink as she turned back into her apartment, the scent of her stogie leaving aromatic wisps behind like a goodbye kiss.

[*Mmm … Nearly the cat who got the canary there, eh, Mabes? Didn't know you had that in you!*]

"*I don't, which is a shame, really…*" She snorted quietly. "*Oh, it was just a little fun, Relly! Can you save her contact info, though? I would love to take her out for a bite some time.*" She thought as she sipped her drink, wending her back through the living room, smoke tailing merrily behind. The coffee was *very* good, but she had something more pressing on her mind, especially after that little *carnivorous* display.

"*I've never felt so … **confident.** So … **powerful**,*" she thought, as a purr settled in her chest. "*Is this who I am now? I think I understand some of that swagger that Volta has…*"

[*Self-actualization is a beautiful thing!*]

Mabel grabbed the ashtray from the table as she passed, and slipped into the bedroom, placing it on her bedside table. She laid the nearly-spent cigar in the vessel as she stripped down and tossed the soiled attire towards the hamper — or in the correct general direction, at any rate, not really caring enough to confirm her aim was true. The feline *did* choose to leave the socks on, giving herself a glance in the mirror as she stood beside the bed.

This was not a dream. Her reality had finally arrived, and she dripped with carnal intent at the sight of herself.

Mabel laid back on the bed and let her paws roam for a moment, relishing the flavors that lingered on her tongue. Her cock stood rigid, demanding her attention, and for a moment it reminded her of the serval with whom she now shared a vice (as well as a place in her dreams). Pink and barbed, it dripped with need as she grasped her shaft and pumped slowly, drawing it out, imagining a slender paw — one that did not belong to her — doing the squeezing and rubbing. She had all the time in the world to enjoy the fruits of Empire Enhancement's labors, appreciating the whole *experience* of her newly-amended body, and she was *absolutely* going to revel in the moment.

"*The doors are locked, right?*"

[*No entry without your express permission, I promise, Mabes.*]

"*You're a doll...*" She sat up and swept her hair to the side so she could unclasp her choker. The metal had become uncomfortably warm — almost scalding, somehow — but she was certain it was just her pent-up desires playing tricks on her senses. The lioness made a mental note to acquaint herself with the base's salon tomorrow if they could squeeze her in, as there was a little more headfur than she wanted in her way.

"*Oooo, maybe an A-line bob? Or a pixie cut? That could be cute!*"

[*Oh, it would be! We'll try some on after you're done taking yourself for a proper test drive!*]

She was so distracted by the pleasure of it all, of existing in a body she actually *recognized*, that she didn't pay attention to where she was dropping her jewelry. She cursed under her breath as she managed to accidentally land it in the center of her stogie's ashen graveyard. Before she could return to the task at paw, an unfamiliar (yet *entirely* familiar) voice echoed within her mind.

A gift of wind and fire will set the demon free. May the lesson be learned, and the covenant honored.

The words from the dream.

"Wind and fire ... *smoke.*" She whispered, realizing the gravity of her little mistake. "*Eneera.* It wasn't a dream...!"

The onyx stone began to shake and shudder within the crystal dish, glowing with an otherworldly golden light; the tinkling sound it made against the tray grew more agitated by the second. It was insistent, like someone desperately rattling a door handle to be given egress.

"*RELLY!* Lock down the apartment!" She didn't know why she shouted that order, why she would want to trap herself in a tight space with a supernatural force; her mouth just spoke the words without a second thought. Every latch in the place clicked in unison, the sound echoing ominously behind the quickening sound of silver in the crystal tray. *"We can't let what's coming go loose!"*

*[Alerting KDARC! Mabes, you need to not be in front of it! Put something between you, and whatever is happening, **NOW!**]*

"Don't need to tell me twice!"

She somersaulted backwards off the bed, landing on the far side before tucking her knees in and bringing her paws to her ears as a roar reverberated through the apartment. An impossibly bright flash lit the entire place like a beacon. To anyone outside, it would have looked like someone was trying to turn their housing unit into a lighthouse.

*Well, it might at least be **slightly** inconvenienced by that. Maybe.* She needed help, but who could she call for supernatural trouble? *Ghostbusters? Is there a queer version of Egon running around the Korps? A **queerer** version?*

This was so far beyond her scope it was terrifying to consider. A demon was quite literally knocking, and she was distressingly short on ideas.

*Do we have any salt in the house? Does the salt thing even work? Those golden retriever brothers were so cute, but really are a pair of idjits ... Also, they are **fake**, and this is real life, Mabel, **real life**, HA HA HA, you know, the real life with demons invading supervillain lairs right as you're getting ... no, get it together!* Her mind continued to race, panic rising to a frantic peak as the whole world felt like it was coming down around her.

"What do we do?" she screamed over the din.

[We're going to be fine, Mabes, I promise! Just stay calm! I'm here, we'll be okay!] The words were soothing to a point, but being at ground zero for an unexpected summoning left little that could be done to assuage the abject terror that gripped her tight.

The cougar held her breath as she awaited certain doom ... but it never came. As quickly as the storm burst into being, it abruptly ended without another sound.

Her ears were ringing, and she was shaking, but seemed to otherwise be okay; the vitals readout on her RCGs provided that much information, at least. Arms and legs were where they were expected to be, and her tail had wrapped around her, so that was five out of five. She nodded, as everything seemed accounted for, and took a deep breath before slowly moving to peek over the bed, before remembering discretion was the better part of valor, so she instead ducked back down when her ears perked to a new noise. It was the voice from her dreams, speaking in the long-dead tongue of an ancient land, in a tone that rumbled through her entire form:

"I am free at last! Who has freed the djinn Eneera from their prison? Let me look upon my savior!"

As before, Mabel understood the words, but could only exclaim, as she stared down into her bedroom carpet, "… *Savior?*"

Chapter 17

Rebel, Rebel

[You speak Sumerian?]

"...That would be a no! I can barely manage *English* some days! I figured you were translating?"

[*Also no! I just now discovered the root language in our database.*]

"Gotcha. Also, just to make sure I note my concern before we gloss on over it, what the *fuck* is KDARC, exactly?"

"It is very rude to converse in front of a guest as if they are not there."

The voice ended the latent bickering before it could begin, and Mabel cautiously peered over the bed at the source of the reprisal. Standing there was a vaguely person-shaped cloud of smoke, like a shadow wreathed in wispy vapor. In place of eyes were two bright spots of golden light, and they were staring intently at the lioness.

The smell of the cigar still hung in the air and was joined by a new sort of scent: like rain on freshly tilled earth, or perhaps a garden, with the faintest hint of a campfire. It was oddly pleasant, and reminded her of many comforting things, but the chaos of the moment would not be denied even by the most powerful sense memory.

"Oh ... sorry. Eneera, right? I um, apologize. I'm not trying to be *rude*, I've just never had someone make such an, uh, *dramatic* entrance from a piece of jewelry before...?" She tried to choose her words carefully, tempering out the impulse to screech in bafflement about the figure who had simply *burst into existence* like a frenzied, phosphorescent nightmare. That, the catamount was certain, would be taken *poorly*.

"I am sorry if my release was ... *boisterous*. When the chance to be free arose, I needed to take it." Again, they replied in the ancient dialect, and again the meaning shaped itself for her, the sounds completely alien and yet intensely familiar. "A thousand pardons, but you have nothing to fear from me; you have my word!"

[*Mabel, we need to wait for support. Please be careful.*]

"We need to keep it calm, I ... I believe ... him? Them? I think we're safe."

[Based on what, exactly?] Relly's voice was skeptical in the extreme, almost sarcastic.

"You have to trust me, Amarelys. I **know** them."

[You know I trust you. I do! But support — **expert** support — will be here in less than two minutes. Please don't do anything reckless!] The skepticism did not leave her voice, but the dragoness didn't *forbid* her continuing the conversation, which the puma took as tacit approval.

"Is there another here? Do you converse with spirits?"

Mabel slowly rose to her feet — modesty forgotten in the moment — as she stood to stare back at the supernatural being. Before she could respond, the cloud spoke again.

"Oh! You are an *Oracle!* Then the speaking is explained. I am honored you chose to release me!"

"What? No! Wait, why would you assume that?" The puma blinked, veering sharply from indignant to *confused*, as she tilted her head at the accusation.

"You are both man and woman, are you not?" An umbral limb gestured to her, every part on display for the djinn to plainly see.

The cat yelped as she covered up as best she could with her arms, twisting to hide what she could. It was a futile task, considering her generous new curves, and her ears flushed red with fury all the while.

"Oh, *buddy,* you've been in that rock for a *very* long time, haven't you? Just because I have a *di*—" She readied herself to launch into a lesson on modern day gender identity, but before she could finish that thought, there was a startling crackle and snap, followed by the smell of ozone.

It seemed that the aforementioned backup had arrived, and all the fur on the back of Mabel's neck stood on end, as the energy of the room shifted. Where a moment ago the being called Eneera was cordial and curious, the djinn suddenly shrank back, their glowing orbs darting about like a cornered animal.

"No ... No ... *Please* no..."

"The entire floor has been locked down. There is no way in, or out, that doesn't go through us." The catamount hadn't even heard the approach of the agent that had suddenly appeared nonchalantly in her doorway. "Nice work, Marl. It's just a little thing, but we all know that trouble comes in all sorts of different packages, hm?"

"Isn't that the truth? Confirmation on the incursion?" The rumbling reply came from the living room.

"Rosa says djinn. Hm. Old one, too, though I suppose they tend to be." The hooded figure pulled down their cowl, and revealed a stoat with curiously pale blue eyes behind a glowing amber visor as she turned to Mabel. "You alright, miss?"

"Yeah, I mean … I'm a little *on edge* given the, uh … situation." The cougar, already at her limit for sudden unexpected visitors, simply stood there, unable to muster a single fuck regarding her current unclothed state. "… I'm assuming you're with KDARC?"

"Got it in one," She clucked her tongue, and pointed at Mabel with a hand that appeared to be missing all flesh. All that remained were bones of gleaming silver, glowing faintly at each joint. "I'm Agent Key; you can call me Penelope. The big lug in the living room is Agent Lock; you can call him Marlon. We'll be your cage mages for the evening's events."

While normally Mabel would have been tickled by the cutesy rhyme or surprised by the Halloween decoration of a prosthetic, she was still processing a *few* other things, so it was lost upon her.

"*So, the choker was a magical artifact. Like a mystical jack-in-the-box, and out they popped.*"

[*Mabes, I didn't know. I thought the listing was maybe a little questionable, but I never considered it was actually—*]

"No, no … it's fine, Relly, I promise. I'm not upset about it, I'm just trying to wrap my head around this."

[KDARC has protocols for handling sudden disturbances like this. It's going to be okay.]

"*I told you, I never really felt unsafe once the lightshow was done, Relly…*" The lioness glanced over her shoulder at the "disturbance."

There was a quiet sort of hiss from the corner, as the indistinct wisp of a being, pulled close on itself. "What trickery is this? Why have you trapped me?"

The words remained clear to Mabel, though Penelope's brow furrowed, as if what they said wasn't perfectly understandable. "… Ah. You are contained presently to confirm you're a *friendly* dust devil, and not something that is going to stir up a mess for us. We mean you no harm, we're just protecting our own."

"I was just freed! You *can't* put me back!" Their voice was a mournful wind as they shook. "Please … I can't go back … No more…"

The cougar's heart ached, as she reached out to Eneera.

"Miss, you may not want to make contact…"

Mabel disregarded the advice. "They're just confused and scared."

As she knelt in front of the shivering creature from another time, she couldn't help but feel for them. She placed a paw on what she hoped was their shoulder, whispering, "No one is putting you back in the stone. I'm here, you're safe. I *promise*."

"Please ... I did not mean to do it..."

"Oh sweetie ... *I know*."

The creature seemed to unfurl, if only barely. No cataclysmic explosion, no dismemberment, just leaning into her touch with the caution of a frightened child.

"Okay, so we're just not listening to the nice lady from the arcana department," came a barely registered voice behind her. "You speak Sumerian?"

"Apparently, on both counts," Mabel shrugged.

"She's funny, Nellie. I like her." The owner of the voice, a burly, near-seven-foot tall black rat, leaned against the top of the doorframe, peering into the room.

"Yeah, well, you like troublemakers." The weasel gestured to herself and then let out an exasperated sigh as she stared up at the rat. "I just wanted some fuckin' pizza..."

"No use having a sook on it. We'll get a slice into ya soon enough."

"Promises, promises..." Penelope clucked her tongue, and turned her attention back to the pair in the corner. "Right, so: Mabel, yeah? We aren't going to harm them, so long as they mean us no harm, but we'd like to bring them to the visitor center at the department to check them in—"

Eneera suddenly wrapped their tendrils around Mabel's paw, glowing eyes wide with panic, "N-no ... no ... please..." A nearly silent whisper, filled with dread. "No more ... Let me stay with you ... Please."

The stoat didn't understand the djinn's words, but she understood the tone well enough. "You have my word, we're not going to hurt you. This is just a precautionary measure, not a big deal." She did not sound angry, but her body language changed ever so slightly, like an unconscious shift in how she was carrying herself.

Mabel's eyes narrowed.

Eneera began to shake so hard that instinctually the catamount wrapped her arms around them in a tight embrace, trying to give them something to ground themselves with. "Please ... do not let them take me away again..." Their voice was a whimper, and she could feel the panic radiating off of them in waves.

Again...

"That's not an option, Penelope." The cougar stated firmly. "They're not going anywhere."

"Listen, this is for your safety, frankly theirs as well, so this is not up for debate—"

The icy glare that the puma gave as she looked back over her shoulder could have frozen the blood in the ermine's veins. "You're right. It's not. They're staying. If we need to figure out how that can happen? Fine. But they're not leaving my sight."

Whether it was the frosty gaze or the motherly tone, who could say, but Penelope was rendered speechless. Marlon's stoic expression shifted only a fraction as his eyebrow rose over his square-rimmed RCGs with the unusually colored lenses.

[Mabel Ramona, if you're still looking to join up, disobeying a direct request by a senior agent is a **hell** of a choice.]

"Relly, I can't just let them go. I don't have time to explain, but please, we have to help ... they're so scared."

[This is beyond the pale, Mabes ... You're certain there's no other way?]

"Absolutely."

[...I trust you, but I expect some explanation when you have the words.]

"Of course. Love you."

[Love you too. I'll see what I can do to help resolve this on the backend, but I know that Jane is going to give me an earful. Nothing by half-measures around here, huh?]

"Whole-asses only I'm afraid. You wanted this, remember?"

[Always will, dear.]

The mustelid did not remain speechless, and she did in fact find some words for the feline who was preventing her trip to the pizzeria, and the hanger was clearly mounting. "Lady, are you fuckin' *nuts?* This sort of situation is fraught at the *best* of times, and you expect us to just, I dunno, let an untrained, quite literally fresh out of the tube, not-even-a-*recruit*, babysit an ancient supernatural being with an unknown power level? *Incredible.* I can see your balls *right now,* and they don't look *that* fuckin' big!"

The catamount's eyes narrowed, but a fierce sort of smile flitted across her muzzle. "I'm glad we're on the same page, then."

"Miss, that is *some* ask. You *gotta* give us more to go on than owly mom-eyes," the burly rodent said with a tilt of his head.

Before Mabel could reply, the racoon was jabbing her finger accusingly in the rat's scarified chest. "Marl! *Do not seriously entertain the completely unreasonable request of the newbie!"* Penelope hissed as the shit-show of an operation continued to spiral out of her control. "You gigantic, soft-hearted dumbass, this shit ain't gonna *fly!"*

"Nellie, I hear ya, but you can't tell me you didn't just *feel* that." Marlon nodded in the direction of the obstinate feline. "Don't be a shit."

"...That could have been anything related to the sudden release of the magical sealing, or ambient candescal resonance, or or—" Penelope's paws gesticulated wildly with each possibility before she was silenced by a single tattooed finger pressed to her lips.

"Or she's got more going on than we knew about," the rat retorted with a shrug, and a sniff. "This is somewheres outside our pay-grade, hun."

"Fuck-me-gently..." She groaned, pressing her forehead against her partner's midriff. "The boss lady is going to pop a fuckin' vein..."

"AHEM! Do you still want my reasoning? Or are you two still busy discussing me like I can't hear every word?" Mabel did not bother to hide her displeasure at being ignored like a quiet child. "Which you will be explaining, by the by, after we sort out the first problem."

"Apologies, miss. First, please tell us why we should be sticking our necks out here, exactly?" Penelope threw her arms up as she turned back to the cause of her consternation.

"They were just set free from a prison, you then proceeded to trap them in a brand new one and then offered to frog march them into yet another one. They're terrified." The catamount's voice had softened its edge. "Do you really think that trying to forcibly transport a traumatized ancient being is safer than having them stay here on my couch, while you get your magical customs officer to come check them out?"

The ermine rubbed at her eyes with one paw and let out a resigned sigh.

"She's got a point, Nellie." The rat seemed to be unflappable.

Penelope, who in fact seem *very* flappable, managed not to curse out loud. The look on her face spoke a string of expletives that would have made a sailor blush as she glared at the cougar and then turned on her heel. "I know! *I know!* I'm calling Command to explain the situation and the *extenuating* circumstances for the request."

"And the *other* thing?" The rat asked before the cat could pipe up.

"Like you said, s'above our pay-grade." she muttered, begrudgingly resigning herself to further pizza delays.

"Attagirl. I'll keep an eye on these two."

The door slid shut behind her, and Marlon squared off to fill the frame, silently observing the cougar and djinn. His face wasn't unfriendly as he stood watch, but he was impassive like a gargoyle or grotesque staring down at his charges.

Not quite so stony, but a certain statuesque quality to be sure.

Now that things had become significantly less tense, Mabel had her own chance to actually observe the rat herself, who was, well, something like a cross between a bouncer at a Goth club and a sharply-dressed boss mob in that cyberpunk TTRPG with the fantasy flair.

Which were the same thing when she *really* thought about it.

Redundancy aside, the ritually scarred, and unusually large rodent, did cut a striking figure for a … wizard? Warlock? Mage? Whatever the title, she wasn't anything like the lioness expected to see, let alone have to be sitting naked in front of. What little modesty she had reminded her to grab the blanket from the bed and drape it about herself.

"Well, Miss, I think you have certainly made an impression if nothing else — a sin for certain."

"Hopefully a good one, if a villain is calling it sinful? That's a positive connotation now, yeah?" Mabel offered a weak smile to pair with the nervous response.

"Remains to be seen, but, for what it's worth? I think your heart is in the right place, and that'll serve you well enough."

"Like the woman said: 'We help people.' They needed help. Not a hard choice at the end of the day." The catamount shrugged a little, adjusting the cloth hanging about her shoulders.

"Dunno what woman you're referring to exactly, but she's right, and you stood up for that, good on you."

The weak smile softened to something real, as Mabel nodded. "Heh … thanks, Marlon. Uh … so what do you think happens now?"

"We wait for what the boss lady says, honestly? Likely going to get what you wanted, but it'll be more than that. Always is, in these sorts of situations."

"And the bit about me specifically? What's all that about?"

The rat shrugged, but there was a twinkle of mischief behind his amber-colored glasses. "Dunno! As I keep insisting, s'not my place! I just lock up when all is said and done, Miss. Nellie and me? We're not admin." He tilted his head down to peer over the rim of his eyewear. "But, between the wall and us? I think everything turned out just how it needed to."

"Mm…" She glanced down to the ethereal being huddled close to her, and ran her paw down their back, idly providing comfort to them both in some small way. "Yeah … I can't say you're wrong."

"So much for 'no interruptions' … Did they install a sign when I was in the tank, or something?"

[To be fair, I am ill-equipped to stop "arcanuse interruptus" on such short notice.]

"Well, Greysmoke, you wanted adventure—" The cougar snorted softly in derision at the thought. "Doesn't get much more fantastical than wizards and mystical creatures…"

[You're sort of speedrunning it right now, dear, but everything will turn out fine.]

"Here's hoping!" Mabel winced inwardly. "Uh … how is the aforementioned boss lady handling the situation?"

[Well, it's going better than I thought it would, but to be fair, I didn't have high hopes. She is … exasperated but agrees with your logic. It helps that Penelope seconded your opinion.]

"Aw! She likes me!" The puma thought with mildly enthusiastic sarcasm.

[I wouldn't go that far, but the pair of them are pragmatic, and Jane trusts their judgement.]

"Well, I'll take it. Gods, what a fuckin' day."

[*Yeeeeeeeeah … happy birthday, sweetheart! Hope it's a memorable one!*]

"First of many, I'm sure, but killer tits AND a magical miscreant roomie from the time before written history? Who could ask for anything more?"

[*I'm proud of you, Mabes. You're a reckless idiot, but you're my reckless idiot.*]

The words were said in such a soft and affectionate tone that Mabel's heart fluttered. Red-tinged warmth crept up the cougar's cheeks, but she managed a smirking reply. *"Familial trait?"*

[*…Girl, you don't even know the half of it.*]

The momentary reprieve was cut short as the door slid open once more, and the burly black rat bouncer shifted his bulk, allowing Penelope to step back into the room.

"So! I explained the situation here to the higher-ups, Mabel. You are either very lucky, or very unlucky. Maybe both; jury's still out," she said with a shrug as she leaned against her partner. "The boss is gonna reach out directly here, didn't want to have to involve another body in this …

discourse. I recommend you don't get lippy with her like you did with me, hm?"

"Okay, when you say, reaching out…?"

[She means now dear.]

In the center of the room, a hologram flickered to life, facing the KDARC agents. Before them stood a short, almost portly raccoon woman, dressed in business casual, and sheer stockings. Long brown hair tumbled around the raccoon's horns, themselves swept-back, similar to a gazelles. The hologram faded out past her knees, but Mabel could easily picture a pair of sensible flats on her feet. The procyonid would have seemed more at home in a government office than the Korps … If it wasn't for her left arm.

It was so disjointed from the rest of her as to be jarring and looked to the catamount like something out of a far-flung sci-fi film. Intricate plates of hard metal gave hints of wiring and a soft green glow beneath, and the handpaw looked more suited to a combat machine than a desk clerk. The incongruity, along with the woman's tired expression, gave her a powerful presence despite her lack of a physical one. Her voice was high and soft, but matter-of-fact as she spoke.

"Signals check. Hello? RIV? Am I coming through?"

"Loud and clear, boss. Mabel Greysmoke, meet Research Director Jane Wick."

"Uh … Hello Director Wick." The lioness stood up, turning to face the projection. "Sorry to drag you out—"

"Let's skip the courtesy contrition and resolve this … situation." Jane massaged her temples and muttered under her breath, "Why is it always RIV…" before turning to address the cougar. "Miss Greysmoke, I haven't the slightest interest in visiting Texas, nor do I care to send any more qualified agents for what amounts to less than a smoke alarm.

"Here is my offer: the djinn is your responsibility. Anything they do, you will be held accountable for. You will have a meeting with your liaison this week. You will not miss it, you will not reschedule it, and if you do not attend, there will be consequences." Jane sighed softly and rubbed the bridge of her muzzle.

"Some ground rules when dealing with extraplanar visitors: no deals, agreements, or contracts of any sort without approval of the appropriate KDARC personnel. This includes but is not limited to blood pacts, sexual favors, IOUs, rain checks on meals, and everything in between. ROSE will be able to put you in contact with our contract expert, and I advise you err on the side of contacting them too much rather than not enough.

"You are clearly a woman of strong convictions, which I admire, but please understand me when I say that, again: anything they do, you will be accountable for. You are now, whether you like it or not, a part of a wider world. Questions, Miss Greysmoke? Another aggressive assertion of blind faith?"

Holy shit she does not mince words.

"…They mentioned, uh … something else? Something I did, I guess?" Mabel was trying her best to remain calm and collected, but the raccoon's brusque manner was keeping her on the back foot.

"Right." Jane's avatar leaned close to Mabel, her eyes blurring momentarily before nodding. "I see. You're leaking."

"Uh! I mean…" She blushed, pulling the blanket closer. "I was sort of in the middle of—"

The raccoon rolled her eyes. "Magic. Anything else is your discretion and not my division's. You're absolutely dripping with candescal resonance right now. You've never shown an inclination before, I'm assuming? I have neither the time nor the patience to go into detail, which I will leave to your liaison in your first meeting. I cannot say for certain why you are suddenly displaying the telltale signs, but a quick theory might be the stress of the situation coupled with your natural instincts popped your cherry. Congrats on the spellgasm, Miss Greysmoke, was it good for you? Again, wider world, all that. I would elaborate, but incidents at RIV have an uncanny knack for interrupting me at the worst possible fucking time." Her tone wasn't cruel, but rather … bored about something that was the opposite of mundane.

For the catamount, at least.

"W-wha … magic? Candescal resonance? Uh … whuh … I'm magic?" Mabel sputtered as what was initially supposed to be a thought, spilled from her muzzle unbidden, "Holy shit … Really?"

"Yes, really. Everyone has that potential, yours is just … louder, at the moment. If you so desire, it is something you can learn to harness, or we can seal that particular crack in the wall. Again, your liaison will discuss all of that with you." The raccoon turned; the prosthetic limb the lioness was too stunned to notice flicked a finger between Marlon and Penelope. "Now, Heckle? Jeckle? My office, tomorrow. Debrief and considerations on procedural updates."

"Yes, ma'am," the silent observers responded in unison.

"Oh, gods…" The cougar felt her sister's paw on her shoulder. The flood of new information was simply more than she had bargained for with her new living arrangements. "Relly … I … this…"

[It's a lot, I know, but I'm here, and we'll figure it out, just like always.]

Her words were joined by the feeling of those gentle arms wrapping around her from behind, more comforting than any blanket.

"Keep up, Miss Greysmoke, and keep that appointment with your liaison. Perhaps if you cannot wait, your new roommate can fill in the blanks. Now if you'll excuse me—"

And, as soon as she had arrived, the raccoon was gone.

"Huh. She cursed a lot less than I thought she was going to." Nellie looked bemused, giving a shrug. "Must be *really* tired."

"I'm sure that's waiting for us tomorrow," the rat snorted.

"Yeah, prolly. Ah well. Now she's said her piece though, time for us to head out." She snapped her skeletal digits, and the energy that had been tingling on the edges of Mabel's perception faded.

The djinn audibly sighed in relief.

The stoat also sighed, but decidedly not in relief. "Dreading asking this, because it could keep us here longer but: Anything else you need to know, Miss Greysmoke?"

"Uh … does everyone in KDARC have a badass prosthetic?" The cougar offered before considering the sensitivity of the subject.

[Mabel!] Amarelys nearly gasped at the faux pas. [What the hell?]

"What? That's two outta three I've met! I'm just asking!"

"Yeah, you oughta see Marlon's dick. It's got settings." Penelope wiggled her eyebrows suggestively, and drew her tongue across her teeth.

"It does not, don't tell lies to the new blood, Nellie." Marlon sighed and rolled his eyes. "I have a perfectly normal dick, for the record, and it does *just fine* without extra settings."

The exchange instantly got a snort out of the lioness. "Heh … Fair enough. Will either of you be my liaison with KDARC, or am I going to be making more friends…?"

"Dunno, that's up to the boss. Marlon and I are field agents; there's specialists for keeping an eye on newbies that don't know a cantrip from a canticle. The fact we were in-house tonight was just a coincidence, lucky us," the mustelid said with a cluck of her tongue. "Any other concerns, before I finally get my pepperoni?"

"No. I'll have Relly reach out if I think of any." Mabel touched a finger to her forehead and flicked it toward the pair. "Enjoy your slice."

"Don't make me regret this. Either of you." Penelope tried to keep up the tough girl act, but she looked far less surly than she had earlier.

"Thank you, Nellie, Marlon … No hard feelings about before, right?" Mabel offered a meekly apologetic smile. "I promise I'm not *always* this much trouble."

"Just sometimes huh?" The rat smirked.

"Uh-huh, *sure*. Don't call me Nellie," the field agent replied as she turned on her heel, hiding a smile of her own as she pulled her hood back up. "And don't mention it." As she stepped through the door, she disappeared from sight instantly, as if the door led to another place that was not the living room.

Marlon dipped his head and gave the catamount a wink before turning to follow his partner. "See you around, Miss Mabel, Eneera. You two keep your noses clean, hmm?"

Without another sound the pair was gone, and left the three occupants of the apartment unattended, for better or worse.

"*…I'm not going to say 'Well…', but I am thinking 'Well…' really fuckin' hard.*"

[Mm. *Thank you for resisting the urge to spout tired dialogue.*]

"*Seriously though, this has to be some kind of record for most unbelievable comic book-level bullshit to happen all at once to a single person not named Parker.*"

[Considering some of those comics are based on actual events? Trans-dimensional-time-displaced-variant invasions are not unheard of, but it's at least in the top ten, sweetie.]

"*Yeah well I—*" Before she could continue to witty repartee, Mabel felt the gentle warmth of the vaporous tendril wrapping around her paw, reminding her that someone else also had had a very exciting day.

"Thank you again for protecting me…" Eneera looked up to her with those glowing orbs, "I … I did not mean to cause you grief."

"You don't need to thank me for doing the right thing, Eneera." Her thumb carefully stroked the ephemeral being and felt them pressing back against her palm.

"You have no reason to trust a djinn, and you know me not. Why risk your safety for me?" The eye lights looked up to her, their voice curious, but still tinged with the hesitation of the perennially punished.

"Maybe I just have a soft spot for misunderstood beings." She touched a paw to where she imagined their cheek would be. It was surprisingly difficult to comfort a cloud of smoke, as it turned out, but she managed as best she could. "Maybe I know you better than you think."

"I am twice now in your debt, kind magician … What is your name?" Their voice remained low, and steadier now, panic fading into relief.

"Mabel works." She shrugged. "Miss Greysmoke, if you're feeling nasty." She realized that the reference would be lost on the ancient Sumerian djinn but just let it go.

"I … It is a beautiful name … 'Mabel the Oracle'…" Eneera intoned softly.

"You know, if I was an Oracle? I might have known to wear more than socks to this little soiree," she snorted, and patted the djinn gently. "Look, hun, a lot of things have changed since you've been gone, no need to be formal with me. *That said,* I am going to warn you: if you refer to me as '*both man and woman*' again? We're gonna *rumble.* I'm a woman, period, and that distinction is *important* to me."

Even without a face, the spirit looked to be noting her words. "Rumble … this means to fight, yes?" They asked the question in English in a sort of halting cadence, their voice still like sand sliding over glass.

She nodded, raising a brow at the sudden change in dialect, though it was hardly the most unbelievable thing that day. "You got it, Dusty! You can speak English now, huh?"

"You gave me the words when you reciprocated my touch. It is much easier to speak thusly, I hope?"

"It is certainly easier for everyone that doesn't speak conversational Sumerian." Mabel's flippancy was an effort to try and mitigate the enormity of how her day was going — and, just maybe, comfort the myth that was huddled at her feet.

"All do not speak the language of Sumer?" The shape tilted their 'head.' "Where *are* we? What is the year? When I was … *punished,* Ur-Nurgal had ascended to his sire Gilgamesh's throne. Does their light still shine?" They leaned closer, clearly startled by the knowledge that the common tongue had changed.

There was a lot of confusion going around to be certain, but the lioness tried to take it in stride. "You are about a mile underground in the outskirts of Austin, in the United States wh— *Wait.* Gilgamesh, as in '*The Epic of*'? *That* Gilgamesh?"

"Then the songs are still sung! Yes, his child is now the king of whom I speak." Their voice sounded hopeful at her recognition.

Mabel was starting to dread what she thought might be coming.

"I know we thought they were old, but I … Relly, closest approximation of a date that will be relevant for them?"

[The timing is speculative, but that would be during the latter part of the Kingdom of Uruk. So nearly five thousand years ago, give or take a century.]

"FIVE THOUSAND? Oh my gods…" The cougar took pride in not just blurting it out, but her surprised look didn't help disguise that *something* was wrong. This being was older than anything she had ever known outside of a textbook and spent all that time … *trapped.*

"H-how do I tell them? How do you **possibly** tell someone that their world is a distant memory…?"

[I don't think there is a good way to share that kind of news, my girl.]

"Gods damnit … the hits just keep coming."

"What do the spirits say?" There was a sweet naivete in their words. It wounded the catamount deeply as she tried to figure out how to tell her new friend such an awful revelation.

"Spirits?" she rubbed the bridge of her muzzle as she caught back up. "Oh Eneera, I'm *really* not an Oracle — I *am* conversing with a friend in my thoughts, but that's … something else. *Listen,* sweetie we need to tal—"

"Then you *are* a magician! It should have been plain to me when you challenged that witch! Oh, how you *glowed!* I am blessed many times over to be released by someone so kind, beautiful, and powerful…" They began to ramble and Mabel squeezed the spot where their shoulder might be to try and get their attention.

"Oh, hun, *please* listen to me, I'm *not*—" she pleaded, but they pressed on, and the excitement in the djinn's voice threatened to break her heart.

"Mother will be so proud of me! A magician choosing to free me will *surely* redeem my transgressions in their eyes—"

The cougar's expression was full of sadness, but she interrupted their excitement to bring them back to the moment, keeping her paw on them. "Eneera. *Please … just stop…*"

Those golden orbs looked up to her expectantly. "Yes, Mabel? I am sorry, I was excited! What do you need to tell me?"

"Oh honey … I'm … I'm so, so sorry, but … it's been almost five thousand years since you were put in the stone." She put her paws on her lips, wishing she could put the words back in. It was too late, though, and what was said needed to be said.

Knowing that didn't make her feel any better when they finally managed a response, their whole form sagging right in front of her eyes.

"Five … *millennia?*" Their voice echoed like a stone dropped in an empty well. Mabel tried to keep her paw on them, but they pulled away, confusion plain to see, even without distinguishable facial features. "*But* … it was not … It was only *supposed* to be a short while…"

"Gods bless, Eneera … I … I'm not a magician, or anything like that, but I'll help you however I can! You're safe here, and I *swear, I—*" The lioness felt like she was the most vile creature on the planet. As she reached out to try and comfort the djinn, they did not pull away but did not look up at her.

They simply sat there in desolate silence.

Eventually, they migrated to the living room, but the mood, unsurprisingly, remained subdued. Eneera sat on the couch (as much as they could be considered to be *sitting* without truly defined limbs), staring ahead at the middle distance. Mabel had positioned herself on the far side, following the steam as it rose from her cup of tea.

"Are you sure you wouldn't like a cup? It's chai…" The small talk was all she could manage, and she hoped they might open up.

"No. Thank you," came the djinn's curt reply.

There was quiet again, and the catamount had to say *something*. She couldn't just leave it like this. She *had* to fix this.

The silence was too much.

They're my responsibility. C'mon, Mabel, you need to comfort them!

"I know this is a lot to process, Eneera—"

Before she could finish, they began to speak again, their voice nearly a growl, as an emotion besides melancholy bubbled up.

"How? How could you *possibly* know? You are a *mortal.* Your lives are as fleeting as they are violent. How could you understand what it is like to know … *nothing?* No *one.* To suddenly be released into a world that is no longer one you existed in? To have … *nothing…*" They stared at her now, each word filled with pain and sorrow.

"How could a mortal understand the curse of being imprisoned in walls from which they could not escape, for a *hundred lifetimes?*" They pressed on as they sunk into themself, as if the weight of their misery had grown too much to bear. "Alone … *invisible…*"

Mabel chuckled quietly at the irony of their word choice, as a chain she did not grasp before linked them together so perfectly across thousands of years. Joined now despite never once knowing the same sky before that night.

"*Sounds awfully familiar, huh?*"

[*Mhmm.*]

"You laugh? Why?" They were taken aback by the sound.

"Because I am not the biggest fan of fate as an idea, but … hard to argue this. Eneera; even if I'm no Oracle, I see that clear as day. I'm a mortal who knows all of those things, and I'm learning to move past them. To grow, *despite* all of it. We are a perfect pair because we can understand *each other*."

"…How could that be…?"

"Come here, darling djinn … I'll tell you a story about a scared boy, and how he escaped his own prison not so very long ago." She sat back on the couch and patted her lap. There was a moment of apprehension from the djinn, as the sentient cloud seemed confused on how to handle her request. "Lay your head in my lap. I don't bite. *No one* is too old to be cuddled, and I have a pair of the nicest thighs modern science can manage, these days!"

Her tea was cold long before she could finish her story, and the late afternoon became the late evening as she finished recounting her tale to the captivated audience. At some point she had traded the cold beverage for a fresh cigar, and the scent of the burning leaf seemed to calm them both after the day's ordeal.

The fragrance from the beginning of the day made itself known once again as Eneera and the stogie mingled and covered them in contentment. As she talked, the djinn was almost perfectly silent, giving her her rapt attention with each twist and turn, their vaporous shape becoming far more distinct. Slowly pointed ears became clear to view, and a muzzle was laid across her legs.

"…And today I woke up, free of that shell for the *very* first time." Mabel left out the *other* happenings of the day. It was her story, after all, and the comedy of errors with Ellen wasn't particularly *relevant* to the narrative, so they were artfully omitted. The lioness paused to take a long draw, and exhaled the smoke upwards, wisps spiraling, wicking her stress away with them.

"So ... you were born in the body of a man, and chose to go through all of that?" Golden orbs stared up at her as she stroked their ears.

"Chose is probably the wrong word..." She tapped her lip with the head of the cigar as she searched for the right one. "I didn't really have another choice."

"You ... *endured* all of that, just for the chance to be happy?"

"Some have endured much worse, for far less. I'm truthfully very lucky, Eneera. How I got here was ... less than ideal, but where I am now? It is *exactly* where I want to be, and if my luck holds out? I'll get to cause some mischief along the way to finding myself."

"But your former life, it is gone?" There was sadness in their voice, seemingly coming to terms with the similarity of their circumstances, at least in one regard. "Does that not make you sad?"

"Not really? Which seems like it should feel worse. It was like I was waiting for my real life to finally start. That life is gone, but nothing of value was lost in the end. I was less than a ghost. Anything I *want* to be from that life? It can be a part of this one, or not. That is my choice to make, now," she stated matter-of-factly as she held their indistinct lobe between her fingertips and rubbed.

"We are not so different." Their translucent paw slipped into hers, fingers twining. "Will I get to choose, like you did?"

"I *promise*. Anything I can do to help? Just ask." They were becoming so comfortable, and that brought her heart a warmth of matronly joy.

"So, you have made a new home, here, in this den of villainy?" The question was so formal Mabel had to laugh. She absently petted the head in her lap, her cigar clamped between her lips, glowing much like Eneera's gaze in the low light.

"Den of villainy! That is a colorful way of putting it! But, yes, they've offered to help me, just like I offered you." She let out of a puff of aromatic vapor, smirking around her stogie.

"But ... if they are villains, do they not only help themselves?"

"Villainy is a perspective, much like heroism is. Let me ask you something, Eneera: If you saw someone steal a loaf of bread from a wealthy baker, but give it to a starving vagabond, are they a villain?" The question was clearly loaded, but it would serve as a litmus test for the djinn's intentions.

"No. The hungry must be fed." They sounded confused at how absurd the scenario was.

"I agree, but they stole the bread! What about the livelihood of the baker? The rule of law is plain to see." The cat *hated* playing the devil's advocate, but she needed to know their feelings. "The thief is a *villain*."

"The baker could make more, perhaps? If they are wealthy, that should be shared! No one should choose material things over the life of another ... Why would anyone be so cruel? It makes no sense..." They sat up, their head tilted in confusion. "Being kind could see you labeled a criminal?"

"It can, and it has before for many. I agree, Eneera — it seems silly doesn't it? That's how it is. The Korps, as I know it, are trying to change that, and other things that should not be. Sometimes it's a loaf of bread, sometimes it's something more ... *drastic*. We want to help those in need, to allow everyone to live as themselves." As she spoke, the puma surprised herself with her passion on the subject of villainy, tapping a finger gently on the end of their muzzle. "And sometimes that entails taking on the mantle of 'villain,' to show there is another way."

She was almost shocked by how easily the recruitment pitch fell from her lips.

[*A villain through and through these days, huh, Mabes?*]

"Mmm ... *seems as though I've been thoroughly corrupted.*"

"Is this what you meant when you said ... make mischief?" Eneera slowly laid back down and nuzzled against her tummy.

"Mhmm." Their warmth brought her comfort she did not know she needed, and she dropped the nearly spent stub into the ashtray to burn itself out. "The ones in charge want things to stay the same. I, and the villains like me, don't. Frustrating them, *deceiving* them, *revealing* how foolish they truly are? With the mockery comes the truth, and each time, they lose a bit more of their power. Then the ones like us? We take it back."

"...I think I would like to help cause that mischief, too." Their vaporous tail swayed into existence and draped lazily across their legs.

"I'm so happy to hear that, Neera..." The lioness began to purr, the day ending so far from where she thought it would but not upset by it — far from it.

Magic lessons? Helping a new friend? A good cigar and a cuddle on the couch? If she didn't know any better, she would think she was still in the tank at EE, dreaming her little dreams.

"Neera..." They repeated the nickname, as they closed their eyes, the lights dimming as they appeared to drift off to sleep. "Thank you ... Mabel."

"Of course, hun ... Dream sweetly."

The darkness did not seem so cruel now, but one thought coalesced in Neera's mind before slumber took them away.

Mother ... Was this what you wanted for me? Please ... don't let me hurt her too...

"A djinn? **That** was what was in that absurd bauble! Oh, thrice curse this obstinate cat's twisting path! Are we sure **she** is not aware of this?"

"We cannot be certain, but we have done all we can do, my dear sibling, to obfuscate the view. All there is to do now is watch and wait."

"I tire of being patient. There is something to be said for direct intervention! Would it be so bad if we just ... **took** what is rightfully ours?"

"You would disobey the laws of the Court? No, dear sibling. You are many things, but you are not so foolish! Come, it shall not be long, now. This new wrinkle may be **just** the fire we needed lit!"

"I do enjoy dancing in the light of a blaze ... The beauty of a flickering flame so ephemeral and yet..."

"Forever."

Chapter 18

Criminal World

"I deserve this."
The walls are so close.
There is no light.
There is no sensation.
"I deserve this."
There are no friendly voices. There is only consciousness.
Only these walls and endless, lonely existence.
"I deserve this."
How long has it been? A moment? A year? A hundred?
A life in darkness, stretching out forever.
There was no speaking. Only the thought.
"I deserve this."
It echoed as a hollow mantra.
But then … there is warmth.
There is hope, if for a moment.
Succor to the sundered spirit.
Then the light.

Mabel awoke slowly from the dream, but it was somehow more intense than a dream; it felt like reliving a *memory*.

The air never moved, surrounded by the still and stale atmosphere. The haunting sound of silence had been ringing so hard she felt it in her jaw. There were no voices, just the single thought. The despair was so tangible her heart still ached in her chest, and then it melted away. The light felt so familiar and comforting. Even as the vision faded, she struggled to remember it at all, flitting away as so much smoke.

The lioness pushed her mane aside as she blindly grabbed for her visor, but her paw found something else first: the choker.

It looked the same as it had the moment it fell into her grasp from the upended little velvet pouch, save for one perfect imperfection. As her thumb pad rubbed at the obsidian medallion, she felt a hairline crack, clean through the center. It was no longer *warm*. She smiled at what that meant; some would say the choker was ruined, but she knew better.

Had it really only been a month since Rose — *Relly* — gave it to her? Had it really been such a short time since the awful night where everything changed?

It felt like a lifetime had passed since, but nothing could have prepared her for what was to come soon after, what sorrow and what absolute *euphoria*. After all that, the previous twenty-four hours had been *especially* intense — but that was, admittedly, an understatement, in the same magnitude as saying the ocean was a bit damp.

She ran down the list mentally as she put her feet on the plush carpet.

She had woken up in her body for the first time in thirty-eight years, and would continue to do so, which filled her with a joy she had never known. *That was very good! Would do again!*

She *came* in front of one of her heroes, in what had to be the most mortifying moment in her existence up to that point. *That one wasn't great; wouldn't recommend it unless everyone involved was on board.*

She'd had an incredible moment of clarity, discovering more about herself and who she wanted to be. *That was excellent! Couldn't say enough good things about it!*

She'd learned that *apparently* she had some magical potential. *That's big news; pretty stoked about it, truthfully.*

...*Oh, right, and there's a djinn asleep on the couch.*

It had been a rich, full day, to be sure. If this was the cost of living a life worth living, then she would gladly pay it. She clipped the jewelry into place and slipped her visor on next, the comforting pink hue followed by a greeting from her favorite dragoness.

[Good morning, Mabes! Did you sleep all right?]

"Mm. I think so. I definitely had some weird dreams, but I can't really recall what about? Huh. But I feel pretty good, otherwise!" She rolled her shoulders with a soft grunt before standing and stretched up onto her tiptoes. Her fingertips tried to brush the ceiling, and the pose elicited a satisfying pop from her back.

"Mmm ... Is Eneera still asleep?"

[They have been awake for nearly an hour. I offered them tea, which they politely declined, and explained they would like to center themself before you woke.] Relly's tone wasn't openly adverse, but the way the dragoness said *"center"* felt off.

The catamount shook her head as she meandered to the bathroom, intending to splash some water on her face and brush her teeth. Along the way, she continued the conversation in her thoughts. *"You're biting your tongue, Relly. Talk to me, please?"*

[*Mabes, I have been around for too long and seen too much, been betrayed too often, to trust without a backup plan, and a backup plan for that. However, I have also been around for too long and seen too much to be overtly hostile to someone who may have been wrongly imprisoned. Korps bases, as you might have guessed, are not inherently keen on uninvited guests as a rule, magical or otherwise, but given the exceptional circumstances, we have little choice but to do the right thing and hope that it is the* **correct** *thing.*]

"So, you're still on edge about them?"

[*I am. I manage the safety of thousands of Korps agents, civilians, and personnel, both on this base and others. Usually, I get the chance to vet people before they enter our base, but in this case … well, it seems it was out of anyone's hands, our mysterious new friend included. You say you know them, somehow? How?*]

Mabel spat out her toothpaste and rinsed her mouth, letting out a quiet, minty-fresh huff of resignation.

"Okay so, it is going to sound a little **far-fetched**, *but given everything that's happened in the last 24 hours? It's* **really** *not, I realize."* The lioness sighed, and rubbed the back of her head before speaking out loud once again. "When I was in the tank, I *dreamed* about them … about *being* them … and I experienced the most awful moment of their entire life — at least, that was how it felt. Even this morning there were echoes of terrible isolation and loneliness. It felt too *real* to be a trick, Relly. Like, we help people, right? That's our whole deal?"

[Of course, dear. If I did not believe you were most likely to be correct, we would not allow them to stay without a more thorough, **immediate** vetting process.]

"I appreciate the caution, but I *know*, in my heart of hearts, I'm right about this."

[Mabel, you are so kind … I hope for the sake of your tender heart you are correct. As always, I trust you, and you have my support.]

Amarelys's lips brushed the catamount's cheek from thousands of kilometers away. [My *favorite* troublemaker.]

The cat hung the towel back up and blew a kiss at the mirror. "Thank you, my favorite big sister! I *also* appreciate how protective you are of your little sister's soft emotional underbelly." She brought her paws up to squeeze her breasts gently, and bit back a little moan. "I have *so* many soft parts these days, *y'know?*"

[Get **out,** you smarmy little shit! I'm your *only big sister!* I started the coffee, there's sourdough for toast, and some more of that cheese you like in the fridge. Eat something, because I have a feeling today is not going to be any less exciting — oh! And don't forget, sleepover with the girls tonight, okay?]

"I'm looking forward to it! You're an absolute angel, did you know that? Love you, sister dearest!" She cackled as she nearly skipped towards the closet.

[Love you too.]

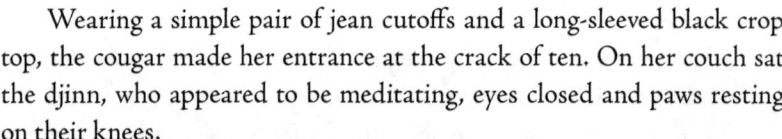

Wearing a simple pair of jean cutoffs and a long-sleeved black crop top, the cougar made her entrance at the crack of ten. On her couch sat the djinn, who appeared to be meditating, eyes closed and paws resting on their knees.

Oh hey! Knees! Kneat!

"Good morning, Neera! I hope you slept okay?" She gave a little wave as she made her way past and into the kitchen.

"Oh yes indeed, Mabel! I slept as the dead and am thankful for it!" They opened an eye and smiled brightly as the catamount walked by, keeping their gaze on her.

Mabel chuckled softly, smirking, as she grabbed the bread from the cabinet.

"Well, a good night's sleep seems to have done your body good, seeing how you have one now, my dear." She dropped a couple slices in the toaster before pouring herself a cup of coffee.

"I do feel whole in a way I have not for many years."

"Feeling hole is a favorite pastime down here, as I understand it! You're gonna fit in just fine!"

"I ... I am not sure I understand?" She could hear the confused blinking in their voice.

"I was just being flippant, sweetie, don't worry," the puma replied with a nose buried in the fridge for the cream and that *delightful* cheese.

"Oh, Relly, can we add some pickles to the grocery list? I would kill for nice spicy dills."

[*Back left, behind the jam. No trans girl on base has less than two jars in their fridge at any time.*]

"Ooo! Hooray for luxury space communism!"

"I'm glad you slept well! I do want to have a little talk about the arrangement here, though; is that all right?" Her ear flicked as she poured her cream — almost half the cup, by measure.

"I agree, our arrangement must be discussed, as well as how I will repay your kindness." Eneera had turned to look into the kitchen, chin resting on their arm, a shy smile on their still mostly hazy features.

Well, will you look at that! Emotive features! Sorta!

"Eneera, you don't have to repay, reimburse, or any other obligatory reward for what I did! It was the right thing to do, so I did it. Completely non-transactional situation." The cougar stirred her coffee, the spoon ringing cheerfully on the ceramic. "Please don't sweat it, okay?"

The djinn nodded, though their gaze cast downwards. "If you insist ... I only wish to reciprocate your act of warmth — both freeing me, and defending me."

Mabel shook her head slowly as she dropped the spoon in the sink, and took a long sip of the mundanely magical tincture. "Well, I appreciate the chivalrous gentleman routine ... gentleperson? I'm sure you'll do what you can to help me in kind, I just don't want you to feel like you *must*." Her brow furrowed as she realized she hadn't even asked her new roommate how they prefer to be addressed. "Neera, I'm sorry; what are your pronouns, dear?" She leaned on the counter — cleavage inadvertently on full display — and unabashedly enjoyed her cup of faintly coffee-flavored cream.

Mmm ... Is there cinnamon in this? Lovely.

Eneera tilted their head as they considered the question.

"I don't know that mortals have a term, as djinn are entirely beyond the realm of your concept of gender. We exist as a wholly other set of societal roles—"

"Nonbinary then? They/them good, or do you prefer something else? We have *neo* pronouns now! You could be a *xe/xem!*" She raised her mug towards the elemental, with a tilt of her head.

They blinked a few times before answering, newly evolved features looking bemused, "They/them is fine ... Are you *always* like this, Mabel?"

"Not *always*, dear ... but we're still pre-first cup, you know." She sipped with a coy half-grin and a shrug.

[You get used to it.] Relly added over the apartment speakers.

The toaster added its own opinion as well, with a spring-loaded pop.

Eneera nodded slowly before responding. "Understood. Thank you, Mabel. I appreciate you considering my comfort. It is ... new to me." They looked down; though still hard to read, they clearly seemed sad, large ears splaying shyly to the sides in a decidedly feline way.

"I suspected as much." The cougar draped a thin disk of the soft cheese over each slice, snagging a smaller piece to pop in her muzzle.

"Relly, is this cheese goat's milk or something? It's so tangy, and like ... vaguely sweet? I've never had anything like it before." She purred as the dairy treat nearly melted on her tongue.

[*I doubt you would have had anything like it before. Korps secret recipe, don'tcha know? But just let out a howl when you need some, dear — always more where that came from!*]

The puma wrinkled her nose while considering the wording of the dragoness's response — licking the residue from one fingertip — before returning the food to its proper places. She called over her shoulder as she did. "Neera, did you want anything to eat? Coffee or tea, maybe? I'm not sure what ethereal beings from another plane of existence eat, if I'm honest."

"No, thank you. Miss Amarelys already graciously offered this morning. I do not need physical sustenance, but I did sometimes indulge. Do mortals still consume honeyed cake?" the djinn replied as their eyes followed her back into the room. "I was quite fond of that confection!"

Their face lighting up at the prospect of sticky sweetness warmed Mabel better than the coffee. "Mm, as we advanced as a people, so did our desserts, dear ... but I believe that classic is still around. If you would like anything, please tell Amarelys or myself, okay?"

"Oh! I would not want to impose..."

Mabel plopped on the couch next to them. "I promise it is no trouble at all! Right, Relly?" she crooned as she leaned her head back towards the ceiling, addressing the all-seeing unseen dragoness.

[None whatsoever! You're our guest, and we want you to feel welcome.]

"See? Of *course* it's not an imposition; not in the slightest! Hey, Relly, could you maybe put something quiet on for us, please? Maybe a little Lindsey?" the catamount mumbled around a mouthful of soft, creamy goodness and crunchy, warm toast, briefly lost in the *flavor*.

Throughout the apartment the sound of piano and beautiful violin began to flow, and Eneera sat up, ears flicking.

"You have a retinue of musicians on call …? Or is this more magic, Mabel?" They began to sway, golden eyes closing, and a smile came over their face. "It … I have never heard anything like it before. It is…" They put a paw to their lips as they considered. "*Enchanting.*"

It was another smile added to the list of those she would have loved to see over and over again.

"Oh, no, it's a recording sweetie, I just asked Relly to … stream … *right*. Before Babylon." She resisted the urge to slap her forehead for her forgetful nature. "Neera, we are going to have to catch you up, but first things first, we're going to discuss our … *deal*, here." She sat her mug and plate down as she made a small circle with her finger.

They nodded, and turned, tucking their legs under them to kneel on the couch.

"Yes, please!" They grasped her paws in their own, now fully shaped, solid, and gentle. "The covenant is made anew, and I will serve you faithfully if you allow it, as thanks for saving me. Twice over now, in fact. I could not ask for a more worthy mortal savior."

As she stared into their countenance, the cougar noticed their eyes. They were no longer glowing orbs, but yellow feline eyes, strikingly bright; like moonlit amber skies over a land from the far-flung past. She mimicked their pose, slipping her knees under her to fully face them.

"Neera, I … I don't know that I'm comfortable with our relationship being … *that*." She sighed and rubbed her thumbs over the back of their paws. "Have you ever been able to decide for yourself? Been *allowed* to choose your *own* life?"

There was no hesitation in their response. "I am a capricious wind, borne on zephyrs! Some of us choose to exist on this plane of the candesca, that of those with whom we make our pacts. For myself, and those like me, there is no greater aspiration than to be a part of the tale of another, lift them up and ease their burdens!"

"Well, we at least agree that raising up our loved ones is a noble goal." Mabel rolled over their words with care, wanting to understand completely. "Now, when you say *'of the candesca,'* how do you mean...?" She asked the question with an arch of a single brow.

"In exchange for my boon—" they began to explain, and her big sister piped up in her mind.

*[Ahh. Here we are, then: **The Deal**.]*

"Let them finish, before you attempt to banish them to Director Wick's tender mercies."

"The mortal to whom I am joined shares her own candesca with me! It is no small blessing, so the gifts I provide shall be great in turn!"

"A ... *pact*. I..." Mabel suddenly looked incredibly concerned and let go of their paws. "What would that entail? What is the *candesca* I would share, exactly?" Her tail swayed slowly behind her; the term felt familiar to her in some way, but she had the sense to clarify.

[Mm ... The very surly director, who did me a favor by showing up last night on such short notice, warned us about this, specifically. Remember?]

"I just want to hear them out! No harm in that, right?"

[...Yeah, until the other shoe drops.]

"They're not wearing shoes, and neither am I, Relly dear! It'll be fine!"

The dragoness let out a low sigh and listened along.

"You are a powerful magician, Mabel, and yet you do not know of candesca?" Eneera seemed taken aback, as if she had declared ignorance of the sky, or fire.

"All right, let me clear this up right now, as last night was ... *a lot*. I am *not* a *magician*." The puma stated it plainly, dismissing the notion with a gesture of her paws, and doing her best not to let herself be disappointed by the truth as it stood — though her voice dropping did little to hide it. "I am not a *witch*, a *warlock*, or *any* other configuration of magic user. I'm not. Or well, I never have been before. I ... I don't know the first thing about any of this!"

"But ... your energy flared bright as the noonday sun! Even today you ... you are *radiant*." Their sand-soft voice became even quieter as they spoke.

*"Are they blushing? Am **I** blushing?"*

[Yes. Do be mindful of flattery.]

"I just acted on instinct, Eneera! I have wielded no sort of magic outside of a video game or a set of dice ... ever! I have lived a thoroughly and *painfully* plain existence until the whole, uh ... supervillainy ... *thing*." Mabel continued to speak with her paws, as was her habit, gesticulating to the immediate space about them. "The only magical energy I'm aware of comes in little blue bottles, or from tapping land cards, for fuck's sake! I just didn't want you to be *taken away...*" She trailed off, as her lack of knowledge made her feel much more vulnerable and unprepared than she liked.

The references were clearly lost on the supernatural being, but they still seemed touched by her motives. "There is more than meets the eye to even the most mundane! You are a beacon in darkness ... I ... could see your light in my prison and feel your warmth!"

If she wasn't already blushing, Mabel would have been incandescent from that praise. She couldn't even muster the will to correct them of their delusions. "Okay. Fine. Let's just take a step back here." She pulled her hair into a rough ponytail as she considered how she fell into this thoroughly fantastical situation. It really was becoming an *alarmingly* regular ordeal.

"Let's say I *do* have candesca, and I *could* share that with you. How would that even work?"

"We would seal our covenant by ceremonial exchange and be bonded. Our spirits would intertwine, and I would be able to manifest fully on this plane, and you would be granted boons equivalent to the gift you will have given me ... if you choose to do so." They sounded excited at first, pebbles skipping across a rock face, before remembering her trepidation and lowering their tone. "You do not have to if you would rather not, and I will not resent the choice. I just ... wish to help."

The things Mabel had shoved to the back of her mind — the fear of closeness, the suggestion of intimacy with another — came rushing forward. Bonded? *Intertwined?* What if she just fucked it up, same as ever? What if this *was* a trick? She had to assume KDARC's arcana was formidable, given the demo she'd participated in the previous night; was the djinn tricky enough to fool it?

*Just **Breathe**. Ask. Learn. Make your choice, after you have the chance to consider.*

"Y-you keep saying 'boons' ... What would that be? Like wishes from a genie? Do we get a song and dance number first?" The catamount stumbled as she tried to recover from the intrusive thoughts, attempting to use humor to dispel her internal struggle. "Never had a friend offer something like this before, y'know?"

[Mabel, dearest sister, you know how everyone keeps on assuming you're trouble?]

"...Yes?"

[It's because you look like the kinda girl who might make a half-considered decision, best of intentions of course, but still…]

"This is me being cautious! This is my responsibility to sort out. If I don't know the details I can't make a decision, right?" she smiled as she felt the paw on her shoulder.

"I am not a 'genie' no … I give no wishes nor perform … musical dances? I am a being of air. My element allows me some control over shaping of that self-same aspect, though the nature of that changes from being to being. One might be able to use the wind to fill a sail, another to provide succor to the wounded. Your spirit would dictate the exact details, and with energy as abundant as yours, I suspect it would be a wonder to behold." There was almost a reverence in their words as they spoke.

"So, the gift itself is … *to be determined*? It's a lot of faith to ask for, Neera. As sweet as you are, we *just* met. What if my only power is *breaking wind*? Which, for the record, I'm no slouch at. How long is this bond for, exactly?"

"Until it is severed. By my expulsion from this world, or … your demise."

The music kept playing in the background, but the djinn's words hung heavy in the air as the catamount nibbled her lip.

"I … I am reticent, Miss, to speak of the end before there is even a beginning, or before I have spoken of the fullness of who I am."

Mabel's heart thudded in her chest. Here it was, the reveal that she abjectly feared: they *had* deceived her, somehow. They took their eyes off of her for the first time since she sat on the couch, and their tail began to sway slowly as her own, like mirrored metronomes.

"My mother was Djinni, yes, but my father was Ifreeti. My realm is air, but not air alone."

"Wind and Fire…" she whispered as the smoke filtered away. The paws smoldering. The terror of the visions. Every last one came rushing back in perfect clarity. She was there in the field once more, watching the horror unfold.

"Maybe I **am** an oracle … Shit."

Amarelys remained silent, but the catamount could feel her close by.

"You were punished for who you were…" She covered her lips with her paws as she intoned. "For an accident, when you tried to help…"

"I *deserved* the punishment I was given…" The words could not be random happenstance. The dream echoed chillingly through her mind as the being stared down at their hands, their muzzle twisted in distress.

"I ruined the life of my mortal partner, as the touch of my father, what mother and I had desperately tried to hide away, made itself known to *all*."

"But … that's not *fair!* You *couldn't* have known what would happen!" Any apprehensions she had were forgotten for the moment, as the injustice of the past seized her heart. Instantly, the lioness only wanted to take that ache away from them, because she *knew* why they struggled. She had felt the pain of that moment in her chest like a dagger, and it bit deep.

"You have a kind heart, Mabel, but it matters not. I knew of my lineage, even if my intent was good. The law of the elements is older than any being, and my punishment was meted. I am the child of air and fire, and could not control my father's blood … I was a calamity made manifest for those I held close … I *deserved* that punishment for the destruction that was rent."

"Stop *saying* that," Mabel snapped as she grabbed their paws in her own, bringing them to her chest. "You were born as who you *are*; you couldn't choose that, and to be punished for that is the same as scolding the stars for shining, or the world for turning. I was there, Eneera, I felt that pain seize you, and all you wanted to do was make it right again." The cougar's passion flared, recognizing Eneera's pain from her *own* past as well as theirs. The shared visions were revealed as faint senses from a kindred spirit, across the ages, perceived and understood completely. "We can only choose who we *will* be, who we *need* to be."

This pairing, the meeting of the two, could not have been coincidental. Whether the machinations of the fates — or just two broken souls, trying to mend, who needed one another — here they sat across from each other. *Echoes.*

There was the sound of a choked sob.

Amarelys broke the silence in her mind.

[*You have to do what you think is right, Mabes. I will love you and protect you just as fiercely as I always have.*]

"I love you too. They … they need us, Relly." Mabel was resolute in her choice. "We have to mend this."

[*I know. Keep making me proud, my beautiful girl.*]

"Eneera, child of Wind and Fire. I will accept your offer, under one condition." The puma held up a single finger, and her voice left no room for dispute.

"I would deny you nothing, Mabel."

"We are *partners* in this endeavor. We do this as *equals*, or not at all."

"But ... what if I hurt you?" The quiet rumble of concern from the djinn did not dissuade the cougar in the slightest.

"Then we will learn from that and heal *together*. You said you wanted to make mischief with me, right?"

"The mischief of which you spoke? Of helping those in need, and vexing those that deserve it! Yes, I do. *Very* much." They nodded, sniffling as a smile lit up their features once again,

"Then let's all three of us make some sweet mischief *together*, Neera. Deal?"

"*Deal.*"

"Relly? Anything to add?"

[Our little gang continues to grow, hmm? Welcome to the family, Dusty!] The dragoness answered with a laugh. [The world won't know what hit it!]

"Excellent," Mabel said with a satisfied smile stretching from ear to ear. This, however, was followed by a tilt of her head, as she realized she was still lacking some rather important information regarding the whole deal.

"So, uh ... what happens now?"

It took the pair only a moment to push the couch and coffee table aside, and gave themselves ample room on the floor. Although they had no "Ash of the Ancient Palm" or "Breath of the Western Wind" available, as the djinn had requested, they were confident the ritual counted intent, and not ceremonial accoutrements. Darkness, the air in the room, and a simple candle — these would be sufficient.

Eneera also assured her that this would not result in the same sort of "*startling commencement*" as their entrance. The puma was less than convinced, and Amarelys made certain her own reservations were noted, but she mentally steeled herself for whatever cacophony might manifest. The cougar removed her RCGs, after once again reassuring her sister that all would be well, and set them on the table. They were in full view of the event, so the dragoness could nonetheless observe and record the goings-on.

"*This is going to be fine, Relly! It's the right choice, I know it.*"

[And I will be here no matter what happens.]

"*KDARC on standby?*"

[Just in case!]

While this was between Eneera and herself, she didn't want anything or anyone else to be affected by her choice. She was nervous, but unafraid. She could swear the air in the room had changed; it felt *heavier*, somehow, almost like it had while Marlon and Penelope had caged them the night before. It was not unlike entering a chamber under positive pressure, and it enclosed them on all sides. It was not *uncomfortable*, but it was impossible to ignore.

Magic is real and is a part of me.

They sat across from each other, flame casting a flickering glow and each took a calming breath, seeking their center.

"Imitate the placement of my paws and answer my questions with the honest heart I know you to have, Mabel." They opened their full-moon gaze, and were met with the dewy verdancy of the lioness's own. "When this is done, we will be united by thought, by spirit and by deed; may our covenant never be divided." The smooth sand of their voice rolled over and through her.

"We will remain separate, but linked intrinsically, correct? You won't be able to manipulate my thoughts or control me in any way." Everything needed to be clear as crystal before Mabel would move ahead. Reckless or not, she was not keen on *losing* herself after finally *finding* herself.

"I could not, but I never would even if I could. Our link will bring us close, but you will never surrender your independence. Thoughts and feelings might be shared but will always be our own."

"I didn't think so, but I needed to be certain, Neera."

"You will share with me what you wish for me to know, and you will even decide my shape on the mortal plane, so I might serve you better—"

She cleared her throat and narrowed her eyes ever so slightly. "Neera ... partners. Remember?"

They looked down with a bashful smile as they corrected themself. "Very well. Then I shall determine my *own* shape. In exchange for your knowledge and a tether to the mortal realm, I will grant my gift to you, however it might reveal itself. You will, in turn, provide me a gift in an hour of great need, befitting your circumstance."

"So, there is more to this than remaining on this plane?" The lioness raised an eyebrow, not discouraged, but certainly curious about the fine print.

"Yes and no. As with all magic, the boon will be equivalent to what you give in turn. I cannot dictate what you can do with my gift, and so you cannot dictate what I do with your own." The djinn responded, gaze levelled squarely upon the feline before them.

"So, this is all about trust, in the end?"

"It is a decision of faith, and I will not think less of you, if this is too much."

"...*This is where recklessness comes into play, huh?*"

[*Blind faith is only reckless if you have doubt.*] Relly stated clearly, but the words were not an attempt to dissuade. [*Do you trust them?*]

Mabel closed her eyes and found her answer with the certainty born of her honest heart.

"Thank you." The puma took one more deep breath, and then a nod of affirmation. "I have made my choice then. I'm ready when you are, Eneera."

The djinn twined their left paw in the lioness's and placed the other on her chest, the rhythm of her life beating against their fingertips. Mabel did as she was bidden, squeezing their fingers with her own; she nearly jumped, feeling almost a static shock when her paw touched their chest. A circuit was a circuit, it seemed, whether electrical or ... otherwise.

There was no heartbeat to speak of in their breast, but there was a pulsing warmth that radiated into her digits. She could have sworn she felt the rumble of a purr, and near-instantly, any lingering fear melted away as their energy twined with her own.

Sumerian words were softly sung, the meanings coming to her again. As they quietly prayed, their eyes began to glow brightly once more.

"The elements four, the sky and the world below. Wind and Fire, we beseech your blessing now." Eneera continued, the words reverberating through her entire body. "Mabel Greymoke, mortal of flesh and bone, she who liberates djinn from stone, and shields from pain, would you share with me your link between heaven and earth?" Their voice was booming but somehow gentle.

"I would," she replied, and realized she had replied in the ancient tongue without thinking. The still air began to stir, and she was thankful she had pulled her hair back. It swirled about the two, rushing around and between, as the djinn resumed speaking over the nascent gale.

"The elements four, the sky and the world below. Wind and Fire, we beseech your blessing now. My boon will be yours, and with this bond, forever shall we be linked. Do you wish my boon to be given?"

"I do." Again, her response came without reticence. The candle — which until that moment she had nearly forgotten — flared briefly, the flames licking their arms. It left no burns, and she felt no pain.

"The elements four, the sky and the world below. Wind and Fire, we beseech your blessing now. May my magic strengthen you, and may your magic sustain me."

"May my magic sustain you, and may your magic strengthen me."

The wind buffeted them, and the flame seemed to burst into rage — an inferno, even — but the spiraling air contained it. The burning light grew smaller and smaller until it was a mere spark floating between the two.

"*Sing with me, Mabel!*"

She raised her voice in song with the djinn, the roaring whipping about and pulling the words from her lips. **"The elements four, the sky and the world below. Wind and Fire, we beseech your blessing now!"**

"The elements four, the sky and the world below. Wind and Fire, we beseech your blessing now!"

"The elements four, the sky and the world below. Wind and Fire, we beseech your blessing now—"

There was a flash that illuminated their eyes, both shining bright as the crescent in the midnight sky. Warm air flooded her lungs, and she felt as if she had swallowed the hot ash of a raging wildfire. It filled her. It changed her. There was no pain, only the blazing fervor in her chest.

Ennera and Mabel let out a gasp at the same moment. As suddenly as it began, all light in the room was snuffed out.

The apartment was silent, save for the panting breath of the two physical inhabitants. Slowly, Amarelys raised the lights and revealed the results of the ritual.

[*Mabes!* Are you all right?]

The cougar exhaled a huge cloud of rich smoke without a cigar in sight, remembering to breathe again, before turning her attention to Eneera.

"I think so? Neera, are yooouuuuu…?" Mabel asked, trailing off as her eyes grew wide.

Where once sat the vaguely feline-shaped wisp, now sat a tall and lanky caracal — almost seven feet of lean, naked felid, crossed legs hiding whatever might be there between. Long tufted ears flicked on either side of slicked-back jet black hair, and their eyes were closed tight. Their fur was the warm brown of the desert sand; markings in black gave natural liner to their eyes and between their light-colored brows, crowned by two *very* familiar onyx-colored horns. Mabel's darker paw stood out plainly on their bare chest. Behind them, a tail batted languidly to and fro.

"Yes, Mabel?" They answered in perfect English, with the barest hint of their former accent, but the voice was still shifting sand.

"Uhh..." Mabel scrabbled to the low table and slipped on her visor.

"...*Relly? Why do they look like they're related to you?*"

There was an uncharacteristically long pause before the dragoness managed a response. [*Do you think? I ... I don't see it. They are **quite** handsome, but...*]

"I'm dead-ass here, sis. They have your jawline, and some distinctly draconic features, like, I dunno ... **the horns?**" Mabel's paw gestured towards her own forehead.

[*...I mean, maybe a little? Lots of people have horns! I'm getting more striking cheek bones, and sparkling eyes pop-star twink vibes, than like ... **familial** feels.*] She offered in the least convincing tone the lioness had ever heard her utter.

"Relly. They're a fuckin' dracaracal, come on now."

[*Mabel. That's not a thing.*]

"Actually, Mabel is not incorrect, Amarelys! I quite like that term actually."

The puma's ear flicked as Eneera spoke to her without uttering a word, interjecting themselves seamlessly into the discussion between the siblings.

*Ah. There's the link. Guess I'm a relay between Neera and Relly then ... huh. I feel like I should be more worried about **another** voice in my head.*

"I chose to mimic some of the appearance of an immortal I greatly admired! You mentioned them by name, actually! The hero Gilgamesh!"

[*...Ah.*]

"This is not a problem, I hope?"

"Not at all! I mean ... devastatingly handsome draconic felines wander into my life all the time! Ha ha!" Mabel remembered to blink, as the nervous giggle turned from thought into actual tittering. "Eheh ... Relly?"

[*Well, who am I to deny someone their ideal form?*]

The dragoness was clearly trying to control the tenor of her response, which Mabel made a mental note to dig into later. [*I'm just happy you're happy, Dusty!*]

The speakers began to play music again, a cheeky plucky bass line.

"Oh! This is David Bowie, yes? Excellent choice, Amarelys." The djinn's words had the flavor of a question, but signaled also that they *knew* they were right, proud of their newly gained knowledge. "Do you think so as well, Mabel?"

"Ah, yeah … uh. Mm. Love me some Bowie," was all Mabel could manage as there was a knock at the door, a very distinctively heavy double-thud. She knew who it was even without the notification in her RCGs; the wolf's presence was, as ever, unmistakable.

The fluttering in the cougar's chest was also becoming a pretty reliable indicator of Volta being nearby.

"*Hey nerd, let us in,*" came the warm, faintly Texan drawl of a certain red wolf. "*We brought pizza and HeroClash! You know, the* **good** *version! Hope you're ready to get your shit wrecked!*"

"Oh, *fuck-me-gently,* they're already here! Gods damnit, I didn't realize how late it got!" The afternoon's activity had thoroughly distracted the catamount's deficiently limited attention. "*Fuckfuckshitfuckballsasscock!*"

Mabel's mind raced as she tried to figure out how she could explain this situation, but before she could consider what she could *possibly* say, she rose to her feet. "*Be right there!* Neera, maybe go ahead and get dressed? I wonder what boon—" The room suddenly rushed past her, and then she was there, at the entryway, the faint scent of rich tobacco and cinnamon spice hanging about her shoulders. "—I … I got." She stumbled across the words as she opened the door, her body reforming from swirling vapor, in full view of the trio waiting to be invited in. She had barely even thought about it; she just was suddenly *there* in a literal puff of smoke.

"…Th-that … that was magic. I just did **Magic**! I did magic like I was breathing!"

[*Mystery solved. I think.*]

"Holy shit!"

[*Holy shit, indeed!*]

The three girls at the door looked very much how Mabel had only a few seconds prior, as they peered into the doorway at their freshly-decanted friend emerging from a purple-grey cloud of vapor — and a stranger who could only be described as a dashingly futch idol-type that stepped from the cover of a queer romantacy novel about fucking a dragon-hybrid with a mysterious past. There was somehow even *more* going on than there was fifteen seconds previously, and the feline tried to roll with it. Hazy wisps drifted from the catamount's paw as she grinned nervously, trying to shake the clinging cloud on her fingertips. Eneera stood behind her, unashamed of their bare form on display, for all to see, smiling brightly at the guests.

"*Oh, oh, oh, what a criminal world,*" Bowie continued to croon, oblivious to the moment.

"Uh … Heya gang … h-how's tricks?" The cougar tried the best casual nonchalance she could muster as she leaned in the doorframe. The smile pasted on her features did nothing to disarm the sudden reveal of her newly-acquired skills, frantically trying to come to terms with the fact that she just became incorporeal.

Ellen and Vixie's eyes flicked about the room, both pairs wide open as their mouths were.

Volta took a moment to inspect the scene. She looked to Mabel, and then to the mysterious, naked feline, and then back to the cougar. She turned her muzzle back and forth several more times before touching a fingertip to her lips, clearly discerning how best to address this new *development.*

"*What a criminal girl…*"

"Surprise?" the catamount chuckled nervously, as she scrunched her shoulders up in a shrug — paws up in the universally accepted gesture of "I have not a *single* clue."

"Mabel? Uh … What the *fuck* did I just *see?*"

CHAPTER 19

RECKLESS GOOD INTENTIONS

The room fell completely quiet as the music came to an abrupt halt. The silence was finally broken by the cougar struggling to play it cool, while simultaneously trying to answer a very complicated question.

"Ha! Well, that's a *long* story, but maybe you should come inside, and we can have a little dialogue!" She made a sweeping gesture as she moved aside, the smell of smoke still hanging in the air. "Goodness, does that pizza smell *delicious!* Is that the little cup pepperonis? Mmm!"

"Mabel, it's been less than twenty-four hours, and not only are you exhibiting some *very* new skills, but did you know that there is a literally horny cat in your apartment, wearing nothing but a smile?" The wolf clucked her tongue. "I'm trying to be patient here — really, I am — but please just stop trying to be cute and tell me what happened."

Mabel's eyes darted around the room, looking for anything that could help deflect the wrath of the wolf. The twins would be no help; they just stood there (one holding the pizza), both wide-eyed at the cat who just reformed from the swirl of smoke. "Volta, sweetie, it's not a big deal! These things happen, right? Just super things, *amiright?* Who *hasn't* had a magical being just pop up in their life and offer them a sweetheart of a deal?" The puma licked her suddenly dry lips, glancing to Ellen for some support, but none was coming from the wide-eyed demivixen. "*Right?* Ha ha…?"

The Hero formerly known as Lawful Neutral slowly shook her head, cringing.

That was it for the Amazon's patience. "Magic beings? *Deals?* Y'all have exactly ten seconds t'clue me in about this whole situation, Kittycat, before I get *mean.*" She crossed her arms under her prodigious chest, her lip curling slightly.

"I do understand the confusion, but I am *supposed* to be here! My name is Eneera, and it is my pleasure to finally meet you—"

The djinn's interjection was quickly interrupted by the surly supervillain. "Not talking to you right now, magical mystery cat! Mabel, you're down to *eight* seconds..." She had managed to shove the Texan twang back down, but the growl in her voice was still very much present. Her brilliant magenta irises bored holes into the lioness, who all but squirmed under her gaze; she ducked inside the door, followed by the spectacularly silent sisters Foxpaw.

"Calm down, cowgirl! I promise it's no big thing, just a little magic is all! Let's just sit down, have some pizza and I'll explain *everything*..." The cat tried to play it off jokingly, but the bravado was so obviously false that Volta cut through it with two words.

"Seven seconds." The wolf tapped her boot in the staccato of impatience.

"This is, err, a little more *complicated* than seven seconds can cover, V..." The catamount sputtered as she backed up, bumping into the corner of the kitchen counter.

She swallowed hard, as her brain struggled to function under the towering lupine. The larger woman was impossible to ignore and completely filled her vision.

*I forgot how large she ... and her breath ... and she's so ... hnng. **Big** a-a- and ... gods be good...*

It was an impossible task to focus when Volta was so close, and the cougar cursed her very gay brain as she stumbled back into a stool. Her paws gripped the seat for balance as she realized something: all the feelings she had pushed down deep? They were, in fact, not very deep at all, and were demanding acknowledgement right that second.

"Six," the wolf rumbled softly.

The lioness's tail stood straight out, and a shiver ran down her spine. She grabbed for the traitorous appendage, lest it be used against her.

[*Uh, Mabes? She seems pretty upset. Maybe it's time to talk **real** fast?*] Relly suggested and sounded genuinely concerned for her little sister's safety at this point.

"Five."

"*Fuck!* Okay! I came home and enjoyed a cigar after our big brunch — yes, I smoke cigars now, that's not the important part — but it did inadvertently release a djinn, Neera here, from their prison of five thousand years, give or take, that happened to be my choker. *Who knew*, right? KDARC busted in, I may have been a little uh ... *reluctant* to follow orders and had a chit-chat with the head of that department, probably not a *great* way to start things — oh! ha ha *ha* I just realized I'm a magical girl now! Also new! — so *anyway* they made 'em my responsibility, along with a mandatory trip to the, uh, Korps School for Magic Queers at some point in the near future. We made nice — Neera and I, I mean — and I had some *real* vivid not-quite-dreams. Then I had some excellent toasted cheese and coffee for breakfast, and then my new roommate and I sang a song, and *now I can turn into smoke, apparently*, and then you showed up. And here we are!" There were hardly any spaces between the words, and her New York shined through for all to hear as she panted, holding her arms out as if to say *"TA-DAAAAAA!"*

Mabel's gaze nervously bounced between the three girls. She received no applause for the performance, but at least Ellen had started *blinking*, finally.

"That's like applauding with your eyelids, right?"

[*Sure, sweetie, whatever you say.*]

The lupine super soldier's eyes narrowed as a brow slowly rose. "So ... you're some kind of cigar-chomping Sailor Moon now? And you're dating hotter Jareth?" She had a paw on her hip and an inquisitive tilt to her head. *"Is that all?"*

"I mean ... I guess I can see the Bowie-esque brow and cheek ... bones..." The catamount quailed under the big bad wolf's glare. "Right, not the point! *I think that's everything? More or less?*"

The barest flicker of a smile across the wolf's muzzle, and instantly the tension oozed out of the cougar's shoulders, spine and well ... *everything*, down to her very clenched ass-cheeks.

Oh thank the gods ... Not gonna have to see Nurse O today!.

"Just to clarify, we are not in any sort of sexual relationship, Miss Volta; Mabel and I are partners, but..." The djinn held up a finger as they attempted to helpfully clarify any misunderstandings.

The puma shook her head, hiding her smile behind a paw, still trying to appear contrite under that slowly less-withering lupine gaze.

Volta pinched the bridge of her muzzle and let out a sigh. "Eneera, right? There is no way you're going to survive living with Mabes if you can't take a joke, so I recommend you focus on filling in those gaps. Speaking of gaps, can you go and put some damn pants on? You're just ... on display, and if that's your thing, cool, but it is *distracting*."

From behind the Great Wall of Wolf, a small voice piped up.

"I don't m-mind..."

And just like that they all began to laugh. All except for the supernatural caracal, who remained confused and even blushed a little, but still managed to smile.

"She stares at me like a parched man eyes an oasis. Why?" They thought as they glanced at their partner with a hint of fear in their golden eyes,

"Oh, sweetie … You have no idea." It was refreshing for Mabel that for once she was not the least informed in the room, and she was going to savor it.

[*Because you look tasty, my dear djinn, and she has a very specific craving.*]

"What do you … oh. Oh? Like with…" The realization finally dawned on their muzzle. They inherited a lot of knowledge from their new partner, and had not sorted through it all, but apparently had just stumbled across the multiple definitions for the verb *to eat.*

[*Yes, my refreshing little breeze, exactly like that.*]

The djinn proved to be a quick study, for being five millennia out of the game. They ducked out to find something to hide their blushing — at the very least — and ideally the rest of their mortal vessel as well.

Mabel snorted and shook her head. She simply couldn't imagine the sweet little vixen like that.

She was too innocent.

"So pretty kitty is magic now! How *psyched* are you?" Volta gave Mabel a friendly shot in the arm, smiling openly now. "Pretty fuckin' hype, I bet!"

"*So* fuckin' hyped!" Mabel rubbed at the spot where she was tagged, but her grin was nearly ear-to-ear once she was certain the wolf wasn't going to tear into her.

The red wolf nodded appreciatively, "B and E is a lot less tricky when you can skip the breaking half!"

The lioness was nearly bouncing, as the possibilities began to flood her imagination.

"Definitely a lot of potential there, Mabel. Any other tricks in the bag yet?" Ellen asked, finally proving she still knew how to speak.

"Not really? Let's see if I can do it again while holding something!" The cougar relieved the vixen of the pizza before she could protest and closed her eyes.

"Wait, Ma—!" Ellen lunged forward with outstretched arms, but the feline and the pie were already gone.

The catamount thought of the space beside the coffee table on the other side of the room, and when she opened her eyes, she was there —

richly scented haze trailing off her as she set the pie down, completely undamaged. It wasn't instantaneous, and it was only ten feet, but it was *fast*, and completely silent. "Ha! *Holy shit*, it worked!"

"It did!" Ellen let out a sigh of relief and a little laugh as she opened the box, taking the first slice, muttering around the mouthful, "And you didn't even singe the pizza!"

It felt unbelievable every time, like a dream from which Mabel couldn't wake, no matter *how* improbable. Having Lawful Neutral there, with her, and looking even the slightest bit *impressed*? That was a high that she could ride into the New Year.

Eneera emerged from the bedroom just in time to see their partner's vaporous shape slip through the air, solidifying in one swift motion. They were wearing a green midriff-baring top and a pair of black leggings that actually had enough stretch to *sort of* fit them, despite being a foot and change taller than the puma.

"Mabel! You are picking up on this so quickly! I *knew* that you were a magician!" They beamed, clapping their hands together in front of them. "Wonderful!"

"Neera, it's just one little trick…" Mabel smiled inwardly, the blush overtaking her cheeks from the compliments, as she shifted the table towards its former spot on the rug. She was all smiles, as visions of supervillain costumes and corresponding shenanigans danced through her head. *But **maybe** I can do more … Maybe … this is it…*

"Yep — if the villainy thing doesn't work out you can join up with K-PARCEL and deliver at the speed of smell! But seriously, I'd *love* to help you practice sometime if you want, Kittycat!" Volta actually sounded a little excited too and laughed as she scooped up Vixie and crossed the room. The wolf gave her a sneaky tickle, making Vixie squeal before tossing her gently onto the couch and shoving it back into position with a single hip check. "Would be nice to have a new sparring partner! I've heard all of the funny noises this one makes." She flicked her head towards the other vulpine in the room, who sniffed, ignoring the baiting commentary in favor of her slice.

The butterflies that seemed to be taking residence in Mabel's stomach — at least any time Volta was around — were stirred into a *frenzy* at the thought of learning more about her powers with the wolf's help.

"So, we brought the pizza and games. D'you have any drinks to help you choke down this incoming humiliating defeat?"

That honey-sweet voice brought the puma out of her reverie, and she tried to hide her blush behind another wall of bravado. "You talk a big game, V, but I've been playing HeroClash since before you were old enough to reach the controls on an arcade cabinet!" Mabel shot back as she flopped onto the couch next to Vixie with two slices and handed one over, sneaking in a quick nuzzle to her hero, who gave a sweet peck on the cheek in return. "Bring it on!"

[There's Cherry Vanilla Dr. Pepper in the fridge, Volta! Help yourself!] Relly was ever the attentive host, and Volta appreciated it, rolling her eyes at the cougar's "trash talk" as she wandered into the kitchen.

"Lessee … OJ … Purple Stuff … Ah ha! Dr. P!" Volta yanked the twenty-four rack from the bottom shelf, and spotted the "excellent cheese" that the lioness had specifically mentioned, giving it a quick sniff. "Isn't this *my* blend, ROSE?"

[Mmhm! Can confirm that it was specially ordered by my sister, for her charge!]

"She has excellent taste!"

The red wolf had to bite her lip so she wouldn't laugh out loud at the thought of Mabel's face as she enjoyed her product, smacking her lips after licking her fingers. *Oh, that is going to be a **fun** topic to bring up, but first, I'm gonna show this cat what a proper tail-whoopin' is.*

"Mabes, should I grab you some ice?"

"Nah. The soda's already cold, isn't it?" the cougar questioned, sounding confused.

"I meant for the bruises from the boot prints I'm about to leave in your ass!" Volta smirked as she cracked open a can and tucked the rest under her arm.

"Yeah, yeah, whatever you got is no match for my Magella mix up game! Come forth for your slice of humble pie!"

"Pft! Don't bring that weak bunny magic in here! Gonna show you what wolves do to easy prey!"

Vixie looked *very* normal all of a sudden.

Eneera watched with quiet amusement, asking Amarelys any questions they had regarding this game, but knew better than to get involved in the brewing storm that rumbled across the living room.

All four girls were — whoever could have guessed? — more than a little competitive, but it turned out that Vixie was actually the one to beat; her command of Lawful Neutral should have been illegal. Volta's True North II looked to be a distant second, as the demivixen pulled off another wall bounce into LN's Speedster super, shaving off the last 20% of Arthur's HP in one brutally efficient combo.

Mabel cackled as the LN victory screen played yet again: the vixen kneeling next to the defeated Canadian Super, making some quippy comment about it being "funny that someone named True North got knocked out by a Southpaw."

The red wolf looked aghast at the screen, before whipping around to stare down at the bottom-heavy menace next to her. "Where the hell did *that* come from, Fangirl? I've *never* seen anyone confirm off of that!"

"M-maybe you should p-practice blocking more, M-Miss," Vixie offered with her usual innocent tone and smile.

Volta let out a barking laugh, taking the loss in stride as she surrendered the controller over to the cougar. She stood, letting out a cute little growl as she stretched. "Fair enough! Guess I know where the bar is set, then, hmm?

Mabel nudged her gently as she sunk into the indentation the lupine's titanic rear had left in the couch. "Where was that Master level game *you* were talkin', V? That looked bronze to meeeee!"

The lupine rolled her eyes as she leaned on the back of the couch between the ever-sweet vixen and the mouthy puma. "Oh, fuck you, Kittycat, you'll see! The real LN can't pull off the moves Vixie does! No offense, Standup."

Ellen was all smiles; even if she had gone 0-for-2 in the mirror match, she was beaming with pride at the clinic her sister was holding. "None taken! If anything, I'm taking notes; she makes me look good!"

Ha … Actual Redline and LN banter … Eee! Internally, the catamount was torn between excitement at the experience and the dread of looking foolish in front of these people that she admired, even if it was only a game. She tried to put on a brave face, snarking to keep cool in spite of her tempestuous feelings, but the cat felt the panic creeping up — especially as she tried to consider how she was going to deal with that cross-up the vixen pulled seemingly out of *nowhere* on Volta's technically impressive True North. *"She is either the sweetest creature on this Earth, or an absolute master of mind games."*

[Two things can be true, sweetheart. Villains come in all shapes!]

"I'm still just *shocked* you main TN2! I didn't take you for the type! He's a classic, sure, but like … he's a *cape!* I just assumed you'd play another bad girl, like Maxima or, like, *yourself?* I mean I would play as *myself* if I had the option, I'm just saying."

The wolf muttered under her breath. "Some of us aren't quite so self-centered … Besides, I've been a fan of his since I was a pup." The lioness smiled at the blush her voice couldn't hide.

"So, like … since last year, then?"

"Up yours!" The lupine growled playfully as she nudged the lioness with an elbow.

"Oooo! Threatening me with a good time, then?" Mabel bit her tongue, ear flicking, as she remembered the girl she was shit-talking could easily put her through a wall if she wasn't careful.

But the puma was not used as an impromptu remodeling method; in fact, the wolf only snorted. "Quit stalling and pick the silly rabbit already. I can't *wait* to watch LN put the boots to her."

"W-well … uhm, I actually p-prefer the barefoot c-costume, Miss V-Volta," Vixie gently corrected, as she looked up to the catamount with the most innocent smile. "G-good luck, M-Miss Mabel!"

"Thanks, sweetie! No going easy on me, all right?" The cougar ruffled the demivixen's ears affectionately, idly shifting through palette swaps before landing on the eighth alternate. Part of her chafed, because it was not the historically accurate choice (which she *always* made), but something about the violet outfit with the pink trim just *called* to her.

"I really do adore that color…"

[You'd look good in it, sweetheart. Purple brings out your eyes.]

Mabel blushed at the compliment for her ears alone before pressing A and selecting the factually incorrect appearance. The two squared off in the opening animation, and the fight was on. As they traded blows, the tempo was precise and measured, at first; but, while the puma was better about blocking than Volta, that was hardly saying much.

Her initial plan was playing it safe, trying to feel out any weakness. Observing the previous matches did inform how she approached, knowing too well that rushing in was only going to put her in a tight spot from which not even the magical Magella could escape. But every carefully planned forward motion found not a single hole in the armor that was the demivixen's defense. Every angle of assault was denied, and after a particularly punishing follow-up to a somersault, Mabel was drawing blanks.

"*I keep getting stuffed, and I can't confirm a godsdamn thing! Fuck **me**!*"

Mabel's dwindling life bar and the ticking timer did the same thing it always did to her: she got antsy, and that made her *sloppy.*

Vixie was leaning forward, the tip of her tongue poking out as she focused on the screen. She was reading every intention of the cougar so clearly she might as well have been Relly, every input matched, until Mabel committed on what she thought was a sure thing. Luke's LN never knew how to deal with her favorite combo — a forward feint that stopped being a punch midway through, and turned into a brutal series of grabs, followed by a throw into several magical traps that she had discreetly laid out seemingly at random, letting her juggle her opponent down through the last few inches of their vitality — and she was willing to bet that Vixie would fall for the same trick.

However, her plan was frustrated. It simply did not work on Ellen's number one fan. In the blink of an eye, Lawful Neutral spun on her heel, letting loose a two-syllable pun that lifted Magella, stopping all that momentum the cougar had hoped to exert. The lapine magic user didn't touch the ground for the rest of the round.

"Oh! Would you look at *that!* Looking *awful* bronze yourself, Kittycat," Volta teased in a sing-song voice. "Should have waited your tuuuuurn!"

"Yeah, yeah … I got greedy. I've just never had that fail with my buddy who mains LN! Live and learn, right?"

"*Shit. That was frame perfect. I stopped trying to play LN because I could never get the timing right on that parry!*"

[*Vixie is nothing if not **incredibly** patient, dear. You could take a lesson from that.*]

"*Yeah … maybe.*"

The second round started with the catamount sticking to the fundamentals, and matching Vixie almost blow-for-blow, remembering to wait her turn; she even managed to eke out the tiniest lead in health, but it wouldn't last.

The wolf played her ace in the hole; pulled her creamy caper; activated her lactic acid trap; even *whey'laid* the unsuspecting Mabel, one might say, and the catamount would grouse about it into perpetuity.

"Oh, yeah, so I spotted that cheese in the fridge! Y'know, I'm a big fan, too." Volta's eyes locked on the screen as she leaned down between the two currently battling, but her smile grew by the second. The predatory grin caused collateral damage as Vixie caught a glimpse and whimpered, dropping her first combo of the night.

"Yeah, isn't it great? That flavor is so delicate and unique, mm. I think I'll celebrate this win with some; if you ask nicely, I'll even share!" The cougar snickered as the rabbit teleported above the on-screen vixen and stomped downwards into a bounce juggle capped with an air throw.

The wolf stopped behind the cougar on the couch, leaning close to whisper softly, the sound sending a thrill down and back up Mabel's spine. "No need to *share*. I do good work, huh?" She licked her lips as her muzzle slipped into the corner of the lioness's vision.

"Haha, yeah! Wait, what?" Mabel's eyes begin to dart between the screen and the wolf. "You do *what* now…?"

"Oh yeah! My milk is really rich — gives it that smooth, tangy flavor. I'm Korps Farms' best heifer this side of the Canadian border!" The wolf's tone suggested she was clearly enjoying herself, as Mabel turned with deliberate slowness to stare up at Volta, the game forgotten completely. (Not that it would have mattered, as the vixen was delighting in in the come-from-behind victory.)

"…V-V-Volta … *cheese?*" Her left eye twitched just enough to be noticed, as the sound of Magella being pummeled didn't even process for the feline. In the back of her mind, she heard a certain dragoness snort trying to stifle herself.

"J'ACCUSE!"

"Guess you couldn't pull a win out of that hat, huh, doc?"

"Whoo! *Winner!* Suck on *that*, kittycat!" Volta howled with laughter as she squeezed the dazed puma's shoulders.

Volta. Milk.

"I … uh … huh…" The cat downed the rest of her can of soda in a futile attempt to moisten her suddenly incredibly-dry muzzle. "G-good game, Vixiedoo." She gave a shaky grin, doing her best to play it off, reaching down and gently rubbing the demivixen's pointed ear. The big toothy smile beaming up at her in response helped provide succor for her smashed ego.

"I think I need a breath of bad air. Neera, tag in! Maybe Ellen can beat someone who's never played a video game before?" The puma shook her head, chuckling as she resigned herself to the fact this would *never* be going away.

"So how long were you working on that one hmm?"

[*Awww, Mabes, don't be mad; the cheese really **was** a coincidence at first! I just kept it around because you enjoy it! Honest!*] Relly teased with her good-natured tone.

"A likely story! *Dastardly creature!*" Mabel turned her nose up with a sniff. Her reddening ears pinned back as she turned up the pout up to eleven. "I'll be back in a bit, y'all."

The cougar grabbed a cigar and the necessary accessories as she slipped away in a fog of her own thoughts, hoping instead to surround herself in the kind of fog that might help her unwind. She needed it, after the reveal that had been sprung on her.

She slid open the balcony door and shook her head, allowing a small smile at the sounds of trash-talking before closing it, and distinctly heard Eneera trying to get in on the action.

"I am confused. I thought you were twin siblings? And yet Ellen moves as one four decades elder."

"I'm the *younger* twin!"

"Ah! A lack of experience surely explains the discrepancy—"

"She doesn't need your help kicking my hiney, okay?"

"There will be an uppance to come, you silver-scaled sneak," the catamount mentally declared with mock indignance. Truthfully, Mabel was not upset, but she was *thoroughly* and *completely* flustered and wasn't ready to let go of her indignance, mock or otherwise. "My own sister! HMPH!"

[*Might I offer something as a poultice for your bruised ego?*] Relly contritely inquired in her sweetest tone.

"...You might."

[*Did you know our very own Volta stars in Milk Maidens 8: Udder Delights? It's a classic in the filles de lait oeuvre, and as a connoisseur of the genre, I think you'll **really** appreciate her performance and ... **production values**.*]

"*...How dare you use my appreciation of fine cinema so brazenly!*" Mabel faltered for a moment as she considered a pair of cute little horns nestled in Volta's auburn locks. "*... Add it to my queue, please? Toward the front?*"

[*Of course, dear, of course! Before or after "Titans with Tobacco"?*]

Mabel's tongue traced over her lip as she couldn't help but think of warm milk, fresh from the tap. "*Before. But ... but do not tell Volta!*"

[*That goes without saying! My lips are sealed, sister dearest. Do you forgive me?*]

"*Mm ... yeah. Can't stay mad at you anyway.*" The lioness couldn't, it was true, but the harmless prank was forcing her to realize that her "*deal with it later*" pile had quickly become precarious in new and exciting ways.

She was an expert at Feelings Jenga. After all, she had years of practice, and decided that since it wasn't going to topple right that second? The leaning tower of messy sentiments was future Mabel's problem.

Present Mabel needed to take stock of the here and now.

Her *busy* morning had melted into a much more relaxed late afternoon, which she appreciated, needing a moment to simply *breathe*. The artificial lighting perfectly imitated the approaching twilight glow, and there was even a faint sound of crickets in the air. She leaned on the railing as she prepared her smoke, the azure butane flame illuminating her features as she toasted and puffed the stick into brilliant, crimson life. A long, cheek-hollowing drag filled her muzzle with rich vapor, and it danced across her tongue. As she closed her eyes she imagined the smoke had filled her from the top of her ears to the tip of her tail — her entire form one with the haze — and as she exhaled, she visualized the stress leaving with it.

She felt physically lighter, and looked down, to see her legs had in fact blurred into a misty form; her torso rested on a hazy cloud.

"*...Huh.*"

Focusing for a moment made her legs become solid once more. Mabel bit her lip and tilted her head, as she pondered. There was no time like the present, after all.

"*Relly, can you make a record for us, please?*"

[*Of course! Would you like me to take video, or just an audio log?*]

"*Uh, transcribe audio for now, please.*" The cougar took another pull and continued.

"*Blessings of the Wind and Fire thus far: Smoke-shifting? Smoke-shaping? Hm ... Anyway, I seem to be able to move quickly in an intangible form, which means I can apparently control my ... density ...?*"

to some degree." She looked at her free paw, and swung it down towards the railing, turning away. She expected a loud clang, but instead, her misty appendage dispersed around the obstacle and reformed.

"Oh, that's handy! Ha!" She wiggled her fingers, gripping the stogie in her muzzle. "Very cool," she muttered around the Maduro. "I didn't even have to concentrate on that..."

[PING]

Her experiment was interrupted by the alert, and it brought her back to reality.

"*A call? From who?*" Basically everyone she knew who would (or *could*) contact her was in the living room — currently locked in a struggle to topple Vixie's streak and win those sweet, sweet bragging rights (and maybe the last slice of pizza, too).

Volta **definitely** *destroyed that pie already.*

[*You have a call from your assigned KDARC Liaison, Agent Alder Irrwisch, they/them.*]

"Uh ... any chance we can push that call back? Given uh—" Mabel grimaced at the prospect of explaining just how many warnings she flat out ignored. "Everything?"

[*Honey, Director Wick explicitly stated you were not to try and reschedule this introductory meeting. You made your choices, and I support them, but you need to be ready to explain yourself.*]

"Ugh ... do you ever get tired of being right?"

[*It can get a little boring, but I'll bear the burden for you, my darling.*]

"...Gee, thanks. Alright, enough stalling. Patch them through."

[*That's my girl.*]

The puma *had* agreed to this but had also sort of hoped she would get the chance to work with Nellie and Marlon again. It was no matter; she plucked the cigar free and stared towards the frame in her RCGs, which instantly filled with the image of a smaller avian with subtle earth tone plumage, and oversized-round spectacles.

"Good evening, Agent Irrwisch! I didn't expect a checkup quite this soon; what can I do for you?"

"Good evening to you too, Miss Greysmoke. The higher-ups asked me to check up on you. I hope you're having a good day so far!"

I mean, it wasn't a **bad** *day ... Just, ahh ...* **eventful***.*

"Oh, absolutely! Just another day in RIV. *Mostly.*" Mabel tried her best to equip a disarming simper.

The hazel grouse sighed, a touch wearily, but not unkindly. "Miss Greysmoke, your aura is *glowing* with untapped energy right now, so much that it's making you look nearly translucent to the mystically attuned. Now then, let's drop the formality: you may call me Alder, and please don't leave out any details as to the *how* of this new development. I want to help make sense of this." They stared over the rim of their large frames, wearing the amber-colored visor much the same as Mabel's other acquaintances in KDARC. "Penelope and Marlon send their regards, by the way."

The lioness took a draw from her stogie, rolling the smoke in her muzzle as she considered. The option of lying was there, of course, but lying to the spooky magical branch of a sprawling supervillain organization seemed ... *unwise*. She *owed* them honesty at the very least.

"I hope they finally got to enjoy their pie! I, uh ... I owe them a lot for this chance. They didn't have to trust me. It certainly would have been a more *intelligent* decision for them not to."

"If the impression you left Nellie and Marl with is any indication, you seem to engender trust in people," Alder offered. "I can tell that you don't make a habit of lying to others. I just need to know what happened today." Their voice was even, calm and soothing. No anger, just patience for the girl thrust into this situation.

So, for the second time that day, she recounted exactly what happened. At normal speed, for a nice change of pace.

Her cigar was nearly spent by the time she had fully explained, and the artificial daylight had progressed into artificial dusk, tiny fiber-optic stars faintly twinkling in the distance. Alder, to their credit, did not interrupt; the avian only sought clarification on a few points, at the end. As she watched the smoke spiral off towards the dome, she nodded, as if to reassure herself that was everything.

"...So now I have the Blessing of the Wind and Fire, and we're trying to figure out what *exactly* that means."

"I should suspect that trial and error might be in order but be careful. Without training, you cannot manage your energy reserves, and that could be ... *troublesome*, to say the least." There was a short pause and the sound of a beak clacking gently together. "So, you have officially bonded with the djinn, and you trust them?"

"I do. Eneera is many things, but they are not duplicitous in the slightest," the feline answered without hesitation. "I trust them implicitly."

"Excellent. We kept an eye out today, as Director Wick and I suspected you *might* roll those dice, and, it seems, your luck holds out. Congratulations."

"...So you knew what would happen then?" The cougar wasn't annoyed per se, but she was a little put out by being so *predictable*.

"Knowing is a certainty. Call it a hunch, Miss Greysmoke. All's well that ends well."

"Mmm ... I won't try and convince you otherwise."

"So..." Impish delight lit up the eyes behind the avian's visor. "*Gilgamesh*, huh? Excellent choice." Alder let out a quiet little chirp, and a laugh.

Why do I feel like there's a joke I'm missing here ...?

"If Gilgamesh of legend looked like a drop-dead-gorgeous androgynous caracal with horns, I suppose so! Not a whole lot of *eyewitness* records from downtown Sumer, but I digress..." She took another short puff and nibbled her lip at the sight of the felid being in her memory, specifically that tail sauntering into her bedroom.

"There is certainly some overlap, given my experiences! Very good! I would very much like to meet you two in person, later next week. For now, we'll continue to monitor the energy fluctuations. I recommend you spend some time in a safe space, figuring out more of what this boon means for you."

"Where would you suggest?" Mabel tapped her ash into the tray beside her.

"Well ... the training grounds in KDARC are beyond you, at present, but the gym facilities have several customizable training chambers. Your friends Agent Volta and Miss Foxpaw would be invaluable with their field experience." The bookish bird, she found out, was practical as they were kindly. "I can tell you're excited about all of this, and I want you to assure you won't be alone on this journey. Relly has cleared a date for us this coming Thursday. I look forward to working together, and be sure to bring Eneera along as well!"

"Absolutely! Best behavior! Villain's honor!" the cougar nodded emphatically. "Thank you for being so understanding, Alder. I was ready to be chewed out for diving headfirst into this."

"Oh, I'm sure you were! This was ... a reckless decision, to be sure, but in the end? I agree that it was the right choice. Just do your best to stay out of trouble until we can properly get together, hm?" The avian teased with a friendly wink. "See you Thursday!"

"See you then, Agent."

[PING]

"I'm starting to see why people keep warning me to behave..."

*[You have a **particular** talent for finding mischief, Mabel Greysmoke. Alder is a kind soul if a bit fast and loose with the rules. They'll be a huge help moving forward.]*

"I got that feeling. *You know, for a cadre of scoundrels, I have yet to meet a deceitful soul here.*"

She plodded slowly back to the railing; it was a lot to take in, all at once. Did she really want all of this? The life of infamy? Nothing ever could be simple again. But it only took a moment of reflection to realize the only possible conclusion.

*Of course I do. I want all of this. The friends, the family, the chance to be **more** ... I want it all.* She smirked as she took another long pull, the warmth from the ember touching her tongue, signaling the last breaths of the flavorsome treat. *It's all mine to take...*

The door slid open behind Mabel. Even though she was still looking out into the starlit night, she knew who it was before they had even said a word.

Ellen joined her at the railing, leaning back against it with her elbows, looking at Mabel with searching, earthy-brown eyes. "Busy couple days, huh?" She smiled as she watched the lioness idly roll the finished cigar in her fingers. "We were hoping we could make this all feel normal, but ... you don't really get to *do* normal anymore." She sounded almost sad for a moment.

"Doesn't seem that way..." Her brow furrowed the tiniest bit as she turned to the vixen, changing the subject. "How long did it take for you to get a handle on your powers? Like, after you discovered them, I mean?"

"So today is ... hmm." She did a little math, counting in the air in front of her. "I'm still learning how to handle them. I'll let you know when I have it figured out; every time I think I've got it, I find a new handle that I haven't even got half a knuckle on yet."

As the cougar exhaled the last cloud of smoke from her spent stick, she watched the cloud rise and had a thought.

What if the smoke was heavy? What if the vapor was dense?

As if obeying her command, it slowly began to sink, rolling across the ground as a warm fog.

"Huh; that's not how *that* works, usually." Ellen raised an eyebrow, "Just figured out something new?"

"Yeah, I think I have." The cougar dropped the last inch of cigar into the ash tray to burn itself out. "Would you and Volta be up for some training after dinner?"

"Sure! What did you have in mind?" The vixen perked up.

"I owe V some Italian."

"And for the training…?"

"Combat exercises," Mabel carefully enunciated with a cocky smirk on her muzzle. She didn't doubt it was growing to be a familiar expression for Ellen.

"I'm willing to bet you've never fought a day in your life, and you want to do combat training, with *Redline*. Say now, do you want to take up mountain climbing too? I hear Everest is a good, safe beginner's climb. They can even airdrop you halfway up, if you want to try it breathless!" She looked incredulous as she reached up to rub her eyes. "Mabe, seriously, though … Volta is a *lot* of lady. Maybe we should take it slow?"

Mabel shook her head as she slipped a paw into Ellen's hand and squeezed gently. "Awww, c'mon Elle! I'm not scared … I'll have you to protect me, *right?*"

Chapter 20

Showing Scars

In the interest of a more enjoyable — or at least less uncomfortable — training experience, the girls decided to hit the gym before they ate. Volta grumbled about the bait-and-switch, but Mabel promised they could do dinner after, and she could have all the garlic bread she wanted. Besides, they had left Vixie and Eneera alone in the apartment, and the catamount was sure they'd be *starving* when they got back.

"Back in the gym together again, huh, Red?" Ellen offered as she stepped through the training room doors.

"That was a *fun* fight!" Volta snorted as she ducked through the reinforced doorway.

"Oh, I remember! That was the fight in the school, right? You decided to try rubberizing yourself, and V ended up knocking you around like a bouncy ball," the puma excitedly recounted. "The footage cutting out was such a bummer!"

"She did a great world's worst piñata impression! I beat the pasta out of you like you were a Tupperware full of Sunday gravy!" the Amazon cackled. "What did that report say? 'I'd only seen that sort of distance before from someone on a tilt-a-whirl!'" She hooted as she rolled her shoulders, swinging her arms back and forth.

"Great. *Great.* Glad you enjoyed that." Ellen's ears splayed out with mild irritation.

"Awww … sad I missed it. Uh. Sorta," the cougar said, looking away with a cough. It *did* seem like the downside of working out with your former nemesis was that they knew the blooper reel by heart. Shaking her head, Mabel straightened out the fingerless gloves Relly had requisitioned with the rest of the temporary workout gear, apologizing that her own locker was not ready just yet.

"Don't worry, I'll have ROSE send you the highlights. Fuck, my jacket smelled like freezer lasagna for *days* after." Volta's laugh trailed off as she continued her stretching routine, leaning against the wall of the training room they had all to themselves. She planted her boot against the wall at a *shockingly* limber height and leaned against her tree limb of a leg. "Dawn got so pissed I let her work get disrespected like that!"

The puma's head tilted as she watched. All pretense of being sly was instantly forgotten before the display of superior flexibility. The wolf smirked knowingly in reply, giving her a cheeky wink before shifting to the other leg. Mabel swallowed hard, and forced a smile, but didn't turn away. "So, you could say you knocked the Stouffer's out of her?"

"Ha! Yeah, I did!" The barking laugh was encouraging but did little to soothe the feline's anxious mind.

"*Ha ha.* I'm half surprised any of that one got published before I ended up defecting," the demivixen snorted derisively, while sitting on the floor and stretching out her limbs. "Bet they didn't have time for the High Tide fight, though."

Mabel's eyes lit up, very nearly twinkling as she whirled back to the vixen, her self-doubt on the back burner at the prospect of a first-hand account of an LN scrap. "There was a High Tide fight I missed!" She plopped down and attempted to mimic the stretches her mentors were doing, having not a clue where to begin otherwise. She quickly realized that her body moved *differently* than it once had. It might have been the excitement of everything, the dunk in the gender fluid, or maybe even something to do with the magic she had released, but she felt better than … well, *ever*. She was lithe and limber in a way she had always dreamed of being, her body moving with a fluid grace that she could never before achieve. Like a cat in more than just *name*. The lioness turned away from that train of thought, lest she began openly weeping in euphoric joy in front of her friends (again). "Did she do that thing where she laughed at all your jokes and cranked your powers up to eleven?"

"More or less!" Ellen leaned back, sticking her chest out as she reached back to stretch her shoulders, and let out a little grunt as she went into the next position. "It's easy to try half a dozen powers, one after another, when your opponent is such an easy laugh."

For the first time in a decade Mabel not only touched her toes, but laid her head on her knee — at least, as well as she could, with her sports bra-encased assets. She played it cool, but internally, she was awash in the happiness that this was her reality now; she just needed to *accept* it. "Does she like, have a thing for you? She did always seem to get real *giggly* around you…"

"She's like that with everyone!" Ellen scoffed, as Volta shot Mabel a look over her shoulder. The fox then slipped into a full split, leaning forward onto her hands and then sliding into standing in a single seamless motion, rolling forward with a somersault, and bouncing on the balls of her feet.

"*Oh* ... Yeah? Th-that's cute! Her laugh *is* kinda infectious, huh?" Mabes looked up at a particularly interesting spot on the ceiling, as her tail stopped its nervous swaying. *All right, then, so that is still on the pile too? Ha, ha, ha ... I'm in* **danger.**

"For someone so well known for thinkin' on her toes, Standup, you sure are slow on the uptake sometimes." Volta rolled her neck, eliciting a loud pop, and a satisfied grunt before she threw a few punches in the air: a snappy left-right, transitioning into a hook. She nodded with satisfaction, before looking back at Mabel and Ellen.

"What can I say? I'm a woman of many talents, Red!" The demivixen winked, having nimbly dodged the point entirely.

Mabel rose to her feet in a *much* less impressive fashion than the former Hero, still drinking in the banter, while trying to keep herself in check.

She was stirred from her reverie by the rumbling velvet of Volta's voice. "When you're all loosened up, Kittycat, why don't we start with you trying out some of your moves? We've got a big open space here, and nice cushioned floors and walls. S'like learning inside a pillow! Gives us a chance to observe your smoke mumbo-jumbo in a few scenarios and see if we can't help you figure out how to use it." The gigantic wolf cracked her knuckles as she motioned to the empty floor.

"Yeah! Time to see your wake-up game!" The vulpine former heroine smiled that winning smile of hers before she continued. "I'm curious to see how you apply that power of yours from raw intuition alone."

The lupine super soldier nodded in agreement. "Yeah, same, actually! You got a smart mouth, let's see if it can do anything besides talk a whole mess o' shit!"

The cat thought she understood the gravity of the situation in which she'd — at her own suggestion — found herself but her anxious mind pressed down even harder on her confidence. Performance anxiety raked down the edges of her bravado.

This was Redline and Lawful Neutral.

She was going to display her "prowess" for *Redline and Lawful Neutral.* They were larger than life, and she was going to try and put on a show.

Whatever that might entail still eluded her, but she nonetheless felt like she was auditioning, somehow — and this was a position for which she was *wholly* underqualified.

"Sure. Sure! I'll just … do the thing. Not a big deal. Fake it 'til you make it, right?" The catamount hopped from foot to foot, nodding, as she tried to convince herself. "Oh, sure, sure. Makes sense…"

[*Deep breath, Mabes, just roll with it. They both know you're new.*] The calm reassurance from her big sister did its best to soothe, as the biofeedback sensation of an unseen paw rubbed her back.

"I don't want to be **new**. I **want** to be useful! They don't need a wet-behind-the-ears—"

[*Mabes.*] Relly's tone became flat, and unamused. [*What did we say?*]

"I know, I know … 'Not a burden.'"

[*Just try your best! This is new for them too.*]

"Okay … I can do that."

The catamount's attention was abruptly brought back to the conversation happening outside of her head, as Volta spoke. "Elle and I aren't trainers, Mabes, but this is old hat for us. If we're moving too quick just say so, okay? I don't want you to get hurt."

"I appreciate that, V, but maybe I'll surprise you!"

"Mm, don't worry about impressing us. We're just testing the waters. You can surprise me by *listening*."

The cougar nodded, closing her eyes and exhaling, as she thought about smoke in the wind. On opening her eyes, she began to disperse — her shape still vaguely there, yet translucent. Her vision was blurred, and she realized that everything was muted, save for her sparring partners. They were clearer, but their voices were muffled, and their movements seemed unnaturally *slow*.

Mabel's whole existence was light as air, and her heart sang. She leapt about on her toes, spinning and joyful. She herself was *not* slow; everything *else* was.

I've sidestepped … I'm there and not! This is **incredible!**

Phasing out of the material plane of existence would have been unsettling for some but having spent so many years as a *figurative* ghost, it didn't bother the cougar quite so much. When she took in another breath, she was standing on solid feet in the center of the room.

The mechanics of it played out in Mabel's mind. To anyone looking on, she would have just blown out a huge cloud of smoke and faded into the purplish-grey vapor. In the span of a few heartbeats — and in complete silence — the cloud spiraled and reshaped into her standard, solid self, three dozen feet away. The only indicator that she had moved was the faint odor of a smoldering cigar and a dash of warm cinnamon.

"Very cool! You closed that gap quicker than in the apartment," the wolf commented, before she turned around and walked towards the wall. "Means you must be able to vary the speed! See? We're already learning!"

A wall panel slid out of the way. On the shelf within the revealed compartment was a massive armament that looked like a cross between a potato cannon and a paintball gun. It would have been gigantic to a person of average size, but in Volta's massive paws, it had the scale of a toy. A hint of pink crackled from her paws, rushing over the launcher's frame in a flash. The smile that blossomed on her face was full of mischievous intent as she turned back to the cat who hadn't stopped grinning since they had arrived.

"So, let's see just *how* quick you can get spooky. The balls are moving at about seventy-five or so…" Without looking, she fired off a shot with a weighty pneumatic whoosh towards Ellen, who deftly caught it with a reflexive reach out.

Unluckily for her, the villainess had dumped a sizable static charge into the ball hopper, which translated to the little fuzz-covered missiles rocking about eight thousand volts, at a hundred and twenty milliamps. It was no different than brushing up against an electric fence; it wouldn't kill anyone, but wouldn't feel wonderful either, unless the recipient of the charge happened to be particularly *into* losing muscle control. There were rumors that the ex-Hero *was*, given how often she tangled with the lupine super soldier. After meeting the pair in person, Mabel was no closer to determining the truth.

The demivixen jumped back and whipped her arm sideways, throwing the ball aside. As she tried to shake the immediate pins and needles out of her limb, she griped at her co-trainer. "ACK! What the *heck*, Volta?"

Volta began to cackle as she chambered the next round of wooly ammunition. "Look, she needs proper motivation! I don't want her to catch, I want her to *fuckin'* dodge!" She swung back to Mabel, her tail wagging with delighted anticipation as she leveled the barrel at the feline.

The cat's eyes were the size of dish plates behind her visor. "*Oh fuck…*"

[*Mabes, I can help! I can estimate the trajectory and display it on the fly!*]

"*Maybe I should try on my own first?*"

[*We're a team! You don't have to do this the hard way, you know? It's okay to use training wheels when you start learning.*]

"I understand, but I need to be able to ride the bike on my own too, **without** you there holding me up! What if ... what if I lose my RCGs, or something?"

[*Mmm ... Suit yourself,*] Relly relented, clearly waiting for the results of the lesson that was about to be taught. [*Good luck, sweetie!*]

"Ah! The dodgeball method," Ellen sniffed, raising an eyebrow to keep a closer eye on the wolf.

The lioness's gaze opened wide in a thousand-yard stare. In the back of her mind, the sound of a rubber kickball echoed through decades past. "*Shit.*"

While Volta was patient with the lioness a *lot* of the time, it seemed this would not be one of those occasions. "Think fast, Kittycat!"

The gun in Volta's hand made a satisfying whomp sound that brought the catamount back to the present, but it was the ball catching her square in the chest like a corporeally manifested exclamation point that really drove home the *physicality* of the endeavor. The thud drove the air from her, and the shock certainly did sell her on the idea that the best defense was simply not to get hit. "O-O-OW! F-FUC-KUH-KUH!" She stuttered as charge ran through her, gritting her teeth, and rubbing the quickly forming bruise.

"Feelin' it now?" The lupine raised a brow, before continuing to squeeze the trigger. "Dance for me, Kittycat!" was followed rhythmic whomp, whomp, whomp as she fired.

Mabel's instincts kicked in at the sound, the second time, and she jumpily sidestepped from the physical plane. The balls passed through her, the charge tickling her vaporous form rather than stinging, thankfully. However, the unexpected change in stimuli caused her to laugh out loud, unprepared for the feeling that fluttered through her. With a sudden shunt back to the mortal world and a solid form, there was no dodging the next shot.

"AIEEEEEEEEHOOOOOOOHOOO, *mama* no!" The tears came instantly as she staggered forward, knees clasped together, tail thrashing behind her. Her eyes rolled back in her head as her legs spasmed out from under her, and she crumpled like a sack of taser-roasted potatoes.

Volta and Ellen both winced at the same time, though whether it was in sympathy for the blow or because she trailed off into sub-auditory whining, grasping her poor, smashed bulge, was up for debate.

"Nice *shootin'*, Tex! I keep telling Nurse O that they really oughta start fitting a steel cap under the hood when they work on those things," Ellen grimaced, her ears pinning back.

"So, uh … really nice job on the middle three … *eesh*." The wolf tried to sound encouraging, and had to bite her lip to not start giggling.

"…New surgery just … dropped … oooogh … haaaaaa…" Mabel forced a laugh as she struggled to breathe again. She hadn't thrown up, which was a win in her book, but the night was young, so that could easily change.

The two veteran supers shook their heads slowly. "Head between your knees, Mabes. Deep breaths," Volta offered, rubbing the back of her neck.

"Yeeeeeah, I think she needs a minute, Red. Can't blast the pasta out of her before she's even had any."

"Maybe, yeah — how y'doing down there? I promise I wasn't aiming for that!"

"I … know. M'fine … It's fine…" Mabel lied as the pain continued to radiate from her core, and up to her clenched jaw. "Just need to not sit still, right? That's the point?"

"No need to play tough, hun. Take a breather. S'fine!"

Mabel knew Volta was trying to be nice, but sympathy was not what she wanted. The cat appeared to dissolve and rolled across the floor as mist before reforming into herself, panting heavily, but steady on her feet. "I said I'm *fine*, V. Really!"

"Relly?"

[Want a hand **now**?]

"…Yes, please."

[Good girl! Let's do this!]

"Ready," the cougar grunted, lifting her visor, and dragged the back of a paw across her eyes to clear the wetness before dropping it back to its rightful place. Her UI lit up; it showed points of concern, highlighting the barrel of the cannon, and flaring up a blinking, dotted indicator for the trajectory of a shot from the current position.

Okay. That's where it'll be. Just don't be there.

"All right, Kittycat, now you've got the motivation. Get movin'!" Volta smirked and fired off another three rounds in quick succession. Better prepared, the balls didn't pass through her; instead, she wove between them.

"Good! *Again!*" the wolf barked as she held the pace.

Wisps of smoke dipped in and out. Over and over Volta fired, and the cat danced between them like a finely scented memory. Relly whispered encouragement, but never pushed, letting her partner make the decisions.

[Good! Remember: breathe, follow the line, and move aside!]

All of a sudden, Mabel felt like she was getting the hang of it. What had seemed impossible became *probable* as the cannon continued to empty in her direction. The balls were still moving quickly, but they weren't as fast to her relative perception of the world in her gaseous form.

Smokeshape? Yeah … I like that. Like I'm a sculptor molding myself…

The rhythm thrummed as the song echoed all around her. In and out, solid to vapor, and back again fluidly; she couldn't hide the exuberant glee in her movements. The catamount didn't manage to dodge them all, but she didn't lose her concentration when the odd one was able to slip through her. When she knew it was coming, she could brush aside the tickling sensation.

The click of an empty hopper signaled the end of the exercise and was music to the puma's ears. Volta howled with excitement, and Ellen whistled loudly, both of them beaming.

"Way to go, kittycat!"

"Good on ya, mabe!"

[That was great, hun!]

The lioness panted, a smile from ear to ear as she put her paws on her knees, sucking in delicious air. "I did it! Holy shit I *did it!*" Her mind was racing as she tried to hold on to each movement, and the *feeling* of this moment, while simultaneously wondering how she could do *more.*

Volta clapped her paws together, before throwing an arm around Mabel in zealous camaraderie. "Hell, yeah you did! I was having trouble keeping up with you! Hot shit Mabes, you're moving like you know what you're doing! Sure you weren't holding out on us?"

Mabel pressed her forehead against the wolf's shoulder, laughing and shaking her head. "I swear! Relly is making it easy, that's all it is!"

[Teamwork, Mabes. I'm only helping you see; you're making the moves.]

Ellen walked up to her as well and handed over a bottle of water. The demivixen placed a hand on the cat's bicep and squeezed. "Well now, that was some impressive footwork; I knew that trick was gonna be good for that! Can't get hurt if they can't touch you, hey?"

The puma drank deeply and was thankful she was a little overheated from the workout, hoping that it covered up the spreading blush she felt through her cheeks and ears.

"Thanks, Elle … I'm trying my best, I promise."

"Hey, this is a learning experience for all of us. Keep it up!"

Volta's tail kept on wagging, "Good warmup! What's next? Maybe hit the bag a bit? Could load up the obstacle course!" She sounded so *excited,* which would have been adorable, if the cougar didn't feel like she had just ran a marathon and now the real race was about to begin.

Mabel's eyes grew wide as she stared at the floor, that arm suddenly feeling like a leaden weight around her shoulders. "*Mmm…*"

[*Mabes, it's okay to need a break. They're not going to be upset, or think less of you—*]

"I don't **want** a break … I want **this**," the puma pleaded with her sister. "I want to be **more**. Please?"

Amarelys squeezed her shoulder in quiet ascent. [*Okay … let's keep going, then.*]

The cougar forced out a little laugh and shook her head. "V, I'm gonna be honest, as much fun as tackling the Aggro Crag in front of my two favorite bad gals sounds, any chance we could do something a little more … *hands-on?*"

Volta stared blankly. "… The fuck's an Aggro Crag?"

"I think that was a low-level terrakinetic from the mid 90's?" Ellen helpfully supplied. "Spikey-costume, always acting like he had a pebble in his shoe?"

"Oh … what the hell does he have to do with an obstacle course?"

"Well, maybe she's talking about scaling—"

"It was from a nickelodeon game show, you *embryos!*" Mabel shouted, throwing her arms up in frustration as she cursed her poorly aged pop-culture reference catalogue.

Volta leaned over to Ellen for guidance once more. "Nicke-whatnow?"

The cougar let out a dejected groan.

"You'd probably remember it better as Nick Jr."

"Ahhh … hm." Volta nodded thoughtfully, before punching Ellen in the shoulder hard enough to send the vixen yelping sideways across the mat.

[*There, there. I thought your reference was very clever, dear.*]

"Thanks." The lioness thought flatly, lip jutting out in a minor sulk.

The wolf snorted softly as she watched Ellen dramatically dust herself off. "What didja have in mind, Kittycat?"

The puma's eyes lit up as she knew *just* what to suggest.

"What about some sparring? A little friendly brawl to *really* give me a *proper* induction into the life of wickedness?" Mabel glanced at Ellen with a smirk, and a little eyebrow raise. "I mean … you *have* to want to hit me at least a *little bit* after how mouthy I was? Maybe a little educational realignment of my tail end is in order!"

The demivixen blinked, but before she could add her two cents, Volta's laugh short-changed her.

"Mabes! Have you even *thrown* a punch before? I love the enthusiasm, but sparring with me isn't gonna go like a HeroClash match," she said, nudging Ellen with an elbow. "Right, Standup? Tell the girl what it's like to go toe-to-toe with me."

Ellen's brow furrowed for a moment as she looked up to the wolf, and then back to the feline. "Yeah, Mabe. I've got years of scrappin' under my spandex, and Red is the only one that gave me any *real* trouble! I mean, I'm no slouch, I definitely got my licks in a *few* times—"

"Yeah! I mean she never coulda *beat* me, but still," the wolf scoffed, "s'a bad idea, Mabes!"

"…Mm." The vixen's ear flicked, "Either way, I just don't think you'll learn anything from diving that far into the deep end, witchy magic or not!"

[*Mabel Ramona, this was not what I had in mind a minute ago when I agreed to you pushing forward!*]

"I learn by doing, Relly! You know that!" The cougar replied. "*It's just sparring!*"

[*You still get hit during a spar!*]

"*And that is an important lesson!*"

[*…How do you plan on learning if you're not conscious for the lesson?*]

"Well maybe you two could show me a thing or two? We don't have to go full tilt or anything—" The cougar smiled like butter wouldn't melt in her mouth, as she played off their pride. "Unless, you're worried that you can't properly rumble anymore, being *sisters* and all…?"

"Oh, I got *no* problem reminding the smartass what our win-loss is," the red wolf's muzzle wrinkled with an eager sneer. "Can't have her forgetting who ruined her perfect fucking record."

The indignant huff of the former hero signaled the bait was taken. "Oh, yah? You wanna try me now that I'm eating food with nutrients in it, Red?"

[*Mabes … I don't think you appreciate the size of the powderkeg that fuse is attached to.*]

"*Oh, but I think I do!*"

[*Mm … can't say I'm not a **little** proud of that mind game you played, but it was pretty sneaky.*]

"*What can I say? I'm just getting into character, is all!*"

"Well, V? Care to weigh in on that claim?"

Volta stepped closer to Ellen, a smile still splitting her muzzle as she leaned down, nearly touching her nose to the demivixen's own. "I'm not gonna take it easy on ya Standup, just so you can look good in front of your *fan.*"

"Don't wanna hear you backtracking that statement when you lose, okay?" The smirk that came with that bravado reminded Mabel exactly what she admired so much about LN.

She *never* backed down.

*"Oh, my gods, this is happening. This is **really** happening."*

"Yeah? You got somethin' better than KONG toy TF up your sleeve this time?"

"I figure I'll wing it. Betcha missed scrappin' with me, huh, Red?" Ellen's eyes lit up, as she raised an eyebrow.

"You kiddin'? Last time I put my boot to a Foxpaw's face, she thanked me for the privilege real cute-like. *You* put up a fight." A slow, eager sneer spread across the wolf's face as her eyes lit up. "It's so ... *satisfying.*"

Mabel learned something new about herself at that moment; she *desperately* needed to know whether Volta would still think she was cute with that boot on *her* face...

M-maybe I'll get to find out ... Her knees pressed together, as she found she could imagine the texture of leather on her tongue with *shockingly* vivid detail. The tennis ball-shaped bruise to the groin did nothing to discourage her sudden thirst, even a little bit. If anything...

It somehow made it *worse.*

It took Ellen's strong fingers grabbing her by the shoulder to knock her out of her stupor. "Well, last time I didn't have *MY* smoky sidekick!"

Sidekick. LN's sidekick. The feline's entire body lit up at the thought.

"Y-yeah! Team Joke and Smoke are here to show you what's up!" The puma was feeling *dangerously* elated, at this point, in several new directions, and was going to need a grin-ectomy after tonight.

"Hey, newbie's got *material!* I'm gonna be out of a job if it gets much better." Ellen shook her head but retained that confident smile.

"You mean you'll be out of a job if it gets much *worse.*" The wolf narrowed her eyes behind her angular visor before rolling them, rubbing the side of her nose with her thumb dismissively. "Right, *anyway*, big talk for a couple of big nerds. Now, Mabes, all I want to see you do is try to avoid me and try to stay out of Elle's way. If you see an opportunity, take a cut; I promise you won't hurt me."

"Got it, dodge the wolf and fox, poke if I see an opening!" The catamount nodded as she bounced on the balls of her feet, shaking out her paws.

"If you need us to stop, the safeword is 'candy.' I am serious like a train wreck here, Kittycat, don't be *stupid!* If I tag you, you're gonna feel it, and I don't need Nurse O giving me shit for messing up all her hard work." With that, Volta rolled her shoulders and squared up between the two. "We'll start on your mark, Standup."

[*Mabel, your top priority is not getting hurt. Everything else is a distant second, do you understand me?*]

"Understood!"

[*This is only a sparring exercise, but even a lovetap from Volta can put out your lights. Please don't make me regret letting this happen?*]

"It's gonna be fine, Relly! I got you and Elle to keep an eye on me!"

[*Ellen is going to be a little preoccupied, sweetie…*]

Ellen got to work without missing a beat. "Did you hear about the girl who was blinded by lightning?"

"Oh, shit. No, who?"

"Vixie, actually, and it turns out it wasn't that bad. All she needed to do was rub 'er eyes!"

Mabel couldn't help but let out a snorting laugh. She was literally facing off with *Redline*, at LN's side, even if it was just sparring. It was like a dream come true! This was like Superhero Fantasy Camp — well, Supervillain, technically — but that quibble did nothing to tamp down her excitement.

A ripple ran across Ellen's body as Pun-For-All did its thing, her flesh and bones shifting, her skin taking on a glossy black shine.

"…We doin' the rubber thing again? *Seriously?*" the wolf scoffed as she got low.

"I told you it was a good idea to save the pasta for later! Gotta keep the spring in my step, you know?"

"Well, LN, I think we can squeak out a win here! You always seem to bounce right back, after all!" her "sidekick" piped up, smiling from ear to ear still, and her previous exhaustion shoved aside by bubbling excitement.

"Oh *God*, the two of you…" Volta did everything she could to suppress her own smile.

"That's *right!* The two of us!" Ellen's feet let out a squeak as she launched herself towards the wolf, who quickly threw up an arm to block, batting upwards as the vixen connected. The deflection sent the demivixen sailing towards the ceiling; as she flew through the air, the wolf took a long step towards Mabel, where she threw out a leisurely roundhouse kick following the momentum of the swat, with a joyful bark of a laugh. "Too slow! Heads up, Kittycat!"

As the boot whistled through the air, the cougar ducked and shifted, but surprised the villainess by making her arms solid. Driving them into her heel as it sailed over her head, she shoved backwards, before dissolving into vapor once again.

The move forced the wolf to bring her boot down hard into a modified axe kick, trying to catch the slippery feline. The distraction caused her to forget about the still mid-air vixen for a second too long, realizing the play just as the former hero was already back on top of her.

"Oh *yeeeeeeeeeah!*" Ellen shouted, dropping an elbow onto the wolf's shoulder with her best heavyweight champ impression. It actually managed to stagger Volta, who looked honestly *surprised* by the power behind it as she stumbled forward. The vixen turned that momentum into a backflip, bouncing and landing a moment before Mabel rematerialized next to her.

"That was *Savage!*" The cougar kept her paws up as she waited for the Amazon to make her next move. She began to giggle when the metaphorical light bulb snapped on above her head. "I wanna try something … Follow my lead, Elle?"

Before the ex-Hero could respond, there was a large snarling presence in front of them, but the smile never left her face. "Do you really think I'm just gonna let you *talk out* a fuckin' plan, you dorks? Come *on* now!" the wolf growled, shouldering the cat bodily out of the way before grabbing the vixen by the arm. She slammed her target on the floor before using the inertia to swing back and launch her across the chamber in the opposite direction, electricity crackling down her arm; she moved the solid rubber figure as if she weighed nothing at all.

"Ha *whoooooa!*" The hero formerly known as LN might not have been able to feel the pain, but she still needed to be able to focus; this was clearly difficult to do when Volta was playing a solo game of handball with her.

It was all moving at such a breakneck pace it could hardly be followed. Relly did what she could, but *Redline* was literally a force of nature. Her limbs sparked, the air was overcharged with the scent of ozone, mingling with sweat and smoke. Mabel had watched the two fight dozens of times, but the wolf was like a terrifying storm of crackling magenta-wreathed limbs, and for her part, Ellen was reacting before Volta could even swing

— clearly better prepared than ever before — and even landed a couple solid blows of her own, as she was tossed to and fro. It was like watching a frenetically animated cartoon, all smear frames, blurred lines and raw speed.

The cougar had never before seen Volta move like this — at what she assumed was full tilt — and with seemingly no effort. She caught Ellen on a particularly weighty bounce and spiked her into the ground. As the elasti-vix came down, the wolf bicycle-kicked her back towards her partner.

The fight was turning into a repeat performance, the puma flinched. It was the gymnasium gastrointestinal exhibition all over again. The lupine super soldier was all surging muscles and exuberant violence, the demimorph was barely holding her own, and Mabel was completely beneath the notice of either one.

No.

She steeled herself, forcing her stubborn legs to react.

I'm not going to just give up. I'm done being ignored. I'm going to show them I was worth being saved. I'll show them I'm not a ... a charity case.

The cat shifted into vapor, swirling into the air to put herself between the vixen and the fast-approaching wall. Ellen braced herself for impact, but instead of ricocheting off the surface, she found herself being caught in a dense cloud of vapor that slowed her velocity, enveloping her as she hit the floor. When she opened her eyes Mabel was grinning down at her, with an arm on either side of her head.

The journey into and out of being a haze of smoke was incredibly calming, somehow, despite their awkward closeness and the high energy of the match. The puma quickly sat back into a crouch, ears reddening as she smiled, rubbing the back of her head. "Hey, LN ... fancy catching you around this side of town." She gave a little snort, her cheeks flushed and warm.

"Yeah, jeez — nice save, rookie." Ellen pushed herself up into a sitting position with the lioness, her words reverberating oddly with rubberized vocal cords, but she still sounded surprised by her partner's quick thinking.

"It seems like you're having problems catching a break! Did you hear about how the cops caught the bakery bandit?" Mabel wiggled her fingers, as she tried to softball an easy one to "The Pun-Slinging Vix with All the Tricks."

Come on, LN, you need more control in your movements. The rubber isn't doing it, but the old adhesive paws can do the trick!

Ellen's brow furrowed as she mouthed the words to herself, and then that mischievous glint showed through suddenly.

"She had *sticky fingers!*"

"BINGO!" Mabel exclaimed as her partner picked up what she had put down.

From across the room Volta watched them, and clucked her tongue. "You two about done bein' gay? We're still sparring, y'know." Her tone was impatient, but playful. "Hardly got my appetite worked up yet!"

Mabel held up a very rude finger in response, as she pulled her trainer back to her feet with the other paw.

"Setting her up would be so much easier if she would just wear her fuckin' RCGs!"

Relly chimed in, clearly exasperated with that particular problem. [*Oh, honey, we are trying, trust me.*]

The wolf had apparently concluded her sparring partners had been given ample time, and her footfalls signaled that she was done waiting. "Y'all can gossip over pasta after I'm done beating your asses!"

"Mix up?" the cougar whispered in her partner's pointed ear.

"I'll take the top!" Ellen nodded with a smirk.

The cat exploded into a cloud of smoke as Volta closed the gap, filling the immediate area around her with dense vapor, and trying to give Ellen a chance to do what she did best: *improvise.*

The wolf coughed and snorted, jumping back with a growl as she brushed at her sensitive nose. As if on cue, two shapes burst from it; the fox went high, and the puma went low.

The attack was well-coordinated, but hardly a surprise to the wolf who snatched Ellen from mid-air, using her as an improvised vulpine flail (impro-vulpined?) to try taking down the lioness in a two-for-one strike. Ellen barely had time to let out a yelp as Mabel dove aside, rolling and popping back up just outside of clubbing range. Volta grunted — almost pouting as she tried dismissively to throw Ellen backwards over her shoulder — but it was too late. She soon realized that while she had let go, the vixen had *not.*

The demivixen's fingers stuck tight to the wolf's forearm; using the momentum from the attempt at flinging her, her legs snapped backwards and then came around like she was on a pair of uneven bars, clocking the wolf on the chin with a solid **thud.**

Volta stumbled, stunned by the unexpected counter.

Ellen released her gluey grasp and landed delicately beside the catamount, on her very much no-longer-rubber feet. "Gotcha on the rebound, Red!"

The wolf's tongue traced her lower lip, and she chuckled. "Well, Standup, I will say *this* … Mabes has made my second-favorite chew toy a lot more interesting to play with. Been a while since you managed to tag me like that!"

Ellen shook her head. "Glad you're enjoying yourself! Stick around, we're just getting started!" She turned to Mabel and held her hand in the air for a high-five.

A *high-five*.

From *Lawful Neutral*.

*If Luke could see this, he would lose his **fucking** mind.*

Their hands connected, and there was a single moment when that satisfying slap rang out. All the universe was right and well and nothing would ever be bad again.

…And then she couldn't pull her paw loose.

The cougar tugged, eyes growing wide. "E-Ellen? Let go!" The panic began to rise as the vixen tugged in the opposite direction.

"I'm trying!" the demivixen laughed.

Why is she laughing? She's going to kill us! The puma's eyes darted between their seemingly holdfast limbs, and the villainess who stood imperiously less than a dozen feet away.

"I swear, if you two had another brain cell between you, you *might* be dangerous," the wolf snorted.

Mabel watched as the wolf's eyes flashed, and she began to lower her shoulder. The catamount instantly recognized Redline going for what Mabel had affectionately nicknamed the "Charge Knuckle Buster," when discussing potential new HeroClash moves with her friends on the message boards. It was a charged dash, using the massive woman's momentum to deliver a supercharged overhand, and was absolutely *devastating* when it connected. She had seen recordings of the wolf putting out the lights of at least five separate Heroes with the move. It was rumored that three of them *still* couldn't enjoy solid food.

It didn't feel like a game anymore.

As she stared down the barrel of the cocked gun that was *Redline*, the terror that gripped Mabel tight radiated into her shaking paws. All common sense told her to run, to get out of the way of that train — but she couldn't flee. She couldn't just *abandon* Ellen to this.

Fear darkened Mabel's face as she stood defiantly, but she wouldn't let her partner get hurt; not if she could help it.

The world slowed down for an instant. Before she could consider her actions any further, she had swung the vixen behind her, turning that paw to smoke to release the stuck hero … and threw up the freed arm to level what defense she could.

She focused on it being solid, closing her eyes tight, meditating on the form of stone that had been super-heated and cooled a million times over.

Dense.

Heavy.

She wanted *obsidian*, she just didn't know it.

She sang the Blessing of Fire without knowing the words, her heart screaming for it.

The next several seconds were a complete blur.

[*Mabel **no!***]

She thrust her arm out, paw first, as vines of wending dark smoke wrapped around and hardened instantly; wicked spikes sprouted, all pointed towards the villain bearing down on her. The thorns of glossy black stone pierced through the wolf's clothing without any resistance, and bit into her stomach. The puma's eyes snapped open as she felt the wet warmth trickle down her arm.

A sudden, brutal knee wrapped in magenta lightning crushed the stonework, followed soon after by the sound of shattered glass as Mabel flew backwards from the force.

The limb disintegrated into gleaming dark shards, and the cougar could only stare at the space where her arm had been, the stone glittering in an arc as she sailed through the air. Wet emerald orbs looked at the wolf, before they rolled back in her head, and the floor rose to meet her collapsing frame in a hard *thud*.

In a moment, what was supposed to be a fun game between friends had instead become a lesson that the lioness would never forget.

"She already has called on the Wind and Fire … I think we may have made a mistake by not stepping in. It's too much."

"The gift was ages old! How could we have known? We wanted to see how that would play out!"

"These mortals are so damned unpredictable. She was an utter coward, the meekest of the meek, and now she's standing up to the half-giant bitch in the biker jacket…?"

"Aye. Isn't that wonderful? So much chaos in their little mortal souls."

"Bah!"

"Relly …? Is … L … N …?"

"Oh fuck! *FUCK!* Mabel! Oh god!" The sound of the wolf's boots slamming into the floor as she bolted over caused the lioness to curl up instinctively. She clutched the smoking stump where her arm had been until a moment ago, shrinking away with a whimper.

Volta came to a sliding stop on her knees, rolling the catamount onto her back with careful paws. The feline's face was twisted into a horrible grimace as she bit back the urge to yowl. The pain throbbed so hard she felt it in her teeth. She could feel the sensation of Relly attempting to step in immediately, but the thought was enough to make her entire body ache.

"Mabes! I'm *so* sorry! I didn't even see what it was before I swung! What even happened? She was there, and then it was you—" Her voice was distraught, a whine settling in her chest as she looked down to the stray she had picked up. Behind them, Ellen scrabbled up to run to the puma and wolf.

"I was stuck to Elle, and I panicked, and I tried to harden my arm … I … I had to stop…" Mabel panted as she grasped at the empty space where her arm had resided until recently. She started swallowing big gulps of air as panic rushed back to the forefront. "My … my arm…" She closed her eyes and choked back tears at the revelation. "It's gone … I— I—" The red creeping up Volta's shirt broke her focus on the pain. "Are you *bleeding?* Oh, fuck … oh, gods … Volta! I'm sorry! I'm so sorry! I didn't mean…"

"Don't worry about *me,* you *stupid fuckin' puma! Mabel!* Your arm is … *fuck!* I *told* you t' stay clear! I fuckin' *told* you!" The wolf didn't sound angry as her words, she sounded … scared. Her paws shook as she looked to Ellen and then back down to the shattered feline. "W-why didn't y' listen? Fuck, fuck, *fuck…*" Volta kept shaking her head, muttering as she rocked back and forth, hesitantly reaching to touch, and pulling her paw back.

Mabel kept trying to catch her breath, and it continued to escape her. Her eyes rolled back in her head again, tears stained pink as the reality of the situation laid on her. *It's gone ... My arm ... I ... I...*

I ... I hurt her. I ... Why did I ...? She could still feel the warm blood dripping down the obsidian despite the heat of the stone. The scarlet seemed almost fake as it ran down the pitch-black glass.

[*Mabes ... your* **arm**...] The dragoness's voice was incredulous. [*Guess I'll cancel the medic...*]

"W-why? What's wrong?"

"Mabel ... You can *regenerate?*" Volta sounded a bit incredulous.

The words snapped the cougar back to the training room floor. "W-what do you...?" She stared down, where her very real arm was there once again, shaking and stained red, and she pulled it away from where she had touched Volta's wound just a moment before.

"Your arm just *reformed?* Holy shit, Mabes, that's like ... that's *huge.*" The wolf had gone from panic to confusion on a dime and the cougar joined her on that journey. "*Goddamn...*" The relief in her voice was palpable.

"I think your new roomie might be *really* good at gifts," Ellen cut in tentatively.

"I ... I didn't know? I ... I didn't know I could do *any* of that..." The pain still vibrated through her, but seeing her paw let Mabel breathe again. However, the panic only subsided for approximately three seconds before she realized the gravity of what she had done, and her heart sank. "*Any* of it..."

*I ... I tried to stop her ... **hurt** her...*

The adrenaline ebbed, and while Volta looked relieved to see the feline made whole, she couldn't help but wince now. The wolf held a paw to her stomach. "Guess you were done fucking around, huh?" She hissed through clenched teeth, shaking her head with a rueful chuckle. "Ah ... *shit.* Got me good..."

"I ... I'm sorry, I ... I didn't mean..." the cougar babbled as she licked her lips.

"Don't sweat it hun! Happens! Still ... should have backed off! You're one lucky Kittycat that's for sure ... Regeneration, without any nanites? You are somethin' else!" The wolf's laughter, a sound that normally made Mabel's heart flutter, did not bring its usual joy. "Dunno why you were *there*, but I'm glad I don't have to sweep you up."

Guilt flared red hot in her belly where the butterflies should have been.

"I just … I didn't want you to *hurt* her! I had to stop you!" The words just spilled out, the dam broken just as her arm had, and the truth rushed forth. "I…"

The relief on the wolf's face melted away.

"*Wait* … You thought I was gonna *hurt* her…?" For a moment, Volta's ears and tail dipped. "You thought that I'd hurt *either* of you?" She stared between her boots, before looking back at Mabel as if she had stabbed her again. "… *W-why* would you think…?"

"You … You were winding up, and … and I panicked … I'm so, so sorry, Volta!" She reached out to grab her paw, but it was the wolf's turn to pull away.

The shattered arm didn't hurt quite as bad as that look of betrayal Volta leveled at her.

"Right. You had to defeat the villain? The *big scary beast* was about to kill your friend? Is that it?" She snorted derisively as she turned away. "That was *completely* reckless, and stupid, and if you pull that shit in the field, you are *going* to get yourself and other people hurt! Or *worse*. This was too much, I should have known better…" Her paw rubbed at her eyes under her visor. "I never should have gone along with this."

"Red, take it easy. She was just trying to defend me…" Ellen interjected weakly.

"Oh, for fuck's sake, Ellen, don't coddle her! She's not even a fuckin' *trainee*! She's *not* your sidekick! You're *not* a team! She begged us to let her play and then she fuckin' *STABBED ME* when pretend got too scary for her." Volta growled and ripped off her tank top, inspecting the extent of the damage. It might have been life-threatening to anyone smaller, but for the Amazon, it was mostly superficial. "She had every chance to call it off if it was too much, but instead she pulled this shit? *Fuck* that. Fuck! *That!*" Her voice went into that low and dangerous register Mabel had heard in recovered footage of the lupine…

When she was talking to *capes*.

"I … I'm sorry. I was just … I was just *trying* to…" the cougar stammered, feeling the heat of shame and guilt rise as the words died on her lips.

"You were *tryin'* to be a fuckin' hero, *that's* what happened! All this, and you *still* see me as a *fuckin' threat*! *I'll save you, Elle!* **God-damnit!**" She spat, eyes narrowed dangerously as her paws clenched so tightly her arms shook. "You're not a *fuckin' hero*, Mabel! You … you don't even know *who* you are … and neither do I." She shook her head, her voice suddenly less angry, instead filling with disappointment as her shoulders sagged and she waved a dismissive paw. "We're done. I'll see you around, or whatever." The wolf stormed away before any response could be uttered. The crash of boots thudding into the distance was punctuated only by the sound of the door sealing with a hiss.

"FUCK!" Mabel slammed her paws on the ground, her whole body shaking. *"I hurt her … I hurt my friend…"* Her claws dug into the padded flooring, cutting furrows in the soft material. *"Why the fuck did I do that? What the fuck is wrong with me?"*

[*You panicked. You didn't mean to—*] The dragoness's voice did not soothe but only agitated her further.

*"Stop. Just stop. This is **my** fault. I did this. It doesn't matter if I **meant** it. I did it. It's the action that matters…"*

"Hey … look, even if Volta doesn't appreciate it, that was some prime boneheaded hero stuff," Ellen said, though her eyes were more full of pity than pride. "I should know, I'm an expert! But … I think she's just scared you'll get in over your head. Honestly, it's probably *our* fault for letting a civvie into a sparring match."

"No. No, she's right, Ellen. I fucked up bad. I got scared and took it too far. Playing at being something I'm not, like *always…*" Mabel looked up to her, eyes glistening as she held back tears and voice still quaking. "What if those spikes went deeper? What if I *really* hurt her?"

"She's got five times as much meat on her as I do, and she's full of combat-medic nanomachines, Kitten. If you managed to seriously hurt her by accident your first time up against her, and I couldn't manage it in two straight years, *I'd* be the one mad atcha. Give Red a day or two to cool off, and then we can try…" The reply was chipper, but the choice of pet name she used could not have been worse at that moment.

The catamount looked away from her, as *that word* burrowed into the worst part of her mind. It was too much. She shook silently as everything attached to it rushed into her. It felt like a gloss over her trauma, the new coat of paint hiding the rot underneath. "Kitten" twisted like an awl, letting the awful feelings pour out.

Too much.

[*Mabes, Ellen is right. You just need to give her space, and we can—*]

Internally the screaming drowned out Relly's words of reassurance. "Y-yeah, maybe. I … I'm not hungry, so I'm just gonna go shower at home.

Thanks for playing along for a moment there, Ellen. It was nice." Mabel refused to look at her as she attempted to stand, and fell back over, feeling all the wind rush out of her.

"Without training, you cannot manage your energy reserves…"

Oh … This is what it feels like to run out of candesca. I am literally tapped out completely. Fuck. She panted as she tried to catch her breath, the sensation of pins and needles running down every nearly useless limb.

"Oh, Mabe, let me help…" The demivixen's fingertips brushed against the cougar's shoulder and she winced at the touch, ears splaying out and tail thrashing to and fro.

"You don't have to *protect* me, Ellen. I'm sorry I suggested you had to in the first place. I'm not your *responsibility* … You don't have to be nice to me just because I'm a fan, you know?" She chuckled bitterly as she shook her head. "You didn't ask for that, why should you? You don't *owe* me anything."

"Mabel, I—" Ellen tried to protest, but the catamount held up a paw. "*Don't.*"

[Mabes…]

"*Relly. Face facts.* **You** *don't need to pretend for me either; I know what a fucking disaster I am. What a colossal waste of* **time**, *and* **resources**, *and … and kindness.* **You're just being ROSE.** *You don't have a choice but to be nice, so I'll just make the choice for you…*"

[W-what …? But Mabes, I'm not—]

"No. It's … it's better like this. I've already taken too much for granted." The lioness slipped her RCGs off and dropped them on the floor, as she finally managed to stand on unsteady feet.

Ellen motioned to grab her paw and the cougar pulled it away before she could, shaking her head.

"*Just … don't.*" Mabel wasn't going to show the hurt or fright on her face to her former Hero obsession, feeling as if she could not handle being a greater disappointment than she already was. The puma gazed back darkly for the briefest moment as she slowly, achingly fled the gym, feeling as if her legs weighed a million pounds each.

Ellen was left alone with a hurt, uncertain expression as she stooped to pick up the discarded visor.

≡

Shame radiated from the catamount as she dragged herself back towards her apartment, feeling like every curious eye was accusing her. Mabel was not alone as she trudged painfully through RIV's residential sector, however; the static was there to remind her just how badly she fucked up.

Oh, is it time for you to melt down, FINALLY? It's better this way, 'Kitten...' You didn't actually believe you were going to make something of yourself, did you? Get a pair of fake tits and suddenly you're not a fuck up? Come on!

She couldn't recall ever being more miserable than on that halting stumble home. Each step was followed by the inner voice, digging into her tooth and nail. It seemed resolute to make up for all the times she was able to ignore it, for all the times Amarelys drove it away and now — now that she had forced her sister away — the static drank deeply of her misery, each syllable tearing off a little piece of her soul.

So now all your queer little "girlfriends" are gone ... just like I said was going to happen.

How long could she take it? The bits of herself flaking away like rust.

You're ruining everything, just like always. You couldn't keep a girl. You couldn't keep a job. You couldn't do anything. What the fuck is the POINT? You're a loser. It's the truth, Joe. Face facts.

She stopped in her tracks.

"Don't ... Don't you *fucking* dare ... *Don't call me that* ... I'm..." She whispered to no one at all, thankful that she was alone on the thoroughfare. *"That's not who I am. H-he..."*

Oh? What are you going to do about it, you fucking basket case? I'm not someone else picking on you, I'm not some fucking bully, or dad, or anyone ELSE! I'm YOU, you retarded fucking pervert! It's all a fucking act! It always has been from the very beginning! Everything you do is just you putting on a show!

Nothing about you is real!

Everyone else is gone because of you! No one else made it happen! Only you!

The nerve had been found, and plucking at it resonated like a sour note in an empty hall.

You only have <u>yourself</u> to blame.

The puma screeched. She broke into a run, not caring about the people around her. "Just fucking leave me *alone!*" Her chest was on fire and her legs dragged, but still she sprinted, trying to get anywhere else. *Anywhere* but where the voice was. But how does one escape themself?

Behind it all, she realized, was a peculiar high-pitched sound, like the whine of an old lamp turning on. It mixed with the echo of her heaving breath and footfalls, and all the while, those vile words continued to pour into her, the malice of her inner monologue. The cacophony inside her belied the perfect quiet of the subterranean street.

I can't leave you alone, Kitten! You want me here! Why would I still be around otherwise? You heard the bitch! YOU don't even know who you are! You can't LIVE without me, because I'm the REAL you!

She lost her balance, cut to the quick, and tripped. She got back up and started sprinting again, oblivious to the scrapes on her paws and knees. She needed to keep moving, lest anyone see her and try to help.

Everyone here is so helpful … I don't … I don't … I can't … Let them see me … Oh, merciful gods, please…

You don't need help. You need to face reality. You need to stop LYING to yourself!

She slammed into the door of the residential sector plaza, tears streaming down her face as she pounded on the button for the elevator, shaking her head as she clawed at the door frame.

Please … Just leave me alone…

The doors slid open and she stumbled in.

They only tolerate you, they don't actually CARE about you. How could they? You only care about yourself! You're self-centered, cruel, and stupid. Why won't you just grow up and face the facts? You'll get nothing except this. It's all you've ever deserved.

"I-I … I deserve…"

Nothing. Ellen doesn't need a distraction like you in her life. A clingy. Useless. Nobody. And as for that wolf…

"Please … don't … I'm … I'm sorry…"

I bet she's crying into Carmen's arms right now. You hurt her. She'll never trust you. You're not worth the metal they put in your empty fucking head.

"Please stop … Please stop … *Please*…" Her paws clapped over her ears as she rocked against the cool metallic wall of the elevator, a whimper trapped in her throat.

Oh, we're not so tough, now, eh? Are you tired of struggling? Tired of living a lie?

"Just have to make it home … Home is safe…"

This isn't your home, you stupid boy. You live here at their pleasure ... They keep you around because you amuse them! They think you're FUNNY! Do you think that's still the case? After you stabbed the one who stuck her neck out for you? How long until you're back on the street, I wonder ...?

Her claws raked down the door as she crashed the other fist into it, unable to manipulate the handle. Over and over she crashed into it.

Or worse ... <u>traitor.</u>

"Shut up! It's not like that! *SHUT UP!*" she shrieked as the door opened and she fell into Eneera's embrace.

You can change the outside, but it doesn't change who you are. A coward. A freak ... A boy who couldn't even manage to be a man. Joseph GODDAMN Greysbell! The <u>brilliant</u> and <u>gifted</u> failure! A disappointment until the very FUCKING end!

"Mabel, what is wrong? Where are—"

She sobbed as she wrapped her arms around them, face buried in their chest. Their hands gently stroked her back as they embraced. The djinn cooed softly and whispered something in a dead language that she couldn't hear over her own panting and moaning.

Just a scared child playing at being what you're not. This isn't REAL.

"Neera ... Please ... I can't anymore ... I..."

MABEL isn't real. They'd be better off without you. Hell ... You'd be better off dead...

She slumped forward as finally the blackness overcame her vision.

"What if this was all a dream...?"
Cold stone. Warm blood.
"What if I'm dead in that alley...?"
Anger.
"Was I worth the time I took?"
Sorrow.
"I'm sorry I wasn't better ... for any of you."
Regret.
"It was a nice dream, though..."

Chapter 21

Learning *To* How *To* Live

There was the sound of the air rushing out of a room.

The static stopped.

The pain stopped.

The panic stopped.

There was only the stillness of silence, and merciful, soothing darkness.

No more unkind words and accusations, just...

Loneliness.

Isolation.

What had been comfortable a moment before was suddenly a crushing solitude, and she realized ... this was the choice she made.

This was what it meant to be alone.

And it *terrified* her.

She floated there, in nonexistence, with only one thought:

"I deserve this."

Mabel could feel a warm breath against her neck, and someone curled up against her. Relief washed over her. She was not trapped in that dark place, utterly alone.

The voice was silent.

Thank the gods...

Her eyelids fluttered open behind the familiar weight of RCGs on her muzzle, where they belonged. (The cougar wasn't sure when they were replaced, but thankful for it all the same.) As she looked down, she could see the mass of messy auburn locks, and two pointed ears that flicked peacefully in slumber. She ran a paw gently through Vixie's hair, and closed her eyes as tears began to sting anew. Red-hot shame flooded her, rushing in to replace the respite of a moment ago.

"…*How long has she been here?*" Mabel thought, but half-expected no response, knowing she *deserved* none.

[*Since last night. Eneera laid you on the bed when you collapsed, and she started crying as soon as she saw you. She curled up with you until she fell asleep, too. She wanted to be sure you knew you weren't alone when you woke up.*] Amarelys's words were kind, but they still hurt to hear.

After everything, she's still here…

"My hero…" The cougar smiled sadly as she rubbed one of Vixie's ears with the utmost care. "*Relly … I really screwed up, didn't I?*"

The answer was bereft of the normal patient tone. [*You definitely made some bad choices.*]

"*Why do I keep doing this?*" Mabel lamented, as she trapped a whimper in her throat. "*Why am I such a self-fulfilling prophecy?*"

[*Because you spent years believing you didn't deserve good things. When they happen, you don't trust them*]

"*…I don't know how to.*" The thought wasn't even a whisper, the admission exposing so very much. "*I … I want to be better…*"

[*Then I need you to fucking listen, Mabel!*] the dragoness snapped, clearly unwilling to entertain the catamount wallowing in self-pitying paralysis again. There was a pause before Relly continued sharing her frustrations. [*When bad things happen, you cannot keep claiming that you should be alone, and then try to make it come true! We want to be happy with you, you stupid girl! You're working on you, and that's fine, but your struggles … They don't excuse how you treat others! Or … or how you treat me.*]

The lioness swallowed hard and stopped stroking the downy soft hair of the vixen. Her sister had never sounded like this before. The voice was raw, and embittered, and had every right to be. In a rare moment of self-awareness, Mabel simply listened.

[*Vixie just wants you to be happy. Just like Volta, and Ellen, and Eneera, and … just like me.*] Another long pause, and the cougar could have sworn she heard a choked sob. [*Mabel, when … when you called me ROSE … took away my name? That hurt worse than anything you've ever said to me … could ever say to me. Worse than anything I can remember … It … It was like you were trying to shut me out again … Like you didn't want me. How could you even … How could you even consider that?*]

"I … I want to be better." Mabel stumbled over her thoughts. "You all deserve better…"

[*It's not about* **deserving!** *Love is not an* **obligation,** *it's a* **gift!** *You could be gone* **tomorrow,** *Mabes, any of us could ... How would you feel if that was how we parted ways?*] The normally even tone of the dragoness was full of concern, and heartache. Wounded by someone who was not only a friend, but family.

Her little sister.

Mabel almost didn't get the chance to say goodbye, to say she loved her. The moment it all changed hung heavy in her heart. Accepting that the end could happen at *any* moment, leaving words unsaid, or worse ... The wrong words left to *fester.*

"Relly I'm so, so, sorry ... Without you I would be..."

[*Maybe you would be.*] She cut Mabel off before the puma could finish voicing the treacherous thought. [*But I would also be, without you, and I don't want* **either** *of those things to ever be true! I forgive you, and you know I love you, but I'm not the only one you hurt, and even if they love you too ... That may not always be the case if you keep letting the fear control you. You need to trust this life is* **yours** *to live, and they want to be a part of it.*]

"I don't deserve you, Relly..."

[*Stop. Don't get on about* **that** *again. We deserve each other! Treasure the gift, and don't lose sight of it just because things get difficult, okay?*] She felt the dragoness's gentle fingers on the inside of her wrist, the small act of comfort that said so very much. [*We'll get through this.* **Together.**]

The cougar tried to choke back a sob of her own now, not wanting to wake the diminutive creature cuddling against her, but the deed was already done. She saw the vixen's sleepy, half-open eyes staring up at her, and felt her hand slip into her paw as a smile spread over her soft and kind features.

"Good morning, sweetheart. Thank you for protecting me last night." The lioness pulled her close, sharing a rumbling purr as she kissed her forehead.

"Mmm ... W-what happened, Miss M-Mabel?" Her still sleepy slurred voice was too precious for words.

"I forgot who I was for a moment, and I did and said some pretty stupid and mean things..." She responded, eyes still wet with guilt.

"*I would rather cease to be than harm any of you ever again.*" The thought was resolute, and without hesitation.

[*There's the Mabel that I know and love. You'd never lie to me. Not ever.*] The pride and happiness was back in her sister's voice.

"Never ever."

"B-but, I *promise* I'll learn to be better, for all of you."

"Th-that sounds good … C-can we have b-breakfast, M-Miss?" The wisdom of the vixen was still unmatched: approach problems one at a time.

"Only if you promise to keep on being so *perfect*, Vixiedoo!" Mabel nuzzled her cheek and laughed as the little demi wiped her tear-stained cheeks.

The vixen blushed a little at the comment and awarded her with that smile once again as she shyly twisted a lock of hair around her finger. "I l-like it when you c-call me that…"

"Then just keep right on being my hero, darling, and I'll keep right on calling you whatever you like!"

"I don't think I'm ready for Cosetta this morning, Vixie! Can't we eat at another spot in the cafeteria?" Mabel called through the frosted glass shower door. "Besides … what if Volta or Ellen is there?"

"Th-then you can apologize s-sooner, right?" she responded, having taken a seat on the sink, doodling on the steamy mirror with a fingertip.

[She's got you there.]

"You're not wrong, hun, but I, uh. I need to properly prepare?" The catamount blustered as she blew water from her muzzle in exasperation. *"Look*, I need to be sincere, and honest, and *thoughtful*." She slid open the door to look at her apology tour's co-coordinator. "I don't want it to feel *rushed*, you know?" She gesticulated with a paw before going back to rinsing the shampoo from her fur, having not previously had the chance to clean after the debacle that was her first training session. "Besides, I would rather not have an audience if I can help it…" She muttered that, thinking about Cosetta glaring at her for being *"la chatte la plus imbécile."* Or, worse still … *What if Carmen was there?*

Did she really want her first impression with Volta's girlfriend to be how *careless* and *childish* she had been, to the wolf who had agreed to help a newbie like her?

No. No she did not.

Mabel had never met the tabby, but her reputation preceded her, and the puma knew enough that she wanted to avoid leaving the worst possible impression on the person who meant so much to Volta.

As if that ship hasn't already set sail, caught fire, and sunk. Fuck.

She shook her head and let the water try to wash away her anxiety (which, honestly, couldn't be removed with a wire brush and a can of Ajax), but the ritual still felt good, and wouldn't leave her nearly as raw. She leaned forward, her tail slowly swaying, swatting at the rivulets that poured down her back.

"*Relly, do we have the stuff for French toast, by chance?*" Maybe she could get a dose of delicious decadent cuisine without the chance of encountering either generation of a feline family who certainly had ... *opinions* about her, by now.

[We actually do! Aren't you just so lucky to have me, hun?]

"*Thankful every moment of every day, my surreptitious sister.*"

"How does 'Mabel's Magnificent French Toast with the Most' sound, Vixiedoo?" the catamount shouted over the spray, cleaning the last of the soap from behind her ear.

"Th ... the m-most what, Miss M-Mabel?" The demifox's ear perked up, and she stopped drawing for a moment.

"Why, powdered sugar, of course, my dear girl!" Mabel poked her head out and quirked a brow with a half-cocked grin to match. "Also, it's Mabes, remember, darling? Don't need to be so respectful!"

"Mmm! Okay, M-Miss Mabes!" she chirped back.

The lioness let out a sort of half-snorting laugh as she closed the door, and held her arms up as the in-unit dryer started, whipping the water out of her fur with wind tunnel efficiency (and as a bonus, tickled in all sorts of fun spots). "Whooo! Okay! So, we want dessert for breakfast, and I think I saw some hash browns in the freezer too. A little juice and some coffee, and we'll be all set! But I bet you're more of a hot cocoa girl, am I right?" She stuck her head out again, fur poofed comically as she pulled a face at the vixen who started giggling at the sight.

"E-extra marshmallows?"

"As many as you like, and sprinkles on top to boot! Let's get you all hopped up on sweets before we try to figure out the best way for me to atone for my stupidity. Can you grab the brush there, dear, and help me with my back quick-like? I can never quite reach all of it, and Relly's a little too short to help!" She giggled as she used a towel to pat dry a few spots.

[Ha, ha. Glad to see your sense of humor is recovering.] She could hear the eyeroll implicit in the response.

"*Can't keep a good girl down!*"

*[Not without the proper restraints, but we can **always** get creative.]*

"Oooo … Mean old dwagoness!"

[You know you love it.]

"…Yeah I do."

The ever-helpful demivixen nodded, biting her lip as she hopped down.

Mabel quietly chuckled as she glanced back to the mirror, the suggestive flowers that had been so delicately "painted" on the glass, a bawdy masterpiece of vaginal lilies and violets sketched with a well-practiced paw.

Mmm … The girl knows what she likes, I suppose.

After they finished the tasks of brushing her fur and getting dressed, Mabel and her tiny vixen-shaped shadow emerged. The catamount had found a two-tone purple and pink hoodie that came to mid-thigh, a black-winged helix wrapped around the side, and a pair of artfully shredded charcoal-colored leggings. Vixie bounced into the room with the same clothes as the day prior, but her blue sundress made her tail and hair pop, and was simply adorable.

Stretched out on the couch with a small laptop on their chest was Eneera, who snapped it closed promptly and rushed over to Mabel. The dracaracal's handsome features were painted with both concern and relief.

"Mabel! You are all right! You emptied your entire vessel, and did not allow Amerelys to assist! What *happened?*"

She held up a single finger to pause the djinn in their tracks.

"First off, thank you for catching me last night. Second, *good morning to you too*, Neera. Third, I'll give you the quick and dirty: I practiced *way* too hard, figured out a few things about the blessings, and then became an absolute … did they use the term 'asshole' in your time to describe someone being untoward?" She spoke quickly, but not as quickly as she might when encouraged by an eight-foot-tall motivator.

"Yes. Typically, in conjunction with its size or cleanliness."

"Okay, cool. Yeah, I was a huge, gaping, shitty asshole." The lioness pressed her head to their chest dejectedly with a pitiful groan.

Eneera's paw rubbed the other cat's back gently, before their chin came to rest on the top of her head.

"You sound repentant. Will they not forgive you for your … anal indiscretion?"

Mabel snorted, unable to stop the laugh that erupted from her, and over the apartment's audio even Relly had a little giggle.

"Eneera, were you just trying to be funny there, sweetie?"

"I have been learning more about this time to try and feel more comfortable, but also to also be a 'fun roommate.' Did the joke 'land'?" They flicked an ear gently and offered a coy smile.

The puma perked up and gave a squeeze to her partner. "Ya did good, Dusty!"

"We're going to do some breakfast, and then the three of you can help me figure out what I can possibly do to fix the mess I made!"

"Your asshole mess?" The smirk on their muzzle was from ear to tufted ear.

"…Yes, my dear Neera. My *spectacular* asshole mess. Now wipe that shit-eating grin off your face, and get ready to stuff it full of carbs instead of smugness, hmm?" Mabel chortled and shook her head.

"Enough talk of derrieres! It is time for the Frenchiest of toasts, and the hashiest of browns! Okay, so we're gonna do this on a per-order basis! Let me get the assembly line set up, and we'll be cookin' in no time!" She patted the short counter for the two as she busied herself in the kitchen proper, concerning herself with getting the stations set up for maximum delicious efficiency.

Delici-fficiency, Mabel thought smugly.

Vixie, for her part, feigned a very convincing interest in the cougar's process, leaning on her elbows and smiling all the while. Behind her, that fluffy tail swayed and brushed slowly against the djinn's own tail and back. Eneera began to blush immediately and could not suppress the purr that rumbled in their chest.

"All right! Who wants…" Mabel turned around, wearing a brand-new apron she'd found in the closet, thoughtfully emblazoned with the phrase "The Chef is Smokin'!", and slowly raised one eyebrow as she stared at the scene. "Some … muh … fuckin' … what's going on *here*, then? *Hm?*" She waved her spatula at the two accusingly, eyes narrowing until they reached full squint. "What's all this?"

"Er … ah … uhm…" The caracal stammered for a moment, staring for assistance from the unassuming demivixen.

Mabel placed a paw on her hip and let her gaze bounce between the two *apparent* delinquents at her counter. She wasn't sure Eneera could sweat, but they looked like they were trying their damnedest. Meanwhile, Vixie met her withering stare with an innocuous, wide-eyed smile, like she had just found a completely unattended pie, and had simply decided she deserved a slice. Or three.

"*Neera … Did something happen last night?*" She sent the thought with a tilt of her head.

"*I … We … Vixie was … She was absolutely **ravenous!** We … we never did anything like that, in my time! She was an Avatar of Inanna made flesh! My mortal form had never been made to feel so … so … **blissful.**" The djinn's memories filled their mind, and due to their link, also began to flood Mabel's.

The unexpected side-effect of the bond made the lioness attempt, mostly in vain, to hide a moan behind a cough, and only managed to stifle it by biting her lip.

The lioness was very glad for her apron at that moment.

"*Gods bless … Ha-haaaaaaa…*" She glanced at the seemingly oblivious vixen, who *clearly* was not so.

[*Eneera! I didn't know you had it in you!*] Relly chimed in.

The djinn hid their face behind their paws, and wilted ears on either side of their swept back horns added to the display of embarrassment.

"*I'm starting to think I underestimated Vixiedoo,*" Mabel admitted with forced, teeth-grit rigidity. A phantom tongue swept the memory of her colon, and her thighs trembled. "*I'm starting to think I underestimated Vixiedoo a **lot.**"

"*She did many things!*"

"*Yeah, I'm getting that! Mmff…*" Her tail twitched above her clenching ring, biting her knuckle as she was educated on a subject she knew next to nothing about, by an apparent *master* of the art.

Mabel couldn't help herself, but soon realized that she *should* have, as the shared sensory recollection of the experience did not abate, and she became weak in the knees from the second-hand analingus.

"*Mmm … So that would be **your** anal-related indiscretion, I suppose?*" Mabel busied herself with the toast, half-supporting herself on her elbows, and got the coffee started, face contorting as she tried to focus.

Her own indiscretions needed to take precedence, but she couldn't stop purring at the shared memory. *Holy shit!* She thought, panting as she threw the tray of hashbrowns into the air fryer, and leaned against the counter, claws scraping the stonework. "Okay, Dusty, *please stop reminiscing!* I need to cook now!" This was very much said out loud, which put the demivixen into a tittering fit.

Vixie kept that smile on her face all through breakfast, absolutely beaming with pride. Despite not hearing the conversation, she clearly enjoyed the apparent results, with not a single ounce of shame to be found.

Breakfast was deliciously decadent, and after a change of pants for both Mabel and Eneera (the cats both claimed the French toast was … *Otherworldly*), the group had made their way to the balcony, so Mabel could have another coffee with the cigar she *absolutely* needed.

Her legs still felt like jelly. *Ponder the implications of that experience later, Mabel; focus on the problem in front of you, not what you wish was behind you.*

Smoke properly lit, the catamount motioned to her co-conspirators at the table and tapped her RCGs to signal the meeting coming to order.

"Now … I have, to put it lightly, *royally, spectacularly,* and *epically* fucked up, and you three are the only friends I have that will currently speak to me." She sighed out a thick cloud shaking her head, "I want to make it right, but I don't even know where to begin. So, I'm looking for solutions! I can't take it back, so how do I … *fix* this?"

Vixie raised her hand, stopping just short of calling out "M-Miss Mabel?"

"You don't need to raise your hand to speak, Vixiedoo, but I appreciate the gesture. What did you want to say?" She slipped her stogie back into her muzzle and perked an ear.

"W-what did you d-do, Miss M-Mabes?" The vixen pulled her legs up onto the chair, holding them by her ankles.

"I…" Mabel's tail whipped behind her slowly in agitation and embarrassment. "I disobeyed and hurt Volta, and when she got mad … I had a meltdown and told Ellen she didn't have to be my friend. I *also* told Relly she didn't need to baby me, and I was…"

"A b-big asshole?"

"That does sound like an apt descriptor, Mabel."

[Summed up your idiocy nicely. Well done, Vixie!]

Being laid bare and so *vulnerable* was never easy, especially by *and* in front of the people she cared about most. The puma rubbed the back of her head and tried to hide her embarrassment with another aromatic plume. "Yes. I was. Relly told me earlier, my struggle does not excuse how I treat my loved ones, so I want to be better, and *if* I stumble..." She paused and snorted derisively. "Already trying to justify excuses. No stumbling! Only earnest attempts at growth, and learning!" She nodded to herself before continuing.

"I need to do something to make amends, and I will take any suggestions you can offer! Honestly, I ... I have only ever succeeded at pushing people away, with Relly and Volta being rare exceptions to that. I don't want to be that person any more..."

"Why would Mistress Ellen and Mistress Volta not forgive you for this transgression? You seem quite contrite." Eneera rested their chin on their interlaced fingers.

"I think I scared her. A lot. And I'm fairly certain dismissing Ellen's kindness hurt her far more than I'd like to admit." The catamount took another long pull from the stick before tapping the ash into the tray. "It was really bad, Neera. They're allowed to be upset. I earned it."

Vixie raised her hand again.

"Yes, Vixiedoo?"

"Y-you said you were t-taking suggestions, M-Miss? Uhm ... d-does that include other stuff?"

"Of course, Vixiedoo! Fire away!" Mabel gestured with an open paw towards the vixen. "The floor is yours!"

"Uhm. S-sometimes ... s-sometimes I don't think you s-see me as a real adult. A-and ... and a l-lot of people, uhm. That ... h-happens to me a lot, M-Miss. And I've g-gotten good at n-noticing, a-and..." Her eyes were firmly rooted to the floor, body angled away. She had, somehow, managed to make herself seem even smaller.

Just like on the sidewalk ... fuck ... The lioness's smile faded, as guilt gripped her. *I kept on treating her like a kid because ... because I saw how sweet and cute she was and thought she was somehow less capable ... Just like the people who made her want to shrink away just like that. I really am batting a thousand lately, huh?*

There was an apology she hadn't realized was needed, and now she had to find the right words with the added pressure of an audience observing her contrition. *I don't **ever** want her to feel like I'm not a safe person for her to be around...*

"...I ... I didn't realize I ... *mmf.*" Mabel let out a sigh, tugging on a fingertip anxiously. "I'm *so* sorry Vixie. You're a grown woman, with grown

woman tastes that I am *very* well aware of now, b-but even if I wasn't …
There's no excuse for my condescending treatment of you, unintentional
or not, it was *really* shitty of me." Mabel bit her lip as she knelt in front of
the vixen to make sure they were eye-to-eye. "I promise I won't talk down
to you ever again … but I want to make it clear, I never intended calling
you my hero to be patronizing. I meant that honest and truly *every* time."

Vixie rolled her lip between her teeth, the corners of her eyes crinkling
with mischief as she very carefully set them to meet Mabel's.

"You can still t-talk down to me w-when I'm the one kneeling,
M-Miss…"

"*Gods*, you're incorrigible, huh?" The catamount snickered and
touched her forehead to the demivixen's. "Is it okay if I still call you
Vixiedoo?"

The vixen nodded emphatically and smiled from ear to pointed ear.
"I'd l-like that, M-Miss Mabes."

"Thank you, sweetheart … I'll never underestimate you again." Self-
consciously, Mabel cleared her throat and glanced at the more physically-
present of her audience members. "Uh, I meant all that earnestly, but …
how'd I do?"

"It seemed quite honest, and vulnerable, as proper atonement should."
Eneera offered with a thoughtful nod.

[Agreed. Just enough self-flagellation to feel repentant, without
coming off as woe-is-me self-pity. Although — a word of advice, for next
time?]

"Please! What can I do better?"

[If you attempt to lower yourself to Ellen's height in order to apologize
to her, she may take that as infantilizing.]

Mabel's jaw dropped. She glanced at Vixie, who was very pointedly
sucking on her lips and looking elsewhere.

"Ah fuck … Didn't even make it ten seconds…" The puma dejectedly
muttered, as her tail curled around her ankle. "Sorry Vixie…"

"W-we'll work on it!" Vixie chimed resolutely, wrapping her fingers
around Mabel's bicep in unflinching support.

"Thanks, hun…" Mabel rubbed the back of her neck, and sniffed
softly. "Please keep on me about this? I want to do better. *Need* to get
better."

"Okay, M-Miss Mabes! I'm sure M-Miss Relly will help t-too!"

[Of course, Vixie! We want this cougar to learn how to be an
exemplary villain, right?]

"R-right!"

Mabel's ears wilted, and her cheeks were warm, but she survived the first apology, which was at least a step in the right direction on the tour.

Overall grade? B-minus. She mused inwardly. *Maybe a C-plus.* A thought which was a totally normal thing that normal people considered when handling social situations.

"Well, that's the first stop down! Now we need to figure out how I can do better for the next two! Any other recommendations?"

"Ooh! W-when I want to help s-someone feel better, I b-bake something for th-them!" the vixen piped up helpfully.

[That's an excellent suggestion, Vixie!] Relly's encouraging kindness seconded the idea. [A good meal does wonders to soothe frustrations.]

"A treat may help them be more receptive to your atonement." Eneera nodded in agreement as they stroked their chin.

The puma sipped her cream that was lightly coffee flavored and nodded thoughtfully. "All right! That's not a bad idea. I can work with that. What do they like, Vixiedoo? You know the two of them best of all of us!" Mabel decided to look pointedly out over the railing, lest her mind wander to the breakfast nookie yet *again* at the sight of the demivixen.

Vixie played with her hair, nibbling her lip as she considered. "W-well … I know M-Miss Volta *really* likes p-pasta sauce and p-pizza!" She sat up, tail waving excitedly behind her.

"Okay, I can work with that, too! Relly, can you find me a good recipe for penne alla vodka? Maybe if I share my favorite sauce with her, I can try to mend that bridge."

[Spicy?]

"Absolutely!" Mabes dropped the barely smoked cigar in the ashtray and tapped a claw thoughtfully on the rim. "Now, how about Ellen?"

"I c-could ask Miss C-Cosetta for an idea? Th-there was a cake Ellen r-really liked when we were l-little." Vixie nodded in agreement with the idea and gave a shy sort of simper when the feline gave her an affectionate kiss on the cheek.

"Brilliant! Maybe don't mention what it's for, though? I have a feeling Grand-mère will be informed of the situation, and I want to fix this before she gets her claws into me." A shiver ran unbidden down Mabel's spine at the prospect of the elder feline cornering her.

[Wise choice, Mabes. You are learning!]

Not the worst way to go admittedly, but still…

"How can I help, Mabel?" Eneera actually sounded legitimately excited about the prospect ahead of the apology committee.

"Whatever you do, don't distract Vixie! I need this cake, or I am sunk! So you are to keep your eyes on the prize and your pants over your thighs, understand? That means *both* of you, until this is all over!"

Vixie pouted a little at that but nodded reluctantly.

"...I will assist you here with your dish."

"Thank you, darling. So, we all have our parts to play, and I cannot properly express my gratitude to all of you for this ... and for saving me again." The puma sniffed softly and closed her eyes. She was going to say she didn't deserve them, but realized that was not what she wanted to say. "I ... I am very lucky to have friends like you."

Mabel suddenly felt arms wrap around her middle, and a cheek against her chest. A moment later that was followed by a lanky arm around her shoulders, and a distinctly draconic paw grasping her own through the view of her visor, the AR-projected dragoness smiling down at her.

"A family is more than blood."

[You know we love you, Mabes. Let's remind those two why they do, too!]

It took about three hours to get everything ready, and a rush delivery from a certain incredibly cute corvid who just *happened* to take the job, but they managed it. The pasta was a standard casserole affair, covered in cheese and a spicy cream sauce, all draped luxuriously over penne in a translucent pink dish that could have been vintage Depression glass, had the real thing included a helix motif amongst the etched floral filigrees.

The cake was unlike anything Mabel had ever seen. It was ring-shaped like a bundt, but lacked frosting; the beautiful golden-brown crust cracked to hint at the shockingly green center. It smelled like the most delicious vanilla-scented treat that she had ever been practically carried towards on cartoon scent lines.

Vixie assured her it tasted even better than that. "M-Miss Cosetta and I t-tested one ourselves! J-just to make s-sure! Ellen is g-going to love it! P-promise!" She made a cute churring sort of noise as the catamount leaned down to kiss her between the ears.

"My hero comes to my rescue again! Thank you for being perfectly wonderful you, Vixiedoo. Now I just need to find your sister ... who *still* refuses to wear her godsdamn RCGs..." Mabel growled softly. "Relly, any recent sightings?"

[She was spotted heading towards the gym, and appeared to stop, and then head back toward Vixie's apartment. When she was not there, Ellen returned to her own apartment and has not been seen since.] The dragoness did not sound surprised, nor did she seem happy about that particular state of affairs.

"Wonderful. I am *completely* responsible for that." The cougar drummed her fingers on the counter as she considered how to move ahead. "Mm. And Volta?"

[She is home with Ms. Rayne, and is set to "Do Not Disturb." I'm sorry, dear.] The way she said that almost sounded like she was apologizing for having to send her to Mordor.

Yeah, that's ... about what I expected.

"...And the hits just keep coming. All right. I'll head to Ellen's first, I guess. Vixie, sweetie, if you want, you are welcome to stay here, or you can head home." The puma stated the plan out loud, just to try and visualize it.

"C-can I come h-help? I *p-promise* not t-to mess it up..." The hurt in the vixen's warm brown eyes almost halted the entire enterprise.

The lioness sighed softly as she pulled her into a hug, "I know you wouldn't, hun, but I need to do this part solo. If Ellen sees you, she might say she forgives me because she doesn't want to upset you. I need her to be honest, so *I* can be honest; does that make sense?"

Vixie nodded sadly, ears splayed out. "Y-yes..."

"I love you very much, sweetie, and I am going to do my best to make up with your sister, because you are *both* very important to me." The catamount patted the smaller woman's cheek gently, then turned and placed the peace offerings into a canvas bag for transport.

Eneera stood in the doorway of the kitchen, looking concerned and conflicted.

"I wish there was more I could do."

"Hey, you were my sous-chef for the sauce, and you can keep Vixie company while I'm gone! Just, uh ... maybe practice how to dampen our link a little, if you're going to daydream about whatever you two get into, eh?" Mabel snickered then and gave her dracaracal a wink.

"Of course." The djinn blushed and nodded. "Best of luck, Mabel. I hope your endeavor to mend your friendship succeeds."

"So do I, sweetheart. So do I." The puma gave them a kiss on the cheek and squeezed their shoulder as she passed by, cargo slung over shoulder, one thought lingering in her mind as the door clicked shut behind her.

If I could do just **one** *thing right … Please let it be this.*

The residential sector of RIV was built for quality of life, prioritizing walkability, so making her way to Ellen Foxpaw's doorstep took no more than a few minutes by foot; not an impossible journey, by any means. She motioned to knock, and then stopped.

"*Ellen. I'm sorry I lashed out at you. You've been nothing but kind…*" She mouthed the speech to herself and snorted. "*She's only a person. Stop putting her on a pedestal; you screwed up, and you need to clean this mess.*" Relly said nothing, which Mabel could only take as agreement.

The lioness was proud that she managed to resist the urge to rap out "Shave and a Haircut" on the doorframe when she knocked. The door itself soon slid open to reveal Ellen Foxpaw, who looked surprised to see that the cat had dragged herself in. "Mabel! Um. Hi."

"Yeah, uh … Hi … Ellen." The puma's green-eyed gaze went directly to the ground, as her free paw rubbed the back of her head. The awkwardness was apparent both in the lack of attempted eye contact from either party, and the way their respective tails nervously twitched.

"So … I just … *Mmf.* Can I come in?"

"Oh … sure." The vixen stepped aside, and Mabel stepped through the threshold, tamping down the lingering feeling of 'Oh-my-gawd-I'm-in-LN's-house!' and tried to not be a total dork.

Just be cool.

"Shoes on or off?" Polite conversation continued.

"Off, please." Polite response.

The door shut with a pneumatic whoosh, as Mabel kneeled to set down her bag and pull off her open-toed pink high-tops. She took a quick survey of the apartment, trying to be discreet, but the domicile was frankly depressing. Distressing. Dour. *Derelict.*

…Does she really live here?

"So, I love what you've done with the place ... Very, um. *Spartan?*" The cougar attempted to hide a sort of half-wince. "But, yeah, about last night..." The most awkward segue since someone mentioned they had a sinking feeling on the Titanic was delivered with startling earnestness.

"Yeah, Mabel, it's ... it's fine." The demivixen clearly wanted to avoid the subject, but it needed to be addressed for both their sakes.

"It is so *not* fine. It is firmly in Badland, approaching Awfulville." The catamount stated her case plainly as she reached into the bag, and removed a smallish foil covered plate with a plastic knife on top. The symbolism of offering it to her from her current kneeling position was not lost on the lioness.

"I asked Vixie to help me with this, and she said this might make you smile ... *Maybe* give me a chance to say what I need to say?"

Ellen peeled back the crinkled aluminum as she sat on the couch and gasped quietly. "Pandan honeycomb..." She smiled at the cake and then looked back at the catamount with her brow furrowed. "I didn't need a bribe to listen to you, Mabel, and Vixie didn't have to—"

"I know. She suggested it, and seemed happy to help, and I wouldn't ever stop her from being her incredibly sweet self." The cat cut her off again and splayed her ears. "Sorry ... I just. I didn't want you to misinterpret the dessert."

Ellen considered the cougar as she sat the cake on the low table and patted the couch next to her. "Well, you came all the way from the outskirts of Awfulville. I guess I can hear you out." Even at that moment, she tried to defuse the tension with her trademark humor.

"I am sorry, Ellen. You didn't deserve my vitriol last night, and honestly? I shouldn't have been so familiar, so readily. You're a person, not some sort of prize I won for collecting box tops, or a conciliatory gift for my bad luck." Mabel sat down, and placed her paws on her knees, musing aloud. "I ... do you ever feel like you just don't have a clue what you're doing? Like, 'What am I *doing* here,' y'know what I mean?"

A vulpine ear flicked ever so slightly. "... Sometimes, yeah."

The room smelled of warm vanilla, with just a *hint* of denial.

"I was trying to just embrace all of this change at once, and I never took into account *how* I was forming attachments to everyone who ... You *were* just being nice, and I cannot tell you how thankful I am for everything you've said and done for me." The cougar smiled sadly. "You called me cute once, even, and I ... You gave an inch and I took a mile. I already had these images of you all in my mind, and that's — that's *unfair*." Her claws bit into her knees ever so slightly as she squeezed.

I need to tell her about "the word."

"You don't know it, but, um. Ki— You also called me 'Kitten'…" Mabel swallowed and shook her head. "It's kind of a loaded word. Lots of … *baggage* there … b-but you didn't do anything wrong! And it was unfair of me to lash out because you stumbled over it. I'm so sorry, Ellen, I just … I wanted to be your friend so desperately, I didn't really consider your feelings in all of this."

The vixen didn't respond right away. Instead, she leaned forward and sliced the ring-shaped delicacy twice, revealing the verdantly vibrant interior, filled with air pockets and smelling just like heaven, or at the very least, a heaven-adjacent bakery. In silence, she carefully plated a pair of slices, leaving one on the table and offering the other to the cat.

"Mabe … The truth is, I'm *used to* people not treating me like a person. I'm — I *was* — a Hero. Fans came to meet a Hero, so I got used to meeting *fans*, not people. It's simpler if I don't think about them in three dimensions, because they only ever knew two of mine."

She paused, pulled a funny expression, and cleared her throat. The cat gave her a wry smile as the vixen continued.

"I've never gotten to know a fan this much before, and there's a point where the whole thing wears thin, and you start seeing the corrugation in the cardboard. It's great for meet-and-greets … but not so much for ongoing friendships. I'm sorry." Ellen reached a hand out and placed it gently on the back of the other's paw.

Mabel sniffled quietly as she nibbled the emerald confection.

"I thought I wanted to be your sidekick. Like, that was the aspiration, once upon a time, but I don't want that. Not anymore. Not really." Bright green eyes looked back at the vixen, sparkling with unspent tears, above a cocky sort of grin. "I want to be a *partner*. Someone you can count on. Be proud of. Not just a fan you need to perform in front of or feel *beholden* to. I'm not going to be a burden. I want to *help* people. You helped inspire that, and I want to … I want to give you a reason to care. I want to be your friend — not Lawful Neutral's. *Yours*." The cougar chuckled softly, and the sound was not bitter or sad, just honest. "I will *always* admire you. Now it's my turn to make *you* admire *me*."

There was the barest flicker in Ellen's eyes, and the feline could not read it.

"Are we … out of Awfulville now, do you think?" the puma asked hopefully.

"I dunno. I think we're between Badland and Awfulville. So, like … Fond du Lac?" A trademark wink and grin completely melted the catamount's heart, and relief washed over her; she was incredibly thankful her tail was hidden by the couch. Ellen chuckled a bit and savored another chewy bite of her sister's baking. "Mm! Well, I will say this about last night: How you got between me and Volta? I know you might have just panicked, but … as panic responses go, that was the same kind of thing I do. Did. *Very* stupid, but *incredibly* brave."

"Yeah, what did you call it … 'bone-headed hero stuff'?" The lioness nudged her gently, and Ellen nodded. "But yeah, I did panic. I just … she was *Redline* again, and everything suddenly felt fight-or-flight." Mabel shook her head.

"Foxpaws bring out the villain in her, I hear," Ellen smirked.

"She's not just Redline any more, though! She couldn't ever be. She saved my life, and not only that … she continues to make it one worth *living!* Why? Why am I still *scared* of her?" Mabel took a much larger bite this time, more to silence her verbal spillage than anything else.

The vixen replied with a shrug and the gentlest of surreptitious eye-rolls. "She's eight feet tall and made of tits and thunder. You've gotta be some kind of stupid to not find that intimidating."

"Well, we both know I'm not lacking for stupidity. Intimidating is fine! I've got almost a foot and a couple dozen plus pounds on you, and I find *you* intimidating, Elle, but here I am." She snorted as she finished the rest of her slice of cake. "I guess I was still scared like she's out to hurt me. Like she would have hurt *you*. She knows that…" Her eyes grew wide, as a realization struck her like a lightning bolt — a brightly magenta-stained one.

"She was upset because I said I trusted her, and then … I pulled that shit. *That* is what hurt her feelings…" she blinked. "Oh fuck. I hurt her *feelings*. She wasn't mad I didn't *listen!* Well, I mean, I'm sure she wasn't *thrilled* by that, or the *puncture wound*, probably … But really … I treated her like a villain instead of … like a *person* … or my *friend*. Oh, fuck…" The cat stood up quickly, and dashed to the door to pull on her shoes. "Fuckity *fuck* fuckin' ball shitting piss ass mother *fuck! Fuck! Me!*"

[*Well that certainly displays the versatility of the word…*]

"Oh, yeah, no, don't mind me. I'll just sit here alone with ... eleven-twelfths of a pandan cake." Ellen polished off her slice as she meandered over, licking her fingertips.

"Carmen is gonna *fuckin'* kill me!" Mabel stated the realization plainly as she held out her paw, and then just wrapped her arms around the former hero, now a budding friend. "I've never even laid eyes on her before, and she's just gonna murder me on the spot."

Ellen returned the gesture and chuckled as she squeezed. "Oh, yeah, she is. Well, hey, at least ya crossed 'make up with Ellen' off your bucket list.' Hate for you to have unfinished business! Thanks for the cake, Mabes. And hey ... for what it's worth? I think you're gonna be the nicest rug they have." The vixen stuck out her tongue and slumped standing there to drive the point home.

"...Good thing I think you're cute too. Smart-ass." Mabel let those words hang in the air for a moment, as she pretended tying her shoes was an activity that required her complete undivided attention.

Ellen took the opportunity to blush herself as Mabel waved and slipped out the door, the feline observed. She took extra care with the heavy casserole the only talisman she could summon against the doom she sped towards. Apologies and pasta were all she had, and she hoped they would be enough to mend the emotional wound she so callously rendered on the wolf.

Chapter 22

A World In The Horizon

Conveniently, the Rayne household was also only a few minutes away. *Inconveniently*, that was not enough time to shake the fear of what exactly she was walking into, nor the struggle she was having to find the words she needed to fix this.

"Relly … I'm going to be fine, right?"

[*Yes, of course. We've got some excellent doctors, and you'd be surprised at the advancements we've made to cybernetic prostheses. You'll hardly miss the original parts!*]

"Relly! I … Please?"

[*You deserve a **teeny** ration of shit, as a treat! But seriously … just be your genuine self. Take a deep breath; you'll be fine.*]

"That's fair. Right. This'll be easy, just … just knock. Be honest. Simple!" The lioness nodded to herself, holding the casserole under her arm as she lifted her paw to knock—

—And found herself unable to move. No … she *was* moving, she realized. It was just so slowly it felt like she was dragging herself through a vat of chilled molasses.

"Her status is set to 'Do Not Disturb.' I *know* that you can see that." The voice embodied the platonic ideal of the *femme fatale*, displeasure dripping from each perfectly enunciated word as the door slid open on its own.

All six-and-a-half feet of Carmen Rayne stood before the puma, but she might as well have been a mile tall, because she *loomed*. Her intimidating presence made Volta seem like a puppy by comparison.

Still, the lioness pressed on. "So, you must be Carmen! It's, uh … a *pleasure* to—" Mabel looked into the eyes of the tabby, which spoke of nothing but violet-tinted violence.

"*Miss Rayne*," she corrected, in the imperious tone of a displeased baroness. "And you must be the little lost stray that my girlfriend picked up last month, then?" Her eyes narrowed to slits, but not once did she blink as she sized up the girl in front of her.

The mountain lioness nodded but did not shrink away from her gaze. *Don't look away. Show her you can take your lumps.*

"You're going to have to have to speak up. *'Yes, Miss Rayne'...*" The tabby leaned in close, running a finger under the cougar's chin. Her expression remained inscrutable, but her tone said more than enough. "...*'Please*, Miss Rayne.' If you even *hint* at continuing your habit of being a little *tête de noeud*, this conversation will be our last. Do you understand me, *Kittycat?*" The nickname was not cute; it was the punctuation of her terms.

Mabel swallowed hard, unable to even pull away from the curve of the impossibly sharp claw. The puma's stomach turned, eyelids fluttering as she felt the furrow running through her fur. Her mind wandered to a dream she once had, and she felt her breath catching in her chest. "Yes, Miss Rayne." Mabel responded, her voice steady despite every alarm in her mind telling her to run.

"She learns quickly! *Good girl.*" The tabby's eyebrows bounced in mild amusement as she leaned in the doorframe, a single finger tapping her bottom lip as she considered the lioness frozen before her.

The cougar knew how badly she had fucked up, and the scope continued to expand. Still she pressed on. "Miss Rayne ... I just want to apologize to Volta ... *Please?*"

Carmen leveled her gaze. "Oh? Whyever would you *need* to apologize? Let me hear it from you, in your words."

"I disobeyed her direct orders, and..." Mabel licked her suddenly too-dry lips, searching for the right words.

"And?" the tabby rumbled.

"Hurt her..."

"Hurt her *what.*"

"I hurt her..." The puma whispered, shame burning in her chest as the simple truth was dragged free. "I hurt her feelings..." She had to close her eyes tightly, unable to look at the other feline's gaze any longer. "I hurt my *friend.*"

Fuck. Don't start crying now. Fuck. Fuck.

Carmen heaved a quiet sigh, before shaking her head.

"Mabel, do you know the most innocent way to kill, after the knife has gone in?" The words were said with such a calm and controlled voice, it sounded as if it was an everyday occurrence for the terrifying feline.

The very idea that she likely *had* sent a chill through the puma. "No, Miss Rayne…" Mabel's ears flagged, as she wondered what would be next? A practical demonstration, perhaps? The memory of the blood running hot over black glass reminded her that it would only be fair. "I … I don't."

"Pulling the blade free." Carmen mimicked the motion with an obviously practiced paw. "Most people think that's the first thing you do — remove the knife — but, if you really want to *help?* You need to be careful and *deliberate.* You need to plan and communicate. Sure, the blade has to come out, but that isn't enough. You need to work with the person you hurt, apply pressure, clean and dress the wound. *That* is what actually helps them. Otherwise, you're just helping them bleed out."

A knife in her chest might have been less painful than the point of the exchange, but still the lioness had to know. "W-why tell me this now?"

"Because retreating back into yourself every time you fuck up, pushing them away when you've already hurt them? *That* isn't helping anyone heal. Not Volta, not you, and not the people who have to try and clean up your mess. It's just pulling the knife and running." Carmen sighed a huff of air through her nose.

"Oh … I … I don't *want* to run anymore. I'm tired of running. That's why I'm here, to try and help heal this, I swear." Mabel returned the tabby's gaze.

"Good."

"And if I can't, well … I'm clearly what needs to go, so it can heal properly."

Carmen sighed once more, shaking her head. "There it is again. *Mabel,* you are not the *knife.* You're a *person.* You say you want to stop running? Stop giving yourself an *out.* You're going to fucking *listen* to me, Mabel Greysmoke, and I need you to *understand* what I am saying." She let out another sigh of frustration. "You need to *mean* it. If you don't think you're good enough? I don't really care to convince you otherwise; I don't know you that well. But Volta? She *cried* for you. *Sobbed* over how you made her feel. So, if you think you might just cut and run, because you're afraid of hurting her more, leave her alone and quit now. I will *not* let you hurt her like this a third time." Her surface was still, but frustration clearly lined every word with an edge.

"I … I won't … Sh-she … means so much to me, Miss Rayne, I—" Mabel shook her head, as she fought to get the words out. "I would rather I had died in that alley than … than to let her ever be hurt…" She meant the words, every last syllable, and the honesty of them shocked her. "I want to do everything I can to *mend* this ... I don't want to lose her, t-to *ruin* this. Please, *please* let me talk to her..." She thought about grasping the tabby's paw, pleading, cursing the stasis she was trapped in.

A tendril of smoke wrapped around Carmen's paw, squeezing with desperation.

"Please, Miss Rayne. *Please.* Give me the chance to fix it ... I *know* you don't owe me anything, and neither does she, but *I'm begging you...*"

Carmen's eyes flicked imperceptibly to her paw before shaking it, dismissing the smoke as little more than a nuisance. "That's what I needed to hear. Let's go, Mabel."

Time started again, and the catamount stumbled forward through the door, catching her bag before a pasta related catastrophe could occur.

"Shoes off. If she wants you to leave, you don't get to argue. Am I clear?"

"Crystal."

"*Bien.*"

To the left of the door sat a massive pair of boots that Mabel knew all too well, and her size twelves were absolutely dwarfed by them. It seemed fitting, given how small she felt at that moment.

"Thank you, Miss Rayne. I know you don't have to do this, and ... I appreciate it." She slid her shoes off and retrieved the homemade gift from the bag; the contents were long since cold, but she knew they could reheat well. (She had *definitely* never eaten an entire bowl cold from the fridge before.)

"I really don't, and I'm glad that you recognize that, but Volta needs to decide what happens next. I'm not going to make the choice for her," Carmen responded coolly.

In stark contrast to Ellen's bleakly barren apartment, the Rayne Residence felt like a *home.* There was soft, comfy-looking furniture, art and pictures were hung on the walls, and the polished hardwood softly glowed in the warm lighting. A family lived there and it showed, from the decor, to the faint smell of delicious cooking that hung in the air, to the smiles in every photo.

*Why does that bat look so familiar? Wow, the tech needed to keep this floor this clean has to be from the future, considering Volta's fluff ... and that couch is **massive** ...* As usual, the lioness's inner monologue lacked subtlety, and was not helped even a little bit by her frayed nerves.

But even with such an idyllic setting, something felt off. She didn't need to be magically-inclined to feel the disquiet, and it caused Mabel's whole body to tense ever-so-slightly, a vague sense of unease at the back of her mind. She bit her lip as the enormity of the situation continued to press into her thoughts — and tried *very hard* not to dwell on it as Carmen walked forward, flicking her tail to indicate the catamount needed to follow.

"What's in the dish?" Was it simply small talk, or actual interest?

"Spicy penne alla vodka … It's my favorite, and I promised Volta some Italian, so … yeah," the cougar answered with a little nod.

"Mmm."

"Gods, I hope she likes it."

"She's asked for seconds of *Ellen's* spaghetti before. You're probably fine."

Mabel considered the vibe of the ex-Hero's general home life and was encouraged by the implications.

It wasn't a long walk to their destination, but it was enough time for the first argument that Volta and Mabel had had to swim to the surface of her memory.

"No! Of course not! But they would just be an innocent victim! I'm not a **monster!***"*

"And I am?" Volta's eyes narrowed.

"…You certainly play a convincing one…"

The cougar swallowed hard, knowing she didn't deserve this chance; after the first time, who could blame the wolf if she just told her to kick rocks, (or kicked her rocks for her?) She didn't relish the prospect of *either* outcome, truth be told, but that was where she stood. It was her responsibility to resolve it, whatever that entailed.

Carmen stopped in front of a closed door, the occupant made obvious the Ontario vanity license plate mounted on the door, reading "V0L7A".

Mabel took a deep breath. *Please, let me know what to say. Please, don't this be broken beyond repair…*

"Always faithful! Ever True! All eyes to the North!" The chorus blared over the cheesy synthesizer sting, and Volta's tail thudded in time with the beat of the show's main theme. (The modified version, of course, the one that had been fully re-recorded with the Hamilton Philharmonic

Orchestra for the much-higher-budget motion picture in the year before that season's production cycle.)

The wolf's discarded spoon rested on the lid of the gallon of *Super Aurora Chunk*, her muzzle buried halfway into the cardboard container, tongue curling scoops of the ice cream. (Real vanilla, loaded with chocolate cookie bits, fudge-covered cashews, and marshmallow swirl; "*Truly Hero-licious*," as the jingle went.) The texture was exciting and soothing, and she relished the sensation of it as much as the sugary sweetness. The chilly treat was disappearing rapidly, but that was okay; there was *always* more.

Under the blanket, it was safe and warm. The wolf hummed along with the lyrics, immersing herself in comforting feelings. The revised theme wasn't a *perfect* recreation of the original, but it *was* catchy, and it always managed to excite her, because she knew what followed after: the colorful montage of her Hero fixation and various guest stars battling against the sinister Colonel Clue. It would end with that week's title card, and a picture of the handsome wolf, smiling warmly at the viewer. Between the bottomless bowl of chilly dessert and the cartoon's warm comfort, she almost managed to distract herself from the twisted knots in her stomach, or thinking about—

No. Fuck her.

The wolf shook her head, dipping her snoot back into the carton. The *point* of blanket fort time was to distance herself from the bad thoughts and shut everything else out except the good ones. Her sole focus needed to be on the solace of her den, and the familiarity of the episode she had watched hundreds of times. She decided this watch-through was for reviewing the authenticity of depictions, cross-referencing the fictionalized versions of the on-screen heroes with the Korps's collected wealth of real-world intel.

True North the Second was fairly faithful, if a *little* less soft-spoken than he had been in actuality. The pitch of the laugh was off, too, but it was more than acceptable. For the others on the show, she had come to find a *lot* of his super "friends" had been remarkably sanitized; Oakes, Hagen, hell … *Tullis's* singular appearance painted him as some proud, compassionate American Patriot.

She tended to *skip* that episode.

As the week's co-star appeared on the screen in a puff of sparkling smoke, she huffed softly, and her ears slicked back. She had forgotten *Magella* was in this episode.

Stupid fucking puma…

Instantly, the catamount was in her head, smiling at her from the couch, looking up at her with those big green eyes, and ... that ... that little toothy smile—

—*Then she was on the ground, staring up again, terrified, pieces of her arm scattered all over*—

The cartoon was forgotten, as was the ice cream. All of it was background noise once again.

Volta tried so *hard* to be careful. Gentle. She didn't *want* the people she cared about to be scared of her. She *wasn't* a monster ... Everything was so fragile, and she did her best, but still that *stupid fucking puma* got in the way. Of course she did. It wasn't her fault she did *that*. Of *course* she retaliated to the attack, that was what she was *trained* to do. Not like that *stupid fucking puma*, just trying to ... to prove herself. Showing off for Ellen...

She was lucky I walked away, and didn't hit her again ... Maybe I should have. She wasn't what all of those people said she was. She thought the cougar had understood...

She rocked back and forth, pulling her giant Carmen plushie to her chest and hugging it tightly. Hugs would be nice. Maybe she was ready for someone to be close now?

Someone knocked on the door.

Her face lit up at the sound, welcoming a new distraction. She quickly checked herself, making sure she was presentable for her girlfriend (maybe Wren too). Her vintage Aurora Squadron sweatshirt was cut to hang off one shoulder, the faded logo still easily legible, despite it being nearly as old as she was. But she wasn't spilling out of it, and these weren't her ratty sweatpants, so she didn't feel like she had to change before answering.

I hope she wants to stay! Maybe she'll watch an episode with me before dinner!

"Come in!" She dipped her nose back into the tub for one last lick, tail thwapping away again as Carmen filled the doorway.

"Hey sweetie, how're you doing?"

The tabby's sweet voice made Volta smile light up, and she couldn't help but yip excitedly at her beautiful partner.

"I'm all right! Do you wanna—"

That smell. The faintest tickle; like cigar smoke, but less acrid, more *spiced*. She always used to *hate* the smell of smoke... The wolf's eyes narrowed as the source of the scent became obvious.

The *stupid fucking puma* was there, in her den, in the safest of spaces, gawking at *her* things. Gawking at *her*.

Any hint of a smile evaporated, and her tail went perfectly still. Every muscle in her body tensed as she put down the ice cream. So, few people had been allowed in her den; in fact, all of them were in her immediate polycule.

Her lip curled ever so slightly.

The *stupid fucking puma* wasn't in the polycule. She never *asked* to be in the polycule. She never even *asked for permission to enter.* Volta didn't *want* her in her room, or even in her *thoughts*, but there she was, with those big, stupid eyes, shrinking away…

*Yeah, now you do the right thing, you and your terrible **fucking** timing. Now you're seeing me how I **want** you to see me. Maybe you'll get the fucking hint.*

The wolf rolled her eyes and paused the cartoon. The growl that settled in her chest let the room know exactly how she felt, as she stared daggers at the *stupid fucking puma*. "What's *she* doing here?"

"She said that she wanted to apologize. Should I escort her back out?"

Volta rose slowly, giving the plushie one more hug before setting it down, her eyes never leaving Mabel's. Part of her wanted to scream, to tell her to fucking *leave* and never come back or maybe find some corner of RIV where the wolf would never see her again. Go *anywhere* else that wasn't her den.

As she stepped closer, those weren't the words she said.

The sad girl look had never looked better, but as she came closer, the cougar realized it might be the last sight she looked upon and quickly needed to come to terms with that.

"What do you want to say, *Kittycat?*" Volta's teeth were on full display two feet above her head, like a serrated Sword of Damocles. To her credit, Mabel's underwear remained unsoiled, unlike some *other* certain super-powered beings when faced with the same view. (Well, not the exact same. She wasn't known for committing crimes in her loungewear.)

Did they rehearse how to say my nickname with the same energy as one would speak of a steaming pile? Gods above and below…

The wolf cleared her throat impatiently, with a sneer. "Can you make it quick? I'm busy." She gestured to the paused image on the screen.

"Volta, I..." The catamount glanced back at Carmen, considering asking her to let them speak privately, but before she could begin the request, the tabby was already shaking her head.

"Right. Volta, I am *such* an insensitive asshole, and you have every right to be furious with me..."

"Mhmm."

"I ... I shouldn't have ignored your orders, and ... uh, stabbed you, and..."

"Mhmm."

"I'm sorry."

"Mm. Anything else?"

"I brought a peace offering?" Mabel held up the glass dish filled with creamy, cheesy pasta.

The red wolf leaned down and sniffed the container. She blinked once before she sniffed a few times more, and her tongue slipped out for just a half a second, tracing her lip.

Okay. Okay. That's a good sign, right? Little blep?

"Um. It's my favorite pasta. Penne alla vodka, and I made it extra spicy ... because I figured ... you *might* like that?" The puma managed to force a smile, the same expression one might use when forgetting how having a face works.

Volta spared a withering glance at the puma before taking the Pyrex, striding back over to her blanketed nest, and settling in. Behind Mabel, the door suddenly closed; the feel of it sliding past her tail made her jump, grabbing the appendage and hugging it to her chest.

"Well? You just gonna stand there like a dipshit fence post?" The wolf motioned to the spot beside her as she retrieved the serving spoon from the inside of the lid and began shoveling the pasta into her maw. "Or are you gonna finish what you started?" She snorted as she grumbled around the mouthful, nestling into the pile of pillows and blankets.

Mabel walked over slowly, sat down where she was bidden, and took in a moment to scan her surroundings. Her eyes quickly grew wide.

This has to be the biggest museum of True North merch outside of Toronto, holy **shit!** *I never would have guessed this in a million years. She's a bigger Hero nerd than I am!* Every surface was covered with posters and shelves heavy with history. The walls were lined with acrylic long boxes stacked four feet high, doubtless filled with every True North comic that the wolf could get her paws on. *Luke's LN shrine looks like a disorganized flea market, compared to this.*

The catamount had to blink as she spied a particularly rare comic sealed in a display case and mounted on one wall. ***Holy shit is that a signed issue of true north true stories with the first appearance of...***

Focus, Mabel. Focus.

"So ... I know that me not listening to you isn't the *only* reason you're so upset with me, and I know the stabbing wasn't appreciated either ... but—"

"You fucking *think?* Why *am* I *really* upset, Mabel? Please, tell me why I feel the way that I do." Volta snapped back, not raising her voice, but causing the cougar to wince all the same.

"I-It's *how* I responded to you pressing the attack. I should have called it off, or stayed out of the way. I ... I treated you like ... like you were going to hurt us. Like I didn't ... *trust* you." Her reply was sheepish because, frankly, she felt even smaller than normal beside the wolf at that moment.

"*Why?*" The wolf asked, her expression neutral, as she sat the pasta down.

"Why what...?" The cougar wilted, withering under the impassive gaze.

"Why don't you *trust* me?"

"I ... I don't have a good answer..."

"I think you *do.* I want to hear you say it," Volta sniffed.

Mabel stared at the floor like the answer was going to suddenly reveal itself in the weave of the plush carpet. "You're so — you're just so *you,* Volta! A giant, striding unapologetically amongst mortals, and ... and I was *scared.* You're powerful, and terrible, and *beautiful,* and ... I feel so *small* next to you. Like I don't belong. I'm *terrified* of you all realizing that I don't *belong* here, and then it'll just ... all be done. I don't feel *worthy.* Of your kindness, your attention ... of your *anything,* really."

Volta nibbled her lip and pulled her knees up towards her chest — as much as her endowments would allow, at any rate — and huffed sharply as her expression softened. "A lot of people have taken advantage of my trust or taken it for granted. I just want you to actually act like it matters. I said I'd help you, because I figured you respected me, because you ... you *liked* being around me. Were you just afraid of me this whole time?" The words were intoned in her quiet voice, the same one she had used back then. They hurt so much more because there wasn't any spite behind them, just a wounded wolf being honest.

"*No!* I ... I don't know why but ... I ... I ... didn't treat you like you deserve, I ... I do know that." The cougar stumbled as she concentrated on not making another fucking excuse.

"I thought ... I thought we had an understanding, you know? But you acted like I was some out-of-control *monster!*" She looked back, ears splayed; the wave of shame made the cat turn away, lest she be shattered by that crushing weight. "It ain't *fair*, Mabel! You can't apologize for doubting me one day and then turn around and pull this shit another! *It ain't right and it ain't fair neither!*"

Stunned silence knocked all the wind out of the feline, as the knife twisted.

Volta's paw grabbed her shoulder, and gripped tightly.

"Aren't ya gonna say anything? Normally I can't getcha to shut up!"

The puma shook her head, refusing to look up at her, but the wolf could surely feel her body shaking as she choked back quiet sobs. Mabel could take abuse, that was easy. But disappointing someone who she admired, who she cared for so deeply? It was just all so much that she couldn't keep it together. *Everything* came tumbling down, because there was nothing left to prop it all up. Any sort of deflection her bravado would normally accomplish crumbled away, and her emotions were fully laid bare all over again.

"I really fucked up, Volta ... I *know* I did. I would do *anything* to take that back. I would rather you never found me in that alley than hurt you, *any* of you, I *swear!*" She gasped and coughed as she struggled to catch her breath, but pushed on. "Y-you *saved* my life, over and over and over again. Your message stopped my spiral, and, and, and, you stopped that ... that ... *man...*" Fat tears rolled down her cheeks as she pushed her visor up, pressing the heels of her palms to her eyes. "All I ever dreamed of since I was a kid was helping people, *being someone better than me*, and ... and I *couldn't* ... And then ... now ... all of this! And you've all lifted me up. Made me *whole*, even. I *never* should have doubted you for even a second." The cougar's deepest fear spilled out as she sobbed. "I'm so *sorry*, please, don't leave!" she wailed, digging her claws into her paw pads to try and keep herself present, before any control was entirely gone. "Please ... *Please*, don't leave, Volta..."

"*I need you to be part of this. Please, just say the words. Please,*" the cat begged herself.

Mabel pleaded in a whisper without shame, just the truth of a wounded heart. "I ... I need you to ... be a part of this. A part of my *life*."

Every word felt like an impossible burden she could have never shared before.

The big wolf planted one equally big hand on her back, rubbing surprisingly gently. "Hey, *hey*, easy, Mabel. Weren't you supposed to be helping me feel better?"

The puma sniffled as she looked back, snorting a bit, as she regained the ability to breathe.

"Yeah … But then you looked at me like a wounded puppy, and I wanted to disappear. V, you are *so much more* than I *ever* imagined, and you're right. You don't deserve to be treated the way I treated you." Her paw came to rest on the lupine one on her shoulder; somehow, despite it all, the cougar gave her a smile. "I have met more heroic people here, within the Korps, than I ever have before. I was always scared to be myself, or to risk revealing any weakness in my armor. Thanks to you, and Relly, and these people who care about me even when I couldn't care about myself, I finally get to *live*." She leaned her head to rest against the mammoth mitt cradling her shoulder and nuzzled against it without a second thought. "I hope I can be a villain just like you, Volta, when I grow up."

Mabel closed her eyes tightly and then began to purr as she felt Volta's chin come to rest on her head. They sat there in silence for a long moment. Nothing else needed to be said in that simple embrace.

"You called me out for wanting to impress Ellen, but you know what? When we started, it was impressing *you* that was on my mind. I need to be worth the trouble I cause, right?"

"Oh, you are gonna need to *really* step up your helpful game to make up that deficit." The warm chuckle that followed made the lioness *want* to get closer. The arm curled around and pulled her close — *made* her get close — and she sunk into it.

"Mm, fair. V?"

"Yeah, Mabes?"

Her heart fluttered as emotions swirled hot and heavy in her chest, words she desperately wanted to say but couldn't; not then, maybe not ever. After a long, *long* pause, she finally managed to whisper something else.

"…Thank you. For everything."

Just outside the door, Carmen clucked her tongue, breathing easier than she had since Volta had come home in tears the night before. The wolf had made her promise not to simply turn the puma away if she showed up, and she kept that promise. Her puppy was attached and had to make these choices for herself. It didn't keep her from worrying, though.

"Wren, we're going to need another plate for dinner."

"Oh my *god*, are you besties now?" the bat smirked as they flicked their wrist, using the rim of the oversized wok to skillfully toss the sizzling produce within.

"Mmm. Not quite." Carmen leaned on the door frame, watching her partner work.

"Still don't trust her?"

"Of course not, but this is at least a *step* in the right direction."

"Eh ... Volta has a pretty good sniffer! She picked *you* out, after all." Wren turned and smiled with a shrug. "Nothing left to do but wait."

To wait ... and hope her backbone doesn't crumble under pressure.

"I suppose so." Carmen draped her arms around the slender bat as they returned to preparing the meal, kissing the top of their head affectionately.

The pair sat together under the blanket, shoulder to elbow, and watched True North foil the villain with the help of his very special guest. Volta was eager to stop being upset at her friend and just continue working on being close. She wanted to trust Mabel, and so...

She did.

Watching the show together was like an act of reverence for the red wolf, and the catamount was all smiles as she seemed to hang on every word. Never once did she discourage Volta from sharing her knowledge, or from being passionate about such seemingly small details. She simply listened as the lupine spoke, and that was nice.

"This scene is really interesting because it's *actually* based on a fight with another villain!"

"Oh, this is the first episode where Arthur uses the Compass Needle like that!"

"Watch the reused frame here from season one! The budget for the show was running on fumes, and it *was* really good art, so..."

The wolf could only smile as the feline leaned against her, stealing bites of pasta before asking questions about other esoteric bits of trivia that only a fan like Volta would know. Minutes before she was so anxious and angry. *Rightfully* so, at this stupid fucking puma, but after this? It was easy.

Mabel *made* it easy.

Even though she was older, she never talked down. She teased, but it never felt mean; it felt like she was inviting Volta to jab back, like she wanted nothing more than to just get Volta *talking*. It felt safe and warm under the blanket again, and the cat fit so nicely there, her head resting against the wolf.

Like she *belonged* there. Maybe she did.

But it was also just nice having her friend back. Volta's tail wagged slowly as the closing credits ran, and she nudged the catamount. "So how close was Magella to the real deal?"

"Ehh … not very? The costume is pretty much spot on, but all the magic she did was too *flashy*. She was tricky, you know? An escape artist! She didn't run around throwing fireballs, because she didn't *need* to. All she needed was her clever little tricks and her wit…" Mabel smiled as she toyed with one of the last bits of pasta in the dish, before looking up to the wolf. "Was still fun though, don't get me wrong! I used to watch this on Saturday mornings when I was a kid — with my own bowl of sugary cereal, not sharing a pan of pasta, to be fair — and it was nice seeing that episode again. Seeing her, and sharing it…" Her ears flicked, and she looked back down. "Mm. So, uh … Talking about nerdy shit! I am seriously *sooooo* jealous of this den you have here. Maybe with a couple less TN2 pinups, but no accounting for taste right?"

Volta growled playfully. "First of all, those are collectible full-body profile diagrams. I'll let you have that one since you were crying like a *second* ago, and if you don't like my merch, my birthday is June fourth, get me something better!" She snorted derisively as she rolled her eyes. "Shit, you *wish* Standup had this kind of quality in her collectibles, talking about taste! You've got none at *all*, Kittycat!"

"Well, you *nearly* knocked all of the taste right outta my head with that *Charge Knuckle Buster*, so I'm lucky I held on to what little I have, I guess!"

"Well, don't be where I'm swinging, that was the whole point of the exer— *Wait. What did you just call it?*"

"Call what?" Mabel played dumb, looking away with pursed lips.

"The move I pulled that you tried to eat, *slapnuts*."

"Oh … Right, that's uh … a Charge Knuckle Buster? It's a Volt Step into the Haywire Hay … Maker. My friends and I came up with names for your moves. Yanno … as you do? When you're a dork who plays too much HeroClash?" Mabel's ears radiated heat that Volta could *feel* inches away, almost glowing in the dark. "Heh…"

Behind the wolf, her tail began to wag at hyper speed, slapping up and down against the cushioned pile. "That is *rad* as *hell*, you fuckin' nerd! I'm stealing that! But it's called a Bolt Dash though, not a Volt Step. Volt is too close to my name, and that's reserved for a signature finisher. The devs never listen to me, though…" Volta grunted in annoyance at the thought.

"Ha! They never listen to me either! I will make sure all of the nerds on the internet know the *proper* terminology. Honestly, I'm sort of surprised you don't have, like, a secret civvy account to slip that sort of information out! You know, set the record straight?" A challenging smirk was on the lioness's muzzle now.

The lupine's tail slowed as she looked away, proving that she had the world's easiest-to-spot tell.

"Oh my god, you *do*!" The cat's paws shot up to her mouth, gasping as if she had an epiphany. "*You're TRUENORTHTRUEFAN!*"

"…No one will *ever* believe you." Volta sniffed and refused to return the incredulous gaze of the cougar, her thick fur covering the majority of her own blush now.

Mabel's paw remained over her muzzle. "Oh, holy *shit*…"

"What?" One eye peeked from under a lid.

Mabel nearly whispered. "I'm ChaoticMewtral…"

"You're—? Ugh, of *course* you are." The wolf rolled her eyes as she shoved the cougar, but her smile remained. "Of *course* you're the asshat who started callin' me a 'cape chaser'!"

The cougar leaned back and gestured around to all of the heroic paraphernalia adorning the walls. "Volta, sweetie, all signs point to me being *painfully* correct in that assessment."

"I don't *chase* capes!" the wolf blustered indignantly. "I *don't*! Except the *one*! The rest chase *me*, okay?" She wrinkled her nose before turning to look away once again with an exaggerated pout.

Mabel began to *howl* with laughter, as she threw her arms around her friend, blankets cast aside in the lunge. "Awww! Don't be like that! I would *never* reveal your secret! Honor among villains, right?"

Volta growled, a soft smile lit up her features. "Oh, you're a villain now, huh, Kittycat?"

The catamount simply nodded before whispering, "How could I be anything else?"

A knock at the door instantly brought the pair back to reality as they broke the embrace. The feline's paw lingered in Volta's for a moment longer before she laid both of them on her own thighs and tried to calm the butterflies in her stomach.

Carmen's voice came through the door, the tone far more affable than earlier. "Girls, dinner is ready!"

The catamount slowly rose to her feet. "Oh! I'm sorry, I'll head out! Thanks for letting me in, Miss Rayne, I ... I really appreciate you giving me a chance."

The portal slid open, and the tabby was there, leaning against the frame and looking nonplussed. "You don't *have* to go, Kittycat. We have a place for you, if you'd like. Wren always makes plenty — gotta keep *this* girl well fed." The tabby gestured to her girlfriend, who was all smiles and wags as she looked up at the cougar.

"You should stay, Mabes! Wren is an *amazing* cook!" The look on Volta's face could have convinced the cougar to do anything she asked.

"Okay! Uh, yeah ... I would like that very much! Thank you," Mabel managed to stammer as she offered to help Volta up, not really considering what little help she could actually provide. Still, the encouraging squeeze from the wolf's paw enveloping hers made her feel that much better about the choice to stay.

Carmen shrugged, the faintest hint of something Mabel didn't recognize flashing across her features before she turned away, "Don't mention it."

The tabby's tone remained inscrutably polite, which Mabel could only take as a step in the right direction. Certainly, there was more left to be done, and it would take time, but it was perfectly clear:

She *didn't* ruin everything.

Dinner was delicious, an incredibly flavourful stir fry with a ton of marinated mushrooms, and a heaping helping of steamed rice fresh out of Wren's comically large wok. Yet again the catamount found herself overfull, toddling towards home content in belly and in mind. Mabel felt like she had accomplished a new beginning to be proud of. She considered what that really meant, and she couldn't hide her elation. She wasn't just making friends; it was so much more. Eneera said it was more than blood, and they were right: she was building a *family*.

And she loved each and every one of them so deeply, her chest ached when she dwelled on it. That made it all feel real. A thought occurred to her, however, as she wandered through the subterranean byways of RIV towards home.

"Relly … *Can you help me write an email?*"

[*Of course, darling girl; to whom are we reaching out?*]

"My parents. I … *I need to tell them some things.*" The lioness nodded to herself. "*I need to know where we stand, and …* they deserve the chance to know me."

CHAPTER 23

VILLAINOUS HEART AND SOUL

The chaos of the weekend ebbed into a relatively quiet start to the week, for which Mabel was incredibly thankful. It was nerve-wracking to right the life she'd nearly overturned, trying to get back on track with her new normal. She dearly hoped the stillness could last a little while longer — but as she lounged on the couch with Eneera, educating them on the finer points of cinema, she wouldn't be holding her breath.

She knew better than that now.

But *maybe* the calm would hold out until at least Thursday and their appointment with their KDARC handler, one Agent Alder Irrswisch. For the *moment*, she would relax herself with award-winning, high-fantasy motion pictures with some of her favorite people.

"Look, I'm not saying you're *wrong* about how he's firing the bow, Eneera, but it is *supposed* to be cool!" The lioness explained the idea, for what seemed like the fiftieth time. "It's not *real!*"

The djinn wagged their finger towards their companion. "Proper weapon discipline *is* 'cool,' Mabel!"

The cougar simply shook her head. "… Wow."

"What? What is wow?"

Mabel didn't even try to stifle her snorting cackle. "I wonder if the stick up your ass got *petrified* in those five thousand years, or did it come that way originally? Did it impede Vixie's moves at all, or…?"

Looking playfully aghast, Eneera threw a pillow at the catamount, who continued to howl as the missile struck her. "We do *not* speak of anal-related indiscretions past! That is *your* rule! *You* made that rule!"

The cougar tossed her hair over her shoulder, giving the best devil-may-care smile she could manage. "Eh. Never been good at following the rules, y'know? That's how I got here, swept up in all of this scum and villainy!"

"Oh! Is that so? I thought it was because *I* scooped your punk ass up out of an alley. Am I remembering that wrong, Relly?" The rumble of dissenting thunder emanated from the kitchen.

[Not at all, Volta,] Relly answered honestly, as she always did. [You did, in fact, do *exactly* that.]

It was now Mabel's turn to look wounded, her ears pulled back in mock indignation, a paw placed demurely on her chest. "I cannot *believe* this treachery! And in my own home, no less!" Her mock pout intensified as she gestured at the wolf in her kitchen. "*Look.* Who invited you over to drink all of my soda and eat all my snacks, you ungrateful pup?"

"You did, *nerd*," Volta snorted as she cracked open the "purloined" pop, before slugging down half in one go.

"That's right, and so I expect you to be on *my side* during these exchanges!" Mabel narrowed her eyes as she stared over the back of the couch, a sly grin hidden by the cushions. "Where is your sense of loyalty?"

"What part of *supervillain* didn't you understand, Kittycat?" The wolf laughed as she heaved herself over the back of the couch, catapulting the two felines a foot into the air. While the djinn primly floated slowly downwards, Mabel ended up flopped sideways, sprawled across the Amazon's lap. As the cougar stared up at the smile on Volta's muzzle, she felt the warmth instantly blossom in her stomach and quickly turned her gaze away before the wolf could catch her stolen glance.

"You evil beast! This is a couch not a jungle gym! Is *nothing* sacred?" the feline blustered before biting her lip. *Settle down Greysmoke … Friends. Don't fu—*

Volta absently stroked the cougar's hair, eliciting a purr from the lioness and derailing her attempt at self-control.

—ck meeeee … Mabel's eyes closed as she leaned into the touch, still rumbling softly. Her heart sped up for a moment at the feel, before the massaging tips soothed her anxiety. *Friends can cuddle, right? They can. They **can**! This is fiiiiine…*

"Alright! So, the big sexy wolf guy just lopped the head off of the orc…"

"*Aragorrrrn*," Mabel slurred through the haze of *purely* platonic affection.

"Yeah, so like, if he's so badass, why even invite the rest? I mean, he sneaks in, dunks the ring in Mount Doom, sneaks back out! No muss, no fuss! Instead, they're going to trust it to those little guys who have to stop to eat eight times a day?"

"It's because he's *tall*, and everyone knows the ... taller you are the more susceptible to ... mmm, *corruption* you are. Hence the hobbits ... which doesn't account for *Vixie*, but that's besides the point..."

"Bet Pippin eats ass like elevenses."

"You *know* Merry's getting that *lemb-ass bred*, but come *on*, Volta, you're *just* as big a nerd as I am, stop acting like you don't understand the subtleties of Tolkien!" Mabel wagged a finger under her nose, eyes now barely visible slits as she stared at her friend ... but the gentle paw combing her headfur could no longer distract her from the red wolf's blatant baiting. "Next you'll be asking why don't they just ride the eagles to Mordor."

"But Mabes, if I don't tease you, I don't get to see you make that face! It's precious when you get all *indignant* like that! 'Sides, *Fellowship* is BO-RING with a capital snnnnnnrk." The red wolf imitated a loud snoring noise to prove her point before letting out an amused chortle. "*Two Towers*, any day of the week!"

"You *heathen!* You say these things to wound me, intentionally!" Mabel covered her brow melodramatically as she slumped over plush lupine thighs, as *ever* certain in lacking a single ulterior motive. "Trolled, by a *supposed* dear friend!"

"Eh. I remember someone talkin' some shit about TN2 recently; was that you, or another mountain screamer with a fat ass and a cigar habit?" Volta scratched her chin — as if she needed to consider a list of all the catamounts she knew, which sadly ended the feeling on the fingers against Mabel's scalp — only sharpened the retort.

"Okay, now *listen here*, you completely correct little shit!" She hid her slight disappointment behind another layer of mock indignation. "You couldn't handle two of me!"

"Oh, is that *so?*" Volta raised a pale eyebrow, the smirk that followed made the cougar's heart nearly leap into her chalk-dry mouth. "I got two paws, and I know how to use 'em."

Mabel was completely unprepared for the flippantly suggestive remark but managed not to start sputtering out loud. Luckily, her sister decided to speak up right then.

[Sorry to interrupt your very *casual* conversation here, ladies — but Mabes, your appointment at the salon is in about fifteen minutes. I know your hair has been driving you nuts, and you mentioned some piercings, too? Don't want to keep the person with the needle waiting...!]

"Oooo … Where ya gettin' holes added, Kittycat?" Mabel could feel the lupine tail thudding against the couch as that mischievous smile continued spread across her friend's muzzle.

Oh no…

"Just my ears! Get your mind outta *my* gutter, V." The lioness chuckled as she sat up, and stood to stretch, trying to further distract herself from the teasing exchange. The *absence* of warmth next to her was staggering, but she resisted the urge to cancel her appointment and dive back onto the wolf's lap.

"Oh, boo! Didn't know you were so *vanilla!* But to each their own, I guess…" Volta stuck out her tongue, the grin not leaving her features; it caused the cat to turn and pretend to be searching for something, *anything*, so she could prevent that smirk destroying what little good sense she had.

*I need so very, very much to ignore that feeling. That feeling? That feeling has never done me a **single** favor.*

Mabel instead patted the dracarcal's knee and tilted her head sympathetically. "Did you maybe want to tag along, sweetheart?"

"Oh, no, no thank you, Mabel! I am invested in this hero's journey now, the arc of his most epic saga, despite the callous disregard displayed for the common-sense wielding of dangerous weaponry! I think it is important that I should stay here and see it through to the end!"

"Fair enough, my budding supernatural dork; no real room on the back of my broom for a cat your size, anyhow! Volta, you gonna stick around? Or what's the plan…?" Idle chit-chat kept everything cool and casual, in the feline's mind; that was something she could do. That was a pillar — shaky and janky though it might be — upon which she could, if she chose, lean.

"Eh …? As much as I *love* watching the Rohirrim ride, I think I'm gonna go for a run and grab a bite to eat." The couch creaked in relief as Volta lifted her weight from its soft surface. She stood, rolling her shoulders as she polished off her soda. With strong fingers, she crushed the can, and then pitched it artfully over to the stainless-steel kitchen sink.

The cat headed to the closet in the entry hall, and began shifting through the outerwear on the hangers. "Oh? Where at…?"

"Mmmf. Prolly Josie's, for some pizza?" The wolf snagged her one-of-a-kind jacket off a kitchen stool and slipped it on with a graceful tug. "I'm in the mood for something hot and cheesy!"

"Ooo, that sounds good…" *Where the hell did I put that sweatshirt? Ah…! There you are!* Mabel pulled the hoodie over her head and chest. There was a moment of heart fluttering, as the fabric slid downward over the swell of her breasts, which distracted her for a handful of seconds.

Her chest. *Her* breasts.

It had been less than a week with this utter euphoric *glee* of her body, and she managed to resist lewdly groping them in front of the wolf. At least *this* time, anyway.

"Y'wanna come with? Best pie this side of anywhere!" The wolf's tail had not stopped wagging since she'd made the crack about the puma's proclivities. It also had not escaped Mabel's notice that the furious wagging sped up *dramatically* at the prospect of imminent pizza.

The comments brought the catamount's mammary revelry to a screeching halt.

"Oh, uh, er … I mean, uh … yeah, I could eat." The puma's tail swayed slowly to the beat of the heart that thudded within her chest. *Not a date. It's **not** a date. Right? It's just grabbing lunch with a friend. Calm your tits, Mabel. People do this all the time.*

"If you start doing that whole, like, 'Well, the pizza in *New York*…' thing, though, I will have to kick your ass. As a matter of pride," Volta said with a sniff.

"I mean, *fair*, but do you need to call me out like that?" The cougar laughed, shaking her head as she leaned against the wall. She was doing her very best to look nonchalant, and she was failing miserably in the attempt.

If the wolf noticed, she didn't make a big deal of it. That was a relief for Mabel.

"I'll shoot you a message and see where you are when I get there, all right, Kittycat? Wanna see your new 'do and accessories!" Volta gave a wink and a wave, and was out the door before any possible changes to the plan could be suggested. "Later, Mabes!"

"Sure! Catch you at Josie's," the cougar replied with a quieting voice, just before the door clicked shut.

*Mm … This pile of feelings is getting precarious. Fuck, who am I even kidding? It's never been anything but, but … **Fuck**.*

"*I am so dumb. So very, very, dumb.*" Mabel dwelled on the thought pointedly as she sat on the tram. The sleek subterranean light rail vehicle was speeding towards the commercial sector; it was affectionately called the "Evil Mall," or just the "EM." Every large base had one, and while it was a commercial sector in name, there was no commerce done in the *capitalist* sense. The EM was one's destination to obtain, to partake, to engage in some "shopping" in their off-time, but not a single dollar changed paws. The goods and services were provided because they were desired and needed, by artisans and craftspeople who *cared*. Queer luxury space communism at work.

[*What's wrong, dear?*] Relly asked coyly, as if the situation was not obvious.

"Nothing, Relly. Nothing. She just ... mm, I ... she always **gets** to me." The feline stared between her feet, at the shockingly clean rubberized floor. "Every. Single. Time. Without fail. It is absolutely without *fail* that I feel like a teenager around her. I'm almost forty, and she's just, she's so, I ... **Ugh!**"

[*You know, we could look into more exciting piercings, if what you want to do is impress Volta, but I mean...*]

Her big sister knew her too well, and sometimes Mabel was just not in the mood to be called out.

I wonder how I'd look with my nipples pierced. Hm. No. **No. Bad kitty!**

"Don't you get started on that! I'm not **trying** to impress Volta! If I want any piercings, they're going to be because I want them, just for myself, right? Don't be a busybody." The cougar's ears flicked back, and she nibbled on her bottom lip with frustration.

[*All right, all right, I'll let it go...*]

"Thank you. I mean, I just made up with her and I don't want to screw it up already by having ... you know, **feelings** all over the place." The lioness stuck her tongue out, pulling a sour expression at the thought of gooey, unchecked emotions. *Whose to say she would even reciprocate...*

[**But** a thought occurs!]

"Auuuuugh! *Amarelys! Let it goooooo!*" The cougar exclaimed out loud and slumped in her seat, causing the dolphin next to her to inch away with a look of concern. The dragoness absolutely would *not* be letting this go.

Mabel smiled and pointed to her visor and mouthed the word "*Sorry!*" and tapped her neighbor's fin, pointed to the small mammal's brilliant blue hair, wordlessly stating "*I love your hair!*" That prompted a purple blush, and a clicky, pitching giggle. The cetacean patted the cougar's knee before going back to her own thoughts.

[*You could, you know, **talk** to her about how you feel? Maybe? Just a little? Not let it, could we say … simmer?*] Mabel could almost *hear* the attempt to put forward the sensation of a disarming shrug in her sister's response.

"Nope. *Too soon. I just want to be friends and not fuck everything up with a stupid crush. I have to. I **need** to. Please, Relly…*" The cat was utterly sincere; she just had no energy left to deal with the situation. "*I **cannot** be allowed to screw this up. It doesn't matter. Not about how many butterflies she gives me, or how she lights up every room she walks into…*" The lioness felt the heat creep up her cheeks, before catching herself. "*O-or anything else! Okay? **Please?**"

[*Mmm. Whatever you say, Mabes. You're a big girl, and you can handle this, however you feel is best.*]

"*Thank you. Can you play some music, maybe? I want to get psyched about this trip!*"

"Hungry like the Wolf" began to play, and Mabel couldn't help but laugh at her incorrigible sibling.

"*Well played. Now that you have **finally** gotten the last word, could you show me the hairstyles you think will work, again?*" The rest of the relatively short ride was akin to a dating app for styling, swiping left and right until there were a few standout choices. Shaved sides, side sweeps, and *bangs, even*, were all in the running — but the cat was confident she would know what she would like, when she sat down in the chair. And she trusted Relly's judgment *implicitly.*

The stylist she was set to work with — who happened also to be a *tattooist* — had the highest satisfaction rating available. At least, outside of KDS's own Demitra, who only worked with clients she chose; even then, she was *legendarily* permanently booked. This was the next best thing, and Mabel was, after all, excited to try something new.

[BING]

[**Commercial sector! Watch your step and have a villainous day!**] A strikingly familiar and yet different voice came over the speakers and signaled their arrival to their destination. The cat gave a little wave to her azure-haired tram buddy before hopping off.

"*Hm. Wonder if I would look that good with different-colored hair. Maybe …? Let's see how our consult shakes out.*"

[*I personally like you in white, dear … Can't really put a finger on why, though.*]

"*Yeah*, it's a mystery, for sure!" The puma laughed as she ran her paw back through her long headfur and wondered just how much she would lose in the name of style. She would never completely lose the white though, that, *that* was a family trademark.

The EM was actually bustling, this close to Christmas — well, "Korpsmas." This situation used to give Mabel off-the-charts levels of crushing anxiety, shoulder-to-shoulder with aggressive devotees to the Church of the Almighty Dollar. Having worked retail herself, it drained all of her energy, sapped her will, and left her just resisting the urge to curl up into a ball and *sob*. But that was a whole gender ago, so much had changed in just a few weeks, and *this* was no shrine to consumer culture.

Now she felt like she belonged in her skin. If any eyes were on her, *good*. She liked the attention. Liked, though … *liked* seemed too frail and small a word.

She *adored* the attention.

She'd spent decades hidden away. After finally breaking free, it was like the first desperate *gulp* of fresh air after being trapped underwater, nearly sucked down by the deadening undertow. Never again would she hide herself, and *certainly* not for the comfort of anyone else. This whole trip was to make her feel even more attractive. That, *that*, was what she was going to accomplish!

Guided by her HUD via Relly's directions to maneuver through the crowd (and resisting the siren call of custom clothiers and boutique boots), the cougar finally made it to her destination. The striking black-and-pink neon barber's pole at the storefront confirmed she had reached her destination: "Get Inked or Dye Trying."

The doors were saloon-style bat-wings. They provided a peek inside, as well as allowing the eclectic musical *vibe* of the place to pour out of the building. Poppy classic country intermixed with deep bass club beats, the buzz of tattoo guns, the whine of hairdryers, and the raucous chime of laughter. It was chaos, but somehow the most beautiful sort of chaos; in truth, it was a cacophony, but the sort she just *had* to explore for herself. Mabel was nothing if not *curious*.

All along the walls were mirrors, and chairs before them. Each was separated by a low wall, with curtains that could be drawn for the privacy of each client. Each booth was decorated to the taste of the incumbent with pictures and records, magazine clippings, even some autographed photos of infamous Korps agents. Each seat was filled, save one, all the way in the back. It was on a raised sort of dais, which looked like something one might be strapped into, but still … *Comfy?* The furniture was all shiny chrome, and bright red synth-leather. It was cluttered but *curated*. It was an artful mess, and Mabel quietly pined for her space in the art studio at school, an eternal-seeming lifetime ago.

The cougar drank it all in. Chit-chat was exchanged; tattoos, stylings, and piercings were being carried out with artful aplomb. Both were loud and proud as one might expect, from an *aesthetic* atelier that prided itself on making supervillains look absolutely, corruptibly fuckable. The cat did her best not to stare but could not help but watch the incredibly-well-hung mare currently having a ladder piercing installed. The equine's eyes rolled back as the artist smirked at the gawking feline, just a bare moment before the horse *gasped* at the jab of the needle plunging through tender flesh.

Without thinking, Mabel's tongue traced her lip. *"Mm. Gods, a hot dog sounds **amazing** right about now…"*

[**Down**, *girl!*]

*"But it's just **there**! Their status does say they're 'looking,' and I am certainly enjoying the view, myself. I'm just doing what they're asking for, after all!"*

It was then that a deep velvet country twang cut through the noise, both inside and outside of the cougar's head.

"Well, *hey* there, sugah! Y'all must be my two o'clock!"

The catamount wiped her mouth with the back of a paw, just in case, as she turned to look at the source of the voice … and then, let her gaze trail upward from the massive bust to the gigantic *smile* that lit up the features of the bovine before her.

"Goddess bless, am I doomed to be surrounded by beautiful, gigantic women?"

[*A fate infinitely worse than death, I'm sure.*]

Mabel ignored the sass and held out a paw. "Hey! Uh, yeah! I'm Mabe—OOOF!" She barely had time to gasp as her arm was yanked, and she was pulled into a bear hug (well, cow hug), the air exited her lungs with a sharp wheeze. "But you can call me, hnngh, *Mabes*," she squeaked out, with the last ounce of breath that hadn't yet been wrung from her chest.

"Well, ain'tchu just the *cutest* little thang! I'm Tammi Lynn, but you can call me Tammi, Tam, or even *Miss* Lynn, so long as it gets a pretty girl to say my name!" She laughed and set down the puma (who wanted to laugh very badly but was still working on the whole *breathing* thing). "I am just so happy to have some new blood here, Mabes! Relly already shot me some ideas y'had, and even just at a glance, I think they'll look great! But c'mon in and have yerself a seat! I'll grab us a couple drinks, and we can work this out!" Her arms — all four of them, in fact — gestured to the rear of the space. She had the usual two of most bipeds up top, and two synthetic ones below; at a glance, they seemed to be made of wire mesh and interlocked plates, covered with ornate designs and filigree. The motifs were echoed in the delicate etchings on her horns. The whole look was curated to be *very* gothic chic, and she carried it expertly.

Those selfsame cybernetic arms came to rest behind the bovine, and pointed Mabel up the central aisle towards the "throne" in the back. As they walked by each space, Tammi continued to gab, talking up customers and coworkers alike — while also keeping her newest client informed of the goings on, who was who, what was what, to say nothing of this, that and the other thing. "So, this *here* is Shelly, and that *there* is her favorite canvas, goes by Davis! Now, the filly you were *eyefuckin'*, that's Sandra..."

The feline didn't even have time to blush as the shop maven pressed on. She always thought *she* was a talker, but even though the drawl was long, this cow could beat her hooves-down in a yak-off. "... and that's everyone! We have so many talented folks in-house, but I am just plain tickled you wanted t'work with *me*, sweetie!"

Mabel was bodily spun back to the entrance as she was gently hurled into the crimson and chrome seat, and blinked, shocked at how quickly Tammi moved. Not five seconds later, she was already digging through a minifridge under her counter space — just a bundle of bright energy wrapped up in lace stockings and Daisy Dukes, the friendliest country gal you could ever hope to meet.

"You want a coke, sweetie? The *real* stuff though, not that icky ol' corn syrup swill you get above ground! Or water? I think I even have a couple beers scooted to th'back here, even. You're not gettin' a tat, right?" She giggled, as she glanced back over her shoulder.

"Oh, er ... no, no ink, but a soda would be great!" Mabel smiled, watching the cow's ropey tail swing before she stood back up.

"Well, that's a shame! You'd look good with a little bit of doodlin' done," Tammi murmured, popping the cap off both glass bottles at the same time, using a groove engraved on either horn, before offering one to her new client. "All right, *all right*! Now, like I was sayin': Relly gave me some ideas, lovely lady that she is, but I wanna hear it from you. How can I help you feel more like *you?*"

The catamount smiled almost bashfully as she took a long gulp of the sugary beverage. "Well ... I like the idea of a page cut, and maybe some bangs? I dunno; I never got to explore this side, when it was relevant, but I think I could rock the scene-adjacent hairstyle. Yanno, sorta, uh, Ramona Flowers with less of a tolerance for dopey asshole man-children?"

"Oh, *absolutely,* Mabes; I am pickin' up whatchyer layin' down! The classic Scott to Ramona pipeline! Do we wanna do some dye, too, go for that *'rawr XD'* vibe?" Tammi pulled up a stool, drained half her soda in one impressively long swig, and stared over her retro-looking rhinestone cateye-framed RCGs with a smirk. "Cause *I* think you could rock some stripes!"

"Mm. I think I wanna try to keep this white — I like that as is — but I need to lose a little length, maybe? Not *too* much, but ... yeah." The catamount toyed with a longer strand and nodded, as much to convince herself that this was still a good idea as a go-to fidget.

"Yeah, I can see that mop getting in the way a bit, *'specially* if you're looking to become an agent..." the bovine mused as she tilted her head, one of her strong, hoof-nailed hands stroking her chin as she considered her plan of attack. "Can't have your view gettin' obstructed!"

"I, err ... w-what do you mean?" The lioness brushed her hair out of her face with the nervous sweep of a paw and looked away, instantly watching her cheeks and ears start to redden in the massive mirror.

"Sweetie, you took a straight shot from *Volta!* If you ain't trainin' t'do the super thing, there are much easier ways to getcher lights put out, if y'catch my drift?" The cow laughed as her synthetic digits spun silently through settings and tools, carefully planning her next steps.

The cougar's blush reached critical heat in moments, the appointment nearly forgotten in the sudden rush of self-consciousness. "Does *everyone* know about that?" Mabel's embarrassment flared to new heights as she covered her face. "Ughhhh ... I am *never* going to live that down..."

"Last time I jump in front of a truck for that vixen!"

[**Mabel.** *That's a lie, and we both know it.*]

"Mm."

"Nah! I'm just nosey! I like t'learn a bit about who I'm working with, so I can best plan out our *style journey,* and I know a few folks in those circles. Y'can't be friends with th'big bad wolf and *not* get into trouble, hun! Don't be embarrassed, I don't know a single soul who could stand toe-to-toe with her and *not* get messed up good and proper-like; she is the *realest* deal." The bovine burped loudly as she polished off her soda, giving a little laughing snort to go with it as she shook her head. "I will say, you picked a *hell* of a sparring partner, sug. Just wanted to start at the top to see the view?"

*And I'm gonna go have pizza — not a date, **not a date**, no pressure — with her after this…*

Mabel forced a smile and nodded. "Yeah, I guess so? Volta is something else, no doubt, though I can't blame eating that knee on my hair getting in the way. That was just me being an idiot, really." Mabel finished her own soda with a glug, and the cow took both bottles, dropping them in a convenient recycling chute near the entrance before returning to give a shrug. "Always been an overachiever, to my detriment," the cougar admitted abashedly.

"I dunno, I don't think y'can dodge 'em all. And sometimes y'just need to take it on the chin to *get it*, y'know? I mean…" The cow smirked as she leaned on the back of the chair. "What did y'learn, in th'end?"

The puma's brow furrowed as she considered for a moment, thumb rubbing the back of her other paw. "Funnily enough? That I have friends, and I need to stop running from that. I just wish I could have figured that out another way." The lioness smiled coyly and closed her eyes. "Y'know, like, *not* getting my arm snapped off by a ton of supervillain…?"

Tammi gave a shrug. "Well now, if wishes were fishes, right? Arm looks fine now, and anyhow, I don't think an idiot would learn that from catchin' a beatin'!" As the bovine spoke, she billowed out a smock with a flourish. The material was covered in little pink helixes filled with stylized skulls and looked more than a little *piratical*. "Now, now, enough of all that. Let's dish about the *important* stuff!" The mischievous twinkle in her eye was unmistakable. "Who do you have that eye on, girl? Anyone lookin' particularly tasty? I mean, that mare you were peepin' loves cowgirl, I can tell ya from *firsthand* experience…" One of the three-fingered hooves not in use wiggled lewdly in front of the catamount.

"Ha! No time wasted…"

[*She's a very busy woman, and she hasn't got all day!*] Relly returned in a singsong voice.

Mabel blushed and giggled a little as the cow began brushing out her hair with one of her synth limbs, with another spritzing water as she went. Apparently she could talk a big game, but there was still no escaping the hesitation to go that next step.

"There are a few folks, but I dunno … I haven't been in a relationship in a very long time. I just dunno what to *do* any more…" The puma blinked as she realized how candid she'd been with Tammi, having known the cow with the outsized personality for a grand total of ten minutes. Mabel felt so comfortable; it was like she had known the woman for years! How could she *not* gossip?

"*Relly, Tammi isn't a super right? Like, she doesn't have some sort of psychic touch, or powers of suggestion, anything like that…?*"

[*No, dear, you're just easy to read. Her only superpowers are her sense of style and an incredibly kind spirit.*]

"Well, sugah, I don't mean who y'wanna settle down with! I'm talkin' 'bout stretchin' those legs! You got all that cake, and y'ain't gonna share? Seems a waste…" The stylist was so *frank* but disarmingly tender, and she never stopped working for even a moment. All four hands moved in a graceful dance of perfect harmony, the soft white hair collecting in small drifts on the checkered tiles as she moved on quietly clicking hooves. "Would be a cryin' shame if *no one* was allowed to have a nibble, is all I'm sayin'."

The catamount felt like she must have been incandescently glowing red by that moment, but the candor the cow brought out continued unabated. "I've never really been, like … *casually* sexual before? I mean — you caught me looking like thirty seconds ago — but I never felt *right*. Like … desirable, I mean? Now that we solved that mystery, I'm just … at a loss?" Underneath the vinyl cover, she pulled gently on her fingertips. The snipping sounds — punctuated by intermittent buzzing — never stopped. The strands fell as snow, and accumulated much as it did all the way back home. "I wouldn't know where to even *begin*…"

"Well, you're *plenty* desirable now, sug," Tammi gave her client a little nudge and a wink. "And I know for a fact I ain't the only one that noticed that. S'there anyone you *want* to see you, like that?" Her brow furrowed a bit in the mirror, clearly having noticed the long feline tail swaying with agitation out of the back of the chair.

"M-maybe one or two …? But … I feel *guilty*. I've just sorta been *thrust* upon them. I still worry … even after everything, what if I'm just too *much?*" The puma struggled, unable to finish a thought, and even her RCGs couldn't stop her nerves. Relly did her damnedest to comfort as always, but the spillways had been opened and the words rushed forth. "I just … What do I have to offer? Everyone here is *incredible* … **She** is *incredible* … and I'm just … **this.**" Her voice dropped as low as her heart sank, but before she could continue the self-sabotaging thought, she was interrupted by a finger touching her chin.

Tammi had inadvertently breached a spot the cougar had been carefully avoiding, and her guard crumpled as she met the cow's gaze. The stylist's conversational talents would have made her a top-notch interrogator, for certain. The cat just couldn't help herself; the contents had been under pressure for so long, it barely took anything at all to cause the dam to burst.

"Mabel, dear…" The bovid beauty had spun the chair around to face her and cupped the puma's chin in a gentle hoof. "Can I give you proof that you are *more* than enough?"

The breath was stolen from Mabel's lungs as she was thrust into those icy pools, and all she could manage was a nod.

Tammi placed her dark-painted lips to the feline's, accompanied by a long, slow embrace that instantly prompted the cat's throat to purr, and her toes to curl. The caress was only seconds long, but it felt like time stopped, as a thick tongue slipped between her lips and was hungrily suckled upon, with her own rough organ playing against the languid muscle. All the heat in her face retreated post-haste, only to regroup much further south.

Oh. Oh … gods…

The cougar hadn't been affectionate like that in so very *long*, she had almost forgotten how it felt. Her eyes grew wet, but the tears stayed hidden behind her lids. There was sorrow and joy in equal measure in that embrace, and her heart began to beat like *thunder* in her chest as she sunk into the kiss; while appreciating the gesture, Mabel suddenly wondered what another muzzle would feel like pressed against hers. Another *particular* muzzle. One with hot cinnamon sweetness clinging to her lips.

As Tammi broke the kiss, the puma let out a tiny moan, and her eyes fluttered open. She was staring into the mirror; the bovid was behind her once again, chin resting on her shoulder, breath hot on her neck. The cat's tail puffed out with flustered agitation.

"You're enough, and if you don't believe me, take a peep of this hot pussy in my chair."

The master stylist had already completed her latest masterpiece. Mabel's bangs rested on her brows, and her face was framed by long strands that faded back around into a tousled mass that just *begged* to have fingers run through it. It was as if Tammi had reached into her dreams and plucked out the most perfect version of her headfur. Ears that had been splayed in sadness perked up once again, and the tears dried up at the sheer euphoric sight of herself. A tentative paw reached up to touch the coiffure, and for the second time in as many weeks, the catamount could hardly believe that this life was real.

She was not a fantasy. She was *right there*. No AR, no fleeting figment of a depressed soul's longing imagination. *Actual. Factual. Reality.*

"*This?* Mabesy Babesy, you are not a '*this.*' You're not a '*that*' or a '*what.*' You're *you*. You're gorgeous, sweetheart, make no mistake. Don't letcherself get hung up so much on who you *were*; let yourself be who you *are*. It doesn't have t'be as complicated as all of that…" The most intensely blue eyes the cougar had ever seen stared into her, and her thoughts stumbled, lost as she briefly was in that gaze. Tammi's hooves held her face still and wouldn't allow the cat to look away.

*Oh, I am painfully gay. I am so incredibly, **painfully** gay.*

"But … th-there was so *much*, before…" Mabel mumbled, shaking as part of her tried to fight this feeling of rightness.

"We all *existed* before, but now? Now y'actually get to *live!* Did you make mistakes? Well, who didn't? Fix what y'can, but don't hesitate now, sweetheart—" Tammi's smile was so kind it threatened to grind the cat into dust. "Don't give yourself the *chance* to regret."

"What if I'm *wrong?* Tammi … I don't want to…" Mabel whispered in response.

*Hurt. I don't want to hurt anyone. I don't want to **hurt**.*

"Shh, shh, shh. Tell me, who are *you* now? Right this second?" Tami knelt in front of the catamount, one set of hands holding the arms of the chair, the other still cupping the round face of her new friend.

"Mabel. Mabel Greysmoke." The feline was barely audible as she closed her eyes.

"And what're you?" The cow leaned closer, and she could smell her breath again.

"A … A cougar?" Her eyes locked on Tammi's, unable and unwilling to move.

"And…?" Their noses were touching now. It took increasing willpower for the lioness to refrain from wanting to just kiss her again.

"A girl?" She quirked a brow, a smirk growing on her features as she remained ignorant, but could not help being playful.

"You're a *fuckin'* villain, Mabes!" A deep rumble shook the cougar's bones as the bovine's smile showed teeth that were terribly, surprisingly sharp. She'd somehow missed them previously, but now her lustful mind wandered, wondering how they might feel buried in her shoulder, grasping at fur and flesh with tender ferocity...

The puma learned, then, that Holsteins could growl: an astonishingly bassy sound that made her vibrate in all of the right places, then gasp out her reply. "I'm a villain..." She repeated the words, rolling them around in her muzzle, savoring them like she would her favorite smoke.

"*LOUDER!* Say it with your chest! Let the cheap seats hear it!" Tammi stood back, and motioned for the cat to stand as she yanked the cover clear.

"*I'M A VILLAIN!*" Mabel shouted as she stood from the chair, laughing madly as fire filled her heart, poured into all of her limbs, and spilled out from her screaming maw.

[**YOU'RE A VILLAIN!**]

"You're a fuckin' villain, and no one can ever take that from you!"

"*I'M A FUCKIN' VILLAIN!*" Mabel threw her head back and yowled, but it was a joyful sound this time, and it rolled through the shop. Soon another voice raised up — not knowing why, exactly, but who in the Korps could resist a good howl? Soon another voice joined, and then another, until the wave of exuberance-without-reason spilled out into the walkway; the primal roar rolled across the crowds and was lifted higher still, echoing through the rafters like a wave of villainous exhilaration.

Below the city of Austin, the Korps did not cower or hide.

No, they *thrived*.

For just a second, Mabel didn't feel like she was pretending. She understood that this was who she was; who she *wanted* to be. Who she *could* be, if she just took those next terrifying steps...

Let go...

"Yeah! Now let's get you stuck, you bad bitch!" Tammi gave the puma a peck on the cheek before turning back to her table.

"W-wait, wha-huh?" Mabel blinked, flushing once again; her fur poofed out all in the same moment, as she stared, wide-eyed, at her stylist.

"*Piercings*, Mabesy, I mean piercings! Y'wanna get stuck the other way, y'need t'at least buy me dinner first, sug! Just the ears today, though, right?" From one forearm slipped a rather sinister-looking needle, while the other grasped a pair of triangular-tipped tongs.

"Well. Well! Well ... you know what, Tammi? Maybe we can go a little further than just two ...? Don't want to be too *vanilla*, after all."

"Oooooh, I like the sound of that, girl! You tell me where, darlin' and I'll get you all shiny..." The cow clicked the clamps together as she raised a brow, clip clopping close as she listened to the desires of the catamount that settled back into the chair.

Stay afraid, but do it anyway.

"Tammi was gentle, but damn, it still stings a little…"

[Don't touch them! It will only make them hurt worse!]

"Mmf. But…" Her piteous mental whimper was just as pathetic as one voiced aloud. It was time for Mabel to make her way to Josie's, which Volta touted as the last pizza place Mabel would ever want to visit, upon messaging the wolf to alert her that she was on the way. The cat snorted to herself as she shook her head.

Mm. We'll see about that. I've lived down south for a dozen years now, and in none of those years have I ever found a slice worth bragging on.

[Look, you were the one that had to get six holes done today!] Relly laughed, playfully berating Mabel for her thoroughly reckless decision that was *totally* not prompted by any urge to gain the approval of a certain wolf.

"It was just the ears, though!" The puma was very glad she held off on any more *adventurous* piercings, based solely on the throbbing in her lobes. *"So many ouchies…"*

[I promise you, if you say **ouchies** *unironically in front of Volta, you are never getting any further with her than you are right now, romantically or otherwise.]*

"Mmm, that's fair. What about with Ellen?" The cougar smirked, attempting to maintain a confident mien as she strode into the dining area, gazing at the various food hall-style stalls on offer.

[Eh … Probably fine there. I mean, she's at **least** *as big a dork as you are. If anything, she might complain you're encroaching on her territory.]*

"I'll take my chances then! 'Sides … got Tammi's contact, didn't I?" Mabel retorted with pride.

[Mmmhm, touché darling girl, and all it took was a little confidence! Building up quite the little black book, huh?]

The catamount blushed a little as she spotted the sign for Josie's 24/7 Pizza. There, leaning on the warmly wood-paneled wall next to the door, was Volta. The wolf was a tower of cool and collected confidence clad in leather and brilliant autumn, every bit the beautiful Amazon, as always.

The lioness found her breath caught in her chest, as it so often did when she got to drink in that sight. When her magenta gaze spotted Mabel, she looked almost surprised, her eyebrows raising and her mouth turning into a momentary O.

"*Oh no...*" The lioness winced, instantly self-conscious, but a sound she never expected twisted her anxiety into bashful happiness.

Volta let loose a very literal wolf whistle as she approached. The lupine shifted herself to get a better look, paws falling to the cougar's shoulders, even tilting her head about to examine the new 'do from as many angles as she wished. "Kitty*cat!* Look at you! Cuuuuuuute ... No. *Wait.*" The younger woman lifted a paw and ran her claws up through the purposefully messy back. The cougar's tail went rail-straight and it took all her power not to let her eyes shut, but she was helpless to stop the purr that began rumbling. Before she could recover, the wolf continued. "Not cute ... *hot!* Holy shit girl, you look *dangerous!* It suits you! And check out the piercings! Did we get anything further *south?*" She leaned in close to whisper the last part, and the feline had to bite her tongue to prevent a giddy squeal at the spicily-scented heat brushing against her sensitive ear.

Should I have, Volta? Keep doing that with your paw, and I'll pierce whatever you like ... I'll get you every ring and stud and chain that you would ever want to suck, or tug on ... The thought intensified the blush on her cheeks a hundred times over.

"Oh ... uh ... no, heh ... er, just the ears ... f-for now ... I mean!" She said the last bit almost apologetically, before trying to slow her rushing lustful thoughts. *Okay, take a step back, Mabel. You're a fuckin' villain, remember? Get a hold of yourself, girl! You're not some horny stereotype!* A deep breath, and she was centered again.

Mostly.

"So! Ellen and Vixie coming along? Or Carmen, maybe?" Mabel hesitated on the last one, lest saying it were to will the tabby into appearing then and there. While the relationship between the two *might* have become cordial enough, the lingering chill was still present in her mind, and Mabel was not sure how to overcome it. That selfsame chilliness might have helped prevent her from just being a babbling *fool* for the entire meal, however.

"Nah! Just us! Rest of the gang was busy, so you get me *all* to yourself! Aren't *you* a lucky girl?" Volta slipped her arm about the puma's shoulders and walked towards the door.

W-what? All ... t-to ... Mabel was so emotionally off-kilter at that moment she couldn't even conceive of where "kilter" *was*, but the wolf pressed on.

"Now, Peps is a handful, but he is *never, ever wrong* about pizza, get it? Just trust the maestro!" The gentle squeeze of reassurance was a tiny gesture, but it kept Mabel present, and not screaming through the corridors of her anxious mind.

"Right! Listen to Peps. Got it." The cat's paw reached up to touch the wolf's, and the slightest bit of static unfurled across her fur, rolling an inadvertent shiver through her body. *This is fine ... It's not a date. Just pizza with a friend! Easy! Just means we can nerd out about stupid Hero shit, and no one will roll their eyes! You've done this hundreds of times! Not. A. Big. Deal.*

She's just a girl!

That you have seen naked...

And have absolutely dreamed about...

And uh ... mm. **Fuck.**

"**VOLTA!** Just the girl I wanted to see! *And* you brought a date! What a *cutie-pie!*" The shout came from behind the counter, and as the tapir beamed up at his favorite customer, a single bead of sweat rolled down the cat's brow.

...Fuck.

"Date? Oh, nah! Peps, this is Mabel; she's a friend!" The wolf laughed, as she nudged the cougar with her hip.

Okay, yeah! Good! Good. She ... She corrected them...

...So why does that feel **worse?**

CHAPTER 24

A TANGLED, KNOTTED MESS

*She's just a friend. That's what I **wanted**. Yeah.*

[*Mabes, are you all right?*]

"Yeah! I'm fine! Just … hanging out with a friend, right?"

[*Really?*]

"Yeah! It's … It's fine, Relly, don't sweat it."

"Then you'll have to remind me to split the check!" the tapir smiled, giving Mabel a little nudge with his elbow before squeezing her paw between his own. "So, Mabel, huh? A lovely name for a lovely lady! The regulars call me Peps, but you can call me Gowan if you like, as in, 'oh, *do* Gowan'!"

The catamount stared down at his paws. Taking a breath, she pushed a grin to the surface as she looked back at the grey-furred snoot and smile of the older mammal. "How about '*Gowan* with your bad self'? You can call me Mabes, and Volta tells me you'll convert me from my heretical devotion to New York pizza?" She grasped his paw in both of hers, features twisted with exaggerated worry, putting on a show for his benefit as much as a distraction to herself. "Can I be *saved*, Gowan?" The puma placed the back of her paw to her forehead, and struck her best fainting, forsaken maiden pose.

"Don't worry, hun! Your salvation from the heartbreak of the greasy common slice is here! Now, let me get a good look at you! *Hmmm…*" He stepped back to take her in, nose twitching all the while as he brought a finger to his lip, tapping slowly before he nodded to himself. "I've got *just* the thing! Go settle in, you two; I'll have your pizzas ready before you can get a good drool going!" He chuckled to himself as he trundled back to the kitchen, no doubt familiar with the lupine's propensity for salivation. It had been quite a while since an older, masculine figure made Mabel feel so at ease, but it was a welcome development.

The outcome of the exchange did leave her curious, however. "Isn't ... isn't he gonna take our orders...?" The catamount blinked and tilted her head as she watched him leave.

"Nah. Peps always brings me pizzas I didn't *know* I wanted, but he's always right. So, I just let him go nuts, 'wherever his muse takes him,' he says," Volta stated plainly. With a shrug, she turned to wander to an empty booth. It was sort of too late for lunch, and a little too early for dinner, but somehow the place was still *packed*. Luckily, the wolf's favorite booth — properly sized for her generous proportions — was just getting wiped down from clearing the previous patron's dishes.

"Ah! Makes sense, I guess ... Oh *shit*, I forgot!" The lioness cursed, before she turned to shout towards the kitchen. "Could we get some mozz sticks and melba, please, Gowan? I'll love you forever!"

"Ahhh, you're from upstate, huh? Yeah, we can do that. But you're gonna love me after this pizza anyhow," he replied cheekily, followed by a hearty guffaw.

"Mozz and ... melba?" Volta quirked a brow. "What the fuck is *that?*"

"*Uh-uh!* Spoilers! It's good, I promise. Who doesn't like fried cheese? No one, that's who! Besides ... don't you trust me?" Mabel batted delicate feline eyelashes in her best attempt at being disarming, trying to gather back up her scattered bravado as best she could.

"Well, I mean, your taste in *capes* is kinda sus, but your taste in women is pretty good. So I'll give you the benefit of the doubt." Volta let out a barking laugh and gave the puma a little hip check before settling into her seat.

Between the comment and her actual girth, the wolf had knocked her friend a little off balance. To the cat's credit, she recovered quickly with a startled yelp. The cougar snorted as she slid into the booth opposite the wolf, rolling her eyes. "Yeah, yeah, you're gorgeous, I know it, everyone knows it ... But you can't sit here and give me shit for *my* taste in heroes with a straight face! TN2 was a goody-two-shoes boy scout!" She brushed her paw through her headfur with an appropriate exasperation, before waving it back dismissively with a flourish of her wrist.

"Oh yeah? And *Ellen* is the picture of badass rebellion? Miss 'Aw-Jeez-Boy-Howdy-You-Betcha'?" Volta inspected her claws as she casually returned the serve with an exaggerated Midwestern accent. "She had *Lawful* in her name, Mabes."

"I mean ... She *did* beat the shit out of her boss that one time ...? That's *kinda* anti-establishment...?" Mabel pretended she wasn't taken aback, but she clearly hadn't thought this argument all the way through. She had been put on the back foot, conversationally speaking.

"Uh-*huh*. And what about the *rest* of her career?" A single eyebrow raised, and the wolf had ended the argument.

"All right, fine. *Fine*. True North the Second, was a Canadian treasure ... *but he was no Magella*," the lioness muttered, knowing she was defeated, but trying despite it all to go down swinging. "No sense of style at all!"

"Uh-huh. Just like *your* comebacks, Kittycat." There was no coming back from that, but as the blush made the catamount's ears grow redder by the second, she wondered: was being dominated so thoroughly by an amazon really so bad?

"I give! *I give!* You win!" Mabel smiled brightly at the red wolf as she smirked back at her with smug satisfaction and idly toyed with the tines of her fork. The butterflies in her stomach were whipped into their usual frenzy at the very sight of her smile.

"*She is so damn **confident**. Gods, how can she always make me feel this way?*"

[*She is a charming specimen, to be sure, but who can say, really?*] Relly likely knew the answer — as did her little sister — but saying it out loud made it real, and neither were prepared to do that.

"I will admit he made some pretty impressive plays, back in the day."

"Okay, and *I* will concede that Magella was incredibly hot."

"I know, *right?* Thank you! Honestly, I wish I spent more time reading and collecting her stuff when I was a kid, but that was a little too, uh, 'girly,'." Mabel shrugged. "No good for a growing boy, according to my dad ... Ugh. Every birthday it was another Manifest Destiny comic, or Skyscrapper figure..." The cat let out a snort, "With Authentic Scrappin' Swing! *So fuckin' lame.*"

Volta rolled her eyes, "Ah, few more and you'd have the Shithead All-Stars..." She made the universally accepted gesture for wasting time with one paw. "*Fuck'em.*"

It felt good to have someone that understood the struggle, so the puma just kept going. "Ha! Yeah, and when Golden Gavel hit the scene? My dad was ecstatic to have such a *paragon* of masculine ideals for me to 'emulate' ... What a fucking fashy tool..." She had snagged a straw from the jar on the table and twisted the paper wrapper off, just trying to keep her paws occupied and the conversation going, mind wandering and not really considering where it led.

"Yeah … I'd rather not talk about *him*, if it's all the same to you." Just like that, the feeling in the air shifted. The wolf's tone changed immediately, and the catamount suddenly realized the faux pas — but it was already too late. The rapid-fire thumping of the tail-wag was gone, and the flatware in the wolf's powerful grip was bent with a quietly staticky squeak.

"Oh, right, o-of course. Stupid of me, I'm sorry … W-wasn't thinking…" The cougar winced as her ears splayed dejectedly, staring at the table between them, misery pushing down on her slouching shoulders.

Welp. There I go! Moment sufficiently ruined.

"It's fine. It's *fine*, please don't … I just … Yeah. Fuck Adam Tullis." The fork, now a mangled ball of metal half-welded to itself, was tossed to the far end of the table with a quiet clink.

"Yeah. Fuck that guy!" Mabel smiled weakly, but when she looked at Volta, there was no smile left — just a low-simmering anger bubbling beneath the brilliance of her narrowed magenta eyes. The silence was *deafening*. Mabel stared at her straw wrapper, idly balling it up and batting it with a fingertip, trying to keep her gaze anywhere but meeting the wolf's own.

The crushing weight of the awful quiet forced her to do something. *Anything.*

"So … I…" Mabel stammered a bit, eyes still solidly on the table. "Err…"

Oh, for fucks sakes, I've forgotten how to form a godsdamn sentence?

Before she could utter another unintelligible syllable, she felt a finger catch under her chin, lifting it with delicacy unexpected from such a massive paw. Volta's soft smile had returned, and not an ounce of malice was to be found.

"It's fine, Mabes. M'sorry if I scared you, just … Let's not ruin the mood by bringing up that piece of shit, okay?"

"Yeah! Sure! Absolutely…" Her caramel-and-chocolate fur hid some of the blush. But only *some*.

Gay. Gay. Gay. Oh, gods, I am so very extremely gay.

"Good girl. Appreciate it, Kittycat."

A gentle thumb stroked the lioness's cheek, and not even a *second* later, her stomach was knotted up and electrified like that unfortunate fork. She counted her blessings that her tail was hidden from view, so it could not betray her more than her half-lidded eyes nor unbridled rumbling purr already had.

I will do every single last thing you tell me to, until the end of time. Just call me a good girl again. **Please...?**

"Oh? We like that, huh?" The smirk was back, as the wolf stared down her nose.

Mabel very nearly nodded, but the welcome sight of a certain tapir caught the corner of her eye, and she cleared her throat.

"Oh *hey*, pizza! Isn't that great? Gowan is here with the pizza! *Mmm*, pizza!" The lioness's fast talk poured out with nary breath or a pause, and her friend simply snorted and dropped the line of questioning, much to her relief.

"You got it, Mabes! So, what I have for you *here* is a thin crust for the base, with some salty feta, roasted tomatoes, and a spicy reduced balsamic I've been working on. Playing with that sweet-and-salty thing you clearly like with that mozz and melba, right?" He gave her a wink as he placed her pie on the wire rack, along with a basket of crispy fried cheese and a sticky reddish-purple sauce.

The smell instantly took her home. It had been years, but the memory was unlocked, and behind that portal came feelings unbidden.

Late nights on Lark Street, laughing and wishing she meant it. Dinner at the Fountain with a girl who never would get the chance to understand why she left. The smiles of friends whose faces she had nearly forgotten, as they all drifted apart. Snatches of moments that were bitter and sweet in equal measure, just like so much of her life before all of ... *this*. The new her. Which was a lot like the old her, admittedly, but just ... *actually* her, finally.

The puma had stared at the steaming food without a word for several heartbeats before looking back up to the chef-turned-server. Her sad smile and wetly shining eyes were unable to be hidden, and she sniffled.

"Thank you, Gowan ... It's *perfect*."

He patted her paw gently and nodded knowingly. "Good food can do more than just make you less hungry, hun, and that is a fact. Don't be sad, though; now you get to give new memories to the meal, hmm?"

Mabel chuckled and dotted her sleeve at her nose. "Yeah. Yeah! I *thought* you were just going to give me a pie, not a new perspective on life, oh sage of the slice!" Her sad smile felt *slightly* less sad as she tried to grasp Gowan's wisdom.

"I'm *very* good at what I do." With another laugh, he turned to Volta. "Your pie is finishing up, and I think you're going to love it! I'll bring some water too, but anything else you all need?"

"Oh, could we get some soda? What do you like, V? Mountain Dew Voltage? Code Redline, maybe?" Mabel quirked an eyebrow, seemingly recovered enough to remember her sass. She made her companion roll her eyes and shake her head, but she still smiled that smile.

"You are a fuckin' dork, Mabes, but uhh … Actually, *do* you have any Code Red, Peps? Please?" Just out of sight there was the faint beat of a hopeful tail-wag to go with those big magenta eyes.

"For you, hun, I'll bring two pitchers!" With that, he was off again — weaving between tables, checking in with customers, and being a genuine delight, as always.

The catamount's stomach growled as the realization dawned that she had not eaten anything besides some toast, and it was quickly closing on dinnertime. Spurred on by hunger, she went to dig in but caught herself: something more important needed to be done first.

Carefully, she chose one of the crispy fried treats from the basket, and dipped it in the melba sauce, before holding it out to the wolf. "All right, Volta, as promised, a treat for my rescuer, and my first villainous associate! I mean, after Relly, I suppose." It was the puma's turn to quirk a brow now as she resisted the urge to waggle the cheese stick at her companion, lest the precious sauce get lost. "C'mon! It's gooooood!"

The lupine's nose flared ever-so-slightly at the aroma before she suddenly lunged forward and snapped her teeth around the offered mozzarella.

The cougar yanked her paw back with an exaggerated "Eep!" before counting her fingers dramatically. "Hey! I just got those done! Nurse O will *do harm unto* me if I go back so soon!"

The she-wolf cackled as she licked the sticky residue from her lip. "Mmm … Okay, sweet and salty, I think I get it! Not bad at all, Kittycat, thanks for sharing!" Her tongue traced her dark-painted lip, as she reached out to nab a slice of the Mediterranean thin-crust pie before them.

"Thanks for rescuing me and all. Least I can do is show a little appreciation and share some junk food, right?" Mabel blushed a bit as she shrugged at the mammoth occupant on the other side of the booth. "I'm just … *really* glad you decided to keep me around. I like spending time together. Like, like friends, I mean! I … I just enjoy your company," the cougar trailed off, tugging on her fingers, before she heaved a sigh. "Sorry for being so awkward … But like … yeah. Thanks."

Volta tilted her head slightly as she smiled back. She couldn't have known the effect the gesture had on the cat — or, maybe she did, and just liked to watch her squirm. "I enjoy your company too, Mabes." She opened her maw wide, dropping the relatively small piece of pie in with a cheeky smile, muttering around the piece as chewed. "Mmm! And no reason not to be friends! Stop sweating it, okay? We watched episodes of True North under the safety blanket and ate pasta and everything. *Relax!*"

"I'll try my best..." The feline drifted to that moment, clinging to the glow of that memory; the two of them huddled close, and just relishing time together. *Gowan is right. New memories for this meal. Enjoy it and stop overthinking every single thing...*

Mabel picked up her own slice and tucked in — doing her best impression of a picky French food critic tasting a rodent's signature dish — just in time for the chef to appreciate the fruits of his labors, three pitchers in one paw and a pan balanced on the other.

"That good, huh?" he smirked slyly.

"Gowan, this is the best thing I have ever put in my mouth in my nearly four decades on this Earth. *Yes*, I know how that sounds, and *no*, I will *not* be changing my answer." She replied before shoving the rest of the slice in behind, and barely resisting the urge to actually say 'OM NOM NOM.'

The tapir chortled as he set down Volta's prize, which was at *least* three feet across, but the table was well equipped for it — as was the recipient, whose tail wagged like a speedboat's outboard motor.

"Something *really* special! Some shaved cactus, pickled habaneros, queso chihuahua, spicy red and a swirl of lime crema! I call it a 'Tickled Prickle Pickle'! Hang a fang on that, kiddo; let me know how *good* I am at this!"

Before he could say "Careful, it's hot!" Volta had already devoured one slice and had plucked another from the tray. Her eyes lit up (equally possibly from pleasure as pain) and tears ran down her cheeks, but she nearly moaned around the second piece. "Another masterpiece, Peps, you are a fuckin' genius!" She began to pant after the following slice and quickly started to drain one of the pitchers of alarmingly red Dew, the water ignored for the moment.

Gowan gave a little bow, clearly enjoying his well-deserved praise, and began shuffling back towards the kitchen. "All the thanks I needed! Enjoy your date, kids!" he called out bemusedly.

"Not a date!" Mabel called back, blushing as the older gent waved a paw dismissively. She shook her head and brought her attention back to Volta, who was polishing off the last of her carbonated beverage. Her throat undulated in an almost hypnotic way — the fluff rising and falling with each gulp — and the puma was mesmerized. It was completely emptied in one go before the canid slammed the plastic container on the table with a hollow thud. She smacked her lips loudly before cutting loose with a belch that was just plain impressive.

Barbarian impressive.

"Braaaaaaaaaaaaaaaawp!" The window next to Volta vibrated quietly in the frame and she smiled with every last tooth in her head, staring down at the cat who was staring, wide-eyed, back at her. A paw absently patted her chest as she blew a faintly pizza-scented kiss across the table, and the cat's eyes fluttered as she sat entranced.

"Scuse me! Did you want a slice, Mabes?"

"Holy *shit*, Volta! Take me now, you sexy Bitch!" The catamount shouted as she cackled, waving her paw in front of her face, before she saw the wolf staring at her with a quirked brow. The grin that settled across her features caused the guffaw to settle into a nervous chuckle. "Uhh ... *heh*..." She jammed a raspberry-smeared cheese stick into her muzzle to prevent any more words from escaping the traitorous hole in her head.

"Take me now? What the fuck is wrong with me!"

"Take you now, huh? I thought we agreed this wasn't a date, Kittycat?" Somehow, her smile became even more mischievous with a simple, looming lean forward, fingers steepled under her chin in the classically-nefarious manner. *"Right?"*

"Err ... uh ... it's not! I was just, uh, it..." Stumbling over her words again, she could only wonder if she would ever be able to have a consistent conversation with the lupine or would forevermore be doomed to nervous spluttering.

"Did you *want* this to be a date...?"

"...W-what? Why would ... you, uh ... What?" The puma's eyes darted around the room as she considered the quickest path of egress from the suddenly *very* hot seat.

Did **you** *want it to be a date, V? I...*

"Mabes, I'm *fuckin'* with you; chill out! Eat some pizza and try to pretend I'm not the hottest wolf you know. I know it's hard," the wolf snorted with a lasciviously villainous smirk. She took another slice, then slid the pie closer to her friend as another pitcher of radioactively reddish liquid was delivered — right on cue, if the telltale belch from the *previous* pitcher was any indication.

*Yeah, easier said than done. Wait ... do I like burps now? That was a joke, right? Who **am** I?*

"I'd make a *similar* crack about being the cutest cat you know, but you're already dating Carmen, sooooo ... *yup*," Mabel shrugged, as she bit into her offered slice. The slightly sweet, floral and citrus notes played delightfully over her taste buds for just a moment, before all the heat snuck up at once and full-on sucker-punched her tongue right out of her muzzle. The flush that instantly appeared on her cheeks was, for a change, entirely related to the culinary indiscretion she had made rather than their previous flirtatious exchange. "Oh! Ah! HAAAAH!" She ignored the cup — there was simply no time — and grabbed the second pitcher, tilting her head back and downing mouthful after mouthful of syrupy-sweet succor until she had half-emptied the vessel in rushed, glugging pulls.

The puma leaned back in the booth — eyes shut tight as she rubbed her belly, tongue lolled in an attempt to expose it to cool air — before she felt the rumble herself. It would not be stopped by any meager attempt at polite decorum; no demure paw could contain this eructation.

"Boooooooouroup!" When she next exhaled it came out in a ragged pant. It felt like she had breathed a plume of fire along with it, and she wiped the sweat from her brow. Her eyes stayed shut as she tried to think soothingly chilly thoughts.

"Haaaaa ... haaa ... 'scuse me...!" She hiccupped, and a little cloud of dark smoke came along with it for emphasis. Soon after came the sound of ... *clapping*, apparently? One feline eyelid snapped open just as Volta started giggling, stopping just short of a standing ovation for the display. Patrons at several other tables began joining in as well with scattered hoots and cheers. It seemed the lioness would be making a scene all over RIV, that day.

Volta guffawed, reaching across the table to give the cougar a slap on the shoulder. "I didn't know ya had it in ya, Kittycat! Fuckin' *nice* one!"

"I don't anymore! It's all in the air now!" Mabel recovered her smile, grabbed a slice of non-five alarm pizza, and tried to hide the non-capsaicin-related blush that reinflamed her cheeks.

"Heh..." The red wolf winked as she polished off the cougar's doomed-to-go-uneaten slice, before working on her next. "So, you think Carmen is *cute*, huh? Did I hear that right?"

The cat nearly choked.

"*Oh gods … Yes? I mean of course?* Volta, I have eyeballs, and I suspect even if I didn't, I would still *know* how attractive Carmen Rayne is? *Fuck,* I mean…" She stared at the table as she attempted to stick the landing. "She's so *hot,* but I wouldn't ever presume to like … I wasn't objectifying, or … Oh *gods…*" She dropped the slice and buried her face in her paws, groaning loudly, and shaking her head. "Please don't tell her I said that? I *like* breathing unassisted, Volta. It's basically the thing I'm best at."

She felt a colossal paw clasp her wrist, and a thumb rubbing gently on the inside, just like she had done before.

Oh…

"It's okay, Mabes … My girlfriend *is* hot. And y'know you're pretty cute too, yeah? Don't sell yourself short, Mountain Mama." The tension was defused instantly by her friend's soft words and kind touch. "Look, I love teasin', but I'll stop if it bothers you, all right?"

"I don't want you to stop, Red…" Mabel smiled at that, and stopped just short of a purr as she tucked into the rest of the meal, leaving the "Pickle Prickle Phucker" or *whatever it was* to the amazon across the way. "I *like* it when you tease me. It makes me feel … *normal.* Like maybe I can manage, somehow? I'm just learning a lot about who I am now, but I promise I'll get there. *Especially* with your help."

"Good, because I didn't really wanna stop!"

"You're a peach, V, truly. A saint amongst the sinners."

"Hey now, I got a reputation. Don't say that too loud, or people will start to talk."

"A reputation, eh? Do they know you cry when Gandalf falls? Oh, yeah, I caught that sniffle, pup!"

"Now *listen* here you little *shit—*"

So went the rest of the meal: laughter at playful digs, bold claims to the power scale of heroes and villains — including more first-hand accounts of embarrassing one Ms. Ellen Foxpaw in combat, amongst other capes — and another gallon of caffeinated goodness, before all was said and done. Mabel was sure she would have to be rolled back home, because not a crumb was left to be found on the table. But this, Peps told them as he bid them to return soon, was what he always intended. The man was all patronly smiles and good-natured back pats, echoing the pats on their full bellies as they wandered out, continuing their previous conversation.

"—So she's lookin' up at me weird, dented forehead and everything, up to her neck in fuckin' concrete, and for a second I'm like, 'oh, shit, did I fuckin' kill her or something?'"

"And that's when you got hit by a truck?"

"No, Kittycat, then she said some cornball shit that summoned a truck. Your goofy ass is lucky I'm still here and not reincarnated into another world. Her goofy ass is twice as lucky, 'cuz Carmen would have actually killed her."

The puma stopped walking for a moment, and turned to the wolf, pouting, eyes wide and sparkling with unspent tears. "Volta…?"

"…*What?*"

"What was the pun?"

"Oh, no. Ohhhhh no. Absolutely not."

"Pleeeeeeease?"

"It wasn't even good. I'm not sayin' it ever is, but it was bad even by Ellen standards."

"C'moooonnn! I never ask for anything!"

"All right, fine. She said," Volta began, but not before adopting the surliest looking frown that a non-muppet face could manage, and dropping into an annoyed monotone, "I've been hammered before, but I never knew I could be this driven."

"That *worked?* Holy shit, the audio was so bad I never knew the punchline she used!" Mabel drank this exclusive account up, unable to disguise the child-like joy lighting up her nerdy brain.

"Yeah, it worked. Turns out taking a running start to kick her head clean off counts as 'reacting.' Next thing I knew, Nurse O was pickin' a U-Haul's shattered headlights out of my ass crack in medbay." Volta grinned, hissing through her teeth. "Still got away with half a filing cabinet's worth of state secrets and a bunch of government credit card data, so Ellen didn't even get to call it a draw."

The lioness snorted and covered her mouth.

Volta could only roll her eyes, unable to ignore the cat's eager expression. "Alright, go ahead and say it, before you burst."

"So would you say you're still *sore* about that pun—" Mabel raised an eyebrow, the shit-eating grin threatening to split her head in two, "Or is it just a *bruised* ego?"

The crackle of electricity between the red wolf's thumb and finger sounded *uncannily* similar to a taser being tested. "Don't you fuckin' start with that shit! Bad enough that I have to deal with Standup on the daily now!"

"Hey, I'm just a stupid fuckin' puma! Gotta keep up appearances, yeah?" The puma-in-question snarked with love, as Volta gave her a playful shove, thankfully sans tasing.

"You're *the* stupid fuckin' puma, Kittycat." The wolf shook her head, but the tail wag that came with her grousing only encouraged the cougar. "Guess I like you that way."

"I can live with that distinction! Mmm…" Mabel mused idly as she slipped a small container from her hoodie pocket. "There's only one thing to really *properly* top off that meal." She withdrew an already-prepared cigar from her travel humidor and offered it to Volta. "I think I know the answer, but … would you like one?"

A small, forced smile and a wrinkle of her nose rendered the dismissive wave of the paw unnecessary. "Not a big fan of smoke."

"*Ah.* I'll just save it, then," the cougar murmured as she pulled the stick back from her lips.

The wolf gave a little sniff and a shrug. "Nah, go ahead."

It was the work of a moment to get the stogie lit; a click of the lighter, a few puffs, and the leaf was burning merrily away. Muzzlefuls of warm vapor did in fact, pair wonderfully with a full belly, and the scent settled her nerves. It truly was hard to be nervous with a good cigar in paw or maw, though Mabel made a mental note that smoking was not going to be something she could do around the wolf.

Her comfort was infinitely more important to the puma than her new favorite bad habit.

"Mmm…" As she exhaled, she made sure to use her powers to keep the smoke away from the wolf's sensitive sniffer. "Thanks for the meal, and the kindness, V. It really helps, like, more than you can realize."

"My pleasure, what are friends for? I certainly can't rescue you from your poor choices in games…" There was that sly smirk again, and this time it *barely* made her weak in the knees.

Progress!

"*Listen here*, you *zygote*, I don't care how 'cool' Fang is! What about Freya? *What about her forgotten love? Kids* these days … *Feh.* No appreciation for the classics!"

The back and forth came so easily as they walked, Mabel didn't realize they had already reached the end of their platonic non-date until they reached the rail stop and Volta leaned down and gave the catamount a hug and a peck on the cheek. The wolf turned as she reached the door to the tram and flashed that smile once again. "Shoot me a message this weekend, all right? Maybe I can finally get that rematch you owe me in HeroClash?"

"You're on, V! Calling for the thunder, and you're not *ready* for this boom!" Mabel's tail still stood up behind her, and she was still blushing, but it wasn't so confusing as it once was. Maybe she wasn't ready for more than this, anyway; that was okay. More wasn't *expected*. As she watched the car zip along the track, she nodded to herself.

"I think I'll take 'cute,' for a start. So that's Ellen **and** Volta who think that, yeah?"

[And me, and Neera, and Vixie, and half of RIV, you knucklehead! Tammi literally made cow-eyes at you and shoved her tongue down your throat!]

"Mmm ... okay. Maybe I can believe it if you say so, Relly."

[Mm. Like you said, it's a start!]

As she pressed on, walking and puffing merrily away, Mabel had a thought. "Relly, did we get a response back from my parents yet?"

[Yes we did, sweetie. It came during your not-date, so I wanted to let you finish eating...]

"That bad, huh?"

[It's not **terrible,** but ... also not great, admittedly.]

The message could not be sent through normal channels, of course. Luckily, the Korps had many ways to both avoid detection, and deliver messages with a minimum of trouble for even the most technologically-unsound individuals. That definitely included Mr. Raymond Greysbell:

Dear Joey,

Your mother and I are glad to hear you are OK, and the rest of the family is glad too. I knew you wouldn't just jump a cop, the story didn't add up, we didn't raise you like that. I don't really understand why all of this is happening, or why the Korps is involved, but we're all just happy you're safe. I guess if you say you're a girl now, that is who you are, but it will take time for us to get used to it, but we'll try.

You always were a little different, but I guess we didn't see it.

As much as we want you to come home for Christmas, I don't think it's safe. There are cars tailing me around town, and mom could swear she heard someone on the phone line the other day.

You'll always be our son, and we'll always love you, no matter what.

Hopefully we can all see each other soon.

All our love,

Mom and Dad

Sent Via Korpsrespondence: Safe and Secure!

All of the wind was taken out of her sails by the contents of the letter. Each new sentence was a (hopefully) unintended jab. To her credit, Mabel was able to contain herself as she stopped for a moment to lean against a wall. She closed the message with a blink and sniffed loudly before taking a long drag and attempting to exhale out her frustration.

It didn't work.

[*I'm so sorry, sweetie. We were very particular about our words, you know?*]

"*We didn't tell them everything, so I have to let some of that shit go. I had a feeling this might be how it would shake out, anyway; I mean … They're old, and … change is hard at the best of times.*" She sighed as she rubbed the bridge of her muzzle. "*The capes are desperate for any leads on the Korps. I'm just glad they're at least keeping their distance, and my family is safe. I can likely thank an intervention from a higher power for that, I suppose?*"

[*Mmm. I'll pass your thanks along.*]

The lioness continued walking in silence for a few minutes before Relly gently pressed on.

[*I know you really wanted to go home for the holidays, sweetheart.*] As Mabel "heard" the words, she felt that invisible paw gently rubbing her back. She didn't respond right away; she just continued walking, gripping the cigar in her teeth, little puffs of fragrant vapor trailing behind.

"*I have a home here, too. Fuck it. Maybe this is for the best. Always next year, right?*" She tapped the ash from her cigar, shaking her head sullenly. "*Mmf … Relly, I really need to get my mind off of all of this, and I definitely don't want to go back to my quarters. Not just yet.*"

[*Well, it **looks** like Eneera just started screening the Hobbit trilogy, so I'm sure they'll be fine if we stay out a little later.*]

"Good. Tell Dusty that I love them, and I'll be back when I'm done." She bit her lip. Normally, she wasn't one to feel like a physical workout, but the evening had left her feeling, frankly, a little pent-up now. Her frustration needed to be vented, and properly hitting *something* seemed the most obvious solution. "Is there anyone open for a new sparring or workout partner? Maybe someone on par with me, skill level-wise? I want to give V and Ellen a break from dealing with me for a bit. Let that wound heal up."

[That makes sense to me, but Mabes, to be very honest, you have almost no training. You're fairly low-tier, all things considered, but I think … one moment. Yeah. She's a trainer, actually, who's looking to spend a little more time on-base, and eager to find a newbie to focus on. Wanna meet up with her?]

"I'm going to ignore that tier ranking crack and say sure! I should be making more friends, anyway! Can't always be bugging the girls anyhow … They have lives to live." It was just shy of self-deprecatory, but the cat hoped she would let it slide.

[Mm. While I don't think it's a bad idea to make more friends, I would hesitate to call it "bugging them." At **any** rate, our potential new friend's name is Mallory — pronouns she/her, specializing in training those with more unique or esoteric powersets. A new set of sparring gear is in your locker, and she's in chamber 3. I'll let her know you're on the way!] The dragoness sounded happy to help as always — possibly more so — her little sister pondered because she was turning her inner turmoil into a positive. It was as close to a healthy coping mechanism as one could find, she hoped.

Since she had decided to hoof it, Mabel had ample time to dwell on the contents of the message. While she had not been upset to begin with, she was *getting* there. She felt a strange sort of warmth in her belly, and it nearly vibrated along her spine. She chalked it up to the anger that simmered within her at these developments.

In her past, she would have railed against how unjust the situation was, and then curled in on herself, a miserably angry husk of impotent rage forced to accept the world as it was. But that wasn't who she *was* any more, and she didn't just *have* to accept it. She could *change* it. Come Thursday, she was going to have something to show Agent Irrswich. She was going to show them how *useful* an asset she could be. She would show everyone: Relly, Volta, Ellen … even Carmen.

She was going to prove, to *everyone*, that she was who she said she was. Who she *wanted* to be.

The cops and the capes want to play like they're doing what's right, like their morals and principles are the only truth in this world? Like they can just do whatever they want, to me and mine?

Not anymore. **Never** again.

Mabel took the last few draws from her cigar, before depositing it in a nearby receptacle to burn itself out.

Never.

Chapter 25

Take Another Shot

The simmering anger at the base of Mabel's skull threatened to boil over as she made her way through the fitness complex. She found herself flexing and relaxing her paws with impotent rage, not at her parents' response, but at the fact that it *had* to be what it was. She could think of nothing better to do with herself than to try and focus on growth (and a little violence) as a pressure relief valve.

Channel that anger into something *useful*.

"You know, Relly, I'm actually kinda excited for all of this."

The cat gestured vaguely to the space as she walked down the aisle of the locker room, pushing her hair back from her emerald eyes with an black elastic band. Her fingers curled into her paw pads. *"I'm done being a burden, for* **anyone**. *I don't want to be* **weak**. *I'm tired of being* **weak**."

[*You were never a burden, you were never weak, and I will fight anyone who says otherwise, including you. Understand?*] Amarelys's tone clearly signaled that she would brook no self-deprecation — not even a little bit — which made the catamount blush.

"Yes, ma'am." Her tail curled slightly around her ankle, but still she smiled at her sister coming to her defense, even if it was against herself. *"I just want to make use of my gifts, make the mischief that I so desperately* **need** *to, and make you all … proud."*

[*I know you do, sweetie, and I know you will! We're already so proud of you, and we all want to help you grow into the villain you want to be! Your permanent locker is the top one at the end of this row.*] The designated spot was illuminated in a soft pink glow that faintly sparkled, which made Mabel laugh out loud as she recognized what her draconic sibling was playing at.

"Oooo … treasure!" Her sister knew precisely how to get her attention; using her RCGs' AR features to gamify the training experience was a trick that would *absolutely* work on the very nerdy feline.

[Mhmmm ... Your very own starter gear. Level 1 Magician, but something a little more practical than robes and a pointy hat!] The dragoness's voice was equal parts jovial and mischievous.

The space was full of bodies coming and going. From the sound of the moaning that hung in the air, along with the humid tang of sweat and steam, there was plenty of going and cumming as well. To her right, a simply *massive* badger was toweling off, smiling and giving a little nod to Mabel as they ran the terrycloth across salt-and-pepper fur. The swell of their muscles (to say nothing of their *other* generous endowments) almost made the cat trip over her own swaying tail, as she did a double-take at the display. Her weakness for large, muscular women was no secret, and her quickly reddening ears and cheeks announced it plainly.

What had the idiot from Fox News said? "Their filthy hiding holes are reefer-dens filled with hypno-slave orgies! When are we going to do something about this subversive canadian influence?"

Psh. Whatever, Boomer.

The Korps was nothing if not *unashamed* about what it represented, and the cougar was slowly getting used to how open about, well, *everything*, everyone was. Acclimation was nonetheless an ongoing process. Frankly, the fearmongering panic she'd seen in the media simply didn't do the Korps's attitudes about sexuality justice; it was so much *more* than they ever could know. Lust, pleasure, and love was *never* in short supply, but also never forced or pressured. Consent, as always, was the most important thing.

Relly sighed wistfully at the sight before the puma. *[When one no longer has to hide their truest self, self-expression becomes a shared joy! Isn't it wonderful?]*

"Mm. Everyone is just so out in the open..." Mabel tried her best to remain respectful, and keep her eyes to herself, but it was impossible to ignore the couple cooling down — or maybe warming up? — on the bench across from her locker.

A titan of a bear was rolling their hips into the plush ass of a lovely-looking dappled blonde-haired lynx, who slowly rose up and down on their thickness, licking their lips as a visible bulge pressed outward from their stomach. Mabel bit her lip as she glanced at the face of the other feline, who made no noise, and stared directly at her with piercing crimson eyes. The puma gave a little awkward smile as she finally broke eye contact and busied herself with the locker, trying to give a modicum of privacy to the "joy" being "shared" a few feet away.

Dressed. Get dressed … Don't stare at the delicious cake…

Luckily, the outfit Relly had chosen was, unsurprisingly, a perfectly picked distraction. Her chosen ensemble featured a striking purple sports bra-tank top with a cowl neck, a pink gradient accent, and strategically placed grey mesh cutouts; a matching pair of leggings with a large black and pink helix wrapped around the right leg. Finishing the look were a pair of back-padded fingerless gloves. A properly sized loadout for sparring was conveniently stashed in a drawstring bag, beside the hanger.

"Oh, Relly … *These are all details from my costume designs…!*"

[*There was some inspiration from there, yes, sweetheart — I know you've been dreaming up costumes in your mind for a* **very** *long time — but these are just workout clothes. You'll get a proper costume when you get your field clearance. You just need to put in the work.*]

Mabel nodded as she ran her fingertips over the slick impossibly-advanced synthetic materials of the leggings. "*Mm … Together.*"

[*Always.*]

With a deeply throaty moan emanating from somewhere behind her left ear, the lioness was drawn back into the reality of the locker room. She could hear the two speed up their joining, but the lack of noise from the other feline was … unnerving. *How could you be going at it like that, and not make a single sound …?*

"…Who's the lynx?"

[*That would be Mx. Jakob Nyarly; they/she. I recommend caution, as a best practice, but they're friendly enough. So long as you don't upset them, of course.*]

"Caution?"

[*Mm.*]

Mabel felt a chill crawl up her spine and took the chance to look back. The lynx's eyes had not left her. Red orbs seemed to nearly glow as their gaze remained locked in on the puma; a smirk grew on their muzzle, pink cock bobbing up and down as she hilted herself on the ursine shaft. As the cougar stared at the back of her locker and pulled her hoodie and top off, a sudden wet *slap* (and low rumbling moan) signaled an arrival of one, while a splatter on the tile signaled the completion of the other.

The lioness closed her eyes and covered her stiffening nipples with her paws as they attempted to betray the thoughts invading her mind.

*Heh … **Very** friendly it seems…*

"Yes indeed, dear — and **perhaps** you will be lucky enough to find out for yourself, one day. Until next time, Ms. Greysmoke."

The response had not been from Relly; the voice inside her mind was … different. *Very* different. Sinister seemed like something of an unfriendly adjective to describe the timbre, but it was not entirely inaccurate. The voice held no evident malice, just deep and rich *uncanniness* as it echoed through her thoughts with the faintest hint of a self-satisfied rumble. It was difficult to conceptualize — especially as the slightly dissonant speech continued to resonate through the catamount's mind — but it was definitely not Amarelys, and *certainly* should not have been there.

All of the hair on the cat's tail stood on end in response to the sudden intrusion, but as she whirled to look back, both the lynx and the bear were gone without a trace; not even a puddle or a hint of musk was left to remember them by. The lioness rubbed at her eyes, and glanced back down the aisle towards the entrance, unnerved.

"How in the hell … Relly, did you hear that voice a second ago?"

The dragoness replied, but her normally chipper tone was edged with something else. [*Finish getting dressed, dear. Remember, Training Room 3! Mallory is excited to meet you, and you don't want to keep the new boss waiting, yeah?*]

Mabel finished donning her new workout gear, but she couldn't shake the idea that she would run into Mx. Jakob again, sooner than she was ready for or would like.

The corridor in front of the puma seemed to stretch on for a mile or more, the brushed steel finish walls broken up by thick sliding doors on either side that were numbered in descending order. As she moved down the corridor, the catamount passed the same room she'd used just a few nights previously with her friends, in her vain attempt at playing supervillain.

*"No. **No.** Not in vain, and definitely not playing. I'm **going** to be a villain."*

[*You already are, dear. We just need to get you comfortable with this new part of you. We'll just keep practicing, learning from your mistakes, and listening to your friends, we'll get there, I promise!*]

Mabel could almost hear the pompoms being shook, and she couldn't help but smile. Her sneakers squeaked quietly, making outsized echoes as she strode down the polished floor; each step took her further away from the bustle of the locker rooms and other amenities the gym offered, formally or informally. Her tail swayed slowly behind as she dragged her fingertips along the wall.

These chambers were for proper application and containment of destructive force Relly had told her. She wondered if anyone — even Volta — could pull the classic Kool-Aid Man entrance through the walls.

Prolly could, if I pissed her off enough. Or Ellen, maybe? Elle seems to have a knack for it. Especially when Volta's throwing her. With a deep breath, the catamount turned her thoughts back to the present. "*So … what do we know about Mallory?*"

[*Mallory does double duty as a field agent and as a trainer. She has years of experience in both roles and emphasizes adaptability. As a big nerd, you might also be delighted to learn this little secret no one topside knows: she's the one who was responsible for ending Vermillion Moonbeam's Hero career nine months ago! And yes, that is **very** related to her sudden interest in staying on-base more often.*] Cheerleader Relly had returned and sounded jazzed to get her charge out there and making connections.

"*Wait … VerMoon … oh! Ohhhh…*" Mabel stopped walking as the realization dawned on her and made her tail twitch. "*Is she gonna, like … uh … me?*"

[*No dear, this is not **that** sort of combat training. Sexual jujitsu is not on the docket today.*]

Mabel wanted to believe she was getting better at discerning when Relly was joking, but you only have to slip up one time…

See: Vermillion Moonbeam.

"*Advanced classes then. Right! Okay! New trainer, new tricks to learn; I can do this!*" The tiny moment of panic passed as the cougar focused, bouncing on her toes and resuming her walk.

[*You can and will! She has a soft spot for weirdos. I'm sure you two will get along splendidly!*]

Finally, she reached room 3. The number was recessed into the door in the Korps's angular chisel script. To the right of the door, a small panel stated the chamber was in use by Trainer Mallory and an M. Greysmoke.

Not an agent. Not yet…

The portal slid open in a pneumatic hiss, the idyllic silence of the hall space melted into what the lioness could only assume was one of those albums made for "meditation" that you'd wake up to commercials for at three AM. In stark contrast to the sounds of rain falling, was the staccato of footsteps hitting the floor rapidly as a greenish-brown blur sped across the room and leapt into the air. Mabel's RCGs identified the flying shape as her assigned anole.

Mallory slammed into a heavy bag that hung from the ceiling, the chain creaking as she drove her knee up into the bag, and with a sinuous twist in mid-air, slammed her opposite heel into the bag hard enough to startle the cougar out of her mesmerization.

With the momentum of the extended spinning heel, the reptile's body whipped back around once more, and her whip-like tail wrapped around the bag, the crack it made louder than a gunshot, and as it coiled tight, the appendage alone kept the trainer suspended above the floor, staring unblinkingly at the feline.

Mabel could only stand there wide-eyed, mouth slightly agape at the beautifully balletic display.

*Right. Supervillains. The key word there is **super**.*

[She's going to make an excellent mother to Little Moonbeam, we're sure!]

"…Motherfucker."

[Yes Mabel, that is how it works.]

"…I meant that as an exclamation, not an observation or declaration. I'm about to get my shit rocked."

[It's an excellent opportunity to learn! Now stop ogling and make a new friend!]

Her big sister would take no more stalling, in other words. The cougar swallowed hard as Mallory considered the cat, blinking sideways. "Mabel, you've been staring straight into my eyes for nearly ten seconds now. Are you feeling all right, or is that normal for you?"

"Oh! Uh … S-sorry," The puma raised a paw in greeting as the door slid closed behind her. "Mallory, right? I just … I wasn't prepared for what I just saw, is all."

"Get used to that. Good first lesson, honestly." Her tail unspooled, the bag slowly recovered from the strangulation as the anole landed on her hands and transitioned with an arched back onto her feet once more, standing in front of the feline and holding out a hand with long, slender fingers. "Nice to meet you, Mabel."

"Pleasure is all mine, Mallory — you can call me Mabes, though. No need to be formal if you're going to be treating me like that bag." The catamount smiled as she accepted the offered hand, and shook.

"Oh, I am going to be *way* harder on you than I am on the bag, Mabes. I suspect you have more brains than the equipment until proven otherwise, so I'll be expecting more from you." The briefest flicker of a smile spread on her pointed muzzle.

Mabel tried to suppress the blush rising up to the tips of her ears. "Uh. Maybe hit me a little less hard than the bag at least, huh? I'm full of blood and I'd hate to get it all over you, yanno?"

"These floors hose off easily, and our laundry service has a *lot* of practice with stains." She fired off pointed banter so fast the cougar wondered how Ellen would fare with the anole as a verbal sparring partner. "Relly said that you're new to this, and that you have a tendency to prefer your lessons with a little physical motivation. I'm happy to oblige, of course, but no sense in getting hurt before the curriculum begins. Let's start with a couple quick stretches, and then we can get to practical applications. My understanding is that you've had no formal training, *and* you just had a whole new suite of powers thrust on you?"

The lioness managed a nervous chuckle and a nod. "Uh, yeah! I'm clay ready to be molded by your skilled paws, my new pal Mal!" Mabel pulled on her gloves, tightening them up. "Just tell me what to do!"

The lack of any sort of reaction to the silly rhyme made the cougar realize her new gal pal Mal was going to be a tough nut to crack.

"We'll see how you shape up then, Greysmoke." Mallory nodded, and motioned for the lioness to mimic her movements, going through a quick rotation of stretches to limber up, prophylaxis against possible problems from an overstrained muscle. There were plenty of opportunities for injury during training; she might as well eliminate cramping from the list, at least. Donning the sparring gear Relly had provided, Mabel was as ready as she would ever be for whatever might be coming.

"Let's start at square one, then. Throw a punch." The anole held up her gloved hands palms out to act as targets. "Show me your form."

Mabel tilted her head, hesitating as she raised her paws as well.

"You're here to learn how to *hit* and *be* hit. Don't act shy about taking a cut," Mallory's eyes narrowed, and a smile slid up along the edges. "I won't."

The catamount nodded and reached back, throwing a quick right jab with no real power behind it; her left paw remained dangling at her side.

Mallory heaved a sigh and shook her head. "Try that again. Give me more; use your body to throw the punch, not just your elbow. Don't be embarrassed, we'll correct the form as we go, but I want to see some effort!"

[Step into the punch! You can do it, Mabes!] Cheerleader Relly had become Coach Relly, but the tone remained her normal encouraging and bright self.

The puma threw another punch, stepping forward, even remembering to turn with her hips to put the extra *snap* into it, just like she had seen in Ellen and Volta's respective techniques. She felt the satisfying slap of her gloved knuckles against her trainer's pad.

"Don't drop right back to idle after; keep your paws up and stay in the fight!" She sniffed softly and brought her hands up again. "Come on, this time, I'm going to swing from your left, so you need to be ready to react."

The adrenaline was finally pumping; getting cracked had definitely awakened something in her. The cat smirked, as it dawned on her — this could be fun, if she just let it! She settled into a shoulder-width stance, and took another swing, this time keeping her left up. As the "counter" came, she ducked under and tossed a left of her own, tagging the anole in the other palm on the sway.

Mabel stared in surprise, tongue nervously tracing her lip. *"Where the hell did that come from?"*

[You're learning!] Relly gave the short answer, but the truth was a little more contrived, the catamount knew: she was learning by observing, and via muscle memory encouraged by the dragoness. Relly was not steering her, but was working on training her mind, while *she* was training her body. *[Keep going!]*

"That's better!" Mallory's voice almost sounded *excited* as she ducked into her own stance, squaring off. "Head on, this time. ROSE will help correct the little things, but she can only work with what you give her. Ready?"

Mallory bobbed in place, then took an almost leisurely step forward. Mabel closed her eyes, and thought about not being in the way of that strike—

—leaving the fist to pass harmlessly through the cat. Since *that* was completely unexpected, the lizard stumbled, recovering quickly to whirl back on her student.

"Interesting. I intended to focus on the fundamentals a little longer, but..." The anole's eyes lit up, a flicker of something besides cool detachment invading her features.

"Oh, I'm sorry, Mal, uh ... Yeah! It's a reflex! I can shift into smoke and that allows me to control my body's density. That's most of what we know so far…" She blushed at the inadvertent activation of her powers; at least doing so *was* becoming completely instinctual, which was encouraging.

"*Fascinating.*" Mabel could see the ideas dancing behind Mallory's yellow-framed ebon gaze. "Let's pick up the tempo. When you're thinking too much, you hesitate. Let's see how that power *adapts* to a little more frantic pace. I'm not going to hurt you, but try to avoid taking direct hits all the same."

The lizard squared up, Mabel did the same, and they picked up the dance where they left off. The puma did her best not to be wherever her trainer was, and as they circled about, they picked up speed.

The puma's form wasn't great, she knew, but the ability to become intangible made up for a lot, missing experience-wise. Each exchange, each move in the bubbling melee was a new sequence to follow. Another step Relly helped cement in her brain.

[Hold your fist at this angle.]

[Keep your eyes forward.]

[Pick your leg up.]

[Low and then high, but don't repeat it. Mix it up! It's a lot like HeroClash — if you're predictable, you end up on your ass!]

Small corrections rapidly led to large improvements in form, and the cougar's confidence grew, accompanied by a feeling of *satisfaction*. Without distracting thoughts, she was absorbing all of the movements intuitively, and the quiet sounds of nature piped into the room kept her from rushing out of step.

Oh … when I can't think … **overthink** … this feels so … so…

Mabel understood the joy she saw on her friend's faces now, when she watched them fight. She *got* it. Anxious energy without the fear. No static. Just reacting and the next choice. Left, left, right, counter, sweep, in, out … It was all happening with a quickness she didn't know she had in her.

The lioness smirked as she shifted instantly into smokeshape and back out, circling Mallory with increasing certainty. She was doing it! She could actually fight! She was *learning* and pushing all doubts from her mind with the action.

But she knew, too, that the anole was throttling herself. She wasn't about to come at the newbie with everything, not yet anyway. As they traded blows, however, Mabel decided to get quippy.

As an LN fan, she felt practically obligated; as a fellow smartmouth herself, she felt *compelled*. "Not too shabby right, *Mally Pally Wally?* Guess maybe I *am* smarter than your average punching bag, huh?" Her green eyes were alight in the cloud of smoke that swirled chaotically *just* out of Mallory's reach, all the while grinning like the Cheshire Cat.

The trainer narrowed her gaze.

Mabel was *pleased* with herself, impressed at how easily it was all coming together. She leaned left, becoming solid to try and throw a roundhouse at her opponent's side. For a normal person, the kick would have been likely too fast to do anything but block, *maybe*.

"*HWAHH?*" the puma yelped and was up in the air from the strike to the underside of her leg. As she attempted to take stock of her new position, spiraling toes over tail, the snap of the lizard's ropey scaled tail wrapped around her neck, and with even less warning than her flight through the air, her entire body went limp, every limb unresponsive and useless.

That was when she realized she had gotten a little *too* confident. In point of fact, she had *fucked up.*

The cougar wasn't fighting a *normal* person. For a Korps agent with hundreds of hours of fighting experience, that roundhouse must have been like honey on a cold day in January: a slow and sweet drip, just begging to be savored.

The noise of all the cougar's weight striking the mat at once was almost laughably cartoonish as she bounced a foot back into the air, and then back down with a *thud*. All the wind was knocked out of her, and she didn't know which way was up, but as Mabel rolled over and gasped from air, she couldn't help but let out a wheezing laugh as her muzzle pressed against the floor. The adrenaline continued to pump, certainly, but her body was demanding a break, and she was glad it was back under her control.

"Good … shot … inf-fallible … M-Mal … ible … Ow. *Fuck me gently…*" She hissed through her teeth.

[*Looks like nothing's broken, Mabes! Just a little too slow on the counter, I think?*]

"Yeah. Yeah, I deserved that one, though. I quite literally **asked** for it…"

[*True. But it was solid banter! At **least** an eight out of ten, I'd say.*]

"The bag is smart enough to not get cocky." Mallory knelt down beside the feline, putting a hand on her shoulder. "You're doing well, but be careful not to taunt an opponent you know is going easy on you."

"Fair…" She laughed weakly as she pushed herself up and into a sitting position. "So that's what it's like being juggled, huh? Can't say I'm a fan." She tilted her head as she considered what her trainer had just said. "You really think I'm doing well?"

"You've no prior training, and you're responding like a natural. Now, whether it's Relly's doing or your own, it doesn't matter; it's encouraging, regardless. You're following my moves fluently and even improvising a little. The attempt at a verbal distraction was well timed, even if ill-advised."

"Glad my mouth is proving useful." She gave a little snort as she tried to roll out the kink the floor had spiked into her ... everything along with the receding pins and needles. "Not like the rest of me there, though, once you wrapped that tail around my neck. That was too quick for neurotoxin, and I didn't feel a *shock*..."

"Good observations. My powers are not tied to either of those things."

"Soooooo...?"

"So how does it *work*?"

"Yeah? I mean, s'hard to counter if I don't have a fuckin' clue what gave me the noodle arms?" Mabel grunted as her back finally popped from the stretch.

"You're right, it *is* hard to counter when you go in blind! Lesson two: analyzing the angles with the tools we have is essential to success. How do you *think* it works?" Mallory gestured towards Mabel, welcoming her observations.

The lioness rubbed her chin, brow furrowing as she attempted to recollect the interaction before the sudden stop by the floor robbed her of her senses. "Does it have to do with the tail around my neck? That was the moment it kicked in, and I, uh ... stopped kicking." Mabel nibbled her at lip as the gears turned.

"You know, in a real fight, you'll have to be quicker."

"In a real fight, I'll likely have more intel."

"An assumption that will get you killed. In a real fight, you may be dealing with someone that neither you nor ROSE have heard of. You will need to theorize, test, and operate without overcommitting to an assumption. So: theorize."

"Mm ... Okay, that was the first time you successfully wrapped your tail all the way around me. Is it like a completed circuit situation, and that just turns *it* on, and *me* off?"

"A good guess, given the information you have so far. But here is where I make my point: if I can wrap *any* limb, not just my tail, around a person, everything from that spot down loses control. If you assume my tail is the only thing to watch out for..."

"Then I'll catch a wristlock, or a pair of head scissors, yeah ... Mm. I bet that's pretty handy in capture and intercept sorts of situations! Also explains the grappling focus ... *hm*..."

Mallory raised an eyeridge. "What's hm?"

"Just trying to consider how I can work *around* that."

A smile blossomed across her features. "Excellent. That is *exactly* what I wanted to hear."

"Always happy to make a teacher proud."

"I'm sure you're both gifted and talented. So, what can you *do* about my trick?"

"Besides not letting you grab me? Hm. I mean, protective gear would likely be ideal. I suspect it has something to do with interrupting electrical impulses?"

"Let's suppose for an instant that you were right. Would you have time to find and equip protective gear?"

Mabel's eyes lit up as it dawned on her. "What if there were no impulses to interrupt?"

The anole nodded, "Go on."

"So, my control of my density goes both ways. Smoke, but also all the way to stone."

"Alright; we'll test that theory. Get hard."

The lioness tilted her head with a cocky half-smile. "Mal, you're real cute, but I don't take orders like that from—"

Mallory rolled her eyes and cut off the cat. "Shut up, and show me the trick, Greysmoke."

"...Yes, ma'am."

The lioness held out her arm, and instantly the flesh shifted, the warm brown fur suddenly glossy black glass, from her fingertips up to her elbow.

"ROSE is reading it as obsidian, is that right?"

"That follows the blessing, I suppose? Fire and Air. Volcanoes and all that." Mabel clenched and unclenched her fist slowly; the highly polished black stone that had replaced her flesh moved without a sound. She was all sharp edges. It literally appeared to be hewn from volcanic glass, polished to a mirror shine. Functional, and strangely beautiful.

"And you said Agent Volta was able to shatter it?" Mallory moved the paw around, inspecting it from multiple angles. "And you reformed the limb? No lasting damage?"

"Yeah ... I'm not sure how I did the second part..." The cat gave a little half shrug as it slowly faded from stone, back to smoke, and back to stone again. "It just sort of happened without me realizing it?"

"I wonder how resistant it really is..." The thoughtful chin rub was implied by the anole's voice, but she made the gesture nonetheless.

"I mean, I didn't have, like, a tensile pressure gauge on when I stood there like a total dipshit, but I mean, it's pretty tough? I think? It is magical, after all." As Mabel stared at her stonework paw, Mallory grabbed her by the wrist suddenly, touching her thumb and middle finger together.

"So?"

The cougar wiggled their surprisingly articulate limb, without any trouble at all, curling and uncurling her fingers. "Working as intended!" She willed the arm back to flesh, and winced as her paw went limp immediately. The numbness that quickly set in was no less disquieting even if she *knew* it would likely happen.

"Now back to stone."

Mabel closed her eyes, but it was as if the paw wasn't there. From the elbow down, the smooth volcanic glass shone, but the paw remained floppy flesh and bone. "Ahh ... I *can't*. Have to be able to use the limb in order to send the impulse, I guess?"

"That follows what we know so far, and that also answers the conductivity question, but now ... we need a good test for the material's durability under pressure."

As the anole released the paw, the catamount was instantly able to turn it back to stone, and back again once more under her control. "Sure. Any ideas?"

Mallory was already moving over to one of the sliding wall panels. "Of course."

Carefully, she removed a set of bars from the alcove, humming pleasantly to herself.

"Uh ... Mal? My gal pally-Mally-wally? W-what's on your mind? Did I do something wrong...?"

"Not at all." Mallory sniffed. She snapped the pieces together, tail holding things in place as her hands worked to create a pair of trestles. "I think hard enough to break *bone* is a good starting point, and we'll work our way up from there."

"Relly?"

[*Yes dear?*]

"*Please tell Nurse O I am* **very** *sorry for unintentionally signing up to be a frequent flyer, and I'll see her soon.*"

The lack of a witty retort from Amarelys made the puma extra nervous as she rose to her feet.

"So, you're … gonna try to break my arm? I'm supposed to stand there and let you *break* my arm?" The feline couldn't dismiss the memory of mashing buttons frantically to beat a bonus stage, except in this case, *she* was the brick in Mortal peril.

"There are other ways we could test its ability to stand up to impacts, but this is both readily available and should be fairly measurable. ROSE will be helping me fine-tune my striking power and watching on high-speed settings from the gym cameras, so we should be able to see immediate effects and any subconscious healing that may take place before I'm able to inspect it personally."

"I'm sorta fond of everything that is attached to me right now, Mallory, thanks! C-can't I just go smoke instead? And, like, *not* get hit? Despite all evidence to the contrary, I'm a big fan of not being hit, turns out!"

"Certainly. We can always save it for another day. There are plenty of non-powered benchmarks I want to gather, but we will want to get an idea of your obsidian's limitations sooner or later — before any *field work*, certainly."

"*Ah…*" The puma closed her eyes and heaved a breath. *Whatever it takes.*

"That makes sense…" Mabel swallowed hard as she stood up. "So, how did we wanna do this?"

"My thought is that we lay your arm across a pair of pressure sensors, and then it's just a straight forward application of force." She snapped the frame into place, and cougar couldn't help but see the simple structure as some sort of torture device she was willingly about to submit herself to.

"It's either this or a hydraulic press, huh?"

"That would most likely be the next choice for this process, yes."

"Well…" Mabel walked over to the stand, before kneeling next to it, and draping her arm across the solid steel piping. "We're already here, and besides that, I like you better than the Crushinatrix…"

"She's a lovely woman, once you get to know her."

"I'm sure."

"Ready, Mabes?" Mallory lifted her knee and hugged it to her chest, first one, then the other.

"As I'll ever be!" She bluffed, before muttering a prayer to whatever gods or goddesses would listen, wishing something, anything, would keep her arm from being shattered once again.

"On three then."

The catamount simply nodded.

"One."

Maybe Athena would help? Artemis? Hekate could be waiting at the crossroads for her...

Anyone?

It felt like time stood still as the anole stepped into position, her hips shifting as she focused on her own task. Mabel focused on steadying her breathing and considering the choices that lead her to this moment, where her arm would again be decimated, but this time by choice.

Her choice.

"Two..."

I was in shock the first time ... what if I feel it ...? What if it doesn't grow back this time ...? Her brow set, and the silence of the room allowed her a merciful moment of clarity;

Then I'll learn to fight with one arm.

A wordless shout rang in the lioness's ear and she clenched her fist tight...

But the sound of shattered glass never came. There was no crack, not even the thud of the limb across her own.

"...Mabel? Care to explain?"

Mabel opened one eye, to look at the lizard. "What? I didn't move, I promise—"

"You *didn't.*"

Her stoneshifted limbs had no feeling, as such, so she couldn't tell what happened; she was terrified to find out. "Okay, so ... why is my arm uh ... *in one piece?*"

"Because there's a *shield* in the way." Her mentor's voice was quietly incredulous, the taciturn anole wide eyed.

"...What?" It was Mabel's turn to be surprised.

[*Open your eyes, Mabes, honey. You need to see this.*]

The other eyelid lifted slowly, and as Mabel turned her head, the aforementioned equipment was affixed to her arm, steady as stone. The scutum was classically Greek, with an owl in the center. It was a smooth and polished piece of armor fit for a museum, or a *myth*.

Pallas Athena, thank you for blessing this cat without an ounce of wisdom between her ears with your protection.

"Oh…" The cougar reached out tentatively, and ran her flesh and bone fingers along the edge of the shield. It weighed nothing in her grasp, but was solid when she knocked on it, and strangely warm as it laid there, affixed without a strap or handle.

"You neglected to mention the ability to form separate objects from your smoke, Mabel…" Mallory whispered. Her tone had changed. There was *excitement* beneath the still surface of her reptilian features as she ran a finger across the mirror-finished surface. "*That* is a skill that deserves some *attention*…"

"I didn't *neglect* anything! I didn't *know!*" The lioness laughed, as she rose to her feet.

"May I?"

"Don't see why not?" The feline removed it from her arm and offered it out to the anole, who grasped it with both hands, arms visibly straining at the apparent mass.

"*Fascinating.* That has to weigh at *least* a hundred pounds … and it *doesn't* to you, does it?" Mallory shifted her feet to accommodate the unexpected heaviness.

"Not at all," Mabel retrieved it with a single paw, seemingly unphased by the weight as she flipped it over like she was handling a frisbee. "Magic, I guess?"

"Best answer I have. Quick math with ROSE reads that as about ten times heavier than mundane obsidian … onyx, perhaps? I'm no geologist," she admitted.

Eneera's voice rumbled softly, as it had when she first heard the words. "*The blessings will be great…*"

The impulsive thought won, and before she could think, she spun on her heel and hurled the shield across the room like a discus. Before she could blink, it struck the wall with a thunderous crack, lodging itself in the padded surface, before dissipating back into vapor.

A slow, very *eager* smile spread over Mallory's features. Deep down, Mabel suspected that she was beginning to see a side of Mallory few others did — aside from, apparently, Vermillion Moonbeam.

"I wonder what *else* you can make…"

Chapter 26

A Deeper Cut

Mabel knelt on the floor, panting softly, as her latest efforts at crafting an obsidian object clattered to the ground. A few seconds later, it wholly *dissipated* in a swirl of smoke.

Her mentor hummed and jotted a note down on her clipboard. "While the size and shape of the blade is certainly ... *impractical,* it makes for an impressive demonstration of what you're capable of."

[*Well done, sweetie! Cloud would be proud!*] Amarelys added a snippet of chip-tuned fanfare to the encouragement for emphasis.

The cougar nodded with a smile, and licked her dry lips. "Right, so, the size and complexity of the object matters. The greater the mass, and the more intricate the pieces, the more candesca it takes! And ... the less I'm able to create before I have to rest, per that reasoning." She slipped into a sitting position with a quiet grunt.

"It certainly appears to be the case. Be sure to make note of anything that might *challenge* that assumption, in future. So, we have successes on a variety of simple weapons, but struggle on anything with moving parts. Fairly standard, I would say, for magical construct powers," she said, with the barest hint of disappointment, "but you do come out above-average on generating constructs with sturdy, sharp edges."

"Mmm..." Mabel took a long pull from the bottle of water and nodded once again. "That sums it up, I think! Relly can help me visualize, but I have to fully understand the object in order to 'make' it, and the more parts I have to concentrate on managing at the same time, the faster I run out of juice."

"Hence why I didn't even have you *attempt* firearms. If you want one in the field, you'll have to bring it with you."

"Yeah, that makes sense. It does seem like the more, uh, *modern,* the item is, the less I can actually focus on it — even with AR assistance. Not sure if that's my mental limitation or the blessing's, really." The lioness gave a little shrug.

"So, your focus then, if you want to use this, is going to be on creating tools that you can create and maintain without too much strain on your candesca reserves *or* your concentration."

"That gives me an idea actually..." Mabel stood up, shaking out her right paw, and clearing her mind.

[*So, what's going on in that pretty head of yours?*]

"Something small and unassuming, but versatile ... Not *just* a weapon."

[*Let me see it, my darling.*]

She opened her eyes and exhaled; a thin stream of smoke spilled forth and spiraled before her. The mystical vapor coalesced into a small, pointed object, composed of the same volcanic rock as everything else she had conjured that evening.

A knife, but also a tool for more than violence...

She could almost imagine seeing a pop-up statistics window in the view of her RCGs when she gazed at it — 1d4, type: piercing, critical range: 19-20; effective both at close range and a distance — and then, Relly made it happen.

Mabel suppressed a snort at her sister's joke and mentally dismissed the image, as she whipped her right paw forward and snatched the blade from the air. The char-black glass edge glinted in the bright lighting of the chamber. It perfectly fit her grip and felt warm against her pawpad even through the glove. A rounded handle started with a ring and led into a blunt edge, until the last two inches or so. After gently tossing it a few inches in the air to gauge its heaviness, she switched to a reverse grip; the weapon felt as if it weighed nothing at all, and the air offered no resistance. It felt like it *belonged* in her paw like nothing else she had made so far.

[*Absolutely **gorgeous**, Mabes...*] The dragoness nearly purred in her ear, and the cougar nodded in silent agreement.

Mallory's expression took on a hint of disdain.

"A dagger, in reverse grip?"

"A throwing dagger, actually, and ... yeah. I always wanted to play a thief, but ... never let myself have it. Too *effeminate*, or some other spoon-fed macho ideal ... That was *never* me..." She stared at the glowing stone that glittered from the base to the tip and knew just how lethal it was. "But this? This is *right.*"

"A ... *throwing* dagger. In *reverse grip.*"

"It's magic!" Mabel pouted. "Let me have this?"

A brilliant flare of orange briefly swelled in Mallory's throat before, with a deep breath, it receded. "I'm putting in my notes that I objected, and that you insisted. Nurse O *will* see my notes."

"Only if I fuck it up!"

The lizard nodded — likely more to say "you will" than "you're right" — but the cat missed the implication, wrapped up in the feeling in her paw.

It couldn't have been more perfect. It was a blade sharp enough to cut the thread of fate.

It *felt* like another missing piece.

"Nothing will stop me from being *me*, ever again." The puma's eyes narrowed ever-so-slightly as she whispered the solemn pledge.

"Nothing or no one."

[*That's my girl.*]

"So, now that you've made it: can you *throw* it?" The words were neither demeaning nor goading, but purely curious, as a teacher might encourage a promising student.

"Hmm, that is an *excellent* question..." The catamount rubbed her thumb along the smooth edge, pondering for only a few seconds before her train of thought came to a skidding halt; that, she realized, was a skill she absolutely did *not* possess. Throwing a knife was hardly like ... hardly like throwing a baseball, say, and being honest with herself, Mabel was always lousy even at that.

*Always **threw like a girl**, heh.*

"Relly, can you call up a target for me?"

[*But of course, my dear!*] Before the thought was finished, a panel slid up with a typical target, a figure outlined with strategic points. A wicked smile instantly spread across the cougar's muzzle: it had a badge. Now *that* was proper motivation for a villain.

According to her HUD, the target was about ten yards away, which suddenly looked like it might as well have been fifty yards. She took a big step closer.

"Nine yards. Much more reasonable!"

[*Mabes ... Have you ever thrown one of those before?*]

"Um. No. Uh … *Help me, please?*" Mabel felt a paw on her own; when she looked down, the silver claw was there, and her smile softened the slightest bit.

[Thumb on the edge like that, *fingers wrapped like you're holding a hammer; not* quite *so tight.]* She felt the biofeedback sensation of Relly's breath on her neck, and a shiver ran down her spine as she nodded. *[Then bring your arm back just past your ear and let it slide from your fingers. We're trying for no rotations here, and not too much power! That blade is sharp, it's not going to take much to bury it.]*

She took a deep breath. "Thank you, Relly." *For everything that you do.*

[Always, Mabel. Imagine you're reaching out to touch the target…]

The lioness's paw came back just past her ear.

[Step forward and point your paw where you want it to go!] The dragoness was still there, projected on the edge of her vision.

The motion felt so fluid, so natural…

The knife sailed through the air, making no noise at all…

…In a spin, bouncing harmlessly off the target with a quiet thud.

Mabel's face instantly began to glow red hot.

"I, err … I guess I can't." She wilted slightly.

[Not everything is going to come easily, you former "gifted child." If you want to be good, we need to practice. Even hitting the target isn't a given for a new learner, darling!] She felt the paw squeeze her shoulder, and the puma nodded in agreement.

"You're right. You're right, of course. Just because it's magical, that doesn't mean it's easy."

"Not too bad for a first throw, but we have some work ahead of us." The anole walked toward her. "Relly, pull up the replay for her, please? Easier to visualize so we can adjust."

The smile came back to Mabel's features as her first knife disappeared, and another appeared in her grasp. A projection of herself from thirty seconds prior appeared in front of her, slowly playing back the motion with various notes, and directives.

As the virtual lioness looped, Mabel ducked around, observing the various angles of the performance. As Mallory constructively critiqued, the feline absorbed every last word, building a checklist in her mind.

"Now," the anole gestured to the target, "try again."

Wordlessly, Amarelys updated her HUD with her character stats in the corner of her vision. Listed at the top were two professions: L1 Magician / L1 Thief.

[The guild welcomes you.]
"Perfect."

"The cat is a quick study, it seems."
"First a spine and now a brain! Growth showing no signs of slowing down at all, hmm?"
"Fah! It's a peasant's pig-sticker, no more. Nothing to write home about. Certainly not as destructive as I had hoped."
"Tell that to the pig, dear sibling."
"Mm. I wonder how loud they'll squeal?"
"As loud as she likes, I shouldn't wonder…"
"When you say it like that, I'm almost hopeful. Almost."
"Her beloved, it is unlike you to despair! We will be rewarded for our patience."
"…Much mischief?"
"Oh, such mischief! A calamity made from flesh and stone! Enough to bring a smile to her highness's beautiful countenance."

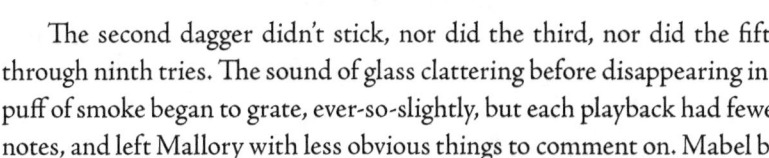

The second dagger didn't stick, nor did the third, nor did the fifth through ninth tries. The sound of glass clattering before disappearing in a puff of smoke began to grate, ever-so-slightly, but each playback had fewer notes, and left Mallory with less obvious things to comment on. Mabel bit back her frustration and visualized her goal just as she did each previous attempt: a dagger quivering in the target.

Finally one did, and another; her muscle memory tightened with every toss, the motion becoming more fluid. She wasn't always on target, and some ricocheted off wildly, but it was *encouraging*, nonetheless. It was a start she could be proud of, and with her two mentors rooting for her, even the missed throws felt like some kind of progress.

Dozens of daggers left her paw that night, everyone the exact same shape and weight, but her aim grew truer with every throw. She lost count of how many attempts she made; before long, she'd completely forgotten that her original goal for the evening was to let off steam. The training however accomplished *precisely* what it needed to, her indignant rage had been soothed.

On what turned out to be her final attempt, the cougar tried to summon another dagger but struggled to shape it properly. Her fingertips vibrated painfully for just a moment, and she couldn't push down the wince, or the quiet noise of discomfort.

[*Mabel, your vitals are showing similar signs to just before the last time you ran out of candesca. I think we should call it for the night.*] The lioness realized just how drained she felt, the adrenaline wicking away her reserves. [*You did great, hun!*]

The half-formed dagger disappeared from her grasp in a wisp of vapor, and she smirked. "And I'm spent, Malibu Calmly. No more magic juice in the tank."

"Fair enough," the anole nodded, and placed a hand on Mabel's shoulder. "Good work tonight. Lots of useful data, and our next steps are laid out. Encouraging developments — you should be proud of that." The cat was rewarded with another half-smile. "This was an excellent first step, Mabes."

The lioness returned the smile and patted the reptile's hand with her paw. "Thanks Mal. I'm glad you were here tonight. I desperately needed this win."

"Been my pleasure, Greysmoke. I hope I see you again soon. That potential deserves to be put to proper use—"

Mallory then said *exactly* what the catamount needed to hear.

"A field agent with your skillset will be incredibly useful to the cause. Keep it up."

Mabel managed a nod without an external giddy squeal. "Yes, ma'am! Give VerMoon my best, Marshmallow?"

Finally, Mabel managed to get a wry half-smirk onto Mallory's features. "Hit the showers and take it easy. There'll be s'more to learn soon enough."

"*Ha!* Can't wait!"

The lioness wasn't previously one to shower in a public space, but she had become far more comfortable in her skin. It stood to reason, she decided, there was no better time to get over that fear. She'd come to not only appreciate but *like* that kind of attention, so maybe it would be fine?

"So, uh … *what's the etiquette here?*"

[*Towels are hanging in the stall, and if you leave the clothes out, they'll be washed and returned to your locker for tomorrow!*] As she'd come to expect, Amarelys always seemed to have the answer.

"*Oh cool! Luxury queer space communism continues!*"

[*It never ends, my dear! You contribute what you can, when you can, and the wheel keeps spinning.*]

The catamount still chose the furthest stall down out of habit.

Baby steps, she told herself, *not cowardice.*

There were others using the facilities, and clearly there were more than one occupant in a few stalls. Judging by the sounds being made, they were clearly having a good time. Mabel took a deep breath. She was still riding high on the adrenaline from the successful training session, so much so that her prudish abashment had vanished completely, replaced with something more…

Indelicate.

"*Let them have their fun! I did what I set out to do and didn't have a single meltdown or tantrum! Like a* **big girl** *who had* **her shit together***, and* **not** *a disaster lesbian working through personal stress and trauma via violent exercise!*"

[*You did! Proud of you, sweetie!*]

Humming one of the harmonies from the music Mallory had had playing during their exercises, she closed the door and began to undress before she noticed the full-length mirror. She decided a spontaneous show was in order, and gave herself a coy sort of wink, taking the time to *really* enjoy the view, purring loudly as she slid her shirt over her head, tossing it into the designated bin.

"Why, hello there, gorgeous…" She cupped her breasts, leaned towards the mirror, and gave it her most lascivious look, lips pouted slightly and brow raised. Her loins stirred unbidden, and for a moment, she recognized why there was so much moaning going on in these showers. Between the exercise high, and mirrors giving the viewer that perfectly *fuckable* look, who could resist? Mabel decided it would be a *shame* to waste the chance.

"*Maybe I could get off real quick, before I head home…*"

[*Maybe no?*] Relly replied in a flustered rush.

"*What do you mean 'no,' Relly? I mean, everyone else is clearly—*"

"*Hello* yourself, Mabel." The lioness recognized the voice instantly, and was very glad the floor wasn't slippery yet, as she exploded into a cloud of smoke, reappearing at the towel cubby and trying to cover herself.

"Holy shit *CARMEN!* I mean … er … *Miss Rayne. Hello.* Hi. Um … Hello. Miss." She whirled around to see the imposing figure of the tabby leaning against the doorway, who was very naked despite wearing a towel as well; laid about her grey-furred shoulders as it was, it hid literally nothing titillating from view. Not her tremendous rack, not the curve of her hips, and *especially* not the turgid length that draped gracefully over her sack and between her thighs, fully free from its sheath. The barbed flesh nearly glistened in the fluorescent lighting, and the puma immediately wondered if she could wrap her lips around the girthy appendage…

"No! Bad Mabel!" She shut her eyes and tried to think of cold things, but the member continued to gleefully sway in the forefront of her mind.

"Uhh … what are you dicking here? *Doing here!* What are you *doing* here … Miss Rayne. Ma'am." The puma winced, and did her best to keep her green eyes locked on the golden tinted gaze of the other feline, and not allow them to roam.

Quite the challenge, given the view.

"Hey, *relax*, Kittycat. I'm just unwinding after my workout — need to stay sharp, you know? Can't be going *soft* in the wrong places…" Carmen continued to lean, but the predatory gaze she held on the cougar somehow made Mabel feel even more naked and vulnerable. Double naked. **Super** naked, even. At least the nickname didn't feel like a curse, that time.

"Oh, of course; can't, uh … be going *soft* where you need to be hard! Errr … in fighting … *shape.*" She sighed softly as she rubbed the bridge of her muzzle, exasperation crystal-clear as she looked back between her fingers. "Holy shit, you're *loving* this right now, aren't you?"

"Mmm. There is *something* about watching you squirm that I enjoy, admittedly…" Her smile didn't seem quite so forced now, but it was still clearly still a perfunctory gesture. "But I digress. Caught some of your session with Mallory, actually. Back in the saddle awfully soon after your last try! I'm happy to see that you're taking our little talk about sticking around to heart."

The cougar nodded as she tied the towel about her middle, her self-consciousness back in full force. "Yes, Miss Rayne … I want to be the best I can be. For y'all, and for myself." She quietly wished she could feel anything but exposed under that warm amber gaze. "I need to be *worth* all the trouble."

"Would you like my opinion?"

Mabel nodded, knowing full well what her opinion would likely entail.

"You're overeager to prove yourself before you've given yourself the time to learn. We already established that you're stubborn; that can be a blessing and a curse, as I'm sure you know. But you seem naturally inclined to *adapt*, and that's why it's all the more important for you to take the time to breathe. Otherwise, you'll become like that last dagger of yours — all smoke and nothing behind it." The tabby continued before the cougar could slip a word in, inspecting one of her claws in the soft lighting. "Speaking of — I'm *curious* about your choices using your new little trick. I don't suppose you've recovered any candesca?"

Mabel allowed herself the tiniest little disarmed smile, as she tried to decide if being read so bluntly was worth the half-compliment tucked in the critique. The cougar *was* a curious thing, all things considered, and wanted to see where Carmen was going with her thoughts. "Oh … what would you like me to make?"

"May I see one of those daggers?" The tabby held out a paw expectantly.

Without another word, the catamount willed the smoke from her paw, ignoring the unpleasant tingling sensation to craft the same dagger she had made so many times earlier in the evening from the curling dark vapor: same length, same balance, and same impossibly-sharp tip. Mabel held it flat in her paw, and offered it up as politely ordered.

Carmen sauntered over to her and plucked it out of Mabel's hand by the flat edge of the blade, flipping it over to grab the handle. The curiously heavy material didn't appear to phase her as she tested the balance, turning it over in her fingers a few times. "I think it's interesting that you chose a knife, after everything we discussed…"

The puma winced at the memory and cursed her fixation on short blades. "I, err…"

"A knife is such a *dangerous* thing … pretty. And *sharp*." The tabby shook her head, tutting softly. "But that's just you, isn't it, Mabel? You *seek out* danger. Every decision is a step towards that, isn't it? Volta tells me you got your powers by bonding with a supernatural being you knew for less than a *day*, and as soon as you got those powers, what did you choose to do first? *Fight*." She spun the knife idly by the ring, her gaze never leaving the puma's. "I wonder … do you court danger simply because you're reckless? Or is there something else going on?"

"Miss Rayne, I don't *want* to be dangerous…"

"How many things did you craft that *weren't* weapons?"

The catamount's ears pinned back, as her tail flicked, trapped in the truth of those words.

"*One.* A blade cuts, Mabel. That is its *purpose*, its reason for being. If you didn't want to be lethal, you would have focused on the shield." Carmen didn't raise her voice, but wielded it with practiced efficiency nonetheless. "*Dangerous* isn't inherently bad, but without control, it'll catch up to you eventually, and what then? You can get lucky with bravado and bluster, a lot of the time. But not always."

"…Not every cut will kill," the cougar whispered, eyes flicking down to the tile between her feet. It had been a struggle to respond at all.

"But it only takes one bad call, doesn't it? One lucky — or *unlucky* — throw, one misstep in a melee." The grey-furred feline snorted softly. "Kittycat, if you want to jump about, throw knives and be *that* kind of big bad villain, I won't stop you; *you're* not my responsibility. But you won't always be working alone, and *that* worries me." She paused, considering the edge of the weapon in her paw. "If you're going to do this? Wield a deadly weapon? You are either going to do it knowing why, or not at all." The tabby stopped the spinning knife suddenly, blade dangling loosely in her fingers. "You don't get to decide after it's already left your hand that you were just playing. That's not how this works. Let yourself take time. No use testing a blade before it's forged."

"Like you said, I'm stubborn." The puma managed a small smile, attempting to show confidence as she stated her case. "No more running. I'm going to do all I can for my family, and for the Korps. Nothing less than my *everything*."

"*Good.* Let that guide you. And … when you throw, you grip too hard. It puts unnecessary spin on the blade." Without any warning, Carmen's whole body tensed, and her lower arm and wrist *flicked* outward toward the puma. Mabel flinched as the knife embedded into the tile wall less than a foot away from her head, splitting through the slick ceramic it like a chisel through balsa wood.

"Loose fingers, less spin," the tabby intoned, a grin widening on her features. "*C'est en forgeant qu'on devient forgeron.*"

Mabel did her best to match the smile before willing the knife to fade, leaving a mysterious crack in the otherwise-pristine tilework. "Thank you … Miss Rayne." She managed not to stutter, and kept her gaze level, but the frizz of her tail made it clear exactly how she was feeling about the display of skill. *Gods above and below, I couldn't have avoided that if I wanted to. She's so damn fast. She wasn't even using her powers this time…*

"Keep practicing, Greysmoke!" the tabby called over her shoulder as she turned to leave. She walked slowly to the door, showing off the only angle the cougar hadn't previously been given the opportunity to admire, and paused just before exiting.

"One last thing — you can call me Carmen." A wink, and the door was closed behind her. Her footfalls made no sound, so it was impossible to tell how far away she actually was.

The lioness gave a long pause just to be safe.

"Is she gone?"

[*Yes, dear, you can breathe again.*]

Mabel exhaled a long sigh as her head thudded softly against the wall. "*Fuck.* She's so intense…" she muttered, rubbing at her eyes. She tossed her towel aside, extracurricular activities forgotten. All she wanted after that gauntlet of conditional approval was hot water to loosen her muscles, and to rinse away the soreness creeping back into them.

[She just knows her worth. I only wish the same for you, my darling girl.]

As the steam rolled over her, Mabel shook her head, and chuckled. "May we all develop the sort of conviction that carries Carmen Rayne."

"So you can conjure solid objects of obsidian from smoke utilizing your candesca? Mabel, that is … *incredible!*" Eneera's eyes sparkled as he sat on the couch, movie paused and forgotten. "I've never seen a mortal able to muster the energy to do that more than a few times without rest, and you summoned *how* many daggers?" The larger tufted ears of the lanky cat-shaped elemental stood straight up, their voice filled with excitement and just a tinge of disbelief.

"Mm. Somewhere around forty or fifty, I think? Honestly, I was just enjoying the motions and didn't think about it too hard." Mabel poured a long dram of cream into her mug before stirring it.

[Sixty-two by my last count, dear,] Relly noted.

"Huh … well, there you go! Sixty-two!" A cigar was already prepped and lit before she put the kettle on, and the catamount retrieved it as she left the kitchen.

"And you are still able to stand! Mabel, I am not trying to flatter you, but you are a wonder!"

She leaned down to kiss them on the cheek before settling in next to the djinn with her cup of tea, and a stogie tucked between her fingers. It was the perfect reward for a long — but *good* — day.

"Thank you, dear, but I'm still no magician. Not yet, anyway." She took a puff and a sip, and purred contentedly for a moment, snuggling in close as she laid her head on their shoulder. "But I'm working on it."

Their arm draped across her back and kept her close.

"Neera?"

"Yes, Mabel?"

"Thank you for bursting into my life. My world is better with you in it." She kissed their shoulder gently, and offered the cigar to them. A purr rumbled in her chest, and her free paw rubbed their thigh, tracing fingertips along soft fur.

Flirtatious, and affectionate, but not seeking more than the warm closeness of her partner.

"You are welcome…" The caracal accepted it and took a long drag before exhaling a ring and then a ship to sail through it, which made the lioness giggle.

"Cute trick…"

Her companion was turning out to be a nerd, just like she was … This all filled her heart to bursting.

Magic. Her life was filled with *real* magic.

"Mabel?"

"Yes, Neera?"

"I think your hair looks lovely." They looked down, and their half-lidden golden eyes were achingly beautiful. The sadness that she'd seen, on the day they met, was completely gone. She blushed at the remark and took her stogie back from their paw, unable to hide the smile while she squeezed close as she could.

"Thank you … Now, where are we?"

"Under the Lonely Mountain … Bilbo has been volunteered into scouting!"

"Oh! This is one of my *favorite* parts…"

And so, the newly minted magician/thief-in-training eventually fell asleep watching a master burglar and his dwarven companions, alongside the comforting warmth of a djinn, and under the watchful eye of a dragon.

Before she dozed off, watching the cigar smoldering in the ashtray, she considered Carmen's words;

*"You **seek out** danger, Mabel. Every decision is a step towards that, isn't it?"*

*Mmm … maybe she's right. Maybe I **do** like danger. But that doesn't mean I don't love these quiet moments all the more for it. I'll give my whole heart for them…*

What better reason could there be?

Chapter 27

Meet Me In The Middle

Despite everything, Thursday did finally arrive.

As Eneera sat on the edge of the bed, quietly observing Mabel riffling through her closet, they pondered the necessity of the task at hand. They did not understand all the fuss over clothing — a uniquely mortal concern — but it appeared to be *very* important to the puma, so they watched, listening to her quiet noises of consideration and dismissal as she inspected her wardrobe.

"Nope ... nooooope ... *maybe*..." Mabel tossed another pair of jeans, darker than the last pair, and with several more tears, and lobbed them toward the bed, on the small pile of clothes that lay there. "Yeah, you can absolutely *rock* that..."

So long as my nether regions are covered, is that not enough?

"Mabel, I do not wish to be a burden to you. Are you certain—"

"Neera, sweetie, I'm gonna stop you right there." The lioness did not turn away from her work as she gently chided the djinn. "You are *not*, and never *could* be a burden for me. You're my *partner*, and I want to help however I can! We can't both be self-deprecatory, and since I was here fir— OW!" Mabel yelped and rubbed at her ear, "Fine. *Neither* of us get to be self-deprecatory," her muttering continued, "unless it's *really* funn— EEE-YOWCH! *TOO HARD!* Relly, you *mean* thing!"

The catamount whined and held her paw over her ear, giving her best wounded innocent pout.

[It's the only way you seem to *learn*, sweetie. Far be it from me to deny you the necessary *reinforcement*.]

The caracal-shaped being covered their mouth to hide their smile at the pair's antics, but the chuckle bubbled up anyway.

"Mmm ... *the point is*, you're not a burden, and that I am certain of. Please don't call my friend that?"

"I will try to keep that in mind moving forward. Please, forgive my faux pas."

The cougar wiggled her shoulders and swished her tail, "*Ooo la la!* Turns of phrase *en Français!* Color me impressed — you are a *quick* study, Dusty!"

"Thank you..." The djinn felt the warmth creep into their cheeks, as they managed their reply. "Your shared memories have made adapting to this new time far less of a hardship, as well as Miss Amarelys helping to guide my studies. There is so much, but I am excited to learn!"

[You're very welcome, sweetie! I'm happy to assist however I can.]

"Love a passionate learner, and I'm glad to hear you two getting along so well! Now, to address the original question: is this a necessity? No, you could very well walk around naked as the day you blew into town, and I'm sure no one would care. In fact, I suspect there are *many* who would enjoy it! *However,* I am not one to let an opportunity like this pass me by."

"And what opportunity is that?"

"Getting to play dress up with my very own life-sized djinni dolly, of course! I didn't get to play with many Barbie-type toys growing up, so you're helping me relive a childhood moment I never got to have! So really, I should be thanking *you!*"

Eneera blinked their large golden eyes, once, before glancing over to the corner where the lioness kept a desk in a tasteful amount of disarray, including some distractingly busty statuettes.

"...What of those? Are they not dolls depicting Miss Ellen?"

Mabel scoffed. "Those are *action figures,* Neera! S'not the same!"

"...I am not sure I can appreciate the distinction?"

"Neither could my ex..." the cougar muttered, before clearing her throat. "*Ahem!* Now, I think that's enough options to start with!" As she stared at the pile, her smile grew as an idea blossomed behind her joyful green eyes. "Ooo! Wait! We could coordinate our fits! That'll be *sooo* cute! Yeah? Yeah. Now, I threw some cute witchy stuff on the pile here for you, let's see what I can do to match it..."

Eneera could only smile, as Mabel's excitement made it impossible to do otherwise. "As you wish."

The puma stopped sorting to place a paw on her chest, and looked back at the caracal in mock surprise. "A Princess Bride quote now! *Goodness gracious,* are you trying to get into my panties *both* ways today, dear?"

The movie was one their partner had eagerly shown them, which made Eneera realize that sharing a film was one of the ways Mabel chose to show her affection, and they were eager to reciprocate the affection with another the lioness's favorite pastimes:

Playfully *suggestive* banter.

"Is this sarcasm, or a genuine request for me to enter your undergarments?" The dracaracal flicked up an eyebrow, and enjoyed watching the teasing puma become the teased, tail puffing slightly as the inside of her ears began to shift from pink to red. "As you mentioned, I am finding the touching of holes is *quite* commonplace here, and I do want to *'fit in'*…"

Mabel snorted and turned back to look over her shoulder. "Well, as we both seem to recall, you and Vixie are fitting in together *just* fine, dear." She cleared her throat as she picked up a tee to "inspect." "*Sadly, no time for a demo!* Back to the matter before us: a proper ensemble for the discerning djinn!"

The caracal allowed themselves a self-satisfied smile, knowing they had successfully "won" the exchange. "I am your doll to dress, Mabel."

The catamount's eyes lit up, and the djinn felt a familiar warmth settle into their chest.

That smile is worth the moon and stars…

The look that Mabel and Amarelys had settled on was decidedly butch leaning, but Eneera's distinctly lanky and graceful frame begged for twinky sort of femme accents.

The djinn did not understand the sensibilities of fashion, but they appreciated how light the clothing was, and how it did not restrict their movements. The long, pinstriped dress pants (tailored for Mabel) were unsurprisingly a little short, but accentuated their height, while the fishnet shirt under the onyx-colored vest showed off what the cougar referred to as "the goods." The burgundy cowl scarf draped over their shoulders was chosen by Eneera, and complimented by both their partner and her sister ("Excellent choice! Helps show off that lovely neck!").

The accessory was something that the djinn recognized, and it was a comfort to see something they knew.

The dracaracal was no closer to *understanding* fashion, but the compliments made them smile nonetheless. Mabel had assured them that the subject of style was simply a matter of taste that needed to be cultivated, and she was certain the djinn's would be *fabulous.*

*Mabel is so sure of my abilities … of my **belonging** here…*

The cougar continued to discuss the inspirations behind her outfitting choices as they made their way towards the agreed-upon meeting place, mentioning a skeleton named Jack, and a wolf called Crow, that were apparently central to two more movies that she would share, and Amarelys was excited to gift them her own favorites and "must-sees."

The subject of the conversation was inconsequential. They could have spoken about anything, and the djinn would have listened with rapt attention. They knew it was important to these people who cared for them as much as they cared in return.

The certainty in that was a comfort that Eneera had nearly forgotten in their time within the stone.

Without a single word, Mabel laced her fingers with the djinn's, pulling their paw up to touch their knuckles to her cheek.

"You're safe, Neera. Never again. I'll **never** let that happen."

"Thank you, Mabel…"

She intuits so quickly, from a flicker of a feeling…

"Ask me how training is going, Dusty." The catamount bumped them with their hip but did not release their paw.

"How is training going, Mabel?" The djinn was learning that rapidly changing conversational paths were a fact of life with their partner, just a matter of how her thoughts oscillated.

"A little off the rails, but I'm conducting myself well enough, I think!" The cougar snickered, bubbling up into a giggle.

[*I don't know that Eneera has gotten to the Industrial Revolution in their studies **quite** yet.*]

While it was true that Eneera's knowledge was limited, the bond with the lioness had given them access to her library of knowledge; while the tomes were many and some *seemingly* useless, they were all helpful in their own ways, and no less precious to them.

"Oh I'm sure they are chugging right along — isn't that right, Neera?"

"Do not be steamed. I am learning as fast as modern engineering permits!" The twinkle in those moonbeam eyes would have melted the heart of even the dourest creature.

Mabel's giggle spooled up into full-throated laughter.

[Gods bless, it'll be good to introduce you to more people that aren't Mabel or Ellen-shaped. Your sense of humor could use some expansion, if only for my sake.] Amarelys's words may have been sour, but the lilting tone of her laugh was sweet indeed.

The chorus of the sisters like music to the djinn.

"Well, Dusty, it seems like your training is right on schedule, and hey—" Mabel stopped in front of the doors leading to their destination: The outer chambers of KDARC. "Looks like we've arrived! *All aboard for Spooky Town!*"

"Wilkommen! Bienvenue! Warmest welcomes to my newest colleagues!" Alder held their arms wide, positively beaming as they ushered the pair into the meeting space, motioning to a pair of chairs opposite a wooden desk, all in the same dark-stained oak. The room was mostly empty save the furniture, the laptop on the desk, and a single pneumatic tube leading to parts unknown.

The avian was simply clad in what could only be called "librarian chic," but they would come to learn they shifted between masc and femme presenting based on the day.

The pencil skirt and long woven cardigan suggested a lunar lean.

"Miss Greysmoke I have met, and you are the djinn, Eneera, is that correct?" They offered their hand across the desk to each as they stepped behind it. "I am Agent Alder Irrwisch, they/them. Please, don't worry about addressing me as Agent; Alder is just fine. It's my pleasure to make your acquaintances in-person!"

The avian spoke with the eloquence of a long-time orator, and with a truly unplaceable accent, a melange that leant an almost lyrical quality to their speech.

Mabel accepted the proffered limb and shook their digits, and the caracal followed suit.

"A pleasure, Alder! Happy to meet you outside of my visor!"

"Yes, I am Eneera. Thank you for the opportunity to find my place here, with Mabel."

"As much thanks goes to Lock and Key, as it does to me, Mix. Their testimonial was convincing enough to allow Director Wick to defer to myself, which I am grateful for, as this is a singularly unique opportunity for each of us."

The dracaracal made a note to thank the ermine and the rat at the earliest opportunity.

The hazel grouse settled back into their chair, clasping their talons before them. "I am sorry that we have to have our first meeting outside of the division proper, but security clearances, and all of that, not to mention the possible misadventures on the way without the correct gear and guidance ... I'm sure you understand?"

"In theory!" Mabel smiled as she settled into the offered chair with Eneera following suit.

"Excellent! We'll try to arrange a proper tour, once we have all met the necessary requirements, but this room works well enough, if a bit ... *bereft*, for my liking." They clacked their beak quietly in annoyance before continuing. "Now then, I know you are both busy, given the new circumstances, so if you please, tell me all that has happened since we last spoke! If I understand correctly, there have been some positively *intriguing* developments vis-a-vis your boon's manifestations, Mabel?"

"Absolutely! The blessing has shown some serious versatility in just how it functions. Relly can forward you my observations thus far as well as training footage, but I'm *excited*." The lioness launched into an animated discussion of the previous several days and a demonstration of her newly discovered abilities — albeit in a much more subdued manner than in the training chambers.

She is so passionate about so many things, but few topics make her light up like her gifts.

The djinn listened intently to Mabel's understanding of her training thus far, her missteps enroute to their goal, and how she was relying on her partner and family for aid. The catamount deferred to Eneera when Alder requested further explanation on their involvement in the process, and the caracal was happy to provide their insight.

"We have mainly been focusing on control exercises, as well as candescal stamina and memory. Mabel, without formal training, has a deft paw for the art, if a little ... *impatience*," the caracal-shaped elemental answered honestly, and glanced at Mabel to see her cheeks reddening. "But she has already shown great promise, and patience is a muscle just as any other. It must be properly exercised."

The meeting went on like that for another hour or more, the avian nodding and noting things, all while the djinn grew more and more curious of Alder themself. The eyes behind their amber colored lenses spoke of experience far greater than their appearance might suggest, as did their energy.

The Alder they chose to present was cultivated in a very particular way, but there was something much more beneath the surface, the djinn was certain. While Eneera was only residing in the body of a mortal feline, their curiosity was *certainly* comparable and suitably piqued.

"May I ask a question, Alder?"

"Please do, Eneera! What would you like to know?"

"When we first came in, you mentioned this situation as a 'singularly unique opportunity.' What did you mean by that?"

"Well, to speak plainly, a bond between a djinn and a mortal has become an altogether *rare* occurrence. Our records are *woefully* sparse, with even the most recent still being several hundred or more years old and lacking depth." They sighed softly, their tone becoming subdued. "What you two represent is essentially the chance for KDARC to preserve and document not only *this* bond, but to better understand *past* bonds, and *potentially* lead to finding out what shaped the current state of the relationship between mortals and the elemental forces … *if* you both still wish to join, that is."

"Of course, Alder. We'll be more than happy to help however we can." Mabel smiled and glanced at the djinn. "Whadya say, Dusty?"

Eneera nodded in assent. "However I can assist, please just say the word."

Alder smiled softly. "I will be sure to, Eneera. Thank you both. Shall we consider it a date, same time and place next week? I am excited to see what you can accomplish with another week!"

It seemed the hazel grouse was just as curious as a cat.

Another week of living and training, another check-in with their liaison, but this time with *activities*.

Alder provided Mabel with several tools to help gauge her progress, and encouraged Eneera, as her partner, to assist.

The span of time the catamount had with access to magic was miniscule in the grand scheme of things, but these exercises weren't about scoring high on a arcana aptitude test (which Mabel *definitely* didn't want to do, and *totally* recognized it was not at all feasible to expect a good grade), but a chance to gauge a proper starting point for the puma's studies.

The first task involved utilizing her candesca to solve a simple puzzle: retrieving a key from the inside of a bottle. Naturally, the neck appeared to be too small for the key. "Now, I'm sure you could figure the mundane solution to this, but I would like to see your arcane ingenuity in action! The bottle must remain whole, as does the key."

Eneera silently watched and smiled as their partner got to work.

Mabel lifted the bottle, considering its weight, and rattling the key inside. She rotated it in her paws, nose nearly touching the glass, as a smile split her muzzle. "What lock does the key belong to?"

"Why does it matter?"

Ebony colored claws tinkled softly against the glass.

"Why wouldn't it?" Mabel kept her eyes on Alder. "A key goes to a lock, a lock secures *treasure*."

"The treasure, then, is the potential for knowledge."

The cougar handed the key to the grouse with a smirk. "Done."

Inside the bottle was filled with dark, fragrant smoke, swirling, but remaining contained within the glass without a cork.

The djinn had watched the smoke coalesce, smiling as tendrils lifted the key, twisting, and turning it so it could slip free. Mabel never once looked up, casually conversing while doing such delicate motions with phantom digits until the key was in her palm.

Her fine control of her own manifestations is already admirable.

Alder chuckled softly and took the key, tucking it into a pocket in their coat. "There are no extra points for showmanship, Mabel, though one might argue for the consideration."

"Awww, well then, I suppose the show is simply for my little audience of two then!" The cougar winked at the caracal. "What's next?"

A flash of something shone even under the lenses of the avian's glasses. The word *puckish* came to the djinn's mind.

"Your next task is no more difficult than the last, just a different application." The avian slid a piece of paper across the desk with a diagram and several bullet points. "This is a cantrip, specifically to generate a small orb of illuminance! If you'll pardon the pun, it is light spellwork, traditional arcanum for the budding initiate." Alder gestured to Eneera, with a nod. "If you would be so kind as to demonstrate for your partner?"

"Of course." The djinn did not hesitate, holding their palm open, and uttering something under their breath. Floating like a delicate seed above their paw was a tiny mote of pale light. "The word is up to you; this is your spell's focal point. I simply said the word for 'sun' in the old voice. The key is to shape the candesca tightly and ignite it."

When they closed their paw, the light was snuffed out.

Alder's fingertips were steepled before their beak, carefully observing the pair, a wry smile barely hidden behind their digits. "Couldn't have explained it better myself."

"Well, I think I can manage that!" The cougar was unconsciously tugging on her knuckles as she spoke, her brow furrowed slightly as she stared at the slip of parchment for further insight. Eneera immediately recognized the telltale sign of her nervousness; they placed a paw over hers and squeezed gently.

The gesture brought her back to the present and reminded Mabel to take a breath in through her mouth and out through her nose, just like they had practiced when meditating. Her features softened as she placed a paw over the djinn's.

"What did I do to deserve a familiar like you?"

"You were kind. Kindness should be reciprocated without thought. Remember: tightly packed, like a ball of clay, and then ask for light." Eneera released her paw and stepped back to give her the space she needed to focus.

The cougar closed her eyes, and held their paw out, palm up.

She whispered her word of focus…

The dracaracal winced as they recognized the flaw in their explanation.

The flash of light that erupted was almost incendiary, filling the room with a light so bright that all the cougar could do was cover her eyes and yowl in surprise as she and her chair fell back.

Eneera caught her just before she would have hit the floor, both of them quietly thankful for their preternatural reflexive response.

"AH! Fuck! *ME!*" The catamount rubbed under her visor, which did little to nothing in this instance, the AR wear unable to react fast enough. "Gods *damnit*…" She blinked rapidly as her pinprick pupils did their best to recover, squinting up at the shape of Eneera. "Too much?"

The djinn held their thumb and index finger just barely apart and nodded. "Just a *little*."

Alder scratched a quick note on the pad before him, still smiling as his full-moon lenses faded from opaque to transparent once again. "That was very informative, Mabel, thank you!"

"Always happy to provide a useful data point," she grumbled, still trying to shake the spots from her eyes. "Maybe someday I'll be able to *see* the results…"

"I'm certain you will! That is the goal of learning, after all!"

There were several more tasks given to Eneera and their companion — all of which were completed — some more successfully than others. Regardless of the results, Alder retained their unshakably pleasant and patient demeanor.

As they prepared to part ways, the bird handed a small leather-bound book to Mabel. "Please use this for guidance in your studies, but don't hesitate to reach out with any questions, please! I will see you both next week."

"Of course! Wouldn't miss it!" The cougar had bounced back from her botched cantrip and slipped the journal into her back pocket. "And not just because I don't want a surprise visit from Director Wick."

"You certainly do not! Her … *distaste* for the Texas heat, and the state as a whole, is second to none! But that won't be a concern," they stared over the rim of their glasses, "so long as you both keep up your end of this bargain, hm?"

"Of course," the djinn intoned, dipping their head in agreement. "We look forward to spending time with you, Alder."

"For sure! Have to claim that … *treasure* … after all…" Mabel's roguish smile faltered as she patted her hips, biting her lip as she felt around, even hooking a finger in her shirt to look down into her cleavage. "What did I *do* with…?"

"With this?" Alder crossed their arms over their chest before lifting one hand to reveal the key tucked between their fingers. "Miss Greysmoke, while I appreciate your enthusiasm for the *art* of legerdemain, you need to pick your marks a little more wisely. Good effort, though."

The catamount's blush was instantaneous and strikingly noticeable even on her softly furred cheeks as her smirk melted from smarmy to sheepish. "I meant no disrespect, of course…"

"None taken, my dear. You'll pick up lots of tricks here, if you stick around long enough." The bird lifted their other hand, revealing another journal.

Mabel hung her head, stepping back to retrieve not *another* journal, but the same one that she *thought* was still on her person.

The djinn couldn't help but be impressed by the display, *especially* considering...

"No magic?" The cougar questioned with a tilt of her head, flipping the book over in her paw before slipping it back from whence it came.

Apt observation. Either it was all mundane, or their skill is far greater than they let be seen...

"A magician never reveals their secrets — nor does a warlock, witch, or any other practitioner worth their component parts." A cheeky wink from the hazel grouse forced the cougar to giggle.

Eneera's response to the display was more measured.

"May I have a moment with Alder, Mabel? I won't be long."

"Oh, of course! I'll wait by the elevator." The puma nodded and exited without question, giving a little wave before the door slid closed behind her.

"What can I help you with, Eneera?"

"There are many advantages to being underestimated, are there not?" The caracal was not aggressive, merely assumptive.

"Indeed! Not knowing the depth of someone's skills allows for improvisation and adaptation." Their air of confidence held no malice, only practiced surety.

"Deception?" The dracaracal's tufted ear flicked, as they raised a brow.

"Not hardly! *Reservation.*" The avian pulled the key from their pocket, the black iron gleaming dully in the warm office lighting. "*Reserving* the right to reveal information when it is most beneficial to my friends, and most harmful to those that would threaten them." Their gaze was suddenly distant, a flicker of sadness quickly passed. "You'll find that old habits die hard, Eneera, as you settle into this new world."

"...Your candesca reveals so much more than Mabel knows ... is *ready* to know..." The djinn fell into step with the ancient dance favored by magic users; of half-questions, and unspoken truths.

"She'll learn when she is ready. Your partner is *exceptionally* bright."

"How long?"

"Hm..." They tapped a fingertip on their chin, considering. "Longer than most memories, lesser than some. *Gilgamesh* was not my peer ... At least, not in *that* life." Another sly smile.

Another unexpected path.

"So, the answer is 'old,' but not quite so old as myself." Eneera chuckled and held out a paw. "Thank you for trusting me as you have."

Alder accepted the offer with the same warmth he had always given, but pretense had given way to comfort. "I'm glad that I was right to trust you, Eneera of the Wind and Fire; I would not have liked the alternative."

"I shall endeavor to be worthy of that trust, and of hers."

"You are her *familiar*, Neera," The hazel grouse leaned close enough for Eneera to feel their feathered cheek brush against their fur but did not release their paw. "She *chose* to give a piece of herself to you, just as you gave to her. You are *worthy*, silly sirocco…"

They speak with such conviction…

"Mm … I would like to know you better, Alder." Eneera's voice barely rose above a whisper.

The facade faltered, if only for a moment. "Who am I to turn away such a handsome caller? Nur ein großer Narr, und ich bin kein Narr."

CHAPTER 28

STARLIGHT THROUGH THE SMOKE

Starshade leaned against the wall, pulling a foot behind to touch her lower back, limbering up in preparation for the evening's activities. As she stretched, she decided she should *maybe* know a little bit about what she'd agreed to, sight unseen — not that the answer would dissuade her, of course, but she wasn't in the mood to find out the new girl was some sort of tank. She always had trouble with the real heavy hitters, and that wasn't really the kind of surprise she wanted before the night of responsible debauchery she'd been looking forward to in the Dominion Club.

"*So, who's the newbie I'm working with, ROSE? Old hat, new convert…?*"

[*That would be Mabel Greysmoke, she/her, a freshly-vilified mountain lioness.*]

"*How fresh are we talking?*"

[*Three weeks or so, practically still wet from the tank.*]

The bunny released her leg and raised the other, her lithe form barely concealed by the tight bodysuit she wore principally to keep her movements unrestricted … and because she liked it when people stared. The shiny black material was broken only by the magenta helix over her heart. "*Holy shit, you weren't kidding, that is **brand** new! Jeeze!*"

[*Indeed. Regardless, she's eager to learn, and has effectively spent the entirety of the last two weeks in training; physically, when awake, and virtually, when resting. She is currently logging roughly fourteen to eighteen hours per day in combat exercises and general applied villainy.*]

"*Wow, sounds like she's got something to prove! Love a motivated girl!*"

[*Seems familiar…*]

"*Ha ha. Maybe a **little**…*" Starshade rubbed the back of her head as she settled onto the floor to continue her routine. "*What sort of tricks is she packing, then?*"

[*Her power set is magical in nature. Recorded skills include the ability to manifest smoke on command, transfer herself via that smoke, adjust her body's* density from vapor to obsidian, and condensing shaped smoke into that same hyper-dense stone.]

[We don't know the full extent of her powers, obviously, but at her current level, your skill set should be a good match for her.]

"Huh … and she just **stumbled** on that ability, or is EE providing witchy HRT these days?"

[Her powers are tied to a KDARC situation, which is why Agent Irrwisch was the one who recommended this exercise. They are curious how you might make her change her approach.]

"Huh! Well, I'm glad Alder trusts me with the new blood! So, her deal is the whole … cursed object-slash-deal with the devil-slash-magical prodigy sort of thingy that they always seem to faceplant into, over in Spooky Town?"

[Astute as ever, my dear. Be warned, however; to say that your partner is impulsive and impatient would be an understatement. Which is, admittedly, another reason why Agent Irrwisch suggested you two pair up.]

"Ah! So, they think I'll be a good influence?" The bunny smiled brightly, ears perking up at the seeming praise. "Because I'm so calm and collected…?"

[Because you're **also** a disaster magnet, Star. You just have more experience working with it at this scale and moving past it. The hope is you'll rub off in the right way.]

"I mean…" Those same ears nearly glowed, as she laid her head against her thigh and muttered mentally. "You're not wrong, but you don't have to just **say it**."

[Don't pout, dear. I'm certain this will all be very familiar to you! The two of you are going to get along like a house on fire. Metaphorically, of course.]

"That happened **one** time! It's not my fault the pyrokinetic couldn't control herself!" The lagomorph rankled as she rose to her feet. "**Never** gonna to live that down…"

[I think you were at least partially to blame, given your fingers were in her cookie jar when it happened.]

"You **indirectly** burn down one **single** building, and suddenly you're a 'potential liability in a team dynamic' and a 'fire hazard'." Starshade rolled her eyes while her head shook with mock annoyance, but internally, she was well aware she wasn't beating those allegations.

[You really do have terrible luck in abandoned storage facilities, come to think of it. Maybe we should consider avoiding them in the future? If only to save K-LAW the headache of all that paperwork.]

"If I can't skulk around warehouses, how will I possibly meet my mischief quota?"

[I have no doubt you will manage it regardless of your location. On that note, however, it does appear that Miss Greysmoke is on her way and already loosened up.]

"Oh? Anyone I know?"

[Nothing so entertaining, I'm afraid. She's just been to the track and the weight room.]

"You act like I've never been the one ran on at the track. Suppose she's all business, then. Boo."

[Her status is presently set to 'Curious,' so maybe you can help her sort that out **after** the training, hmm?]

"Oooh! I do love an eager beaver..."

[She's a cougar, dear. Why don't we focus on the situation at hand before you skip to the fun part?]

The alert light above the door flashed red for a moment, and then went solid green as the telltale hiss revealed the topic of the conversation in the flesh. Mabel Greysmoke rolled her neck from side to side as she walked into the room, the barest hint of sweat glistening on her fur under the white light. Her outfit — a sleeveless, cropped and behelixed hoodie pulled over the violet singlet — was far more modest than Starshade's chosen attire, but still revealed plenty of soft curves. The knee-high tabi and padded fingerless gloves pulled it altogether, just screaming villain-in-training. It was a good look, and she carried it well.

As the cougar closed the gap, the bunny realized that while the predatory feline was shorter than her, she was far from small. The lioness was stocky, solid, and broad-shouldered. The agent-in-training clearly had a powerful physique lurking just below the softness, with every intention of honing it to a razor edge.

"Oo ... big kitty."

[Technically, mountain lions are the largest of the small cats. They can still purr, you see.]

"...Good to know."

As Mabel's much larger paw enveloped her own to help her off the floor, the bunny stifled a nervous giggle.

"Hey there! Starshade, right?" Her voice was a warm, friendly rumble, and it made the cottontail's ear flick as she imagined what it would sound like saying other things. Perhaps even demanding other things...

"Mhmm! And you must be Miss Greysmoke; nice to meetcha! ROSE was telling me you just figured out your powers! Smoke magic, huh? Really cool stuff!" Starshade bounced from "impractical"-heeled boot to heeled boot, burning off the nervous energy of meeting a new friend-shaped person.

"You can call me Mabel, hun, or Mabes if you like. And yeah, uh, just sort of had them fall into my lap — or more accurately around my neck, if you can believe it." The cougar's shy little smile lit up her face, as she rubbed at the back of the aforementioned neck. "Thanks for agreeing to spar me sight unseen! Alder said our powers were a good matchup, and I'm eager to throw paws with someone who isn't an eight-foot tall lightning elemental, a *frighteningly* stoic anole, or the world's punniest Swiss Army dipshit."

Starshade snorted, wrinkling her nose. "Well, I can't bring the thunder, but I am *well* known for my dipshittery! Regardless, really going for the gold, huh?"

The catamount raised an eyebrow and pushed her hair back from her eyes with an elegantly-donned headband. "Nothing in half-measures, darling. Hope that's not a problem…?"

"Not at all! You wanna learn by diving into the deep end, I get it! Hope I can keep up!" The rabbit chirped cheerily as she squared up with the puma. "You ready to start?"

Mabel nodded, the feral glint in her eye impossible to miss. "Absolutely! Relly, give us a bell?"

Underneath the calm surface, the cottontail was taut like a bowstring. The brief of the lioness' abilities suggested that they outclassed Starshade's own in raw power, but real-world experience was worth far more to effectively wielding a power, and Mabel had never been in the field against live opponents. She simply wouldn't know the *angles* that the rabbit did.

The triple ding signaled the start of their scrap, and the cougar wasted no time, ducking low to throw a left and then a quick right, clearly feeling out her opponent. Starshade dodged easily, hopping back in a smooth motion, which elicited the faintest smirk from the feline, a warning easily read by the certified field agent.

"Let's see what she's got!"

The cottontail's ears flicked as the not-even-subtle-a-little trap sprung, Mabel dissolved into smoke and disappeared into the swirl. Starshade blinked, not really expecting either the speed at which the puma melted into incorporeality, nor the sheer spectacle of the act, her distracted mind racing at the sight of *actual* magic at play.

*"Holy shit, that is **cool** as **fuck**!"*

[*Fight now, admire later! Behind!*]

"*Right!*"

The rabbit leapt into the air, long limbs launching her in a perfectly arching backflip. The move handily dodged the flying knee of her opponent, suddenly on her rear, and the momentum allowed her to bring her heel down directly on the cat's bare shoulder in a beautiful, sweeping crescent. The counter-blow drove the puma into the ground with a heavy *thud.* Mabel grunted as her face struck the mat, and her claws bit deep into the stitched flooring with faint *ripping* sounds, the weight of the rabbit pressing between her shoulder blades.

The whole exchange happened in less than five seconds.

"*Thanks for the heads up.*"

[*Always!*]

"That was a clever trick, but maybe showing your hand a little early? Let's go again!" Starshade rolled backwards off of the floored feline and popped up, eyes bright and eager as she bounced on the balls of her feet.

The lioness rolled onto her back. She snorted softly as she kipped up, the motion sinuous and showy. A growl crept along the edge of her voice. "Yeah, okay, I'll give you that one. Won't happen again…!"

"I'm glad you think so!" the cottontail beamed. "Learning is the point, right?" Her peppy exterior belied the more serious internal conversation with ROSE.

"*I barely caught that.*"

[*Well, she's only going to get faster, but now you've seen it in action.*]

"*How much more can she do?*"

[*Do you really want to spoil the surprise?*]

When their eyes met again, Mabel's lips were pressed into a thin line, and her tail swayed slowly behind her. "Yeah, sure. Ready for another?"

"On your mark!" Starshade bounced from foot to foot as the pair squared up.

The moment the signal beep sounded, the cougar exploded into a cloud of thick smoke, the scent overwhelmingly cloying as she swirled about the rabbit. The move did accomplish muddling several of Starshade's senses, but her hearing was hardly hampered. The suddenly solid limb swinging upward made just enough noise that the lagomorph managed to activate her *own* trick, and…

VANISHED…

…reappearing a heartbeat later in a crouch *well* under the catamount's attempted roundhouse, leaving nothing for the move to connect with but stardust. The rabbit's powerful leg lashed out as she spun, hooking into the side of the feline's ankle, and flipped Mabel over like a hundred-kilo-ish pancake. The cat nearly made a full rotation in mid-air before crumpling to the floor with a surprised yelp.

Mabel's ears flushed as she pinned them back. The barest hint of a snarl played on her muzzle just long enough for the rabbit to see that she was losing her cool.

"She's already frustrated. Not a great start."

[She's pushing herself hard. She's looking past you, and three steps further still. Rookie mindset just needs adjusting.]

"Guess I'll have to show her I'm here. She needs to focus on the moment."

[You got it.]

"So the smoke bomb is cool, and *would* be super effective once you're already stuck in it, but you can't assume that it will disorient your opponent so much that you can leave yourself open with a big swing." Starshade offered as she watched the smoke rise to the ceiling as the air filters powered on.

"Your instinct to end a fight quickly is great, but you don't know me that well! You need to play it safe, so you can be sure you can land that hit. You had the right idea in the first round, I think you just need to wait your turn!"

"Okay, **that's** kinda scary. She, like, **just** got these powers, right? It's wild how easy she makes it look already. It took me years to get the fine-tuning on my teleporting right."

[Mhmm. It may be, in part, the benefit of her familiar's experience and, of course, my own assistance. The popular opinion is that it may also be a function of hyper focusing on the technical aspects of supers and such for so long. She's accidentally molded her thought process to be uniquely suited to utilizing her abilities.]

"...So being a big nerd means she just **innately** understands how superpowers work? I call bullshit."

[I don't think you understand **quite** how much time she spent studying capes and crooks, dear.]

"Maybe, but even being a natural, she's getting flustered quickly. It's a bad habit ... well, outside of the bedroom, I mean."

[Or the Dominion Club?]

"Bedroom in the symbolic sense! A bathroom stall is as much a bedroom and ballroom as, er ... betwixt the..."

[*Maybe for the moment we focus on the increasingly-agitated magic predator, and not the poetic room for balls between thighs? Unless you* **want** *to be made her bitch?*]

"*Do you think—*"

[*Focus, you stupid slutty bunny. Teach now, get stepped on by Mommy* **later.**]

"Mm." The cat was staring very intently at the floor, the noncommittal grunt of assent speaking volumes more than she did. Mabel melted into vapor, reforming into a standing position and straightening her gloves, iridescent claws glinting under the lights. "All right. Makes sense. Again?"

"Sure! On your mark!"

The bell rang once again, and for the first time that session, Mabel did not make the opening move. She began to circle slowly, and waited for her opponent to attack, keeping her paws up as she swayed. The more experienced villain could tell that she was outwardly trying to appear limber and loose, but the tightness of the muscles in the puma's neck betrayed how tense she really was.

Starshade took the invitation and started with a quick-stepping side kick that the cougar brushed aside dismissively, taking the opportunity to step in and toss a tight right hook of her own. The bunny intercepted the blow and planted her deflected foot, bringing the opposite knee up with blinding speed, which Mabel barely blocked. The cat was knocked on her back foot by the strike and took to the defensive as the rabbit's long legs went to work, utilizing her reach to press her advantage, just waiting for the puma to try her luck with a counter.

To her credit, Mabel had dialed back the aggression, but the impatience was bleeding through the cracks. The catamount obviously wanted it to be her turn, so apparently decided to *make* it her turn. She exhaled a stream of smoke that swirled into the Platonic ideal of a classical round shield, made of perfectly-smooth obsidian. The polished glass looked strong enough to deflect a bullet, but Starshade was hardly a straight shooter, and not about to throw herself against the bulwark.

As the shield was shoved between them, rather than another kick, the lagomorph *lunged* forward and grabbed the edge of it. With surprising strength, she pulled the aegis towards her, using the leverage to vault over it with her legs spread wide. A crotch flying at one's face at high velocity wouldn't be unusual in any Korps activity, but *this* time, it was an unfortunate circumstance for Mabel.

The lioness grunted as the rabbit's thick thighs clamped around either side of her head. Before she could let out more than a confused, "Mmf?", Starshade arched herself back toward the floor, planting her paws on the ground, and used all of the momentum she had swung to once again catapult the catamount into the floor.

Knees squeezed gently as the rabbit took her time releasing her opponent, grinding the puma's muzzle against her leather-covered mound, before finally rolling backwards off the feline's chest, straddling her hips instead.

[I know you're trying to show her how to wait for the opening, but did you have to rub her nose in it?]

"It's an excellent incentive!"

[For you, or for Mabel?]

"That was much better! The shield was just the *tiniest* bit telegraphed, though — need to be ready to change your plan on the fly! You just need to loosen up, Mabes." Starshade leaned down, and pressed her muzzle gently to the lioness's own. She smiled as she broke the kiss, letting her tongue flick over her bottom lip. "Don't be so … *rigid.*" She wiggled her hips, before giving a wink and standing up slowly, giving the cat a view to remember.

[For you, then.]

Mabel's paw slowly came up to her lips as she laid on the floor, recovering from the whirlwind that had just fallen upon her, both physically and emotionally. She was struggling to verbalize anything, simply nodding as she rose to her feet before giving a cough, and a sniff, *trying* to get her head back in the game. "So you *improvised* a Frankensteiner on me, or do you just keep that one in your back pocket?"

"I've spent a lot of time learning, just like you, and from all over the place! Unorthodox or not, sometimes you just need to bust out a pro wrestling move! They're flashy and intimidating — perfect for when you want the option to disable and *not* hurt your opponent."

The cougar looked thoughtful for a moment, considering the words of the field agent, before responding with a sniff. "So far we've got: be patient, be loose, and be a nerd who likes wrestling. Did I miss anything?"

Starshade pursed her lips in thought, tapping her chin before shaking her head. "Nope, that sums up the lesson so far!"

"…Well I'm *one* of those at least." Mabel smirked and rolled her shoulders. "Ready when you are, long-ears!"

"Hey, she cracked a joke!"

[There's hope for her yet! Going to clean her clock for the nickname?]
"Oh, well, **obviously**, yeah."

Seven more times it rang once again, signaling the start of another round between Starshade and her *very* determined sparring partner...

...Who had not managed to take a single round.

Mabel was *clearly* trying to control her emotions, but failing miserably, and had fallen into pacing rhythmically: five steps to the left, then five steps to the right, over and over, as she silently waited for the rabbit to ready up for round eleven.

"You almost got me, that last one! But, uh." Starshade hadn't *easily* taken a round in the last seven, but it didn't seem as though the cougar could see that, so focused was she on winning. "Do you need a break, Mabes...?"

"Nope," the feline responded curtly, fingers flexing and relaxing, making her gloves squeak softly in protest. "I'm good."

"Are you sure? Because you look a little ... frustrated."

"I'm *fine*, Starshade. It's all part of the process, right? Getting my ass kicked is the only way I'll learn. Tch..." Mabel tutted softly and shook her head. "I'm not upset with you, if that's what you're worried about."

"But you *are* upset."

The puma stopped moving and heaved a sigh. "How could I not be? Like ... I'm doing everything I can to get better, but it feels like I'm making no progress! I just keep on getting my shit rocked by *everyone*! By Volta, or Elle, or Mal, and now you! I was hoping that maybe I stood a chance here, *maybe* I was making *some* headway, and I just ... I don't see any of this growth you all keep talking about. I'm eating as much mat today as I was on day one!" Her exasperation was clear as she rubbed at her muzzle. "It's ... it's fucking *infuriating!* I don't want to waste this gift, and *yet*, here I am ... spinning my fucking wheels, and whining about getting nowhere, *again.*"

Starshade's ears dipped down as she walked closer to her partner. "Mabes, you sort of set the game to the highest difficulty, when you've never played it before. If it's too much—"

"It *can't* be too much! I've wasted so much time getting here! I ... I can't ... I can't *wait* for some nebulous moment when everything's perfect and I finally *feel* ready! I've been doing that my whole. Fucking. *Life!* I have to push through this! I don't have any other *choice!*" The cougar snarled, but when the cottontail winced, her features fell with the weight of immediate regret. "You … you don't understand, Star; you're so *young.* I'm so far *behind,* and it's … I can't just…"

Starshade reached over and placed a paw on the cougar's shoulder, unsure of the right words to say.

Mabel shook her head as if to knock loose the rest of her thoughts, her voice dropping to a barely audible whisper. "I *can't* wait … I don't have the *time.*"

The rabbit squeezed gently. "So that's why you're pushing yourself past the breaking point…"

The catamount sniffed loudly, before clearing her throat. "A muscle only grows strong from being torn and repaired, right? Well, I'll snap every *single* fiber in my body a thousand times, if it means I can be useful even one *second* sooner. Maybe this *is* too hard, and maybe I am just being stubborn … but we don't give up. Villains *never* give up."

Starshade bit her lip. In its *entirety,* as coined by a particularly brutal shithead cape back in the 90s, the saying was, "Villains never give up, until they're dead." The Korps had taken to using the first half as their rallying cry, and Mabel clung to it like a lifeline as she fought back frustrated tears, shaking her head before slowly levelling her gaze on the rabbit, jaw set and green eyes alight with new determination. "So no, I don't need a break. I need to get *better.*"

Her sparring partner nodded slowly, as she understood that this cat was no different than her in that regard; they both desperately *needed* to be useful. It was as integral to their existence as breathing.

"*Heh … we're going to be scooping up her pieces a lot, huh?*"

[*That's funny coming from you. Nurse O has your emergency contacts on speed dial.*]

"*Wasn't a complaint! Just wondering about the kinda mess she'll make.*"

[*You do* **adore** *a mess, after all.*]

The cottontail allowed herself a tiny smirk.

"*Is she a hugger?*"

[*Most definitely.*]

Starshade pulled the catamount into an embrace, pressing her forehead to Mabel's as she squeezed tight. "I promise, I'm not holding back. I would *never* disrespect another villain like that."

The smile the cougar flashed was all predatory daggers. "Good girl … because I won't ever hold back." The smile faded slowly, into a softer expression as she let out a quiet chuckle. "Maybe I *could* use some water, and maybe we can watch the replay of that last round? I think I was onto something there."

The rabbit smiled brightly as she bounced towards the cooler, shouting over her shoulder. "You were! You just hesitated for a second too long!"

"Yeah, turns out a cute girl looking up at me with surprise really activates some instincts that I wasn't ready to deal with in the moment."

"Oh?" Starshade tilted her head as she snagged a couple bottles. "Horny?"

Mabel raised an eyebrow as placed a paw on her hip, a lopsided smirk slinking across her muzzle. "In a manner of speaking … more *feral*, though. *Hungry* is a better word, I think."

The rabbit's ears stood up for a second as she let out a nervous laugh, but her thighs pressed together for just a moment at the tone the feline used. "O-oh! Well, I mean…"

"Don't worry, Star," the catamount guffawed. "I like you too much to eat you."

"Awww."

[*There, there; I'm sure she doesn't really mean it.*]

Mabel's eyes narrowed as she focused on the rabbit's center, watching her sway and twist to better predict the next move that was coming, and defend accordingly. When she blocked she kept in close, waiting for the chance — taking the opportunity for throwing out quick retorts both physical and verbal — but taking care also not to overextend, lest Starshade put her on the ground for the sixteenth time.

The cougar couldn't help but smile as the cottontail seemed to be moving slower — not because of fatigue, or even her RCGs giving her any kind of reflex-enhancing edge, but because she was *learning*. Starshade's fighting style relied heavily on kicks, like a looser, much more fluid take on tae kwon do. Recognizing that meant her studying was doing the trick. She was getting *better*.

The rabbit, however, remained rascally.

[*Very good! Keep working the mix-up game!*]

"I'd love to, but she's making it really hard! I can't find a gap between those legs she keeps fucking throwing!"

[I'm sure you could if you asked nicely, dear. She is a **very** accommodating girl.]

"Ha ha." Mabel ducked and blocked high as the rabbit swung low. With a momentary shift to smoke, the sweeping strike passed through harmlessly, leaving her opponent ripe for a counter — a chance she would surely take.

"That's bait."

The tiniest little perk of her opponent's ears, the most subtle of twitches, brought the flicker of a smirk to the catamount's muzzle.

Be patient.

Starshade was not an easy read, but she was a joyful soul. When she was happy, a smile wasn't the only tell; Mabel swayed left, and the lagomorph was suddenly...

GONE...

...and nothing but twinkling light remained as the feline brought her leg up.

Be loose.

Mabel didn't follow through with the punishing axe kick she would have thrown an hour before. Instead, she grabbed her knee, tucking up to roll backwards, eyes lighting up as she watched the rabbit reappear above her. She wrapped her arms around the rabbit's hips, claws dragging along before clasping together just below her belly button. The catamount purred, her lips brushing against her opponent's cheek as she whispered: "Gotchaaaaaa..."

Newly-earned muscles and freshly-pumped adrenaline allowed the cougar to heave the ninety kilos of rabbit up into the air with ease, throwing those infuriatingly long legs up and over her shoulders. Mabel spun to catch the rabbit by her armpits mid-tumble, and sat down hard, driving the bunny into the mat with authority. The satisfying thud — and following gasp — was instantly added to the cat's mental highlight reel.

[A sitdown facebuster is certainly an inspired choice! Poor thing hit the floor like a sack of potatoes.]

"**Spinning** sitdown facebuster! Gonna call it the Black Stone Diver! Whatcha think?"

[We'll workshop it!]

The cottontail just laid there for a moment, arms draped over Mabel's legs, her head inches from the puma's crotch. A low and thin groan escaped her lips, before she finally spoke, shakily pushing herself up to look at her opponent.

"Told ya … you're … getting better. *Ow.*"

Mabel tilted her head, running a fingertip up Starshade's throat, before tucking under her chin as she leaned close. "You know what? I'm starting to believe it…" She chuckled softly before planting a delicate kiss on the end of the bunny's blunt muzzle. "I didn't hurt you, did I?"

The rabbit slumped back down, laying her head against the ample thigh of the cougar as she managed a weak giggle, eyelashes fluttering flirtatiously — or still recovering from the toss, it was impossible to tell. "Not really, but if you want to kiss it better I wouldn't *mind*…" Starshade's fingers walked slowly up the puma's leg, her smile filled with sinful implications on just what sort of kiss she had in mind.

"Is she always like this…?"

[Only with the ones she thinks are cute.]

"Ah."

Mabel grasped the rabbit's paw and forced herself to smile through the sudden prey-like rattle of anxious nerves. "As much as I would *love* to play doctor, Star, some bunny just beat my ass for an hour and a half, and I'm a little sweaty and a *lot* exhausted."

"The first part's not a dealbreaker, *but* if you're too tired, maybe I could get a raincheck?" Starshade looked up at the feline with doe-like sweetness, perfectly masking the otherwise illicit intentions. "Pretty please?"

"Well … how could I say no to that?" The cougar gave her paw a squeeze, before her legs melted into smoke, gently laying her sparring partner down, before whirling towards the door with a rumbling purr of a chuckle. "See you later, Twinkletail."

[Left in an awful big hurry there, hun, everything okay?]

"I just think all the training is catching up with me, is all," Mabel grunted softly, rolling her shoulder with a wince and walking quickly towards the nearly deserted locker room. "Neera is going to read me the riot act for going too hard. *Again.*"

There was a pause for a moment, the only sound was the cougar's softened footfalls on the polished floor.

[Mabel. You know I can tell when you're lying, right?]

The feline could hear the unamused frown in the dragoness's tone, but she clearly had no interest in opening up, and said as much plainly. "Yes, Relly, I know. But you **also** respect me enough to do me the courtesy of pretending to believe it and giving me space. Please?"

[*Mm. She does like you; you know that, right? Is that the worry?*]

Mabel sighed and looked down at the locker handle she grasped in one elegantly-clawed paw. "Yyyyeah, maybe, and I do have a weakness for clever cottontails. I just … I'm just … I'm not ready for … hmm. What does my public profile status say right now?"

[*Lesbian. Single and Curious.*]

"Can we remove the second bit and just set me back to 'Not Looking' for now, please?"

[*Done.*] Her sister paused and pressed gently once more. [*You're certain you d—*]

"Yes, I'm certain." The cougar put an end to the hushed discussion as gently as she could. There was no telling what cracking open that particular door might let out. "What I'd like now is a shower, a big fuckin' greasy burger, and maybe a cigar for dessert. I appreciate your concern, but I'm okay, Relly. I promise," she lied.

Thankfully, Relly dropped the subject, and Mabel finished stripping her sparring gear and padded delicately towards the showers in silence.

She didn't have time to be not okay. This life was too important.

CHAPTER 29

READY AND WILLING

Never once has she treated me like a servant. Always she asks if I am comfortable; her concern for me is clear.

She treats me like a partner, rather than as a tool.

*I worry about how quickly she is developing. Not in the sense that I fear she will do something **wrong**, but because it may simply be too much for her. This has all occurred so very rapidly, but she seems to be taking it all in stride — as if entirely remaking her whole world is something for which she was already prepared.*

*She reminds me of you in many ways, truly; stubborn and strong, but admirable, and aware of herself. Always watching. Smiling, as if she knows something more than she dares reveal too hastily. She is most certainly mortal-born, but ... something about the **joy** in how she wields her power is so free-spirited, I am given to wonder. Her very being is playful and mischievous. I was never worried the gift would be wasted upon her, but I could hardly suspect how she would make it her own.*

Every day she works with me, trying to hone her form and control. Her natural instincts have given her an adaptability that borders on fantastical; it is incredible to watch how she has developed, and how she approaches any given obstacle. With paws so deft, it is like she is spinning a potter's wheel with her candesca. Each step forward is another throw of the clay, another pigment of glaze to daub on for the firing. That is not to say there are no mistakes; she gets discouraged for a moment, but then comes at it again from a new perspective, almost pleased with the idea of a new puzzle to solve. Her mistakes become intricately woven into the whole; something to overcome becomes her motivation, rather than the goal she originally sought. She lives to prove them wrong...

But herein lies my concern: that the greatest threat she faces is not a foe she has yet to face, but rather, her own determination...

Maybe it is because she did not think highly of her world before? Or of herself ... This lack of care for her well-being is a most disconcerting trait. She grinds herself to the bone, and the cracks are beginning to show, but no one can seem to get through to her — not her sister, nor her friends, nor me...

*What is she really running from? Her past? Her future, perhaps, and the mortality it represents? She would never tell me ... but she **cannot** run at a sprint forever, and I only hope that we can get through to her how important rest truly is. How important **she** truly is...*

She would never make demands of me. There are no commands given. There are questions posed, suggestions made, choices offered. She listens to me. I am treated as family.

I've never known another mortal like Mabel Greysmoke, and all I want to do is keep her safe ... to prove to her she is worthy...

Mother, if this is what you wished for me, I am thankful. The term we have begun using is "familiar," and that comforts me. Being a part of her has ... healed me, and I only wish to do the same for her.

I don't know that I will ever not miss you. But we have mischief to make, and I know you would be proud.

Wherever you might be.

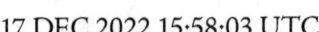

17 DEC 2022 15:58:03 UTC

RE: Agent Candidate — Greysmoke, Mabel

TO: Commander Celia

CC: Director Wick, Jane

Commander, per your request, my thoughts on the new recruit, and their charge:

In the past two weeks, I have met with her twice — alongside her djinn —who has taken the title of "familiar." Eneera is old stock and very powerful, but endlessly friendly and inquisitive. I sense no ill will from them, and I am incredibly curious about the nature of their being. Given the opportunity, I have spoken to them regarding their history, and I think they would make an ideal candidate for either or both of the Division's History and Demonology branches, and they have expressed interest in helping however they can — but I digress.

Mabel Greysmoke herself is a unique specimen amongst mages. Her magic comes as easily to her as breathing, and her candesca is a curiously deep well, at times almost beyond her powers to contain. She has managed adequately to date, but monitoring will be necessary. Her natural abilities have proven highly adaptable in both matter conjuration and manipulation, and she is likely to be an excellent field asset, given the opportunity.

She does struggle to cast traditional, formal, or ritual spells. Her energy is too unruly in that regard, but she has a potential knack for artifice and enchantment given a flair for artistic expression. Her spellwork is likely otherwise to improve, given my assessment to date. Of note, is that she has a particularly stubborn drive to learn and grow.

She is, in fact ... *"reckless,"* I suppose would be the most accurate word. Her impatience does worry both her familiar and myself, and I should suspect that there are more close to her who are concerned as well.

We all know too well what the chill of candescal retreat is, and she pushes herself to the brink every single day. We do not need *another* practitioner of the arcane destroying themselves upon the wheel of knowledge and betterment without concern for their well being ... Wouldn't you agree, *Director?*

Mabel shows great promise and incredible tenacity and has both embraced our mission and welcomed our guidance, *to a point.* I will tentatively give my support for a recommendation of Agent clearance, and initiation to KDARC proper, with provisions outlined in the attached document.

Signed,

Agent Alder Irrwisch, KDARC

P.S. She thinks herself a thief in the making, Mistress Celia, and could be an impressive one with the proper training. But I don't suppose that would interest you...

[So, the decision has been handed down! Mabel is cleared for Field Agent status, and I think you girls should give her the good news! It will mean a lot, coming from the agents she respects and admires most in the world.] Amarelys announced in delight, her tone unmistakably bright even over the portable speaker. [She has worked so *hard* at this, and really, I'm so incredibly proud of her.]

[My little sister...]

"Still not *technically* an agent," Ellen reminded.

[You are now. Welcome to the fold, Agent Foxpaw.]

"Wh— how come I don't get any pomp and/or circumstance? You aren't gonna seek out someone I look up to to tell me?"

"I can if you would prefer. Volta, would you like to tell Ellen she's an agent now?"

Volta rolled her eyes, and with apparently great effort, turned to face the fox beside her. "Hey, dipshit. You're *Agent* Standup now. Be honored." Ellen grumbled ineffectually as Relly continued.

[Now then, as I was saying, her two favorite agents can share the good news!] Relly resumed her cheery tone. [What time works best for the both of you?]

"She only started training … what, two, three weeks ago?" Ellen quirked a brow as she stared down at the little Pinktooth device, hesitation plain to hear in her voice. "I have some reservations about putting her in the field so soon…"

[Her provisional qualifications are as a stealth operative and tactical field mystic. So, no direct combat hopefully, although we have been utilizing the subconscious training program most nights to help fill in the gaps in case need arises. She really wants to help, Ellen. She *needs* this…] The dragoness trailed off a bit, but there was pride in the words that followed. [Her whole world was turned upside down, and she rolled with it. She deserves the shot.]

"Subconscious training? I can see the Keanu Reeves yiff in my head."

[…Do you mean 'gif'?]

"Pretty sure the creators said it's pronounced with a 'y.' Yiff. Like the peanut butter."

Amarelys suddenly became thankful Agent Foxpaw strenuously avoided her RCGs, because she would be unable to hide communicating the mental sensation of how hard she had just rolled her virtual eyes. […Regardless, yes. While time in 'dream training' is no substitute for the real thing, it is recognized as a useful supplemental resource.]

"I think she's ready enough. No one's gonna be able to stop her, anyhow; that cat's stubborn as her ass is fat." Volta spoke up, claws tapping idly on the table.

"But *that's* what worries me…" Ellen's brow looked uncharacteristically furrowed. "Why *aren't* you throttling her, Relly? Why allow her to work herself so *danged* hard without intervening? You have the keys, you should be taking them away if she insists on doing 105 just to try to prove herself!"

[We all work hard, Ellen! Mabel sees it as just trying to catch up! I'm not going to *stop* her and I'm *absolutely* not going to do it without her consent!]

"And we're gonna just ignore the blood on her knuckles and the bags under her eyes? She needs to learn the discipline of *self-care* before she learns more about *self-defense*. The weight of exhaustion is going to send her into a brick wall eventually, and I don't want to give I-told-you-so's while Nurse O scrapes her off the ground ... *or worse.*"

[Ellen, stop being so dramatic ... She's a little tired, yes, I know that, but she can handle herself. Volta, you trust her, don't you?] The dragoness bit back on her indignance, but sought someone to join her side. [Is she doing a lot? Yes. We can work on slowing down when she's *ready* to.]

"When she's ready to...?" The wolf's claws stopped tapping anxiously, as she struggled with how to say what was on her mind. "Feels weird sayin' this so often these days, but Standup's right. It's almost like you're ignoring her well-being just so you don't have to tell her '*no*' ... but that can't *possibly* be true, that would be *wildly* irresponsible for someone operating with the combined thought capacity of a small country. It's not like you to enable someone's self-destructive tendencies."

[It's not that I don't want to tell her no, it's that she can't hear it — and by the way, those 'tendencies'? Are something the both of you have as well, and I don't care to point out the examples, of which there are many. We all have had our growing pains, we can't belittle her for that!] Relly caught herself just short of snapping, but the turn of the conversation was unexpectedly frustrating.

Why aren't they just happy for her?

"The first thing the Korps did upon my arrival was assure me that I didn't *have* to put myself in harm's way anymore."

[You *don't*, and neither does *she!* This struggle is her choice! She wants to *help*...] Amarelys's voice unexpectedly faltered as she continued, and Ellen shot the uncharacteristically quiet wolf beside her a look. [She ... *she's trying so hard to be better ... for all of us...*]

"Relly, do you really believe that she's ready for the field? What if she runs into another super? What if someone like *Strong* gets involved?" Volta did not look up from the spot on the tabletop she was focused on. "*Technically*, I'm sure she could manage light field work ... but we can't guarantee light won't turn into *unbearably heavy out there*, and I *can't* believe **I** have to tell **you** that!"

[Well, we would step in ... if ... *if* ... *it*...] The device went silent.

The wolf and the fox waited, and the sudden quiet was broken by a soft sob.

[I let it go because I *love* her … because she was so *proud* of herself … every *bruise*, every *ache*, every *single* ounce of pain, she felt proved she cared … That she was *worth* caring for … She wants nothing more than that … how could I tell her to stop?]

"Relly…"

[I … I thought that *maybe*, if she reached what the goal was in her mind … *maybe* she would finally listen when I said it, and *believe* me.]

"…Tell me right now you don't think it would be a bad idea to let her have agent clearance before she learns to listen to her body, or even to *you*. You tell me that right now, and I'll sign off on it. *Hell, I'll bring the cake.*"

[I … I *know* you're right … I just … *I can't break her heart. I don't have that in me…*]

"Well," Ellen said, looking thoughtful, "what if you didn't have to do it alone?"

The catamount was sprawled out on the couch, nursing a large glass of nanomilk and a severe candesca-depletion headache. Her entire body felt like it was made of crumpled aluminum foil, such that with every minute movement, she could feel herself *crinkling*; her punishment for overtaxing her magical abilities, or so Eneera had suggested earlier, forbade her from any physical exertion.

"*Psh … Just wanted me to stay in tonight so they could go have coffee with Alder,*" she sulked, crossing her arms under her chest. "*Lucky witch-bird.*"

Well a little headache isn't gonna slow me down … And mental exercises aren't **physical.**..

"*Relly, you up for some mind games? A little dream sparring just to keep me sharp?*"

There was no response internally or externally from her sister.

"Relly? Hello?"

A loud, single rap on the door startled her from the apparently one sided conversation she was attempting to have. "Hey, who's there?" she called out, but got no reply.

Okay, so no one is going to answer me now? Cute.

The single knock repeated itself.

No doorfeed … Maybe the network is experiencing some issues? That would explain the sudden absence of a sister in my head … The catamount grunted as she shifted her legs from the couch and, with a few unbecoming noises and a little more effort than she cared to admit, pushed her glow stick-impersonating joints into a standing position.

A third loud bang of impatience made her wonder who it could possibly be. Everyone she knew was occupied that night in one manner or another, and she was *trying* not to dwell on being lonely by focusing on something *useful*.

"Hey, Charla, if that's you, hun, I didn't order anything, and I'm kinda in rough—"

The door slid open with the telltale pneumatic hiss before she hit the release.

"Hello, Mabes."

"*…Shape.*"

There she was, in the flesh. Not augmented reality, but *actual* reality. Her smile was warm, and her mossy eyes were alight with impish delight at the ruse she had just played.

"Surprised to— *OOF?*" The dragoness couldn't finish her smug little gloat, as all the air was forced out of her lungs by two-hundred- plus pounds of feline missile.

The puma nearly tackled her as she hugged her close, squeezing as tightly as she could. She said nothing, just sniffled quietly as her head was buried in the leather bustier of the silver-scaled sweetheart, who began to laugh as she stroked the feline's hair with her free arm, leaning down to kiss between her ears.

"I've only been gone for thirty seconds, Mabes…"

"Shut up, and keep hugging me, you draconic sneak!" She wrapped an arm about the lithe reptilian neck and planted a big peck on her cheek.

"Guess we're chopped liver, huh, Standup?"

"Liver *is* a good source of iron, and other minerals for muscle building and recovery…"

"You sound like that commercial you were in for that diner. The one with the best liver and onions in Milwaukee?"

"Y'know, it was actually in West Allis, but like … who would ever admit that if they could help it?"

"Damn, that bad, huh?"

"Eh, ups and downs. They got Liberace *and* Jeffrey Dahmer—"

"*Hello?*" Mabel interjected, leaning to either side of her sister, her eyes wide with delighted surprise, "Volta? *Elle?* What the hell are you *three* doing here, I thought you were busy tonight?"

"Turns out Vixie had a thing," shrugged Ellen, "so I'm here."

"What about you V? I thought you were busy too?"

"Plans changed, Relly asked if we wanted to come over," Volta sniffed, "turns out we did."

The cougar stepped aside and ushered them into the apartment. "Well, I'm sorry things didn't work out, but lucky me, huh? I was going a little stir-crazy, and company will be a welcome distraction!"

The cougar winced as she turned towards the kitchen. "So, what would you all like to drink? Should I break out some snacks—"

Mabel stopped when she felt Relly's paw on her wrist.

"Can we just sit for a moment?" She led her little sister to the couch and placed the wrapped package she was carrying down on the table. The dragoness settled into her seat and patted the spot beside her. "Please?"

The catamount blushed, eyes flicking to the box before plopping down beside Amarelys. "Oh, sure! O-of course!"

Volta and Ellen settled into the armchair and the other side of the couch, respectively. The pair said nothing, which was unsettling in a way she did not miss from her previous life. The lioness was getting emotional whiplash as the vibes in the room seemed so ... *serious.*

Why does this feel like a break-up?

"What's going on, girls...?" She licked her lips, and forced a smile. "Did I do something?"

Relly pulled the feline into another warm embrace, nuzzling gently, "You're not in trouble, Mabes." She cooed into the feline's ear, who visibly relaxed in the dragoness's arms.

"Okay, good ... I was just scared I fucked up again during a training session or something." Green eyes danced around the room, looking at each of her guests. "Trying to avoid that, y'know? Did a whole apology tour not too long ago? Remember?"

"You didn't fuck up, Mabes." Volta shook her head as she leaned forward, resting her forearms on her thighs. "Not like you're worried about, at any rate."

"...The fact I fucked up at *all* is worrying all the same, V." Mabel snorted, and bit her lip. "Can I maybe get a straight answer?"

"Mabel ... we need to talk to you about your training. It—"

"I'm training as hard as I can!" Mabel cut in. "I *know* I'm not the greatest candidate, but I want to do something with this gift, and I keep having to stop because of my stupid body, and *I'm sorry*—"

"*Mabel.*" Relly put a paw on her knee. "Everyone knows you're trying your hardest, but that's the actual issue here." She looked at the demivixen and the wolf, who nodded. "You're trying so hard that you're ignoring everything your body is telling you."

The cougar looked confused, letting out an incredulous laugh at the accusation. "I'm literally resting *right now!* What are you *talking* about? Holy shit, y'all came in here so somber, I thought I was about to get kicked out or something! *Gods...*"

"*Bullshit,*" Volta spat. "The only reason you stopped tonight is because you can hardly *move.* You're not *resting,* Mabes, you haven't slept more than six hours in the last three weeks. Relly told us your routine, and I'm kinda pissed that *none of us* stepped in sooner, honestly. You need to give your body *and* your mind the chance to recover, and you're not." She sighed and rubbed at her muzzle. "We're not doing you any favors by letting this slide."

"Volta's right, Mabe. It's okay to work hard, but you've got to be *smart* about it. You're trying to rush to the finish line, and if you keep going like this, all you're gonna do is burn out! I am speaking from *experience* here! I'm talking about 'sixteen hour days on a peanut butter sandwich' sort of experience! No one expects *or wants* that from you."

"I'm a grown woman gang, a big girl even!" Mabel rolled her eyes, "I can handle a little soreness with some ibuprofen, and the lack of sleep with judicious application of caffeine! This is literally nothing to worry about, and you got me all fucking wound up! Come on, this is my fuck up? *Bettering myself?*"

"Shut the fuck up, Mabe."

Everyone turned to Ellen, silent and wide-eyed at the outburst.

"*You're a big girl?* Let me guess, you know what's best for you? We're not your real mom?" she snarled. "You got these powers *three weeks ago,* Mabel, you *impossible* jackass! You think you're the one person whose career won't come to a sudden stop because you didn't slow down when you needed to and now you can't bend without screaming? You want that to happen before you even start a career? You think it can't happen to you? That the people with experience, the people you yourself claim to look up to most, don't know what the hell they're talking about?" The vixen was standing now, and ran a hand back through her hair as she looked up to the ceiling for the strength to carry on. "You really are a stupid fuckin' puma if you're going to just *disregard* the advice of every single person in this room, and I *know* a few more outside of it, who have told you to *slow. the hell. DOWN.*"

The catamount was struck speechless, if only for a moment, staring up wide-eyed at her former Hero, now clearly wounded friend. "... You don't swear, Elle..."

Volta had covered her muzzle with both paws but remained silent.

"I do when someone I care about is acting like a total *shithead*." Her eyes narrowed as she glared daggers sharper than anything the amateur could conjure. "There is nothing *noble* about suffering like this. You're not going to make up for lost time by throwing yourself directly in the chipper! What's the point in all that, if it just ends up with you dead?" Ellen trailed off and shook her head. "I won't stand by and watch you grind yourself to paste."

"So, what does that mean? I just *take it easy*? Fucking, *how*? Ellen, I don't know if you *realize* this, but I'm about two decades older than *most* of the fuckin' roster here!" The feline was clearly shaking as she pressed on. "I can't *afford* to slow down, or be hurt, or *anything else* that will keep me from this! I wasted my whole life being fucking *scared*, and I'm finally *not* anymore, and you want me to *wait*?" She sniffed loudly and glared back at the demivixen. "You don't know what it's *like*, to not only live in the wrong fucking body, but to have that body be so fucking pathetic, some shithead could just ... just *take* what he wanted..." She swallowed hard, and looked to Volta, pleadingly. "V ... I ... You get it ... *right*? Why this matters...?"

"Mabes..." The wolf sighed, rubbing her knuckles as she lifted her gaze back to the catamount. "I *do* get it, and I don't disagree with what you want ... but what's the point of getting agent status if you're just going to become another name on the memorial wall days after?"

The frustration had reached a boil now, and the vitriol spilled over as a frustrated yowl. "At least I'll be *worth remembering*—"

Mabel's next tirade was stopped by a power claw grasping her jaw. "Worth *remembering*? You think *dying* is what is going to make us *remember you*?" Relly would not let her look away from her eyes as the tears spilled down her silvery cheeks. "You promised me! You fucking *promised* you would listen! That you would grow ... That you would *live*..."

The cougar tried to turn her head away, but the grip her sister had was like iron.

"Mabel Ramona, we are *trying* to keep you safe and help you actually *reach* your goal and stay with us! You are the most stubborn creature under the fucking sun, and that says a lot, because I know a *lot* of creatures!" Amarelys nearly growled the last words, which turned into a pained sob. "We love you, and want you to succeed, but not at the cost you seem so *desperate* to pay..." She slipped her free paw into Mabel's, who stared down at their interlaced fingers.

"Please, Mabes ... I'm sorry I didn't stop this sooner ... I ... I was being a bad friend ... a bad *sister*, by allowing you to push yourself like this." Relly brought the held paw up to her cheek, and Mabel felt the moisture mingle with her fur. "You want to help *so badly*, but you can't help anyone if you're not here ... *with us*. We're not *just* your friends, Mabes ... *We're your family*. You picked us, and we picked you..."

Mabel, famously stoic in the face of a crying dragoness, began to weep.

"Relly ... I don't *want* to go! I ... *I just want to be useful!* I have waited so long ... I ... I..." She pressed her forehead to her sister's. "I ... I want to *live*, and this feels like I'm *finally* doing it ... you mean so much to me, and I just wanna be—"

"Mabes, if the next words out of your muzzle are gonna be 'worth it'? I'm gonna shove my fist so far up your ass I can help you pick better ones." Volta was looming now, and leaned down, nearly touching her nose to the trembling and sniffling feline as her voice dropped to a gentle rumble. "You've *always* been worth it, with or without powers, *dipshit*. Being an agent isn't a badge that means we suddenly acknowledge you because we *already do*."

She knelt down and enveloped the pair with those powerful arms, flicking her head to the vixen to join the embrace.

Mabel choked back her tears for long enough to whisper, "I'm s-sorry ... I ... I never meant to worry you..."

The red wolf laid her chin on top of the cat's head and let out a quiet chuckle. "Well, we're always going to worry about you a *little*, Kittycat ... you're a stupid fuckin' puma, after all."

Ellen had managed to get a hand on Mabel's shoulder, standing awkwardly beside Volta. "Besides, Vixie's been missing you these past couple weeks. Relax, take it easy, actually hang out a while with the family you wanna protect, y'know?"

Amarelys, speaking without saying a word, shared a vision that would have terrified Mabel in the past.

But it never could when her big sister held her so close.

It sounded like *bliss:*
[*Forever.*]
"*Always and forever.*"

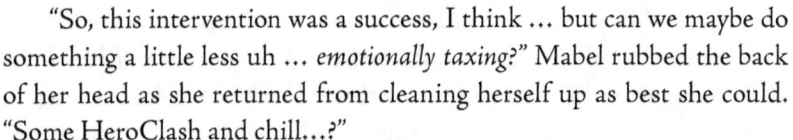

"So, this intervention was a success, I think ... but can we maybe do something a little less uh ... *emotionally taxing?*" Mabel rubbed the back of her head as she returned from cleaning herself up as best she could. "Some HeroClash and chill...?"

"Well, we actually had something else we wanted to talk about," Relly smiled, as the wolf and the vixen returned to their seats. "Aren't you curious about that?" She pointed to the neatly wrapped box that still sat on the table.

"I mean ... I'll admit that I sorta forgot about it, what with the crying and the hugging and all that." Mabel sat on the table next to the package, running a fingertip along the pink ribbon. "But you know me, *love* a mystery box..."

"Now you sound like *Vixie...*"

"Shut!" Ellen huffed, as a blush crawled up her furless cheeks.

The puma was relieved by the return to normal, chuckling at the antics of the enemies-to-sisters. "The girl likes to find her way into a warm and dark secret or three, I've been told."

The dragoness leaned over, smirking as she said in a perfectly audible stage whisper, "She's a *professional* arse-iologist."

Mabel snorted, trying to stop her giggle from getting out of control not only from the unexpected wordplay from her big sister, but the mortified look on Ellen's face.

The cougar did not succeed, and neither did Volta.

"HA! Holy shit — *tongue spelunkin'!* That's *exactly* what she does!"

Ellen, who was quickly going past pink to a dark crimson, quietly huffed, "Can we focus on the box on the table, and not my sister's—"

"Anal indiscretions?" Mabel suggested with a wink at Relly.

"She certainly isn't *discrete* — and neither are those noises she yanks out of folks via their backdoor!"

Another round of cackles, another shade closer to purple for the vixen.

"Okay! *OKAY!* Yes, my sister is a big fan of … butt stuff … *SO.* The box — the *present* — I mean? Remember?"

"Yes, girls, let's stop teasing our recently promoted *official agent—*"

"Wait, Elle wasn't an agent already?"

"Long story, Mabes, just let her finish."

"I feel like I— *ope.*" The cougar stopped short as she watched Relly rise to her feet and looked imperiously down on her. "S-sorry."

The dragoness raised an eyebrow, nodding as she continued. "As I was saying … to *celebrate* our *up and coming* agent and provocateur…"

Mabel's brow furrowed as she glanced between the three and then over her shoulder.

"My sister, *Mabel Greysmoke.*"

"W-what?"

"*Provided* that she adheres to a strict regimen requiring proper rest and downtime when recommended *or* requested, Mabel Ramona Greysmoke's status as a field agent will be approved. As a recently recruited civilian with recently developed powers, she will be restricted to missions of a *minimum* level of risk — that means no combat! As her training continues and she proves herself in the field, clearances will be revisited." Amarelys leaned down now, her voice still deathly serious. "Can you handle that, *trainee?*"

The lioness looked to Volta, and to Ellen, who wore the smiles of proud parents watching a child walk across the stage, before nodding enthusiastically. "Fuck yes I can! *Of course!* I … err … Yes. Ma'am. I can do that. Thank you. Ma'am."

Relly's smile lit up her face. "Then open the box."

Shaky paws carefully untied the ribbon, lifting the lid, before she let out gasp. "You … *you…*" The package tumbled to the floor, and its contents spilled out, the violet material seeming to glow on the polished dark wood as the waterworks started anew. "You did it … You *really* did it! You made *my* costume! *I love it!* I—" She buried her nose in her draconic sibling's neck. "*I love you!*"

The two embraced, laughing and crying together until Amarelys tucked a finger under Mabel's chin and pressed her lips to the puma's. "I love you too, my darling girl. We'll show them all what proper mystical mischief is, soon enough!" She purred, touching her snout to the cat's nose. "*Greysmoke.*"

The cat began to laugh through the tears, pressing her forehead to her sister's chest, nearly overcome, that familiar paw rubbing her lower back. "Now, dry your eyes, and let's see that cute behind in that skirt!"

Mabel sniffed and nodded, her smile dipping to something between shy and nervous. "Okay, sure…"

"Oh, shoot! I have to go help Vixie! She made cake in case this went well — which it did!"

"Ellen, I could just call her?"

"It's *a lot* of cake." The demivixen smirked, and headed out the door before anyone could stop her.

"Oh … well, maybe I should wait to reveal the costume until Elle gets back?" The puma's ears splayed slightly.

"Oh? And make us wait for *our* private viewing, Kittycat? Don't you want to show off for us?" the wolf rumbled, a pale eyebrow lifting as she leaned forward. "Pretty *please?*"

There was a puff of smoke, and when it cleared both cat and costume were gone. The bedroom door closed behind her, and she leaned back against it, smiling, and blushing.

"Well, I'm glad I resisted the urge to start stripping in front of her…"

*[She's only **slightly** disappointed.]*

"…Shut up."

[Fine, don't believe me. Not like I'm in her head, too, or anything.]

"Mmf."

Mabel said nothing else, though her thrashing tail and pink ears were very loud indeed. She tried to focus on slipping out of her lay-around wear and into her night-on-the-town ensemble.

A deep hood, silver chains, supple leather, fishnets…

Every piece was something she had inspected, designed, and *re-designed* in her mind over and over again, and as she pulled on the fingerless gloves that fit her perfectly, she realized…

Each was a part of who she wanted to be seen as, *if* she could be brave.

If she could be who she *wanted* to be.

This is so much more than the component parts…

As she tightened the last strap on her boots, she nibbled her lip pensively. *"I'm afraid to look…"*

*[Then let **us** look for you! Get out here!]*

The cougar took a deep breath and stepped towards the door, dissolving into smoke before reforming on the other side, with her eyes closed. "So … whadya think? Am I *cloak-and-dagger* hot, or a ren faire reject?"

The lack of response was … *disconcerting.* She sheepishly opened one eye. "Uh … girls … *hello?*"

"Oh, *Mabes…*" Relly stood there with a paw to her lips, smiling softly, with freshly wet eyes.

Volta's tail was wagging, and her cheeks were just a little redder than normal. All she could manage was a quiet, "Holy *shit…*"

"…Good, then?" the lioness asked, tail curling around her leg as the smile crept up her features.

"Yeah! I think I did pretty good work there, *if* I do say so myself!"

Sitting on the back of the couch for maximum pansexuality was a projection of a familiar bat, with dark hair, long lashes, and lips painted bright blue and pulled into a self-satisfied smirk. "Solid ideas — the materials were *all wrong,* of course, but…" Wren mused before the holo-light image suddenly appeared in front of the cougar, leaning this way and that. "The *vibe* was pretty easy to read, but I made some little tweaks and improvements to get it where it needed to be!" He pointed his finger up and moved it in a circle. "Give us a turn, and let's see the back! Wanna make sure that skirt falls in the right spot — just enough ass to be distracting, yeah?"

The feline did as instructed, trying to decide if she was mortified or flustered and settled on both.

Morti-stered? Fluster-fied?

"Tail up, c'mooooon!"

Mabel's blush intensified as the virtual bat leaned close to inspect his work, *apparently.* "H-hey, Wren! Haven't seen you in a hot minute!" She flashed a look to Relly, who shrugged.

[*He's one of the finest designers in RIV, and* **volunteered** *to assist besides! His only request was to get to see it on you as soon as you … what did he say … "squeeze that fat ass into those combat panties," I believe were his exact words.*]

"I knoooow! *Someone's* been too busy for me to raid their closet *or* discuss costume ideas…" He clucked his tongue, before glancing back to Relly. "I'm assuming you all had the talk, and she's gonna behave now?"

The dragoness and the wolf both nodded, their eyes not leaving the cat.

Mabel sighed quietly, "Yes, I'll be a good girl, and not *try* to find new ends of the candle to burn."

"Good!" Wren's smile was as bright as his white fur, and wicked as they came.

The bemused cougar rolled her eyes, before looking back over her shoulder. "So, it really looks good…?"

"Of course it does! I helped make it!" The bat rolled his eyes. "Turn around and look at the projection if you don't believe me."

Mabel once again did as she was told. Standing there was a villain — *her.*

Greysmoke.

"Well? What do you think, Kittycat?"

"What do I think…?" The catamount smirked and traced her teeth with her tongue. "I think, Volta darling, that after a mandatory week of rest? The mischief can *finally* commence…"

CHAPTER 30

TAKING IT BACK

The locks had been changed, and the police tape was still across the doorframe, but they were barely a deterrent for a feline with her skillset. She had practiced picking locks with nothing but smoke, feeling the pins and solidifying the vapor precisely to trip the tumblers without showing signs of entry. Sure, she could have just slid under the door while in smokeshape, but that would have been too *easy*. She had to wonder, though, whether the validation of her skills was worth a trip all the way back to Lubbock, just to return empty-pawed...

Mabel stared at the barren walls of the apartment she'd once called home and snorted derisively at the view. The noncommittal beige paint, the crack above the bathroom door, the scuffed linoleum in the kitchenette. They hadn't even bothered to replace the ratty carpet. The space within was hollow, and the air felt motionless and stale.

Like a mausoleum.

It occurred to the lioness that — clad as she was in her nondescript hoodie and jeans — she didn't look all that different from the last time she was there, either. Save for the glowing pink visor across her eyes, or the tits, or the ass ... all of the blessings bestowed by EE, both apparent and otherwise. So, just the clothes were sort of passingly similar, really.

Had it really been less than two months since she'd fled? It seemed like *years* had passed.

The apartment never felt like a home, though; not really. Not until Amarelys came into her life. Still, it was so *empty*, it was as if she'd never been there at all. The police had clearly gone over every last inch with a fine-toothed comb, trying to find answers that were not there — and, truthfully, never could have been. The cougar imagined them tweezing fur, and dusting for prints. There had been some sheets in the laundry she hadn't gotten around to before she left, too, there'd be *plenty* of DNA on those...

The dejection radiated from the catamount in waves as she stalked around the empty studio. *"Wow, they really cleaned the place out, huh…?"*

[That'll happen when you are accused of colluding with a terrorist organization, hun. I'm sorry,] the dragoness replied sadly.

Her consternated expression seemed thoroughly unconvinced of the necessity. *"Gods damnit … What an incredible waste of resources."* None of her meager belongings remained; not a single scrap of paper was left behind. It was her first trip outside of RIV since she'd been rescued, and she was spending it in this … this *monument to the utterly unremarkable,* finding nothing but echoes of the unhappy ghost that had once resided there.

She paced the circuit of the room, stopping before the bathroom. The mirror was still bolted on the door, still smudged as it always seemed to be, no matter how many times it was cleaned. Her gloved pads ran down it, activating melancholy memories of the last person she'd seen in it. The boy left behind.

[What were you hoping to find, love? You never did say.]

"Nothing much. It doesn't really matter, y'know? All of it is likely going to rot away in an evidence locker somewhere, now. Mmph…" She pulled her hood back and ran a paw through her hair in exasperation. *"I don't know why I bothered. I just hoped for one good memory from … from before it all. I didn't even get to finish filling it up…"*

[Oh … Your sketchbook.]

While she'd only drawn in it a few times around the dragoness, it held incredible importance to her. The contents were fantasies, a record of dreams, a piece of the one who was. *"Mm. They took so much from me; what's one more thing, right?"* She sat on the floor where her dingy old couch had once been and hung her head between her knees in defeat. *"I just feel like … this was the one thing I wanted to keep, even if it was from then. Not everything was awful, right?"*

[Mm-mm … There were good times here, but those are long past.] The comforting voice of her sister was joined by invisible fingers kneading her shoulder. Mabel reached up instinctively, and felt the phantom digits twine with hers.

"It's all right. It was just paper, y'know …? They can't take the important part." She tapped the side of her head, forcing a smile. *"We know what was here. He's gone for good, and I won't miss him … but I'm very glad he stuck around long enough to meet you."*

The cougar brushed one melancholy tear aside with a sniff.

"Ah, well. Into each life, right? Anyway, how long until our ride arrives?" It was always safe to bet on the puma to change the subject if she was uncomfortable, and she was definitely feeling overwhelmed by the visit.

[You have an hour before pickup is scheduled. In the meantime, would a little recreational thievery soothe your wounded soul?]

"Maybe ... what did you have in mind, dear sister?" She rubbed at her nose with the back of a paw and gave a small smile.

[Well, there is a cigar bar a couple blocks over, and it seems the owners are **very** conservative...]

"How conservative are we talkin'?"

[Let's just say they're **outspoken** fans of Germany circa '38.]

"Ah. Well I'm not going to pass up the chance to fuck with a fascist AND get myself a treat or three."

[That's my girl. Two birds!]

"One stone," chuckled the cat. "Thanks, Relly. But you know what? Before we go..." She whispered, the weak smile shifting into a smirk as she withdrew a silver cylinder from her front pocket, and began shaking it, the telltale rattle making plain what it was. "How about we lower some property values, and give the sad boy a proper sendoff?"

The quiet chuckle from Relly was all the approval she needed, before she began to "ruin" the ancient, chipped paint with brilliant magenta memoria.

Joseph Greysbell
Born: August 1st, 1984
Died: November 2nd, 2022
HE DIED, SO SHE COULD FINALLY LIVE

"I mean, I had no other choice! Their smoke detectors didn't look up to code!" Her impish grin split her muzzle as she clenched an unlit cigar in her teeth.

[You **had** to test them! Safety first, after all! How could you have **possibly** known they were in working order? Shame we forgot to reconnect the security systems, those sprinklers going all night is going to ruin all of their stock...]

The giggle that joined the thought was as far from innocent as could be.

"Damn shame! I'm sure it'll be a struggle to recover, but I guess they'll just have to pull themselves up by das bootstraps, eh?" She giggled while wiggling the cigar and her eyebrows. The laugh trailed into a sigh, as she popped the stogie back into her muzzle. "Thanks, Relly … I needed that distraction. I'm trying not to let the sketchbook get me down. You'd think some cigars and some property damage would cheer me right up! It's just…"

[Just what, sweetie?]

She rolled the cigar between her thumb and forefinger pensively as they strolled down the near empty street. "I had started a drawing of you — well your vixen shape I mean — one night when I had a little insomnia and didn't want to wake you. It was supposed to be a surprise, but … I just never got to finish it. Kinda stupid to be moping about that, yeah?" She shrugged but stopped as she felt the dragoness's claws wrapped around her wrist.

[Mabel Ramona, don't you call my little sister stupid! It's okay to be sad about losing things! Yes, they may **just** be objects, and you do have the memories, but it is okay to have attachments … things you can hold can be important.] Invisible fingers twined with the puma's own. [I wish I could have seen it, but maybe you'll try again …? For me?]

The squeeze Amarelys gave Mabel's paw said so very much, with the tiniest gesture. "I'd like that, but only if you'll come model for—"

"Did you hear something?"

[I did. It came from up the street a bit further. About three blocks, maybe four.] A waypoint marker lit up in the cougar's view to the north. [No radio chatter, and no video feeds to access.]

"Then I think it's time to stick my nose where it doesn't belong." The cougar tossed the cigar aside, shifting to intangibility with practiced ease.

[Please be careful.]

"I'm **always** careful, darling!" She took a deep breath before exhaling into a cloud of smoke.

Stepping sideways is still a trip, Mabel thought idly as she moved. She was unable to feel her legs propelling her, but instead felt the ground *flowing* in what, after many hours of practice, had become an incredibly familiar sensation. Physically, she was still *mostly* on the correct plane of existence, but Eneera had explained that taking the shape of smoke propelled part of her to the elemental plane — overlaid with the material world, yet intangible for all but the spirits of the song.

She'd always had a quiet step, but with the djinn's blessing, she had become the utter absence of sound. A wisp on the wind and the flash of glowing eyes were the only indicators she was anything more than vapor. Her view shifted along with her, and everything became faintly desaturated and blurred, like looking through frosted glass, and noises became muted, like listening through water.

Stretches of chain link, darkened store fronts, and utility poles sped by in a matter of moments. As she got closer to the marker on her display, the drowned-out sounds grew louder and more distinct.

Arguing…

She stepped back into her world, tucked herself against a wall, and leaned around the corner. Her heart caught in her throat an instant later as the source of the commotion revealed itself. In the back of a parking lot, half trapped in shadow, two figures struggled, one pressing the other up against the hood of a parked car.

"Listen, I'm not fuckin' stupid. Only one reason you'd be dressed like that!"

"I wasn't d-doing anything! I'm just c-c-coming home from the club!"

She ducked back, focusing on analyzing the scene via a still Relly had captured, and not the simmering rage in the pit of her stomach.

The police officer looked to be a German Shepherd in her early thirties. Her blonde hair was pulled back into a ponytail, and her surly muzzle was twisted with sadistic glee. She was lean, but well-muscled — but how strong did you *really* need to be when you had a gun pressed against someone's back?

The lioness felt Amarelys gripping her shoulder, keeping her present.

Scanning her badge number, Relly was quickly able to pull up a file confirming the puma's suspicions. Mabel's eyes narrowed to knife-edged slits as she reviewed the police dog's greatest hits, which happened to include the words "accused," "sexual assault," "harassment," "brutality," and "*dismissed.*"

"*Dismissed? Because women can't be violent dickheads?*"

[*Three separate times.*]

Mabel shook her head, lip curling, and ear flicking as the interrogation continued.

"Oh yeah? Which one did you *grace* with your presence?"

"AHHH! *Heat!* I was dancing at Heat tonight!" the skinny figure whimpered as their arm was wrenched upward.

Mabel didn't feel her claws digging into her palm.

"That disgusting strip club off 289? What a filthy fuckin' hole. Just like *you…*" She laughed at her own joke, and the puma felt her stomach turn.

The victim was just a kid, couldn't have been more than eighteen or nineteen. Feline, a Russian Blue maybe, or at least somewhere in the family tree. Visibly queer by the stereotypical standards, and their outfit did not dissuade from that queerness. They were scrawny.

Effeminate.

Weird.

*An **easy** target.*

The hollow sound of a face hitting the hood of a card echoed in the open air of the lot, followed by a choked sob.

"I j-just wanna go *home! I didn't d-do anything, I swear!*"

"Didn't do anything or *anyone* I bet. Y'know ... I think a night in the tank is in order. You've been so ... *uncooperative.* Maybe it'll teach you to mind your superiors, *you fuckin' whore.*"

"N-no! Let go of me! Pleaseeeee ... Somebody help!" Their voice was thin, pleading.

The only light in the building above them shut off in response.

"Oh my **God**, you're a fuckin' tranny?"

A growl began to rumble deep inside the lioness, and she shook with barely contained rage. Mabel clenched her teeth, claws digging reflexively into the stucco she'd braced herself against.

[Mabel, extraction is inbound and has a combat-trained op onboard.]

Blood was thudding through her veins, pounding like war drums in her ears.

"*It'll be too late if we wait for backup. We **can't** let this happen.*"

She knew protocol dictated that she should have asked for clearance to engage, before making a move. She was, after all, still a trainee and this was supposed to be a non-combat op...

She decided, under the circumstances, that she would ask for forgiveness later.

Amarelys agreed.

[Don't forget your training.] Relly's voice was firm, knowing full well that her sister's conclusion was a forgone one.

*The **only** one.*

Mabel took a deep breath as the wrath seared within her breast. Somehow, she managed a response, her tone perfectly calm and collected. "*I won't. Besides! I just wanna **talk** to her...*" The menacing noise that rolled up through her betrayed any delusions that it would be a civil discussion. Her tail whipped behind her, the cougar unable — or simply *unwilling* — to disguise her intentions. "*Going to have a **Nice. Little. Chat.***"

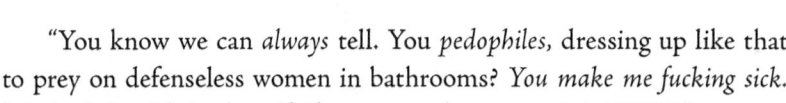

"You know we can *always* tell. You *pedophiles*, dressing up like that to prey on defenseless women in bathrooms? *You make me fucking sick.* Maybe I should rip this off, *if you wanna be a wo— AAAGGH!*"

Mabel had sidestepped once more, and in a burst of smoke she was behind the cop. The dog's words were cut short by the fingerless glove grasping across her trachea, claws digging in along either side, much like the point of the knife that pressed upward and under her ballistic vest. "What was that, officer? I think I heard a threat, but I can't understand you when you're *gurgling* like that..." She giggled in her pointed ear with venom-laced sweetness, before her voice fell to a growl. "Tsk, tsk ... **Drop** the gun, and no talking. Not a **single** sound, or else I'm going to give you a few new holes to breathe with. Nod if you understand, *shitstain.*"

The catamount motivated the Shepherd to comply with the subtle press of a dagger. She nodded quickly and dropped the gun between her boots, lifting her paws up slowly. "Now kick it under the car..." Her vitriolic sarcasm laden with contempt as the cop did as she was told. "Oh! She *can* listen! Maybe you just don't know what '*no*' means?"

Mabel felt the heavy swallow in the throat against her palm, as she forced the dog to step back, and away from her victim. "Don't worry, I'm just going to teach you about *consent.*"

The catamount looked at the terrified cat who didn't dare turn around, still shivering against the police cruiser. "*Run.* I don't want witnesses." She felt the cop shudder in her grasp as the realization of just how much trouble she was in became apparent.

Good. Hold on to that feeling...

The civilian muttered a hurried "thank you," and then scrambled off in what the cougar only could assume — what she *hoped* — was the direction of home and safety.

Scared. Bruised. Not ... not dead. But now for the TERF...

"ETA on pickup, Relly?"

[*Seven minutes. Police response in less than fifteen.*]

"Plenty of time to do this right, then..."

"Just you and me now, sweetie ... and my *knife*, of course. Pretty little thing she is ... You *like* pretty little things, *isn't that right?*" She felt the growl bubble up against her paw still pressed to her throat. "Oh! Are we feeling a little *frisky?* Wanna try your luck with someone who isn't *fucking defenseless?"*

The cop's body tensed against her; the telegraphed body language spoke clear as a bell, and the villainess was going to ring it. "Oh, *please, try* and be a *hero!* Let me get you on the evening news," she hissed, egging her on. "*Do it.* Give me *another* reason to put you on the fucking ground…"

Or in it.

The officer wound up and thrust back with an elbow. Mabel could only roll her eyes at the pointless attempt at violence. If she wanted to try her luck, well…

Who am I to deny her raison d'être? she thought with a sneer.

The canine caught two things at that moment: air where Mabel was once standing, and the cougar's own elbow crashing into her head, sending her rocking sideways with a grunt. Before she could react, the lioness's heel slammed into the back of the Shepherd's knee.

The dog crumpled from the force of the strike, but the follow-up that landed between her shoulder blades audibly drove the breath out of her. With nowhere else to go the momentum slammed her muzzle into the bumper of her cruiser with the sickening crack of shattered teeth.

The satisfaction Mabel felt was *palpable* as Kandusky moaned, slumped against the car, coughing up a glob of blood, and bits of enamel. She put what she hoped was *extremely* painful pressure on her wrists, before she was unceremoniously shoved off the vehicle by the catamount's boot, letting the dog's limp form land on the concrete with a thud. The Shepherd was forced to look up at the sinister face of his assailant, her sharp teeth peeking through a feral grin, illuminated magenta within the shadow of her hood.

"*Zip ties,* huh? So *kinky,* Officer … Kandusky, is it?" Mabel straddled her, squatting down so she could get a good look at who was in charge here. She pressed one paw to the wheezing cop's chest while the other idly spun a knife with a well-practiced paw, the edge making a low, eerie whistle as it cut the air. "Good to see the Lubbock PD is still upholding the long tradition of being such *predictable fucking monsters.* Protect and serve? Pfft … right. Only your best interests, right, *Officer?"*

"W-what do…" The officer's eyes went wide; the blade was no longer spinning in her paw, but was instead quivering in the poured stone, the edge grazing her cheek as it flew by. It clearly took a second for the pain to register, so sharp was the knife, and red blossomed in a razor thin line across her face. As she opened her mouth to cry out, the villain backhanded her with a closed fist, contempt twisting her lips into a snarl.

"*I said No.* **Talking! Gods,** y'all never can listen when a girl says no, huh? *Typical* ... All of you stormtroopers are *exactly* the same. A pattern cut from the same piece of masochistic cloth." She leaned in real close, her maw inches from her muzzle as she plucked the dagger from the earth. "I *talk.* You *listen.* I *ask?* You *answer.* That's how this works. If you do that, *maybe* you get out of here intact. *Mostly.*"

She began twirling the knife anew, switching from forward to backward grip as she locked eyes with the canine. "What to do, what to do! Caught you in the act, didn't I? I *suppose* I could try to turn you in, but ... *that* doesn't matter, does it? A girl in a pink visor won't get a fair shake, and besides! You'd just get off again. Little Miss *Victim*, '*Oh, the big mean perp threatened me! I had to use force!*' Isn't that right, *Mary?*"

The canine stared up at her, eyes flicking between the knife and her captor.

"I asked you a *question.* **Speak.**"

"Th-they were resisting ... a-and ... I ... I couldn't..."

She could smell the reek of fear pouring off her. At least, she hoped that's what it was.

It wasn't. It was the other thing, pooling on the ground under her.

"*Oh my gods ... Do they* **all** *do that?*"

[*Pretty frequently, yes.*]

The canine shook her head emphatically. Her eyes grew wetter by the second, just like her pants. Tears ran rivulets through her fur.

The lioness sighed in frustration at the cowardice on display, seeking satisfaction and finding only disappointment for the second time in as many hours. It was *too much* to accept, and she was going to take it out on the dolorous dog.

I'm **going** *to do this right...*

"I fucking *hate* bullies, Kandusky! Can't fuckin' stand 'em!" Mabel couldn't stop the tirade that erupted out of her. "You're all alike! You want to feel *powerful*, but you're *not!* You're *weak.* Which is why you prey on those who're *weaker* ... You want to pretend you're a good guy, right? Heroine, just like Fatal Thorns, or fuckin' *Dazzler*, I bet, saving the world from *evil?*" She snorted, tracing her tongue over her lip as she shook her head.

"You've been *playing pretend*, and now? A real threat, someone *stronger*, is here, and what do you do? Piss all over yourself. Real heroic behavior,

Officer." Mabel lifted the Shepherd's chin with her knife. "Heroes don't *sexually assault* victims … *What do Heroes **do**, Kandusky?"*

"Th-they help … b-but but! They all *asked* for it! They *wanted* to be tr—"

The obsidian tip dug in to draw out a wordless whine, stopping the excuse in its tracks. "Ah ah! Mary Mary, so *contrary!* The only thing I hate more than a bully is a *lying bully!"*

She exhaled through her nose, and clucked her tongue.

"You know, the thing is? I imagined this whole *villain* thing playing out differently for me." The puma let out a dramatic sigh, pulling the dagger back, wiping the blood on their formerly clean and pressed uniform. "Like, I was going to come over here, beat you half to death, maybe do a little monologuing, wrap it up with some cackling, just the good stuff, you know? Greatest hits, fear of the gods, all that … let you *bleed*. But, *no* … you're just a **spineless** piece of shit." Her empty paw clenched into a fist before snapping back open, claws a flash of purple in the warm streetlight.

The mountain lioness grasped the dog's slowly swelling muzzle, forcing the canine to stare at her as she snarled. "You're not even worthy of my **scorn**." She slammed her head back with a sneer of disgust on her face. *"Pathetic."*

She began to sob, then beg; the sounds, unfortunately, did not satisfy like Mabel had hoped they would. There was an itch that they would *never* be able to scratch…

Because they weren't *real*.

"Please … d-don't kill me … I have k-kids—"

[*No children, no adoptions, not dependents. A string of flings, but none serious enough for a break from the dating apps.*]

"So no one would miss her…" Mabel didn't think she could be more enraged, but the excuse ignited something in her. *"Manipulative bitch, 'til the very end…"*

The canine was such a sniveling mess the mewling pleas only infuriated her further. This cop was not the one she wanted; no, she couldn't have the one she *really* desired under her knife. The chicken eluded her, but … *two birds…*

The flash of inspiration prompted a thin and wicked smile to slowly spread across the catamount's features. All the pieces fell into place, arrayed as a revelation before her:

*You work with what you have, but good art? It **always** sends a message…*

The cougar bit her lip as a shiver ran down her spine, the thought of what she could *do*, what she could *say* with the urine-stained canvas before her, and her despondency faded.

"**One** *thing is going to go right today...*"

[Three minutes, Mabes.]

"Can you make it five? I promise it'll be worth it."

[Done.]

"Love you."

[Love you too.]

"*Kill* you?" Mabel put a paw to her chest, as if pained by her entirely valid assumption. "I'm not going to *kill* you! *Goodness*, officer, don't be silly! A corpse is a terrible messenger ... Well ... save for *one* sort o' message, I suppose!" She quirked a brow. "Do you *want* to be my *sticky note*, Kandusky? I probably don't even *need* a pen and paper..." The flat of the knife smacked against her nose. "This can be my quill, and you're *full* of the right ink for *this* message ... you could finally be a victim like you *always* wanted..."

She shook her head immediately but remained silent.

"Awww. Well, if you *must* keep breathing, I need you to deliver these words to someone for me, since he's not accepting visitors!" She whispered in her ear, a short message, but of the utmost importance. "Got that? Repeat it back to me."

Another empty headed nod as the canine repeated the directive word for word, through the tears. "For ... D-Dwight DePain..."

"*Excellent!* I'll know if you don't deliver it! I'll come find youuuuu..." Her voice was unsettlingly chipper as the cougar patted the canine's cheek gently twice before the third turned into an open palmed slap. "Now, I did say I wouldn't *kill* you; I am a woman of my word, after all..." She leaned in close, voice dropping low once more as the dagger pressed into the dip of her neck. "But I *didn't* say I wasn't going to *hurt* you. I'm **definitely** going to do that; can't have you assaulting any more innocent kids, y'know? And I have *just* the thing to dissuade would-be-rapists..."

The malice in her eyes was pure. Purposeful. *Righteous.*

"P-please ... *no*..."

"Oh, you want *mercy*..." The leather of Mabel's gloves creaked audibly as she grasped the handle tight. "Letting you live is all you get."

"*Say* ... D'you think those zip ties can be used like a tourniquet in a pinch, *Officer?*" Before she could respond, the lioness had already looped one over her muzzle, and cinched it tight. "Guess we're gonna learn *together*, Mary Mary…"

The combat op on the VTOL was a face Mabel knew *very* well, a lithe anole with soft brown-green scales. They quietly watched out the window with their bubble-visored RCGs, sitting together in relative silence … for all of about three minutes, before the puma had to put a stop to that.

"Going to *really* enjoy my ill-gotten gains when we get home. Earned a nice smoke, if I do say so myself."

"Successful mission, I assume?" Her reptilian co-passenger sounded as cool and dry as she looked.

"Absolutely! A wonderful op to really *cut* my teeth on, Mal."

"Brief said this was a B and E with some personal stakes. I take it the mission evolved?"

"Just a little message delivery added on! Not a big deal. Barely *any* combat!"

"Mmm … Otherwise, everything went well?"

"You know, it did? It *really* did. Real peace-of-mind stuff. Didn't find what I came for, but got what I *needed*, y'know?" Mabel leaned back in the seat, closing her eyes for just a moment, a contented purr beginning to rumble.

Mallory raised a scaled eyeridge as she tilted her head. "You got a little something-you-needed on your hoodie."

"Huh?" The lioness looked down and scoffed. "Oh! Heh! Clumsy me! You always *hear* about the spray, but you don't believe it until you see it! The PSI is no joke!" She sighed and shook her head ruefully at the crimson splash across her fit. "Need to remember to angle it away, next time…"

Another hoodie ruined by the cops. Gonna start sending them the cleaning bills…

"…What kind of message were you sending, if I might ask?" Mallory leaned in close, her interest shining through her less-than-emotive expression.

Violence always accrues interest.

Keep your paws to yourself.

"All Cats Are Beautiful, naturally!" the cougar demurred, and gave a cheeky wink as she clucked her tongue.

The reptile graced her with another small smile. "Relly already sent over the footage — are you ready for an expert's opinion, or would you prefer to revel in a job well done a little longer?"

"Of course! Always love your feedback, Marshmallow!"

The anole leaned back into her seat, thumbing her chin thoughtfully. *"Do you want to be my sticky note,* eh? You have a flair for the dramatic, certainly. Above-average knifework this time, you correctly judged whether an additional objective was within your capabilities and acted accordingly. You *did* go out of your way to delay oncoming backup, which … well, I've met plenty of first-timers who did *worse.* Competently done, Greysmoke. I look forward to seeing more of your work."

The cougar beamed with pride. "Thanks, Mal! I aim to please! Glory to the Overlord, and all that!"

Friendly banter made the rest of the trip fly by, but as Mabel idly practiced one of the knife tricks Mallory had shown her recently, she smiled to herself.

"Maybe I will grab a new sketchbook tomorrow…"

[*I'd love that, Mabes!*]

*"What can I say? I'm feeling **inspired**."*

[*By the by, I already sent the video to Volta and Star for you, dear.*]

"Thanks, Relly, you really are the best big sister a girl could ask for."

[*I know. Shall I add Vixie to the list as well?*]

"…Really? You sure it's not too graphic?"

[*She is **very** enthusiastic about the more villainous activities!*]

"By 'enthusiastic,' do you mean…?"

[*Oh, like Niagara.*]

"Right, yeah. Go ahead and send it to her, too." The catamount allowed herself a satisfied smirk. Mischief made, and stopped a rapist from *ever* considering that path again.

She couldn't *quite* put a finger on it, but she was confident about that assumption.

"In local news, yet another police officer was assaulted by a member of the terrorist organization known as the Korps this evening. Though left alive, they are in critical condition and are currently under observation at CMC. The nature of the attack is too graphic to discuss on the air, but our thoughts and prayers go out to that brave officer!"

The TV powered off with a click.

It was a miracle that he could clasp the controller, truth be told; his body was still broken beyond belief or relief. Weeks in traction, with the hope to eventually regain some mobility. It was slow going, and he had only managed to remain suspended by the various cables and pulleys, and playing on the sympathies of the nursing staff who treated him like a hero for being injured in the line of duty. But his beak was still wired shut, too, after that mountain of a bitch had crushed it with her forehead.

But he was safe here. They wouldn't come for him here. *Too risky.*

"Detective DePain?" A voice came from the doorway, one the rooster didn't recognize. "I was sent over to give you a message. Kandusky was just assaulted by the Korps and wouldn't calm down until I promised to give it to you, and *only* you."

The cock's eyes grew wide at the mention of the Korps, and their terrifyingly specific interest in *him*. They grew even wider as the hastily-scribbled note was held before his face, and he read:

We both know what really happened. The truth will be heard.
Or I'll come digging for the bones she didn't break.
NYK.

"It really didn't make much sense, but I wrote down everythin' she said to! That psychopath lopped off her fingers, so she couldn't do it herself, y'know?" He held up a paw with the index and ring fingers lowered, with a grimace. The young officer paused for a moment as he considered the contents of the message.

"What's it mean, sir? This talk about what '*really happened*' … and who the hell is NYK?"

His beak could not open, but he began to scream anyway, his monitors blaring as he struggled inside the rack. He was trapped. *Trapped.* The Korps knew where he *was* and he was *trapped!*

"*I have to leave! I have to get out! Oh god! Oh god!*"

The nurses ran into the room, trying to calm him as his eyes rolled wildly in his head, screaming in a strangled squawk. After a moment, he felt a sharp *jab* in one thigh, and his words began to slur as they poured from his beak. Still he screeched until he went limp in his restraints, his mind filled with images of magenta-eyed monsters, twisting and crushing his body past recognition.

Finishing what *he* had started.

Mabel brushed at her ear, a sudden warmth tingling ever-so-slightly. "Mm…"

She did finally get her smoke, as soon as she was off the landing pad, giving one to Mallory as well to celebrate the small victory. The reptile accepted a light and puffed contentedly as she went about her own business, after confirming their weekly training session.

A real unspoken perk of hands-free communication via RCGs was that she was never interrupted, never precluded from dedicating her fullest attention to the lighting and savoring of that first puff. With a deep drag, any lingering tenseness in her shoulders began to melt away. With another long exhale, she let it go.

[NEW MESSAGE]
Volta
That was fuckin' *brutal*, Kittycat! Dangerous looks *good* on you!

The cougar couldn't help but blush and shake her head, imagining a tail wagging a mile a minute while watching the recording, cheering her on all the while. Maybe *Carmen* had even cracked a smile when she was inevitably shown the footage, though she suspected her dramatics might earn her a lesson in brevity from the tabby.

Eh … constructive feedback is better than dismissive apathy. I'll take it.

The walk home was meandering and blissfully uneventful, which gave her ample time to properly enjoy the victory cigar, discarding it in the nearby ashcan before entering the building. She gave the otter at the desk a cheerful wave as she stepped into the elevator. While the doors closed behind the puma, a thought occurred.

"Relly … Did I go too far?"

[Only you can decide that, Mabes, but I will say you saved that kid. What you did will change their world for the better, and that's something you can be proud of. I know I'm proud of you … Kitten.]

The catamount tried to quietly hold onto that moment, her heart so full, accepting everything that happened and the word Amarelys had chosen to use. It felt like it used to, before that night … Like when the people she loved had used it with her.

Back when it wasn't *poisoned*.

She suddenly began to shake uncontrollably, the last drops of adrenaline having finally wicked away as she leaned back against the smooth metal wall. What she did struck all at once, and she slid downwards until her tail was on the floor. She was a *villain* now. It wasn't just a word anymore. This wasn't playing at being in a comic book, or a video game; she *hurt* someone. That was a choice only she made, and she did it *willingly*. She could have *killed* her…

Would that have been so wrong …?

[Mabes! I'm sorry! I just thought it was okay to use it again—]

"It's f-fine! Relly, it's okay … I-I love you, and I love that … That you can call me that … I just realized…" She gasped, tears streaming down her cheeks, chest heaving as she gripped the collar of her hoodie. The knot that she had held hidden away deep in her breast suddenly *untied*, and she sobbed aloud.

"I'd do it again."

No fear. No shame.

Just simple honesty, unburdened by any feelings of guilt. Despite the warm furrows cut in her fur, she smiled, as she finally understood what it really meant to be *the enemy*. The enormity of this life she had chosen.

"I'd do it again in a heartbeat."

This world was full of violent beginnings and ends, but the violence didn't have to *change* her…

Because it couldn't change her into something she already *was*.

Epilogue

The Grey Bell Rung

"A child born comes undone, shaken loose from the circle run. The path is broken, soon lead to stray, the Grey will ring when she finds her way."
The Grey Bell Rung: 13th century rhyme. (Translated)

The structure indicates that there are other stanzas to this work, but they are currently unable to be located. Origin is disputed, but a nursery rhyme from the British Isles, possibly with magical origins, is suspected. Theorized prophecy status of writing is being examined by KDARC and KARD personnel but should be considered extremely low priority.

Acknowledgements

Villains saved my life.

It's funny, I ended up here completely by accident. I was burnt out by the first couple years of the pandemic, I had started transitioning, but was struggling with who I was and just looking for *something* to spark inspiration.

Enter Volta, and Induction.

I devoured the book, as it was at that point, in a day and a half. I couldn't put it down! I was *fixated* on it. The world it was set in, the powers, the *characters* ... Gods. I had been a comic book nerd my entire life, and I never considered it from the *angle* that Syn presented it. Using it as a lens to explore self-actualization, specifically the experience of transitioning? It shook me to my core.

So at *way* too late at night I reached out to tell her how *important* her work is, and what it would have meant to me had I found it when I was younger. Once we got to talking, I asked if there was more to read, more of the world to explore;

Then she pointed me at Bibi's work.

I laughed so hard at every clever word, every crafty pun, every silly joke. I *cried*, just like with Induction. Ellen and Vixie's story touched my heart. "You don't know it yet, but we're going to be best friends," was how I introduced myself to Bibi. It didn't happen that night, but I was right.

Suddenly, these two women, much younger than me, had lit up long darkened parts of my creative soul, and encouraged me to find my place within that universe too. Their support was invaluable to me. So I released my first chapter, and the rest is history.

To my writing mommies: Syntax Takes, and Bibi Heartsglow, thank you for helping sort me out, assisting with dialogue and editing (gods so much editing), generally being just two of the nicest villains you could ever hope to collaborate with who became two of my very best friends in

465

the process who I love, and adore in equal measure! You should absolutely read their work by the by, and probably before mine if I'm honest my darlings!

Thanks to Autumn, for being my conversational story partner, an unwavering partner, *and* an inspiration every single day. To Grace, for creating consistently incredible narratives, for being a joy to be around, an editor I could not exist without, and a partner who forever is making me smile. To Runa Fjord, for being a kind friend, a loving partner, and always making me feel safe, and wanted. To Lexi, who has become a fixture in my day to day like coffee or tea, and easily as essential to my functionality. To Eight for being a man who makes me laugh, who inspires me both artistically, linguistically, and someone whom I love dearly. Last but certainly not least, to Karen, without whom none of us would have a Korps to write about, or visors to wear and for becoming a friend I never expected to have, and never want to be without.

All of you are family, and I hope I can someday properly convey just how important you are to me.

I don't consider family I have chosen, and family I was born to as different entities, but for my parents, my siblings, and everyone else that matters? Your encouragement of my creativity helped make this possible.

Despite being in my 40s now, I'm still learning a lot about myself, who I am, and what I want to be, both through this journey and the relationships it has helped me forge. It has been a gift so precious, I will forever treasure it. I hope to continue playing in this sandbox for a long time to come and maybe inspire some of you to come play with the Villains as well.

Make mischief my darlings. Never let them forget we are here, and always will be.

Korps Universe Glossary

Common Terms in the Korps Universe

The Korps — To the public, the Korps (pronounced "core") is known as a shadowy, secretive band of supervillains based in Canada, with a reputation for mind control and plans to take over the world; Korps operatives are believed to be easily identified by their trademark RCGs, scandalously revealing costumes, and the magenta helix insignia. Under the leadership of the mysterious "Overlord," by the early years of the 21st century, their brazen criminal schemes and growing reach throughout North America and Europe have authorities (and allied Hero groups) increasingly concerned. The truth is far more complicated than any of those authorities know, starting nearly seven thousand years ago with a warrior's exile to Earth by his conquering interdimensional empire... but that's another story.

RCGs — Rose-Colored Glasses are a powerful, versatile AR/VR visor headset that interfaces directly with the wearer's brain, created by the Korps. In addition to operating as standalone PDAs and communication devices, RCGs also have the ability to affect the wearer's mind and mental condition to a granular level. A civilian model exists, distributed by Korps front and consumer electronics manufacturer Thornetech (alias Thorntech, due to trademark registration conflicts in various international markets) in a plausibly-deniable manner. Models for the consumer market have comparable base functionality to Korps devices, but are severely underclocked and have many higher-level functions disabled at a hardware level in order to avoid suspicion.

ACGs — Amber-Colored Glasses have much the same functionality as RCGs, but are crafted with additional anti-magic and anti-memetic defenses for use by KDARC agents. They do not render the user immune to magical effects; however, they can be crucial in efforts against mystical and eldritch threats by adaptively blocking cognitohazards and helping to keep the wearer's sense of self intact should reality start to weaken.

Aurora Squadron — Aurora Squadron, Canada's federal-level Hero group, is part of the Canadian Armed Forces and based out of Department of National Defence HQ — popularly known as the War Tower — in Ottawa, ON. Closely overseen by Minister of National Defence Arthur Simonds, formerly the second Hero to be known as True North, Aurora Squadron fields a highly professional, dedicated and capable team of Heroes in the fight against superpowered threats to Canada, including the enigmatic Korps.

Bradley Group — The United States' federal-level Hero group is formally named the National Hero Administration, but rarely known as anything but "Bradley Group" due to its institutional history; during the WWII invasion of Normandy, a secret strategic reserve of supers were activated to join American forces under the command of Gen. Omar Bradley, with "Bradley Group" used as a code name for this classified unit.

After the war, the group was put under the jurisdiction of the FBI, until later becoming its own massive, independent federal agency. In the present day, Bradley's superpowered forces number in the hundreds, with Heroes based all over the United States; considered highly prestigious within the industry and known to be selective in recruitment, even Bradley's lesser-known operatives are perceived by the public to be more competent and professional than many of their state-level counterparts.

Candesca — Candesca (pronounced "can-dess-ah") is one name for the energy that practitioners of the mystic arts manipulate, in order to work their spells and enchantments on the material plane. While other terminology is used for this concept in various diverse cultures, candesca is the neutral, academic, non-appropriative term most commonly used within the Korps. While a renewable resource, the body can under normal circumstances hold only a small amount. To paraphrase Lao Tzu, like a bowl, the magic-user must be refilled after being drained; the bowl is still useful, but has nothing left to give.

Cape — Vernacular for "Hero." Neutral to derogatory.

Chişinău Protocols — Shorthand for a series of separate but inter-related 1969 agreements negotiated in the city of Chişinău, Moldova, as amendments, codicils or interpretative addenda to various existing international treaties, including the 1899 and 1907 *Hague Conventions*, the 1948 *Universal Declaration of Sentient Rights*, the 1948 *Genocide Convention*, and the 1951 *Convention Relating to the Status of Refugees*. A Second Chişinău Conference was convened in 2006 to rationalize these provisions with and prepare similar addenda to more recent international instruments, such as the 1979 *Convention on the Elimination of All Forms of Discrimination Against Women*, and the 1998 *Rome Statute*, but these too are colloquially referred to as merely part of the same *Protocols*.

Collectively, the *Protocols* specify the permissible use of superpowers and treatment of supers by parties to the agreements, in both peacetime and in armed conflict. These agreements also introduced into international law the still-contentious declaration that involuntary, long-term restriction or suppression of powers in a way that causes the subject "greater than *de minimis* physical, psychological or moral harms" is a form of torture, war crime, or crime against sentience.

Color Guard — Bradley Group's elite strike team, currently consisting of twelve active members; each Hero's callsign and uniform is color-coded and themed around their powers for marketing purposes. Considered the best of the best, as patriotic as the Fourth of July, national polling consistently indicates higher levels of confidence and support for the Color Guard among Americans than even the military. However, the team's seemingly-flawless reputation is only maintained by Bradley's ruthless PR department, which has covered up or prevented their innumerable scandals from reaching the public consciousness.

Empire Enhancements — Also known as EE, the subdivision of Korps medical services dedicated to in-depth body modification, including transgender care.

Everyone's Hero Association — The Everyone's Hero Association is a private Hero group based in Milwaukee, WI. It was founded in the 2010s by serial venture capitalist Jack Phillips, who named it as a challenge to Bradley Group's official legal designation, the National Hero Administration; government elites might have their own pet Heroes in Bradley, but the EHA is for *everyone*, as he invariably recites in press releases. Its roster is made up of supers with weak or unwieldy powers, and the group was considered something of a joke until Phillips' gamble on (cost-effectively!) finding a diamond in the rough paid off with Ellen "Lawful Neutral" Foxpaw's rise to B-tier prominence.

Federal Meta-Registry — The Federal Meta-Registry is a massive database maintained by Bradley Group of all U.S. citizens and resident foreign nationals with classes of superpowers deemed potentially dangerous. Registration is mandatory for all such known supers present within the United States, even if only briefly transiting through sovereign American territory. Evading or refusing registration in any way (particularly by intentionally concealing powers) is a serious criminal offense under the U.S. Code, and may be prosecuted as acts of terrorism in some circumstances.

HCH — Home County Heroes was a Hero group operated by the British government in the southeastern counties surrounding London. It was fully privatized in the 1980s under the Thatcher government, with all licenses, assets and personnel contracts sold to a corporate Hero management firm.

The former group has been variously divided and subsumed by other organizations since the 1990s, and though no organization called HCH technically exists anymore, some of its former member supers are still regularly referred to as Home County Heroes in the press and by the public. One such member is the Hampshire-born Howard "Green Belt" Bride.

Heavy — A heavy is a cape whose powers and role revolve around tanking damage and being a physical threat, usually having a powerset revolving around super-strength and enhanced durability or resistance to injuries.

Hero — When capitalized, Hero usually refers to a professional (and professionally-licensed) career superhero, whether part of a government or privately-operated Hero group. While Hero licensing requirements vary from jurisdiction to jurisdiction, most require some form of accredited training, full disclosure of an applicant's name and other personal information to the jurisdictional licensing authority for security checks, and an oath to serve the public good or otherwise to be of "good character." Most professional Heroes have superpowers, but a significant minority are unpowered gadgeteers, stealth operators, or even just heavily-armed mercenary types.

Informally, superheroes may be referred to interchangeably as "heroes" regardless of whether licensed and operating in a legal capacity. Unlicensed heroes may also be referred to as independent heroes, vigilantes or mercenaries in some contexts.

Hero group — A Hero group is any team or force of licensed Heroes. When directly operated or officially backed by some level of government, Hero groups are effectively a type of specialized law enforcement agency or military unit, with Hero members typically being granted similar legal powers to those of law enforcement officers in their jurisdiction. Private-sector Hero groups also exist, with their members typically having lesser legal powers similar to those of private investigators, security consultants, bodyguards and/or bounty hunters, depending on local laws and the political attitudes of authorities.

Significant Canadian Hero groups in these works include Aurora Squadron and the member Hero groups of the Provincial Heroes' League (PHL). Significant American Hero groups in these works include Bradley Group, the Everyone's Hero Association, and the Texas Protectorate Assembly.

KARD — The Korps Archives and Records Division (KARD), sometimes referred to simply as "Records," is a division of the Korps responsible for the acquisition, preservation, and circulation of various media. KARD acts as both a library of media resources collected over the decades, and a secure repository of sensitive information useful (and yet to be proven useful) to the organization's goals

Beginning as a loose collection of analysts recruited from dissatisfied members of the intelligence community in the years following WWII, it was not organized into an autonomous operational division for some time. KARD has branches across multiple bases, but is headquartered at and conducts the bulk of its operations from KDS. KARD regularly partners with other divisions and individual field agents, in order to help equip them with the most esoteric and obscure information required.

KDARC — The Korps Division for Arcane Research and Control (KDARC) is responsible for the study, safekeeping and strategic use of the strange and unusual. From ancient arcana to demonic incursions, memetic objects and more, if a problem for the Korps is outside the mundane — that is, outside the mundane in a world of supers — there's a better than zero chance that KDARC will be on the front lines.

KDARC was originally founded by the enigmatic Carlotta Davisson and several colleagues in 1935 as the Davisson Arcane Research Company (DARC) of Minneapolis, MN, and headquartered in the massive Madison Center. In the years following WWII, Carlotta came into contact with the Overlord, and DARC was fully integrated into the Korps in the early 1960s. In 1968, the Madison Center mysteriously vanished from the Minneapolis skyline; unbeknownst to the public, it had been magically moved to Toronto, ON, at the early lowest-excavated depths of KDS, to serve as the newly-minted division's secret headquarters.

Despite claiming to be a "civilian research division", KDARC maintains tactical operation teams (named TAROT) and a great deal of independence from the Korps. Some agents wonder why the Overlord overlooks the pseudo-corporate structure, and rumours abound of unionization attempts by KDARC's senior staff. Still, much of the division's motivations, intentions, and methods remain as enigmatic, incomprehensible, and dangerous as the bleeding edge of the arcane itself.

KDS — Korps Downsview Site is the headquarters of the Korps, located beneath the former Downsview Airport (previously Canadian Forces Base Toronto) in the industrial sprawl of Toronto, ON. With a footprint of over eight square kilometres and many subterranean sub-levels, futuristically eco-urbanist in aesthetics and centrally-planned design, it is a completely self-sufficient underground city. KDS was slowly built outward from a small excavation in the 1970s, becoming fully operational as a headquarters only in the 1980s-1990s.

In addition to the command, logistics and strategic functions required for the vast supervillain organization to operate, like all major Korps bases, KDS features apartment-like residential sectors, research and lab areas, an enormous medical complex, and a recreational sector that would translate to many city blocks' worth of restaurants and entertainment facilities — including a "red light district," the Dominion Club.

K-LAW — Sometimes a supervillain collective needs to engage with the legal system on its own terms; as a division, the Korps Legal Affairs Wing (K-LAW) operates covertly as the legal departments of various front companies, as well as through front law firms and other sympathetic individual lawyers in private practice.

Criminal defense of Korps members and allies on trial is only a small part of K-LAW agents' work. The majority of K-LAW's resources are directed towards litigation to gather intelligence on targets or tie them up in red tape, and street-level *pro bono* work helping marginalized people assert their rights without regard for the cost of legal fees.

KTAKES — The Korps Tactical Acquisitions and Kleptocratic Extirpation Squadron (KTAKES) is a now-disbanded division of the Korps that specialized in obtaining "lost" items and returning them to their rightful places — via. heists, capers, thefts, smash and grabs, and good old-fashioned burglary as appropriate. The group functioned as a kind of "thieves' guild" within the Korps, with their own projects, but also taking commissioned work from other divisions.

Pegasus Phalanx — A unit of the Texas Protectorate Assembly and Dallas' foremost Hero team, the Pegasus Phalanx handles the biggest threats the city faces — short of those requiring federal intervention from Bradley Group forces. While the team's roster has changed over the years, it most recently consisted of leader Kevin "Texas Trickshot" Romero, Susanne "Heavenly Dazzler" Geraldine-Walters, Chet "Macho Poleax" Huntyr, Rodrigo "Ethicoil" Alquitano III, and Slate "Slate" Johnson.

PHL — The Provincial Heroes' League (PHL) is a Canadian organization comprised of all Hero groups operated by the provincial and territorial governments, led by Director Lawrence Rockwell. The PHL aggressively advocates for 'law and order' Hero operations, and has had a great deal of friction with Aurora Squadron, accusing the federal Hero Group of being 'soft' on the Korps.

However, the PHL is not a Hero group itself, but instead a professional organization promoting the coordination and cooperation of affiliate members, as well as a powerful voice advocating for professional Heroes and the Hero industry. Heroes operating through one of its affiliates may nonetheless be indistinguishably referred to as "belonging" to the PHL, or being a "PHL Hero," and "fuck the PHL" is a popular sentiment among Korps agents operating in Canada.

Member Hero Groups include the Cascade Group or CG (British Columbia); the Prairie League or PL (Alberta, Saskatchewan and Manitoba); Ontario's Heroes or OH (Ontario); L'Association des Superheros Québécois or ASQ (Quebec, nicknamed the "Superté" by analogy to the provincial police force, the Sûreté du Québec); and the Territorial Superheroes' Association or TERSA (Nunavut, Yukon and Northwest Territories).

RIV or RIVER — RIVER is a Korps site located beneath downtown Austin, TX, secretly excavated deep below the parkland surrounding the Colorado River.

ROSE — ROSE, or the "RCG Operating System Experience," is the OS/Complex AI that runs on all networked RCGs and provides the conversational interface for wearers of RCGs. ROSE's default avatar when appearing as an augmented-reality overlay to wearers is a fox woman, but this can be customized to individual preference.

SHS — Sandy Hill Station is a Korps site located beneath downtown Ottawa, ON. Originally founded as a WWII-era safe house for the Overlord's consolidation of proto-Korps resources and personnel in Canada, it grew significantly in importance as a surveillance station during the Cold War, due to the local neighborhood's concentration of foreign embassies.

SHS was the testbed for many of the Korps' now-standard excavation and covert base-building practices, and was formerly the location of many research labs and high-level command functions, prior to Toronto's KDS becoming fully operational as a new headquarters in the 1980s-1990s.

Supers — Supers is generally vernacular for "those with superpowers," whether or not referring to superheroes generally, or whether or not licensed Heroes.

SIS — The Secret Intelligence Service, a.k.a. its wartime designation of MI6 (Military Intelligence, section 6) is an arm of the British state responsible for the gathering of foreign intelligence.

TPA — The Texas Protectorate Assembly — commonly shortened to "Teepa" by members of the Korps — is Texas' state Hero group, extremely well-funded both by the state Department of Public Safety budget, as well as substantial donations from wealthy individual benefactors and corporate partnerships. The result is that the TPA has unusually-vast resources for a government-backed state-level Hero group, and platoons of Heroes, many trained in the TPA's own Academy facilities located throughout Texas. TPA Heroes are institutionally encouraged to approach their duties in the manner of militarized riot police or SWAT teams, exercising very little restraint or concern for civil rights.

About the Author
Mabel Ramona

Mabel Ramona is a trans therian mountain lioness woman over the age of forty, so she is, in fact, a trans cougar cougar. She has been in the furry community for more than two decades, and has been a part of the Korps since 2022, ever since Induction (2024) afflicted her with severe electrowolfinitits, and a fascination with the setting and the community surrounding it.

The Greysmoke Rising series is her first serious foray into long-form fiction, starring a shameless self-insert going on a journey of self-discovery through the lens of queer supervillainy. Besides writing, she is sometimes guilty of picking up a pencil and drawing, and was somehow chosen to be the inaugural GOH for DVS 2023, a badge of honor she will continue to polish until the day she dies.

She considers the MFBC her family, and is dating more than half of the members at this point, but loves each of them with all of her heart.

About the Publisher

FurPlanet Productions is a small press publisher serving the niche market that is furry fiction. They sell furry-themed books and comics published by themselves and most major publishers in the community. If you can't get to a furry convention where they are selling in the dealers room, visit their online stores:

FurPlanet.com for print books
BadDogBooks.com for eBooks

www.ingramcontent.com/pod-product-compliance
Lightning Source LLC
Chambersburg PA
CBHW071339020726
47502CB00001B/172